This edition contains the complete and unabridged texts of the original editions. They have been completely reset for this volume.

This omnibus was originally published in separate volumes under the titles:

Restoring Hope © 2013 by Valerie Knupp
Finding Faith © 2014 by Valerie Knupp
Creating Chance © 2014 by Valerie Knupp

Published by Valerie Knupp

The text herein is a work of fiction. Names, characters, places, and incidents either are the product of the author's imagination or are used fictitiously, and any resemblance to actual persons, living or dead, events or locales is entirely coincidental.

ISBN: 978-0-9899029-3-9
Printed in the United States of America

Contents

Restoring Hope

1

Finding Faith

_____

255

Creating Chance

_____

487

RESTORING HOPE

By

Valerie Knupp

Dedication

This book is dedicated to my father, Billy Mike Knupp, the man who gave me a twisted outlook and the gift of quick thought, making writing a free flowing process. I only wish he were still on this earth to read it. I think he would have enjoyed seeing his daughter's name in print.

Prologue

He had no idea what day it was, much less the month. His eyes didn't want to open, and even if they did, he questioned whether they'd see the way they should. Even with his eyes closed, he knew that the room was spinning around him, the world turned upside down, making the room appear to be a fog. The only certainty was that his head, his heart and his body were in terrible pain.

How long had he been here? Where *was* here? That thought brought more clarity with it, and his memory started to return. How much had he had to drink last night? Had he hurt anyone? He wasn't certain, but for the moment all he could think about was how could he 'kill' the pain. He tried to rise and forced his eyes open; slowly glancing around, his nostrils filled with the smell of … what? What was that smell? It was putrid, whatever it was … like old cigarettes, the copper of dried, yet fresh blood, and old fermented wine. Realization poured over him; it was he who smelled like this. The room around him was nearly dark. Still, his eyes struggled to adjust to the low light and dust particles that hung in the air, evident even through his hang over. He needed to pee. That was going to take precedence over his unwillingness to move. He swung his legs over the side of the dirty mattress, sheets askew and sticking to his sweaty body, then tossed the blankets aside. Struggling to his feet, he began to make his way through the room, tripping over clothes and piles of food bags with names like McDonalds and Burger King on them, stepping on the newspapers headlining the latest killing spree. What was the name they were calling him now? He wondered, sparing a glance at the newspapers, averting his eyes toward the window not really interested in what the media thought of him anyway.

The curtains hung off the rod slightly, allowing for a small amount of light to seep around them and into the hotel room. The effect made the scene around him even more unsavory, as the glow merely displayed the chaos of his life. This life – not the one he had cherished, but this new ugly one. The life he was living now made him want to do these ugly things, driving him to think those thoughts again. This life drove him into the darkness looking, hunting…, this life would no doubt win, consume him, unless. *Unless what?*

He made his way through the clutter to the bathroom and stood in front of the dirty toilet, hands trembling as he relieved himself. He slowly zipped his pants, flushed, and watched his fluids spin around and then down, out into the city sewer. He moved to stand over the chipped and stained sink, which was as rundown as the rest of the hotel room. As rundown as his body felt. Rusty water stains snaked from the faucets into the drain, making a trail that seemed to naturally disappear into the pipe and from there into the dark city. He found this ironic, as those rust stains and his bodily fluids were much like him, finding their way back out into the dark city.

Looking into the mirror through his blood-shot eyes, now he realized that he saw only pieces of the man he used to be. His eyes – once blue and sparkling, hinting of a happier day – were now gray and dull. The lines in his face once there from smiling where deep and taunt, his shoulders once held high and proud stooped and ached. Looking at his reflection through the cracks in the mirror, which had most likely been delivered by some hooker or drug addict during a few hours of paid-for passion, he started to see the way. The answer was there right in front of him, he realized, though it was in pieces, parts, and fragments. But he had a chance to have it all again, if he could put all those pieces together. If he could just change, focus, and plan. His life – this one that consisted of pain and chaos – must end, and a new one – a happy one – could replace it.

He just had to make some minor changes. In his mind, a plan began to form.

Chapter One

The Jackie Cooper Mercedes Benz lot was displaying balloons and incentive signs for the special of the month. The signs flapped frantically in the Oklahoma wind, seemingly begging a buyer to come in and see what deals were being offered. As he pulled the black SL550 convertible onto the lot, he thought that the dealership must have just opened; there appeared to be no other customers in sight. It was Wednesday, though, and perhaps that meant it was a low volume sales day.

If that was true, then this should be easy.

He pulled into the parking lot and pulled into one of the spaces near the front steps. Before he could even get his long frame out of the car, a sales person was bounding down the stairs from the showroom floor. The man was obviously the typical, car salesman; flashy, and sporting a gold chain necklace. Thick, and probably fake. He had on a cheap – but shiny – pair of black, loafer-style shoes, and had the overly whitened smile to match.

"Good morning, sir," he called out, waving. "My name is Ben, but most folks remember me as Benz. How can I help you this fine, sunny morning?"

It was difficult not to notice the partial comb over flapping in the wind, seeming to dance in unison with the signs, and even harder not to laugh at it. This was the first step to regaining his life and it was time to begin to act like Jack again; he straightened his face and answered politely enough.

"Well Benz, my name is Jack, and I need to swap out my convertible here," he said, pointing to the car he'd just exited, the door still standing open. "I'd like to get a more practical car, as my wife and I are planning on settling down here."

"Okay, well I am sure we can work out a deal. That is one beautiful car you have there. I'd hate to part with it if it was up to me, but what are you thinking? A sedan, wagon, SUV? We have them all," Benz said with a gleam in his eye. He swept his arm out across the air, gesturing to the lot, which shone with all of the newest models.

Jack nodded, humored by the man's stupidity. Benz had clearly ran out when he had seen Jack pull onto the sales lot thinking this would be a big sale based on the current vehicle Jack was driving. It was obvious Benz didn't realize the plan was to move out of the luxury vehicle and into a practical one. It was necessary to eliminate this vehicle and settle into something less noticeable with a good sized cargo area. "I was thinking maybe a Honda or Toyota from your used car sales lot, actually," he answered quietly.

"Ohhhh," Benz exclaimed, trying desperately to hide his disappointment in the request. "Are you certain? I would think after having the finest in luxury, you might be disappointed in such a choice." Noting the darkness that fell over Jack's face, Benz continued, "But we aim to please all of our customers. Let me walk you back to where the used cars are, and we can see if any of them interest you."

He set off toward the back of the lot, and Jack followed, seeing that Benz had a slight imperfection in his gait. It appeared that one leg was shorter than the other. Mentally noting that this minor disability might be helpful later, Jack followed him having no problem keeping up with Benz, but found he was struggling to pay attention as Benz rattled on about how long the dealership had been in business, his years of service, and the numerous monthly awards he'd received over the years for top sales performance. Jack's mind, instead of listening to the salesman, had already wandered on to his next steps. He would eliminate Benz, so that there would be no witnesses and, well, because it had been two weeks and the need was raging. After that, he would begin working towards the day that he could settle into this new life with his wife, his love, and everything else. Benz would be a necessary casualty so that he could move forward. Jack knew he must succumb to the darkness while he put the rest of his plan in place. Benz would help him get through.

Benz stopped suddenly, spinning around to face Jack again, interrupting those thoughts. "As you can see, we have a pretty wide assortment of used cars. Why don't you tell me what style you're looking for and we can narrow down the selection?"

Jack looked around at the cars in front of him. As Benz had said, there was a good assortment. While his preference was actually to keep the car he had, he realized his life could only be good again through numerous personal sacrifices. Giving up a luxury automobile would be nothing compared to the reward he would have in the end. He noted a few cars that would meet the 'look' he was striving for – not overly successful, a subtle color, with minimum to moderate mileage on the odometer. Appearances were going to be incredibly important; being low key and blending in were a primary part of the plan.

"I think a mid-sized or large SUV will do," he said, thinking that the additional trunk space might be useful. "And anything with around 50,000 miles should be satisfactory. I'd prefer a silver or beige color. You know, easy to clean," he explained. What he was really thinking, of course, was that those colors would blend in on the road. He looked back at Benz and smiled, knowing his smile was difficult for anyone to resist. If he played his cards right, the guy would be in the palm of his hand within minutes.

By the age of five or six, Jack had learned that he had something special – a charm that, when applied, could easily win over anyone. At about the same time, he'd discovered his darker side and realized that he had the ability to apply looks which could immediately invoke feelings in others. Feelings of fear, joy, seduction ... they were all quickly within his reach, just through an adaptation of his facial expressions. Over the years Jack had crafted this skill to encourage people to behave as he desired them to. He could quickly gain trust or was capable of easily making someone uncomfortable. Most people would say he had charisma and charm. Jack thought of it as a means to manipulate necessarily, and this was one of those times.

He'd also realized that he could make these changes so quickly that most people didn't even realize what happened. They never knew that anything had changed, until it was too late.

Once he recognized this incredible ability, he had worked diligently to hone it to perfection. Over the years, he'd gotten really good at adapting to the situation or the personality he was trying to manipulate. On almost every occasion, he got exactly what he wanted.

Benz looked at Jack a bit quizzically at the request for the SUV, and then turned to look at the sea of cars, trucks and SUVs. "Okay, then let's take a look at this one over here. This is a Toyota Sequoia, it has ..." He paused for a moment, as he leaned over the windshield to see the details on the tag, 58,520 miles on it. Came from a single owner, a single mom from right here in Tulsa. Her youngest went off to college this year, and she traded this in for her dream car."

Walking over to the silver full-sized SUV, Benz used his dealer key to pop open the lock on the key storage device. Opening up the driver's side door, he stepped to the side and clicked the door opener to unlock all the doors. Then he dropped the keys into Jack's hand and walked around the rear bumper to the passenger side.

Jack reached in and moved the driver's seat back to accommodate his 6-foot frame and climbed in to settle behind the wheel. Benz joined him in the passenger seat and began to show Jack the features of the SUV, covering everything all the way down to the nine cup holders. Then, jumping back out of the car, Benz walked to the rear of the vehicle. Jack joined him as he pulled down the seats and showed the cargo space.

"Great for vacationing with the missus. In fact, my wife and I had a vehicle similar to this a few years back." Suddenly, looking somber he continued, "That was before the cancer took her, of course. You should definitely take the missus on lots of trips," he finished, a look of sorrow filling his eyes. Then, returning to his sales pitch, he continued to explain how the seats folded completely flat.

Jack looked into the back of the vehicle, wondering to himself how well Benz would fit in there later. When he spoke, though, it was to offer platitudes. "I'm sorry to hear about your wife. You alone now, or are your children in the area?

"Ah thanks, it's fine. Kids are all grown and busy with their lives. Just me these days," Benz answered, plastering on a smile.

Looking at Benz with his most sympathetic face, Jack decided he knew more than he'd hoped for and needed to change the subject. He didn't want to get personal with Benz; nothing good could come from it. Tipping his head towards the car, he said, "I think this will do just fine."

Benz barely contained his surprise at this sudden sale, but recovered gracefully. "Okay, well let's take her for a spin."

But Jack shook his head, his mind already made up. "That won't be necessary. I think this will do nicely for me and my wife. I see there's a dealer warranty, and I'd like to go ahead and do the deal on this car. Why don't we talk to your manager about trading in my car?"

Suppressing a sigh, Benz looked up at Jack, taking in his expensive clothes, nice shoes and manicured hands. "Of course," he said. "I'll have the car pulled around and cleaned for you while we work out the details." Benz suppressed his obvious disappointed, the deal being made was not going to be a favorable one from a commission perspective as he had originally hoped. The car being traded far out priced the car being bought.

"Don't bother," Jack stopped him. "The car seems to be in quite good condition." Secretly, Jack was smiling at the red nail polish spots on the carpet inside the car—an obvious spill from the prior owner. How much more perfect could that be? Closing the hatch he followed Benz into the showroom to meet the finance manager.

An hour later, Jack was pulling out of the dealership in his newly purchased used SUV. The dealer had provided him with a note to pick up a cashier's check for $60,000 in two days. A fair deal, he felt, though he had paid well over $100,000 for his car just a little over a year ago. Had it been that long since his life had been turned upside down? He hadn't expected the dealer to be able to write him a check and realized that once the money cleared, he would have completed everything necessary before eliminating his current identity. Dr. Jack Tyler would no longer exist. Then he could begin the rest of the plans necessary to restoring his true life.

Pulling out onto the street, Jack made a right turn to head north on Memorial Avenue. He had already conducted an Internet search for schools offering programs that would teach him a new profession. It was all part of the next phase of the plan. It was show time, time for him to begin his transformation. While he didn't relish the idea, he knew he had to leave himself behind for now.

If there was even a chance for Hope, it required a metamorphosis. He had to learn to live in a world that held little to no interest for him.

He'd already started exploring the programs and realized that he could complete them and be in his new profession in just three months. This timing was perfect, really, as it gave him the time he needed to practice his new lifestyle. That new life would provide cover and the perfect place for finding and putting the pieces all back together.

Chapter Two

"Agent Wells, it's a pleasure. How was your flight?" Chief of Police Harding asked, greeting one of the FBI's finest agents. He grasped the man's hand and pumped his arm fiercely, noticing the agent's tall, muscular frame, and thinking to himself that the guy could obviously hold his own.

The agent returned the greeting, sweeping his eyes over the large parking lot and the police headquarter building in one glance, and just as quickly returning his gaze to the chief. "Chief Harding, thank you for the invitation to work with you on this case. How can I help?" he asked.

Harding faced Wells, with the sun glinting off the dark pupils of his eyes, standing 5'10", with thick arms, broad shoulders, and a slight paunch around the midsection that came with too many greasy meals, late nights, and passing the age of fifty. He looked up at the younger man, who he guessed was mid-thirties, stood 6'2" and obviously only ate healthy, high-protein foods. Harding immediately respected the Agent, knowing he would have the type of discipline to remain focused under pressure. The necessary attributes of a good person to have on your side. Making eye contact, he started laying out the high-level details.

"We have six bodies, all same MO. The method of killing is always the same. There's a lot of rage, violent deaths all of them. Either a knife or saw was used with an unusual skill level, very clean, though we haven't yet identified the weapon of choice. He leaves nothing behind, and the bodies were all carefully cleaned with bleach afterward. No specific victimology, and this is where we're stuck. We're not going to be able to catch him until we know who he's going after. We need your help on the profiling." The chief shifted his eyes away as the roar of a motorcycle came racing into the parking lot, abruptly stopping about 25 yards to the east of them.

"Perfect timing," Harding stated, nodding to where the motorcycle stopped. "That's Detective Max Nichols, lead investigator on the case. Nichols can fill you in on all the case files, victims, and evidence, or lack thereof."

The two men started heading towards where the motorcycle had come to rest in one of the motorcycle parking spaces near the front entrance of the police department. As they got near the cycle, Wells began to take in the bike – an impressive ride that any man would love. He knew little about sports bikes, but admired the details of the silver and black Kawasaki Ninja ZX-14R. As the rider dismounted, propping the bike up expertly on its kickstand, Agent Wells prepared to shake hands with the rider. He drew back when that rider removed the helmet, freeing handfuls of long, rich, flowing, dark auburn hair.

"You must be Agent Wells. Max Nichols. Call me Max. Welcome to beautiful, sunny California," the woman under the helmet and attached to the hair stated, extending her hand and offering a firm handshake.

Wells quickly recovered from his surprise and returned the handshake, replying, "Mark Wells." He dropped his gaze slightly, taking in the beautiful, confident creature that was Detective Maxine Nichols.

Watching the exchange the chief smiled to himself.

Wells collected himself and brought the meeting back to order. "Detective Nichols... Max, my pleasure. I understand you have a serial on your hands. Chief Harding tells me I might be able to assist in profiling your un-sub. I hope I can help. I'm at your disposal for the next forty-eight hours. Ready to get started when you are," Wells stated, staring into the detective's rich emerald green eyes.

Max returned the gaze, sizing the man up in a similar fashion, noting his all-American good looks, excellent physical shape, blue eyes, and dark, thick, hair, which swept slightly to the left across his forehead. He had a sharp jawline that exploded into a perfectly white smile. *Okay, he'll do,* she thought to herself. Quickly pulling her hair back and nesting it into a pony tail, she pulled off her leather jacket and nodded towards the entrance. Climbing the steps two at a time, she arrived at the double doors and turned back to the two men who seemed to be falling behind. As she entered the building, her mind drifted to the case. She had six dead bodies on her hands, and while she wasn't originally thrilled about the FBI swooping in, she knew she needed input, and fast, if she was going to catch the killer. She hoped like hell that dreamy, Agent Mark Wells would be able to see something, anything, that she had missed, so she could lock the bastard away forever.

Chapter Three

Jack smiled to himself as he continued down the street. The sun was shining, though the news had called for rain. He didn't care for rainy weather, but he did have to admit that rain had some advantages. Everything needed water to survive, after all. Rain also did useful things like destroying evidence in a murder. That was a *major* advantage. The day was sunny, traffic was light – the benefit of middle-of-the-day travel, though it didn't much matter, as Tulsa never really suffered long traffic delays. The worst he had seen was over on 71st, where it seemed every business was packed into one area. The uncongested traffic patterns allowed him to be nimble in his activities, and that made him feel safer and at ease in his surroundings.

When he had been looking to relocate, one of the allures of this area was the city for hunting and the country for disposal, having little to no traffic issues was an added benefit. As he slid down the street, and pulled into a Walgreens, he was making a mental list of supplies he needed. He'd already spent some time planning and practicing the look he needed. He'd even gone to night clubs in California before leaving to make sure he knew how to behave in the situations he would likely face. It was imperative that the persona was believable.

As he approached the store, the automatic door slid open, and he felt the draft of wind caused by the external air forcing in against the heating system. Grabbing a small basket by the handle, he immediately headed over to the cosmetics department and began putting items in the basket. The Internet was a very helpful device, he'd realized, and very important for his plans. He'd spent quite a bit of time studying the cost and variety of mascara, face creams, lipsticks and eyeliners, and he put that research to good use now. Once he started school, classmates or – hell – even newfound friends might be close enough to notice that sort of thing, and he needed to make sure they stood up to the critical eye of a woman.

His persona, after all, had to be impeccable, or he'd be caught.

With his items selected, he headed to the checkout counter, where a plump woman stood smiling, her face pleasant, but lost behind acne. Paying with cash and thanking her, Jack collected his bag and returned to the car.

His next goal was the school itself, but first he'd stopped by the house. When he first arrived in Tulsa, he'd sought out a modest home with a few specific requirements. It had to have a basement and some privacy, but not enough to cause suspicion. He didn't want anyone wondering why a man like him would want to live too far from the ease of the city. He ended up buying a ranch style home just outside the city in a connecting town called Catoosa. His house sat on two acres with a private driveway and a basement, which had been separated into two rooms. He hadn't required the basement design, but he sure had been pleased to discover it. It appeared the prior owner had designed the rooms for specific purposes – one a family room and the other for canning fruits and vegetables.

He had much different plans, of course, but the layout was perfect.

Turning into the driveway, Jack slowly pulled the SUV into the garage. As the door closed behind him, he got out of the 'new' car and walked through the sparsely decorated garage, absent of the normal tools a man would have displayed in the space. The only masculine things here were the paint cans and brushes in the corner, under the built-in workbench. There was also a shovel and some gardening gloves in the corner. It was all quite intentional to not have much in the garage; he did not want to seem overly manly to any potential visitors. That was necessary to support his new image and the overall plan.

Entering the house through the door just off the kitchen, he headed left past the living room and guest bedroom, entering the master bedroom. From there he continued on into the bathroom. The area had his and her sinks; he smiled at that. They would not likely live in this home together for very long, but knowing that they would be back together soon made a sense of warmth begin to burn in his stomach.

Setting the bag on the counter in front of the mirror, he began peeling open the packaging, tossing the torn cardboard in the pink waste can against the wall. Moving back into the bedroom he opened the door to the double mirrored closet, and stood briefly admiring the contents. It wasn't so much that he actually appreciated the items neatly organized on the hangers inside. More that he appreciated the cleverness of his plan. This was real, and it was all beginning today.

Selecting a light pink tank top and a white button-up dress shirt, he closed the closet door and laid the clothes out on the bed. Now he removed the polo shirt he was wearing, pulled on the tank, and slid his arms into the dress shirt. Returning to the mirror, he admired the look as he fastened the shirt. The jeans were tight fitting and allowed just enough masculinity to make him look attractive rather than ridiculous. Considering his shoes, he opened the door again and took out a pair of Andrew Dyker wing tips in gray suede. He'd picked them up on Melrose before leaving California, along with most of the clothing inside the closet; he thought today would be the perfect time to try them out. Sitting on the edge of the bed he pulled on the shoes admiring the fit. He stood to slip on a gray belt then took in the whole ensemble, smiling. Perfect.

Back in the bathroom, he applied some gel to his hair, spiking it up on top. Next he applied a single fine line of eyeliner on each eye. He hand was steady, his mind completely focused on completing the task. A thin layer of lip gloss completed the look he was striving to achieve. The subtle change was perfect for where he was going today. The other makeup items would be for a more dramatic effect if needed.

He stood back and stared at himself in the mirror. Was it convincing? Realistic?

Yes, he decided. He looked at the rest of the items on the counter and then scooped them into his vanity drawer, arranging them in straight lines. Then he grabbed up his keys from the counter and retraced his steps through the house, glancing at the clock on the wall and noting that it was only two o'clock.

Perfect, he would be at the school before three o'clock.

Returning to the garage he climbed into the SUV. Pulling out of the garage and heading back down the driveway, he glanced in the mirror instinctively, verifying that the garage door had closed. A moment later he was turning the SUV back out to the highway. Passing the Hard Rock Casino, he noticed the neon sign indicated that Diana Ross would be playing there soon. This made him wonder for a moment what had happened to her, not having heard anything of her in years. In fact, he'd nearly forgotten that she existed. Shrugging to himself, he returned his focus back to the road.

He followed the road to the split at highways 412 and 44, listening to Pink piping through the speakers and watching for the Broken Arrow Expressway. From there Jack followed the highway past Clary Sage Cosmetology School getting off at Sheridan and looping to the right to pull into the parking lot.

Show time, he thought, taking a quick, approving glance in the mirror. As he got out of the vehicle and locked it, he inserted a slight sway to his gait. He exaggerated the sway as he walked across the parking lot, the excitement building inside of him. It wouldn't be long now.

In front of him, the school was polished and bright, with lots of windows and doors. He walked in and immediately gave his million dollar smile, bright teeth flashing at the two girls behind the counter. Glancing up, they both immediately returned his smile, though theirs seemed genuine.

"Hi there, welcome to Clary Sage. How may we help you today?" a blonde with short cropped hair the tips painted a light red, said, glancing at the girl next to her.

Jack took in both girls without allowing them to notice even the slightest display of male to female interest. The fact was that his interest in

15

them was only how they could help him. That made the pretense he was presenting much easier to be convincing.

"I'm interested in applying for classes for mani and pedis," Jack replied with a slight bat of his eyes, giving the first hint as to why a strapping, handsome man such as himself would ever want to take those classes.

"Oh, of course," the blonde replied, seeming to suddenly understand. "My name is Mandy, and I can help you with all of the details, including any financial aid needs you might have." She reached out and handed him a brochure, and continued, "I'd love to give you a personal tour and answer any questions."

"Mandy, that would be wonderful," Jack replied, laying on just the right amount of excitement.

"Fantastic." Mandy smiled and held out her hand. "What is your name?"

"It's Thomas. Thomas Jennings," he lied, returning her handshake with a weak grip. Coming around the counter, Mandy began explaining the layout of the school, taking him through the expansive lobby the various rooms, explaining all of the training programs offered at the school. She was thorough, covering the school's accreditation and attendance policy, and even describing the final testing requirements upon course completion. Then, leading Jack into a small room that looked more like an office, she offered him a seat and asked if he would like a bottled water or herbal tea.

Accepting an herbal tea, he settled into the chair.

Mandy left for a moment then returned with the tea, handing the cup to Jack. She settled into the chair opposite him and put a file folder on the table between them. She opened it and started going through each of the papers inside. There was a cover letter welcoming the potential student to Clary Sage, the school mission statement, an enrollment application, and financial aid documentation.

"Now the hard part – money. How do you think you'll be paying for the program? We do offer financial aid, which can fund all or part of the program. Once school is over and you're working, earning an income, you can set up a repayment program at a very low interest rate. Almost all of our students get at least some of their school covered through financial aid. It's a very simple process, and we offer assistance in filling out the paperwork."

Jack clearly did not need the money, but he also did not want to stand out. He needed to fit the role of the person he was presenting himself as. He listened intently as Mandy explained options to him.

Mandy stopped and smiled, allowing Jack, aka Thomas, to take it all in. Not seeing any confusion on his face, she continued on. "We also have grants that can help cover some parts of the program completely. I really like to encourage all students to apply for these, as it's a great way to get a good portion of the program taken care of without any repayment required."

Jack let his eyes drift over all of the forms. Looking up, he put on what he hoped was his best glow. "I'm so excited. Once I fill out the application, how long before I can get started?"

Mandy returned his excited gaze, "Well, your timing is very good. We happen to have a new class starting the week after next, and it still has two openings in it. I should tell you, though, that it's an accelerated program, for full-time students only, and completes in just over eight weeks. If we had your application back no later than tomorrow afternoon, we could get you started in that class. Or we have a part-time class that starts in four weeks."

Mandy seemed just as excited as he was, she was apparently pleased that he was ready to enroll immediately. He assumed class vacancy was frowned on and that her boss would be thrilled that she had enrolled another new student.

"Were you considering full time or part time?"

"Oh, I want full time for sure, and I think I could have my application back tomorrow to be sure I get it in on time. Will you be here tomorrow morning?" Jack was struggling to contain his real excitement. He truly thought he would have to wait much longer to get into a program. Being able to complete this part of the process in such a short period of time was even better than he had imagined. This was setting the timeline for the entire plan, and he could not have been more pleased. *Soon, he thought. Soon.*

She blushed, flattered at the fact that he'd asked. He was adorable, and though she was certain he was not interested in her in *that* way she still could hardly take her eyes off of his. "Yes, I'll be in starting at nine o'clock. If you bring this back to me, I'll make sure we get you started, Thomas. You're going to love our school. The program goes quickly, and the instructor, Melody, is excellent. You'll love her!"

"Okay, fabulous," Jack beamed. "I'll be here first thing, then, just to be sure it all gets processed on time." He jumped up, giving Mandy a quick hug. "Girl, you have no idea how excited I am."

Mandy returned his pats on the back, clearly comfortable with him. Walking Jack back through the lobby, she waved her fingers at him as he bounced out the door, and then said to her co-worker who had just come back into the room, "Why do all the super cute guys have to be gay?"

When he got back to his SUV and closed the door behind him, Jack let out a sigh. *Well, that went well*, he thought as he tossed the folder on the seat next to him. His stomach was telling him he had missed lunch. Later there would be some unfinished business with Benz. Benz was someone that knew him as Jack and that was not acceptable. Besides, the darkness was starting to rage within, and he needed something to tamp it down, so he could keep his focus.

Replaying the meeting with Mandy in his mind, he thought it important that he apply for some sort of funding. Having credit run on his new identity wasn't his favorite idea, but she did say that almost all the students did it. He didn't want to stand out in any way. He certainly didn't want to march in there and act like he could pay for the whole thing himself. This definitely didn't go with his new persona. Sighing at that, he moved on to thinking about where he wanted to eat.

Chapter Four

Max and Agent Wells had spent several hours going through the six case files, working diligently with all the victim crime scene photos lining the table between them. They'd discussed each victim, where they were last seen, financial records, and family information. Finally, deciding that it was time to grab a bite, they both stood, stretching their legs and backs. Max tossed the Styrofoam cups that had held their numerous refills of the burnt station house coffee in the trash, "I know a great place to grab lunch," she said as she turned to face Agent Wells.

"I'd like to see the first victim's house and the dump site," he said as they walked out the doors and down the steps. Pulling keys from his pocket, he dangled them at the detective. "Looks like I'll be driving."

She smirked. "Of course, while my ride could hold you, I'm not sure you could hang on tight enough. Besides the Federal Government has deep pockets and they seldom share," Max smirked, pushing a rogue strand of wavy hair behind her ear. "We can go visit the dump site on the way to the first victim's house, AFTER we eat." Leaving the lot, Max smiled, knowing she could have checked out a police cruiser. The fact that she didn't even offer made her feel like she'd pulled one over on Agent Wells, and for some reason that made her happy. Though she had no idea why, she wasn't going to investigate it any further. For the moment, being happy about it was enough.

Leading him out towards Venice Beach, she began to recap what they knew. Six bodies – two males, four females, two black, four white. Was this meaningful? Doubtful, she thought, but it was still something they had noted together. There was no sexual assault on any of the victims and no appearance of sexual motivation or failed rape attempt. So whoever killed them wasn't doing it for sexual satisfaction. The victims were from various social areas, all seeming to have been grabbed from random locations and from what they could gather from the witnesses – those last seen with the victims – there hadn't been any trophies taken. All personal items were left with the victims.

From there, it was a matter of detail. Each victim had been stripped of all their clothes, cut from just below the throat to the pelvis, and internally explored. They were cleaned excessively with bleach before they were dumped, this final act wiping out any possible evidence. The clothes had been deposited into the grave with each body. Nothing appeared to have been kept.

Max pointed Wells toward a diner near the Santa Monica pier, and they circled the block once before finding a place to park the rental car. As they walked the half block to the diner, Max could feel Wells watching her. She knew he was checking her out. For a moment she wondered what he was thinking about the physical attributes of his newfound colleague. She knew she had Hollywood looks, yet she seldom thought about it. She suspected that he was wondering how she'd ended up chasing killers, that always seemed to be the first question people wanted to know the answer to.

As they entered the diner, a few heads turning briefly in their direction. After assessing the attractive pair focus returned to their dining mates, newspapers, phones, or food. After asking for a table for two, Max followed a young woman to a booth at the back of the room. The diner was what you might expect – walls covered with photos of movie stars personally autographed in thanks to the place for great food or service. The pair took their seats and accepted the menus offered by the hostess.

Max was absorbed in the menu for a moment, then tossed it down and blurted out, "So, Wells, what's your story?"

Taking his time, using the menu as a reason to delay the response, the agent tried to decide whether he wanted to play cat and mouse with detective Maxine Nichols or not. He found her intriguing and did not want to put her on the defense. Before he could decide to play it cool with her, better to gain her trust than toy with her just because of her good looks, the server appeared at the side of the table - an unsuspecting rescue from having to provide a response for now.

"What can I get the two of you to drink today?" she asked.

Wells nodded indicating to Max to answer first, and she turned to the waitress. "I'll have a Diet Coke," she answered, distracted briefly by the pierced eyelid on the pretty server. *What a shame,* she thought, wondering why beautiful young women felt compelled to put pins through their faces.

"I'll have an iced tea," Wells said, looking at the girl. "And I think we're ready to order." He didn't want to waste time. He wanted to get to the victim's home. With little time to work this case he needed to come up with a profile and fast.

"Go right ahead, then. I can take your order now."

"Okay," Max started, ordering a veggie burger and fries. Wells followed suit.

Once the food arrived, Max pushed up the sleeves of her long-sleeved, police-issued LAPD shirt and reached for the ketchup sitting at the edge of the table next to the salt and pepper. Applying an ample portion of ketchup to the burger and on her plate next to her fries, she looked over at Wells and toasted him, raising her sandwich in cheers towards him.

"*Bon appétit!*" she said, smiling.

Wells added some ketchup to his plate as well and nodded back in appreciation of the gesture. Catching the scent of seasoning, he suddenly realized how hungry he really was, and took a nice-sized bite out of the burger. He looked across the table at Max and noted that she was deep in thought. He took the opportunity to observe her noticing how her full lips seemed to kiss off every bite of fry. Not wanting to stare, he looked back down at his meal, and began eating as he realized just how stunning she really was.

Max knew he had been watching her. After chewing through three or four bites of her veggie burger, she dropped the sandwich back onto her plate and took a sip of her Diet Coke. "So?" she asked with a lopsided grin.

"So?"

"So, I believe I asked you, what's your story?"

"Oh, *that* so."

"Do you always avoid questions like this?" Her green eyes sparkled across the table mischievously.

"No, not usually, you seem to be bringing that out in me," he offered, teasing her. "I guess there's not a lot to say. My father was a cop, and you probably can guess the rest from there. Runs in the genes, I suppose. Grew up listening to his stories about chasing the bad guys and it seemed like the right thing to do. I graduated high school, went to college and studied forensics, then applied to the FBI academy right after graduation. Completed training at the academy and the natural place for me, given the forensics training was profiling. I love and hate it, if you know what I mean. How 'bout you? What's your story?" He leaned back, feeling pretty good that he'd just lobbed a question right back at her.

Max studied him for a few seconds, thinking. She *did* know what he meant, probably all too well. "Me? Not much to tell either, probably more of a rebellious story than following in the family footsteps. No cops on my side. Actually doctors, both parents. So, when I told them I'd applied to the police academy, they were, well, not so happy. I think they pictured me in children's medicine or something, and that's so far from who or what I wanted, it's like they never really knew me."

Biting into another fry, chewing slowly and swallowing, she raised her gaze up to his blue eyes. "Married, kids?" She had already noticed that he wasn't sporting a wedding ring, though it didn't hurt to ask. She'd seen him watching her on a few occasions, though this had happened a lot throughout her life, and with most men she seldom gave it much thought. This man was making her somehow feel more aware.

"No, not me. You?"

"Ha, no way, not ready for anything like that. Why haven't you? You seem like the marrying kind to me."

21

"Guess I haven't met the right woman. I know that sounds cliché, but it's true. Oh, and the job makes it rough – travel, crazy hours, at the drop of a dime, I'm off to somewhere else for another horrible crime. Not a lot of women want to share those end-of-day stories, much less have them wrapped around their children." He paused for a moment, as if wondering if what he just said was true.

"Your dad did it though, right? You turned out okay."

"He did, it's true, but the marriage didn't survive it. Parents divorced when I was twelve, had every other weekend with the old man."

"So it made you cautious about marriage. Natural, I guess," she acknowledged, finishing the last bite of her sandwich and sucking a drop of ketchup off her right index finger. Taking a napkin from the dispenser, she delicately wiped her hands and wiped a crumb from her lips. Then, taking another long draw on what remained of her Diet Coke; she pulled out some bills from her back pocket and plopped them down on the table. "It's on me. You ready to roll? Crime scene is waitin'."

Wells enjoyed watching Max clean herself up, as he sucked down the last of his tea. He thanked her for lunch and followed her out the door.

Walking back out into the sunshine, the pair were caught by the smell of salty air and the cool ocean breeze. They headed back up the block to where they'd parked the car and climbed in, with Max telling Wells to head down the street and then pull out onto the Coast Highway. The day was gorgeous, and people were enjoying the beach in a variety of ways – surfing, beach volleyball, jogging, and walks on the sand. Seagulls swayed over their heads in unison with a colorful kite here and there. Traffic was typical – stop and go at each of the lights, cars whipping in and out of the driveways of the homes crammed along the road, purchased by people eager to have front-row seats to the ocean view. Wells took in all of these observations waiting for the next set of instructions from Max who rode next to him seemingly doing the same.

They drove in silence for a while, and then Max directed him to turn right onto Mulholland Drive.

Here the road became more interesting, curving upward with sharp twists and turns. Wells imagined it would be quite a fun drive in the appropriate sports car. He forced the thoughts of the two of them driving along with the top down enjoying the day and was grateful when Max interrupted him five minutes into the climb up the mountain side, pointing through the windshield.

"Just ahead on the right is Camp Shalom. It's a retreat where organizations can have team-building challenges or have weeklong camping events – everything from horseback riding to ropes courses. Past that about a mile there is a big tree on the left. We'll pull off there and then hike in about 100 yards."

Wells nodded, noting the iron name over the entrance as they passed the camp. The area was devoid of traffic. There were rock cliffs and undergrowth all around, but there was no sign of human life or homes – no mailboxes or driveways indicating any homes sitting away from the road. It was the perfect place to leave bodies. This revelation made his stomach churn a little, the burger feeling heavy now. No matter how many crimes scenes he covered, he always had the same feeling.

"Pull over here," Max said, directing him to the tree and the small turnout on the opposite side of the road.

Signaling to the left and feeling a little silly about it, since there was no one on either side of the road to acknowledge the indicator, he pulled across the yellow lines and rested the car under the tree. Putting the car in park, he released his safety belt and pulled on the car handle. Max was already outside the vehicle and heading into the underbrush, so he followed quickly behind her. He certainly didn't want to get left behind up here.

"He dumped them out here, just down this incline and in the cluster of trees. No reason for anyone to ever find them, I suppose, if it wasn't for a couple of kids sneaking out from the camp to fool around. They stumbled on the site and about shit themselves. It was just after midnight when I got the call. Crime team unearthed all six of the bodies before dawn – shallow graves just deep enough to keep most of the animals away. Rain had unearthed a hand and the kid, male, tripped over it, fell down, flipped on the flashlight to see what the hell had grabbed him, and got the surprise of his life." Max paused for a moment as she took a glance at Wells, giving him a moment to take in his surroundings. Their eyes met and he nodded for her to continue. "I had hoped that we would get a break, given the number of bodies and the fact that they were all intact, but there was no DNA on any of them. They'd been fully cleaned up, clothes lying beside them in the grave. They were all still wearing their jewelry. One of them, victim number three, Jason Sampson, still had on his Rolex. The bleach had ruined it, of course, so we have a pretty solid time of death on him. It's pretty clear that robbery isn't the motive."

As she talked, Max continued to hike into the brush, dodging the brambles careful not to flip the branches back into Wells' face as she went. Suddenly, though, she came to a halt.

"Right here," she said, sweeping her arm in a semi-circle. "Laid out in a row, neatly placed very close to each other."

"Any signs of remorse when you found them? Hesitation marks in the cuts?" Wells asked. He already knew the answer but felt he had to ask.

If he'd overlooked something in the photos, this was the time to know about it.

She shook her head. "None, they were neat. Nothing to indicate that he'd loved them or had regrets," Max said knowing he would understand.

Wells nodded, looking around and going over the facts in his head. If the un-sub had felt bad about what he did, the victims would have been covered in blankets, or lying with their arms crossed over the chests, or had their eyelids closed. There would have been something that showed the killer had cared about their modesty or feelings.

"We know he spent some time with each of them, but there was no sign of sexual assault on any of them. This guy is pissed, inflicting a tremendous amount of pain, but I can't figure out what he's so angry about."

Wells was already heading to the car. "Okay, let's move on to the first victim's grab point and home. Then I want to drive by each of the others. In the order they happened." Wells hoped something about these facts would help confirm his preliminary thoughts and needed to be sure he had not missed anything in the case photos.

Joining him on the climb back out of the brush, Max briefly paused when she reached the car. She took one final glance around always hoping something here would speak to her. Opening the passenger car door she climbed in and buckled up. "Head on up Mulholland. First victim, Kelly Tompkins, lived in Calabasas. We'll go by her home. Then I'll show you the last place she was seen, which is where we believe he grabbed her."

Wells followed the curves of the road, feeling the engine pull a bit as they climbed higher before starting the drop back down into the valley. He'd heard of the fires up in these areas, and took in the thickness of the dry underbrush. That kind of stuff would no doubt fuel a fire very quickly, he thought. That led him to the next logical point, and he wondered if they would have found the bodies at all if there'd been a fire before the discovery.

Maybe that was the un-sub's hope. No bodies, less chance of being caught.

After considering the possibility for a second, though, he discounted it as too unpredictable. More likely, the un-sub didn't expect anyone to stumble into the brush on the hillside for any reason and felt safe placing the bodies there. They were never intended to be discovered. Still, though, it made it seem like the un-sub had some knowledge of the place. He filed that thought away and turned his attention back to the road in front of him.

With Max instructing, Wells wound the rental through a neighborhood until she asked him to pull over. He saw a large two-story home, adorned with a cactus garden wrapping around the front porch and up the side of the driveway, which led to a two-car garage. He guessed it to be about 3,000 square feet and imagined that the price tag for that kind of place in California was probably above a half a million dollars. She'd been well off, though he wasn't sure that had anything to do with her death.

On the house, the now-sagging crime scene tape was still attached to the front door. Obviously, no one was staying here at the moment. He remembered that the victim was married with two children. Her husband was an executive at some firm in Los Angeles and had been in Dallas on a business trip during the disappearance. His alibi was good, and he had been eliminated as a suspect.

Wells heard a dog barking next door and quickly determined that this was definitely *not* the grab site. The homes were too close together and too close to the street. There were dogs barking and children playing, and this particular house was too far down the road with signs indicating a security system to be a good spot. The un-sub couldn't have snagged her without someone seeing it happen. And according to the file, there hadn't been any sign of break-in or any reason to believe the un-sub had ever been in the home.

He continued past the home. There was no need to stop or go inside – he already knew there was nothing to see.

"Okay, next stop, Starbucks," Max said with a big smile, showing off her perfectly straight, white teeth. "Coffee sounds good, and we believe that's the grab spot. Kill two birds with one stone, eh?"

Wells returned the smile. Considering the types of detectives he'd worked with before, he was glad to find Max as casual as she was. A guy could definitely get a rougher deal. Wells navigated the rental onto Ventura Highway and followed her directions once again, spotting the familiar Starbucks logo up on the left in a strip mall next to the Albertson's grocery store. Going back over the case file in his head, he remembered that Kelly had last been seen at about 10 am at this location. He pulled up in front of the Starbuck's; in much the same way Kelly might have done the day she went missing. The parking lot was expansive and empty at this time of day – few vehicles and fewer potential witnesses.

Max was once again out of the car nearly before it could stop. Wells followed, and they headed into the coffee shop, where they were greeted by the barista.

The young man behind the counter was most likely a college student, based on his age and hairstyle. Max ordered a tall vanilla latte and turned to Wells with inquiring eyes, asking silently what he wanted to drink.

"Tall Pike, please," he said, slowly turning his gaze to the area around him. It was a typical Starbuck's, complete with coffees, cups, and pastries for purchase. The tables were aligned perfectly for the student or executive to drop in and log onto the wireless service. So what was so special about this place that their un-sub had decided to nab his first victim here?

Handing the kid a credit card, Wells flashed his badge and asked, "On a typical week day, how many people come through here around 10 am?" He'd already seen that there was only one person in the coffee shop now, a kid hammering away at a laptop in the farthest corner from the door.

"It depends," the barista answered, a little taken back by the credentials flashed in front of him. "But by then, most people have come through. It can be pretty quiet at that time, maybe one or two people in here at a time. The morning rush really dies off after nine o'clock," he finished, handing the Pike to Wells and turning to finish up the latte. Putting the lid on the cup and adding the cup sleeve he asked, "Do you need your receipt?"

"Yes, thanks. Oh, and one more thing, do you usually work the morning shift?" Wells added.

"I do, every day except for Friday and Saturday."

Wells knew it was unlikely that the un-sub as skilled as the one they were searching for would make simple mistakes, but he needed to see if anyone stood out. "Have you ever seen someone in here that was different, didn't fit in or stood out in some way?"

"This is about that woman, right?" The kid waited for a response, and when Wells didn't answer, rushed on. "Lots of people stand out, but mostly the students. You know crazy hair, clothes, and piercings. Everyone else that comes in usually wear business clothes. No one ever did anything that made me like freak out or anything. But I've already told the cops all that."

Taking the receipt, Wells thanked him and picked up his coffee. Max turned with him from the counter, but then suddenly swung back around to the kid.

"Is there anyone who always came in here then suddenly stopped?"

The kid thought for a second, then shook his head. "Not that I can think of."

Max thanked him and carrying her Latte in her right hand proceeded back out to the car. It was now four o'clock and the sun was starting to fade. Wells didn't expect to get much from this interview, but he was still disappointed.

"Next we head to Encino. Vic number two, Danny Alonzo, was snagged from outside his apartment. Least that's what we think. It was late at night, and he was returning from his night job. No one saw or heard anything. He left his job and dropped a co-worker off at his apartment before arriving home. We know he made it, because his car was in the drive, keys still in the ignition."

From there, the process was the same with each of the following stops – Max leading Wells through the order of events; showing him each of the locations where the victims had lived or were last seen. They returned to the LAPD building just after 8 pm, stepping out of the car and heading toward the building. Wells stretched his long legs and followed Max up the steps. It was dark now, and the night air was crisp with the ocean's cool edge that can only be felt in Southern California. In the distance, a siren rang out just as the doors to the building snapped shut, locking out the sound and the night air.

"What's next?" Max asked, heading for the coffee pot on the table at the back of the office.

"I'd like to take the files with me this evening, if that's okay. With any luck, I'll have a profile for you in the morning." Wells studied Max, wondering if she was going to deny him access to the files. He didn't know why she would, but people got funny ideas in their heads, becoming territorial especially when the FBI came in on a case.

Max regarded him for a minute, and then nodded, conceding that he could have the files overnight. "What time do you want to meet back up in the morning?" she asked.

Wells smiled, grateful for the time with the files to gather his thoughts and the idea that she trusted him enough to allow it, "Eight o'clock work for you?"

"Yep. Well, I guess that's it for tonight, then."

"It is, but tomorrow we'll have some direction. Remember, this is my specialty." He grinned, picked up the files, and then looked at Max. "You need a ride home or anything? It's pretty cool out there tonight, and you rode in on your bike."

Max tossed her hair back and laughed. "I ride that bike in every day, unless it is raining really hard. Thanks for the offer, but I'll be fine." Grabbing up her jacket and helmet, she tossed back the last of the cup of coffee she'd poured, crinkling her nose at the taste. "Eight o'clock sharp, then."

"Yep," he said. They turned and walked silently out into the night, each heading to their respective modes of transportation. Wells watched as

Max headed to her motorcycle and a twinge of concern began to mount for her. As the primary investigator for a serial killer case and a beautiful young woman, his chest pulled just a bit at the idea that the killer might target her as a victim.

Leaving the parking lot he followed the directions to his hotel and pulled into the Hilton Garden Inn parking lot where he had reservations. He hadn't checked in yet. It had been too early – he'd gone right to the police department to talk to them. Popping the trunk, he collected his overnight and laptop bags, looping the laptop bag strap over the roller bag he pulled it through the parking lot into the hotel lobby. He'd traveled a lot, lately, and this was becoming routine.

With the case and the events of the day still rolling through his mind he was a bit distracted when he was instantly greeted by the woman behind the counter.

"Good evening sir, do you have a reservation?" she asked, looking up over the reading glasses sitting on the tip of her nose, her wispy grey hair swept back in a bun.

He pulled his thoughts out of the memories of the burial site and smiled, "Yes I do, last name is Wells," he replied handing her his driver's license and FBI-issued credit card.

She looked at the computer and clicked a couple buttons. "I see your reservation here, Mr. Wells. Staying for two nights?"

"That's correct."

After typing in the computer for a few moments, she said, "Okay, you're all set," and slid the room keys to him in an envelope. "You're on the third floor, and here are two complimentary bottles of water for you to enjoy during your stay. Breakfast is served from 6:00 am to 10:00 am right over there in the Americana Grille."

Wells thanked her, tucked the water bottles into the pocket of his bag, and headed left of the reception area to the elevators, pushing the up arrow. Riding the elevator up to the third floor, he exited and was guided by the sign posted on the wall indicating that room 311 was to the right. He slid the room key into the key guide, a green light flashed identifying his key, the door clicked, and then he was in. Looking around the room he noted it was the same as every other hotel room he had stayed in recently.

Dropping his laptop bag onto the bed, he reached to flip on the light. He would only be in town for two days, but he quickly unpacked the items from his overnight bag, filling the closet with his things. As he entered the bathroom to lay out his toiletries he washed his hands, leaning down to rinse his face to wake himself up for the long night of reading.

And it was going to be a long night. He needed to go over every file again, to ensure that the profile was accurate. He couldn't afford to overlook any details. Having an accurate profile could be the difference between a closed case and a cold case, for Detective Max Nichols and the city of Los Angeles. This case was already starting to turn cold, as the killer's pattern looked like it had changed. The killing spree had been fast, with numerous murders in a very short span of time, and now it appeared to have suddenly stopped. Why? He hadn't put his finger on it yet, but he had a theory. With any luck, his work tonight would confirm his suspicions.

Chapter Five

After leaving the beauty college, Jack returned to his home to complete the application. He knew it was critical that he get the details correct. He wanted to make sure that there were no mistakes. Leading this new life included remembering certain aspects like a new social security number. He needed to keep it all straight. The name was the easiest part — he'd gotten to pick that — but the rest had to be provided, and newly memorized, while attempting to forget the ones he'd used for the previous thirty-five years of his life.

At six o'clock, he settled down at the kitchen table and began the tedious process of completing the paperwork. An hour later he realized that he was hungry. Jack understood the importance of keeping his strength and nutrition up. For a moment he remembered a time not very long ago, in a land with the sea nearby where none of that mattered. For a time he allowed himself to lose focus on such matters. More recently, of course, he'd found a new purpose in life. Remaining fit was important to him again. He needed to be strong and healthy to ensure he was worthy of his new life. Smiling, he rose and began to prepare a chicken breast, applying rosemary, salt, and lemon, and placing it in the oven to cook.

Next he began working on a salad. As he was cutting the lettuce into small pieces, the glint from the edge of the knife caught his eye. He paused, his mind flitting to Benz. Recognizing the feeling in his stomach, he told himself to push down the desire that had plagued him his whole life. It was too soon. The funds for his car hadn't yet been transferred, and until they were, he couldn't take care of the car salesman.

Thinking for a moment about what it would be like when he *could* take care of Benz, and the feeling he got from those thoughts, made him grow warm on the inside. Struggling to return his focus to the preparation of his meal, he decided a glass of wine would complement the food nicely. Reaching into the wine rack next to the pantry, he retrieved a wine glass from the cupboard and poured a glass of Pinot Noir. The red of the wine returned his thoughts to Benz and the others.

"You don't need to. There are other ways," he heard a small voice saying.

"I know," he said out loud, without even realizing. Then the light sound of the chicken sizzling in the oven forced his thoughts back to cooking.

After finishing his meal and straightening the kitchen, Jack settled back at the table with his second glass of wine and began studying the papers, double checking everything he'd written, and comparing each number and date to the driver's license he carried with the name Thomas Jennings on it. Pleased that the forms were accurate, he returned the documents to the folder Mandy had given him and set it on the counter next to his car keys. He'd be ready to leave in the morning, to meet her and complete the process.

Heading back to the master bedroom, Jack caught a glimpse of himself in the mirror, still wearing the pink tank top and white dress shirt. He thought he looked ridiculous and believable all at once. The clothes themselves made him want a shower, and he began stripping out of them. Tomorrow would be a big day. There were things he needed to prepare, and it would take some time to get everything in order before he started. He needed supplies, and the preparation had to be perfect.

Most importantly, he had to stay safe. If he got caught, they'd never be together again.

The shower felt good on his skin. It soothed him and made him feel cleansed of the person he was going to become. The person he had been living as most of the day. Thomas. Not that he had any issues with homosexual men. In fact, he could really care less about any of that. He believed in science, and how people lived their lives had never impacted him. He only cared what people would think of *him*. And Thomas would make people think of him exactly the way he needed them to.

This new persona would most certainly divert attention away from any questions. And that was the important part.

Before settling down into his bed to flip mindlessly through whatever was on the news, he decided that he would go down into the basement and survey the area again. Pulling on a T-shirt and the jeans he'd worn earlier, he left the bedroom and walked back through the house. Opening the basement door, he thought of the way he would conceal the entrance. It would be simple to confuse people about what was here. Basements were fairly rare in Oklahoma, so no one would think there was a basement at all, if he built the cover out properly. By the time anyone figured it out, he would be gone, and he would have his life returned to him.

When he opened the door, the basement felt dank, cool even. He figured that was good, and smiled slightly. Using a fictitious name, he had shipped some things to the house and those items were stored in the basement. Nearly everything was in his new identity now, allowing the trail from his past life to essentially stop in California.

In fact, he thought that finding Jack Tyler in Oklahoma and associating him with any of the things that he'd done in California would be nearly impossible. He was careful, always careful. His meticulous care forced him to plan ahead. He had most of the medical supplies he would need. He had practiced the procedure again and again. His medical background afforded him the sources he needed to secure the necessary supplies. He thought his plan would work exactly the way he envisioned. He merely needed to complete the basement and everything would be ready.

He could purchase the rest of what he needed for preparing the basement from any home improvement store. As a boy, he'd spent many summers helping his father and grandfather around the house, and those painful years had taught him many capabilities. He would use his basic carpentry skills to prepare the room for the restoration. It wouldn't take him long.

Looking around, he considered the various aspects of his plan, making sure that everything still made sense to him. The main room in the basement maintained the look of a small family room. A sofa pulled out into a bed against the wall to the right of the stairs, and a floor lamp sat next to the sofa. In the far corner was a walk-in freezer, which Jack had purchased when he first moved in. Because many Oklahoma residents had a heavy interest in hunting, it was common for people to have large freezers in their homes for storing meat. No one had asked any questions. The freezer settled tightly into the corner, measuring 6 feet high by 48 inches wide and 6 feet deep. He remembered special ordering it from Sears, and how narrowly it had made it through the double-door basement entry and down the steps. Despite the struggle to get it through the door and installed, it was perfect for what he intended to use it.

There were a few miscellaneous paint cans in the corner, and a small flat-screen TV mounted on the wall near the sofa. The only other furniture was a small kitchen-style table with two chairs. In the room to the left of the stairs was the utility room, which included the washer and dryer, hot water heater, and furnace. That entire section was bare of any flooring. The back room, which had been used for canning by the previous owner, was smaller. It would be perfect for lining with washable wall panels. There was already a sink in the room and plumbing out through the floor. In the middle of the room sat a canning table, previously used for preparing fruits and vegetables, approximately 6 feet long and 3 feet wide. He would have bought something similar if it wasn't already there. The table was made of stainless steel, and therefore it fit perfectly into the plan. It glistened with a shine, nearly as pristine as any operating room he'd ever used.

His mind flashed quickly through the numerous operations he had conducted, briefly reflecting on the feeling of cutting into a human body. Being a highly skilled, happily married, and successful surgeon had

33

afforded him a good lifestyle, and it had kept the dark side at bay. But then ...

"Jack? Jack, what are you doing?" He heard the voice in his head, and suddenly he was just a boy again, twelve years old and standing in the woods behind his father's home. The dead cat was still warm in his hands. The sound of her voice startled him, as he had been so focused on what he was doing, the feeling of the warm blood washing over his fingers, the knife shining in his fist.

"Hope! What are you ... I'm, I'm sorry." Suddenly tears streamed down his cheeks. He felt afraid – afraid of getting caught, afraid of Hope telling his parents. But mostly he was afraid of Hope being mad at him.

"Jack, why?" Hope looked from him to the cat and back again. The look on her face showed her confusion, hers eyes big and starting to fill with tears.

"I ... I ..." The tears continued to flow. Jack dropped the cat and fell to his knees beside it, turning away from the cat and turning his back to Hope, not being able to stand the look on her face. He squeezed his eyes shut and the tears washed down his cheeks.

"Jack?" she said as she slowly approached him. Looking down at the cat, she turned her head from it and focused on her friend, her best friend, the boy she had known and shared every waking moment with for as long as she could remember. None of this made sense. Had he done that horrible thing to the cat? Had he found the cat this way? "Answer me, Jack. What happened?"

"Hope, go away!" he shouted at her, pulling away, turning further from her eyes, those beautiful eyes, the eyes that knew everything about him, everything, except for this.

"No, Jack, I won't go."

"Hope, go, please go. I can't, I can't do this ..."

"Can't do what, Jack? I want to know what you did or why you did this. Tell me and we can fix it together." Hope held her ground, pleading with the broken and sobbing boy on the ground.

Suddenly he felt that there might be a chance. She wasn't running away. She said they could fix it together. How? Why? Could she mean it? Was it a trick? She had never tried to trick him before. Well, at least not over anything important. They were always tricking each other over silly things, but never in a mean way.

"I can't help it. It just happens to me," he stammered, stealing a glance her way.

"Jack, what do you mean it just happens? What happens?"

"I mean, I have these feelings and I can't stop them. The only thing that makes them go away is doing ... is doing *that*," he said, his eyes

34

darting to the cat lying on the ground in a matted heap of fur and blood. The intestines were hanging out of a gaping wound in the middle of its stomach, its eyes bulging from the head.

Hope looked down at the cat and then quickly averted her eyes. "Jack, I can help you. You don't have to do this. Not if you don't want to. There has to be another way. We'll find it together, and no one will have to know."

The tears beginning to subside, then, and Jack looked quickly up at Hope's face. Her eyes caught his before he dropped them to the ground in front of him again.

"How?" he asked softly.

"I don't know yet, but we'll figure it out. Come on, Jack, let's go. We'll clean you up and then figure it out."

Getting to his feet, Jack kept his eyes on the ground in front of him. He felt weak, his hands and knees shaking, and then he felt his body shudder. Suddenly he was trembling all over, barely able to control his body. Hope kept walking beside him, saying nothing until they reached the creek. Jack struggled to pull himself together and gain control of his trembling legs.

"Wash off your hands, Jack."

Without questioning what she said, he did as she asked, watching the blood wash away from his hands, downstream with the cold spring water.

Jack looked around, realizing he was still standing in the middle of the basement. The memories had come in a flood, and were bittersweet. Hope had taught him how to control his dark side. Together, they had built a plan and stuck to it, and it had worked. It had worked for a long time, and things were perfect. Being a surgeon had helped him. Until that day. The day of the terrible accident, and now he needed to focus on gaining his life back. Doing just that, he forced himself to look around the room one final time.

Deciding he was well prepared, he climbed back up the steps and closed the basement door behind him. Suddenly, he realized how tired he was. The memories had exhausted him, and now he could think of little more than getting to bed. Heading to the master bedroom, he stripped off his clothes, dropping them into the hamper inside the closet. Falling into bed without even turning on the TV, he fell further into a fitful sleep, his dreams filled with images that flitted through haunting faces of past victims, operating rooms, and the many successful surgeries, thankful loved ones, necessary body parts, sunny days during a happy time in California, gay men, and images of his beautiful Hope.

He woke feeling nostalgic and determined, and headed off to the shower to prepare for his day. For the next several months, maybe even up to a year, his lifestyle would make a drastic change. But he figured he'd already gone through the most difficult time. This should be easy by comparison. Reflecting on the past year, he thought that anything would seem easy. In that year, he'd gone from being a well-respected surgeon in Beverly Hills, a loving husband and father, to a widowed, angry killer. He had been forced through loss back to the tormented and broken twelve year old boy. Well not any more.

He could make the transition from that to a gay single man in a snap.

Forcing down the thoughts about how he got here, he let the shower cleanse him, shampoo and soap washing down his muscular body and into the drain. Jack allowed himself to imagine that the cleansing of his body was rinsing away the thoughts, forcing the memories back out of his mind and pushing the dark feelings away. Those feelings were starting to press down on him, making his skin nearly itch with the need he could never truly explain or deny, and he was glad to find some relief. The operating room had given him an outlet, but that was no longer part of his life, and the feelings were getting harder to control.

"Focus, Jack," he said out loud, almost startling himself. "Thomas," he restated, and smiled. His stomach growled reminding him it was time to get the day started with a healthy breakfast.

After again carefully choosing from his newly purchased wardrobe, Jack dressed and headed to the kitchen, where he whipped himself up a veggie omelet and washed it down with a Veranda Starbuck's coffee, made in the Keurig that occupied a space on the counter next to the refrigerator. Finishing up, he cleared the dishes and took a final look around ensuring the kitchen was immaculate. Returning to the bedroom, he stood observing himself in the mirror. Stunning, he thought, and collected his jacket remembering that the weather report yesterday had called for light rain. Once again, he returned back to the kitchen where he grabbed the folder with the completed application and snapped up his keys. He found himself almost chuckling at the thought of going to cosmetology school, but it was necessary, as this was how he'd meet the right kind of donors. The plan required up-close exposure to a variety of women. This program and new profession would ensure he had lots of variety.

Backing out of the garage into the daylight, he squinted. It was still early, only nine o'clock, but he wanted to get the application in to ensure he could get into the next class. He also had much to do. He wanted to get started today and needed to get the supplies for preparing the basement.

As he headed out past the Casino and read the neon sign, he noted that Tuesday was ladies night. For a brief moment, he thought this could also be a possible solution, but quickly discounted the idea, realizing that the women at the casino would never do. Gambling was often tied to smoking and drinking – behaviors that his Hope would never have indulged in.

Continuing through town, he found he was pulling into the Clary Sage parking lot with little recollection of how he'd gotten there. This made him a bit nervous, but he shrugged it off, getting out of the Toyota and heading into the lobby to find Mandy behind the counter as she'd said she would be. Her smile was immediate and genuine when she looked up and saw him approaching.

"Thomas, great to see you," she said.

"I've filled out the application, and I'm so excited. I can't wait to get started." He returned her smile, sliding the folder across the counter to her. "I think I have it all filled out correctly, including the financial aid parts."

"Well, I can look it over and call you if there are any issues, but it should be fine," she offered with confidence. "We're so excited to have you joining us here at Clary, and I know you'll love our program. Once we get your approval, I'll call to confirm your start date and time, okay?"

"Oh, girl, I know I'm going to love it here," Jack gushed, batting his eyes slightly and dropping his wrist, once again acting the role of Thomas. "If there's anything I need to do, just let me know. My cell number is on the application and that's the easiest way to reach me."

"Great, Thomas, don't worry about anything. I'll be in touch real soon," she replied, smiling.

He waved good bye and tossed a smile over his shoulder, then headed back out to his car, consciously applying just a little sway in his hips. Mandy watched him go smiling then shrugged and picked up his folder and started looking over the pages and keying them into the computer program to complete the application and enrollment process.

Jack climbed back into his car and headed down Sheridan to 41st street cutting the car up toward Home Depot, checking off the mentally prepared list of things he would need to get started. With only one week before his classes would start, he needed to get the majority of the building done on the basement quickly. When he started school, he'd be spending his time studying for his exams, and wouldn't have time to do any building. It was important that he pass his exams with flying colors, so that he could find work in his new trade quickly, without any unnecessary delays.

He also knew instinctively that he would not be able to control the dark impulses much longer. Staying focused on the end result was critical to ensuring he did not make any mistakes, there was no room for error if he was ever to have his life back.

Entering the home improvement store, he grabbed one of the flat bed carts with the vertical metal bars providing separations for large long building materials. Heading directly to the building materials aisle, pushing the flatbed along, and listening to the front wheel wobble as he walked, he began looking up and down the aisles for bath panels. Cutting through a few aisles, he finally found what he was looking for and, after thinking about the color, he chose pure white panels. He had previously measured the canning room and had determined that twelve 4x8 panels would allow him to completely cover the walls and ceiling. And make for easy cleaning. /he counted out twelve and loaded them onto the cart.

He also loaded up two sheets of plywood. Next, he gathered cases of bathroom caulk and construction adhesive. He grabbed two large rolls of duct tape, some rope, a circular and jig saw, a drill, and a hammer. He couldn't decide if he would need nails, so being unsure he put a box of ten penny and a box of small finishing nails on the cart too. Heading to the paint department he selected a gallon of off white interior that would match his kitchen, a gallon of acrylic outdoor deck paint and several large rolls of plastic drop cloth. He proceeded on to the hardware department, seeking out some heavy duty concrete bolts for securing the stainless steel table to the floor. Originally, he had thought it was not really necessary, but decided, better safe than sorry.

With each item he laid on the cart, he grew more excited. By the time he was ready to check out, he was nearly unable to focus. When the clerk asked him if he'd found everything, he pulled himself out of his excitement and felt his heart rate slowing back down. He nodded to her and laid his small items out on the counter for her to scan.

Then he noticed that the clerk was looking at him a bit funny, and realized how this must look. He had to remember that he was posing now as an obviously gay man. He smiled with a hint of girlishness at her. Seeming to have her suspicions answered, she giggled a little and continued to complete the transaction, accepting his cash and providing him his change. A few moments later, he was pulling the cart up next to the SUV. He would now get the chance to try out the folding seats and use the back area. Loading in the panels which barely fit, he was forced to load them at a slant from ceiling to floor across the back. He nestled all the other items in under and around them. Next, he took the rope and opened the package, securing the panels in as they would have to ride hanging out the back about a foot for the short trip across town.

Once certain that he had everything secured properly, Jack pushed the cart to the cart return area across the parking lot. After checking his load once more, he opened the door and entered the vehicle.

Inside, he sighed, knowing that the feelings surging inside him were going to get stronger and stronger. He would have to do something soon. It had already been over a month since he'd last given in to the need, and without his medical career and Hope by his side, there was only one way to satisfy the darkness inside. It was important that he fight this as long as possible. He also realized that losing control would put everything else at risk, and that he would never allow. Better to satisfy the craving than let it get out of control.

Chapter Six

Agent Wells had studied the information in every file until the wee hours of the morning. He'd spent his time marking the individual facts about each victim, location, and the order in which the bodies were laid out at the dump site. He'd then taken all of that information and related the aspects within the different situations. There weren't many factors that stood out, really, but he had completed the process. At about 4:00 am he sat back, looking at what he had.

Then, nodding to himself in a manner of gaining his own agreement for the profile he'd developed, he gathered all the gruesome photos and case contents, and put them back into their respective folders.

Looking over towards the nightstand next to the bed, he saw that the digital clock read 4:15, and yawned, thinking he could get two hours of shut eye before heading back to meet Max and deliver the profile. She would have her hands full with this one; there was no doubt in his mind. Slipping out of his clothes and sliding in between the cool sheets, he set the alarm on his phone for 6:30 and clicked off the lamp. Sleep came quickly, but behind his eyelids were images of gaping wounds and blood, so much so, that in his dreams he imagined the coppery smell.

The fitful scenes were blurred with pictures of a motorcycle-riding seductress engaging him in passionate lovemaking. His mind was drawn between the two scenes, the murderous images seemingly pulling him back in every time he began to allow himself the freedom to be seduced.

Then the alarm went off, and Wells glanced around, trying to understand where he was. It took a moment for him to get his bearings, but then he hit the clock for a seven-minute snooze, turned flat on his stomach, and went back to dozing. When the alarm sounded again, he clicked the off switch and snapped on the light swinging his feet over the side of the bed and onto the floor. For a brief moment, he thought of all the other feet that had hit the floor on this hotel room. Immediately resisting where his mind headed with that line of thinking he stood up stretching his long, muscular legs, crossed the room and pulled out the clothes he had packed for the day. After showering, which felt amazingly refreshing, he dressed and then finished the preparation for the day with a final review of the files he had left sitting on the desk across the room. Packing everything back into his briefcase, he scanned the clock. It read 7:07. Just enough time to grab something from the complimentary breakfast. Grabbing the hotel key, car keys, shouldering his gun holster and picking up his briefcase, he exited the room and proceeded to the elevators. He could already smell the savory scent of coffee and bacon.

After enjoying the omelet the cook proudly prepared and downing three, much needed cups of coffee, Wells headed out into the morning light. The California sun was up, but there was a light chill in the air, causing him to shudder slightly as he clicked the remote to open the car and place his briefcase inside. He glanced at the palm trees that lined the parking lot and gave himself a moment to think about how nice it would be to live here. Then he pushed the thought away. He'd never been a dreamer and now certainly wasn't the time to start.

When Wells arrived at the LAPD station, he noticed that the sleek motorcycle Max had arrived on just yesterday was already sitting in the space. He wondered if she'd had as restless a night as he had, and smiled slightly at the memory of a fitful two hours of sleep that had been filled with ugly images, washed away by visions of that seductress on the motorcycle.

"Stop it," he muttered under his breath, realizing that Max was that seductress.

Inside the doors, the guard at the desk nodded his approval for Wells to go on in. Apparently, seeing him with Chief Harding and Detective Nichols yesterday had been enough to give him free rein, at least for now. Heading to where they'd spent the day working yesterday, he found Max standing at the coffee machine, and felt a slight sense of deja vu.

"Good morning," he said, walking up to her.

She jumped, spilling a bit of coffee out onto the table in front of her. "Jesus, Wells, didn't your mother tell you not to sneak up on people?" she snapped.

"Oh, sorry, I thought you heard me walking up," he apologized.

Mopping up the mess, she shot him a look. "No, I didn't, and damn it you startled me."

He watched, amused, as she cleaned up the coffee and refilled the cup. After stirring in both cream and sweetener, she stomped back to the desk where they'd spent half the day yesterday. Filling his own cup up, he followed her, noting to himself that she obviously wasn't a morning person. He set his briefcase on the table, opened it, and pulled the files out, laying them down in front of her.

She settled down into her chair, her demeanor indicating that she'd shed the frustration from the earlier coffee incident. "So how was your night?" she asked, eying the files. "Did you make any progress on our unsub?"

"Yes, I'm ready to present you with a profile."

"Great, mind giving me a preview before we get with the chief?"

Wells looked at her and nodded in agreement at the recommendation, "Sure. After looking through the individual details on each case, it's obvious that each of the victims are random attacks. There's absolutely nothing in common with any of them, not a single connection. Their shopping, friends, texting, and phone habits are different. The obvious things we would expect to be present in terms of economic, race, gender, or social equities are all missing. The only connection is the manner in which the victims are eviscerated, and the very careful precision with which the incisions were made. The clean wound tracks were most telling to me. There was something there that I couldn't put my hands on at first, and in my initial assessment I kept feeling like I was missing something. I finally decided that I was probably wrong. I'd assumed that the clean wounds were about remorse, or possibly had been cleaned as a part of the process during the cleanup of the kill site. I had basically considered that the body was treated as just a component of the location, and therefore cleaned as a result. Since we haven't been able to see any of the actual locations where the murders took place, this is still a question, but I personally believe that the cleaning of the body is very intentional. It would seem impossible for that level of precision to happen in each case without intent. This brought me back to remorse, but the suffering each victim endured continued to leave me unsettled. I then realized that it's *more* than just intentional. Those wounds were intentionally cleaned as part of the ritual or act, not out of remorse, but out of requirement. There is an absolute need for perfection." Wells stopped as Max took in what he'd stated so far.

When she nodded, he continued. "I believe our un-sub is a white male, between thirty and forty years old. He's meticulous, and this leads me to believe that he is, or at least was, high functioning, likely a professional. Possibly in the medical industry, maybe even a doctor or vet. There's a precision to the incisions that an unskilled person wouldn't be able to execute, especially given the fact that each of the incisions were delivered perimortem, and there were no signs of sedatives or painkillers in the blood stream of our victims." He paused, swallowing at what he was about to say. Max already knew it, of course, but it didn't make it any prettier.

"The victims would have been struggling, yet the wounds are perfect. This means he's talented and enjoyed the process of killing his victims. He has no remorse and is driven to get inside the victims. There's no sexual motivation. He's an absolute narcissist, and his needs, goals, and plan are all that matter. Given the fact that no trace evidence was left at any of the scenes, he's been doing this for a while, and either has periods of inactivity, or he moves on to new hunting grounds. These victims are most

43

certainly *not* his first kills. Even with the first victim, the wounds showed no hesitation. That doesn't happen, and with this level of skilled execution, I think he's had a lot of practice. He's strong, remains in good physical health, and is easily accepted in the mainstream. There is likely some trigger that set him off on this specific spree. Find what that is, and you'll find your guy." He paused again before continuing with a final thought. "I'm concerned, though, that your un-sub has already moved on."

Max had been sitting watching Wells as he delivered all of this information. With the last line she raised her eye brows. "Why do you believe he's moved on?"

"He was progressing, with shorter time between his kills, and now he's off his cycle. If you look at the timeline, he was getting progressively quicker and quicker. Less time was elapsing between kills. He never went backwards, taking more time between kills. But now more time has elapsed since the last two kills. To be more specific, I counted the number of days between the missing person's reports for each of our victims and the estimated time of death to gain the time between kills. He was previously escalating. I believe this means he's stopped or moved on. He could have been picked up for some other crime, but I doubt it. If he stuck to his timeline, he should have taken another victim three weeks ago. Given the fact that we discovered his dump site, I think you'll have to work off the cases you have until he kills again, and we have no idea when that might be. Nor do we know *where* that might be, or where he might seek to dispose of them. He killed successfully for quite a while without being detected. I suspect finding him again will be a challenge."

Max's disappointment showed on her face. "So we've gone cold," she said with a certain level of frustration in her tone.

"I can't say for sure, but I'm afraid that is a possibility." He hated telling her this knowing she was eager to find the un-sub, and they both knew solving a cold case was much less likely.

She thought for a moment, and then grinned. "*Or* I can go looking for people in the medical profession that recently left the area, or have suffered some major event – divorce, death, things like that. Maybe I can get a list together."

Wells watched as Max displayed a new level of energy, smiling to himself. "Shall we go tell the chief?"

Shrugging Max stood up. "May as well go get it over with. He's going to be thrilled."

Chapter Seven

Getting back to the house Jack backed the SUV into the open garage about half way and then unloaded his supplies against the far wall. The basement did not have an outside entrance which was ideal for providing cover, but not for getting supplies through the basement doors. Jack remained unworried as they had delivered the freezer and gotten it down there so he knew it could be done. He made numerous trips slowly working everything through the narrow doors and down into the basement. Looking around he took in his payload including the medical and taxidermy tanning supplies. His eyes scanned over the bottles of bleach he had been purchasing each time he went to the grocery store. He had decided to buy a bottle per week rather than buying several at one time. He now had eight of them. Perfect. Heading back upstairs he reached for a Coke Zero from inside the fridge and guzzled some of the bubbly drink down. Then he headed back to the bedroom to change into some work clothes.

Once he had on a pair of work jeans and a long-sleeved t-shirt, he headed back downstairs to start the makeover on his new surgical room. Pulling out an extension cord, a carpenter's pencil, and tape measure, he opened the jig saw box and installed the smooth-edged blade, perfect for making clean cuts through the bath paneling. Measuring the first wall and then marking the panel accordingly, he worked away at installing the panels onto the walls, fixing them into place using the adhesive. Normally, he would have trimmed off the edges with a baseboard, but he didn't want the boards overlapping anywhere. He needed to be able to hose the walls and floors down, and know for certain he hadn't missed any areas.

Hours must have passed without Jack realizing, because the sound of his stomach growling broke through the work noises. It was the first time he actually looked around, and when he did, he realized that he had most of the panels cut and fixed to the walls. There was only one more bottom panel remaining. He had worked from the ceiling down, making sure everything flowed top to bottom for easy rinsing. He still needed to apply the caulk, but decided that could wait for another day, and headed up out of the basement after admiring his handy work one last time. *Oh yes, this was going to be good*, he thought. This was the perfect place to complete his work. He felt his stomach tighten; not much longer now, and he would be reunited with Hope.

When he got upstairs, he took a look at the clock on the oven and was surprised that it said 8:33. Where had the day gone? He didn't feel like cooking a big meal, and fixed himself a pre-made salad instead, with a few

45

raw vegetables and some cheese. He made a conscious note to remember to eat a little better tomorrow, as he needed his strength. He also needed to get some real exercise tomorrow. He liked to stay in shape, and had been letting himself slip lately. He had a lot to do over the coming months, and he wanted to be at the top of his game for Hope. He couldn't let her down. Not this time.

Tomorrow he would pick up the cashier's check for the sale of the car and deposit the funds under his new identity, so that no one could trace a relationship from his old identity to his new. Money wasn't really an issue, of course, as he had plenty of money from the sale of his home in California. Besides that, moving from California and the type of lifestyle he'd led there as a prominent surgeon, and relocating to Oklahoma meant he had a lot more money than he reasonably needed here. He'd moved the funds around over the last several weeks, cutting the connection with his previous identity. He had researched and spent a good deal of time learning how to manage accounts off shore in the Caymans. Once the car transaction was complete, Jack's identity would simply cease to exist. There would not be a single paper trail leading to him in Oklahoma. He'd made sure of that. He didn't think anyone was looking for him, but if they were, he didn't think they'd ever find him here. Dr. Jack Tyler had simply disappeared.

Finishing off his salad, he suddenly realized that he was very tired, and headed into the bathroom to shower off the adhesive smells, sawdust, and dirt. When he was done, he settled into his boxers, slid between the sheets, and clicked on the TV, flipping through channels until he found the news. He sat replaying his day with nothing really capturing his attention until they started a story about a serial rapist sexually torturing women across the city.

He was repulsed by this. What kind of man took sex from women? He could picture the man sneaking in through windows or doors, though, and he felt a stirring in his own groin. But his excitement wasn't sexual in nature. The stirring he felt came from imagining himself taking one of those women and bringing her here to be with him, feeling inside her body as the life in the organs began slipping away. But he'd never have sex with any of them. That would be cheating.

When he started paying attention again, the story had ended and the newscast had moved on to the weather. The report said it would be windy tomorrow, but nothing remarkable; no tornado warnings or anything that would disturb his plans. Before nodding off, he wondered when he would hear from Mandy about his first day of class. He hoped it was soon.

46

Chapter Eight

"Well, damn it," Chief Harding shouted, slamming his big fist down on his cluttered desk. "You mean to tell me that this bastard has beaten us?"

"Sir, with all due respect I think we can still get him," Max stated with more conviction than she actually felt.

"Chief Harding, I think it's worth it to apply a couple of resources to check out the medical angle. While it might be a long shot, it's still your best chance at finding this guy. I'm officially here until tomorrow, and I'd like to offer my help until I leave," Wells added.

"I don't like it at all; Nichols, but I'll give you the support of our forensics database analyst for one week. Then you're off this case and onto an active one. If Wells is right, we're wasting our time, and I can't afford to have detectives working cold cases." the chief finally answered.

Max nodded, knowing not to push the offer. One week; that meant she had to work fast. If she could uncover any leads at all against the profile Wells had provided, she might be able to get Harding to let her stay on the case. Without any leads, though, she knew for sure that this was a cold case. And if that happened, it would be moved out of her department. Max had certainly worked many cases, but for some reason this one was important to her. Usually there was so much more to go on, at least a minor trace of DNA, but with this one the killing was methodical and the burial site told Max there was something different about this case. She couldn't shake these feelings and because of them she felt compelled to see it through to an arrest.

"Don't make me regret this, Nichols," Harding boomed at her, waving his hand and dismissing the two from his office.

After leaving the office they preceded down the hall until they were out of hearing range, "Well, that went really well," Max said.

Wells found her demeanor to be more sarcastic after dealing with the chief. The man was gruff and barely gave opportunity for either of them to speak. "He's just being realistic," he stated trying to defuse the situation a bit

"I know, and that means I have to work fast."

"Well, let's get after it," Wells said, slapping his hands together. "I'm all yours for the next day. Where do we start?"

Max led Wells down the hall and onto the elevator. They went up two floors, where they found a young man, apparently rocking out to some good tunes through ear buds properly poked into each ear. As they approached, he unplugged his right ear and raised his right hand as if asking them to stop.

"Oh no you don't, Nichols," he said to Max before she'd said a word, "You're not coming up here batting those big green eyes at me and thinking I'm going to stop, drop, and roll like I always do. I've got my orders, and that's not going to work this time." He shook his head, but Max smiled.

"Aw, come on Bobby," she started. Wells watched her obvious eye batting while she continued as if she hadn't heard him. "This time it is different. This time I have the chief's support. I've got one week, and I need you to work your data magic."

"Man, here we go. Okay, what do you need?" Bobby offered, surrendering easily.

Max grinned and gave him that *don't pull my chain* look. "First we need to see a list of any medical licenses that *haven't* been renewed or were suspended in the last year, including veterinarians. Keep it to Los Angeles County to start with. We can narrow our search after we see what this pulls up. We also want to research medical professionals who've gone through a divorce or loss of an immediate family member. If we can find people who're on both lists, that narrows our search, right there."

The young man bounced as he started pounding the keyboard in front of him, still bobbing to the music in his left ear. "You got it, Detective, give me a few hours. I'll let you know what I find as soon as it's available." He popped the ear bud back into his other ear, dismissing them, and went to work.

Max looked at Wells. "What do you think the list will net?"

"It may be quite long, honestly, and we'll have to really narrow it down. Look for people who live closer to the grab or dump site. If we get lucky and there's crossover to both lists, we could have something really solid to work with. Once we have that list, I can forward it over to the FBI and have the names run through our database. I'll check for any federal crimes, just to see if there's anything else we might have overlooked."

Max nodded. "Bobby said it'll take him at least an hour, want to grab lunch?" she asked, looking at her watch. She was surprised to see that it was already 12:30, but that made it a good time to grab a bite to eat.

"Sure, lead the way."

They headed back down the elevator and out to the parking lot, where Wells had parked in visitor parking near the front of the building. The sun was shining and the spring air felt nice and warm. Wells sucked in the warmth and raised his face to the sun, taking it all in, while Max watched him, enjoying the fact that he truly seemed to be soaking the air, breeze, and sunshine into his tall, muscular frame. As much as she hated to

48

admit it, she enjoyed his company, and his story yesterday had made her want to relate to him, though it seemed they'd come up a bit differently. His hair was shining in the sun now, and the dark curls that just barely swept the nape of his neck moved softly with the breeze. She found herself wanting to wind her fingers into those curls, and felt herself blushing at the thought.

Agent Wells drove through downtown, passing City Hall as Max directed him to Engine Co No.28 – a downtown favorite of hers that offered American dishes, including a special spicy fry recipe. The ride in the car on the way over there was quiet; there was an obvious attraction in the air that neither of them could deny, though neither wanted to talk about it either. The silence was only broken by Max directing Wells on each required turn. Each took quick sideways glances at the other when they felt it safe to do so without being noticed. But neither said anything.

Once in the restaurant and seated in a comfortable booth, Wells broke the silence, "What's on your mind, Detective?"

Surprised by the directness, Max felt off of her game; she was used to being the one in control. She paused for a moment, and then decided to talk about the case first.

"I'm trying to get my head around why our un-sub would leave. It seems to me that if there's a trigger to start his killing spree, there must be a trigger to stop."

"It could be the discovery of the dump site," Wells offered.

"Maybe, but my gut says there's more to it than that. I'm sure we're missing something here, it's just a matter of figuring out what it is."

Silence wrapped around them again. The server approached, a big strapping man that looked less like a server and more like he could have been a firefighter on a real engine. After taking their orders, he disappeared, reappearing almost immediately with their drinks. Once they were alone again, Wells eyed the beautiful detective across from him and continued the conversation.

"I don't believe that's what you were actually thinking, though it *is* a good thought."

Max huffed. "Really, Mr. Smarty Pants, and when did you get to be a clairvoyant?"

"Okay, maybe not. Well, let's talk about something else then. Yesterday you told me that your parents were disappointed in your career choice. How do they feel about it now?"

Studying him closely, the detective wondered where this was leading and how much she would share with him. He was already making her feel things she hadn't felt for a long time, and she had no idea why. They'd only spent a day together, so she was chalking it up to raw physical chemistry and convincing herself that she shouldn't allow sexual attraction to get in the way of reason. That meant giving him the safe, careful answer.

"My parents are okay with it. I think they may even be a little proud, but it took a major crime to shift their thoughts."

"How so?"

"Two years ago I was on a child abduction case. After a really difficult search, we recovered the child. A child everyone thought for sure was dead." Listening intently Wells recalled his time on the flight to California. He had studied her profile and a brief case history on the plane, and knew there was more to the case than she was offering. She'd nearly died in the recovery of that child. He'd read it carefully, taking in every part of the case, fascinated that she'd given that much to the case. Of course the file hadn't said that she was female. Everything in the file had led him to believe that Detective M. Nichols was a male. He should have pulled full name and photo. He would not make that mistake on any case in the future. It was always important to know as much going into a situation as possible, and he had failed to do that this time.

"Impressive. Sounds like a great outcome."

"Yeah, we were all pretty excited. Handing that boy back to his mother was worth everything we went through trying to find him. Getting a death penalty conviction for the kidnapper was icing on the cake."

Agent Wells started to respond, but the waiter appeared with their food, setting it down in front of them, the aroma reaching up and teasing his senses. He knew it was due to lack of sleep, but he felt like he was starving. This always seemed to happen as if his body naturally knew it needed more fuel.

"Wow, this looks fantastic." He nodded to the heap of meatloaf and spicy fries on the plate in front of him, then glanced at her plate. "And so does yours," he laughed, looking at the matching plate sitting in front of her. He hadn't noticed it before, but they'd ordered the same thing.

Max gave him a flirtatious, approving smile, and before she realized it, her eyes had locked with his in a rich, blue, green reflection of mutual attraction and lust. Breaking the gaze, she looked around the restaurant. "Cool place, huh?"

Wells grinned, realizing that for just a moment he'd rattled her strong resolve. His eyes followed her gaze around the packed restaurant, where nearly every table was loaded down with a variety of city and business workers from the nearby buildings.

"Yes very cool. It is all very...," he paused slightly, hoping to draw her gaze back to him, "...interesting. Especially the people."

Looking again into his eyes, Max realized they needed to stop this one way or another. They were never going to get any work done otherwise. So in her typical fashion of absolute directness, and before she could stop her mouth, she blurted out, "Agent Wells, what's happening here?"

Wells was taken by surprise, not used to a woman addressing something so directly. He took a bite of the savory meal, buying some time to think of the appropriate answer. He matched her gaze, which hadn't wavered since she asked the question.

"I'm not sure, Detective Nichols," he said, playing on the formality in which she'd asked the question. "I can only say that I'm here on professional business, and have nearly concluded what I was sent to do, but I always enjoy the excitement of a new case and helping in the possible apprehension of a serial killer. But in this case …" He paused, taking a drink of his iced tea. "I can also say that I'm enjoying this case for other reasons as well. I know that I'll be disappointed when I return to Washington and I find myself hoping for other opportunities to see you." Leaning back, he waited to see what she would say.

"Wells, this is ridiculous. We've known each other for barely thirty-six hours," she recanted almost chastising him as if his assessment were not mutual.

"I know that, Max. But you asked, and I can only tell you how I'm feeling and what my thoughts have been. And frankly, I can see in your face and eyes that you feel the same way."

"I … I … I don't know what I feel. Look, let's try to just stay focused on the case. You leave tomorrow, and we'll probably never see each other again."

"I know." Wells acknowledged that fact, his eyes dropping to his food.

They continued eating their meals in silence, both enjoying the food less now. When neither of them was able to clear their plate of food, Wells paid the bill and led her back out into the sunlight. The day was truly beautiful, and for a minute they stood on the sidewalk looking at one another. After a moment, a smile crept up on each of their faces. Max considered his comment, *"find myself hoping that I'll have other opportunities to see you."* Her stomach fluttered at those words, and she fought to not allow them to control her.

Back at the headquarters, they took the elevator back up to see what Bobby had discovered. When they arrived on the second floor, he greeted them with a smile, filled with extra-large white teeth.

"Well, my favorite and most beautiful detective returns," he tossed out, making Wells laugh out loud. "I have some interesting data for you right here on this thumb drive. Let me show you." Popping the thumb drive into the computer USB slot, he once again started hammering away at the keys of his computer. "Okay, here's the deal. There are a *lot* of doctors in Los Angeles County," he said dragging out the word lot. "I sorted the data first by active and by city. There are several tabs on the files for you to parse through and manipulate. The next tab contains all of the inactive licenses. I included the date the license expired, was suspended, or was revoked. Tab three includes some info on malpractice suits. I threw that in since it might mean something. I separated out nurses, vets, techs, and hospital workers. I did *not* include in my search janitors or housekeeping." He paused for a moment, waiting for them to get the joke, and then sighed at the silence. "Even without those, it's a very big number, but I figured with the city reference I allowed you to narrow those down if you want to focus in on certain areas."

He looked between the two of them, then continued, "Using the same list, I also included the information you wanted for recent losses of immediate family members." Finally, he handed the flash drive over. "I hope it's what you want."

"It's perfect, Bobby," Max said. Then, looking at Wells, she shrugged. "Looks like a long night ahead."

"Indeed it does, so let's get started," he quipped.

Thanking Bobby for the thumb drive, Max and Wells returned to the first floor, planning to set back up in the room they'd used the day before. As they walked through the station, a few fellow officers gave out their hoots and hollers to Max and sideways glances at Wells, as if sizing him up. Wells did not appreciate the behavior, but he noticed that Max dished it right back. He also observed that she was obviously well liked, recognizing that the teasing was only offered to those who fit in, and she clearly did. He expected that the kidnapping case she had spoken of earlier helped solidify her place on the team. She had gone to great lengths and put herself at risk to save that little boy, but she had done so in a manner that followed protocol and reduced risk for others. That part set her apart from your run of the mill detective. This woman had Hollywood beauty, sex appeal and stones. All of these attributes made it incredibly difficult to get her off his mind.

After putting on a pot of coffee, Max took the files on the drive and emailed them over to Wells so they could each work the files separately, which would allow them to work more quickly. Pulling up the first file, Max took note of the fact that there were over two thousand physicians alone. The number was daunting when she considered all the other medical professionals and veterinarians. It seemed that they'd be looking for a needle in the haystack.

A second pretty alarming finding was that the divorce rate in the medical profession was very high, with around fifty percent of the names marked as divorced, some of them twice. They would definitely have to break the data into more sub groups.

"Let's do this to start with," she suggested. "Focus on removing all the females and put them onto a separate tab. We'll only look at them if it feels like we're not getting anywhere with the males. Then break the men down to those divorced within the last year, and cross reference to see if anyone from *that* list is on the list of expired or suspended licenses. You work on the males with license issues and I'll work on the males with relationship issues. Then we can compare our files. Deal?"

Wells was scanning the data as she talked. "Deal," he said, nodding in agreement. He was already starting to parse through the data, setting up filters so that he could sort out the males versus females.

It took some time, but eventually they had the list down to a total of sixteen hundred. They filtered that by divorced and unmarried, and brought it down even further to just over a thousand. The file with males, who had suspended, revoked, or non-renewed licenses took them to just under three hundred. Now they had some data to compare.

Max got up to refill her coffee and grabbed Wells' cup as well, offering to refill his too. He looked up. It was the first time they'd paused in nearly three hours. They were now ready to really get into some data, and it was a good time to take a break.

"Thanks," he said, accepting her offer. He caught her eye briefly and felt the slightest increase in his heart rate, recognizing that familiar feeling from his dreams the night before.

She returned a moment later, setting the coffees down on the table and leaning over his shoulder to see the file he was working. He now had the data lined up to compare license numbers as the single point of reference. He decided to run a pivot table against the two fields and see if he got a count in each one, and their eyebrows went up when they saw the data showed a total of nine matches for recent divorces and licenses that were no longer valid for whatever reason. Looking through the list, they noted one was a chiropractor, and decided to drop him off the list for now.

Eight remained on the list, none of which matched up to recent family losses or malpractice suits.

Still, they decided to follow the same process for all the other medical professions, to get a complete list of people in the medical profession, who could have the skills required to commit the murders. Starting back in, they found this data even more challenging as the gender was not listed in every case. Given the profile was a male un-sub they would want to separate out the males from females. They agreed to separate out those that they could not identify in the data quickly and realized that if they needed to, they would simply have to go through it later one by one.

They were halfway through the process when Chief Harding came through the door, taking up the whole frame. "What are we learning Nichols? Any luck with data being a guide?" His gruff voice and scowl displayed his frustration, which obviously hadn't subsided since hearing the news that the killer had likely moved on.

"We're narrowing in on a few people to look at, sir. Our focus right now is on medical professionals with recent losses, malpractice suits, or other life events that might be triggers to have set him off on the spree," she answered quickly.

"And how is *that* coming along?" he barked, looking between Max and Wells.

Wells jumped in at that point. "Slow, but our goal is to have some solid leads for Detective Nichols by the end of the day."

"Good," the chief barked. "Nichols, you've got one week. Find the bastard."

Before Max could reply, the doorway was empty, the chief having moved on.

Wells noted the wrinkle on her brow and said, "Hey, it's a long shot, but we're going to give it our best."

Max looked up, leaned back, and stretched, thinking. Glancing over Wells' head, she saw that the clock on the wall showed 7:30. "Let's take a break; I need a change of scenery. Oh, and what time is your flight in the morning?"

Wells studied her for a minute. "A change of scenery, eh? Okay, how about this? Let's move this effort to my hotel." Before she could say anything, he held up his hands and offered an explanation. "Look, there's room service, plenty of room to work on these files, and we get out of here. That way we can work right up to my 8:45 am departure time."

As he was saying all of this, he was trying to convince himself that capitalizing on the extra time and the luxury of room service was all he had in mind. He finally decided that whatever else he had on his mind didn't matter, as they actually *had* to keep working. And they needed food. Convincing himself of that, he further concluded that his idea was a practical suggestion, nothing more.

Max was about to protest, but then stopped herself. "Okay, Wells, but no funny business," she said, giving him a look that said 'don't you dare,' while wagging her index finger at him.

"I promise." Wells smiled, making an X with his right index finger across his heart. "I'll drop you back by here to get your bike on the way to the airport."

Max began gathering up the files. Wells cleared away the cups and pushed the chairs against the metal table. She joined Wells as they headed towards the front door. Stepping out into the night, the air was refreshing after being in one place for the past six hours. Max felt the stiffness in her body and observed Wells stretching his back, apparently working the soreness out. As they climbed into the car, they started talking about the eight physicians on the narrowed-down list. There were two that had stood out most, as their offices or homes were in closer proximity to the dump site. One was in Woodland Hills, the other from Malibu. Either of those could have easily driven up from the freeway or Pacific Coast Highway to dump the bodies.

"You know, I think we should look at the make and model of their vehicles, as well as their family history. The un-sub will have had a vehicle that could transport a body. It's weak, but it could help narrow the search. Plus, family history may tell us something."

Wells glanced over as he continued to navigate the car towards his hotel, but agreed with the thought. "Worth a look. Why don't you call Bobby and have him run them. In fact, have him run all of them while he's at it."

Max was already dialing Bobby on her cell phone. She spoke into the phone, describing the added data she wanted, waited a moment, and then thanked him, saying something about him being a doll. Then the call ended.

"He said he should have it in about an hour. He'll email it over as soon as he does," she told Wells.

Pulling into the hotel parking lot, Wells found a space that allowed him to park close to the door. They walked together into the hotel lobby and headed past the front desk while nodding a greeting back to the hotel receptionist. At the end of the hall on the right was the elevator, and Wells punched the button to take them up. Once in front of the room, Wells scanned his key card and opened the door, standing back to allow Max to enter first.

Walking in, Max looked around the room and suddenly realized that they were alone in a room with a bed. Heading over to the desk, intentionally ignoring the bed, she set her computer bag down and started setting up. Wells presented her with the room service book and turned the page to the menu.

"I say we order a variety of stuff we can snack on, and a fresh pot of coffee," Max said, looking over the menu.

"Sounds great, go ahead and order." Wells was already unpacking his laptop bag, ready to get back to work.

After ordering a variety of appetizers and the coffee, Max hung up the phone and sat down at the desk. Pulling back up the files, she began pouring over the data again. Wells joined her on the opposite side of the desk, and both worked in silence until a knock at the door brought them up out of the data. Wells went to the door and led a young man in pushing a cart displaying several platters with warming lids on them. The smell of cheese poppers and coffee immediately filled the room. By now it was 8:30 pm, and Max realized how hungry she really was. Lunch seemed long ago and neither of them had finished their meal after the sensitive conversation.

Setting the food onto the counter where the in-room coffee maker sat they each filled a plate with a few items and stood for a minute marveling at the view outside the window. As Max turned back towards the desk, Wells took her plate from her and set it on the desk. Her eyes raised up to meet his, and as he stood looking down at her, he could not resist the temptation of the thoughts that had been floating through his conscious and sub-conscious mind, wrapping her in his arms he drew her to his chest. Before she could collect herself, he was pressing a kiss onto her mouth. The feel of his lips and his hands on her lower back took her breath away. She pushed against his chest, but he held his grip until she relaxed into the kiss. Max responded to the gentleness, then, and the kiss turned passionate as she felt her lips part to accept the soft sweep of his tongue. She wrapped her arms around his neck and drew him in closer, enjoying the strength of his arms and his firm body against her own.

Finally pulling back, Wells looked into her eyes again and smiled at her beauty. Max returned the smile, but just as Wells leaned down to kiss her again, his cell phone rang, the face displaying FBI HEADQUARTERS. He picked up the phone, grimacing.

"Agent Wells here," he said quietly.

Max listened to the one-sided conversation as Wells recanted what they had thus far discovered, apparently bringing his director up to speed. She heard him say, "I'll see you tomorrow afternoon," ending the call and turning to face her.

Before he could say anything she said, "We should get back to work."

There was an air in the room as they settled back into their chairs, but neither spoke of what had just happened. Each choosing instead to begin the tedious process of sorting out the data the way they had agreed. They continued to nibble on the appetizers, occasionally sneaking glances at each other. At ten o'clock, they had more data to merge and compare. This time, the list they got was much longer, including over seventy people as suspects.

Sighing, Max pushed back from the desk.

Wells sensed her frustration. She was facing a daunting task of having to work through a huge list of suspects in less than one week if she was going to gain her boss's approval and keep the case active.

"So, let's prioritize the most likely un-sub first, using everything we know about our guy. That way when you start working the leads, your chances are better."

Continuing on, Wells outlined the profile again and focused in on the triggers that might start a vicious spree. "He's angry, literally ripping these people apart, but meticulous in his process and precise with his cuts. Talented even. He also cleans up afterwards, leaving no trace of evidence, making him an organized and methodical killer. So he's rational. But something set him off and something else made him stop, or I'm totally wrong about the timeline being meaningful."

Feeling energized by Wells' input, Max started reprocessing some of the data. "I think doctors, or more specifically surgeons, would be our most likely candidates. If you think methodically, they have to have a lot of training, due to the nature of their jobs, and the precision of the incisions seems to point that way. I would think vets next, for the same reasons, followed by surgical assistants and vet techs."

Wells was nodding in agreement, rising from his chair and leaning over her shoulder as she worked. He could smell her hair and her skin, which smelled faintly of vanilla. Every time she moved, his senses were assaulted with her fragrance. It was intoxicating, but he forced himself to concentrate on what she was saying. They had work to do, after all.

After several different manipulations of the data, Max remembered that Bobby was going to be sending over a file. Checking her email, she saw that he'd already done so. Pulling the email up, she began comparing some of the names on her list. Nearly all of the surgeons had either a sports car or a SUV. Some had both. The list became less specific as she drilled further down, using the logic they'd discussed.

Wells had sat back down. After two hours of working on this he pulled his chair up beside her, and they leaned back in their chairs, staring at the computer screen. They had a new list now. It was prioritized according to profession, geographical proximity, and possible triggers, and was sorted from 1 to 112. There were, of course, more if these didn't pan out, but this was the starting point. Max would have to work through each one of these, hopefully finding something that helped her identify her un-sub. It was a start, and more information than she'd had that morning.

Wells and Max looked at each other and smiled. For the first time today Max felt like there was a possible solution to finding the killer. Their eyes locked, and the kiss from earlier seemingly still burned her lips.

Standing up, Wells poured two fresh cups of coffee and handed one to Max. Their hands touched briefly, and she felt a fluttering in her stomach. Thanking him, she took it and drank the warm liquid. It was now almost one o'clock in the morning, and she was beat. Tomorrow was going to be another long day if she wanted to find this guy. Setting her coffee aside, she looked up at Wells, she knew she should leave now, but she was not able to pull her eyes away from his.

"Not much more we can do tonight. I guess I should go and let you get a couple hours of sleep."

"Max, we left your motorcycle at headquarters," he reminded her, smiling.

"Oh, damn, I'd totally forgotten that. I'll just call for a cab."

He shook his head. "Look, stay here with me. I'll sleep on the sofa, and you can have the bed. We'll both get some rest, and then I'll drop you off in the morning." He meant what he was saying, but after the kiss they had shared earlier, he wasn't sure he could live up to his words. His nostrils were still filled with the smell of her hair, which had not left his senses from earlier.

She shook her head back. "I really don't think that's a good idea. I really should go," she said, starting to gather up her laptop.

Moving around behind her, Wells took her hands from the computer bag and turned her to face him. "Stay with me. I want more time with you." He pulled her in to him and began kissing her this time more deeply, more passionately.

Resisting at first, she tried to pull herself away, but found that she couldn't stop the desire that was welling up inside. Her body was responding to his touches, his kiss, and she found herself pulling him in closer. His hands gently drifted over her body, stopping and pressing on her lower back to connect their bodies completely. She could feel his passion pressing against her, and this sent an electric charge through her entire body. She heard a soft moan, and then realized it was coming from her. Her lips parted, and she returned the probing kisses. His hands came up into her hair and gently caressed her neck.

Leaning back, he looked deep into her eyes, seeing the desire they shared. He began unbuttoning her blouse and slowly moved her to the bed, laying her down gently and sliding his warm, muscular body against hers. He enjoyed the contrast in her femininity and incredibly toned body. Slowly they removed each other's clothing, and after he produced a condom from his wallet, they spent the next couple of hours engaged in sensual lovemaking. At first, their connection was timid, but it became erotic and finally settled into gentle and tender caresses and kisses, as they repeatedly brought each other up and over the edge.

At about four o'clock, exhausted from their hours of research and passion, they began to doze, their arms and legs intertwined.

Six o'clock came all too soon. Wells propped himself up on one arm to gaze down at Max, taking in her beauty. Her hair was tossed, and a wavy lock swept across her brow. Pushing it back with one finger, Wells gently kissed her lips and then unwrapped himself from her and slid out of the bed.

She woke as he pulled away. "Where are you going?" she whispered.

"Shower."

"Um, may I join you?"

"I'd love that."

Slipping from the covers and wrapping a sheet around her body, she followed him into the shower. They spent a few minutes taking in the beauty of each other's bodies in the light of the bathroom. After lathering each other in playful fun, they rinsed and helped towel each other down.

"No fair, you actually have clean clothes to put on," she complained at him, gathering up the clothes she had come in.

Getting dressed in silence, they each packed away their work and belongings and prepared to leave the room. Then they stood facing each other, just inside the room door. Wells started to say something, but Max placed her finger over his lips and kissed him gently.

"I know the game and so do you," she whispered.

Wells knew she was right but hated the idea that he might never see her again. They each grabbed a bagel from the hotel breakfast area and headed out into the day. The air was crisp outside; the morning sun had not yet taken the chill off. Max hugged her body as if to lock out the morning cold as they drove back to the headquarters where her motorcycle was parked. There was a moment of joint silence before she leaned over and gave him a quick kiss on the cheek. He felt the warmth of her lips and knew he wanted much more, but could not for the life of him picture how to work that out. Feeling frustrated with the circumstances, he looked down at her, taking in her green eyes and trying to read what she was feeling.

"Will you let me know if you catch your guy?" Wells asked, studying her face.

"Sure thing. Take care, Agent Mark Wells." Max got out of the car, pulled her motorcycle jacket tight, strapped the laptop bag to the motorcycle seat, and pulled on her helmet. As she slid her leg over the bike, she waved her fingers at Wells in farewell. Then she rolled the bike away from the parking strip, and fired the starter button. With a quick tap of the gear peg, she pulled away and tore out of the parking lot.

Wells sat staring out the windshield and watched her go, not wanting to accept the fact that he might not ever see her again. Finally, he put the car back in drive and pulled away from the Los Angeles Headquarters, on his way to LAX to catch his flight back to Washington D.C.

Chapter Nine

It had been two days since Jack submitted his application to Mandy. He'd spent his time on the renovations to the basement, trying not to focus on the dark feelings that were burning inside him or the anticipation of the phone call saying he was accepted to the program and could start next week.

This morning he'd been working on the caulking, wanting to make sure he had the seal perfect. Looking around, he was pleased with his work. No room for error. It had to be 100 percent washable, but he thought he'd nailed it. He'd always prided himself in running a very sanitary operating room, and this couldn't be any different. Perfection was to be achieved, nothing but the best for Hope.

He was so absorbed in his work that he barely heard the phone ringing. When he did, he answered, careful not to get any caulking on it.

"Thomas?" a voice on the other line asked.

"Yes, this is Thomas," he replied, throwing in just a hint of flirtatious lisp.

"Hi, it's Mandy from Clary Sage, and I have great news for you."

"Oh, girl I can't wait, Please tell me," he said, grinning. He'd started to worry about this, and was glad to hear from her.

"Well, we have you all approved and set up to start the accelerated classes next Monday. Your instructor's name is Melody. You'll love her. She's the best. Also, we have your financial aid all approved, so you'll have some more papers to sign on the first day. But all the new students go through that information during orientation. There's nothing for you to do right now. Just be here at eight o'clock Monday morning, okay?"

"It sounds perfect. I'll see you Monday. Thanks for all of your help, Mandy." Jack hung up the phone, and a smile crept up on his lips. This was going to be way too easy. The only thing he had to do was ace the class. With his acceptance in the program, he would have the means to a variety of women, allowing him to choose the perfect mate. Now all he had to do was get the rest of his identity scrubbed, so that every aspect of his life could be lived as Thomas.

He'd completed all the financial transfers from the sale of his convertible, making sure the paper trail on Jack died in Los Angeles and couldn't be traced to Thomas. But he did have one last piece of unfinished business. There was something he *must* do.

Tonight, he would do it tonight.

"Hello, can you tell me if your salesman Benz is working today?" Jack clung to his cell phone, waiting anxiously for the receptionist on the line to answer.

"One moment please …Yes, he'll be here until seven o'clock tonight, and he works tomorrow too," she finally said.

"Oh perfect, thank you." Jack clicked off the line. *Perfect,* he thought as he descended the basement steps. Checking his watch, he saw that it was now 5:30. All he needed to do was make sure the basement was all set.

The room was complete, and everything was ready. The caulk he'd purchased was supposed to set in thirty minutes, and it had been four hours since he had finished the application. Checking to make sure that it was dry, he applied a light spray of water to it and wiped it away. The caulk stayed in place – definitely dry. He proceeded to thoroughly scrub his hands, making sure there were no remnants of caulk on his skin or under his nails. He definitely did not want to leave any trace evidence where he was headed.

Moving out of what had once been the canning room, now converted to his new surgical room; he walked across the floor over to the supplies in the opposite corner and took a look at the items on the built-in shelves. Everything was perfectly arranged and labeled. Lifting the amber-colored bottle marked Chloroform; he drew out 5cc into a syringe – enough of the chemical to induce sleep for at least an hour – and dropped it into the tube, then capped it. He pulled surgical gloves from an open box, also on the shelf. Tucking the gloves into his pocket, he headed back up the basement stairs.

In the kitchen, Jack flipped on the light and headed down the hallway, turning on the lights as he went. In the bedroom, he laid the gloves and syringe on the nightstand while he pulled on tight-fitting jeans, work boots, and a tight, long-sleeved shirt, remiss of any buttons or snaps. You could never be too careful; he would never wear anything with items that could be pulled off. He wasn't expecting a struggle, but he had to be especially mindful of that sort of thing now. Double checking himself in the mirror, he pulled on a jacket, picked up the syringe and gloves from the nightstand, and put them in his pocket.

He headed back through the house, turning the lights back out as he went, and collected his keys from the counter. Once he was in the garage, he walked around to the back of the SUV and opened the hatch, and then crossed the garage to the workbench, where he'd placed the rolls of plastic sheeting and several rolls of duct tape. Taking a roll of each and a carpenter's knife to the back of the SUV, he carefully rolled a strip of plastic out to the carpet, where the seats were folded down flat. He cut the sheet just large enough to cover the floor and halfway up the walls of the storage area. He then used duct tape to hold the sheet in place.

Finally satisfied that he had the area covered, he closed the hatch and returned the plastic and knife to the workbench, putting the duct tape in a small satchel stored behind the seat. The satchel contained his surgical instruments as well – scalpel, blade, forceps, speculum, stethoscope, and scissors. Having them in his car meant that he was prepared for anything that might happen. He had similar instruments and more in his operating room.

With everything set he climbed his long frame into the driver's seat and hit the button on the garage door opener mounted on the visor. Remembering something, he climbed back out of the SUV and went back to the trunk area again. Lifting the hatch he reached inside and slid the interior lights to the off position, closed the hatch, and went back and got back inside. By the time he was backing out of the driveway, it was already 6:15. It would take him twenty minutes to get across town and find a place adjacent to the dealership where he could watch and wait. But tonight he'd be able to relieve the darkness inside him, and that alone was calming. Tonight would give him what he needed to control his urges until he was out of school and could begin the restoration of his life.

The anticipation of the hunt was almost as exhilarating as the kill. The radio was playing some familiar tune, though he couldn't quite recall who sang it. Even so, he found himself humming along as he drove. He headed down Memorial Avenue and stopped as lights changed, tapping the steering wheel as he drove. Pulling into a strip mall across from the car lot, he pulled through until he was facing the dealership in a way that allowed him to see the entrance doors. Hoping he would be able to see from his parking spot, he wondered if employees left through those doors or if there was some parking in the rear of the building specifically for employees. He sat tall in his seat now and watched eagerly, waiting for Benz to complete his work day.

Jack's eyes barely blinked. Like an animal waiting on its prey, he held his vigil. Thirty minutes into his watch, he saw a man starting across the parking lot and recognized the slight limp of the car salesman. Immediately alert, he turned the key in the ignition and backed out of the parking space, idling in the strip mall exit and preparing to drop in behind Benz as he left the dealership. After a moment, a white, two-door Mercedes appeared at the dealer entrance, making a right out of the lot and heading north on Memorial. Jack pulled out into the opposite lane of the white car and followed, staying two cars back. The white car made it easy to follow, especially with the dealer plate on the rear.

Continuing to keep the car within view, but back far enough to avoid recognition, Jack watched as the car signaled the intention of getting onto the ramp for the Broken Arrow Expressway heading east. Sliding over to the right lane, Jack followed the Mercedes onto the ramp, remaining a car behind. Benz continued on to the Elm Street exit and followed the ramp off to the right coming to a stop at the light. Jack exited too, but changed lanes to avoid sitting right behind or beside the salesman.

When the light changed and the traffic went forward, Jack laid back slightly, allowing some distance to grow between the two cars. Benz moved over into the left lane, pulling in front of Jack and going through the light at Washington Street. Jack got lucky and caught the light just as it was turning yellow, then eased off the accelerator slightly to keep pace with the Mercedes. The turn signal indicated that Benz would be turning left at the next street. Jack carefully peered through the windshield and saw that the street sign read W. Toledo Street.

Not wanting to lose him, Jack followed cautiously into the neighborhood, watching closely as the car disappeared around the curve at the end of the street. Edging on very slowly, Jack caught the car turning right again onto another street. He didn't make the same turn, afraid that he might look suspicious, but drove on past, narrowing his eyes to see where the car had gone.

He smiled when he realized the street was a dead end. Perfect. Nowhere to run. Continuing to the end of the block, he turned the SUV around in the last driveway and pulled forward, slowly approaching the street Benz had turned on. Down the street, he saw the car pull into the house at the end and enter the garage. The garage door was just closing.

Knowing from the conversation they'd shared at the car dealership that Benz lived alone, Jack decided that he could drive to the house without really being noticed. After all, it was best to catch the man off guard, before he was settled in. Jack pulled into the driveway, then reached behind the seat and pulled his black medical bag forward. He opened his satchel to remove several items: a rag, rubber gloves, scalpel, and shoe booties. He slipped the booties on over his shoes, then pulled on the rubber gloves and slid the scalpel into his back pocket. Folding the rag into a perfect square, Jack depressed the plunger on the syringe, saturating the rag with Chloroform. Last, he grabbed the roll of duct tape and stuffed it into his jacket pocket.

Exiting the car, he walked up to the door and knocked. A moment later, he heard the door lock disengage, and saw a surprised Benz opening the door. Before Benz could speak, Jack forced the rag over the salesman's mouth, pushed him through the doorway, and kicked the door closed behind him, while looping his arm around Benz from the back and pulling the stunned man's back tight against his chest. The car salesman was so surprised he didn't even have a chance to put up a fight. Jack held him tightly and let the Chloroform do its work.

Benz grabbed momentarily at the arms that held him. He fought against the chemical, and Jack knew he was feeling the burn in his throat, as he watched the man's face indicate the panic that was setting in and the desire to stop what was happening. But as the drug took over and as he began to lose consciousness, the last word he managed to mouth to Jack was "Why?"

Jack let the man slump to the floor. Looking around the home, he took in the modest furniture, few pictures on the walls, and immaculate kitchen. The home was neat as a pin. Jack approved of Benz's single and simple lifestyle, with no wife and the children all grown, off living their lives. Benz had been doing this right. That wouldn't help the man in any way now, but Jack did have respect for a man who understood how to keep it simple.

Cautiously pulling back the curtain, Jack peered out to see that the street was quiet. After ensuring the street was clear and all was quiet outside, he looked around the room. There was a giant clock with a barn and landscape painted on it, hanging over the living room couch. It read fifteen minutes to eight. Most people should be home from work and safely in their houses, but he would still need to be cautious. Jack took a few minutes to explore his surroundings. Only the living room light was on, which was perfect – people would assume that Benz was settled in for the night. Jack never brought anything with him that wasn't completely necessary, but sometimes, like now, he wished he had something to conceal his victim. He usually grabbed people in the dark, off the street or from an open area. It was rare for him to go inside someone's home. He really did not like it, as there was a chance of being seen or leaving behind evidence. In this case, though, he didn't have much choice. Coming into Benz's home without any supplies was necessary. He would have to improvise with items from within the home.

Noticing an area rug under the coffee table, Jack decided he could remove Benz in this. Of course, the easiest thing would be to just kill him here, but he really wanted to try the surgery room in the basement. He also wanted some time. He knew he had to make this one last until he finished his training at the school, as he had to remain focused on school and not allow the darkness to cause him to lose that focus. The school was the means to his goal, and there was no room for error. It was important that he keep the dark feelings at bay for just a little while. It wouldn't be too long now before he could begin reclaiming his life.

Deciding the rug was perfect; he slid the coffee table away and placed it next to the opposite wall. He then rolled Benz onto the edge of the long side of the rug. The Chloroform would last a while longer, but he reached into his jacket pocket and retrieved the duct tape. No use taking chances. Holding Benz's hands together, Jack applied the tape in tight loops, and then did the same with his feet. He then made two loops around Benz's head, covering his mouth, careful not to cover his nose. Rolling the rug into a tight tube with Benz securely inside, Jack applied the duct tape around each end then moved the table back in front of the couch. Looking down, he saw that there was a slight hint of where the rug had been. Shrugging to himself, he decided it didn't really matter, as there would be no indication of when the rug had been removed. Benz would simply disappear, and no one would know why.

Hitting the button on his key remote to open the hatch on the SUV, Jack took another peek out the front window. It was solidly dark out now – safe to get going, time to get Benz out of the house and into the vehicle. At approximately 160 pounds, Benz wasn't a real challenge for Jack. He intentionally maintained his health and worked out regularly, so that he could handle any situation. Lifting Benz up inside the rug, he took a moment to balance the weight properly, and then pushed open the front door with his foot quickly before exiting the home. Jack stepped carefully down the two steps on the front porch and lifted the rolled rug into the back of his SUV, pushing it in diagonally with the tip of the rug pushing slightly between the two front seats. Closing the hatch, Jack returned to the home, took a quick look around and ensured he had the duct tape and rag in his pocket. Before leaving the house, he locked the front door and pulled it closed behind him.

Entering the car, he slid off the gloves and shoe booties, putting them back into his satchel, and then backed out of the driveway, heading down the street and only turning his headlights on when he was about to turn onto the next street. Jack worked his way back down Elm and onto the Broken Arrow Expressway, opting to head west. The turnpike would be a little faster, but he hadn't purchased a pass and didn't want to stop at any toll booths or have the cameras at the toll stations record his movements.

Driving cautiously, Jack was on high alert as he drove, keeping his speed limit right at or under the posted roadway signs. He navigated his way back on to Highway 169 and then took the ramp to Highway 412 heading him home. It only took him twenty-four minutes to get home. He hit the remote control garage door opener. He pulled in, waiting for the door to close behind him before getting out of the SUV. Opening the hatch first, Jack went into the house, turning on the lights and opening the basement door so that he could carry the rug easily down into the basement.

Then he returned for his cargo. When he had the rug safely in the basement, he laid it down on the floor of the main room. Carefully removing the scalpel from his back pocket, he cut the tape from around the ends and rolled it open. For a moment he thought Benz might be dead from being confined in the rug, but then he saw the reflexive movement of his eyelids. He was still alive, thank goodness.

Lifting the man up, he carried him into the operating room and laid him on the surgical table. Then he pulled his stethoscope from the wall, where it hung with the other tools of his trade. Listening to the heart rate of the man, he confirmed that Benz was still unconscious enough for prepping. Using the scissors from the tray, Jack proceeded to cut away Benz's clothing and the duct tape he'd applied to his hands and feet. He then secured him to the table, using clear plastic zip ties through rings that had been applied to the underneath of the table. Jack wasn't sure what the rings were actually for. He'd assumed they were for hanging vegetables for drying. But he knew exactly what he would use them for now, and that was really all that mattered.

Once Benz was secured to the table, and all his clothing removed, Jack covered the lower half of his body with a disposable hospital operating sheet, leaving the man exposed from the waist up. Looking around, satisfied that things were as they should be, Jack walked back upstairs to shut the car and make sure the house was completely secured. He didn't want to be interrupted. Closing the hatch to the SUV, Jack retrieved his keys from the ignition and then headed back inside, clicking off the garage lights and pulling the entry door shut behind him. He then went around the home checking all windows and doors. *You can never be too careful*, he thought to himself.

Once he was certain the entire house was safely prepared, it was time to return to the basement. The pain he'd felt for the last few days was slowly being replaced with excitement. Before descending the steps, Jack pulled the door closed behind him. Soon he would need to build out the faux wall in front of this entrance to keep it hidden. For now he was alone, and it didn't matter. All that mattered was Benz on his table and the fact that the Chloroform should be wearing off.

***

As Jack entered the room, Benz, who was just starting to awaken, blinked in an effort to clear the fogginess from his head and eyes. His head was killing him, and he could not figure out why his arms and legs would not move. Jack leaned over him, "Hello Benz. Did you have a nice nap?"

Benz blinking furiously now as recognition started to seep into his mind and he remembered the handsome man wanting to exchange his Mercedes for a far inferior vehicle. Recognition soon began to shift to fear as he started to recall through the dull, throbbing in his head this man, *what was his name...*, Jack, standing outside on his porch. Beyond answering the door he could remember nothing else. Shifting his eyes around him he saw the overhead lights and the stark white walls oddly paneled in what appeared similar to bathtub wallboards. Realizing he was strapped down to something, he tried to pull free, but was unable to move. Trying to speak, he struggled with the soreness in his throat and the tape over his mouth.

***

"Benz, no need to worry with small talk, we just have fate now. Just know we were brought together by circumstances. It really is nothing more or less, I assure you." Jack had moved over to the corner of the room, where a shelf held neatly folded operating scrubs, booties, and scrub caps. Jack proceeded to disrobe and change into a set of operating scrubs, complete with a scrub cap covering his hair. He pulled booties on over his shoes. Returning to the surgical table, he pulled forward a rolling surgical tray and stood admiring the shiny tools, which he'd laid out perfectly. Finally, choosing a number 5 scalpel from the tray, he leaned down over Benz.

By now, Jack was no longer concerned with the panic in Benz's eyes or the manner in which he struggled to speak. He was merely focused on the task at hand. Embracing the darkness far outweighed any compassion he might have felt for the man who had shared the story of losing his wife.

Even as a child, Jack had enjoyed taking life while the victim squirmed for its freedom. Unlike many killers, Jack's needs weren't sexually motivated in any way, nor was it about the act of inflicting pain. Jack cut people because he had to. Doing it while they were alive, alert, and awake meant that the blood would still be coursing through their veins, and this was the part that fascinated him most. Then, once the blood all ran out, the heart would stop. At that moment, he would feel a twinge of remorse. Fleeting and sudden, then over.

But never enough to stop.

For a moment, he reflected on that day when Hope had found him with the cat, how she had promised they would find a way together. And they had, but that had been taken from him. Not for long, he thought firmly. He would soon have that back. It all would start on Monday with getting through school. Then he could find Hope and have his life returned to him. Everything would be good again.

Jack returned his thoughts to the man in front of him, leaning over as Benz watched in horror, struggling against the zip ties holding him down on the table. Without thinking about it, Jack took the scalpel and made a long incision from the top of the man's chest to just above his pelvis, straight down the middle, and right through the hard core of his navel. Benz writhed against the pain and the restraints, screaming, as the blood began to ooze out of the wound.

Jack wanted to do it now. But he fought the urge to reach deep into his body and touch all of those parts, knowing that if he did, it would then be over and he would once again have the darkness hovering around him. In fact, he thought, he showed the most restraint he'd ever allowed himself. Instead of reaching in, he reached out to the tray, selected the sutures, and slowly began sewing Benz back up. Benz had fought hard and now watched in horror as each stitch was applied to his chest. Once Benz's body was back intact, Jack inserted an IV drip with saline and antibiotics into Benz's left arm.

Benz would survive this round, and Jack could do this a few times before he needed to finish the deed.

Taking a few minutes, Jack cleaned the surgical tools meticulously, and scrubbed his hands, then returned the tools to the tray in perfect order again. Feeling slightly relieved of the pain inside, he peeled off the gloves and stripped out of the scrubs discarding them into a laundry basket. He collected the rest of his clothing, ready to return to the real world. Double-checking the IV and Benz's pulse, though shock had rendered the man unconscious, satisfied that he would live, Jack headed back upstairs. He was exhausted and hungry as the euphoria slowly cleared from his mind.

Deciding it was too late to eat a heavy meal; Jack selected a can of soup from the cupboard. He committed to eating healthier tomorrow, before he could spend any more time with Benz, but this would do for now. Pouring the soup into a bowl he popped the creamy broth into the microwave and tossed the can in the trash can under the sink. Suddenly feeling chilled and remembering he was naked, Jack walked through the dining area and down the hall to his bedroom. Pulling on workout pants and a t-shirt, he heard the microwave sound that his soup was ready, and he returned to the kitchen.

Jack carefully removed the soup from the microwave. Setting it on the counter next to the sink, he poured himself a glass of water. Carrying both items to the dining room table, he sat down facing the front windows. The curtains were drawn closed, blocking the view of the woods beyond his driveway. He liked that view and enjoyed the wildlife that could be seen frequently playing in the trees or foraging for pecans. When he was a boy he would have had to hunt them, but he no longer needed animals. These days he could just enjoy the beauty they possessed on the outside. Besides he already knew what they possessed on the inside.

He finished his soup and looked around the room, anticipating a time when he would share this place with Hope. Granted, the house was nothing like the lavish home they'd owned in California, but Hope had always told him that as long as they were together, it really didn't matter where they lived. And he believed her. Full and relaxed, he collected the bowl and glass and walked over to the sink to wash them out. The clock on the stove read 11:33. Yawning, Jack turned out the lights and headed to bed.

***

Benz woke and shivered uncontrollably from the pain, blood loss, and exposure. Looking down, he saw that he had no more than a paper sheet covering him. His arms and legs ached from the inability to move, and the zip ties tore into his flesh. He felt like he couldn't fully breathe either, with the duct tape still covering his mouth. It was dark in the room, and even though Benz's eyes had long ago adjusted to the darkness, he desperately looked around the room hoping for some way to escape. He worked through the pain in his head trying to understand why he was here. *That man, what was his name?* He tried to remember once again through the haze in his head. He had sold him a car. Why was he doing this to him? Terrified he struggled to understand that he was strapped to the table. He couldn't move, and there was no escape. He fought to stay awake, but found himself drifting in and out of consciousness.

Chapter Ten

Max rode home through the cool morning air, the force of the wind against the motorcycle waking her up. Thoughts of the night with Wells flooded her mind as she whipped in between cars down the palm tree lined streets. Arriving home she pulled into the drive of her California style bungalow and grabbed her things, pulling the bagel from her pocket she nibbled on it as she entered her home and walked down the hallway to her bedroom.

She stripped out of her clothes and pulled on her thick terrycloth robe. She then slipped into bed and pulled the blankets up around her shoulders. Sleep took her immediately, but her dreams were torn between images of strong hands roaming over all the right places on her body, blue eyes that seemed capable of knowing her every thought, and bodies buried in shallow graves, split open down the middle, with their insides hanging out.

She was ripped from her dreams when her phone rang. Looking over, she saw it was the chief. She needed to brief him on the progress she and Wells had made the night before, but she wasn't quite ready to, and rolled over to look at the clock instead. She'd been asleep two hours, and it was time to get moving. As she made her way to the shower and climbed in, she found that she had only one thought on her mind - it was time to get to find this killer.

Out of the shower, teeth brushed, she ran her brush through her long wavy locks and quickly dressed, passed through the hall adorned with family photos, and entered the open kitchen, putting on a pot of coffee. Retrieving her laptop from near the front door, she set it on the kitchen table and let the computer boot up while she got a cup of coffee. Then she settled down at the kitchen table, ready to start going through the possible suspects. As she pulled up the computer files, she pressed callback on her cell phone, ready to return the chief's call.

He wasn't in a good mood. "Nichols, where the hell are you and what have you found?"

"Good morning to you too, Chief," she replied with a bit of sarcasm in her voice. "I've got a lot, actually. We have the files narrowed down to the most likely suspects, and I'm starting to work through them now."

"Is Wells still with you?"

"No, sir, he left a couple of hours ago."

"Well, keep me posted."

"I –" Before she could respond the call had dropped. The chief had hung up on her.

Sighing, Max returned her attention to her laptop. Starting with the list of surgeons, she found the first name in the LAPD database. She needed to map these out, so that she could go and talk to these people one at a time. Pulling out the first twenty names, she began the tedious process of mapping the last-known work and home addresses. For a brief moment, her mind drifted, wishing Wells was here to help her with interviewing these people, but she pulled herself back into focus. She didn't have time to allow her thoughts to drift to the night before, or the man responsible. She had a killer to catch.

After a little over an hour, Max had her list mapped out, and she knew who she wanted to call first. She sent the information to the printer in her bedroom, and hoped that her guy was on the short list of most likely suspects. Then, before heading back to the bedroom to change into real clothes, she sent an email over to Bobby, letting him know that she was going to interview these people. You could never be too careful, and since she was going out on her own, she wanted someone else to know where she was. Taking a quick pass at her now dry hair with the brush, she quickly applied some mascara and then pulled on shoes. Moving down the hall again she walked through the living room to the entry way stand and collected her keys and her gun holster belt, checking the 9mm Glock; and slid the belt over her shoulder. Leaving behind the helmet, this was a job that required her car. She grabbed up the list from the printer and exited the house through the kitchen into the connected garage, hitting the garage door opener button mounted on the wall.

She climbed into the leather seat inserting the key into the ignition listening to the low rumble of the Honda Civic. Engaging the clutch and dropping the gear in to reverse, Max backed the car out of the garage into the sun and down the driveway past her motorcycle.

The first person on the list was a Dr. Henry Solomon. The good old doc had gotten a divorce just before the killings started and had a malpractice complaint against him, though it had been settled out of court. Also putting him at the top of the list was the fact that he worked and lived near the dump site in Chatsworth canyon. Either the divorce or the malpractice complaint could have been enough to trigger him, sending him into the killing spree. Having both made him the top pick. Max worked her way out to the Ventura Highway. It was almost noon now, and stopping by his office might be the best shot of actually talking to him. Visiting him at his office might also be enough to throw him off, if he had anything to hide.

Thirty minutes later, she pulled into the parking lot of the medical center where Dr. Solomon practiced medicine. When she got into the building, Max glanced over the directory and found Dr. Solomon's office on the second floor. The elevator was just at the end of the hall. Max entered the car and selected the floor. As she exited, she saw the sign on the opposite wall that indicated suite 204 was to the left. As she entered the office, she removed her badge from her gun belt and walked up to the counter. Flashing her credentials, she asked the red haired, thirty-something, woman behind the counter if she could speak with the doctor.

The woman's eyebrows rose immediately when she saw the badge. She looked up at Max and then back to the badge again. "Umm, okay, one moment please. He's with a patient." Getting up from behind the counter, the woman disappeared down the hall. A few minutes later she returned and said, "He'll see you in about five minutes. He's just finishing up."

"Thanks." Max proceeded to look around the waiting room, curious about the doctor himself. The place was tastefully decorated in modern décor, with local contemporary paintings adorning the walls. Everything was clean and colorful, the tables layered with magazines including *Time, Parenting,* and the *Local Scene.* As Max stared at a painting on the wall, the door opened beside the patient check-in counter and the redhead asked Max to follow her.

She stopped in a consultation office and before closing the door and leaving Max alone in the room said, "The doctor will be right with you."

Moments later, the door opened to reveal a man wearing scrubs. He was slightly grey at the temples and wore small round glasses. He stood about six feet tall and was in good shape. Max immediately assessed his physical capability of committing the crimes for which she was about to question him. Deciding that he would be more than capable, she extended her hand and introduced herself.

"Detective Max Nichols, Dr. Solomon. I was hoping to ask you some questions."

"Of course, but what is this regarding?" he replied with a bit of irritation in his voice.

"I'm investigating a series of murders that happened over the past several months, and was hoping you could help me," Max offered, studying his reaction to the statement.

He looked a bit shocked, "I'm sorry, I guess I don't understand. Murders? How is it that I might be able to help with something like that?"

"I understand you recently underwent a divorce." Max intended to press on him to see if she could get a rise out of him.

"Yes, but what does that have to do with your case?"

"Is your wife still in the area?"

"Yes. Look, Officer, I'm more than willing to help, but I would like to understand what all of this has to do with me and my ex-wife."

Max ignored his demands for answers and continued, "I also understand that at about the same time, you settled a malpractice case for a fairly substantial amount of money."

The doctor was becoming increasingly irritated, "Yes, I did! Officer, I'm sorry, but I'm not sure what you're implying or what all this is about. I don't think I like your line of questions."

Max acknowledged that she had raised his blood pressure just a bit. That was exactly what she was hoping for. Now she wanted to see if she could get him to say something special.

"It's Detective," she stated, correcting the fact that he had attempted to minimize her. "That's a lot of pressure for one person to handle all at one time. Would you agree, Doctor?"

"Yes, but nothing a few months in the Bahamas didn't correct," he snapped.

"You took a trip? When was that specifically?"

The doctor looked like he was thinking for a second. "I left just after my divorce. I needed some time, so I bought a sailboat in Nassau and spent two months sailing around the islands. I returned to work a month ago. My patients needed me, and with the alimony and malpractice payout, I needed the money."

"Can anyone confirm the time you were away?" Max pressed on.

"Yes, my staff, my lawyer, and I have all of the expenses, including the boat purchase."

Max paused. If the doctor was really out of the country, it wasn't possible for him to be the killer. "Would it be okay with you if I validated your timeline with your receptionist before leaving?"

"Yes, one second I will have her come speak with you."

Max waited only a moment before the doctor returned with the receptionist.

The doctor handed her a folder, "My expenses from the trip. Janice can give you whatever else you might need. I have a patient," after accepting Max's card he left the room.

Max asked the receptionist about the doctor's travel timeline and confirmed he could not have been the killer. Handing the receptionist her card, "Please thank the Doctor, for his time. If I have any further questions, I'll be in touch." The receptionist took the card and shook her head as she led Max out of the room, obviously confused by the whole exchange.

Max rode the elevator down and exited the building, heading back into the sunshine, frustrated and grateful all at once. At least she could check this guy off the list completely. She knew some would be a lot tougher. She was already thinking about the next person on the list – a doctor who had lost his mother. Knowing the loss of the mother/son relationship had led to plenty of serial killer sprees in the past, especially if there was any abuse during childhood, Max was hopeful that the next visit would indicate something. Pulling out of the parking lot, she worked her way back to the Ventura Highway.

Doctor Jackson Dailey was further out from the dump site, but still close enough to be reasonable. His office was closer than his home, and again it made sense, given the time of day, to go there first. Though none of the victims had any connections to each other, Max wondered if one of the people of interest had used their exposure to patients as a means to hunt their victims. She made a note to try to tie this together later. She pulled into the next medical building parking lot, amused that it was somewhat similar to the last one and thinking that her next few days would be filled with sterile hallways, waiting rooms littered with magazines, and elevator rides with boring music piped into the speakers.

Dr. Dailey's waiting room was much busier than the last one, and Max wondered if this had anything to do with the malpractice suit Dr. Solomon had settled. Los Angeles County was huge, but small at the same time. Word of a doctor making errors definitely got around. Not that it mattered; she'd already crossed Dr. Solomon off the list and could let him go.

Following the same drill, she produced her credentials at the window, and the two receptionists shared a glance, the blonde one informing Max that the doctor was booked with appointments today. Max smiled and replied that it would be important for him to make time, so that she didn't have to take him downtown with her. This tactic usually worked, and it did this time as well. The dark-haired receptionist, named Becky based on her name tag, left briefly and returned, inviting Max to come through the door and into the back office. She led Max to a patient room, and the doctor appeared immediately, extending his hand.

"Dr. Dailey," he said in an introduction of himself. "I understand you need to speak with me. Is there something wrong, Officer? My wife and kids are fine, right?"

Accepting his grasp and realizing the doctor had assumed there must be a personal emergency involving his family; Max quickly put him at ease. "I'm sorry to have caused you concern for your family. They're fine, I'm sure. I'm Detective Max Nichols, and I'm actually here on official police business. I'd like to ask you some questions. It shouldn't take too long."

Max spent the next few minutes walking through similar questions with Dr. Dailey. In this case, the man had buried his mother and then taken his father into his home to care for him. He seemed genuinely focused on his family. His mother had been ill for a long time and unresponsive for nearly a year. Eventually she'd required extensive care. Max didn't see any indications that this man was her killer. He had offered his surgery schedules freely, and given that his surgeries often started very early in the morning, she was hoping to count him off the list by tying his hospital schedule to dates and times when the victims had gone missing. If he was in surgery when even one of the victims disappeared, there was no way he could have committed the crime. She was certain that there was only one killer, and if he didn't commit one of the crimes, then he hadn't committed any of the crimes. She left the meeting feeling confident that she could cross him off the list.

Returning to the car, Max pulled out the list of dates for the disappearances and quickly compared them to Dr. Dailey's operating schedule. He'd been in surgery on two of the dates and times when victims were last seen. As she suspected, then, Dr. Daily wasn't the killer.

Moving down the list, she identified the next name, and then pulled out of the parking lot feeling signs of hunger and frustration. She decided to pull through Jack in the Box to get a couple of tacos and an iced tea before heading to the next interview.

Chapter Eleven

Jack had slept peacefully for the first time in weeks, and it felt good to be rested. Keeping his promise from the night before to have a healthy meal and work out before visiting Benz downstairs, Jack went into the guest room just opposite the master, which he'd setup as a gym, complete with leg press, free weights, a tread mill, and boxing bag. After a full hour of working out, he hit the shower. His muscles felt good, his mind was clear. Pulling on sweats and a t-shirt, he headed to the kitchen, where he prepared himself a vegetable omelet, wheat toast, and a cup of black coffee. Clearing his plate, he took a moment to enjoy the feeling; this was the best he'd felt in weeks. Having Benz downstairs was enjoyable, but knowing that he was close to bringing Hope back was the real reason for his light heart.

Jack finished cleaning up the kitchen, and then took a few measurements of the basement doorway, drawing out a plan of how to make the basement entrance appear to be a pantry. There were two good things about this plan. One, it protected him from discovery if or when he had any guests, and given that his social life was about to become enhanced, this possibility was more likely. He also knew Hope was certain to love the extra storage for food items. Before he started though, he needed to go to Home Depot to buy the necessary supplies.

And before he did that, he wanted to spend a little more time with his current guest.

Heading down the concrete stairway into the basement, he wondered how Benz had done overnight. He considered whether he would need to give him any nutrients through his IV, and decided that unfortunately, with school starting in just a few days, he wouldn't be able to keep the salesman around that long. This made him feel slightly sad, but he knew it was the way it had to be for now. Pushing down those feelings, he entered the surgical room and found Benz awake. Checking the IV and discovering it empty, he removed the bag and replaced it with a full one.

Seeing Jack enter the room, Benz immediately started to struggle against the restraints. Jack could see he was weaker now, his teeth chattering from the cold and loss of blood. Fear cloaked his eyes as Jack entered the room, which seemed to escalate the chatter and tremble even more. Trying to plead and beg for mercy came out as mere noises, gurgles and grunts, the duct tape restricting any means of forming words.

Jack went through the ritual of applying his surgical scrubs, gloves, and booties, and then stood over Benz looking at him, checking his wounds and deciding what to do next. Considering the amount of time he had remaining between now and the first day of school, Jack was deciding how long he could keep Benz here before he had to dispose of him. In the end, he decided that he couldn't think about that now; today it was about enjoying the time he had left.

Rolling the surgical tray closer to the table, Jack selected the suture removers, and one by one, pulled out the stitches he'd applied the night before. Benz struggled hard, but Jack ignored his thrusts, muffled screams and grunts, remaining focused on the process and his own personal needs. Some minor healing had already begun, keeping the wound from immediately falling open. Jack returned the suture removers to the tray and picked up the same scalpel he'd used the night before. Looking at Benz, he saw the fear rising as Benz realized Jack was about to cut him again. The panic rose, and the salesman writhed on the table to no avail. Moving slowly, Jack carefully reopened the wound in the man's torso.

This time, Jack spent a little more time sliding his hand into the opening and feeling the pumping, slippery organs inside. The excitement rose in his chest. He felt Benz resisting the pain and crying out under the duct tape. Before long the man passed out from the pain. Blood flowed from the wound, pooling around Benz's body on the table. Jack was careful not to allow too much blood loss, knowing if he did that Benz would die tonight. He wasn't ready for that to happen.

Slipping his hand back out of the wound, he cleansed the area with a saline and antibiotic solution, and then carefully began the process of sewing up the wound again. Benz remained in an unconscious state as Jack went about cleaning up and putting everything back exactly as it had been. He'd always been an excellent surgeon with careful organizational skills, and this was no different. He'd managed a tight operating room, displaying top surgical skills as one of the best in his field. The canning room was no different; he managed it in the same careful fashion, maybe even more so, as he had to keep the level of bacteria and evidence as minimal as possible.

He checked the IV again and made a mental note of when he'd need to change it out. Considering for a moment the advantage of buying a baby monitor to allow him to hear his captive from upstairs, he quickly discounted the idea as too risky. If anyone was visiting, there was a chance they might hear noises coming from the basement, and that wasn't acceptable. Besides, after Benz, he wouldn't be holding anyone for a long period of time. He wouldn't need them to remain alive for very long. After taking what he needed he would discard them quickly.

Disposing his scrubs into the laundry bin and thoroughly cleansing himself of any possible blood, he dried off and put his sweats and t-shirt back on, then headed back upstairs. He would make the run to Home Depot and begin the work on the pantry. He must get that finished before starting school. Upstairs again, he carefully closed the basement door and then pulled on a light jacket from the closet near the front door. He slid on his tennis shoes and headed out to the garage with the list of supplies and sketch he'd made earlier.

Jack spent the rest of the week continuing to spend quality time with Benz in the basement, each time getting a little more invasive, opening the wounds, exploring a little deeper into the organs inside Benz's body, and then stitching him back up until the next time. Benz was weaker with each experience, despite the continued administration of IV fluids. His body now was ravaged with fever likely due to infection in the wound that was time and again opened and closed with each of Jack's visits. Jack noticed that Benz no longer struggled or fought against the assaults to his body. Benz's eyes indicated defeat; he had given up on surviving and now simply waited for the day when the painful invasions would end.

When not in the basement, Jack worked on the pantry design, enjoying the physical demands of the job. The pantry was almost finished and he was scheduled to start school on Monday, just three days from now. Having already planned where he would dispose of Benz, he'd decided that he wanted to do it on a weekday rather than a weekend, to minimize the chance of hunters stumbling upon him. He knew he needed to end his time with Benz, and while this revelation made him a bit anxious, he had to move on. And the decision was getting him that much closer to having Hope back in his life. Tonight would be the night to finish the task. Once Benz was gone, he would focus entirely on his school. He hoped that his time with Benz would be enough to hold his desires at bay until he could start building his life with Hope once again.

He only needed to add the trim to the pantry, which was now the perfect cover for the basement entrance, opening from the left side and swinging outward to permit entry to the concrete stairwell, with the hinges hidden. He'd built in shelves that would appropriately house various sizes of cans and boxes, and even put one on the bottom that would accommodate larger kitchen appliances. He knew Hope would enjoy this, as he remembered her complaining about this in the first house they'd owned in California. The memory brought a smile to his lips. Standing back and looking at his work, he was proud of how this had turned out. The trim he'd purchased matched the cabinets in the kitchen, which would provide further cover to any visiting eyes. Feeling good about the work, he decided it was time. The sun was about to set, which meant if he got started now, he would have some time with Benz before he had to drive him out of town.

When Jack first moved to Tulsa, he'd spent time with a realtor, and each house's surroundings were an important part of his decision. He looked at the surroundings near the homes, assessing rural land that showed the most potential for the disposal of unnecessary parts. He was very pleased to see how quickly one could get outside the city and into a rural area. Tulsa was fairly spread out, and all the surrounding areas offered thick trees and heavy underbrush – perfect places for his needs. Jack remembered reading of Tulsa when he was a boy in one of his medical magazines. He had always pictured what it would be like here, so moving here had made perfect sense. On one house-hunting trip, the realtor had taken him east of Tulsa to a small rural community called Inola. They had gone down a road called Lock and Dam, and Jack had seen several adjacent roads winding off into the trees, thick with weeds and brambles, proving they were hardly ever used. Jack remembered thinking this was the right place – a small town where nothing ever happened. No one would ever think to look for bodies buried out there.

Of course, the realtor had no idea that Jack was more focused on the surroundings than the three-bedroom ranch style they'd gone out to view. He had committed the drive to memory and could clearly picture each turn in his mind. As the sun set he would be ready to take that drive again.

It was nearly dark outside now. He needed to get started, so he wouldn't be rushed. This was his last time with Benz, and it needed to carry him for a while. But, before he could spend that quality time, he first needed to prepare everything for transporting Benz. There couldn't be any signs of ever having a body in his car. Every step of the process required thinking ahead. Jack had no way of knowing if the police would ever look in his vehicle, but he needed to know that his tracks were covered well enough that he would always have enough time to leave if necessary. Opening the pantry, he entered the basement, closing the door behind him and heading to the surgery room. Pulling out sheets of plastic, he carefully laid them onto the floor in the main room just outside the surgery room. He set the duct tape onto the tray of the rolling surgical stand and looked down at Benz.

The man was nearly gone. Despite the IV, he hadn't eaten in days, and had been slowly fading away. The repeated attacks on his body had made him shut down emotionally. His eyes were now devoid of any recognition, all hope had left his body, and no longer did he seem to respond to the visits from Jack at all. Benz was, for all intents and purposes, already dead. Jack knew Benz realized he was going to die and had likely already resigned himself to that idea. He probably even welcomed the fact and wished it would come sooner. Jack's daily visits, where he repeatedly opened up the salesman's body and slid his hands inside, then sewed the man up, had delivered pain no one should ever endure. In the days prior, Benz could be heard quietly praying for the pain to end. Jack had assured him that he would only die when he allowed it.

Jack knew what Benz must have thought throughout the last few days, and at this point, giving the man peace was the natural next step. Leaning over Benz, he whispered, "Thank you for providing me a few days of satisfaction. I know the feeling is not mutual, but you see, the pain you had to endure has given me great pleasure, and for that I am grateful to you. Benz, it will be over soon. I can't keep you here any longer. Tonight, you'll be free." For a brief moment, he saw relief, maybe even gratitude in the man's face.

Turning, he put on a full set of surgical scrubs. Picking up the suture remover, he removed the sutures from Benz's body for the last time, and then used the scalpel to open him up again. This time he used the tissue scissors to cut the tissue of Benz's abdomen in two circular shapes on either side of the original incision. Once the organs were exposed Jack reached his gloved hands deep into the cavity of Benz's body and eagerly felt inside. One by one he touched each of the vital organs caressing them, in complete awe of the significance of each function. He gently squeezed the heart, feeling each beat, a euphoric feeling coming over him as it slowly stopped pumping. He watched as the blood slowed until there was nothing flowing. Benz had struggled but died as the blood flowed out of his body, and his heart stopped while Jack held it in his hands.

Jack leaned back, his own heart racing while Benz's stopped, as if his heart had taken on the pace for both. Forcing his breathing to slow and trying to regain control, he took out the stethoscope and listened for a pulse in Benz's neck, satisfied that the man was now dead. Using the surgical scissors, he cut the ties that had held Benz captive to the table since being brought here days ago. Disposing of the ties in the waste can, Jack began carefully washing down the body, removing any possible evidence, the bloody water swirling down the drain in the floor under the stainless table. He finished with a bleach bath, washing the body and table again and again until the water flowed clear down the drain, and the areas around the wounds had been bleached clean to the point of being nearly absent of any blood. Finally, he poured an ample amount of bleach down the drain, to make sure that there were no signs of Benz ever having been there.

Now Jack lifted the man from the table and lowered him onto the plastic on the floor, wrapping the body tight in the plastic wrap, and securing the ends with duct tape. Confident that the body was secure in the wrap, Jack lifted the bundle up onto its end and then onto his shoulder so that he could carry it up the stairs and out to the SUV.

Once in the garage, Jack laid the roll on the floor of the SUV, confident that the plastic would hold the body still. He pulled a tarp off of the shelf over the workbench and spread it over the plastic roll, concealing the body as a precaution. He didn't think anyone would look in the back of his car, but if they did they'd see only the tarp.

Going back into the house, Jack checked the time. He'd spent more time with Benz than he realized, and it was now nearly eleven o'clock. This was perfect. It was getting late, and most people would be settled in for the night. He would need to drive very carefully; at this time of night, the police would be looking for people who had been drinking. Before making that trip, he had to go one more time into the basement. He gathered all of Benz's clothes and placed them in a plastic bag. Back upstairs, he grabbed a bottle of water and his keys, returned to the garage, slid a shovel under the tarp next to the bag of clothes, and was ready to go.

Backing out of the garage, Jack headed east onto Highway 412. Setting the cruise control at exactly 65, he drove for fifteen minutes before seeing the sign for Inola. Tuning right at the Fiesta Mart about an eighth of a mile before the exit ramp that led to the small town, he passed the Dollar General on the left and liquor store on the right, just as he remembered, then continued down the Lock and Dam road out into the darkness, leaving the lights behind him. Driving three more miles into the night, he saw a road off to the right that had grass nearly growing over the path. No cars had passed him in the last two miles, and the houses had gotten farther apart. This was the place. Jack turned the SUV down the unpaved road and killed the headlights. Working his way slowly down the path, he found himself appropriately concealed in the trees and pulled the car off the road.

Before stepping out of the car, he slid on gloves and surgical booties. Retrieving a flashlight from the glove box, he popped the trunk hatch and retrieved the shovel from under the tarp. Then he began working his way out into the woods, using the flashlight to help guide his way. Most people would look for the path easiest to travel, but Jack wanted the most difficult path – the least likely for anyone else to travel. As he got further into the thicket, he found a small opening that looked like a site where deer may have been bedding for the night. Pulling back some of the brambles; he began digging up under the brush there, preparing the final resting spot for Benz.

The soil was soft due to the recent rains, and after about thirty minutes, sweat beading on his forehead despite the cool air, Jack decided that the hole was deep enough. Returning to the vehicle, he pulled the plastic roll, with Benz inside, out of the car and hoisted it up onto his shoulder, retrieving the bag of clothes with his left hand, while balancing the body with his right. He carried both back into the woods, carefully watching his footing so as not to slip.

When he arrived back at the opening, he laid the body face up in the hole with the clothes beside it. Then he filled in the hole and pulled the brambles back over the disturbed dirt. Finally he assessed the area with the flashlight, ensuring that everything looked natural and undisturbed. Returning to the car, he placed his gloves and booties in the satchel and slowly pulled the SUV back down the dirt road. Looking both ways and seeing no sign of any cars, Jack flipped on his headlights and pulled out onto Lock and Dam Road, heading back out to the highway.

He felt both peace and sudden fear as he headed towards the city lights, seeing Tulsa coming back into view. Having Benz over the past few days had kept his demons at bay, and that made him feel peaceful. The fear wasn't of being detected, but rather driven by the fact that he knew he'd have to contain the darkness by himself for several weeks. He knew this would be a struggle, and he hoped that focusing on getting his license to provide manicure and pedicures would be enough to keep his mind off of his needs. *"Focus on the plan Jack"*, he silently told himself.

He spent the weekend finishing up the pantry trim, cleaning his car inside and out, giving a second bleach bath to the surgery room, and making sure that everything in the house was perfect for Hope. He went to the grocery store and shopped for canned and boxed goods to fill out the pantry shelves, giving them the perfect look of a stocked kitchen. He grabbed two more bottles of bleach ensuring that he kept that supply stocked. He even bought a blender, bread machine, and food processor to put on the bottom shelf. He spent Sunday evening preparing his wardrobe for the week and his transformation to Thomas – the persona he would have to retain throughout the next several weeks.

On Monday morning, the alarm went off early. Jack got out of bed eagerly; ready to begin the journey that would bring his beloved Hope back to him. After a quick work out and hot shower, Jack dressed in a colorful button-down shirt and jeans. He spiked his hair slightly with gel, and intentionally applied a little too much cologne. Giving himself an approving look in the mirror, he walked down the hall through the living area and into the kitchen to have a healthy breakfast. Downing his coffee, he cleaned up and then checked the time. He would be a few minutes early to school, showing the appropriate amount of first-day excitement.

Arriving at the school, he was greeted and led to the classroom, where the first hour of class was spent on introductions, an overview of the course curriculum, and school policy. When all eyes in the class turned to Jack, he introduced himself as Thomas, offering a general background of having grown up in several places throughout the United States. Thomas was the only male in the room besides a small Asian man, whose family owned a nail salon inside a local grocery. He was not all too surprised by the demographics of the group and was pleased with the arrangement.

Before the day was out, Jack was already forging friendships with some of his classmates. The charisma that he'd always had would ensure that Thomas was a big hit, just like Jack had always been. Settling into this new persona, he thought that things were going just as planned.

Chapter Twelve

Max had spent four days interviewing the surgeons on the list, and so far nothing had popped. Everyone either had a very strong alibi or just didn't meet the profile Wells had outlined. Max knew she was running out of time. The chief was losing his patience with her, and had started telling her they needed her on the latest big case. Someone was driving down the highways shooting passengers on city buses, and they needed as many men – and women – as they could get on finding that killer or killers. She couldn't stand the thought of being pulled from working her current case. She really needed a break but couldn't afford to stop working. It would most certainly mean the chief would pull her, and this killer would get away with killing six people – something she was not willing to accept. Taking a deep breath, she forced herself to continue on.

The next name on the list was a Dr. Jack Tyler. It was about nine o'clock in the morning and she thought she would head to the hospital where he conducted most of his surgeries. Dr. Tyler was Doctor of Internal Medicine and Cardiology, often performing emergency splenectomies, appendectomies, gallstone removals, and heart surgeries. Through the process of interviewing now more than twenty people, she'd learned that most of the surgeries were conducted early in the morning. She was hoping to catch him just following a surgery.

Reading over the notes she'd taken, she saw that Dr. Tyler had lost his wife and four-year-old daughter in a car accident, a certain tragedy that anyone would find devastating. She wasn't even sure how *she* would handle such a horrible loss. Arriving at the hospital, she parked and entered through the main entrance, then approached the information desk, asking the volunteer behind the counter about Dr. Tyler while displaying her credentials.

The elderly woman seemed a little rattled by the display of the badge, but she quickly recovered and called security to help the detective.

A security officer arrived a few moments later. "Hello, Detective, may I help you?"

Max glanced up at the tall, dark-haired man and nodded. "I'm looking for a Dr. Jack Tyler. My records indicate that he's a cardiac surgeon at this hospital."

Shaking his head, the security officer, whose name tag read D. Reynolds, said, "Now that's a real tragedy. A real talent, that man. He received the Patient's Choice Award two years in a row, had everything going for him. Last year, Dr. Tyler lost his wife and child in a car accident. Took a leave of absence and hasn't come back. I'm not sure where you'd find him. Last I heard, he wasn't doing well. Then again, after a loss like that I don't know who would be."

Her gut churned with excitement, and she thought she might finally be on to something. Thanking the security officer, she headed back out to the parking lot. Once inside the car, she checked the address in her file for Dr. Jack Tyler's residence. Peeling out of the parking lot, she headed in that direction.

As she pulled onto the street, her excitement dropped. The house had a 'sold' sign on the front lawn, right in front of the lavish home that the Tyler family had shared – a beautiful Tudor style house, right out of the 20th century, with a sweeping, curved driveway. The house appeared to be unoccupied, though, and Max quickly jotted down the real estate agent's phone number. Maybe the agent would be able to tell her where Dr. Jack Tyler was living now. Dialing the number on her cell, Max connected with the real estate office

"Coldwell Bankers, how may I direct your call?"

"Yes, I'd like to speak with Janet Brinkley please."

"One moment please."

As Max waited she thought, *"Where are you, Jack? Are you my guy? Did you kill six people and bury them up in the canyon, Jack?"* Max heard a brief pause, followed by some soft music, and then a new voice on the line. "Good morning, this is Janet."

"Good morning, Ms. Brinkley, my name is Maxine Nichols. I'm a detective with the Los Angeles Police Department, and I have some questions for you regarding the sale of the home of Dr. Tyler."

"Detective? Oh, um, yes, how may I help you?"

"Can you tell me how long ago you closed on that home?"

"Yes, the final closing was about a month ago."

Max's heart sped up. That would match roughly with the last murder. "Did you help the seller, Dr. Tyler, buy another home locally?"

"No, I'm afraid not. Dr. Tyler was really suffering from the loss of his family and said he wasn't prepared to buy another home."

"Do you have any idea where Dr. Tyler is living now?"

"No, he never gave me any forwarding contact information. When he's ready, I hope he'll contact me to purchase a new home. He definitely needs the tax write-off."

"I understand. One more question, can you tell me how the funds for the proceeds from the sale were handled?"

"I'm sorry but I can't give out that kind of information".

"I know this is unusual, but I really need to contact Dr. Tyler, you don't have to tell me specifics. I can get a warrant and bring you downtown for questioning, require you to provide copies of all of your sales contracts,

I really don't want to do *all* of that," Max stated in her most sympathetic voice.

"Well, ummm... they were transferred to his Bank of America account."

"Great, Janet, thank you. You've been very helpful."

"May I ask what this is regarding?"

"I'm afraid it is a police matter. Thank you, Ms. Brinkley." Max disconnected the call without giving the woman a chance to ask any more questions.

After disconnecting the call, she hit speed dial to contact the chief. When the chief picked up, she could barely contain the excitement.

"Chief, I may have found something. I have a doctor who lost his wife and child in a tragic accident. He's off the grid, sold his home about a month ago and seems to have disappeared. I'm going to have Bobby do a trace on his phone, bank accounts, and credit cards, to see what I come up with."

"Good work, Nichols. Keep me posted on what Bobby finds." The call disconnected without another word, and Max shook her head. That was all the recognition she was going to get until she actually found him, evidently.

She bit her lip and called Bobby, wanting to get on this lead before it went cold. "Hey Bobby, it's Max."

"Max, I know that sugary voice anywhere. How's your doctor search going?"

"Well, that's why I'm calling. I may have something, but I need you to run some more info for me on a Dr. Jack Tyler. He's an internist specializing in cardiac surgery. Credit cards, banks, the works – focus on recent activities and any purchases around the dates of the crimes. Plus any activity that might indicate where the good doctor is *now*."

"You got it, my detective beauty. I'll email you as soon as I have something."

Max checked her watch and decided she had time to run and get a cup of much-needed coffee while she waited. For the first time in days, she was excited that this case might have some hope. Pulling back out of the neighborhood, she headed to the closest Starbucks – one of the swanky ones you found in expensive neighborhoods.

That thought brought another with it – one of the vics was last seen at a Starbucks. She wondered whether Dr. Jack Tyler was a frequent Starbucks patron. Thinking she might be on to something, she picked up her cell phone again.

"Bobby, I need one more thing. A photo of the Tyler, can you send it now?"

"Sure, Max darling, anything for you. It's hitting your email now."

Max checked her phone and saw the mail flag blinking. "Thanks, Bobby, you're the best."

Max headed into the Starbucks, opening the email and downloading the photo attachment. She glanced down and saw that the doctor was polished and handsome. *Very* handsome. Dark hair and light blue eyes, charming looking actually. Not exactly the monster one would think capable of killing six people by cutting them right down the middle, peeling back pieces of skin from their abdomen, and cleaning them with ample amounts of bleach.

Still, it was worth a try. Approaching the counter, she ordered a Venti Pike with room for cream. Once she had the drink, she showed her credentials and asked the young black woman – who had her nose oddly pierced through the middle – if she recognized the picture.

The barista took the cell phone and looked at it for a moment. "Oh, yeah, I've seen him in here before, but not for a while. He used to come in here almost every day. He was an early bird, always came in real early."

"What was he like?"

"He was good, seemed real, you know. Like kind – gentle almost. I know he was a doctor, 'cuz he would come in here with his scrubs on sometimes. Always ordered a Venti Pike, black. His name was Jack. I know, because we write the names on the cups. Is he okay? I heard about the family. It was on the news, and I haven't seen him since."

"I'm not sure. I was hoping to talk to him. Thanks for your time." Picking up her cup, Max headed over to add some cream and sweetener. Then she headed back out to her car, hoping Bobby would have some information for her. But he hadn't sent her anything, and she decided to head home to get her laptop booted up.

Pulling into her drive and then into the garage, she gathered up the papers scattered around the passenger seat and headed into the house, dropping the keys and her holster onto the stand next to her helmet. Immediately powering on her computer, she waited for the wireless to connect and then opened her LAPD email account. She noticed right away that she had new mail from Bobby.

"Thank goodness," she murmured. The sooner she got into this, the quicker she could find this guy.

Diving right in, she pulled open the bank statements first. The accounts were lucrative, and showed all the normal activity – utilities, random purchases, and mortgage payments up until about a year ago. Then the accounts got sporadic, the balances dipping. Most of the monthly bills were on automatic payment, so those seemed to continue, but the normal payroll direct deposits stopped. The credit card purchases charged directly to the checking account suddenly changed from high-class eateries to fast food purchases and liquor stores. Jack Tyler was obviously hurting, and his accounts showed it.

Then a large sum was deposited – over $1 million in proceeds from the sale of the home. Then suddenly, the bank account was closed with no paper trail of where the funds had gone. How could one move more than $1 million with no paper trail? Max sat back, frustrated. Now she was sure this was her guy. He'd fallen apart for a while and now was off the grid. It matched the profile, and the timeline was right. But where had he gone? What was he up to now?

And how could she find him?

Opening up the file regarding background information, she found no living relatives. The wife, Hope, and the daughter Faith had perished in an accident involving a semi on the 405 freeway. The truck driver had fallen asleep and crossed into their lane, flipping the car and crushing down on it, killing the mother and child instantly. Dr. Tyler's mother and father had both died years before, and he'd been an only child. Hope's parents had also both passed. Hope's sister Mindy Prescott appeared to be living in Arizona with a husband and two kids, and reaching her might be the only way to learn more about Jack Tyler. Max thought about calling the sister, but if Jack was her guy and he was living nearby, he could be tipped off. Deciding she needed to drive over to Arizona, a quick calculation said that she could be there by evening. Maybe he had relocated near Hope's sister.

At that point, Max picked up the phone and called the chief again. "Chief, this is our guy, but he's in the wind. I want to make a run over to Arizona and talk to the sister-in-law. She's the only living relative. Bank accounts are closed, and house has been sold. Wife and daughter dead. He went into a drunken stupor for a while after the accident. I think he must have killed our six vics, and I don't know what he's up to now. But we have to find him before he kills someone else."

The phone line was silent for a minute while the chief took this in. Finally, he broke the silence. "Roll with it, Nichols, but I think you need to take someone with you in case our guy is over there. You start showing up there asking questions; it could be risky if he's in the area. Take Officer Cortez, I'll let her know. She'll be ready to depart in forty-five." Then the line went dead again.

Filled with the first sign of hope in a while that she might catch this guy, Max packed up her laptop, stuffed some clothes and toiletries into an overnight bag, grabbed her Glock and keys, and headed off to the headquarters to pick up her partner for the trip. She wasn't sure she loved the idea of taking someone with her, but she had to admit the chief was right. She needed to be careful. Trading out her personal car for a Crown

Victoria police-issued vehicle, she logged the mileage per protocol and went to find her road mate. Inside the building, she went to the second floor and found Cortez ready to roll, with a bag tossed over her shoulder.

Lorraine Cortez was a thin, Hispanic woman with sharp features and beautiful, clear, olive skin. She'd earned a reputation as a serious cop who wouldn't take any crap from the guys, despite her looks. Max had never worked with her, but she respected her just the same. Only a couple of years on the job, Cortez had collared her share of perps and pulled down a kingpin from the east side drug ring in an undercover sting. She seemed to be the real deal.

The woman threw her head back in a tough nod as Max walked in. "Heard we're going on a trip. What've we got?"

"Possible murder suspect, the six dead bodies found in the Malibu canyon. I have a potential lead, road trip to Arizona to talk to the sister-in-law, only living relative."

"Okay, I'm ready. You can fill me in on the way."

"Deal, let's go."

The trip to Arizona was mostly uneventful. Max and Cortez had gotten acquainted with each other, sharing their stories of how they each joined the police academy and why they'd wanted to. Cortez had described growing up in the hood, how she was sick of the violence, and had vowed to help put a stop to it. She'd seen a lot in her young life. At just twenty-four she'd lost two cousins and a brother in gang war. Her own mother was an addict, and her dad was long gone. It had been a rough road, but somehow, through perseverance, she'd managed to come out on the good side. After graduating the academy, she'd work as a beat cop for a while and then grabbed the opportunity to go undercover on a drug raid – a dangerous role she'd navigated very well. Her work had netted the shake down of one of the biggest meth dealers in East Los Angeles and gave Cortez a name in the precinct and a likely promotion to detective soon. Max shared her story too as they continued to drive, making their way out of Los Angeles and out into the desert.

The six-hour drive over to Phoenix had them pulling into town just after dark. They decided to check into a hotel and then go by the sister-in-law's house, thinking they would arrive before eight o'clock, when the family would be home. Finding a Hampton Inn, they booked two non-smoking rooms on the second floor and rode the elevator up to drop their bags in their respective rooms. Meeting back at the car just moments later, Max noted the time was a little after seven thirty. Cortez navigated on her iPhone as Max drove through the city streets. About twenty minutes later, they were pulling up in front of a Spanish-style stucco home, with a cactus garden lining the walkway up to the front door.

The two women exchanged a glance and then nodded at each other indicating their individual readiness before exiting the car. It was possible Dr. Jack Tyler was inside this home, and they needed to be prepared. Max unclipped her Glock in her holster, with Cortez following suit. Approaching the house, the women stood on either side of the door as Max rang the bell. After a few moments, the porch light came on and the door swung open, offering a beautiful, blonde-haired, blue-eyed woman, standing about 5'5". She gazed out at them with a questioning smile.

Max did a double take. Bobby had sent photos of Jack Tyler's wife, and this woman could have easily been her twin. There was no doubt they were looking at Hope's sister.

Displaying her badge, Max started, "Good evening, Mrs. Prescott, sorry to bother you so late. I'm Detective Max Nichols, and this is Officer Lorraine Cortez. We were hoping we could ask you a few questions regarding Dr. Jack Tyler."

The woman at the door appeared shocked for a moment, looking from one woman to the other. "Jack? Is he okay?"

"I am not sure, ma'am. That's why we're here. We're hoping you can help us fill in some blanks," Max replied, feeling both relieved and disappointed that the man they were seeking wasn't at this particular home.

Backing away from the door and gesturing for them to come in, the woman said, "I'm not sure I understand, but please come in."

As they entered, they were overtaken with the smell of homemade bread and something that smelled like meatloaf. Max suddenly realized she was very hungry, and that she'd barely eaten all day.

Then a man suddenly appeared from what Max assumed was the hallway, interrupting her thoughts. "Honey? Oh, I thought I heard someone at the door," he said.

"Paul, these ladies are from the LAPD, and they're asking questions about Jack."

The man looked surprised. "Jack, really?"

Max reintroduced herself and Officer Cortez to Paul, and then accepted the offer of a seat on the couch. She'd learned over the years that sitting could help put people at ease, and she really needed these people at ease. Feeling very certain they were alone, except for perhaps the kids down the hall, Max opened the dialogue.

"Mr. and Mrs. Prescott, thank you for talking with us. First, let me say how sorry we are about the loss of your sister and niece. We are investigating a series of crimes in California, and we were hoping you could tell us where Jack is living now."

Mrs. Prescott looked at her husband and shrugged. "Please, call us Paul and Mindy. As for Jack, we haven't seen him in a while. After the accident he wasn't doing so well. We tried to help, even tried to get him to come and stay with us for a while, but he wouldn't have anything to do with it."

"How long have you known Jack?"

"Gosh, I've known Jack my whole life," Mindy replied. "We grew up next door to each other. Hope and Jack were friends since they were very young. Jack was always at our house. Our parents were friends, played cards together, that kind of stuff. But his dad was gone a lot, traveled with his job. Hope started dating Jack as young as seventh or eighth grade. They got really tight one summer and just never separated after that. Always having a really … interesting bond."

Max noticed that the woman shuddered when she said interesting, and narrowed her eyes. "When you say 'interesting,' what does that mean?"

"Oh, I don't know. Jack was a charmer, handsome and sweet, but for me there was always something strange about him. I never really understood my sister's fascination."

Max and Cortez exchanged a glance, and Mindy continued.

"I don't know what it was, but I know my sister loved him. And there's no doubt that he loved her. He made a wonderful life for her. They were very happy, especially after Faith came."

Max nodded, and then went back to something Mindy had said. "You said Jack was always at your house as kids. Did you or your sister spend much time at *his* house?"

"I wasn't over there as much as he was at ours. Hope spent a lot of time over there, but I think they spent that time in the woods rather than in the house."

"Were there any issues with his family life? Were his parents stable?"

"I always wondered about his mom. We never talked about her much, and it seemed like she might drink a lot when his dad was gone."

"I see. And when was the last time you saw your brother-in-law?"

"It's been a few months, now. He started drinking and took a leave of absence from work. Things got really dark for him then, and as much as I hate to say this, I didn't want my children around him. Not when he was like that."

"When you say he got dark, how do you mean?"

"He was acting strangely, not just with the drinking, but with something else. He seemed … I don't know, sneaky, not wanting anyone in his home. I assumed it was because he wasn't taking care of the house.

92

One day I went to his home, he told me to go away and just leave him alone. I didn't know how to help him, so I honored his wishes and left."

Max took a deep breath, but made up her mind. Mindy had obviously noticed some strange behavior in her brother-in-law, and Max didn't think the woman would be opposed to answering a more personal question. "Mindy, what can you tell us about Jack's history? Did you ever know of Jack hurting anyone or did you ever have reason to think that Jack was capable of hurting anyone?"

Surprised by the question, Mindy looked at her husband before answering. "I don't know. Like I said, Jack was always a little off to me. Everyone else was so taken by him. Too much so for me, I guess. I never thought he was as genuine as other people did, but could he hurt someone? I don't know the answer to that. I know he never hurt my sister. He was loving and kind to her. He was a little strange as a boy, spending hours in the woods alone. He had very few friends until high school, except for Hope, but she talked him into joining the football team and he got stronger, gained more friends and developed socially. His good looks always carried him, and the girls loved him. But I don't think he ever dated anyone besides Hope. One summer, when they were about twelve, Hope started pushing him to read everything he could on medicine and sciences. By the time he was a freshman in college, there was no doubt that he was headed to medical school, with Hope as his biggest cheerleader. She was constantly telling him that he could do it, and he did. Right out of college he went to Stanford medical school on an academic scholarship. His grades were off the charts. Hope went with him and helped him work through everything. They were married as soon as he started his residency."

"Okay, this has been very helpful, Mindy. Just one more question. Do you have any idea where Jack would go? He's sold the house and hasn't returned to work at the hospital."

"I'm not really sure. He grew up in California, but there isn't any family left there. So, I really don't know. Without Hope I'm not sure what Jack would do."

Max handed her a business card. "I'd like to thank you for taking time this evening, and again, I'm sorry for the late intrusion." Both Max and Cortez stood to leave.

"Detective, is Jack in some sort of trouble?"

"I'm sorry, we don't really know. He's disappeared, and it's all a bit mysterious. We'd like to talk with him and know that he's okay. If you happen to hear from him, please let us know."

"I will." Mindy and Paul led the officers to the door, holding hands to comfort each other.

Thanking the couple they heard the door close behind them. Once outside, Cortez gave Max a knowing look. "This is your guy, Max. Now we just have to find him."

"I think you're right." Climbing back into the car, Max looked over at her temporary partner and added, "But first things first. I'm starving, and that house smelled great. Let's eat."

Cortez flashed her beautiful, white smile. "Not going to get any complaints from me," she answered.

They Googled restaurants, and quickly found an Italian pizzeria nearby. When they arrived, they rushed in, took in the garlic aroma, shared a glance, and grinned in mutual approval. Max asked for a private table, wanting to talk about the case without the other patrons overhearing them. Though it was after nine o'clock, the restaurant was still pretty busy. Max took this as good a sign at a chance for great food. After all, people didn't crowd into a restaurant with bad food.

After ordering some pasta, garlic knots, Caesar salads, and glasses of red wine, the women tore into the food, savoring the bread and wine first. Cortez washed down a bite of bread with a swish of wine, and then opened the conversation.

"So this Jack has some secrets. Did you see the way Mindy shuddered when she said there was something off about him?"

"I sure did. I wonder what secrets Jack had as a boy that she couldn't put her finger on. I also thought it was interesting that she talked about him spending hours in the woods. What was he doing out there? And then she kept saying things that indicated a turning point. That *'one'* summer, suddenly Hope was pushing him. If he had these tendencies as a boy, Hope may have found out and then pushed him to turn his desire to hurt things into helping. If he liked cutting things, it would make sense for her to push him into med school."

Cortez thought about this for a moment as she tore off another piece of bread. Just as she was about to say something, though, the rest of their food arrived. They each received a creamy dish of penne pasta with sun-dried tomatoes, capers, and artichoke hearts, and it smelled delicious. As the server walked away, Cortez spoke again.

"Do you think someone who has the urge to kill can control his feelings in that way? Would it be *safe* for him to be a surgeon, or could he just flip one day and start killing his patients? Seems like that might be a bit of a stretch."

"I know, I know," Max agreed, shaking her head her thick locks swaying with the motion. "Something about the fact that there was a change that one summer," making air quotes with her fingers, "is really bothering me."

"What about another road trip? We could head up to Ojai where they all grew up. Maybe we could take a look out in those woods. I know it's been a long time, but maybe there's some special place that was Jack's killing ground back then. It's a long shot, but it might be worth a try. Could be some neighbors around there that still remember him, and they could tell us if there was anything weird going on. Missing pets, that kind of thing. That's usually where these guys start."

Max liked the way Cortez thought. "You might be onto something with that. Maybe Hope caught him and decided to help him. We don't have enough for a subpoena, but if we could get the new owners of his old house to let us stomp around out there, we might stumble onto something. We have to find him before he kills again!"

By the time they finished up their meals, they had agreed they would get up early to grab a quick breakfast, so they could be on the road to Ojai by seven o'clock. Even with the early start, they would not get there until after three o'clock with stops, not leaving them much time to go through the woods. They would have to hurry, so they would have enough daylight to explore Jack's playground if offered the chance to do so. Bidding each other good night in the hall of the hotel, they went off to their separate rooms to settle in for some rest.

When she got into her room, Max called the chief and gave him an update before changing into a pair of men's boxers and a t-shirt. Once she was in the bed, she settled back against the pillows and laid there for a moment thinking of Wells. She was enjoying Cortez's company, but wishing that Wells was crawling in bed with her, remembering the warmth of his skillful hands on her body. Forcing those thoughts from her mind, she chalked them up as silly. After all, they'd only spent one night together, and he lived across the country. She had considered calling him when she got the lead on Jack Tyler, like he had asked her to, but she decided it would only delay the inevitable. They lived worlds and jobs apart and there was no way a long distance relationship could work out. She punched her pillow and allowed her mind to settle down into images of Jack Tyler as a boy in the woods. That was far more important than missing Wells. She had a case to solve, after all. Slowly, she dozed off to sleep.

Morning came too soon, Max quickly showered then packed her sleeping clothes, ran a brush through her long hair, dabbed on makeup and decided she looked good enough. Collecting her things she took one last glance around the room, ensuring she had not left anything behind. Cortez was already in the breakfast lounge, and looked fresh as well. Her big brown eyes connected with Max as she dropped her bags next to the table.

"How'd you sleep?" Cortez inquired.

"Good morning. I slept hotel good, how about you?" Max replied with a slightly tilted smile.

"Good, once I got settled. I couldn't stop thinking about Jack Tyler, though. We need to know a little more about his parents. Usually there's some abuse or something that sets off these behaviors. Do we know anything about that?"

"We don't. Although Mindy said the dad traveled a lot and the mom was home alone, possibly drinking. There could have been some abuse from his mom, or Jack may have had some abandonment issues with his dad, if he was rarely there."

Cortez nodded, thinking. "That may be what set him off as a boy, and if you're right about Hope knowing and helping him, that would explain the bond between them. Maybe she knew he was abused, felt sorry for him, and decided to help."

Max considered what Cortez was saying. She believed they were on the right track, convinced this was the right guy. Now, she just had to find him and prove it before he struck again.

"He *will* kill again. With Hope gone, and the fact that he's not working at the hospital, which has been his vehicle to channel his desires, he won't be able to help himself. All the controls they built have been taken away. The question is... how or why did he suddenly stop, since we know he was escalating? What changed?"

"Maybe he found another woman to replace Hope. If a new woman is creating enough of a distraction right now, it might be enough to keep him from killing anyone else. Or maybe he stopped only because his kill site was discovered."

Max shook her head. "I don't think so. Mindy said he'd never dated anyone besides Hope. This is a girl he'd known since he was born, practically. I doubt he'd be able to settle for anyone else, or keep it together socially. As for the kill site, he was already off his pattern when we found it. I think he'd already stopped. I think he's just moved on. I think he's still killing, but now he's somewhere else."

On that note, the women grabbed an extra cup of coffee for the road, tossed their room keys on the counter in the lobby, thanked the hotel clerk, and left. They had to find this guy's story – and him – before he killed again.

After fueling the Crown Vic, they were on their way, discussing the case throughout the trip back to California. Max had emailed Bobby, requesting the childhood address for Jack Tyler. Bobby sent the information back right away. Cortez resumed the role of navigator, giving Max the directions from her phone.

By two o'clock they were pulling into the small, quaint town of Ojai, the streets lined with unique eclectic shops. This was a beautiful little town, and Max had always loved it, often coming up here on her days off just to enjoy the tranquil, peaceful setting. There was a place called Boccalli's on the outside of town – a restaurant that sat in a beautiful location, and was a hot spot where bikers of all sorts stopped on weekend rides through the beautiful mountains. She particularly loved that you could sit and eat outside under the trees. During the summer months the place was always busy – a definite favorite for local and weekend visitors. Max could imagine growing up in this beautiful little town and wondered of the life Jack had here.

As they drove through town, she pictured Jack as a boy, walking along these streets, going to these places. The car followed the winding road further north. As they continued climbing up the road, the terrain began to change, and soon they were in a mountainous area, driving through a thick forest of tall trees. Max assumed they must be getting close and began looking for addresses. Finding a mailbox at the end of a driveway with the number they were looking for, Max slowed the vehicle down and pulled into the winding drive. Orange trees, not yet in bloom, lined the driveway that led to a large home with a Mediterranean flare made of Mexican stucco. They wound up the drive and arrived at the house, which sat nestled against a brace of trees that led deep into the hillside. Within those trees was the likely childhood playground for Jack and Hope. Max could see why a boy would want to play out there. The beautiful foliage looked like the kind of place you would hike and climb for hours. The area was truly beautiful, and the trees would provide any child the perfect playground, with room for imagination and mystery. And privacy, if the child so desired.

In fact, she thought, it was the perfect place to practice killing. There were plenty of places to hide. The trees draped low, and in some areas were thick almost appearing elusive. Any number of animals certainly lived in those trees and no doubt, when darkness set in, coyotes would be heard howling as they raced after their prey.

Pulling around the circular driveway to stop just in front of the walkway that led to the door, she saw that the house looked deserted. A garage was attached to the two-story home, which had beautiful flowers lining the walkway and surrounding the house in planters. But there weren't any cars around. Someone had a green thumb, at least, and had spent a number of hours loving this flower garden. Walking up the path, Cortez rapped on the door using the ornate door knocker, and waited. After a few moments, the big door swung inward and a small, elderly woman who must have peaked seventy stood peering at the two officers through small silver-framed glasses and the lines on her face.

"Good afternoon, ma'am, I'm Detective Max Nichols, and this is Officer Lorraine Cortez. We were hoping to ask you a few questions," Max said, pitching her voice to a softer tone.

The woman smiled at them, pushing the wrinkles on her face up around her eyes. Her silvery hair shone in the afternoon sunshine. "Well, hello," she offered. "I don't believe I've ever seen two more lovely policemen in my life."

Max and Cortez each pushed back a laugh at the comment – policemen, really? "Thank you, ma'am, could we come in for a moment?"

"Oh, dear where are my manners?" The woman stepped away from the door and let them in. "May I offer you some lemonade?"

Max graciously accepted the offer for the cool drink. They'd been driving for a long time, and giving them lemonade would set this old woman at ease. "Yes, that would be lovely, Mrs...?"

"Please, call me Vivian. I'm no longer married. My husband passed more than a decade ago," the woman said, cutting Max off and offering her guests to take a seat in the living room, before heading off to the kitchen to get the drinks.

As they waited, Max and Cortez checked out their surroundings. The home was nicely decorated with what looked like expensive antiques. There was ornate woodwork around the ceiling and a beautiful mahogany mantel over the fireplace at one end of the room, while at the opposite end a large bay window allowed a view to the backyard. Off in the distance, Max could see the woods. The carpet was a dark paisley design that looked quite expensive. Jack's father had been in software sales in the early days of the Internet boom, Max remembered, and by the looks of the home, he must have done well.

Then Vivian returned carrying a pitcher of lemonade and three glasses filled with ice cubes. Setting the tray on the coffee table, Vivian poured the lemonade and handed a glass to each of the women, then settled into a winged back chair opposite them and smiled.

"Now, to what do I owe the pleasure of this visit? I don't get many visitors these days." A look of sadness passed briefly across her crystal blue eyes. Max gulped, she hated the idea of this woman being all alone, and it made her question her own life. *Would she end up alone like Vivian?* Returning her thoughts to the woman across from her, Max continued, "We're curious about a family that lived in this home years ago – the Tyler's. Did you know them?"

"Oh yes, the Tyler's. We bought this home when Mrs. Tyler passed away. Mr. Tyler was already gone. Jack was the only one still around, and he'd become a successful doctor down in Los Angles. He didn't have any interest in moving back up here. We'd always admired the home, so when the opportunity presented itself, my husband couldn't resist."

Max could hardly contain her excitement. "So you knew this family?"

"Yes, we had lived about a mile from here for years. This is a small community, everyone knows everyone. As a teenager, my daughter babysat for Jack when he was a little boy."

Max contemplated this. She was talking to someone who knew Jack fairly well. "Really, what can you tell us about the Tyler's? She asked hoping to gain more insight to the type of boy Jack was and possibly how he was raised. Any insight into Jack might help lead her to where he was now.

"Well, they were a bit of a strange family, what with the husband gone so often. I never quite understood the arrangement. Mrs. Tyler, Janice, was a beautiful woman, but she was alone far too much. I suppose it only stood to reason that she would find ways to get through the long, lonely stretches when her husband was out of town."

"Oh and how would she do that?" Cortez asked her voice tense with suspicion.

"Well, there were rumors. Mind you, I didn't pay too much attention to those. But there were always suggestions that she had some male suitors coming around when the mister was out of town. People said that some of them weren't very nice, and I always worried for little Jack."

Finding the opening she was hoping for, Max jumped on it. "And what kind of boy was Jack?" she asked.

"He was a dear little boy. A little on the softer side most times, gentle with my daughter, and kind, but there were times where he seemed ... different."

"Different? In what way?" Max probed further as her mind processed her thoughts. *Now she was getting somewhere. Hope's sister Mindy had said similar things. How different was Jack exactly?*

"I can't really say, other than ... well, at times, it seemed like he was lost inside his own head."

"Vivian, we were told that Jack spent a lot of time in the woods behind this house. Have you or did your husband spend much time in the woods?"

"My husband did a bit. He liked to walk along the stream and enjoy the wildlife, but I never spent any time out there. I focused my time

99

in the gardens. I know there's a play house off in the woods that Jack used to play in when he was a boy. Both he and his friend Hope, who he later married, went out there to play for hours. My daughter really enjoyed babysitting for him because he was always off exploring somewhere. They were only about four or five years apart in age, and she never had to do much to entertain him. Not like kids today, who never want to get outdoors, what with all of the electronics and such."

"Vivian, would you mind if we took a walk out to that play house? We'd like to see where Jack played when he was a boy."

"Oh, dear … what is it you're looking for? Is Jack okay? Has something happened to him?"

Thinking it might play out better with this woman to be subtle, Max offered, "Jack's missing. He wasn't doing very well after Hope and their daughter Faith died, and now he's disappeared. We're trying to find him, and knowing a little more about his boyhood might help us figure out where he would go."

Vivian shook her head in despair. "I heard about the accident, a real tragedy. Those two were so in love. They were inseparable as kids, all the way through high school. I don't know what you might find out there, or even if that play house is still standing, but you're welcome to go take a look. It sits out about 200 yards or so into the thickest part of the trees, just north of the creek."

Standing up, Cortez placed her drink – now empty – back on the tray. "This is very helpful, Vivian. It's not very likely that anything out there *will* help us find Jack, but it's worth a look."

Max followed suit, placing her glass back on the tray as well. Thanking Vivian for the drinks, saying they would let themselves out, Max and Cortez walked quickly through the room and back out into the sunlight, heading past the garden and into the tree line. They walked through the trees single file, with Max taking the lead, and could hear the rustle of the breeze and soon the trickle of the creek Vivian had spoken of. Before long, Max caught a glimpse of what appeared to be a small building, nearly overgrown with brush. That had to be it.

"Cortez, look up ahead," she muttered.

Cortez peered into the distance and caught sight of the building as well. "Looks like we found our play house."

The women approached the building cautiously. They didn't have anything with them to help them clear the way, but they joined forces in pulling away the brambles that had nearly overtaken the building. After a few minutes of tugging and tearing at the vines, weeds, and brush, they'd pulled back enough of the bramble to expose the small door. Max couldn't help but think that they were looking at something right out of a

Huckleberry Finn novel. A dream play house for most boys. They bent to pull on the door and got it open after a few tugs.

"Have I told you I hate spiders?" Max asked Cortez, who looked like she was none too pleased about the small, dark building. She pulled out two sets of small, dark gloves, and handed one pair to Cortez.

Cortez looked at her curiously

"Always got to be prepared," Max explained.

Ducking into the small door frame, Max stepped into the main room of the play house. It was nearly empty, except for a small beanbag that had seen better days, with tiny holes bitten in it from mice. The once white, and now graying, beans spilled out over a toy gun and a soiled, tattered cot that sagged in the middle. Cortez ducked in behind Max, hesitating a moment while her eyes adjusted to the darkness. Max watched as Cortez took in the surroundings, carefully avoiding the spider webs that swept between the corners. Something scuttled across Max's shoe and down into a hole in the floor board, causing her to shudder and suppress a scream.

While Max was wiping away spider webs, Cortez shook her head at her partner, but continued to look around, climbing up a built-in set of stairs that led to a small loft at the far end of the little building.

Standing on the fourth step, poking her head up to peer into the loft, Cortez saw that the area was empty except for a small stack of magazines and a rusty old Swiss Army knife that had long been abandoned.

Collecting the knife and the magazines, Cortez lowered herself back down to the main floor. There was a page folded back in the magazine that really caught her interest.

"Max, check this out." She handed the magazine over, pointing to the page in question. "He studied this page a lot, based on the obvious wear."

Max took the magazine and looked over the page Cortez had flipped open, her eyebrows raised. The magazine article was about the proper procedure of conducting a heart transplant, and the pictures were detailed close-ups of each step in the process. One photo was of particular interest to Max – the photo showing the initial incision, straight down the abdomen. Exactly like the six victims.

"Cortez, this is our boy," she said quietly. "Now we have to find him."

Continuing to look around, Max thought for a moment about the rodent that had scurried through the floor board, and wondered what else might be hidden under the boards of this little house. Kneeling down, ignoring the thoughts of spiders or worse, she pushed on the ends of the boards, trying to see if any seemed particularly loose. At one end of the building, she found a board that was different than the others.

She looked around for something to use on the board, and grinned when Cortez leaned over her shoulder and offered her the Swiss Army knife. Taking the knife, Max pried on the board until it gave way. When she pulled it to the side, she could see down to the ground below the playhouse. Under the floor board, barely visible through the leaves and dirt, was a metal box. Holding her breath, Max reached down and pulled the box out of the hole, setting it on the floor of the play house. She sat staring at the box and anticipation grew of what might be inside. She was hopeful and yet almost afraid of what she might find. There was a small padlock holding the box closed. One swipe with the knife opened the hasp, and the lock dropped off. Max gave Cortez a questioning look, then reached to remove the lid.

Inside the box was a deck of playing cards, some rubber gloves, a knife that was much bigger than the one Max had used to pry the lock open, a change of clothes that were now moth eaten and appeared to be those of a young boy, and a series of small, random bones. None of the bones were large enough to be human. They also didn't belong to a single animal, given that there were three unique sets of jaw bones.

"His trophies from his early days of killing," Max breathed out. They'd definitely found their man. Now she would just have to prove it.

She reached in to pull out a small folded paper that looked like a letter, and opened it. The words were too faded to completely discern what the letter had said, though she could make out a signature from Hope. Reaching into the small side pocket on her gun holster, she fished out an extra-large evidence bag, and carefully placed the box with all of its contents, magazines, and Swiss Army knife into the bag, sealing it with adhesive evidence tape.

"I think we have enough here to have reasonable suspicion that Jack Tyler committed our murders," she said. "Now we have to find him."

Stepping back out of the play house, the women both furiously brushed at their hair and clothes, stripping away any webs and leaves.

"This place gives me the creeps. Let's get out of here," Cortez offered first.

"No arguments here," Max replied, quickly making her way back through the brush the way they had come. Then she stopped. Out of the corner of her eye, she'd seen what appeared to be something carefully carved into a tree. She jetted off the path they'd forged on their way into the playhouse to get a closer look, and motioned for Cortez to follow her. They stopped, staring, in front of the tree.

Before them, carved into the wood, were the words, 'We can do it together. I promise.' A heart circled the words, and under the heart were two letters – J and H. The initials had a unique look, as if each had been carved by a separate hand. Jack and Hope had made their solemn vow right here in the woods, where it all began.

"Hope definitely knew Jack had a problem, then," Max said. That confirmed her suspicions.

"She must have been helping him," Cortez agreed. "Maybe trying to fix him."

Max nodded. She'd convinced Jack to make medicine the vehicle for channeling the impulses to kill. As a surgeon, Jack could cut people open and touch their organs without it being a bad thing. If his impulse didn't require killing, but was a fascination with the internal organs, then the doctor gig was the perfect outlet. Hope and Jack had found a way to keep him from hurting animals, and ultimately people.

"And when Hope died, the outlet was damaged, and ultimately the channel was closed. He slipped right back into his old ways, no longer denying his impulses, and there was no one there to stop him. Only now he was an experienced surgeon, capable of much worse things than a little boy practicing on animals," Max said, concluding her thoughts out loud.

Cortez let out a low whistle as she read the carving in the tree. Pulling out her cell phone, she snapped a photo of it, and they returned to their path and exited the tree line with the evidence bag in tow. Max went back up to Vivian's door and tapped lightly.

The silver-haired woman returned to the door, smiling. "Well, how was your adventure?"

"We found a couple of items that we think might be useful," Max replied, holding up the bag. "I was hoping we could take these with us to have our analyst look over them. There may be something in here that'll help us figure out where to look for Jack. Once we're done with them, we can return them to you."

"Oh I don't care what's in that old building. If you think it'll help you find Jack, please take what you need. I don't need them returned. I've never even seen anything out there."

"Thank you, Vivian, this has been very helpful," Max said, offering her a business card. "If you think of anything Jack may have said that might indicate where he would go one day, please call me right away."

"I will. I sure hope you find him soon. He must be lost without his family."

Max thanked her one more time and then waved good-bye, heading back to the car where Cortez waited. As they left Ojai and headed back towards Los Angeles, Max grew more anxious about their findings.

103

They were definitely onto something and it was only a matter of time before they caught up to Dr. Jack Tyler.

Getting back to police headquarters after seven o'clock, Max and Cortez went directly to talk to the chief. After walking him through everything they knew, and the fact that they needed forensics to try to recover the letter, they grew quiet. He leaned back in his chair, forming a steeple under his chin with his thick fingers.

"Good work. Get that letter down to forensics, along with the knife. Let's find out if there's any blood on that blade, and if so, what kind. I'll let you keep working this for a couple more days, and if you can get a lead on your guy, we'll make this case active again. If we can't get a lead on him, we'll have to wait until he strikes again. My guess is that our guy can't just stop, and as soon as he kills again – no matter where he is – we might be able to pick up on the lead. Get Bobby to load this up on the national database. If he strikes somewhere else, hopefully we'll hear about it. Cortez, you stay on the case with Nichols."

"Yes, sir," Cortez responded, excited to keep working the case.

"Thank you, sir," Max stated, suppressing her emotions as she turned to leave.

The women left the office and stopped outside, the door closing behind them. Max let out a big sigh. "Well, we bought some more time. Let's get these in and see if anything in here tells us where our boy went. While forensics is trying to recover the letter and run blood analysis on the knife, we can go through the magazines to see if there's anything else in there. Maybe we'll get lucky and find a specific story about a special place. Jack might have been harboring some childhood dream of moving to some other state." Cortez nodded to Max as they headed down the corridor to the forensics department.

The forensics lab was led by an unusual man named Porter, with bushy eyebrows and unorthodox ways for getting things done. Despite the oddities, Max really respected him. He ran a tight ship, and she'd built a relationship with him over the years. He knew she didn't ask for unnecessary favors, so when she came knocking on his door he was generally willing to help. After first complaining about short staff and heavy workloads, of course.

Today would prove no different. He fussed at her for a few minutes, then picked up the phone and called in two of his forensics specialists, giving them sharp directions to drop what they were doing and see if they could find anything useful on the items Max had brought in for review. They would study the bones and give some insight into what animals they had belonged to, how they had died – if that was possible to figure out – whether their blood was on the knife, and, of course what the letter had once said.

Having not eaten since the breakfast at the hotel, Cortez and Max headed down to Engine Co. No.28 to get something for dinner. When they entered the building, the smells and memories wafted over Max as she remembered the last time she had been here, it was with Wells. At that time they barely knew each other, but it was here that those first hints of attraction had developed. All heads turned as the two attractive women entered the restaurant. People stared as the hostess led the women to their table. Max was further tortured by her memories as they were seated at the same table where Max and Wells had shared lunch.

Cortez noticed a shift in Max's mood and wondered what had just happened. Cautious not to pry, she let it slide by not asking what was up. A few minutes after ordering Max seemed to be back to normal, starting to talk about their last two days. After tearing through their food and paying the bill, the officers decided to meet back at headquarters at eight o'clock in the morning to see what the lab had come up with and then spend some time working the magazines. Returning to the parking lot, they said their good-byes and headed for their respective vehicles.

Chapter Thirteen

Jack had been enjoying school. He was making friends, and with his attention so focused on studying, he rarely felt the darkness nagging at him. The instructor was fantastic, and he had made fast friends with her. They had fun days where they did silly things and often were pulled in by the stylist to practice on each other. Jack had never had so many people fondling with his hair, hands or feet in his life. He had been uncomfortable at first but quickly accepted it as a necessity.

Leaving school each day, he would return home, eat, workout and hit the books making sure that when it came time to test he was well prepared. Each night he would fall into bed exhausted, and his mind would run through the random clients that came in to have their nails done by the students at discount prices. So far no one specific had caught his eye, but he knew all he had to do was remain patient. She was out there. He knew it, and it was only a matter of time. His job for the moment was to remain focused on completing school.

Chapter Fourteen

The next morning, Max got up early, not having been to the gym in several days, and in desperate need of a workout. After over an hour of aggressive boxing and free weights, she hit the locker room for a shower before meeting up with Cortez. She grabbed a large cup of coffee on the way in, and entered the room where she and Wells had worked the case together over a week earlier. Cortez was already settling in at the table.

"Hey, good morning," Max greeted her. "Ready to go see what the lab has for us?"

"You know it," Cortez replied, grabbing her own coffee off the table and following Max to the lab.

Approaching Porter, Max smiled, trying to tame him before he started in on his usual tirade. But he shook his head warningly.

"Nichols, it's too soon for anything yet. This is Los Angeles. Do you know how many crimes happen every day?"

"I know Porter, I know, but I also know you can work magic sometimes. You can't blame a girl for trying." Max batted her long eyelashes and flashed a huge smile full of beautiful white teeth at the grumpy, old man.

"Yeah, I know what you're up to Nichols," Porter said, wagging his finger at her. "Come on; let's go see what we have." He waved for her and Cortez to follow him into the lab. Approaching one of the two lab techs, Porter nearly shouted, "John, what do we have on the knife and bones?"

The man jumped, but grinned when he saw Max. "Yes sir, I actually do have a few things for you. The bones are from at least three different animals – two cats and a squirrel. There could be more, but it'll take a bit of time to sort through them. Looks like at least one of the cats and the squirrel was killed with some sort of knife. There's sharp scarring on some of the bones. My initial analysis suggests they were cut down through the abdomen with the knife, going deep enough to strike some of the breast and rib bones and cause the scarring. More time with the bones and I'll be able to confirm this. Maybe even match the scarring to the knife. I've also identified that there was animal blood on the blade and down inside the hinge. I confirmed the blood is a combination of feline and rodent, which is consistent with the bones."

"Can you check for prints on that knife? We might be able to match to our suspect," Max said quickly. If they could prove without a doubt that it was Jack killing those animals, it would strengthen her case.

"I'll see if there are any prints to lift, sure. Give me until tomorrow to do that part." Obviously done with his report, he turned back to his work station.

Porter then shouted out to the other lab tech, "Jose, where are we on the letter?"

The young Hispanic male appeared with the letter vacuum sealed in a plastic bag. The writing on the letter was now obvious, and Max flexed her hands. He'd obviously done something to the letter to lift the ink to the surface. That meant they'd get to see what Hope had written him. Obviously something important enough to keep.

"Here you go, sir. I was able to get most of the writing to appear. There are a couple of spots that are too damaged to repair, but I made you copies of what I have. I can try to do some more work on the missing elements, but I think you can figure out what the message is from what I have so far." The tech handed Max a copy of the letter in a file folder.

Looking at the techs and Porter, she grinned. "You guys are the best. Call me if you come up with prints before tomorrow morning, otherwise, we'll see you then." Max accepted the folder, glancing at Cortez, and the women rushed out the door.

Back up in the meeting room, Max opened the file folder and took out the copy of the letter. It appeared to be written by a young person, with a few words spelled wrong, and read:

Jack,

I know you are scared. I am too but I know together we can be stronger. I wont let you down. I have an idea on what we need to do. You will have to promise me that you will listen to me and fight hard to stay with the plan. One day we will be together and you will be special. We can use the play house to study and prepare. _____e will go away together and live happily ever after just like in the farie tales. I believe in you and us and will always love you like you always love me. We have to keep this secret. No one else can ever know. I brought you some books today. You need to start to study these and let the pictures help you. Let me help you. One thing you have to promise is to

---

Your Best Freind Forever Hope

The blanks in the letter were areas where the damage had been too great, but the overall message was clear. Hope had known Jack had a problem, and she'd vowed as a young girl to help him.

Max and Cortez looked at each other across the table, Cortez speaking first. "You nailed it. Hope *did* know. There's no real evidence here, but knowing about the animal bones and Jack going off the deep end after her death, this guy is absolutely our killer."

Max nodded, but still wondered about one line in particular. *What had Hope asked Jack to promise her? What exactly was the plan he had to stick to? Was it that he wouldn't kill anymore, or that he would keep it only to animals, never hurting a person? How could all of this help lead her to the where Jack was now?* Max feared these answers might never be known, unless Jack would answer them one day, and she needed to find him before he *did* kill again. Max wondered what had happened that drove Jack to kill, she pictured these two young kids trying to work through something as challenging as containing the urges to kill and a tight feeling formed in her chest.

Sighing, she turned to the next problem. "Well we still don't know where he's gone. Let's read these magazines page for page, see if there's an indication of where ole' Jacky boy may have gone. These might be our only chance of getting a lead on where he is. With his bank accounts closed, no family connections, and quitting his job, we don't have any place to look for him. And I don't want to have to wait until he starts dumping bodies again." Max picked up the magazine with the photos of the heart surgery and started flipping through it. Obviously, Jack had spent a lot of time studying this particular magazine. Maybe the answers lay here.

Cortez picked up another magazine. Starting with the cover, she read line for line from cover to cover. After two hours, Max threw down the magazine she had been reading through, frustrated. Nothing was jumping out at her. It was like she was looking for a needle in a haystack. Cortez too showed her frustration, leaning back in her chair shaking her head.

"I have no idea what I'm looking for. Why couldn't this guy have underlined the next location in here?" Cortez scoffed, somewhat joking.

Max laughed at her frustrated humor. "I know. I was hoping this would be easy. Let's get some fresh coffee and dive back in. I need some air and a walk. My ass is numb from sitting in that hard chair." Standing and stretching her thin, muscular frame, Cortez joined her, walking out of the meeting room and down the hall. Two officers were heading their way, including a tall black male Max recognized as Officer James Wilson, and a Hispanic man that Max didn't know.

"Yo, Cortez, hear you made the big time working a multiple with a girl dick," Wilson cat called after them.

Cortez shut him down. "Don't be jealous, just because Max here has one and you don't." The women laughed all the way out the door, while the Hispanic male patted Wilson on the back and said, "You just got told."

The women shook their heads at the ridiculous ways of some of the male officers. Part of the hazard of being a female cop was standing up to such interactions. Walking up the street to a coffee house frequented by the whole force, Max soaked in the sunshine, though the air was still brisk. She was ready for summer, preferring warmer temperatures. It felt nice for a moment to shed the case and the demons that came with trying to constantly think like a killer. Cortez fell in line beside her, also enjoying being outside and stretching her legs. They walked in silence to the coffee house, both churning through their own thoughts. After ordering their drinks, they pulled up stools in the window booth that faced the street and looked out at the people passing them.

"If there aren't any leads in those magazines, where do we look next?" Cortez finally asked.

"I don't know," Max admitted, shrugging. "We're out of leads until he either strikes again uses a credit card, or some other financial tie, or we get a tip. Adding his profile and the specifics of how he kills to the national database will help us if he lands somewhere else and kills there. Hopefully, other precincts will be looking for similar crimes. I can do the same once a week or so, but I hate that we may be waiting for him to kill someone else before we know where he's gone. That means we're not doing our job."

Cortez looked out the window, her eyes shining with the sunshine, her sharp features tense, deep in thought. Suddenly she stood up, saying, "Well then we better find something in those magazines. Let's go figure out what we're missing."

Max smiled at her enthusiasm, grateful for the help and motivation. "Okay, let's do this."

They walked back to the headquarters with a rejuvenated energy, their heads cleared by the fresh air and coffee.

When they got back into the meeting room, Cortez said, "I have an idea, let's write down every city in those magazines. Just make a list and catalog the associated page numbers. At least we'll see if there's some sort of theme. Then we can look at any stories that cover that theme." Stopping, she looked to see what Max thought of the idea.

"I like it. Let's do it. I didn't really understand those articles anyway. At least this way I feel like we have a strategic approach."

They spent the next several hours listing every city in the seven magazines, noting duplicates, and then noting the publication dates and page numbers. When they were done, Max looked up at the clock on the wall and was shocked to see it was already seven o'clock. Where had the day gone? They had a long list, but there were some cities listed more often than others. Los Angeles was listed the most times, followed by New York City, Phoenix, then Miami, and then on to cities with smaller populations, like Baton Rouge and Tulsa.

"I think with this list we can contact the local authorities and see if any recent crimes match our case. We can also go onto the database and look for possible matches, narrowing in on these areas. He was a kid and would have been open to suggestion. It makes sense that he would have gotten his idea to move from something he'd read when he was young. It's going to take days if not weeks to let everyone know and go through the database. I hope the chief lets us stay focused on this. My gut tells me our guy is either here in the city, still waiting to strike again, or has moved to one of these places. He studied these magazines for years, dreaming of these places. I think we'll find him in one of these cities. The question is which one, and how?"

Chapter Fifteen

Jack had spent the past two months deep in his books, studying and learning the proper techniques for giving manicures and pedicures, applying nails in the various hottest styles – French tips, half-moon, two-tones, and pink and white – all coined as nail art. He had worked on the relationships with his fellow classmates, most of who were female, and had pulled off the perfect impersonation of a gay man. The girls were constantly trying to hook him up with a male friend of theirs, though he'd always decline, saying he didn't have time for a relationship. On several occasions they'd all gone out for drinks after school, sharing stories about their clients. He was fitting in well, just like he'd hoped.

He was getting practical experience, through his training, and was becoming very confident this had been the right decision. Working on the clients he had seen a lot of woman, and he could sense that with more exposure he would be able to find the perfect one. He just had to keep looking. Jack had always applied himself and had a level of dedication unusual for most people – a skill Hope had helped him develop. In this case, the dedication was in his desire. Or rather … not desire, but the *need* to have Hope with him again. There simply wasn't room for lack of focus, not if he was going to accomplish his goal. With that in mind, even the darkness had been manageable. He'd absorbed himself in the nail school activities and friendships so deeply that he'd hardly thought of his internal need. It certainly wasn't gone, but for now he had to stay focused on the goal. And that was enough to keep the need buried.

Melody had proven to be a perfect instructor and a good friend, promising Jack – as Thomas – that she would help him find work as soon as he graduated. He had professed a strong financial burden and said that he needed to get to work quickly. None of that was true, of course, as Jack had ample means, but no one could ever know that. No, his desire to get working quickly was for a much different and more urgent matter. He soon would have his life back. He was going to put the pieces back together. She was out there. The perfect fit; he just knew it. Completing his classes had just gotten him that much closer to finding her.

The time had flown by, and he would be graduating tomorrow. It was hard to believe that he'd met the 600 hours of study required in the state of Oklahoma. The only thing left was taking the exams to get his license, and securing a place – or ideally two – where he could apply his new training. He'd already scheduled his exam date in Oklahoma City, where the Oklahoma State Board of Cosmetology was located. It wouldn't be long now until he found her and brought her home.

115

The next day, Jack showed up ready for his graduation. This was a true turning point in his life, and he was taking it seriously. He'd dressed for the occasion and the part. Everyone had decided that after the graduation ceremonies, they'd go to dinner and then to Club Majestic for a night of dancing. Jack had never been a good dancer, so he spent the last couple of weeks in between studying, watching videos in the evenings of gay men in various gay clubs throughout the world. This had helped him prepare for both the evening of dancing and also how to behave in such a setting. He'd even gone out one night by himself, to a male club called Maverick's, just to get a feel for the environment and to watch how the men interacted with each other. He couldn't afford to blow his cover now. He was way too close for that.

Jack was enjoying the graduation celebration. The school had provided cap and gowns, and they had laid out a red carpet and a platform for each student to walk up and accept their diplomas. Some of the students had brought their family members, and Jack spent time being introduced to several of his classmates, significant others.

The week before, the whole class had worked on the evening plans, and they had agreed to meet at the Olive Garden to have dinner. The drinks had started flowing there with everyone having a glass of red wine with dinner. The festivities were wildly fun. Jack was relaxed, enjoying the time with the students he had grown close to over the past couple of months. Everyone was in good spirits, telling favorite class stories, until it was time to head to the club. Jack had avoided riding with anyone, saying he might get lucky tonight, to which everyone had laughed. He met up with the group outside the club after circling the block a couple of times looking for a parking space, finally finding one a block away just past an alley in front of an old abandoned brick warehouse.

After paying the cover charge and receiving a stamp on their wrists, everyone went in, with Melody wrapping her arm inside Jack's. Jack really enjoyed her high energy and infectious smile. He considered her a friend and liked her company. Of course not in any romantic way, that would be disloyal, but spending time with her was pleasurable and had made the time go by faster. They approached the bar and ordered their drinks, the music pumping and the bass so loud it seemed to vibrate inside his chest. Jack bounced along to the beat, trying to look natural. It wasn't long before he was approached by a younger man, probably in his early twenties. The kid started flirting with him, making his interest apparent, and Jack had his first challenge. All he had to do, of course, was flash that beautiful smile – the one that made just about anyone fall in love with him.

It worked like magic. Within minutes the handsome and well-built, though small, young man with sandy brown hair and blue eyes, was swooning over Jack.

Melody flashed her bright smile and winked at Jack, leaving him to flirt as she was pulled onto the dance floor by a few of the other girls.

Jack tossed back his drink and ordered another, allowing the liquid to loosen him up. Before long the young man, who had introduced himself as Gary, pulled Jack out onto the dance floor. Jack was able to successfully carry the beat, while displaying some suggestive moves. Unfortunately, this only further interested Gary, and the younger man moved closer to him. In response, Jack could feel the familiar darkness rising up inside him, and gulped. If he wasn't careful, Gary was going to get lucky tonight. He just didn't realize how.

Jack offered to buy Gary a couple more drinks, pretending that he too was drinking more, but he actually only ordered Coke for himself. The music was so loud when he placed the order Gary couldn't hear. Jack wanted to have his wits about him from here on out. The dancing and drinks flowed as fluently as the music. Jack and Gary continued to dance wildly with Melody and the girls, the group randomly dancing together in playful abandon. It was getting late, as was evidenced by the packed dance floor with sweaty, intoxicated patrons.

Gary was hinting at leaving together, which met with Jack's thoughts perfectly. As Jack led Gary out the door, he flashed Melody a smile and held a thumb and finger to his ear, indicating that he would call her. Melody laughed, giving him the thumbs up as she watched the men disappear out the door.

Outside, the night air felt good on Jack's sweaty body. Gary was clinging to his hand as they headed down the street, away from the sound of the pumping music into the darkness. When they got further down the street, Jack invited Gary to come home with him. He knew the younger man would accept and wasn't surprised when he did.

The men rounded the corner and passed the alleyway where Jack had parked. He unlocked the doors to his SUV and watched Gary climb into the passenger seat. Then he opened the back door and reached into his lab bag where he had a syringe of Chloroform and a rag carefully tucked away. There was no time to apply gloves, so he depressed the syringe into the rag, dropping the syringe back into the bag pocket. Closing the door and looking to be sure no one was around, Jack climbed in behind the steering wheel and leaned over as if he was going to kiss Gary. His companion was completely compliant, but instead of Jack's lips coming into contact with the young man's mouth, it was the chemical-soaked rag that stole his breath away.

117

Jack held Gary back against the seat, watching as Gary struggled against the rag for a few moments and then slumped against the window. Jack propped him up and leaned his head back in the seat, to make it look like he was just settled back against the head rest. Once he was confident his sleepy passenger looked natural to anyone outside, Jack pulled the SUV out and headed towards the highway entrance and home. Jack felt excitement surge in him as the darkness swelled at the opportunity that had so naturally presented. His mind raced as he considered the risks. This was not how it was supposed to be, yet Gary had made it so...*easy.*

Carefully watching for any signs of police while making sure he maintained his speed, Jack felt the excitement growing inside him. This was an unexpected treasure, and while it wasn't in his plans, it had played out so naturally that he couldn't pass it up. This would be the last time before Hope came home, and he could return to his normal life. He knew Hope would understand. She always had in the past, and there was no reason to think this time would be any different.

As he drove, Jack considered the consequences of his spontaneity. People had seen him with Gary, but they hadn't talked to anyone other than his classmates. He'd been careful not to tell anyone that his name was Thomas, he had paid cash for everything, and he didn't plan to go back to this club any time soon. Gary had told him he was new to town, and didn't really know anyone in Tulsa. This information seemed to minimize the risk, as it was unlikely that anyone would report Gary missing for the time being.

Jack wondered suddenly what it might be like if anyone *did* report him missing. There had been a newscast on Benz missing two days after Jack had taken him from his home. The police report had said he'd last been seen leaving work and then disappeared from his home. It had gone on to say that there was no sign of forced entry and no sign of a struggle. At the time of the report, Benz was still zip tied to Jack's table in the basement. He had watched the report, but he had not felt any specific need to hurry. He was certain no one would trace Benz to him. He had immediately determined there was no need to change course and had fully enjoyed Benz. However, he recognized that he would need to move faster with Gary, since he had just been seen with him.

Gary had said that he had just started working as a waiter two days ago. He had spoken about not yet having made any friends at work, and that this had been his first night out to the club. Even with no friends or family in the area, there was a chance that an employer might report him missing. But even if they did, would the police spend much time on a missing man who had just moved into the area? He didn't think the employer would even report an employee missing. Waiters and waitresses

118

came and went. Jack decided that given the short employment, the employer would most likely think the new employee was unreliable, and had simply quit without giving any notice. His thought process gave him comfort.

It wasn't even worth worrying about, really. Smiling to himself, he concluded that he was safe and could proceed. The excitement of his decision welled up inside him, causing his heart to race just a little bit faster.

When he arrived home, Jack pulled into the garage and quickly went into the house and opened up the pantry door, exposing the basement stairwell. Returning to the garage, he opened the passenger door and pulled Gary out, lifting his sagging body up onto his shoulder. The young man had a small frame, but was muscular, and Jack struggled with getting him balanced properly as he navigated the stairwell. He accidentally knocked Gary's head against the wall on the way down. Gary responded mildly with a groan, but between the chloroform and the alcohol, he nodded back out.

In the surgery room, Jack disrobed Gary and placed his nude body on the stainless steel table, which Benz had previously occupied. He thought about it for a moment but decided that he couldn't afford to keep Gary. A disappointment, but he really couldn't risk it. Additionally, he decided he would need to be especially cautious; with Gary being a gay man, there could potentially be other risks. Though not likely, Gary could be positive for HIV. He would need to be extra cautious with any blood contact. Putting on his surgical clothing and gloves, Jack carefully zipped tied Gary to the table.

Gary was beginning to wake up, and at first he smiled at the sight of Jack standing over him. As his vision slowly cleared, though, he became aware of the fact that he couldn't move his arms or legs, and that he was in a very strange place. Jack hadn't yet placed duct tape over his mouth, and Gary struggled to speak, swallowing hard in an effort to wash away the drugs in his system.

"Thomas, what are you doing?" he gasped.

Ignoring the question, Jack pulled the rolling surgical tray toward him.

Gary's eyes searched the room wildly. His eyes fixed when they saw the scalpels and various tools on the tray. He began to struggle against the zip ties, screaming, "Noooooo! What are you doing, Thomas?"

Jack didn't enjoy hurting people, really. It was the touching of life and the witness of death that he required. He didn't like hearing Gary's pleas. He grabbed the roll of duct tape off the shelf and applied a six-inch strip over Gary's mouth, quieting the frantic man. Then, selecting the scalpel off of the tray, Jack made a perfect slice, opening Gary right down the middle just like he had Benz. Gary thrashed about on the table against the pain and restraints. His eyes bulged from his head and he cried out unintelligible pleas through the duct tape. Blood poured out, and Jack's heart raced as he watched the flow. Choosing the retractor from the tray next, Jack used the tool to separate the incision, allowing him access to the tissue and organs inside Gary's chest and abdomen.

By the time Jack had the retractor in place, Gary had passed out from the pain, but Jack hadn't even noticed. He was fixated on placing his hands inside Gary's body. With Benz, he had to resist going too far at once, as he wanted to keep Benz alive. But this time there was no need for personal restraint. Gary would be dead soon, and Jack could do what he wanted. He took the rib spreader and used it to push Gary's ribs apart, allowing him a complete view and access to all of Gary's organs. The feeling of euphoria rolled over him as he carefully explored the now-dead body on his table.

Jack was enjoying his time with Gary so much that he lost track of time, and when he next looked up, he realized it was nearly four o'clock in the morning. Deciding he had to move Gary quickly, he began the process of cleaning up and prepping the SUV for transporting Gary out to the Lock and Dam road. Since no one had stumbled onto Benz, Jack thought he had the perfect place to dispose of Gary as well.

When Jack arrived at Lock and Dam, he found the area much as he had before – no one around. The townspeople of Inola were sleeping tight in their beds. Retrieving the flashlight and shovel, Jack made his way out into the woods, finding his way to Benz's resting place from memory. Soon he was in the familiar clearing and began digging under the brush and trees near where he had buried Benz. Once he'd dug deep enough, he returned to the SUV and lifted Gary out in the standard plastic roll. He carried Gary through the woods and deposited him and his clothes into the hole, just like he'd done with Benz and the others in California. Next, he carefully replaced the soil, making sure the body was fully covered. While he was there, he fanned the flashlight over the entire area, looking to see if anything had been disturbed by humans or animals. But everything seemed to be in order. No one had discovered the site.

Satisfied, Jack returned to the car, loaded the shovel and flashlight, and then climbed into the driver's seat to make his way back home.

Jack awoke to banging on the door, followed by the doorbell ringing. Not used to having visitors, he'd never even heard the doorbell ring before, and it took a moment for his mind to recognize that there was someone at the door. His night had been long, and he'd fallen into bed quite exhausted. Shaking off the fog, he climbed out of bed and pulled on some pants before navigating his way down the hall. Going through a mental checklist, he thought that he'd left everything in proper order after returning from Inola just a few hours earlier. It was safe to have someone in the house.

He thought.

As he approached the door, he saw Melody standing on his front porch. She'd been here once before when he hosted a study group, but he hadn't expected her to show up unexpectedly.

Opening the door and smiling, he greeted her, "Girl, don't you know when a guy has to sleep?"

"Good morning, lover boy. Is your guy still here?" she giggled, looking around the house.

"I'm not that kind of guy, really! How dare you," Jack teased back as he led her into the kitchen area.

"Okay, I really am sorry to barge in," she said as she settled into a seat at the dining room table. "But I have some great news and couldn't wait to tell you."

"Really, do tell."

"Well, I have a friend who owns two salons in Tulsa, one out on 191st and the other in mid-town. She's looking for someone to work both locations. I immediately thought of you because you were saying you needed a lot of hours, and I think this will give you those hours without having to deal with two different manager styles."

"OMG, this *is* fantastic news," Jack exclaimed with flair.

"I thought you'd be happy. I want to set up an appointment with you and her tomorrow. Will that work for you? Then if you hit it off and she hires you, you can start setting up and work under her license as an apprentice until your exam in a week."

"This just sounds too wonderful," Jack said, beaming at her. "Have you eaten? All this good news is making me hungry."

"Sure, you want to go get something? IHOP is just down the street, isn't it?"

"It is. Just let me grab a shirt and some shoes. I'll be right back, honey." Jack sashayed out of the room and down the hall to dress quickly and add some gel to his hair. He hoped she wasn't wandering around his home, and his heart thumped at the thought. What if she found something? What if he'd forgotten to close the pantry?

He rushed back to the kitchen to find Melody still sitting at the table, enjoying the view. His mind settled then, and he grabbed his keys.

"Okay, I'll drive. My car is behind your garage door," she offered, standing.

"You're a doll. Shall we?" He waved his arm toward the door in a sweeping motion, inviting her out the door.

Melody had grilled Jack during breakfast about his date the night before, but he dodged the questions, saying he wasn't a kiss-and-tell kind of guy. Melody had accepted it as a good enough answer, and the conversation turned to the possibility of him working for her friend. She had placed a call and set up a meeting for Jack the next morning. He was very excited, and had chatted about it nonstop for the rest of the meal. Then breakfast had ended, and Melody had dropped Jack back off, waving good-bye.

He went inside and immediately went down to the basement to verify that he'd appropriately cleaned up the night before. Things looked to be in perfect order, but he didn't trust his state of mind after his time with Gary. He went through the process of cleaning it again, bleaching every nook and cranny. Once he was satisfied with his work, he walked back upstairs to shower and settle in, awaiting his interview in the morning. He spent some time selecting his clothing for the occasion. He had a ten o'clock meeting with the owner, at the midtown location. The 191st Street shop was a bit of a drive from Catoosa, but in a way this was really good. He knew police looked at patterns, and considered location heavily in an investigation. Working at salons that were far apart and one that was far from his home was a good strategy.

The morning came, and Jack followed the usual routines, readying himself for his interview. He wondered if the salon owner, Samantha, would ask him to perform any specific manicuring demonstrations to show ability to do the job. He wasn't worried though. He knew he was ready, and this seemed like a better option than having to answer fake questions. Either way, he knew he could do it.

Pulling up in front of the address Melody had given to him, he saw a bright red sign over the door for The Beehive. There was a contemporary drawing in the sign, depicting a woman with chiseled features and a big beehive hairstyle. *Clever,* Jack thought to himself, considering the contrast between the 60s and contemporary. The windows had writing in big white letters, displaying the various services provided, which included manicures and pedicures.

Jack took a deep breath and headed into the salon, the door chiming as he entered. A tall, brightly dressed woman came from a back room, while two other women gave pedicures to patrons seated in the recliner chairs with bubbling water at their feet. The salon was tasteful and clean. Jack approved of the layout and could picture himself working here.

122

When the woman approached, he introduced himself. "Good morning, my name is Thomas; I have an appointment with Samantha."

An infectious smile broke across her face. "I'm Samantha. Good morning, nice to meet you, Thomas. Come on back here to my office where we can chat."

The next forty-five minutes were spent discussing Jack's recent graduation, station rent fees, and how money was shared for the services offered. Samantha talked about the flow of traffic between the two salons. The 191st Street location had much better foot traffic, while this location had more repeat business and people on a fixed income. Jack figured he would get a good cross-mix of the population, which was exactly what he needed. He wasn't interested in social status. He *was* interested in specific attributes, and finding those was all that mattered to him. So this would work out perfectly.

By the end of the interview, Samantha was charmed by Jack. He'd used his smile and charisma to draw her in. He left the shop with a set of keys to each location and an assigned work station, which he was free to start setting up right away. She'd given him a work schedule that split him between the two locations. Samantha had sent him to the 191st Street location to meet the other salon workers. She told him to go ahead and set up there as well, as soon as he had time. He had gone directly over to the other location and after meeting everyone, he'd spent an hour hanging out with the girls that worked there, making sure he would fit in. Feeling very comfortable with everyone he had bid his farewell telling them he would see them soon.

After leaving the second shop, he called Melody on his cell and thanked her profusely. Things were coming together so smoothly. Doors were opening and setting the plan in perfect motion.

Chapter Sixteen

Max and Cortez had spent two weeks working the magazine leads before the chief pulled back their hours. The man now named The Freeway Killer by the media had ramped up his activity, and more innocent people had been killed while absentmindedly riding the buses across Los Angeles, innocently reading a book, listening to music, or working emails. The mayor was all over the case, and the six unsolved murders had gone cold. The media and city focus had been replaced by this active killer. The chief said – in no uncertain terms – that Max and Cortez needed to get on the Freeway Killer case and quit working the cold leads.

Before being pulled back, however, they'd successfully transferred the details of the case into the national police database and contacted over fifty local precincts, inquiring about any similar activity. While they'd come up empty handed. Max still had hopes that she'd get the call one day, telling her that they'd found a match in another city somewhere in the United States, and Dr. Jack Tyler had been located. This wish came with a dread, as it would likely mean another body or bodies had been found. Ideally, they would get something that could really link this guy. Then they could use the media to help find him.

To Max's frustration, they hadn't been able to run any news reports with the doctor's photograph, linking him to the crimes even as a person of interest. They didn't have any solid connection of Jack Tyler to the murders. Max had suggested they put his photo out as a missing person, but no one had officially reported him missing, and there was no crime in leaving of your own free will.

Both Max and Cortez were frustrated with the lack of leads, and had been forced to settle back into their normal routines and assigned cases. They saw each other in the headquarters, but were currently working on different assignments. Each missed the partnership. Max had recommended Cortez for the detective's exam. She wanted to see Cortez apply next time it was offered, and had told the chief that Cortez had natural instincts, and with the success of the drug case had a proven track record. Her skills were certain to be an asset to the team. Max had offered to mentor Cortez as needed to help her pass the detectives exam. The thought of mentoring Cortez made Max think of Wells. Not that she and Wells had been on uneven footing, but she admired his skills as a profiler and found it very interesting.

Max thought of Wells often and considered calling him on occasion, but she always resisted the urge to do so. Given the distance between Los Angeles and Washington D.C., she considered the pursuit of the relationship fruitless. The idea of a long-distance relationship was ridiculous in her line of work. Still, though, she couldn't help but wonder if Wells thought of her, or if she'd just been a one-night conquest. The night had seemed so natural, though … She'd been with other men, but this had been different. Very different. Even different from the man she'd nearly married – her college romance. They'd been comfortable together, sure, but they'd grown to that point over time, not fit perfectly from the moment they met.

Any time her mind went to thoughts of Wells, she would force herself back into work.

***

Back in D.C., Wells was working his own cases. There was a stack of files piled up in front of him that required profile reports, but his mind often drifted to the long locks of auburn hair and the full lips that had kissed him with an incredible passion. He would frequently caution himself to not allow those thoughts to lock him in, as he couldn't envision how their paths could really cross again. Max was in love with her job, and if he was truthful with himself, so was he.

He had spent some time working the list of leads on the un-sub that Max was looking for, in his spare time. He had not had much time to spend on it, but he had parsed through it a few times and as he narrowed down the list he emailed his thoughts to the chief. He wasn't even sure if Max got them and he'd secretly hoped the information would have sparked her to call or email back. On a few occasions, he had called Max then hung up when he had gotten her voicemail, never leaving a message.

Considering calling again, he stared at the phone for a moment and decided against it, returning his thoughts to his files.

Chapter Seventeen

Jack had started working for Samantha, and forced himself to settle into his role as gay manicurist. The girls he worked with loved him, swept in by his natural charm. At the 191st Street location, he shared the time with Vietnamese sisters Ly and Anh, and their three cousins Cam, Kim, and Hong, who also worked the midtown location. They spent hours chattering and giggling. Jack couldn't understand them when they spoke in their native language but watching them was always fun, and occasionally they would work at teaching him certain words or phrases. The sisters loved the playful disposition he displayed and teased him mercilessly - he enjoyed their company. It was a pleasant atmosphere, and he was gaining the experience he needed. He'd taken his exam in Oklahoma City, traveling there with a couple of his classmates. He was still awaiting his exam results, which he should be receiving any day now. He felt confident that he'd done well, as the tester had given him good cues, and he hadn't had any issues during the test.

Now, with his shift having just started, Jack was standing at the front counter when a beautiful young woman walked in. Jack's heart nearly stopped when she looked at him and smiled, her beautiful blue eyes sparkling. *Oh*, he thought, *they're perfect.* He couldn't believe his good fortune. He tried not to show his eagerness to help her when she asked if she could get a pink fill. Instead, he greeted her with a warm smile and casually led her across the salon, offering her a seat. Settling her into his nail station, he put on his face mask, using it as a bit of a cover to observe her without much notice. He began making small talk with her, sneaking peeks whenever he could to get a glance at those eyes. They were the perfect shade, and had those little flecks of grey. *Yes, this was right.*

After carefully removing the previous nail cover, filling her nails, then applying the pink polishing crème, he gave her nails a final buff to make them shine, and led her back to the wash station. She dried her hands then proceeded back to the front of the store. At the checkout counter, the young woman handed him a credit card, giving Jack a chance to ask for her ID. She handed him her driver's license. While waiting for the credit card to process, he carefully memorized the address. He hoped it was current. Smiling, he handed it back, thanking her stealing a final look at those eyes. His heart fluttered.

When he finished up his shift, Jack returned home to get some supplies. First, he restocked his doctor's bag in the car with a fresh syringe and rag. Next, he lined the trunk with plastic, *just in case*. He wasn't going to risk everything he'd dreamed of and planned for by taking shortcuts. He would check out her house tonight and then decide how to proceed, based on what happened.

Once it was dark, he headed out to the address, navigating the SUV through neighborhoods until he came upon the right house. He would have to wait, as he knew nothing about this woman, other than that her name was Angela. He didn't know if she lived alone, but in looking at the house and knowing how striking she was, he doubted it.

After a while, he saw a car pull into the drive, and a man got out and entered the house. Jack thought that this was probably her husband. Realizing the husband would offer a challenge he did not want to take, he began thinking back to their conversation and other options. He remembered that she'd said she liked to jog in the park. He'd passed a park just a block earlier, and wondered now if that was the park she'd meant. He watched the house as long as he dared, not wanting to be seen sitting on the street for too long. Deciding the occupants were settled in for the night, he started up the car as he contemplated his next steps. He didn't have to work until noon the next day, so he thought he would come by here in the morning to see if he could catch her heading out for a jog. Pulling away he pictured those beautiful eyes looking at him. He could hardly wait to see them again.

Jack returned home slightly disappointed. He wanted so badly to begin the process. But he knew he had to be careful, or the whole plan would be ruined. And he'd never be with Hope again. Wanting so desperately for her to come home, he forced himself to calm down and focus, deciding this time could be well spent preparing rather than remaining disappointed with the evenings events. He pulled back the pantry door, opening up the stairs to the basement and descending into the darkness, flipping on the light at the bottom of the steps.

The room had slowly taken on more of a medicinal smell. Specialists said that smell was the strongest sense in terms of association for memories, and for him, the familiar smells of alcohol, bleach, and the coppery remnants of blood comforted him and made him feel safe. From those smells, he could imagine the smell of Hope's hair – the shampoo she'd used that hinted of jasmine and lavender. The memory made him want to buy some the next time he was at the grocery, and he made a mental note to do so. He wanted her to have everything she needed when she returned.

Going into the corner of the main room, Jack dug around, looking for a box of canning jars that had been left behind. Finding what he was looking for, he pulled out two of the smaller jars and found their matching lids and seals. Taking the jars into the surgery room, he set them on the table next to the sink and applied a small amount of bleach to each, then carefully scrubbed them until they shined. He soaked the seals and worked away any food residue until these too were in perfect shape. He carefully rinsed out the bleach and then applied alcohol to each jar swirling it around to ensure it washed away any leftover bleach. Finally, he thoroughly dried each jar, and then filled them with a mixture of 50 percent alcohol and 50 percent formalin. Sealing the lids tightly, he viewed the fluid in the jars and gingerly placed them on the shelf over the sink, next to the chloroform and other chemicals he had for his work.

That should do nicely, he thought as he scrubbed his hands meticulously, cleaning every nail on both hands with a small brush as if he was preparing for a surgery. Satisfied that he'd set things up perfectly, he returned to the main floor to prepare something for dinner. He made sure to close the pantry door behind him. After finishing up his dinner and cleaning up, he headed to the bedroom.

Jack could hardly sleep in his anticipation of the morning. Waiting wasn't something he had ever enjoyed, though working with Hope had helped him master the ability to control his impulses, making them work for him rather than them driving him to do things he would regret. Taking a quick shower, he was up and leaving the house very early. He couldn't be sure what time Angela – *was that her name?* – would go running. He knew that some people ran very early in the morning, and she might be one of them. He could only hope that she would show up to jog, and that he would see her easily in the dark. He decided to wait closer to the park and avoid the possibility of being seen sitting on the street.

The park was small, and there weren't many trees, making it easier for him to find a spot where he could see the street from the angle which she would most likely come. He wished he had some coffee, but had resisted the idea, not wanting to challenge his bladder. He needed to be able to wait as long as necessary. The location he'd chosen in the park also gave him a good view of the street to see any drivers in oncoming cars. Should she be leaving her home in a vehicle, he might be able to see her in the car, and then he would be able to follow her. Excitement filled him, but he forced the tingling to settle as he waited and watched. After waiting nearly two hours, he finally decided that he'd been wrong. She wasn't a morning runner after all, or she'd decided not to run this morning. He'd have to come back tomorrow, and the next day, until he worked out her schedule.

He knew exactly what to do. After all, he'd done it many times in California.

Jack spent three days watching the park and the house. He'd followed a car one morning, but realized it must be a neighbor after the woman stopped at the local market and got out to go inside. This morning he was sitting in his usual spot, where he had a view of both the street and the park. He'd started to become frustrated with the whole thing, but had been physically tempering these emotions, forcing himself to remain patient, when suddenly he sat straight upright. A slender woman came running into the park, heading down the path just east of him, into the stretch of trees that dropped down by the creek. He was certain it was her. The path would wrap around and come back up in front of his car, unless the woman turned around, but the park loop was only about a mile around. He was pretty sure most people would complete the loop.

He had intentionally nestled his car just at the end of the tree line, before the expanse of the park opened to picnic tables, swings, and slides. This spot provided some cover, while still allowing visibility to the street and park entrance. It was perfect.

His pulse began to race as he waited for the woman to come into view on the path. He found himself nearly holding his breath as he waited, until he finally saw a bobbing movement on the path. Pulling on gloves and removing the syringe he'd prepared days earlier, he sat with his eyes fixed and ready. It was early, and still a little before full daylight. The sun had started to rise, but the park was still cloaked in a darkness that lingered, especially in the forested areas. Jack was counting on that darkness to cover him as he grabbed her and got her inside the vehicle.

A few more moments passed, and Jack could see her approaching. Popping the trunk latch, he stepped out of the car and hid himself perfectly behind a tree, right at the edge of the path. He would be able to see her from here, and as soon as he was certain this was the woman from the salon, he'd grab her and be able to look into those eyes… *Hope's eyes.*

The woman rounded the last bend and was on the final incline, heading right towards him. He could see her clearly now and there was no doubt that this was her. Depressing the syringe into the rag from his pocket, he waited until she ran passed him. Then, stepping out from behind the tree, he cleared his throat, causing her to stop at the sound, startled. Just as she started to turn to see who or what had made the noise, Jack looped his arm around her neck and pressed the rag over her face, pulling her back against his chest. She fought against him for a few moments and then went slack in his arms as the chemical entered her body.

Jack laid the woman out in the back of the SUV and covered her with the tarp he'd loaded three days earlier. Once she was secure in the back, he shut the trunk door. Resisting the temptation of looking into her eyes, he quickly hurried into the driver's seat, reminding himself that there would be ample time for that soon. He pulled out of the park gate just as the sun was peeking over the horizon. As he drove, he removed the gloves, shoving them deep into his pocket while paying close attention to the posted speed limits. Arriving at his home, he pulled into the garage and quickly closed the door behind him. Opening the trunk door he pulled the tarp aside and lifted the woman out and cradled her body as he entered the house, delicately balancing her as he opened the pantry and the secret door that would allow him entrance into the basement. The excitement inside him surged as he realized that his plan was finally coming together. He was almost euphoric as he laid the woman on the metal table.

Removing her clothing, he zip tied her to the metal table in the same manner as his prior guests. Today, though, his mission was quite different. He would wait for her to awaken, as he needed to see those eyes one more time to be sure. If they weren't perfect, he would still have some fun with her, *BUT* if they were perfect...

While he waited in an effort to temper the excitement in his chest, he got himself ready by pulling on his surgical gear. Just as he was preparing the instrument table with the required tools for the task, the woman started stirring. She let out a few moans as the effects of the chloroform began to wear off, followed by attempts to raise her hands, most likely in an effort to rub her head, as chloroform was known to leave the patient with a wildly painful headache. When she found that she couldn't lift her hands, she fought harder to wake up, thrashing her head about. Fear was no doubt setting in.

Jack leaned over her, lowered his mouth next to her ear, and softly asked her to calm down. Her eyes opened, and recognition slowly settled on her face, followed by a look of fear and puzzlement as she tried to understand what was happening. All Jack saw were her eyes, though, and could think of little else. *They were perfect, beautiful, a perfect match.* Moving to the shelves behind him, he pulled a portable light off the top shelf and carefully mounted it to the instrument tray, plugged it in and pulled it over the woman's face. He leaned in and looked closely at the exact shape and color of her irises and pupils. Once again, he felt the excitement surge through him. Hope, he was looking into Hope's eyes! He thought he would never get to see those beautiful eyes looking back at him again, but there they were.

The woman was awake enough now that she was starting to cry and attempting to scream. Not wanting to hear any of her questions or screams, he tore off a strip of duct tape and secured it over her mouth, immediately silencing her to muted and muffled moans. She stared at him, and he intentionally blocked out all parts of her face except for her eyes. She was crying, and he didn't like that; didn't want Hope's eyes crying. He attempted to soothe her, talking gently, telling her not to worry – that soon they would be together and she would never need to cry again.

As he continued to try to calm the woman, he lifted the round, closed-blade speculum off the instrument tray and inserted it into her right eye, forcing the lids to remain open. The woman's back arched upward as she thrashed against the pain. He had only removed an eye as a surgeon once before, when he was a resident doctor in the ER. He clearly remembered the experience and just like on that day, his mind flashed to a time in the woods behind his parent's house when he'd done this to a cat. He'd been about ten, and vividly recalled spending time looking at the series of five or six muscles and how they had seemingly wrapped deeply in the back of the head. He had finished the act by slicing into the eyeballs and remembered being fascinated by the lens, which had reminded him of the shape and size of an M&M candy. He remembered that for a brief moment he'd been tempted to taste it, but had resisted the urge. Instead he had spent some time simply enjoying the jelly-like substance inside the eyeball.

He wouldn't be cutting the eyeball open this time though. This time the eyes were perfect whole. Drawing his thoughts back to the present, he returned to the shelves behind him and retrieved the two canning jars. Setting the jars onto the tray next to his scalpel, he removed the lid from the one on the right, carefully applying a prescription label and with a pen marked the jar 'Hope Right.'

Jack had carefully prepared for the type of tools he might need. Before moving to Oklahoma he had purchased some specialty tools that he felt might be required in executing his plan.

Jack lifted an evisceration scoop, which was the perfect tool for completely removing the eye from the socket. The tool was normally used for Endophthalmitis – a very painful disease, usually caused by fungi and bacteria. As Jack leaned in over the woman again with the scoop in his right hand, she screamed through the tape on her mouth thrashing her head back and forth. Jack realized he needed to contain her head, to avoid damaging the eyes during the surgical process. Retrieving the duct tape, he applied a strip across her forehead and around the entire table binding her head in place to the table. Now, with the woman contained, and the attempts to move her head restricted, though her pain and terror showed on the features in her face, he could begin the procedure. She continued to buck against the restraints, and her muffled screams continued. Jack became oblivious to her reactions or the torture he was injecting and carefully used the scoop to extract the eye from the socket, passing through the speculum. He then took the scalpel and cut the muscles and optic nerve that were keeping the eye from completely falling from the socket. Once the eye was free, Jack studied and admired its beauty, then gently lowered it into the solution of formaldehyde and alcohol.

The woman had writhed through most of the extraction, and as shock took over her feet twitched at the end of the table. Jack noticed them only momentarily before removing the speculum from the right eye and inserting it into the left eye, forcing the left lids open. He repeated the procedure on the left eye exactly the way he had on the right eye and at some point during the procedure, the woman's feet stopped moving. She'd completely lost consciousness.

Now with two jars properly labeled as 'Hope Right' and 'Hope Left,' Jack double checked the seal on each to make sure the eyes were stored safely. He stood in front of the shelf, staring into the jars, with Hope's eyes staring back at him. His heart raced as he stared into the beauty of his wife's eyes. They were so perfect. He then looked back at the woman on the table and stifled his excitement at the next steps. He needed to finish this. Jack found himself explaining to the eyes that he was only doing these things to bring them together again, at which time he would be able to return to the medical profession, once again stopping the darkness from controlling him. After finishing his explanation, he watched momentarily nervous, waiting until he was certain Hope's eyes had given him approval to finish his task. Returning a loving nod to the eyes facing him from inside the respective jars, he smiled before turning back to the table where the woman lay unconscious, two gaping holes where her eyes used to be.

The woman's breathing was labored; she remained unconscious. But the removal of her eyes alone wouldn't kill her. She could easily live like this, but that was never the plan. Even though nothing else about this woman was a match to Hope and all he wanted from her was her eyes, there was far too much risk to even consider allowing her to survive. Besides, Jack had a need that must be fed. This woman had donated her eyes, yet there was so much more she could offer. So much more she could do for Jack.

Returning his attention to the surgical tray, he lifted the scalpel and made his signature incision down the center of her torso, then used a sternal saw to cut right through the sternum. Next, he inserted the retractor to push open the chest. As he dug his hands deep into the cavity, he couldn't help but think that Hope was watching him. She had watched him only once before, the day when they were kids so long ago. He was glad this time, for he didn't need to feel ashamed of what she was seeing. She knew, and she accepted him as he was. Hope had saved him all those years ago, and it was being with her that would save him again. The thought of this gave him a warm sense of pleasure. He'd nearly forgotten what it felt like to feel pleasure, but today he was happy. This really was going to work.

Jack spent time touching and feeling inside the woman even after her heart stopped pumping blood to the other organs. Suddenly he became aware of the time and realized he needed to finish up here, as he would need to go to work soon. He couldn't mess up his job, not with it being the source for completing his plans.

Jack carefully cleaned up the surgical tools with the same precision he'd used during every surgery he'd ever performed as a highly recognized surgeon. He then washed down the woman's body, cleansing it fully with bleach to make sure there was nothing on the body that could be traced to him. Satisfied, he turned his attention to the room and washed the walls and floor, making sure everything rinsed to the drain in the center of the floor. Then, taking his scrubs off, he deposited them into the laundry and realized he had three pairs in there now. Those were evidence, and he needed to handle that. He stuffed them into the washer with bleach and detergent.

Heading upstairs in the nude, he went straight to the shower, glancing at the alarm clock on the nightstand as he passed. He had enough time to shower and get something to eat. He'd have to deal with the disposal of the body tonight after it got late and it was safe to do so. On the way home from work, he thought, he'd fill his SUV up with gas. That way he could go straight out to Lock and Dam Road without having to make any stops along the way.

After his shower, Jack dressed quickly and prepared a smoothie and some toast for breakfast. He was famished from his morning, but had little time for anything else. After finishing up his toast, he went back into the basement to take one more look into Hope's eyes, telling them he would be home soon. He pulled the basement door shut, and sealed the basement with the pantry. Then he headed out for the day at the salon. He whistled as he drove feeling especially light hearted today.

Jack disposed of the ravaged, eyeless body just after midnight. He'd carefully assessed the area out at Lock and Dam and was pleased to see that nothing had been disturbed. He had paid special attention to the road heading into the area, checking to see if there had been any recent travel, and then, noting nothing out of the ordinary, he returned home, feeling confident that there would be plenty of time to complete his plans without being disturbed. He just had to wait it out until the right opportunity presented itself again.

Over the next two weeks, Jack spent his time carefully observing his clients at the two salons, though he didn't find any likely donors. His disappointment was starting to overcome him when a woman entered the midtown salon, where he was scheduled to work until four o'clock. He watched as she asked for a pedicure and was led to the back and seated in one of the pedicure chairs. He'd just started applying a full set of nails on a repeat client that had come in a few minutes earlier, and almost forgot where he was as he stared at the woman. Trying to avoid notice, he soaked in the shape of her frame and the graceful way she moved through the room. Her hair was the wrong color and her eyes, well, those didn't matter. But her posture, the way she moved… Without even standing near her, he was positive that her height was exactly right. Oh, she was perfect!

Careful to not pay too much attention to her, Jack put on his Thomas persona, flamboyantly laughing and joking with his client. He knew keeping up this façade was imperative; if anyone came around asking about a missing woman, he needed to be the last person they would suspect. He tried to focus, but he couldn't help stealing occasional peeks at her as he held his client's hand, using a purple brush to dust off the fingernail powder. He kept it together for long enough to apply a new set of beautiful, red, shiny fingernails, then moved his client over to place her nails under the nail dryer, setting the dryer timer to five minutes.

He rushed back to his seat, glancing at the woman again. She was nearly done, and his shift was over. He busied himself tidying up while keeping an eye on the woman. He needed to get over there and stand next to her before she left. To his delight, he'd just finished cleaning up his station when the woman stood up, thanking Anh for the pedicure and handing her some money. He worked his way to the front of the salon, finished up by straightening all of the nail polish in the stand near the front of the door. He stalled for a bit, taking the payment from his client, telling her to come back again and then said his good-byes to his co-workers before strolling out the door.

Just outside, he stalled again, pretending to be texting someone as he waited for the beautiful woman to exit. She came out the salon door moments later, passing him as she headed towards her car. He was parked beyond her, at the back of the lot where most of the employees parked, giving him an opportunity to pass her. As he walked after her, he carefully observed her, forcing down the excitement. He assessed her height to be a perfect 5'4". A perfect fit.

Finally walking past her, he said, "Honey your nails look lovey," overly emphasizing the gay male attributes he had so successfully adopted.

"Oh, thank you," she replied, looking down at her feet before opening her car door.

"See you next time." He waved and headed to his SUV. He sat in his vehicle long enough for her to pull out. Then, carefully staying back, he followed her out of the parking lot and out into the street, allowing the few cars moving down the street to separate them. He paid close attention to her car. It was a Silver Camry, with a license plate holder that read 'Indian Nation.' He recited the license plate number to himself over and over, wanting to remember it in case he lost her.

For a moment the sun got in his eyes and he thought he *had* lost her, but then he saw the car turn left. He quickly navigated the SUV into the left lane, almost missing the opportunity to make the turn when a red pickup slid in between them. In the end, the truck provided the perfect cover as she got on the highway, heading for Owasso.

The car continued travelling towards Owasso. Jack remained behind the vehicle intentionally staying in a different lane allowing a car or two in between. Road construction nearly separated them as they wound through cones and narrowed roads near the Tulsa International Airport. They travelled for several minutes, before he saw the red turn signal. She was going to exit at 89th. She must live in Owasso, he decided.

The car got off the freeway and made a couple turns, heading into a modest neighborhood with smaller, single-story, ranch-style homes. She pulled into the driveway at the first part of the curve – one of the smaller homes on the street, the roof was a rusty brown shingle, a white barn-style cross-stitch over the front entry, and a corral-looking front porch. The entry was remiss of any flowers, and the grass was still brown from the winter frosts.

Jack drove past before she exited her vehicle and continued on down the street. As he checked out the neighborhood, he noticed some sort of industrial building backed up to the housing addition. That might give him access to the back yard without being noticed, which would be ideal. He decided to take a look around on the next block to see what was there as well. Wrapping around, he saw that he could enter the parking lot to the industrial building from the parking lot of the pharmacy. Following the parking lot around, he saw that he could pull all the way through to the back of the building to come up just behind the backyard fences for the houses on the other side.

This was perfect. The only concern now was whether or not this woman lived alone. The house showed some signs of disrepair, which could mean that there was no man around. Or it could just mean their financial resources were limited. Not knowing who all might reside inside the home, he would need to proceed cautiously. Jack decided that given the time of day and the fact that it was still daylight, the best choice was to wait until later. For now, he'd drive across town to put some distance between himself and the area, so that no one would associate him with having been in the area on this particular day. After driving for 10 minutes, he pulled into a restaurant parking lot having deciding that it was likely going to be a long night, and he should get some dinner.

After allowing himself plenty of leisure time with the meal, he finished up and then called Melody to check in. It was important to keep up the charade that was supporting his plan.

"Hey girl, I haven't talked to you in at least a week. How the hell are you doing?"

"Thomas, honey, how's my favorite graduate doing?" Melody replied.

"I'm good. I still can't thank you enough for connecting me with the salon. I love it, and am perfecting my fabulous skills every day," Jack replied with an intentional lisp.

"Oh, that's so great to hear. I miss seeing you every day. We need to get together for lunch or something soon, or another girls' night out. What happened to the guy you met at the club? Have you heard from him?"

"Girls' night sounds fantastic, but of course I'll settle for lunch with you anytime. As for the boy, no. I think he had a boyfriend, actually. Besides, you know me. I'm not ready to settle down with just one cowboy." Jack laughed at his own words.

"Well I'm going to find you a man. I promise. We'll get you to settle down one day, just have to find you the right one," Melody teased.

"Okay, well when you pick him out let me know. Give me a call to let me know your schedule, so we can make a plan. I know you're a busy woman."

"Okay, let's try to get together next weekend, maybe round up a few of the other girls too. Miss you, Thomas, mu-wah," she said, blowing him a pretend kiss through the phone.

"Miss you too, dear. Talk to you soon, kisses." The call disconnected, and Jack smiled to himself. He actually enjoyed Melody and would truly miss her, but once he had Hope home with him, there would be no reason to carry on the façade.

It was now fully dark outside and approaching nine o'clock. That meant it was time to try to gain access to the woman's backyard from over the industrial fence. He headed back towards the house. The first thing he had to do was try to figure out whether this woman lived alone. If she did, it would certainly make things easier. Otherwise, he would have to follow her for a while until an opportunity presented itself. If that happened, he needed to get close enough to get her into his SUV without anyone seeing him. He'd done it several times in California and was confident he could do it again. Through the excitement of finding her, he really was hoping he could get into the house tonight.

He already had everything he would need if she was alone. Turning back onto 89th East Avenue, he pulled into the parking lot of the pharmacy and headed to the back of the industrial building. There were no cars in the parking lot, and the lights were now all off, with the exception of a few parking lot lights and exterior lights near the entrance that appeared to work on motion sensors. He turned his headlights off to conceal his car and reduce the chance of anyone seeing him pull around to the back. Then he followed the fence line along the curve of the street, trying to align to the house. He pulled his car in behind the dumpster to provide some additional concealment, and pulled a syringe, rag, and a small Swiss Army knife – a childhood favorite – from his medical bag, tucking them into his jacket pocket. He slipped on gloves, hair cover, and booties, and then got out of the car.

He walked over to the fence, checking the homes on the other side through the slats in the boards, until he identified the smaller brown house with cross fencing trim over the back sliding glass door. He recognized that as a perfect match to the front of the house. This was the place. He pulled himself up over the back of the fence, just far enough to look into the yard for dog houses or toys – indications of pets or children, which could get in the way. He saw neither. The backyard had similar disrepair as the front, further providing hope that there was no man living here. There were weeds on the edges, and it looked like no one had trimmed the grass all summer. There were no flower pots or anything showing that the woman gave any specific TLC to the yard either. It seemed almost sad to him, that the graceful creature he'd observed at the salon had no one appreciating her. It pleased him to think that it wouldn't remain like that for much longer.

Feeling fairly safe that he could drop down into the backyard, Jack swung his body up onto the fence and slid down into the yard, dropping low to the ground. He stayed still for a few moments, hearing a dog barking a few houses away. Once the barking stopped and the dog had settled down, he thought it was okay to move closer. As he approached the house, he slid along the side fence and then hid behind the only tree in the yard, which was nestled up close to the back patio. He could see a single light on in the back of the home, casting a small glow out onto the yard on the opposite side. He assumed the light was coming from a bedroom, which meant she was likely, still awake. He would have to be careful, not wanting her to hear him. Continuing to slide along the side of the house, he approached the window, knowing he couldn't be seen by anyone on the inside with the lights on. He peered through a small slit in the curtain and saw the woman lying on the bed, apparently watching TV, based on the flashes of light flickering across the walls and ceiling.

Careful not to make any noise, he tried to look around the rest of the room, seeking any indication of who else might be in the room or home. The rest of the house was dark, except for a small glow through the sliding back door, possibly from an oven clock or some other appliance in the kitchen. As he took in the contents of the room, he noticed that the closet door was open and he could see clothes on the inside. Peering more intently at the items in the closet, he saw shoes and dresses. He saw nothing that obviously belonged to a man. He looked at the items on the dresser and saw a small, delicate jewelry box atop a lacy dresser runner and a few other items, none of which were masculine. Next he focused his attention on the nightstand. He noticed that there was only one. *Interesting,* he thought, as he realized that this was the ultimate indication that she was sleeping alone. An ideal situation.

He had one final task, and that was to try and check out the other bedroom. He was pretty sure by the size of this home that it was only a two-bedroom, so he began to work his way down the side yard along the house to the next window. This one was a single window, and he could barely see into the room. The mini-blinds that covered the window were just barely turned open. There was a small nightlight in the hallway, providing just enough illumination to give him a view of the room once his eyes adjusted. He saw what looked like a queen-sized bed with a comforter designed with some kind of flower that he couldn't quite make out. The bed was empty, though, and there were no pictures or toys to indicate that the room was occupied. Very sparsely decorated, it looked as if this room was rarely used.

Jack thought for a moment and decided that it was safe to proceed. He was going to get lucky tonight, if he could find a way in. Testing the window for this guest room, he found it locked. Returning along the house to the back again, the way he'd come, he went to the sliding glass door. He gave it a nudge and realized it was locked, but not very well. He could slide a knife up in between the door frame and the wall and lift the latch. Reaching into his pocket, he pulled the Swiss Army knife out and flipped it open. Sliding the knife in between the frame and the door, he began working. It took him a few minutes, but he heard a click as the hasp sprung free from the latch.

Resisting a smile, he slid the door open just enough to slip through and closed it again. He was in. Allowing his eyes a moment to adjust to the darkness of the room, he decided that the best thing to do was find a place to hide and wait. The woman was in bed – a good sign that she would be turning in early. He wouldn't have to wait much longer. Thinking the guest room would give him a place to stay while listening for her to settle down for the night, he slid through the small dining area, past the kitchen and down the hall to the left. The guest room door was a few feet from the master bedroom. Here he would have to be especially careful, since the master door was open. Sliding slowly past the picture mounted on the wall in the hallway, he waited until the TV went to commercial and the volume seemed to increase, and then slid into the guest room. Holding his breath, he prepared himself in case she had sensed someone in the house and came looking. He waited with the syringe in his hand, ready to depress it into the rag if needed, but heard nothing. He checked the time on his watch and saw that it read 9:45. He hoped when the news came on, she would turn out the lights and doze off. He waited patiently, listening for the show to end.

The TV show ended; she'd been watching *The Mentalist*. Jack had recognized the storyline, having watched it on occasion. He liked to watch some of the cop shows, only his motivation was different than hers. He liked to watch and learn what not to do. Now the news started, and he heard movement. The woman got out of bed and came out of the bedroom, heading off down the hall. Jack stayed in the shadows of the guest room, watching the kitchen light come on and hearing a cupboard open and close, then the sound of water. The light turned back off then, and she came back towards the master bedroom, carrying a glass of water. Even in the near darkness, Jack could see her perfection. It was amazing. He was in awe for a moment, nearly forgetting why he was here. Focusing, he listened and heard the sink water running, and assumed she was brushing her teeth. Then light footsteps on the carpet, blankets moving, and the TV went off, followed by the lights going out. She had turned in for the night.

Jack waited another half an hour. The house was silent, and he could hear every move, listening as she pulled her covers tight around her and turned in her bed. He waited several minutes after he heard light breathing and knew it was time.

Stepping out of the shadows, he pulled the syringe from his pocket and depressed the plunger into the rag. Entering the master bedroom, he approached the bed, where he could see through the darkness a slight lump under the covers. As he got closer, moving silently across the carpeted floor, he could see her head resting on the pillow facing the opposite direction. Leaning over her, he pushed the rag over her mouth and in one quick move splayed his body out over hers, pressing her into the bed and immobilizing her with his weight. Her petite body had no chance against his strong, long frame. Struggling against the pressure Jack felt her losing control as she fought against the weight on top of her. Moments passed with the rag crushing against her mouth and nose. He felt her trying to avoid taking any breaths until she could no longer resist, and gasped for air succumbing to the burn of chemical in her nostril and throat. Next, her head would begin to ache. She stared into the face of the man through the darkness. Her eyes registered a vague familiarity as she looked into her attackers eyes, but before she could completely pull the recognition together into words the darkness took her and her body went limp then still.

Jack waited a few more seconds, making sure that she had a good amount of Chloroform in her system for the thirty to forty minute drive ahead of them. Now that he had her contained, he took a moment to consider how he would get her into his vehicle. It was too risky to take her out the front. The driveways were all short, with the houses set close to the road. Someone would very likely see them. He wondered whether he could slide her over the fence, dropping her gently over onto the ground, and felt certain that he could do so without hurting her. As he thought this through, one thing became clear: he didn't want to cause her any bruising. Her body needed to remain the flawless perfection it was. He decided he'd wrap her in one of the blankets for extra precaution, then dispose of it in the dumpster before leaving.

Rolling her in the comforter from the bed, he carried her out to the back patio and laid her on the concrete while he closed the sliding glass door. He took a moment to listen for any noises and look around for any lights that had turned on or other changes that may have taken place. All he saw or heard was the quiet.

The night was clear with a few stars in the sky and a light breeze that felt refreshing. The stars shining reminded Jack of days when he and Hope would stay out late, lying under the stars telling stories to one another. He looked down at the blanket roll at his feet and smiled; they would have nights like those again. Picking the blanket up, he stayed in the shadows as he made his way to the fence at the back of the yard. He checked the parking lot for any motion, cars or indications that anyone had come along while he was inside the home, but saw nothing out of the ordinary and lifted the blanketed woman up and over the fence. The woman couldn't be more than 110 pounds, and though she was knocked out cold, the blanket made her easier to handle. He lifted her up, gently not wanting to harm her.

Once she was on top of the fence, he carefully allowed the roll to slide to the other side. He let go, and heard the bundle connect softly with the ground. Hoisting himself up after her, he took one more, quick look around before pushing himself up and over the fence, landing next to the slumped woman. The blanket had slid off and her head dangled forward, evidence of her unconscious state. Wrapping her quickly, he lifted her and headed to his SUV, where he opened the back hatch, slid her in onto the plastic, and pulled the tarp out from under the cargo door to cover her quickly. With her body safely on the plastic, he took the blanket and threw it in the dumpster, totally aware that he must open and close the lid quietly. He hurried back to the vehicle, backing away from the building. Removing the gloves and hair cover, he stuffed them into his pocket as he pulled around through the parking lot. He waited to turn on the headlights until he was closer to the exit, and then made his way to the highway heading towards home.

Back at the house, Jack carried the woman into the basement, realizing now that he didn't even know her name. Absent mindedly shrugging to himself, he realized that it really didn't matter. He went about securing her to the table without her waking up, and took a few minutes to prepare her properly. He'd already stripped her of all clothing, taking his time while she still was in a deep sleep to examine all aspects of her body. It was nearly perfect. The only issues being that her hands and feet were way too large, and her hair coloring wasn't right. She also had a large nose, and the positioning of her features was too broad.

Well, details, he thought. The torso was perfect, as were her breasts, nice flat belly, and the pubic region and legs were really a perfect match. Before securing her to the table, he'd rolled her over and examined the arch of her back and buttocks. Yes, this would all work. He had forced himself not to become sexually aroused. This woman wasn't actually Hope. Not *yet*... He had to be careful. He was dedicated and wouldn't allow anything to test his loyalties.

Preparing the items needed, Jack set to work in the room. He paused for a moment as she stirred briefly, to take in the beauty of her slender torso. His eyes paused momentarily, on her breasts and the perfect nipples, puckered against the cool air. Taking a deep breath, he continued on. *Not yet,* he chided himself. He had work to do first. With the tray set, all he had to do was wait until she awakened before he could begin. It was true that he really didn't need her to be awake, but he enjoyed it so much more that way. Then, not wanting to listen to her if she got upset, he decided to go ahead and apply duct tape to her mouth. She stirred again.

***

Feeling very heavy she tried to pull herself awake, but something seemed to be pulling her back into a restless sleep. Thoughts of hands and darkness entered her mind, but they seemed far away. And then fear set in as she again tried to force her eyelids to open. She could see light and someone. Her head pounded as she tried to think about what was happening right now. Trying to roll over and sit up, she felt as if someone was pulling her back down. Fighting the urge to allow herself to return to sleep and let her headache settle, she forced her eyes open again and as the blur cleared she saw a man standing over her. Suddenly realizing it was a doctor, she felt relief. She must have been in an accident. The hospital, that was where she was, of course, but what happened? Had she been in an accident? Letting her eyes adjust, she shivered from the cold. Focusing on the doctor, he was tall, and handsome, and he had on surgical scrubs and gloves. Had she had surgery? Looking about the room, she saw the light and tray. Lowering her eyes she suddenly realized she was completely naked on the table. Why would she be naked? Looking back at the doctor she was going to ask, but then suddenly she realized she had seen this man before. The parking lot somewhere, *where was it*? She could see her feet at the end of the table, toes. *The salon*! She had seen this man in the parking lot at the salon, but that did not make any sense. He worked at the salon, he wasn't a doctor. At that moment the fear welled up inside her and she struggled to get up. Her hands and feet were bound with something, and when she tried to demand what he was doing she realized she could not speak. There was something covering her mouth. Any sounds she made came out garbled and unintelligible through the tape.

***

With the woman fully awake now, Jack decided he could begin. He had taken extra precaution and applied two strips of duct tape across her calves and thighs, and across her forearms, ensuring she would be unable to move against the procedure he was about to perform. He tried to calm her, telling her not to worry, and that it wouldn't be long. She didn't seem all that interested in listening, though, and continued to struggle against the tape and zip ties, so he didn't waste any more time on conversation. As he picked up his bone saw, her eyes grew wide with terror, and like the others she screamed under the tape covering her mouth. Her eyes followed him straining to see what he was about to do as he moved the light to the end of the table. Her body went completely taunt as he made a quick incision with the scalpel at about two inches above the ankle bone, in a complete circle around her leg. Then he took the bone saw and began to saw through the tendons and muscle.

After a few good thrusts back and forth, he came to bone and pushed and pulled as if taking a limb off of a small tree. Jack was so focused on the precision of his work that he barely noticed the woman writhing in agony as he cut through her leg. Once the foot and ankle fell free, he set to work on the left ankle, adjusting the light so he could see, and making sure he was precise in cutting at the same place and at the

143

same angle as the other leg. Blood from the severed limbs spurted and poured off the end of the table onto the floor, pooling around Jack's feet, his surgical booties absorbing the crimson puddle.

By the time Jack moved to her hands, the woman had passed out from the pain and blood. She would likely bleed out before he was finished, he realized. That was okay, though, as this time he wouldn't be reaching inside to touch the wonderful organs. This time he would preserve and keep the beautiful parts needed. Following the same process, Jack removed both hands and stood back, admiring his work. The woman was dead now, having lost nearly all of her blood through the wounds. In the final moments, one of her arms had caused an arterial spray on the wall. Clean up would take some time, but first he had some work to do to preserve the torso and legs.

Jack had fervently studied the effects of body preservation, and while no single science seemed to preserve a body forever in its pliable state. He had found through some experimentation that with the combination of cryonics, embalming and taxidermy he could preserve a body for a very long time. After several experiments on animal carcasses, he had a cat that was still in good shape for – now – well over six months. He had attempted the process several times in the past and hadn't been successful, but he had finally happened upon a formula that worked well. The animal looked as good as any prize mounted on a wall, but it was still somewhat pliable, like a living creature. It was truly amazing.

He had to keep the specimen in a cold, dry place, of course, but had kept it out with him for several hours during the week, to test the effects of the elements. So far there were only minor signs of decay, but to Jack it was perfection. Storing the torso of the woman in the walk-in freezer would preserve it until he could finish his work. He had not performed this on a human, but there was no reason to expect it would work any less favorably. Excitement filled him.

Taking special care, he wrapped the torso in cloth similar to what the ancient Egyptians had used for mummification, and stored the body carefully in the freeze for now. Double checking the temperature, he placed his hand lovingly on the door before turning to collect the hands and feet, which he threw into an oversize baggie, sealing it shut. He then began the process of cleaning up. Spraying everything carefully, he washed the blood off of the walls and pushed the pools of blood towards the drain with the water pressure. Once the majority of the room was washed down, he applied a heavy application of bleach, scrubbing and swabbing all the areas. Carefully, he cleaned and polished every tool, using a surgical scrub brush to get into every crevice. He cleaned for hours until the room sparkled and his sinuses burned from the smell of the chemicals. Satisfied, he removed all of his surgical clothing and threw it in the laundry, then hosed his own body down with bleach to ensure that all possible blood was washed away.

He dropped the baggie with the hands and feet onto the shelf in the freezer, at the far end from the body, and decided that he could wait to dispose of these later. No need to make a special trip to Lock and Dam just for those. Besides, he was tired and thirsty. Checking the clock, he saw that he'd been busy for hours. It was nearly four o'clock in the morning – no wonder he was tired. Heading up the stairs and closing the basement door, he entered the kitchen. Grabbing a bottle of water from the refrigerator, he went to shower. Even though he had bleached himself, he now needed to feel clean - shower clean - not surgical clean. Refreshed after his shower, he dropped into bed not even bothering to pull on any clothes, only taking time to set his alarm for work. The covers and pillows enveloped him as he dropped into a hard despite short sleep.

Chapter Eighteen

Jack had visited the freezer several times over the past two weeks. He hadn't opened the freezer not wanting to risk any damage to the body, but just being near it comforted him. Now he was standing over another woman. *Oh*, it had taken time, but he'd finally found the right fit, while giving a manicure and pedicure to this woman. He'd hardly been able to contain his excitement when he saw the size of her hands and feet. Even the fingers and toes were perfectly shaped. And the veins in her hands were exposed just right, running down her wrists and across the back of her hands down to her fingers.

He'd struggled to focus on the manicure at the time, as he filed her nails down, dust from her layered over his hands and up his arms. The excitement of having the flesh from such perfection layering over him was nearly all consuming. He knew he'd finally found the right match to the rest of the body in his freezer, and had ultimately followed her for several days, keeping a careful distance, and making sure never to be seen. She was married, and it had been difficult to find her alone in a place that was safe enough to get close without being seen. Finally, though, he'd caught her just before closing outside of a small dry cleaning shop in Catoosa, ironically, and conveniently very near his home. She'd dropped off her clothing in the small strip mall after the other nearby businesses were already closed, leaving no one else in the parking lot. As she came out, obviously having retrieved some clothes which she carried by the hanger, the shop worker flipped the closed sign around, and waved good-bye. She walked to the back of her vehicle and opened the trunk to put her clothes inside. After assessing the shops for any signs of video surveillance, Jack had sped up behind her and pulled her into the SUV, drugging her. The trunk lid on her car had conveniently blocked them from view.

He closed the trunk of her car careful to not leave any prints and then pulled away before anyone had passed by. It would be a while before anyone questioned the car parked in front of the shop; by then it would be too late.

Now she was lying on his table fighting, cussing and swearing through the tape on her mouth, and writhing against the zip ties to no avail. This one had some spunk. While amusing, it caused him no real concern. She wasn't going anywhere. Not today. Not ever.

Following the same procedure he'd performed just a couple of weeks before, Jack carefully removed her feet and hands, in precisely the same order. At first, the pain had caused her to fight hard against the restrains, forcing him to work very carefully to keep each incision and

147

amputation precise, but otherwise things had gone perfectly. Like the woman before her, she too had calmed sometime before the first hand was removed, the artery in the wrist spurting the final pumps of blood loss that brought on death.

Quickly, not being able to resist the temptation of seeing and feeling the organs inside her body, he took the sternal saw and cut down the middle of her torso, breaking through the breast bone and ribs. She was already dead, though, and he found the experience a little underwhelming. He always got more gratification in being able to feel the organs as they stopped beating or pumping. He truly loved the feeling of holding life and yet experiencing the death, but he had more important things to focus on today and therefore moved on quickly.

He spent little time with her, not wanting to leave the recently removed hands and feet unattended for too long. He needed to get to them soon, and he moved quickly preparing them. After wrapping them, he gently placed the wrapped package into the freezer, right next to the body. He resisted the desire to look at the body, and closed the door quickly, ensuring that it didn't remain open for too long. It was important to preserve the ideal temperature inside. He also took the baggie of unacceptable parts out of the freezer, and laid it on the shelf near the door.

Next he meticulously cleaned the body, just as he always did, using bleach to remove any possible trace evidence. He then wrapped the body of his latest victim in plastic, preparing her for disposal. Her name had been Lily. She was a nice enough lady despite her feisty demeanor, but she was now serving a much greater good. She would be a part of greatness beyond anything she'd ever dreamed. She may not have realized the greatness she had been rewarded, but he certainly did. Stripping off his surgical scrubs, gloves and booties, he washed himself and the body thoroughly with bleach. After drying her, he lifted the body and carried her, minus her feet and hands, to the car, laying her out in the back and covering her with the tarp. He prepared everything for the trip to the Lock and Dam Road.

As he entered the bedroom his cell phone rang, startling him. Looking at the display, he saw Melody's name, and then, hesitating for a moment, he clicked the answer button.

"Hey girl, what's shakin'?"

"Thomas, I have been meaning to call you. Hey, what do you think about going out and shaking our money makers on Saturday night? Some of the gang and a couple of the newbies in the class are talking about it. It should be a blast."

"Sure, just let me know the game plan. I'm in," Jack replied, throwing in a bit of a lisp.

"I'll get all the details, but we're thinking of Club Majestic again. The music is pumping. Probably just all meet up somewhere. I'll call you tomorrow and let you know the 411," she chirped.

"Sounds wonderful, love you! Ciao." Jack hung up the phone, then took a deep breath and laid the phone back down so he could get dressed. It was getting late, after ten o'clock. He needed to gather his tools and head out to dispose of the body.

Jack returned from the Lock and Dam Road after taking the woman's body out and digging a hole next to the others. He'd deposited her, along with the hands and feet of the other woman, and both sets of clothes, all into the same grave. After carefully covering the grave and taking a surveillance of the area to make sure nothing appeared to have been disturbed, he'd returned home to begin the most important part of the work. Restoring the pieces ... pulling the parts together to make everything right once again.

Taking the torso and legs from the freezer, he laid the body out onto the table and began carefully stitching the new, more appropriate sized feet onto the stumps where he'd removed the others. The work was tedious, but he wouldn't accept anything short of perfection. And he was willing to take his time. He worked with expert precision, using the most expensive sutures, made from polyester. They were non-absorbent and had good tensile strength, capable of holding the knots well while slipping through the tissue with ease. He wanted to make sure everything aligned and looked as natural as possible. Though it was unnecessary as he could have clipped them, he carefully reattached all the ligaments and muscles.

He had been working for hours when he finally had the hands and feet sewn into their proper positions on the body. He lifted and bent each foot and hand, admiring the way they flexed. He could see the graceful abilities each held. His heart fluttered for a moment as he admired the body in its entirety. It was getting close but things weren't right yet. The hair coloring and facial features were wrong. Suddenly he knew what he had to do to correct those. It was late, and this would have to wait until the timing was right. But he would continue to focus on the plan. He knew the right one was out there he just had to find her.

For now, he would leave things as they were. He cautiously covered the body in the cloth, wrapping every part with a tenderness and love. The feeling was overwhelming and one he had missed terribly. After completely reapplying the cloth, he put the body back into the freezer, being ever so gentle as he laid her flat on the shelf inside. Double checking the temperature, he gently closed the door. He had been working for hours and had totally lost track of time. It was the middle of the night.

Chapter Nineteen

Max had been working long hours on the Freeway Killer case. They had some strong leads now and were narrowing in on a suspect. During her off time, she had created an investigation room at her house to work the Dr. Jack Tyler case on her own. She hadn't told the chief of her off-hours endeavors, but she couldn't let those people lay cold for years without any explanation as to why they had been killed. She'd removed everything from the wall in her living room, and the wall was now covered with a sheet pinned up near the ceiling and filled with the pictures of each victim, the places of their abductions, homes, and the autopsy photos. She'd pinned the sheet so that she could pull it down quickly if she needed to, for any unexpected guests. So far it hadn't been an issue. No one had come around, and she studied it frequently.

Every hour of free time she continued to work the case. At least once a week, she checked VICAP and NCIC for any related crimes or trends in missing person's reports that might match her case. Her instincts told her that Jack Tyler would kill again. It was just a matter of when, and if he would do so in a single location or if he was out traveling the world, killing people in other countries. So far nothing had turned up. The number of missing people was, sadly, too large for her to track every single one. He could kill a person on the other side of the nation and bury the body in a random spot, and it might never be tied to her case. There would have to be a pattern of missing people, or victims found with identifying markers and buried in shallow graves in a remote area for it to be tied to and match her case. She silently questioned, *"Would this actually happen, and how would she feel about it when it did?"* Not able to answer the question she continued to study the sheet covering her wall each time she had a chance.

She sat on her living room sofa stared at the wall and sipped on a glass of red wine, and found herself wishing a body would turn up somewhere. It was the only thing that would give this case an opportunity to draw to a close. She knew in her heart that Dr. Jack Tyler was the killer. But he'd seemingly completely vanished, and until he turned up again, she wouldn't get any further. After a moment, she chastised herself for even thinking such a thing. Forcing herself to stop thinking that she hoped for that exact thing to happen, she returned her thoughts to the wall.

Her eyes moved to the lists that she had complied over the weeks since she and Cortez were taken off the case. She mentally checked through the commonalities in all of the murders. He'd used bleach to clean each victim, leaving no trace evidence. There had been no sexual assaults, and no specific victim type, with both males and females found. Each victim had been savagely opened and explored with the precision of a medical professional. All wounds had been applied perimortem, with the victims being split open while still alive. Their organs had been explored until pain and trauma brought on death. The amount of suffering was immense, unfathomable, *"How could a person do this to another? Where are you Jack Tyler?"* she silently asked.

Her eyes then travelled to the lists of cities she and Cortez had made from the medical magazines young Jack had spent endless hours studying. Max was certain that Jack had absorbed each and every word. But that didn't answer the biggest question.

"Where are you now, Dr. Tyler?" she asked out loud before taking another sip of her wine, allowing the red liquid to swirl in her mouth and ravish her taste buds before she swallowed it.

Getting up from the sofa, she walked into the kitchen and poured the rest of the wine into her glass, emptying the bottle she'd been nursing over the past few days. She put the bottle into the recycle bin, then glanced at her watch and sighed at the time. She hadn't been able to sleep over the past few weeks, between the Freeway Killer and thinking about the six bodies – no, not bodies, *people* – who had lost their lives for what appeared to be no reason. Suddenly realizing she was exhausted, she looked at the clock. It was past midnight now, and six o'clock would come soon. Deciding she needed to at least try to get some sleep, she headed off to the bedroom, only to lay awake for a long while unable to get the images of Jack out of her mind.

Max found herself watching the clock until nearly two before falling into a fitful sleep full of fast cars racing up to buses, cities racing past her, one after the other, and a man with dark hair and blue eyes leaning near enough that she could almost see him clearly…Jack always eluding her. He always faded away before she could make him out.

The radio alarm sounded way too early, and Max rolled over and hit the snooze button longing for a few minutes of thought free sleep. After the third time, she finally pulled herself out of the bed, stretching her small, muscular frame as she headed into the bathroom. *Another day,* she thought to herself.

Maybe today would be the day she caught the bad guy.

Chapter Twenty

Jack had been patiently waiting for the day the perfect girl crossed his path. He hadn't seen her yet, but he had a sense that it would be soon. He was able to remain patient simply because he knew what was waiting for him at home. There was a calm feeling inside him that he hadn't felt for a very long time. There were times when anxiousness would start to grow. When that happened he would sit quietly near the freezer in the basement and a unique calmness would quickly overcome any impatience he felt.

While he waited, he passed his time working. He'd enjoyed another night out with his old classmates and a few new people from the most recent class. Everyone had danced, drank and laughed a ton. He'd been careful not to allow any men to approach him in the same way Gary had, though. He was too close to having his life back in order to risk it on a spontaneous moment of self-gratification, and an easy victim would have been too tempting. A few men had asked him to dance, and he had indulged them briefly, then cut it off, saying he was out with his "girls" for the night. This had worked, allowing him to enjoy his time in the role of Thomas, letting off some steam and getting some good exercise in on the dance floor. He'd returned home late and had fallen asleep on the couch next to the freezer in the basement.

Now he had the next two days off from work and was looking forward to working out and having some free time, though he knew that each day delayed his quest, stalling his ability to finish the plan. He made some coffee and gathered the newspaper up while flipping on the TV to check out the local news. Over the past few weeks, there had been stories on each of his victims, as local missing people. Most were brief, and so far there had been nothing connecting any of them together. No bodies found, so the people were all just single missing person reports, and nothing more. He had been pleased with this, knowing he still had plenty of time to finish his plan.

He was shocked when he removed the rubber band from the newspaper and folded the paper open to the front page to find a spread with a photo of three of his victims. Benz, Angela and the last woman, Lily, were all staring back at him from the front page of the *Tulsa World* under the caption, "Have You Seen Me?" Jack's heart rate increased as he read and re-read the article, his mind racing with the potential consequences of the victims being lined up together. Reading it for the fourth time, he noticed there was no mention of Gary, which he considered good, and also attributed to the fact that Gary had been new to the area. Nor was there any mention of the woman from Owasso. He'd never known her name, and since she was from a different town he quickly assumed that the police hadn't made any connection. Deciding that the missing connections were good, not all of his victims had been connected, this detail had to add some difficulty to any investigation.

Jack carefully scanned the page, then went back and re-read every detail several times. So far, the police had no leads and had been unable to make any connection between the missing people. Jack smiled, as he knew they'd never get what they were searching for. The people hadn't known each other, and there was no repeat behavior to track. As he continued to read, trying to find any other important information, a news cast came on the TV asking the same question as the paper.

Jack's head jerked up at the news anchor's voice. It was smooth, soothing actually, and he suddenly realized he'd never really paid attention to her. He listened intently as she reported that police were asking for any information on the disappearance of these three people, pointing to the photos behind her, which matched the newspaper article identically. She continued on, saying police were trying to determine if there was any connection between the missing people, but that none had been identified. Then she gave a phone number – the tip line to provide any information. Jack suddenly realized that he'd been holding his breath, but that it was only partially because of the news report. The other reason was because of the woman staring back at him from the TV screen.

She ended her news report with, "Jessica Jenkins, reporting live Channel 2 News."

Jack mumbled under his breath, "Reporting live," and scowled when the station broke away from the newscast and moved off the woman. He wanted to see more of her. Her face was flawless, the shape familiar. He waited as patiently as possible until the commercials had ended and the news returned, only to be further disappointed when they went to weather, leaving him waiting even longer. He sat mesmerized, he was anxious and excited waiting for her to return. Finally, there she was in front of him again. He grabbed the remote control and hit the button, engaging the DVR to record. Now he would be able to watch her any time he wanted to and he would be able to study her closely. As the cameras zoomed in on her face, he made sure the record button in the top corner was blinking. After several minutes he clicked the DVR button again, stopping the recording. He then selected the recording he'd just made and played it back, watching intently with the remote aimed directly at the TV, waiting for the perfect spot. Then, just as the camera zoomed in, he clicked the pause button, allowing her face to nearly fill the whole screen.

Jack got up and went over to the television, kneeling down to look at the frozen image on the screen very closely – her fully formed lips, hair the perfect color of natural blonde, her small nose that tipped up ever so slightly at the end, and the way her head tilted to the left when she smiled … even her perfect white teeth fit. Her complexion was flawless, and had that honey warm look that tanned easily in the summer. The smile drew Jack back, reminding him of when Hope got her braces, and how shy she was at first, demanding that he not tease her. He'd thought she was beautiful even with the braces, and never once did he tease her. He also remembered the day she got those braces taken off, and how it had nearly made him stop breathing; her teeth were suddenly perfectly straight, the white gleaming against her golden skin. On that day, he saw the most beautiful creature on earth, and today she was back on his TV screen, staring back at him.

He suddenly realized that his two days off from work at the salon were a sign. A miracle really, because they'd shown him where she was. Now all he had to do was find her and bring her home.

Chapter Twenty-One

It was just before dawn, and the two hunters had parked their truck along Lock and Dam Road. They were dressed in their full camo gear, guns propped against their arms, with barrels pointed safely at the ground, heading down the dirt path that led out into the brush and trees. The brothers had never hunted here before. But they didn't see any signs that warded them off, and thought it looked as good a site as any. Deer season would end soon, and time was running out to stock the freezer. Avid hunters, the two had hunted all over the Rogers County area. Denny, the older brother, had already gotten his deer for the year but had agreed to help his younger brother David try to nail one more before time ran out. Neither of the young men were natural killers; they hunted only for food. Both men had kids to feed, after all, and deer season was as good an opportunity as any to stock the family up on good meat, jerky and the likes for the cost of ammo and a hunting license. Each year, they went out and took down one deer each, enjoying the meat during the rest of the year. Today they hoped to meet that goal of stocking the freezer and began the walk down the road looking for the perfect place.

Part of hunting was a trust in the silence between the brothers. They used hand signals to communicate, not wanting to scare off their prey. A few hundred yards down the road, they found a small opening that led to a clearing, and decided to start there. Finding themselves in the middle of the clearing, David pointed to an area that looked like deer may be bedding down here at times. They both noticed a bulk of brambles and thick underbrush that grew up and around some of the trees and nodded in agreement that they could wait inside that thicket without being detected, Denny signaling with a flip of his index finger to go under the brush and David nodding his acknowledgement. As David worked his way in, his foot dropped into the soft soil causing him to swear under his breath. He pulled his boot out shaking off the dirt then took another step forward. Denny was laughing at him, holding back the sounds and grabbing his gut, showing his amusement at David's plight. The brothers continued to push their way into the brush with David continuing to lead the way, lifting and ducking under branches and brambles, careful to not allow their clothes or guns to get snagged. As David got further into the thicket his other foot dropped into the soft soil this time seemingly landing on something hard. Once again, he cursed, thinking they should have continued on until they found a tree they could settle up into.

Denny laughed out loud this time as he watched his brother struggle in the soil, "Bro, what is up with you this morning?" he inquired, keeping his voice low.

As David pulled his boot up out of the soil, something caught his eye through the early morning darkness. It was… plastic or metal? "Man this place… there is something in here," he responded.

Reaching down, he grabbed the item which was now lying next to his soiled boot, lifting it up to his face to get a better look. It was a baggie with something inside, but what it was he was not sure. It looked like someone had left their food out here or something. He first wondered if another hunter had been here recently. Maybe someone had attempted to lure some animal or had brought some bait out here for fishing down at the creek, which he knew was about a quarter of a mile further down the dirt path. Letting his eyes settle on the dirty bag. He squinted to get an even better look, while trying to hush his brother who was behind him prodding him to keep going. He held the bag up between their two faces peering through the dirty plastic. An eerie recognition came over the brothers at exactly the same time, seeing the finger nails and toes of the severed hands and feet that were the contents of the bag.

"What the hell?" David shrieked, dropping the bag.

The two young hunters began quickly backing out of the thicket. David's hands were shaking as his foot again dropped into the soil. He was struggling with calming his stomach. Losing the battle, he bent over just outside the brambles and threw up the eggs and bacon he had eaten before leaving the house with Denny.

Denny was already reaching for his cell phone.

"911, what's your emergency?" asked the dispatcher.

"Yes, um, my brother and I are hunting out at Lock and Dam Road, and we found … we found a plastic baggie, and … well, ma'am it has body parts in it," he said, swallowing heavily.

"Sir, did you say body parts?"

"Yes, ma'am, it looks like hands and feet."

"What's your name, sir?"

"My name is Denny. Denny Parker. I'm with my brother David."

"Okay, Denny, please stay on the line while I dispatch an officer out to your location."

"Yes, ma'am."

Denny held on the line listening as the dispatcher continued to speak with him telling him when she had made contact with someone, and that they were on the way. She had asked him a few more questions, including if they were both okay. He could tell she was merely trying to keep him calm and on the line while they waited. He looked over and saw

David had taken a seat on a log a bit away from the thicket where the baggie now lay. He tried to focus on the questions the dispatcher was asking him as he worried about his brother. In the distance he could hear a siren getting louder as it got closer, and felt a sense of relief as the sound grew closer.

Denny told the dispatcher the police had arrived and disconnected the call, putting his phone back in his camo vest. David was looking a bit better now and rose as the lone officer approached. More sirens could be heard in the background, and soon fire and rescue were also on the scene.

Inola has a strong volunteer fire department, like most of the small towns scattered all over Oklahoma. Within minutes several volunteers were standing around. The officer, a young man probably not much older than David, with a name tag clipped to his chest shirt pocket that read D. Metz, worked his way into the thicket.

Pulling out an evidence bag, the officer lifted the baggie with a leather-gloved hand and dropped it in. Coming back out of the thicket, officer Metz held the baggie up to take a look at it and nodded his head in realization that in fact these did appear to be partial human remains. He had never seen anything like this before. Having graduated from the Academy just two years earlier, working in Inola, he usually only handled drunk driving, a few domestic disturbance calls usually by the same drunk drivers and traffic offenses. Pulling his radio mouthpiece off of his shoulder strap he depressed the button and spoke the words for his boss to come on the line and then outlined what had happened. The local police chief responded that he was en route and had already contacted Rogers County Sheriff.

Over the next hour, more officers arrived and cordoned off the area with yellow crime scene tape. Denny and David went with an officer to the police station, where they were questioned for details and then released. The Investigation Division of Rogers County took over the scene, and began a search for any other body parts. Leading the investigation Detective Adair was a tall black man, skin so dark it nearly glistened, taking on a hint of blue. He sported a Mr. "T" Mohawk making him stand out. He was a serious man and was careful to not run on too much speculation, but he was working on the possibility of the rest of the body being somewhere in the area. The Sheriff barked out orders to the team to pair up and search through carefully, warning them about destroying possible evidence, and instructed them to go slowly. Another detective and a crime scene analyst were assigned to the area of the thicket where the baggie had been found. Adair had been informed that the brothers who had discovered the baggie containing the hands and feet had mentioned their boots sinking into the dirt, and his instincts told him they were on the right track. The detectives working the thicket soon called out to Adair, showing him the soft soil and indication of recent activity. Instructing them to get shovels from the fire and rescue team, they returned to begin carefully sifting through the soft soil removing it gently. After several minutes the analyst held up his hand and called out, "got something!"

Standing over the shoulder of the young man, Detective Adair watched as more soil was removed. What appeared to be a body, wrapped tightly in plastic and bound at the top and bottom with gray duct tape was revealed. Together they lifted the plastic roll out of the dirt and laid it out on a tarp that had been rolled onto the ground behind them by one of the fire and rescue team members. The CSI took several photos before beginning to remove the plastic, gently cutting through with a box cutter. Pulling back the plastic revealed the partially decayed body of a young male.

"Damn it all to hell," Detective Adair said out loud as he reached for his phone to call the coroner to get over to the scene ASAP. The hands and feet had been clearly female.

The team continued to dig which revealed more bodies. After spending nearly twelve hours out at Lock and Dam a total of five bodies had been recovered, two males and three females. Each body had been carefully placed on the tarp on the ground and photos had been taken. Detective Adair contacted the FBI and asked them to come in, indicating they had a potential serial killer. He was connected with Agent Mark Wells and began explaining the situation in Oklahoma, multiple bodies buried in a remote area just outside of town. Wells got a tingling in his stomach as he imagined the area. Requesting photos to be sent to his phone immediately, he began wondering if this could be the same un-sub as the one in California that he had worked with Max on. He couldn't help himself for hoping so.

After receiving the photos Wells pulled together a group of agents to meet him in the conference room. Projecting the photos, he began to deliver the details he had so far. After answering any questions the team had and instructing them to be prepared to depart in two hours, Wells concluded the briefing and returned to his office. Clicking open his contact list on his cell phone, he scrolled down to Max Nichols's name. Standing there for a while, he considered his next move before hitting the green phone key. With a nagging in his stomach he reconsidered, clicking end before the call had connected. He scrolled to Chief Harding's name, deciding that he must follow protocol.

160

Chapter Twenty-Two

Max was sitting in her living room, looking at the murder board on her wall again. Cortez had come over to work with her, and they were half celebrating. They'd apprehended the Freeway Killer at last. It was nice to just relax for a minute, but they knew they had work to do. Max had spent the last two hours catching Cortez up on her work over the past several weeks – how she'd continued to work through the cities where Dr. Jack Tyler might strike next.

Max sat waiting for a reaction from Cortez not sure if she would approve of the continued quest to find Jack Tyler. She relaxed when Cortez said, "Well, I am impressed."

They still agreed that Jack had either moved to another state or, he was responsible for more of the current missing persons that piled up each day in LA. Max had set up a notification tracker in the database to advise her of any crimes that matched the criteria of these victims, but nothing had hit yet. She'd also taken all of the cities and prioritized them by common aspects, such as terrain. She was looking for places that had areas where he might hide or get lost. As she'd continued to study the list of cities compiled from the magazines they had recovered from Jack's playhouse, she'd slowly rearranged the order according to which was a most likely new location for Jack. She'd moved three cities up on the list because the location offered close proximity to a city, but also had quick access to rural areas that would serve well for disposing of bodies.

The cities that had made the final list were Phoenix, Tulsa and Albuquerque. On a map of the USA, she had placed red circles around each of those and now shared her rationale with Cortez. Phoenix was a big city surrounded by desert. Tulsa was a mid-sized city surrounded by rural farm land, and Albuquerque was another mid-sized city surrounded by mountain and desert. They were ideal for Jack's activities. Narrowing it down without more to go on, though, was going to be tough. And knowing which city they *thought* he'd gone to didn't get them very far. Not until he did something wrong.

They talked about the possible cities, snacked on cheese and crackers and drank wine, enjoying the evening.

Cortez took a moment to explain, "I am grateful that you trusted me with this," waving her hand toward the wall of evidence. "I learned a lot working with you and personally haven't stopped thinking about Tyler either."

As they continued to discuss the case, and aspects of the job, and the male officers that gave them a hard time, across the room, Max's laptop sat on the kitchen counter, the email box flashed new incoming mail. As she enjoyed another glass of wine, she remained unaware that she had a notification from the database of a recent discovery that matched the search criteria she had entered, just outside Tulsa, OK in a town called Inola.

Max and Cortez continued to talk, looking through the case files for any new clue. Anything they'd missed. Maybe there was something that they'd overlooked. Suddenly a cell phone rang, and they both reached for their own.

Max gave Cortez that "It's mine" look as she hit the answer button, not taking the time to look at the caller ID. "Detective Nichols" she said into the phone.

"Nichols!" the chief nearly shouted into her ear. "Sorry to bother you. I know we just ran back-to-back shifts for weeks, but I got a call from our FEEB friend, and you might be interested." Max sat up. He was referring to the nickname local police often called FBI agents. She was definitely interested now. "Remember Agent Wells? He has a serial in Oklahoma that looks like it might match your dump site serial. Round up Cortez, I want the two of you to fly to Tulsa tonight. Wells specifically asked for your assistance on the case."

Max was stunned. This was the break she'd been waiting for. She stood, and was pacing back and forth now, with Cortez staring. Her mind raced. Jack was at it again, somewhere near Tulsa. Tulsa was one of the top three. Her eyes darted to the wall and the three red circles. She was right, her instincts were right. As this all settled on her, she realized the chief had said *Agent Wells*. Her heart raced, and she realized as she listened to the chief bark out orders to her that she had been holding her breath. Glancing at Cortez, she decided there wasn't any reason for the chief to not know that Cortez was with her, but Max had not acknowledged that Cortez was sitting in her living room, it just kept things clearer without him asking questions.

Finding her voice and calming her thoughts, "I'll find Cortez, sir. What do we know?"

"Not much. Five bodies, some of the work looks to be a match, but he's evolved. He's amputated limbs on one of the bodies. They're just starting the investigation. The bodies were just discovered there about fourteen hours ago. Wells will meet you and Cortez there. Now go nail that bastard!"

"I'll do everything I can, Chief," Max replied, her heart racing.

"Keep me posted every step of the way," he finished. Then, as usual, the line cut off and he was gone.

Cortez looked at Max. "What the hell was that all about?"

"You won't believe this," Max replied as she walked over to the murder board on her living room wall. She picked up the red pen and circled TULSA three times. "I was working with Agent Wells of the FBI on this case before you and I got paired on it. He came in for a couple of days, helped with the profile and some of the research. The chief just got a call from him and they've discovered more bodies. And guess where they are?" Not waiting for Cortez to answer, she continued, "In a small town just outside of Tulsa." She tapped the word TULSA again with the pen, then turned back to Cortez.

"Let's go. We're heading to Tulsa, first flight out. Go home, get some clothes packed, and bring your laptop and service weapon. Be sure you're carrying your LEOFA License", referring to the license *Law Enforcement Officer Flying Armed* that allowed officers entrance onto an airplane with a weapon under certain circumstances. "I'll pick you up in an hour."

Cortez looked shocked, "Max this is…" her voice fading off, quickly standing and grabbing her keys, she headed out the door without saying a word.

Max knew what she would have said. This was an interstate case. A case to build a detective's shield on, a chance not many got offered.

Chapter Twenty-Three

Jack immediately performed a people search for Jessica Jenkins. He couldn't get her address but did locate a phone number. He decided to try something, and dialed the number. When the woman answered, he almost couldn't talk, already certain he was speaking with her directly.

"May I speak to Jessica Jenkins, please?"

"This is Jessica."

"Ms. Jenkins, I'm terribly sorry to do this, but my name is Thomas and, well, I'm with Rainbow Florist, and we have a delivery for you. I would normally never call the recipient, but unfortunately we've attempted to contact the sender without any reply for over twenty-four hours. I'd really like to get your delivery to you, but the address we have leads to an empty lot."

She laughed, sounding delighted. "I don't know who would be sending me anything, but you can deliver them to my home. My address is 1619 W. Apache in Jenks."

Jack bit his lip. "Oh, well I see the problem here now. We have 1916, and that address doesn't exist. Again, I'm so sorry for having to ask you and potentially ruin the element of surprise, but we'll get these out right away."

Jessica thanked him and said good-bye, and Jack sat back, hardly able to breathe. He stared at the address he'd written on the paper in front of him. He was so close.

Without realizing it, Jack had been sitting staring at that address for a really long time. When he finally did realize it, he turned on the TV, hoping to catch the news and potentially see Jessica Jenkins live again. As he waited, a breaking news report flashed across the bottom of the screen, and the station icon flew in from the left, leading into the news report.

In the new screen, a male anchor with a receding hairline sat at a desk with a stack of papers in front of him. "We're sorry to interrupt your regular programming, but we come to you this evening from Inola, Oklahoma, where local authorities have made a grisly discovery. Details are still coming in, but according to sources, several bodies have been discovered in shallow graves just off Lock and Dam Road, west of the city limits."

Jack felt his body go cold, and he barely heard the rest of the report. They'd found the bodies. And if they for some reason compared this to the cases in LA …

His mind immediately went to the options he'd previously laid out: he could leave now and finish the plan elsewhere, or he could fly to the

Cayman Islands and disappear. He'd spent a few weeks setting up an International Business Corporation to host his offshore account for a fictitious company, giving him access to his money at any time, and complete privacy protection. He had several identities ready, two of which had been associated with the offshore account. He could quickly assume either of them if he needed to disappear again. He could get out of the country and become a completely different person.

But he needed to have Jessica before he could move on. She was perfect, and what were the chances of finding anyone else like that? He couldn't... *wouldn't* leave without her. *No!*... He would not let Hope down this time. He would be there for her, and he would not get caught. He would *not* fail. He would simply need to work fast. With that thought, a sudden realization set in – he didn't have much time. Returning his focus to the TV, he saw photos of police swarming over the area out at Lock and Dam. Yellow crime scene tape marked off the road around the clearing, where the deer slept at night and Jack had laid his victims to rest. He watched with a sense of urgent anticipation at the scenes wishing they would pan in closer so he could see more details. He felt anxious and eager at the same time, feeling somewhat conflicted by the excitement of knowing they had found his special spot. Those feelings quickly passed and turned to anger. Why did they have to find it so soon? He just needed a little more time. His eyes remained fixed on the TV as the report continued.

In the background, the anchor continued on. "So far, the police have no leads on who may have committed these horrible acts of violence. Now we'll return to your regular programming." The camera panned back, and there sat Jessica Jenkins, looking as beautiful as ever.

Jack knew what he had to do. Pulling his laptop up, he looked for more information on Jessica Jenkins, performing searches on her name and Tulsa, Oklahoma. He scrolled through the search results returned to him by Internet Explorer and saw one that looked promising – the link to her online biography. Clicking the webpage open, he found a story detailing her life, including where she was born, where she went to school, and now where she worked. He scanned the details of the page and leaned back when the he came to the end. No mention of a husband or children; Jessica Jenkins was single, and would therefore likely live alone. Smiling, he started to formulate his plan. First he needed to go see where she lived, so he could determine what options he had. Looking at the clock, he decided he could do that right now.

Chapter Twenty-Four

Max and Cortez waited at the airport for the next flight to Tulsa for over an hour, with Max pacing up and down in front of the boarding gate. They'd spent nearly forty-five minutes going through special security checks to get clearance to board the plane with their service weapons. Their weapons were checked since they weren't actually transporting a prisoner, but they would be able to retrieve them immediately upon deplaning. It had taken a lot longer than Max liked, and that further delayed their trip.

In the end, the only flight they could get had a connection, with a two-hour layover in Dallas before their final leg to Tulsa. After retrieving their service weapons at gate security, Max turned to Cortez.

"We'd better eat while we can. Who knows when we'll get a chance once we get to Oklahoma?"

"Not going to get an argument from me," replied Cortez, as she followed Max through the terminal in search of food.

It was getting late, but most of the restaurants were still open. After wandering down the terminal for a little while, they selected Friday's. Asking for Cortez to order her a coffee, Max excused herself to go to the rest room before sitting down. Looking at herself in the mirror, she silently made herself two promises: one, to catch Dr. Jack Tyler and two, not to be distracted by Agent Wells. Running her hands through her thick, wavy mane, she took a final look at herself in the mirror before heading back to the table, where Cortez sat with menus and drinks in front of her. During the meal they discussed everything the chief had told Max on the phone. Max pulled up her laptop, logged onto the airport Wi-Fi, and downloaded all the crime scene photos the chief had forwarded to her while they were inflight. They looked through each one carefully and recognized the grisly similarities to the dump site in Malibu.

After finishing their meals and paying the server, they headed to the gate, where the status displayed on schedule and boarding in thirty minutes. They approached the boarding gate counter and once again checked their service revolvers, receiving gate check tags. While they waited they sat in silence each running the case through her head and picturing what they would be facing when they arrived in Oklahoma. The Chief had arranged for a car and a local officer to meet them at the airport to escort them to the crime scene. After boarding the plane, they settled in anxious to be on the ground in Tulsa.

The pilot announced the upcoming landing, and the wheels dropped, making a loud noise when they engaged. Looking out the window, Max saw that it was late now, and the city was lit up with lights that spread out and slowly diminished into the night the further you looked past the city. She wondered where Inola was out in that darkness. She knew it was reported as east of Tulsa, but she couldn't identify from which direction they were approaching the airport. The landing was a single, quick and smooth bounce onto the tarmac before the brakes pushed them forward against their seatbelts. Grabbing their bags from the overhead storage and laptops from beneath their seats, they anxiously waited to deplane. After collecting their service revolvers they moved through the airport. Max flipped open her cell phone, restoring the service, and dialed the contact number Chief Harding had emailed her while they were in flight. Speaking for a moment into the phone as they continued to walk through the airport past the baggage claim to the airport exit, she turned to Cortez, "Our escort is waiting at the rental car area."

After getting the car and meeting up with Officer Parker, a young man who could not be more than twenty-five and who had been assigned to escort them out to Inola. They departed the airport and headed onto the highway, following the dark blue car marked Rogers County Sheriff in bold white letters down either side. They drove for about a half an hour, with Max and Cortez trying to get their bearings in the night. Passing the Hard Rock Casino, Cortez called out the possibility of trying their luck at the slots or craps tables after catching and arresting Tyler. They laughed an artificial laughter that helped to mask the tension that mounted the closer they got to their destination. Turning off the highway, they drove into the darkness with the sheriff's vehicle seemingly the only other source of light and life. Max clocked the trip as just over five miles from the main highway before they pulled off behind other police vehicles. There were lights set up, but it appeared the investigators were packing it in for the night. These people had been working the scene since early the prior morning, looking for any evidence that could possibly be found. It was now just after midnight and the air was cold. Officer Parker led the two women up to Detective Adair and introduced them.

"Welcome to Oklahoma, Detective Nichols, Officer Cortez," he said as he shook each of their hands. "I'm sorry we're meeting under these circumstances."

"Thank you, nice to meet you too, Detective. The feeling is mutual," Max responded, accepting Adair's strong grip. "Let's just get to the scene. If you could walk us through how the bodies were found, that would be great."

Detective Adair spent the next thirty minutes covering the burial site, showing exactly where the bodies were discovered and explaining how the hunters came upon the body parts. After answering their

168

questions, he offered to take them over to where the local team and the FBI agents had set up their operation. They agreed, hopping into the car, and after just a few minutes they found themselves in the small town of Inola. It was obvious that the local residents had been tucked in for hours, evident by the absence of any glimmering lights in the windows of the small homes that lined the street. Arriving at the City Hall building, Max observed it included a small court room that had been turned into temporary Investigation Headquarters. As they entered the building, they saw that the investigating officers had covered one entire wall with photographs and lined the room with tables. One person was standing in front of the room, giving a rundown of each of the photos.

Max felt her stomach drop when she realized the person was Wells.

"We thought we had four bodies, but we actually have a partial fifth body," Wells was explaining as he pointed to a photo of two hands and two feet in what appeared to be a kitchen storage baggie. "These hands and feet match each other, but they don't match any of the bodies we have."

Pausing when he saw Max and Cortez enter the room, Wells stared for a moment before returning to his explanation. "While we have a body where the hands and feet are missing, these," he tapped the photo, "do not *match* that body. This means there's another body that we have yet to discover." Stopping again, Wells turned his attention to Max and Cortez. "Ladies and gentlemen, I've asked for some additional help from California, and I see that they've joined us. This is Detective Maxine Nichols and Officer Cortez. I personally worked with Detective Nichols on a case that had some very similar characteristics. We have reason to believe that the un-sub may be the same person here as in that case."

Everyone turned and looked at the two uniquely stunning women, and Detective Adair immediately asked, "What makes you think these two cases are related?"

"Max, uh Detective Nichols, do you have your case files with you? If you could share your victims' photos, place them up here along with these please," Wells answered, pointing to the murder board.

Max glanced at Cortez as she rested her laptop bag on the table in front of them and began removing the case files she'd brought with her. She walked up next to Wells, avoiding any eye contact with him as she felt his gaze on her. She struggled to keep her emotions off of him and his presence, which seemed to fill the entire room. She began taping the photos to the wall under the photos Wells had just been talking about. She lined the victim photos up in the order in which they were killed, and as she was taping them up, she began describing the case known facts.

"We have a total of six victims. There was no sexual assault on any of the victims. They were all buried together – though in individual graves – in a remote area in the Malibu canyon, just north of Los Angeles. The victims' clothing was placed in the graves with their bodies. The victims were both male and female, and each was killed after an incision was cut down their torso, cutting completely through the sternum. The incision was executed with a high level of skill and allowed the killer to have access to the internal organs while the victims were still alive. The organs were touched … massaged perimortem. None of the victims were given anything for pain, and there's no doubt that they all suffered greatly, ultimately dying from the trauma and blood loss. Each body was precisely cleaned with bleach postmortem."

A young, pretty, black woman raised her hand. "Agent James," she said, indicating her name. "Were any of the bodies mutilated by the severing of body parts?"

"No, that does appear to be a deviation, but everything else fits. We also have reason to believe that our suspect might have relocated to this exact area. Our case went cold, but after weeks of investigation we believe the killer is a well-known surgeon from the Los Angeles area, named Dr. Jack Tyler. He may have relocated to one of several locations. The Tulsa area is in the top three of our list."

"How did you identify Tulsa as a possibility?" Agent James asked.

"We believed the precision of the incisions required a level of skill that only someone with medical training could have executed. On that theory, we identified several medical professions and began narrowing down that list, specifically looking for someone who had an event that triggered them and set them off. Dr. Jack Tyler suffered a loss – a trauma he didn't recover from and ultimately disappeared. When we investigated his past, including his childhood home, we discovered his childhood trophies – animal carcasses and some medical magazines that had been lovingly studied."

Max added some more photos to the board – pictures of the items they'd discovered in Jack's play house. "We created a list of cities from within those magazines. Tulsa was on the list, but more importantly we felt it met the profile of possible locations, having the flexibility and convenience of city life, along with quick access to a rural area as a possible dump site."

As Max talked, Cortez taped Dr. Jack Tyler's photo on the wall next to all the others. Tapping the photo, she said, "We believe this is your suspect, but we also assume that he's using a new identity. Like your case, there was no physical evidence to directly link Tyler to any of our bodies. He's a person of interest, and we really want to speak with him. But we do *not* have enough to put him at any scene, and therefore have not put out an all-points bulletin to bring him in for questioning. We need something to tie him to these bodies, any of these bodies," Cortez said, motioning her hand to the photos on the board.

Wells, who had been quiet and stood back while they shared their theory, stepped forward now. "Ladies and gentlemen, our first order of business is to find the other body. If we find her, maybe we find our guy. There are certainly enough similarities between these two crimes to consider the possibility that the un-sub is the same. If so, he may be escalating, which led to the severing of the hands and feet. Or there might be another reason for his change in MO. Understanding what he's doing with the remaining body might lead us straight to him." The room, filled with local, federal and out-of-state officers fell quiet as they all took in the information.

"We'll know in the morning whether the bodies here in Oklahoma had any sexual assault, or if the killer used bleach to clean the bodies. Those two things would certainly tie this case together with the case in California. The Chief Medical Examiner's office has committed to getting us preliminary results by morning. Full autopsy results won't be available for a few days, possibly even weeks. We've asked for immediate identification against missing person reports, and we hope to have these very soon as well. Once we have them, we'll focus our efforts around how the victims spent their last days and hours, to try to find any connection between them. For now, it's nearly two-thirty in the morning, and I'd suggest we all get some rest. Tomorrow is going to be a busy day. Let's reassemble at eight o'clock, right here."

At that, everyone began to slowly pack up and depart the room. Soon, only Detective Adair, Agent Wells, Agent James, Max and Cortez remained. Wells offered to lead Max and Cortez to the nearest hotel, which was back in Catoosa near the casino they'd passed on their way out to Inola. Max consciously tried to not allow anything she was feeling show to Cortez, but she caught Cortez watching her as she hesitated to accept Wells offer. Max hoped that Cortez would chalk it up to her desire to stay and keep working to track Tyler and hoped Cortez would not ask any questions.

Max hadn't thought about Wells being in the same hotel, and she instantly reacted to the thought of it. Her stomach dropped and she felt her pulse quicken. She needed to focus only on the case, but his presence was hard to ignore. She caught him watching her occasionally and somehow felt exposed and warm under his watchful eye. She wondered *why* he watched her. Was he feeling the same things? Was he hoping for a repeat one night stand? Chiding herself as having a childish reaction to seeing

Wells again, she accepted the offer and followed Cortez, James and Wells out the door into the night.

Chapter Twenty-Five

Just before the ten o'clock news was about to start, Jack headed over to the address he'd written down for Jessica Jenkins. Knowing that she would be on the news at ten, he thought that this was the best opportunity to get into her home. Once he was in, he'd wait for her to return from the news station, and then take her.

And then, of course, he could finish the plan. As long as he got her quickly enough. Time was critical now. He couldn't spend days following her around; tonight had to be the night. Before leaving, he had ensured he had everything ready, double checking his stock. Confident he was set he made the trip across town into Jenks, a more elite town which literally connected to Tulsa.

Once Jack got to the house, he drove by, scoping out the neighborhood and checking to see where he could park. He also looked for a way to enter the home. The neighborhood was nice, and the homes were placed a good distance away from each other, each with a good acre for a yard. Jessica's home was mostly made of brick – a two-story with nice landscaping, despite the time of year. Obviously a landscaper cared for the yard, as Jack was fairly certain that Jessica's schedule didn't allow for her to keep the yard this nice.

He decided to park the vehicle a block over, to keep it from being seen on her street for any longer than necessary. He walked down the street, paying careful attention to neighbors, dogs and the street lights as he walked. The air was brisk, and he felt chilled under his light jacket. Maybe it was the air, or maybe it was the excitement that was mounting. He wasn't sure but he welcomed the fresh air. When he got to her house, he took a quick look around, then slipped on his gloves and slid up the side yard. Trying the back gate and finding it open, he pushed in, ducking into the back yard. Once inside, Jack laid his back flat up against the brick wall of the house, certain he'd gotten in undetected, and continued sliding down the side of the house through the back yard. He checked the two windows he passed to see if either showed any indication of a security system or happened to be unlocked. Neither had a sensor, and there hadn't been any signs in the front yard about a deterrent for a potential burglar. Continuing to move around the parameter he made his way to the opposite side.

Jack noted a garage door that allowed access into the back yard and appeared to enter the house from the attached garage. He smiled to himself, as this was the perfect entry. He was prepared to take the door knob apart with his pocket knife, but found, to his surprise, that the door was unlocked, giving him immediate entry into the garage. As he'd hoped, there was another door that led from the garage into the house. Slipping on the booties and hair cover, he opened the door and found himself inside a mud room, followed by a laundry room and kitchen. He turned the other way and found a hallway, where he thought he could wait until he heard the garage door opening. Then, he found a doorway, and stood perfectly still; with a determined resolve uncommon to most people.

It wasn't long before he heard the sound of the garage door opening, a car entering and the door closing as the car engine was killed. Pulling the syringe and rag from his pocket, he depressed the plunger, depositing the chemical into the rag, and slipped back into the mud room just behind the door. He heard the car door close and the sound of high-heeled footsteps approaching and, as the door opened, stepped quickly behind the anchorwoman, wrapping his arm around her neck and slipped the rag over her nose and mouth. Her purse and keys hit the floor as her arms flailed up in an effort to push him away, but he knew it was useless.

***

A terror she had never felt before filled Jessica as she fought and kicked her legs backwards, but his arms were strong, and his was grasp tight around her face. She felt her arms and legs going numb, and as if her vision and hearing were slowly being taken from her. She continued to try and fight against the sweet, yet pungent odor filling her mouth and nose and the grip on her body. It was only moments before she knew she was losing. Unable to gain control of the grip on her, she slowly faded away.

***

Her body fell limp, and he gently lowered her onto the ground. Grabbing up her keys he returned to the garage and climbed into her car discovering the garage door opener mounted on the visor. Opening the door and exiting with the car, he lowered the garage door and drove over to the next block. Parking her car behind his SUV, he changed vehicles after grabbing the garage door opener from the visor. He pulled his car into the garage using the opener and closed the door behind him. Spreading the plastic out in the back of the SUV, he re-entered the house and lifted Jessica Jenkins up and carried her outside to the garage. For a moment he studied her face as he laid her down in the back of the vehicle. *Beautiful*, he thought. He covered her unconscious body with the tarp after carefully securing her hands and feet with duct tape. He opened the garage door and backed out watching the door close as he drove away into the night, his heart racing.

174

***

Jack arrived home quickly, pulling the SUV into the garage. He popped open the rear hatch to lift Jessica out and carry her down into the basement. With familiar precision, he removed her clothing and strapped her to the stainless steel table, then carefully prepared her for surgery. With an amazing amount of excitement, he realized that this would be his last surgery. There was work following this surgery, of course, to perfect everything so that Hope could come home. But this was the final step.

And this time he had to make a change. As much as he enjoyed the lack of sedation in his patients, he didn't want this beautiful face crying. It was important that she was at peace during this process, and she needed to stay hydrated. Connecting an IV drip to her hand, he administered both a saline and a twilight sedative. Then, after waiting the appropriate amount of time, he began preparing his surgical tools. Realizing he was missing something, he climbed the stairs and went to his room, where he had a wig head that he'd gotten during his classes at Clary Sage. He'd nearly forgotten about it, but decided it would be perfect to assist him during the procedure.

Returning to the basement, he began the procedure. Taking his scalpel, he made incisions at the neck and then parted her hair and made an incision along the part. Working methodically, he made the fewest number of incisions necessary, ensuring that he minimized the damage. Once he was done, he slowly pulled back at the incisions, peeling the beautiful face and hair away from the victim and snipping away at the arteries that supplied blood, nerves and underlying fat to separate it from the body. He put the face and hair onto the wig head temporarily, for safe keeping, and turned back to the woman.

To his delight, Jessica was still alive. Her breathing was labored, but she was alive. He removed the IV from her arm, as it had served its purpose – to prevent her from crying on that beautiful face – he took his time to enjoy her before she died, oblivious to the grotesque, bloody mess where her face had once been.

Opening her up as he had the others, he stuck his hands into the cavity, feeling the life leave her body. His time with her was short, as the trauma from the removal of her face and scalp had caused too much blood loss, but at least his needs had been satisfied. For now. He cut the zip ties holding her body to the surgical table, then washed her down before laying the dead body out on the a roll of plastic and dropping the remote control for her garage alongside her, ultimately sealing her away with duct tape.

After hosing down the table and cleaning it of all signs of Jessica Jenkins, Jack went to the freezer and gingerly lifted the body from the storage, bringing it into the surgical room and gently laying it on the table where Jessica Jenkins had been just moments before. Beginning again, he followed the same process and removed the face on the body from the freezer. When the work was completed, he slowly lifted the face from the wig head and fit it onto the head of the body, replacing the face he had just removed. Once it was aligned, he used the underlying fat from Jessica Jenkins' face to shape the cheeks and nose. When it was finally set to his satisfaction, he began stitching the incisions closed.

He had worked tirelessly. It had taken hours to make the changes to the perfection Jack demanded, but he'd wanted only the best for Hope. When he completed the procedure, he stood back, looking at his work and at how beautiful she looked. She was perfect – her hair, nose, chin and cheekbones perfect now. She looked just the way he remembered her. As his eyes travelled down her body, he felt an excitement he hadn't felt in over a year. He could now prepare the final steps in the restoration.

With the face in place, it was time to apply the final pieces. To fully restore his beloved Hope, he needed to add the window to the beautiful spirit she'd been. Looking over at the shelf, he turned and collected the two Mason jars with the beautiful eyes in them. He'd been waiting to truly be able to enjoy gazing into these eyes, and now was the time. He cautiously removed them, one at a time, and worked to insert them into the eye sockets of the face he'd just built. He worked steadily, making sure to properly stitch the rubber band-like muscles so that the eyes would work the way they should.

Jack applied his combined taxidermy/embalming method of tanning to restore and preserve the look so that Hope's face and body would be perfect, preserving the body while keeping the supple feel of real skin, and the ability to overcome some of the issues with rigor in a deceased person. He worked for hours, laboring over his creation to get the look and feel that he required. He would, of course, still have to follow the storage process, keeping the body cold most of the time. This saddened him slightly. But it was the only way, and he was grateful for the opportunity to have Hope back with him, even if there were minor sacrifices to be made. The process was long and tiring as he worked focused on precision.

Exhausted from his work, Jack finally put the body in the freezer before thoroughly cleaning up in the room. He then loaded Jessica's faceless body into the SUV for disposal, along with the unsuitable face, nerve and fat scraps. He couldn't go to the Lock and Dam Road, but he really didn't care any longer about the police finding the body. He knew they could not track the body to him, and besides he had what he needed now.

Deciding that heading anywhere in the direction of Inola was out of the question, he headed towards Keystone Dam, figuring there were plenty of places he could drop a body around the lake. He drove until he found an outlet on the east side of the dam that was free of any people, boats on the lake, or cars in sight. After disposing the body in the water behind a thick layer of brush and tossing the extra parts out into the lake, pretty certain the fish would take care of those quickly, he worked his way back to the SUV and then home, exhausted from the night's events.

Jack had fallen into a deep sleep as soon as he returned home and had awakened with a start, dreams of police coming as he and Hope ran off into the distance. Shaking off the dream, the images soon fading into the back of his mind, he smiled to himself. While running may be exactly what he and Hope would do, he had plans right now. Getting up and stretching his long muscular body, he pulled on a pair of jeans and then tugged a t-shirt over his head. Bare feet padding down the hall to the kitchen, he pulled a bowl out of the oak cupboard and dumped Raisin Bran in, followed by milk, and ate greedily. As he made a pot of coffee, immediately enjoying the aroma from the coffee beans, he tried to remember if he'd eaten the day before or not, but finally shrugged. It really didn't matter. He finished the bowl of cereal just as the coffee chimed readiness. He opened the cupboard again and pulled out his favorite cup, which said 'World's Best Daddy.' It made his chest ache every time he used it, but he would never throw it away, as it reminded him of Faith, making him feel as if she were still part of his life. Filling the cup full of the freshly brewed drink, he turned toward the pantry and let himself into the basement.

When he opened the freezer he stared in amazement, then lifted the body out and carried her to the surgical room. He laid her gently on the table, then returned upstairs to the master bedroom, where he opened the other closet and stood staring for a long moment at the clothes. Deciding today needed to be a celebration; he selected a dark blue dress that was simple, but elegant. He pulled out a pair of heels in a satin that matched the blue of the dress, and then went to the bathroom, gingerly carrying the items, to pull out the makeup kit. Next, he went to the shower and retrieved the shampoo and conditioner, then grabbed the blow dryer that was under the sink and the brush from the drawer. Hands full, he headed back downstairs to the basement, hanging the dress on a nail in the wall and setting the shoes on the table under the shelves.

He pulled out the adjustable hose that he'd used to wash down the room and guided it over the body with a tenderness that he only had for Hope. He bathed the body and washed the hair, being especially careful not to get too much water around the incision areas. After rinsing the body, he went out to the main room for a towel, and then proceeded to carefully dry the body and hair. Taking the blow dryer and brush, he slowly dried her hair, styling it with a part in the middle, exactly the way Hope always liked to wear it. Pulling a small can of hair spray from the makeup bag, he sprayed just enough hairspray to hold the hair in place.

With her hair styled, he began to dress her, carefully pulling the dress down over her hair so as not to mess it up, then rolling her gently to the side so he could zip the dress along the back. Next, he pulled the dress down over her hips and then laid her back on the table, moving down to her feet, where he carefully slid the shoes on. His heart raced as he slipped the first foot in and realized it was a perfect fit. This was almost his own version of the children's story Cinderella, he thought, smiling at the beauty lying before him. Returning to her head, he slowly and methodically applied makeup – first the light base that Hope always wore, followed by mascara and lipstick in the perfect shade of pink. Hope was a natural beauty, not requiring much makeup at all.

Once he had the makeup perfectly applied, he lifted her from the table and carried her out to the main room, seating her on the sofa and gingerly manipulating her into a seated position, propping her up with a pillow behind her back. Looking at her carefully, he realized that something was missing, and raced back up the stairs, taking them two at a time. He quickly gathered what he needed and returned to her, pulling out the diamond necklace and putting it around her neck.

As he leaned in, he resisted the desire to kiss her, telling himself that it wasn't time yet. He wanted everything to be perfect first, just like it had been... *before.* He placed the matching bracelet on her right wrist, seeing that it covered the sutures perfectly, and finally, with his heart beating nearly out of his chest, placed her wedding and engagement rings on her left ring finger, whispering under his breath, "With this ring I thee wed." As the wedding set slipped over her knuckle into place, he leaned in and ever so gently placed his lips over hers.

Without even realizing it, the tears began pouring down his face. They were tears of joy, relief and love. He had missed her terribly and looking at her now renewed his belief that he could have his entire life back just as it had been. Jack leaned back and looked at Hope, who was as beautiful as ever, her eyes shining back at him with love. He ignored the jagged incisions around her scalp and hands, and the fact that her head sat a little lopsided. To him she was perfect. He decided he could afford some time with her before heading into work for the day, and settled onto the couch next to her, wrapping her in his arms.

After an hour of sitting and holding onto Hope, Jack tore himself away from her, knowing that he would need to put her away for the day. It saddened him, but he promised himself to be grateful, knowing that she would be there waiting for him when he returned from work. He moved one of the chairs from the table into the freezer and then carried her over and gently seated her in the chair, allowing the shelves to prop her up. Then he kissed her lips tenderly.

"I love you, Hope. I've always loved you," he vowed, before tenderly touching her face with his hand. Turning to close the door behind him, he whispered, "Rest darling, and I'll see you when I get home tonight."

Once back upstairs, he turned on the TV to see what was going on with the investigation of the bodies he'd buried out on Lock and Dam Road, or whether there was anything about Jessica Jenkins that he needed to worry about. He knew deep inside that it was only a matter of time before the police made the connections, and he needed to leave before that moment came. There was little he needed to take with him, other than Hope, and he'd already figured all of that out. Today he would quit his job, giving notice at work so that he could focus on getting out of Oklahoma safely if he needed to. After all, he didn't need the money. Deciding he had better check the news first, he settled into his chair and flipped on the TV.

The news only briefly touched on the bodies in Inola, but it was filled with concerns for the missing anchorwoman Jessica Jenkins. The Tulsa Police Department and the Oklahoma Bureau of Investigations were working closely with the Rogers County Sheriff's Department and the FBI, the reporter said, trying to determine if there was any connection between her disappearance and the recent murders.

Yes, he decided, it was time to leave. He'd envisioned having more time with Hope before having to separate again, but he knew it was for the best, and in the long run they would be together forever. Turning on his computer and opening up the desk drawer, he looked through the various identities he had and selected a passport in the name of Jackson Phillips. Putting it to the side, he logged onto the Internet and searched for tickets to the Caymans, leaving within two days.

After securing a ticket which, unfortunately, had a layover in Houston, he searched for cold storage rentals in the Fayetteville, Arkansas area. Finding a place that had commercial cold storage, he called and spoke to a woman, making sure the space was acceptable. Using a credit card in the name of Jackson Phillips, he placed a deposit on a storage unit that was 9 feet high by 4 feet wide and 7 feet deep. He explained to the woman that he would be in the next day to pay for the next three months, at which point she had explained that he would be granted a passcode to the privacy entrance for twenty-four hour access. With that setup Jack went through a mental list of his plans, making sure he had not forgotten any small details.

Jack leaned back from the computer, thinking through the details. After a few moments, he decided everything was in place. The drive to Fayetteville was less than two hours long and with the proper provisions Hope should be able to make the trip easily. He knew she was fragile, so he would need to take even better care of her now than he had when they were in California. He would never let anything happen to her again. Never again would anyone be allowed close enough to harm her. No one would ever be able to take her from him again.

Feeling good that his plans were secured, he headed off to the shower and to work for the last time.

Chapter Twenty-Six

When the team arrived at the hotel, Max and Cortez had checked in, saying good-night to Wells and Agent James. But Cortez must have caught a glimpse of something off in Max as they rode the elevator, causing her to ask, "What is up with you?"

Max was startled by the question. "What are you talking about?" she joked, throwing on a petulant look and working hard to not show how she was feeling. The truth was she was loaded with emotion. Between her desire to find Jack Tyler and Mark Wells being in her presence, she was struggling to keep it all together

"Um, just ever since we got here you seem off your game. What's up?"

"Oh nothing, I must be just tired. I promise to be on my game in the morning."

"Yeah, okay, I understand," Cortez threw back at her.

The elevator doors opened then to reveal Agent Wells standing there with an ice bucket in his hand. Max stood back as Cortez, stepped out pulling her suitcase behind her.

Looking back and seeing Max and Wells both frozen in their spots, Cortez asked, "Are you coming or what?"

Max realized she'd just been standing there staring, and now the doors were about to close on her. "Or what," she muttered. "I'll see you at seven o'clock downstairs, Cortez."

Cortez gave a confused look. She glanced between her partner and Agent Wells, then shrugged and waved her hand, "Okaaaaay, seven it is."

As Cortez rounded the corner, Wells stepped forward, grabbing the elevator doors as they tried to close, and allowed Max to step out.

"Max, how have you been?" he asked.

"Mark Wells. I'm good, though I'd rather not be chasing a serial killer in Oklahoma," Max replied, not sure what to do or say to him, and again chastising herself for immediately admiring his strong jaw, muscular shoulders and good looks.

She watched as Wells took her all in. She wasn't sure if he realized he had done the top-to-bottom gaze. *What was he thinking?* Her hair was tossed from the wind making it fuller with the waves flowing past her shoulders and circling her face. Her light green eyes looked at him with a certain resistance.

"Max, I wanted to call you like a hundred times, and just didn't know what to do or how to make it work," he offered her with his hands splayed out to his sides.

"It's okay, Mark. I understand, and I know what you mean. Look, I'm tired. It's been a long day, and tomorrow's coming soon. We have a case to focus on, and I really don't want any distractions from catching this guy."

With a deflated look on his face, Wells nodded and pushed the button for the elevator, raising the ice bucket in salute. "I'll see you at seven, Max. Sleep well."

"You too," Max replied as she pulled her suitcase away and turned the corner, following the arrows indicating her room was to the left.

As he waited for the elevator car to return to the floor, Wells watched her until she turned the corner. When the doors opened he stepped into the elevator and pushed the button to the floor below, cursing under his breath at his inability to handle the situation with Max better. His inability to pull her in and make her understand that she was all he thought about besides work and the number of times he reached for the phone to call her was more than he could even admit to himself. Exiting the elevator and wandering down the hall to the ice machine, he decided when this case was over that he and Max Nichols would have a much needed talk. Scooping the ice into the bucket, he smiled at the thought.

Max slid the hotel room key into the door and watched the green light illuminate. She then pushed the door open and flipped on the lights. Seeing Mark Wells was something she'd pictured a million times, but then when she was standing there in front of him she couldn't muster anything more than *"see you in the morning"*. Sighing, she dropped her laptop bag onto the desk and unpacked her clothes quickly into the drawers, and then spread her toiletries out onto a hand towel on the counter in the bathroom. Tired, she slid out of her clothes and pulled a tank top over her head, and slipped into a pair of men's boxers, drew back the covers, set the alarm on her cell phone, and crawled into the bed.

Unable to sleep, all she could think about was Wells and Jack. She lay staring up at the ceiling trying to decide what she was to do with her feelings for Wells. She could not deny seeing him and being near him had filled her with emotions she thought were under control. She kept trying to convince herself that all they had was two days and a single passion filled night, but that one night had amounted to more than she had felt any other time. The problem was she had no reason to believe it meant anything to Mark. His eyes drew her in. Every time he looked at her it was as if he were pulling at her. *Why?* She would have to figure out what he wanted from her, but the case had priority now. Finding Jack was the single most important thing she could do right now. For all she knew, he was still killing people. She had to stop him and she had to do it soon. Her mind flitted between the beauty of Agent Mark Wells, the darkness of Dr. Jack Tyler, and photos of dead, bodies as she drifted off to sleep.

The alarm went off in what seemed like ten minutes. Max threw the covers off, rubbed her hands over her face, and slipped out of the bed. Deciding not to consider what might possibly be on the floor, she went into the bathroom in her bare feet, turned on the shower and looked forward to the steam of hot water. After her shower she headed back out into the main room and pulled her clothes from the drawer when she heard a phone ring in the room next door. Though she was initially annoyed at the paper thin walls in hotels, she stopped suddenly when she heard his voice.

Wells was on the other side of the wall. He'd been sleeping right next door all night. Running her fingers through her thick hair, she cursed under her breath and returned to the bathroom where she finished getting ready, thinking maybe a cold shower would have been more appropriate.

Showered and refreshed, Max collected her laptop and files. She stepped out of her room she was stopped in her tracks as Wells exited the room next door to her. They headed to the elevator after making the obligatory good morning statements to each other, and as they approached the elevator they found Cortez already entering the elevator car. She stuck her hand out, stopping the doors from closing, and invited them to join her for the ride down. They entered the elevator, saying good morning to her, and then stood silently for the rest of the ride.

Exiting when the doors opened, Cortez and Max headed off to the coffee station. "Okay, for real, what am I missing?" Cortez asked when they were alone.

"It's a long story. Just let it go, Cortez," Max warned not wanting to share something she herself barely understood or had yet figured out the proper place for it.

Throwing her hands up in compliance, Cortez poured her coffee and walked away to set it down on a table.

Soon the other agents filled the breakfast room, spreading out at the tables and milling about the room, devouring a variety of items from coffee cake to the hot egg and sausage sandwiches in the warmer. Wells had selected a seat at another table but could not keep his eyes from drifting over to the table where Max and Cortez sat. After thirty minutes, he stood up, signaling that it was time to go. Everyone gathered up their coffee cups and equipment as if on cue and began heading to the cars outside to make the twenty minute drive back to Inola.

Arriving back to the City Hall in Inola, the team immediately began to assemble and work out the case files. Wells took charge, along with Detective Adair, addressed the group.

"Good morning, everyone. We have a lot of work to do. If we're going to find our un-sub, we need to see if there's any way to connect our victims. Let's review what we know at this point. This morning we received the preliminary results from the coroner. We have the identities of all of our victims. There was no sexual assault, and each victim was cleaned with bleach. This definitely makes a very close similarity to the murders in California. We believe he'll have a fairly specific hunting ground. We need to look at anything that might tie any these victims together. One more thing – we do not believe there will be any connection between the California victims and the Oklahoma victims. There is no reason to believe any of the victims are related in any other way than having come across the path of our un-sub."

"Sir," Agent James asked, "why not just put Tyler's photo out as a person of interest and flush him out, bring him in?"

"We're afraid he'll run. If Tyler is our guy, and we do believe he is, then we know he's assumed another identity. He's a man of significant financial means, and we have no reason to believe that he won't immediately assume yet another identity, leaving the area to move on and kill elsewhere. We're prepared to put his photo out there if we can't tie something together quickly, but we'd rather do this ourselves. Tyler is smart. He has a sadistic side, but he's not a sexual sadist. He also has narcissistic tendencies, hence becoming a surgeon, and this has manifested into somewhat of a God complex, allowing him to justify his need to cut people. Basically, he is a narcissist who manifested into a surgeon. He will protect his image." Wells paused, letting everyone soak in the information. "Okay, we also have another issue. We have a missing anchorwoman, Jessica Jenkins. We believe we're looking for her still alive. We don't know if her disappearance is related, but if it is, we need to work quickly to narrow our leads. There is plenty of work to do and one of these details is going to tell us how to find Tyler and possible Jessica Jenkins."

No one said a word, though assignments were handed out. Detective Adair agreed to take on the difficult task of notifying the next of kin for each of the victims. Agent James was sent with him to help conduct the interviews with the families.

Meanwhile, Max and Cortez were asked to start pulling as much information as they could about each of the victims. Max first printed out photos of each victim, numbering them in the order of reported death, based on the coroner's report. She added their ages as she went – Victim #1, Benjamin "Benz" Callen, 60; Victim #2, Gary Collins, 31; Victim #3, Angela Perkins, 28; Victim # 4, Sylvia Franklin, 28 (hands and feet only); Victim #5, Lilith "Lily" Nathan, 32 (missing hands and feet) – and applied them to the murder board, assigning their names to each and aligning them to the photos from the burial site out on Lock and Dam Road.

As she applied the last photo, she stood back, looking at the total visual devastation Tyler had caused across two states. Max and Cortez agreed that they would begin working on the female victims first. Max was troubled by the photos. Something was niggling at her, and she could not let it go.

Suddenly, it dawned on her. "Wells, I think I know what he's doing," she offered with an energy she hadn't felt in a while.

"What have you got Nichols?" Wells asked as all eyes in the room turned to her.

"I think he's making a body from the others. The missing eyes," she said as she pointed to the photos both dead, and alive, of Angela Perkins. Continuing on, she said, "The severed hands and feet." She pointed to the photos of Lily Nathan. "We have various other body parts missing or present. I think ... I think he's rebuilding his wife."

The room was silent for a moment as everyone soaked this statement in. All eyes were on Max and the photos as she pointed to each. Heads started to nod as the others began to make the connection Max was exploring.

"What about the male victims? How do they fit in?"

"I'm not sure. I admit that part doesn't fit." Her eyes dropped in disappointment that those victims did not match with her theory. "But, I still think I am right," she said standing her ground. "Hope was his world. Without her, he crumbled. His narcissistic personality will somehow believe he is capable of *restoring* her."

Cortez jumped in before anyone else could say anything. "Maybe they simply got in the way, or maybe he couldn't control his urges, and those were just thrill kills, keeping him in balance while he worked at restoring his wife. We know he's been killing since he was a child, though being a surgeon seemed to keep it at bay. But the loss of his wife Hope and daughter Faith was the trigger that set him off – without Hope, he wasn't able to keep from killing. I think Max is right. He may believe that if he can restore Hope, he can control his urges and have his life back again. He just thinks he has to ... rebuild her. It's sick, but it makes a certain kind of sense."

Wells walked up and said, "Max, can you pull up a picture of his wife and get every detail you can about her? If this is true, we need to work very fast, as he may be getting close to finishing his project. And once he's done, he'll disappear again."

From the DMV records, Max pulled up a photo of Hope Tyler, who had been a vibrant-looking woman with interesting eyes and small features. Establishing a connection to the local printing device through her print settings, Max sent the photo to the printer and rushed to retrieve it, placing it up on the murder board next to the victims. Max began working to find the similarities. She began pulling up the driver's licenses for the other victims, starting with Angela Perkins. Max noted that the eye coloring matched that of Hope. Next, she pulled up the driver's license for Sylvia Franklin and compared height and weight. There was a nearly identical match. Sharing what she discovered, she wrote those comparisons on the murder board under each victim. Then, glancing over at Wells as she printed Hope's name under her photo, she noticed a flicker in his eyes, showing that he approved of her assessment of what potentially was driving Dr. Jack Tyler. This made her feel good. She felt the connection to him in that moment. She smiled at him briefly, acknowledging that she had noticed before she returned her attention to the files.

Settling back in behind her laptop, she began digging into the personal history of the first victim. Cortez helped her, and together they worked diligently, separate, yet together, comparing names of friends, work history, and married with kids or not. After a few hours, though, they'd found nothing that would connect the female victims together. The women didn't have anything in common. Stopping for a moment, they both grabbed coffee and then immediately jumped back into the information, this time attacking financial records and credit card purchases. If they could connect these women in some way, they may be able to narrow Jack's hunting grounds, and if they could do that, they could close in on him.

While Max and Cortez worked with the team back at City Hall, Detective Adair and Agent James had gone to the home of Benz's daughter. After notifying her that her father had been found and immediately dashing her hopes that he would be found alive they had spent another thirty minutes asking her if he had mentioned any unusual people or new friends in his life. She could not recall anything unusual and spoke of his pride as a car salesmen working for the local Mercedes dealer. After asking if there was anyone they could call for her, they had left her to deal with her grief and the need to make funeral arrangements.

Leaving there they worked their way through the families of the victims. Agent James had proven to be an effective partner and had superior interviewing skills, making any family member she was addressing feel very comfortable. After two more interviews, they stumbled onto a coincidence. Two of the women within days of their disappearance, had appointments to have either a manicure or pedicure.

Not sure if this was an important finding or not, Agent James called it in to Agent Wells.

Wells hung up the phone, his eyes excited, as Max looked up at him. "We have a report from Agent James and Detective Adair," he said intently. Everyone's eyes turned to him, and the room, which had been a buzz as everyone worked against the clock, fell silent. "Agent James just reported that two of our victims had recent appointments to have their nails done," he said, pointing to two photos on the board. "Angela Perkins and Sylvia Franklin. We don't know where these appointments were, as neither family knew the name of the salon, but this is the first lead we have had that could potentially connect any of these victims. Let's see if we can find where these women went to have those services. It might just tell us where they went after that."

Max and Cortez were already digging through credit card purchases and now, with a specific purchase type, they had a renewed energy about their efforts.

"We're working that angle and will shift our focus to those specific types of charges," Max offered. Wells nodded, telling them to do it as quickly as they could. For a moment their eyes locked before Max returned to the records.

After looking through the purchases on the credit cards for a connection, Max found a purchase on Angela Perkins' activity for a location called the Beehive. Immediately opening up a Google search engine, she looked up the name in Tulsa, Oklahoma, and found two different locations, both indicating that they were salons providing beauty services including manicure and pedicure. Bingo!

Waving Wells over to her computer and showing him the credit card statement, she asked Cortez to look for any similar activity from Sylvia Franklin. But Cortez came up empty. There was no activity anywhere around the date of her disappearance for the Beehive.

"What if she paid cash?" Max offered.

Wells looked at Max and Cortez, nodding. "She could have, and it's a possible connection. Go check it out. If we can connect them to this location, then we may know where he's hunting."

Max jotted down the two addresses for the salons, printed out photos for the female victims, and grabbed up her phone and keys. "Let's go," she said to Cortez, who was already gathering the folder of names and credit card activities. As they were walking out the door there was a subtle nod between Wells and Max that Max was certain Cortez picked up on.

Once they were in the car and heading out of Inola toward the highway, Cortez dared to joke, "Okay, I know you basically told me to back off, but what's the deal between you and Clark Kent? I mean it's like there is an electric current running between the two of you."

Max sighed. "Look, let's just say we had a moment, okay?"

"Looks like the moment is still in play, girlfriend," Cortez replied.

"Yeah, well it's not." Silently, Max found hope in what Cortez said, but still did not want to share her feelings with anyone. Still trying to sort everything out and with no clue on how Mark was feeling, she really did not want to get into a big discussion.

They rode in silence, Max driving and Cortez staring out at the open country that displayed the complete contrast to Los Angeles. After a while Cortez broke the silence. "I can't believe this. It's hard to believe there is this much open land just moments outside of the city. You know, I had a cousin that had lived on a farm in Texas. I spent a few summers there. I had kinda forgotten the feeling of freedom open land offers." She continued on by telling Max of those summers, playing in the creek, running through open hay fields, and fishing off the dock. She stopped when the casino came into sight.

Pulling out the paper Max had written the addresses on, she said, "Looks like the midtown location is the closest. I think we should go there first."

Max nodded in agreement to the suggestion, and Cortez plugged the address into the navigational system on her cell phone. Max took the exit and followed each turn as Cortez called them out. Within a few minutes, they were pulling into a strip mall with cars parked in front of the variety of storefronts. Max and Cortez took in the surroundings. The parking lot was stacked three rows deep. Looking at the vehicles in the lot it appeared they were in a moderate part of town.

Entering the Beehive, both officers flashed their badges to the young Asian woman behind the counter. "My name is Detective Nichols, and this is my partner Officer Cortez. We're with the Los Angeles Police Department and are currently working a case with the local authorities and the FBI. Can you tell me who is in charge, please?"

With wide eyes, the young woman nodded and quickly scurried to the back of the salon. Looking around, Max took in the store, then gazed back out to the parking lot, trying to think what Jack Tyler would see if he was looking in and watching women from there. The salon was thick with chemical smells from hair dyes to alcohol. To Max it reminded her of a near medicinal smell. Before this recognition could fully form, she turned back around to see a small, thin and attractive Asian woman heading towards them. *This must be the manager*, she thought.

Extending her hand to the officers, the woman offered through a controlled accent, "Hello, my name is Kim. I am manager on duty. My boss Samantha not here right now. How I can help you?" Her face exhibited a look of concern and confusion.

Accepting her offer, they each shook her hand. "Kim, I'm Detective Nichols, and this is Officer Cortez. We're investigating a series of serial murders in both Los Angeles and Oklahoma, and we have reason to believe that at least two of the local victims may have visited your salon just prior to their disappearance. Could we show you some photos to see if you recognize any of the victims?"

Nodding her head with a bit of apprehension, the woman glanced down at the first photo – one of Angela Perkins. Her eyes widened as she nodded her recognition. Next, Max showed her the photos of Sylvia and Lily. Kim pointed to the photo of Lily. "She come here. This one go to our other location."

"What about this woman? Have you seen her before?" Max asked as she showed the photo of the missing anchorwoman, Jessica Jenkins.

"Oh yeah, she on Channel Two News," she quickly acknowledged.

"What about in here? Has she ever come into one of the Beehive locations?"

Kim shook her head. "No, I never see her here."

"Have you seen anyone unusual around lately, maybe a man sitting in the parking lot for too long?"

Thinking for a moment before answering, she replied, "No nothing like that."

"What about men in the salon? I assume you have male clients that come in to get a manicure?"

"We have a few males that come here, most are regulars, though, been coming a long time. The only other man is Thomas. He work here."

"What can you tell us about Thomas?" She asked thinking maybe they were onto something.

"He work both places, just like me and my cousins. He funny, but he no like girls."

Max and Cortez had exchanged a look at the offer of Thomas working both locations, but Max felt her excitement falter at the thought of him being gay. That didn't fit the profile. They could still check him out, but Max was certain their un-sub was heterosexual.

"Thank you, this is very helpful. Can you please contact your boss and let her know we're on our way to the other location, and that we'd like to speak with her too?" Kim nodded, accepting a business card from Max and agreeing to call if she saw anyone that looked suspicious.

When they left the salon, Max immediately called Wells to let him know that they had confirmation that all of the dead women were customers of one or the other of the Beehive locations. Hanging up, Max looked over at Cortez, "He's been here watching the woman from these locations. The question is what is the connection between the two locations? It would make more sense if there was only one."

"What if he hunted in two locations to throw off anyone looking?" Cortez offered. "Having a bunch of woman missing from a single location is way more likely to be noticed."

Max nodded, agreeing this seemed logical, but she still felt like they were missing something. Something was off, if she could just put her finger on it. Returning to the car Max could not shake the feeling that there was a small matter they were overlooking.

Cortez once again navigated as Max made her way back out to the highway, heading South to 191$^{st\ Street}$, where the second Beehive salon sat. This was clearly a higher-class part of Tulsa, as the parking lot for this salon was filled with newer, high-end vehicles. Also located in a strip mall with a similar parking arrangement, it seemed someone could park their car deep in the lot and watch for specific women to exit. The variation in the locations might explain the differences in their women victims, who came from within different economic lifestyles.

This time when they entered the salon they were greeted by a tall Caucasian woman who immediately extended her hand. "Samantha, Officers. Kim called me and said you were on your way. How may I help you?"

Max immediately offered her a business card and accepted her handshake, as did Cortez. "Sorry, for the quick request to meet with you, but we're assisting in the investigation of the murders of several woman here in Oklahoma. I'd like to show you some photos that Kim acknowledged were customers of your salons. These are some of the victims, and we're looking for any connection."

Samantha nodded and looked through the photos, confirming that the victims were patrons of her salons. She showed visible signs of concern at the implication that each woman was dead. Max then showed her the photo of Jessica Jenkins, explaining that she was reported missing. Samantha said that while she knew the anchorwoman from the local news station, she wasn't a customer at either location.

Cortez jumped in then, inquiring, "Have you seen anyone around lately that may have acted strangely, perhaps showing too much interest in any of these women? A man sitting in the parking lot too long or possibly a customer that seemed overly interested in any of these women?"

Hesitating for a moment as she thought, she finally said, "I can't think of anything that jumps out, but our clients sign a registry, which would indicate any male patrons that may have been here at the same time as these women." Reaching for the notebook on the counter, she offered it to the officers. "You're welcome to take it with you if you think it could help."

"Thank you. Do you have something similar at the other location?"

"We do, and I could have it faxed to you if that would help."

"Yes, that would be very helpful." After placing a call to Wells to get the number and letting him know to expect something, while informing that they were on the way back in, Max offered Samantha the fax line for the Investigation Headquarters in Inola. She took the time to inform Wells that there was only one male employee, but that he did not fit the profile, explaining that he was openly gay. Before hanging up Wells had agreed it did not fit. Max again felt the disappointment she felt each time it seemed they were onto something it failed to pan out.

Offering their thanks for the cooperation, Max and Cortez exited back out into the Oklahoma air. The air was cool with a bitter wind, making it feel colder than the temperature would have indicated. Max hugged her coat tightly around her.

Chapter Twenty-Seven

Jack had been working at the 191st Street location when Kim called, saying some officers were on the way. His heart raced as he considered leaving now. Realizing that was too risky, it would be too obvious. So far from what he could gather from the conversation he overheard, it appeared they were just fishing. Reminding himself that he must remain calm, he'd decided to wait until he saw them in the parking lot, then went into the back room and began unpacking supplies. From here, he could hear parts of their conversation, but not be seen. He wanted to hear if they had any clues on who specifically they were looking for, and was pleased to learn that they didn't yet have a connection to him under the name of Jack or Thomas.

After the officers left, he came out of the back room and listened as Samantha told them the questions she'd been asked. Knowing the police were looking for a male client or man possibly stalking women in the parking lot, he felt comfortable that he could leave town tomorrow, before anyone realized he'd been right there under their noses. When Samantha described the situation, he'd participated in the conversation, feigning his best horrified expressions as Samantha had shared the horrible deaths of some of their favored clients. Suddenly he realized that he couldn't give notice as he'd planned; while he respected Samantha and really didn't like leaving her high and dry, he knew his sudden notice would raise suspicions. And he couldn't afford that.

He needed to get out of town, and quickly. Of course, when he didn't show up for work the next day, those same suspicions would kick in. But at least he'd be long gone. He would finish his shift, as planned, and then never return here again. By the time anyone figured out what had happened, he and Hope would be gone.

Chapter Twenty-Eight

Returning to Inola City Hall, Max and Cortez gave the others an update on their findings at the Beehive Salons. All the female deceased victims had in fact been clients at these locations. No one reported anything suspicious, and they now had the registries to see if there had been any male clients that possibly frequented on the same days as the women. Neither salon was familiar with Jessica Jenkins, and how, or if, she tied into this was anyone's guess.

Max took the registry that had been faxed over, and Cortez took the book provided by Samantha for the 191st Street location. They agreed they would note any male names in the book for thirty days prior to the disappearance of the first victim, and focus on any men that appeared more than once, or had been there the same day as the murdered women. With luck, they'd get a hit.

As the women were working their way down and compiling a list, Wells stood up and addressed the team again. "Ladies and gentlemen, I just got a call from the Tulsa Police Department. A woman's body was discovered by a fisherman, and I'm afraid it matches the physical description of Jessica Jenkins. The body's out at Keystone Dam, about thirty minutes west of the city. No positive ID yet, but I think Detective Nichols was onto something," Wells paused before continuing, gulping. "The victim's face and hair have been removed."

A quiet fell over the room as everyone sat, looking at Wells. "I've asked Detective Adair and Agent James to head out to the location. They're en route now, and will send photos of the crime scene as soon as they get there."

Max slammed her hand on the table. "Damn it!"

Wells looked at her, and it pained him to know that in some way she blamed herself for not finding Jack Tyler sooner. "Take a walk, Detective," he said to her, hoping she could see in his eyes the concern he felt inside.

She stood up kicking her chair back with her foot and walked out the door allowing it to slam behind her.

Waiting a couple of minutes, Wells followed her, walking up to her and laying his hand on her arm. "Max, there's nothing you could have done to change this. Tyler is a sick bastard."

Trying to ignore the tingling his touch gave through her clothes, she asked, "How are we going to find him, Mark?"

"We will. I promise you. We *will* get this guy. We follow the evidence, and we get our guy."

They stood facing each other for a few more moments; their eyes locked and held. Wells was the first to break the silence, never releasing the lock on her eyes. "When this is over, we need to talk."

"Mark, I don't know what there is to say, really."

"Lots, Max, there's lots to say," Wells stated before taking her by the elbow and leading her back towards the door. When they returned to the room together, Max could feel Cortez watching her has she returned to her seat and started working through the registry, again looking for connections between the two salons. Once finished, she and Cortez compared their lists of names. There were only two that repeated. Neither had gone to both locations, nor had there been any male patrons on the days any of the women had disappeared. Agreeing they should look at these men anyway, they began working through them one by one, looking at driver's license photos. If Dr. Jack Tyler was one of these men, they would have him. Deciding to collect all the male names from the registry back a full sixty days, they spent the next two hours going through the records for all men holding Oklahoma driver's licenses. They concluded none of the men were Jack Tyler under an assumed name. They had just come up empty.

Max sat back in her chair looking at the murder board, then stood up and moved Jessica Jenkins to the spot of Victim #6. When she did, the photo of Jessica Jenkins and Hope Tyler sat side by side. A chill ran up her spine at the resemblance between the two women.

"Oh my god," she murmured. "Wells," she called out, turning to stare into the room.

Cortez and Wells both came over to her and joined her standing in front of the murder board. She pointed toward the photos. "They looked almost exactly alike. I hadn't noticed it until I put their photos side by side." Wells and Cortez were both nodding, and Max continued. "What if the reason this one is different is because she was a public figure? What if he was sitting there in his Lazy Boy recliner, drinking beer, and just saw her on the ten o'clock news? His sick ass sees her and recognizes the resemblance to Hope and decides he's going to take her. That's why she was never in the salon."

"It makes sense," Wells agreed.

"He wouldn't have to find her. She was right there in front of him every single night. She was a public figure, could be easily traced and followed. He could have grabbed her from anywhere. She was the missing piece to the puzzle," Max finished.

Chapter Twenty-Nine

Jack's final shift as Thomas had ended without incident, and he had left waving good-bye to his friends and co-workers, knowing he would never see them again. He placed a final call to Melody on his way home, checking in chatting about the new students she was teaching and the possibility of a dinner next week. He knew it would never happen. It saddened him slightly to say good-bye, as she had been a good friend and a source of companionship during his time here in Oklahoma. But that time was over.

Arriving at his home in Catoosa, he immediately took two blankets from the guest room and went to the freezer, depositing them on the shelf. He'd decided that extra protection was required when transporting Hope. Wrapping her in the frozen blankets would help with transporting her to Arkansas. He would leave his SUV behind, renting a mini-van for the trip instead, so that there was no connection. The trail for Thomas would die when he abandoned the van. Once they found out about his identity as Thomas, it would lead them here, and they would find the room. Then they could trace the van, but by the time they found out where he'd gone, he would have disappeared with his new identify.

All he had to do was safely secure Hope until he could return to her.

He arranged for Enterprise to deliver a white minivan to his home at five o'clock, then he returned to the garage to move the SUV to the street. He'd park the van in the garage, where he had easy access, and then enjoyed the rest of the night. Tonight would be all about spending time with Hope, as it would be their last night together for a while. The thought of having to leave her behind, even for a short while, tugged at his heart, but he pushed those thoughts away, deciding not to let them interrupt the evening they would have together.

After the van was delivered and carefully stowed in the garage, along with a suitcase with some clothes, he printed boarding passes and then made dinner for two. He carried the beautiful plates to the small table downstairs, lit a candle in the middle of the table, and went back upstairs to retrieve two wine glasses and a bottle of wine. Once everything was perfectly laid out on the table, he opened the freezer and carried Hope, with her chair, out to sit in front of the plate and glass of wine he'd prepared for her. He offered her a gentle kiss on the cheek, ignoring the chill on his lips, then sat down opposite her at the table.

For the next hour, he told her how much he loved her and of his plans for them to be together forever. He explained why he needed to leave and compared it to one of his speaking trips when he was a surgeon. He wouldn't leave her for long, he said, devouring his meal and teasing her for eating like a bird. Hope had always had a small appetite compared to his – a trait he'd always found endearing. It seemed that some things never changed.

After pouring himself another glass of wine, he asked if she would like to join him on the sofa where they could cuddle. Of course she agreed. As he settled her onto the sofa, he brushed a lock of hair from her eyes, just like he had always done. He joined her, wrapping his arms around her shoulder and waist and drawing her close to his chest. He sat holding her, sharing his plans and recanting stories of when they were children playing in the woods together, their first kiss, their prom, and when he'd asked her to marry him.

Finally he decided it was getting late and kissed her gently, then went upstairs to get her a night gown from the dresser. It was made of beautiful white lace – the exact one she'd worn on their honeymoon. Tonight, he would make love to her the same way he had on their wedding night – gently, taking his time with her, allowing her to enjoy the moment as much as he had.

Chapter Thirty

At the Investigation Headquarters, Wells had received photographs of the body found out at Keystone Dam, and the preliminary reports, which indicated that this was in fact Jessica Jenkins, despite the missing face. The body was wearing a ring on her middle right finger, which matched a ring Jessica had been wearing the last time she was on air, and just before going missing. To him, and given Max's suggestion that Jack Tyler was somehow trying to restore the body of his wife Hope, this was enough evidence to indicate Jessica Jenkins had been taken specifically for her resemblance to Hope's face and hair color.

Wells didn't want to tell the task force of his mounting concerns – that with a face in place, the reconstruction was likely complete, which meant time was running out to find this guy before he took off again. He'd rebuilt his wife, and that probably meant he was ready to move on. They needed to move quickly. Wells was weighing the risks of putting Tyler's photos out as a person of interest, because the minute Tyler saw his own photo, he was going to run. He just wasn't sure if waiting gave them any advantages though, and his frustration was growing.

Suddenly, Max had an idea. *Benz,* she thought to herself, grabbing her files from California. "Cortez, help me look. What kind of car did Jack Tyler drive in California? We never found his vehicle."

"Mercedes, I think."

"Exactly. Benjamin Callen, they called him Benz. He worked at the Mercedes dealership. Maybe that's the connection there."

Cortez quickly pulled up the records on vehicle registrations for Dr. Jack Tyler and found a convertible Mercedes. She jotted down the VIN number and cross-referenced it to the available inventory at the Jackie Cooper dealership. "Nothing, but they could have sold it already or even traded it to another dealership."

Not hesitating, she picked up the phone and called the dealership, asking to speak with the inventory manager, looking at the clock and noting the time was nearly eight o'clock, Cortez waited for the woman who had answered to come back on the line. After about thirty seconds, she heard, "I'm sorry, but our inventory manager has gone home for the day. Is there someone in our sales department who could help you?"

"Yes, my name is Officer Cortez. I'm with the Los Angeles Police Department and I need to speak to someone in charge please." Wells and Max stood by waiting to see what Cortez would find.

After another moment the call transferred, clicked, rang, then a voice greeted with, "Hello, my name is Steve Tatum. How may I help you, Officer?

"Mr. Tatum, I'm investigating a series of murders and am looking to see if you accepted a trade on a Mercedes convertible lately. It would be a high end vehicle over a hundred thousand. I have a specific VIN number that I need you to reference."

Cortez heard a small pause before the voice came back on the line, "Unfortunately, I don't have access to those files. Our inventory manager will be back in at nine in the morning. I could have him call you the minute he gets in. I will say, we did have a car that fits your description, but I am not sure how we moved it or what the particulars of the deal were. It was a very attractive car, I just happened to notice it wasn't here anymore."

After giving the phone number to call back on, Cortez hung up. "Damn it, I was afraid it would be too late to find out anything tonight. We'll get a phone call first thing in the morning."

Wells looked at the clock. "Let's take a break. No one has had anything to eat since breakfast. We can't do anything about the body at Keystone until we have a full confirmation, and we can't do anything about the car lead until morning. Let's go eat and get some rest, so we can get right back at it tomorrow. Our best chance to find this guy is tracking down that car and any leads the coroner might give us on the Jenkins woman."

With that, everyone started packing in their files and laptops.

"Detective Adair offered, "There's an IHOP right off of 191st Street in Catoosa, the exit at the casino. Let's go there. It's right across the highway from the hotel where you are all staying."

Max and Cortez exited the City Hall building and headed to their car. As Max was about to get into the car, Wells called out to her coming over to her side of the car. "Good work today, we're getting closer."

Max looked at his face, and for a brief moment their eyes locked. Then she turned away. "I'll see you at the IHOP."

"See you there," Wells replied with a smile before heading to his car. As he walked, his mind went back to the reflection of the beautiful green in her eyes. Jesus, she was beautiful. He knew they had a lot to talk about. Max was clearly frustrated. He was confused by her actions and found them endearing at the same time. He wanted to hold her and tell her that he had tried calling many times and hung up. Did she even care? Had she called him and done the same? There were so many questions to ask... *after they caught this guy.*

Max climbed in behind the wheel and looked over at Cortez, who had been watching the exchange between her and Wells. "I don't want to hear it," she said before Cortez could start in with a line of questioning. Cortez threw her hands up in a surrender stance at the comment and smiled at Max, who nodded at her and started the car.

They drove mostly in silence, with each of their minds processing the events of the day. Arriving at the IHOP just behind Agent Wells and his team, they parked and followed everyone inside. Max had thought she was not hungry, but the minute the doors opened and she was assaulted by the smell of bacon, she realized she was famished. The bacon smelled decadent, despite the hour of the day.

Wells told the hostess the size of the party, and they waited briefly as tables were pulled together to accommodate the group. Once seated, Max could feel Wells' eyes on her, and occasionally she dared to look at him, catching his glance. Each time their eyes met, one of them would quickly look away. The conversation was light at first, but found its way to the case and the findings the day had brought. Max felt excited and frustrated all at once, as it seemed they were getting closer to finding their perpetrator, and yet she still had no idea what name Jack was using or where to look for him. She looked forward to questioning Dr. Jack Tyler, picturing the day she would be seeing the monster face to face and wondering how it would feel trying to understand what made him tick.

Chapter Thirty-One

Jack had slept well after making love to Hope. He'd become very sad when it was time to put her back into the freezer, but she had calmed him down, her beautiful eyes assuring him that it was for the best. Everything he was doing was done for her, to ensure that they could be together forever. He was pleased that she understood, and he had fallen into a deep sleep dreaming of their life together.

When he woke, the sun was shining. Quickly waking up he'd finished packing, looking around the house for anything he thought he might need or that Hope would need once he was able to return for her. He had decorated the home thinking they would share it together, but it was just a home. And they could settle somewhere else and build a new one together. Right now the necessities and getting away together were most important.

Now he was in the shower, applying a bottle of graying hair dye. He didn't want to be recognized at the airport or storage facility, and graying out his hair was just the first step in his disguise. There was no room for errors now. Stepping out of the shower and toweling off, he looked in the mirror that hung over the sink, studying the new look. After a few minutes, he decided it was enough of a difference; no one would immediately identify him as Jack Tyler. It would take time for people to put it together, and while that was happening, he could disappear. Of course, this was assuming anyone even knew they were looking for him at all. And he still wasn't certain of that.

As he dressed he flipped on the news to see if there were any updates on how the police were progressing on his victims, including Jessica Jenkins. He wasn't surprised to see that Jessica's body had been found so quickly. Even though positive identification was pending the coroner's official report, the newscaster continued stating that the body discovered was presumed to be Jessica, based on a piece of jewelry that matched a description to one she was known to be wearing. He shrugged; it wasn't like he'd really spent much time trying to conceal it. He listened intently as the news person stated that the police were trying to determine if there was a connection between the Jessica Jenkins murder and the bodies discovered out on Lock and Dam Road in Inola. The news reporter then asked for anyone with information to come forward, offering a phone number to call.

Jack sighed in relief. He took this to mean they had no leads at this time. Clicking off the TV, he collected a few toiletries and packed them into a small suitcase, along with some additional clothes. In a separate suitcase, he packed all of Hope's clothes, toiletries, a blow dryer, and makeup.

After packing, he went to the basement and opened the freezer, gingerly lifting Hope out and placing her on the sofa. He would need her body to soften for a few minutes so that he could lay her out in the van. The idea of having Hope ride next to him in the passenger seat was very appealing, but he knew it was too dangerous. He needed to resist the desire to have her near him in the open. He would need to lay her down to ensure she was concealed, and so that he could protect her with the cold blankets he'd put in the freezer the night before.

Next, he went into his surgical room and began collecting his supplies. He wouldn't be able to take these things with him, but he could put them into storage until he returned. He certainly didn't want to lose them. His plan was to be gone for no longer than necessary, and leaving all of this behind here in Catoosa was not a solution he could accept. He loaded the scalpels, forceps, bone saw, the miscellaneous other tools, and his suture kit into a single box. He then unscrewed the table light from the stainless steel table and placed it on top of the other items. Next, he collected the perfectly labeled drugs from the shelves, wrapping them in tissue to ensure they wouldn't get damaged or broken, and placed them into another box, along with the syringes, duct tape, and zip ties.

Taking stock of his surroundings, he thought that he had everything he needed for when he returned from his trip to the Cayman Islands. One by one, he carried the boxes upstairs and out to the garage, where he loaded them behind the driver's seat. Next, he went and got the final overnight bag and Hope's bag, bringing these out to the van as well. He stood in the garage, looking around trying to decide if there was anything out here that he would need. He ultimately determined that the answer was no. He could purchase anything out here at any hardware store when he was ready. With everything he would need carefully stored in the van, it was time to leave. Opening the back of the vehicle, he laid the tarp out flat across the carpet, folding half of it to one side.

Leaving the back of the van open, he returned to the basement and checked on Hope. He was able to gently manipulate her limbs, which meant the combination of chemicals he'd applied into and on her body was working as he desired. He retrieved the blankets from the freezer and took them up to the van, laying one out flat on top of the tarp. He then went to get Hope, and, with an intense and overwhelming tenderness he carefully carried her up the stairs and to the van. Laying her onto the tarp on her back, he slowly worked her into a flat position, then covered her with the second frozen blanket, and pulled the other half of the tarp up over her, making sure she was concealed. Last, he gently tucked the blankets and tarp around her body to ensure the blankets retained the cold for as long as possible. It was a two hour drive, and he needed to be sure that she would be safe for the entire journey.

He made one pass through the house, looking for anything that would indicate where he'd gone. Next he double checked his travel documents. He didn't want any scenes at the airport. Suddenly, remembering that he'd used the printer to print the travel documents, he returned inside to remove the printer. He wasn't sure if anything could be retrieved from this type of printer, but he also wasn't willing to take the chance. After stowing the printer on the floorboard of the passenger side of the van, he slid on his jacket so that he could turn the air-conditioner on high for the trip. It would make Hope more comfortable. Climbing in, he pulled out of the garage and down the driveway, glancing back in the rearview mirror at the house in Catoosa. He felt a momentary twinge of nostalgia but put it away and made his way to the highway, heading east to Arkansas, away from Oklahoma and the police who were no doubt hot on his trail. Or soon would be. As he drove, he promised his covered passenger that he would deliver her to safety within two hours and return for her before she could even miss him.

Chapter Thirty-Two

The team of FBI agents, detectives and officers had devoured their food and slowly dispersed from the IHOP restaurant, wandering out into the night in groups matching the cars they had come in. The table had dwindled down to Agent Wells, Agent James, Max and Cortez, who were settling up with the server. As they rose from the table, Wells indicated they would meet in the lobby at six o'clock, to hit it hard the next morning. Stepping out into the night, the air was refreshing as the aura surrounding Max and Wells was so thick it could have been cut with a knife. Seemingly pulling the air with them, they headed to their cars.

Getting into the car and starting the engine, Max could feel Cortez's eyes on her again. "What?" she snapped. "Why don't you just say whatever's on your mind and get it over with?"

"Well, now that you asked," joked Cortez, "I was wondering when you and Wells were going to deal with this thing you have between you." She made air quotes with her fingers when she said 'thing,' smirking.

Max rolled her eyes and laughed. "Thing, really?"

"Uh, yeah, really."

"Look, Cortez, that thing you're talking about never was a thing, and even if it was, it was dead a long time ago."

"Could have fooled me. Doesn't look dead to me."

Max rolled her eyes again, but deep down she knew Cortez was right. She just hoped she could get through this trip, arrest Dr. Jack Tyler, and get out of here soon before she found herself in his arms again, an action that certainly would lead to heartbreak.

Arriving back at the hotel, they found Agent James and Agent Wells standing in the lobby talking. As Max and Cortez approached, they heard Agent James say good night and turn towards the elevator. Cortez, called out to her, "Hey hold the door, I'm right behind you!" She tossed a wink to Max and darted off in the direction of the elevators, to join Agent James on the ride up to her room, leaving Max and Wells standing alone in the lobby together.

Max looked at Wells, and for a moment they just stood there and stared at each other, neither of them saying a word. Finally, Wells broke the silence.

"Well, we got a lot of ground covered today."

"Yeah, I guess so," Max replied, not feeling quite so certain.

"I know it's frustrating, but we'll get this guy."

"I hope so." Max said not quite feeling the confidence that Wells displayed.

They slowly started making their way to the elevator doors. The ride up was silent, and as the doors opened to let Wells off at their floor, he turned to her and struggled to speak. "Max, I …"

"Mark, you don't need to say or do anything."

"You don't understand."

"I think I do."

"No. What I am trying to say is …" his words trailed off.

"It's okay, Mark. Really."

"Max, it's not okay." Not being able to articulate his thoughts, he leaned in and pulled her to him to gently kiss her.

Max was surprised by the sudden move, and found herself fighting; but rather than pulling away from him, like her logic wanted her to do, her reaction to his touch was to kiss him back. His lips pressed down on hers and enveloped her in a swirl of emotion. She found her hands threading around his neck and pulling him in even closer. The passion of the kiss intensified as their bodies pressed close together, until Max caught hold of her emotions and pulled back.

Before she could say anything, Wells brushed her cheek with his hand. "That's what I wanted to say this whole time. Good night, Detective Nichols." And with that, he exited the elevator, leaving her standing there in a daze.

Realizing she was standing in the elevator alone, and that this was her floor too, Max stumbled out of the lift and headed to her room, both relieved and disappointed that Wells had already entered his own. Her head was spinning with questions. What was it Agent Mark Wells wanted from her? What did she want from *him?* Could they have these one-night stand encounters and just leave it at that? Obviously not, since they were both still thinking of each other. But could they have a long distance relationship? Would she even be willing to, knowing how crazy both of their schedules would be? Entering her room, she quickly undressed and fell into the bed, exhausted at the thought of it all. She lay there, again her mind swirling with images of her and Wells tangled together in sheets and sweat. She fell into a deep sleep with no resolution to all of the thoughts and questions.

Chapter Thirty-Three

The morning came far too quickly for Max, and as the alarm on her cell phone went off, she opted to snooze it once before crawling out of bed. As she showered, her mind vacillated between the case and the kiss in the elevator the night before. *Awkward,* she thought to herself as she pictured meeting in the lobby downstairs. She prayed that Cortez would be slow to roll this morning, or she'd pick up on it immediately and be full of questions. Laughing to herself, she blamed Cortez for leaving her alone with Wells.

Arriving downstairs, she found that the breakfast area was crawling with people. There must have been more people checked in than the night before, and she wondered what was going on in Tulsa to draw such a crowd. Then she saw a t-shirt that gave way to the answer: 2013 National Fishing Competition, with an exaggerated drawing of a big fish snapping on a fishing line, and a man on the shore reeling it in. The shirt indicated the next three days as the dates for the big event. Max hadn't heard of this event, but there were obviously some serious fishermen and women in this room. Amused she looked across the room for anyone from the team.

Navigating her way through the crowd, she found Cortez at a table and dropped her laptop bag over the back of the chair, freeing up her hands so that she could work her way back to the coffee station. Waiting patiently behind a man with the fishing shirt on, Max glanced around the room at the crowd, then proceeded to fill a cup with the dark roast. Turning around to head back to the table, she plowed right into Wells, nearly spilling her coffee.

"Good morning," Wells said with a sly smile on his face, his blue eyes gleaming at her.

"Sorry. Good morning." Not able to say anything further, she pushed passed him, taking in the clean, fresh scent of his still-damp hair. Despite her efforts to ignore his smell, she found that she couldn't tune it out, the scent instantly taking her back to that morning in Los Angeles when they'd showered together. Her senses seemed to be on overload, and she realized there was so much she wanted to tell him. But for the moment she could not seem to speak.

Wells smiled as her long flowing hair had brushed against his arm as she passed, ever so slightly tickling him and immediately arousing his every sense. He was quickly reminded of her beauty and her seemingly lack of knowledge of the fact that, had she desired to, she could have easily been a Hollywood heartbreaker. She was a strong, assertive and intelligent woman, but none of that came from the beauty that could certainly make her hell on wheels. She was instead natural, fun and strikingly beautiful, but humble, all characteristics Wells found intoxicating.

Wells worked his way over to the group and noticed that all seats were taken except for one at the table with Max and Cortez. *Perfect*, he thought to himself. Walking up, he asked if it would be okay if he joined them.

Cortez looked up as she took a bite from an English muffin. "Looks like it was saved for you." She glanced towards Max, throwing off a big smile.

Wells slid his tall frame into the seat as he set his coffee and plate of fruit and muffins down. Max jumped up quickly and headed back to the food station, grabbing some fruit and a blueberry muffin from the bar. She returned to the table, making eye contact with Wells as she sat down, unable to ignore the statement Cortez made. Wells and Cortez were engaged in some conversation, and she found herself relieved to just sit in silence listening and eating while they talked.

As Wells and Cortez spoke, sharing ideas on Jack, eyes would drift to Max. Max smiled and tried to avoid the subtle hints by both of them in their obvious attempt to gloss over the tension that was evident at the table. Max was relieved when everyone was finishing up their meals. Everyone began to gather up their belongings preparing to head back to Inola, where they hoped new leads would deliver them something more on Dr. Jack Tyler.

Arriving at the City Hall, everyone piled out of their cars. Detective Adair and some of his team were already assembled in the make-shift investigation room, and as the others arrived and settled in at their respective tables, Wells moved to the front of the room, where the gruesome photos of the victims remained pasted to the board.

"Everyone, if we could have your attention," he started, drawing an immediate silence in the room. "I've received official word from the coroner that the body found in the lake is in fact that of Jessica Jenkins. Fingerprints provided a positive identification. We will need to conduct the official notification to the family. They've already been asking to see the body, which I strongly recommend against given the condition of the head, so we need to find a way around that."

Before Wells could continue, Detective Adair said, "My team and I will handle the notification."

"Thank you, Detective. We also need to view the tapes from the cameras at the parking lots of the two salons. The local PD will be providing the tapes to us within the hour. We'll be looking for any cars that

210

seem to frequent the area. Run the plates on all of them. Qualify any employee vehicles that should be there. I requested a list of all employee vehicles from each of the locations in the strip malls. That information was emailed to me this morning, and I've printed out lists for you. Finally, we should have feedback from the car dealership this morning, which may confirm Detective Nichols' theory that Jack Tyler may have traded his vehicle in for another model."

Pausing for a moment to let this soak in, Wells continued, "Team, we have a lot of possible leads that can help narrow this down. Let's move quickly now. I've split the work up so that we can move faster. Nichols and Cortez, you work the car dealership angle. Then you can help with the tapes. The rest of you work the video feeds from the parking lots; anything remotely out of the ordinary report it. If you see any of our vics on those tapes, or if Jack Tyler shows up on there, report it" Wells tapped the photo of Dr. Jack Tyler that was taped on the board, with 'POI' written under it, signifying person of interest, "Report it."

Max grabbed one of the employee rosters that was circulating the room, as did Cortez. Scanning the lists, she saw Kim's name there – the Vietnamese woman they'd spoken with – as well as several women with matching last names, likely all relatives. She also saw the name of Thomas Jennings, probably the gay employee Kim had indicated worked at the salon. His name appeared on both lists. Max stared at that for a moment considering this. He was an employee at both locations, so he *should* be on both lists.

She continued to review the list, looking for anyone else that might appear on both location lists of employees. After spending thirty minutes comparing the names, though, she didn't find any other employees on both lists. Apparently none of the other businesses had any employees that worked at both strip malls. Frustration welled up as she realized that she'd yet again come up empty handed. Max had been hopeful that there would be multiple duplications on the lists of names for people who would potentially fit the profile. So far all she had was a gay male who did not fit the profile.

Cortez was still focused on the employee list when her phone rang. She answered, spoke for a moment, and gave thumbs up. Max looked at the clock to see that it was just after nine o'clock, which meant that the car dealership was keeping to their promise of getting back to them first thing in the morning. Cortez spent most of the time listening to the person on the other end, and took notes as she talked. Then thanked the person for their time and asked for a direct call back line, just in case she had any further questions. Finally she hung up and looked at Max, her eyes shining.

"Bingo! Jack Tyler traded his convertible Mercedes for a SUV, and guess who his salesman was?"

"Benz?" Max answered before Cortez could say another word.

"Yep. The car has since been sold at auction and is now proudly in, of all places, Los Angeles."

Max shook her head, shocked. Finally they'd tracked Dr. Jack Tyler to Oklahoma, had a connection between the two cities where similar crimes had been committed, and had a direct connection to one of the victims. Adrenaline raced through her veins. She waved Wells over to fill him in on their discovery.

Wells listened intently and agreed that there was now enough of a connection to get Tyler's photo out as a person of interest. "I'll work on the BOLO notification. We can line up a media conference. It's time to get the public involved. You start a trace on the vehicle he traded into. We can add that to the BOLO wire. If Jack Tyler is in this city, he's in for a surprise. We're going to find him."

He rushed off, and Max and Cortez hovered over the computer, entering the vehicle identification the dealership had given on the new vehicle. It was a silver Toyota Sequoia low profile, sufficient enough in size to hide a body, an SUV that would easily fit in anywhere. The car was still running with temporary registration tags. After a few minutes of digging, they learned that in Oklahoma the buyer was given a temporary paper license plate and required to register the vehicle within thirty days. That time had clearly elapsed, but according to Detective Adair, it wasn't uncommon for new car owners to take more than the allotted time. The car had not yet been registered, leaving blank any name association to the vehicle. The car had been bought with the cash from Jack Tyler and then never registered under any name.

Max had been hoping that if Jack had assumed an alias, this would be the lead to giving them that information, but it looked like he'd thought of that too. The vehicle had been sold to Jack Tyler, but there was no trail of Jack Tyler in Oklahoma, or anywhere for that matter. And as of this point, he hadn't yet switched to his alias. Once again, they'd hit a dead end. Max pushed back from the computer in frustration. Again, she found herself struggling with what to work next.

The tapes the local PD had promised first thing showed up late, arriving well after noon. All of the delays caused them to miss the midday news. The report would hit the six o'clock news instead, as well as the local paper the next day. This information further frustrated Max, though Wells tried to calm her through his eyes as he looked at her across the room. He locked in on her, and as their eyes connected he nodded subtle assurance to her, Max smiled back at him.

212

With the tapes to work on, everyone buckled down sorting through them. Agent Wells asked for one of the officers to have lunch brought in. It was likely to be a long night, and with the case starting to turn hot, he wasn't planning on stopping until they had Jack Tyler in cuffs.

Max and Cortez began going through the tapes as well, initially frustrated at the grainy picture. It was taking longer than desired due to the poor quality, and in some cases it was difficult to even determine if a person on the feed was male or female. The tapes that had been requested contained the past forty-five days of feeds from the surveillance company. The process of going through these was very slow. This was not going to be an easy task.

The food was delivered around two o'clock, and everyone stopped to grab a sandwich from the box of food and drinks. Max rubbed her eyes, already tired from straining to look at the video. With Cortez's help, she'd recorded a number of plates that they'd now cross-referenced to the employee sheets, as well as look up for owner details. This seemed somewhat fruitless to Max, as the car Jack was driving didn't have a plate at all, unless he'd stolen one. And so far, none of the vehicles recorded had been a silver Toyota. The parking lot cameras only covered about half the lot, though, picking up the store entrances and the first two rows of cars. The third row was not in the view of the video at all.

As they nibbled on their sandwiches, Max said, "Our Jack is smart. If he was hunting in those parking lots, he wouldn't park where the camera would see him. So unless he walks into the view of the camera to enter a store, we're not going to see him on these tapes."

Cortez nodded in agreement. "And if he's changed his look or comes onto the frame wearing a hoodie or a ball cap that would make it impossible for us to identify him."

"Okay, let's take a new approach then. You start looking up the plates we've collected so far, and I'll continue looking at the tapes. We can switch when the eye strain becomes too much, but let's focus on stolen plates." Cortez nodded in agreement to the plan, taking one last draw on her Diet Coke and moving back toward the computer. Max handed Cortez a report of stolen vehicles and license plates that had been earlier provided to use in her review.

Around them, everyone started settling back into the work. Max started back in on the tapes as Cortez began checking registration records for the plate numbers they'd recorded. The process was laborious and unrewarding, and before they knew it, they'd gone through an entire week of video and found nothing significant. Max looked up at the clock, and saw that it was just before five o'clock. The media was starting to gather outside, preparing for the live news conference at six o'clock. Wells had a

TV brought in from the adjacent police office, so they could air the statement in the room. Everyone was anxious for the report to run, and the room seemed to have a renewed buzz.

Wells walked up to Max. "I want you to join me in making the statement."

Max looked up at him in surprise. "What? Why?"

"You have the most intimate knowledge of our un-sub, and I think it's important for people to realize that we're tying this to California. I want you to assist in delivering the conference."

Max looked at Wells, their eyes locking for a moment. "Okay."

Max had participated in news reports in the past, but this was significant. Their chance to catch this guy likely hung on this report. She felt honored that Wells trusted her. They worked together to setup for the conference.

As the microphones began to appear in front of the City Hall building, Wells and Max worked preparing their statements. Wells warned Max not to engage in questions with the media. Right at six o'clock they stepped out of the office in front of the press. They had agreed on the point that the report would transition between the two of them, and they covered the facts several times, making sure they covered the details they wanted people focused on.

Wells stepped up to the podium and began. "Ladies and gentlemen, my name is Agent Wells and I'm with the FBI. This is Detective Maxine Nichols of the Los Angeles Police Department, Homicide Division. We're here tonight to ask for your help in locating this man." Wells held up a photo of Dr. Jack Tyler, facing it toward the cameras. "We believe this man has information related to the recent murders of the five people whose bodies were found out by Lock and Dam Road here in Inola, as well as that of Jessica Jenkins, discovered at Keystone Lake."

Max stepped forward as Wells stepped away from the podium and added her own piece. "We also believe that Dr. Jack Tyler, a well-known surgeon from Los Angeles, has information regarding six more murders in California. Dr. Tyler has been missing for several months, and we need your help in locating him. He was last seen driving a Silver Toyota Sequoia with Oklahoma temporary tags."

Wells stepped forward again. "Anyone with information regarding the whereabouts of Dr. Tyler should call our tip line immediately. Thank you."

Stepping away from the podium, both Max and Wells re-entered the building, declining to take any questions from the reporters, who shoved microphones in their faces and hurled questions towards them.

Wells looked at Max and smiled, "Well done."

"Yeah, whatever," she threw back at him with a bit of a grin. "Now, let the fun begin. The tips will come in claiming everything, including the sighting of Bigfoot."

"I know, but one of those crazies might just be the one that gets us our prize."

Chapter Thirty-Four

Almost immediately following the live conference, the phone tip line started ringing with all kinds of information, none of which was valuable. Several hours later, the ten o'clock news aired the conference again, and a few minutes after that Max's cell phone rang. Looking at the display, she saw a 918 area code and recognized it as a local number, though not one she'd programmed for anyone working on the investigation team. Answering the phone, she listened as the woman on the other end identified herself as Samantha, the owner from the Beehive Salons. She seemed almost frantic, and Max had to take a moment to calm her down just to understand what she was telling her.

"The man in the picture on the news, it's my employee Thomas," the woman muttered, her voice rushed.

Max paused feeling her stomach drop, "Are you sure?" She asked nearly dreading the answer. She should have trusted her instincts. She had felt she was missing something, and here it was, the gay guy right in front of her the whole time.

"Yes, I'm positive, but he's different now. I mean he's gay, and he wears a little bit of makeup and, well, he's different for sure, but I know that's him."

"Okay, my partner and I are coming to see you right away. Where can we meet?" Max struggled to keep her adrenaline from consuming her. She had moved past the fact that she should have pushed the connection with Thomas, but now she had a solid lead. A witness saying she knew Jack Tyler. They had to move quickly...*very quickly*.

"I'm at home. You can come here," she said, giving Max her home address in Broken Arrow. "Oh and Detective, he didn't report to work today."

Max hung up the phone and gathered everyone around to tell them about the call. By the time she was done, Cortez was already heading to the car. When Max started to follow her, Wells called out, "Nichols, be careful, and call us the minute you have an address on him. We'll meet you there. We all go in together. No heroics."

Max looked back at Wells, and they both paused for a brief moment before she let the door close behind her. She knew he was warning her to be safe and to stay calm. That look would carry her throughout the night. Once in the car, Max and Cortez rode to the address Samantha had provided, discussing the possibilities this new information offered. When they arrived at the address, they got out of the vehicle and approached the house, Max leading the way. Ringing the bell, she found that she could barely stand still, shuffling between feet as they waited for the door to be answered. This was the lead she'd been waiting for on this case, and she could hardly wait to follow it. Before long, the salon owner opened the door, looking stressed. She had her hair pulled back away from her face and worry shrouded her eyes. This wasn't the same confident woman they'd met the day before.

"Come in," she said, stepping away from the door.

Once they were inside, she led them into the living room, where they each took a seat on the stylish sofa and chairs. Max pulled out a file and laid out a few photos of Dr. Jack Tyler on the coffee table between them, not bothering with preliminaries.

"Is this Thomas?" she asked.

Samantha picked up the one in the middle and nodded. "Yes, it's him. Did he kill all those people?"

"We don't know that for sure, but we definitely need to speak with him right away. Do you have an address on file for him?"

Samantha hesitated for a moment, but then nodded. "Yes of course. I keep all my employee files here in my home office. Let me go pull it for you."

Max and Cortez sat in near silence as they each took in the surroundings. The house was well decorated. Samantha had an obvious decorator's flair. It had shown in her salon, and it showed here too. The furniture was modern and colorful, with pieces of glass art distributed around the walls. Everything had a curve to it, which made the room feel as if everything was flowing. Cortez nodded at Max in approval of the room, and Max smiled back at her.

Samantha returned to the room with a folder in her hand. She pulled out the application Thomas had filled out and handed it to them.

"I apologize, but this is the first time I've noticed that he only wrote in the city. Apparently he never put his street address on the application."

"Do you run any background checks?" Max asked, already knowing the answer.

"No, I never do. Most of my employees come to me through referral."

"Was Thomas a referral?"

"Yes," Samantha answered, sounding almost excited now. "My friend Melody's an instructor at the beauty college here in town. Thomas was one of her students. She raved about him."

"Would Melody know Thomas's address?"

Samantha nodded. "I think she's actually been to his home before. They're good friends. They go out dancing occasionally. You know, girls' night out."

Cortez jumped quickly to the next question. "Could we get Melody's number from you? We need to speak with her right away."

"I can call her for you. I know it's late, but under the circumstances …" she trailed off.

"That would be very helpful," Max indicated.

Samantha pulled out her cell phone and quickly selected from the contact list, pressing send and waiting for a connection. After a couple of rings, the line obviously connected as she began to speak, asking if Melody had watched the news. She shook her head at Max and Cortez at the answer, and Max, growing impatient, motioned that she would like to speak with the other woman. Samantha told Melody that there was someone that wanted to talk with her, and handed the phone over to Max.

Taking the telephone from Samantha, Max spoke into the receiver, "Melody, I am Detective Max Nichols with the Los Angeles Police Department. We need to speak with your friend Thomas right away.

Melody started to protest. "I don't understand."

"I know this is confusing, but we don't have a lot of time. All I can tell you is that he is a person of interest in several local and out of state murders."

Max could sense Melody's sudden revelation as the words settled in.

"We need to know if you have Thomas's address. We need to speak with him right away," she finished.

"I've been there before, yes, but …, Oh hold on a second, let me see. I wrote it down somewhere the first time I went there." Max heard rustling of papers and then Melody came back on the line. "I can't find it, but it's in my GPS. I entered it in the first time I went over there. I just can't believe Thomas would have anything to do with anything like murder. He's sweet and a good friend."

Max nodded to Cortez, indicating that they had an address. "Melody, I know this is tough, but we need that address. We're on our way to your house. Don't talk to anyone before we get there, especially Jack … uh Thomas. What's your address?"

After jotting down the address, Max thanked Samantha and headed to Melody's house to pull Jack's address off of the GPS and talk with her a bit further. On the way, Max called Wells, letting him know that within the hour they would have an address for Jack.

Max drove as fast as she could to Melody's house, arriving in about twenty minutes. They pulled up in front of a modest brick home in a neighborhood of similar houses. Walking up the drive, Max and Cortez exchanged a look of both excitement and concern, fearing they might be too late. Knocking on the door, the two again waited impatiently as they heard footsteps approaching from the inside. Then the door opened, and they were greeted by an attractive woman in her mid-thirties, wearing sweat pants and a sweat shirt that advertised Oklahoma University. It appeared that she'd just pulled on the clothes, most likely due to the late hour.

Still, at least she was there and ready to give them what they needed.

Max greeted her, quickly introducing herself and Cortez, and apologized for the late hour. "We're very sorry for coming so late, but we do need to see if we can get that address from you. It's very important that we see Thomas as soon as possible."

Melody acknowledged the statement with a nod and led them to the vehicle to show them the recent history on her car's GPS system. She had already written down the address and handed it to Max. "I went there twice. Last time I was there, it was the morning after we went out dancing. Thomas had taken a man home with him that night, and I stopped by the next day. We were only there for a while and then went to get something to eat. Why do you need to talk to him?"

Max and Cortez exchanged a glance as they both made the connection that Gary was likely the man he'd taken home. "He's a person of interest in the abduction and murder of five people here in Oklahoma and six others in California."

Max watched as the color drained from Melody's face, her hand fluttering to her neck and twisting at the necklace. "Thomas is my friend. How could he know anything about those murders?"

Not answering her questions, Max continued to probe. "Do you remember the name of the man Thomas took home with him the night you went out?"

"His name was Gary. He wasn't there when I showed up in the morning, but Thomas said he'd already left."

Without confirming anything, Max continued, "We have reason to believe that Jack, or Thomas, has information about the murders, and that's exactly why we need to speak with him. When was the last time you talked to him?" Max tried to wait patiently, not wanting to push Melody too quickly yet not hardly able to wait for her responses.

Melody looked back and forth between the two women before offering, "He called me a couple of days ago and asked if we could get together soon for dinner or a night out. I mean, doesn't that prove that he has nothing to do with this? Why would he call me if he had anything to do with those people?"

"We can't be sure until we speak with him, but we believe his name is actually Dr. Jack Tyler. He's a well-known surgeon in California. Was there any behavior you thought unusual at any time?" Max asked.

"Jack? A surgeon?" The three having returned to the living room, Melody took a seat on the sofa, obviously shaken by the news. "Nothing stands out. He was a great student, got along with everyone and has been a very good friend to me, as well as a model employee for Samantha."

"I know this is unsettling, but we really need to go. Is there someone you can call to keep you company?" Max continued to try to contain her eagerness to get on the phone with Wells and get a team headed to the address, but realized she had a responsibility to ensure Melody was okay. She was clearly shaken that her trusted friend could be this person, and leaving her alone was not an option.

"I can call my sister. She lives just a few minutes away," Melody offered, still clearly shaken by the news.

Max and Cortez waited for Melody to call her sister and then offered their thanks and darted out the front door. As soon as they were on the front porch, Max pulled out her phone and called Wells. "We have an address. You won't believe this. The address is in Catoosa, less than a mile from the IHOP and our hotel. He's been right under our nose this whole time." After giving Wells the address and agreeing to meet the team in the IHOP parking lot so they could all go in together, Max started the car and turned around, heading back through Broken Arrow, pointing her car towards Catoosa.

They arrived in the IHOP parking lot in what had to be record time, and Max found Wells, Agent James, Detective Adair and his whole team, as well as the Inola Sheriff's Department waiting there. After a few minutes, they agreed to go up the driveway together and fan out across the front of the home to cut off any escape routes. Detective Adair's team would head towards the rear of the house, Wells and James would go to the front door, and Max and Cortez, along with the Inola Sheriff's team, would post along any windows and corners of the house.

If Jack Tyler was inside that home, there was no way he was getting out without walking right into a member of law enforcement.

With Wells leading the team, the row of cars headed up the same driveway that Jack must have travelled any number of times. They brought with them a large cloud of dust, which sheltered their activity from the neighbors, and pulled onto the grass surrounding the home. Then officers began exiting their vehicles and taking their respective posts. Max and Cortez walked up the drive past the SUV, peering through the windows as they passed, with guns drawn. They stopped on opposite sides of the garage entrance, their eyes on each other. Once everyone was in position, Wells and James approached the front door, knocking loudly.

"FBI, Dr. Tyler, please open the door," Wells called out.

Waiting a few seconds, Wells knocked again and tried to peer through the window in the door. There was no answer, though, and the silence from inside hinted that no one was home. Or that Jack was hiding, Max thought to herself. They would need a warrant to enter the home, and that would take time.

Detective Adair spent a few minutes on the phone, securing the warrant, and then returned to where Wells and the team anxiously waited. Max wanted to get into the home and forget the paperwork, but she knew that if there was anything inside that would connect Jack Tyler to the murders, they had to do this by the book.

"We should have the warrant within an hour," Adair said. "I have a friend who's a judge, and he'll sign it the minute it crosses his desk. Being drawn now, then it'll be taken directly for signature and brought here."

Wells nodded and gestured to everyone else, and they started moving to sweep the area on the outside. As long as they were outside the house, they might as well see what they could find, and anything in the open was fair game. A search of the trash netted nothing that connected to any of the victims. Then they discovered a burn pile, but nothing was salvageable. The garage didn't have any windows in the doors, so they weren't able to get a visual to the inside. The silver SUV Jack had traded for the Mercedes was in the driveway, but it was locked. So it too was off limits for now. They just had to wait.

An hour and a half after Detective Adair had called to request the warrant, a car appeared in the driveway with the document.

Adair accepted it with a nod and quickly read it over, then looked up. "This gives us access to the house, garage, vehicle, and any property. We're good to go. Break the door down." He nodded to the sheriff, who had pulled out a battering ram.

Within a few minutes, the doors were open, and the FBI and police were swarming the home, calling out "clear" as they entered each room. Jack Tyler was definitely not home. Max struggled not to show her disappointment as she went from room to room, trying to get a feel for the life Jack had led. He wasn't home, but this was the closest they'd been. And maybe they could find something here that would lead them to him. The home was nicely decorated and well-tended. In the master bedroom, she pulled on gloves and one by one opened the drawers and closet. Both sides of the closet seemed to be only partially filled. On the left was clothing for a man, and on the right was a woman's clothing. Max wondered if it was possible that he was living with someone. That had to be impossible, though; there was no way Jack could pull off the crimes he had with someone in his immediate life.

So why did he have a woman's clothing in his closet?

Wells entered the room as she was looking through the dresser drawers. "What'd you find?" he asked.

"Both the closet and dresser seem to be only half filled. And get this – they have a woman's clothing in them, too."

Wells looked at her with clear surprise on his face. "Maybe he had a girlfriend?"

"Melody told us he took a man home with him one night from a bar. His name was Gary. Guess we know now how that victim fit in. She never mentioned a woman being here or any girlfriend."

"Could he have had one, and she didn't know?" Wells continued, "We need to find some physical connection to Tyler. Right now we have nothing but circumstantial evidence."

Nodding, Max continued to search the room and bathroom. Finding nothing, she moved to the guest room and then to the kitchen. Searching through all of the cupboards, she found all the normal kitchen dishes and appliances. Then she opened a long cupboard next to the door that came in from the garage and found a well-stocked pantry. Something seemed off about the pantry, and she closed the doors and went out into the garage, wondering. The garage was almost bare, though, and she frowned.

Then, looking at the garage floor, she noticed two sets of tire tracks. One set was narrower than the other, and the total wheel placement front to back was different. She turned to Wells, who'd followed her.

"Mark, take a look at this," she said, pointing out the two different wheel markings.

Wells nodded. "There've been two different vehicles in here. This might explain why Jack is nowhere to be found, and the SUV is out front. I'll get the CSI team in here to take pictures of this and see if we can get make and model off of each." He headed out to get one of the techs to come gather the evidence, and Max turned back to the garage.

It didn't take long to realize that there was nothing else interesting in here, and she started back into the house. As she did so, she noticed what appeared to be a void between the garage and kitchen that didn't make sense. Standing in the door frame to the door between the kitchen and the garage, she stared into the void, narrowing her eyes and trying to understand what she was seeing. Going back into the kitchen, she opened the pantry again. The void would be behind this pantry. Studying the stocked shelves, she turned and looked at the door frame. The distance was definitely off. Something was strange about this pantry. She began taking a few of the canned goods off of the shelves and setting them on the counter. As she was unloading one of the bigger rows, Wells approached again, looking at the pantry items on the shelf.

"Is there any reason you're unloading the kitchen shelves?"

"Yes, look at this. There's a void here. The width between here and the garage door isn't right. The pantry is too shallow to take up that much space." Max showed Wells what she was referring to by motioning between the pantry and the garage doorway. "Look at the difference between where the wall ends and the door starts. The pantry has the ability to be another 2 feet deep, but it is not."

Wells looked at what Max was referring to and quickly moved to help her. He glanced at the other cupboards in the kitchen. "You're on to something, Max. Look at this. The construction is slightly different on this pantry. The wood used on the inside isn't the same, looks like it was added later."

By that time, Max had the pantry completely unloaded and was poking around in the back. "Look, right there," she said, pointing to the corner. "It looks like a hinge."

Wells pushed where Max was pointing and the wall moved. Then he pulled on it instead of pushing. A moment later, the wall gave and swung open. He glanced back at Max, then pulled the two walls apart.

They stood facing a door.

"In here," Wells shouted out as he reached to turn the knob on the door in front of them.

As the door opened, Max and Wells stared into the darkness of the basement stairwell that faced them. Wells ran his gloved hand along the wall until it passed over a switch. He flipped it into the on position, and light flooded the stairs into the room at the bottom. Moving forward, they drew their guns and slowly moved down the stairway into the basement, Wells leading the way. Cortez appeared behind Max moments after they landed at the bottom, and soon the room filled with other officers. They found themselves in a room with a sofa, small table and large freezer, and they looked at each other, all recognizing the strong odor of bleach. Max tried to calm her racing heart. This was it. They hadn't found him, not yet, but they'd found where he murdered those people. She was sure of it.

Ahead of them was another door, and they cautiously proceeded forward. Wells reached out and turned the knob, swinging the door inward, and the smell of bleach nearly overwhelmed them. He flipped on another light, and the room lit up, displaying a stainless steel table sitting in the middle of what appeared to be a makeshift operating room.

"Clear," Wells called out, once again holstering his gun.

All the officers relaxed their stance, and Wells and Max moved into the room. She noted that the shelves were clear of any items, but it was obvious that this room had been used. Wells ordered the CSI agents to test for prints everywhere, as well as check the drain and all surfaces for any trace evidence.

Moving out to the main room again and over to the freezer, Max opened the door with some apprehension, glancing over her shoulder at Cortez, who was on her heels. The light came on in the inside of the freezer as the door swung open, and Max glanced in. She was almost relieved to find it empty. She hadn't realized until that moment that she'd been afraid they might find another victim, though she was pretty certain Jessica Jenkins had completed the process of trying to put his wife back together. She exhaled softly. Behind her, Cortez let out a sigh too.

Staring into the freezer, there was no way not to consider what and who had occupied this cold room. Max pictured his victims inside and the baggie with the hands and feet laying on one of those shelves. *Had he stored any of the victims in here? Was he keeping the parts in here? Was Jessica's face in this freezer once?* The coroner had not said anything about any of the victims being frozen. He took the parts he needed and then buried the rest.

Max turned to Cortez just as Wells approached. "Damn it, he's in the wind," she claimed, considering the missing clothes and the lack of anything in this freezer.

"Not necessarily, he could pull in the drive at any moment," Wells returned.

"No, he ran!" Max nearly shouted as she turned for the stairs, taking them two by two. With Wells and Cortez right behind her, confused by her outburst, Max hurried through the kitchen and returned to the master bedroom, staring at the closet again. She ran through the door to the bathroom, opening the drawers again.

"Look," she exclaimed, pointing into the drawers one by one. "Everything one uses on a daily basis is gone. Razor, toothbrush, comb, gel, toothpaste – all of it is missing. The only items left in these drawers are the things someone would leave behind if they were in a hurry and didn't need every day. And the closets, his and hers, are both partially empty. He took what he needed for 'them' and left with *his version* of a restored Hope."

Wells and Cortez stared down into the drawers, taking stock of the contents. Q-tips, lotions, dental floss, cotton balls … there wasn't a single item that was a must-have on a daily basis.

"Shit," Wells exclaimed, quickly turning from the room and heading out to the team. He gave directions to the CSI team to speed up the results on the car tire treads. "We need to know what kind of vehicles those treads go on. We have reason to believe the suspect has left the area."

The CSI agent responded that they hoped to know the make and model of the car that had left the other tread marks within the hour, and Wells nodded. "As quick as you can," he muttered. "We need to get after this guy."

Meanwhile, Max stood in the living room, taking in the activities of the crime scene investigators. Detective Adair was leading the collection efforts, and every detail of the home was being covered. He had emailed photos of fingerprints from within the home, to be compared to Jack Tyler's prints. He looked at Max and nodded in acknowledgement.

"We should have some information soon on the prints. If this guy is Tyler, we'll have a positive ID. My team is supposed to call me as soon as they have something."

Max looked at him and offered a small smile. "Thanks, Detective," she said, trying to not show the frustration and despair that was starting to creep over her. She had missed him at the salon, and now she may have lost him here. The house made her skin crawl, and for a moment she had to choke back the bile that built in her throat.

Wells entered the room and looked at Max with an understanding look on his face. "Max, we *will* find this guy. If it's the last thing we do, we'll track this bastard down. The CSI team is working on the tire treads, and while it may not be 100 percent conclusive, we'll get a list of vehicles that are a potential match. We're also canvassing the neighborhood. Agent James is talking to the closest neighbor right now. We're hoping maybe he saw something."

Looking at Wells, their eyes met and locked in. Max nodded not feeling the confidence her gesture indicated. That moment when their eyes connected there was a comfort that transferred between them. Max could read Wells. Cortez walked up then, and the three of them stood there for a moment, then headed back out into the night towards the car and some of the others. They'd made it as far as Wells's car when Detective Adair came rushing out.

"We got it," he said, not able to contain his excitement. "The fingerprints are a positive match to Dr. Jack Tyler."

Max sighed. "That's good news."

Wells jumped in. "Exactly. Now we know that Tyler is our guy, and with the surgical room in the basement, I'm certain we'll be able to connect him to the victims. Any idea how soon we might get tread analysis?"

"It depends. It might be morning before we get that. The team is processing those photographs now, and they have been informed to advise me the minute they have any information."

"Agent Wells, sir," Agent James said, approaching the group.

"Yes, James?" Wells responded. "What do you have?"

"The neighbor seems to be a bit of a voyeur. You know, the Gladys Kravitz type," she offered, referring to the nosey neighbor in the 1970's television show *Bewitched*. "He says that yesterday Enterprise delivered a white van to this address. He knows because the rental company had a car with the company logo on it. He saw that van leave early today and never saw it return."

"Good work, James," Wells praised. "Detective Adair, can you tell your team to narrow the tire tread search against only vans? Also, can you contact Enterprise and see if we can get the rental information, ASAP? Whichever gets us the answer faster, we go with."

"I'm on it," Adair said, quickly heading off.

Max, Wells and Cortez waited together discussing their options. Max decided it was early enough in Los Angeles to bring the chief up to speed so she made a quick call to him. He did his typical barking out commands, demanding her to keep him informed and then as usual hung up on her. She sighed, he sounded disappointed when she told him she had let Tyler get the slip on her at the salon. "Great," she muttered under her breath before returning to Wells and Cortez. As she walked up, Adair was coming up from the other direction.

"I have a little bad news. The rental company isn't open again until five in the morning. In the meantime, the team has matched the tires to a very common tread – 17-inch wheels that could fit several models of vans."

"Okay, thank you, Detective," Wells replied, unable to contain his disappointment. "What else are we finding inside the home?"

"Not much so far, I'm sorry to say. We have a lot of evidence that will likely tie Tyler to the murders, including some blood in the drain trap. Most of it was contaminated by the heavy use of bleach, but I think we have a good sample. All we need is to tie him to one of the victims, and we've got him. Unfortunately, we haven't found anything indicating where he may be headed. We do have a trace on his cell phone, but there hasn't been any recent activity, and the signal is showing somewhere near here. I have a team looking for it. I'm pretty sure he dumped it."

After a few moments of silence, Wells, Max and Cortez realized they were stalled until they had the information from the rental company. In the meantime, Jack was hours ahead of them and they had no idea where he was headed. With the search of the house winding down, they were running out of things to do as they waited.

Finally, Wells broke the silence. "I recommend we get four hours of shut eye. Tomorrow, as soon as we have the vehicle information for the rental, we can get a BOLO out on the van and track him wherever he's gone. I'm not giving up yet. But I need to sleep if I'm going to keep my eyes open tomorrow, and so do all of you."

Returning to the hotel together, the three of them boarded the elevator, along with Agent James, and rode up to their floor in silence. Wells and Max headed in the opposite direction from Cortez to their respective rooms, while Agent James stayed on the elevator for another floor. They agreed to meet right at five the next morning, hoping that Detective Adair would have some news from the rental car agency as soon as they opened.

When Max got to her door, she was surprised to see Wells stopping with her. He leaned close enough for her to hear his heartbeat, and whispered, "Stay with me tonight?"

Somewhat shocked by his request, she shook her head. Leaning in to him and looping her hand up around his neck, she pulled him down to her and placed a gentle kiss on his lips. "I'd like that but, we only have a few hours. And we need to be fresh. I'm hoping tomorrow is a long day."

Wells feigning a pout in protest then leaned back down and pulled her into his arms, giving her a deep, passionate kiss before releasing her and turning to his own door. He looked at her one last time before slipping into his room and closing the door.

Max entered her room too, still savoring the kiss on her lips. All she really wanted was to crawl into his arms and sleep for the next few days, but she knew they couldn't do that until Jack Tyler had been stopped. Dropping into bed after merely pulling off her socks and pants, not even bothering to pull on her sleep clothes, Max fell into a restless sleep, her mind imagining catching and facing the monster that Jack Tyler had become.

Chapter Thirty-Five

Jack had arrived in Fayetteville a little more than two hours after leaving Oklahoma, and had gone straight to the storage facility. After he filled out the necessary paperwork, the elderly man behind the counter offered him directions to the specific refrigeration storage rental. He proceeded through the storage facility, following the rows of mini-garages down and around to the back. He was pleased to learn that the cold storage was at the rear of the facility. He had asked for a corner space, seeking the most privacy possible. As he worked his way past the other rows, he paid careful attention, looking down each one for signs of anyone else accessing their storage lot. He didn't see anyone and assumed that was because it was mid-day. Feeling good about the fact that he was apparently alone, he continued looking for the storage number. He also made a mental note that mid-day provided privacy, even though it was daylight. No one seeing him was more important than the concealment of darkness. He would be back here in a couple of months and wanted to remember this.

Arriving at the storage unit marked 7373, he smiled up at the numbers. When asked his preference of available units he'd chosen this one because he saw those numbers as a lucky sign. Not that he was a gambling man. In fact he had never stepped into the casino that sat within walking distance of the home in Catoosa. But he still occasionally found himself looking for the odd things that could be considered omens. This was a good omen, he was sure of it. Pulling the rear of the van up as close to the door of the storage unit as possible, Jack jumped out and removed the bag on the seat next to him. He'd purchased a heavy-duty combination lock from the man at the counter. It would be used to keep Hope safe. Tearing away the packaging, he tossed the empty box back into the driver's seat and opened the locker door.

Stepping into the storage room, he quickly assessed the temperature and made a minor adjustment, setting the thermostat to the optimal temperature. Before paying and accepting the rental lock or signing the rental contract, he'd asked what happened during power outages, and was happy to learn that the backup generators would keep Hope safe even during power failure. Short of a complete failure of the refrigeration system, this should be a perfect place for her until he could return. The storage room was equipped with built-in shelves on one wall that would serve perfectly for laying Hope down flat.

Returning to the van, he looked around again and noticed the surveillance cameras. He made sure that the van doors were up against the wall offering a block against the cameras positioned throughout the facility. He took one more look around to make sure that he was out of sight. Then he gently pulled back the tarp and the now thawing blanket, lifting Hope's body from the floor of the van and carrying her into the storage room, where he carefully set her on the middle shelf. Her body laid perfectly on the width of the shelf, and he tucked her arms close to her sides.

Bringing the blankets in, he laid one over her, covering everything except for her face, and stood staring down at her for a few moments before returning to the van, this time to retrieve the boxes of supplies, chemicals and surgical instruments. Finally, he put the bag with Hope's personal clothes and toiletries in the room. Once everything was inside the storage room, he closed the door behind him.

Now he moved over to stand next to Hope. He took the other blanket and folded it several times, transforming it into a small square. He lifted Hope's head, placing the blanket in a pillow-like manner so that her head could rest on it. In his mind, it was very important to make his wife comfortable. As he cared for her, he covered the moment with loving words and promises that he wouldn't stay away any longer than necessary. Before turning away from her, Jack leaned over and kissed her lips and softly brushed the hair from her forehead.

All he saw was the beauty that Hope had once been. He did not see the stitches, or the strange way the face sat over the eye sockets. To anyone else the strange sight would have been a horror. Repulsive and terrifying, but to Jack she was as perfect as Hope had ever been.

Leaving the storage locker was the hardest thing Jack had ever done. He had to force himself to stay focused on the next chapter. Carefully programming the date of his wedding anniversary as the code for the padlock, he double and triple checked the security of the lock. Once satisfied, he closed the van doors and walked around the van, ducking the cameras and sliding into the driver's seat. Pulling away, he left the storage unit and Hope behind.

He exited through the gates of the storage facility, smiling at the sign advertising 24-hour access. He could come back any time, once he returned. All he needed was the access code he'd been given after filling out the paperwork. He'd paid for three months advanced rent, not thinking he would be gone that long, but not wanting to have to worry about any payment issues while out of the country.

Heading through town, Jack began seeking the perfect place to leave the van. At some point it would be detected, and he only needed it until tomorrow morning when his flight would leave.

While Jack was safely tucking Hope away in storage, the task force in Oklahoma was pulling together information on him that would lead to the discovery of his home.

Jack had ditched his cell phone already, tossing it out the window before ever getting on the interstate in Oklahoma. As he drove along the street, he saw a Dollar General along North Gregg Avenue and pulled in, deciding to buy a throw-away cell phone. After gathering everything he needed, he proceeded to the checkout counter.

Placing the phone, a ball cap, and a pair of reading glasses with the minimum level of magnification in them on the counter, he paid with cash and then asked the clerk if she had a phone book he could borrow. Seeming a little annoyed, the twenty-something reached under the counter and handed Jack the small book. Flipping through the yellow pages, he committed to memory the number of a local cab service and, thanking the clerk, grabbed his yellow Dollar General bag. Seeing a dumpster at the side of the building, he pulled the printer out of the passenger side of the van and tossed it in the dumpster under some of the trash, then climbed back in the vehicle and continued down the street.

When he saw a small diner just off the road, he decided that it was a good spot to park. There was a wraparound parking lot and the place sat a bit off the road. Pulling into the lot, he drove to the back and parked in one of the spaces. Pulling out the new cell phone, he installed the battery and sim card, then powered it up and dialed the cab company, requesting a ride from his current location, giving the diner name as the pickup address.

Pulling on the hat and glasses, Jack waited for the driver to arrive. He collected his travel bag, travel documents, and laptop from inside the van and locked it up. The cab arrived about ten minutes later. As he saw the black car with yellow checkers in a triangle on the door pull into the diner parking lot, he approached the driver, requesting to be taken to the airport rental car center. The driver helped him load his bag into the trunk, and Jack climbed in the back of the car, keeping his laptop with him.

The ride to the airport was fairly short, taking only ten minutes, during which the driver never spoke. Jack was relieved to be left alone with his thoughts. As the car moved across town, his mind cycled through a checklist, making sure he had thought of everything. Mostly, that he had Hope safe in a place where she could stay until he returned. He pictured how he had left her, and sadness overcame him.

Paying the driver cash, Jack gathered his belongings and headed inside the rental center. He approached the Hertz counter and asked the clerk for a compact car for a one-way rental to St. Louis. Handing over a credit card and the driver's license, both in the name of Jackson Phillips, he secured the rental and headed out to the parking lot. There he found the White Chevy Aveo in the appropriate spot, placed his bags in the trunk and got in the car, quickly adjusting the seat and mirrors.

Once he was out of the parking lot, he took off the glasses, so as not to impair his driving vision, and made his way out of the airport, headed north. It was a five and a half-hour drive to St. Louis. To be safe he would make only necessary stops.

He arrived in St. Louis, just after six o'clock. It had been a long day, but everything was going according to his plan. He found a fueling station and filled the car with unleaded gasoline, paying with the credit card of his newest identity. Finally turning into the rental car return center, Jack put the glasses back on and pulled into the rental return. He asked the return agent to leave the charges. Receiving the receipt, he thanked the agent and headed to the shuttle van area, where he waited for the shuttle to the airport terminals and hotels. He carried his bags onto the shuttle and informed the driver that he was going to the Hilton Garden Inn then settled in for the ride. As he focused on his new cell phone, he smiled at the thought of how easily he was slipping away from the authorities.

Arriving at the hotel, Jack checked in, requesting a late checkout the following day, which was granted. He would be allowed to stay in his room until two o'clock. After making those arrangements, he proceeded to his room and ordered some room service, not intending to leave again until it was time to head to the airport. In less than twenty-four hours, he'd be on a flight to the Caymans, and they'd never find him. Or Hope.

Chapter Thirty-Six

Max rose before the alarm even went off, tired of tossing and turning. After she showered and dressed, she grabbed her laptop and hurried downstairs, anxious to get the day started and find out what the rental company had on the vehicle. Being the first one downstairs, she enjoyed the coffee and silence of the room. Apparently the fishing tournament was either over or they were already headed to the lake. As a child, Max had fished with her grandfather and remembered going out in the wee hours. According to her grandfather, fish would bite best before it got too hot. Based on that memory, she was betting the fishing teams had headed out a while ago.

After about twenty minutes of silence, Wells showed up, followed very shortly after by Cortez. As they were getting their daily breakfast and coffees, Wells's phone rang. Max looked at the time on her cell phone and saw that it was just a couple minutes after five. She held her breath, hoping that this was the call they were waiting on.

A few minutes later, Wells hung up. "Got it, we have the make, model and license plate number. We already have a BOLO out on the car and Tyler in all fifty states. Let's hope he didn't expect us to find out what vehicle he is driving right away. Anyone spots the vehicle, they're directed to arrest him on the spot."

Max looked at Wells and then to Cortez, nodding her head. "Once we get a hit on the vehicle, what's the plan?"

"If he's left the state, the immediate orders are to extradite him back to Oklahoma. In the meantime, we're waiting for the preliminary results on blood found in the drain trap at the house. We're hoping to have some information before noon. The CSI team is conducting a lab comparison of the blood found in the trap against the DNA of our six victims. We've requested a rush on the results, and Detective Adair has a personal connection to the coroner, so he's pulling some strings to get the confirmation of the connection between Tyler and the victims. When we find him, and we will, we can bring him back to face trial here."

"What about the crimes in California?" Cortez asked.

"Once he's convicted in Oklahoma, he could be forced to go to California to stand trial there," Max replied before Wells could, citing the interstate laws.

"So basically, both states get their day, just not at the same time?"

Wells nodded. "That's correct, but let's not get ahead of ourselves. We need to locate Tyler first."

Max couldn't sit around waiting on the BOLO to hit, so she and Cortez headed back to speak with Jack's employer Samantha, in the hopes that she or one of the other employees had heard Jack talk about going somewhere specific. After talking to each employee and then going over to speak to Melody again, though, they'd come up with nothing more than a handful of new names of fellow students that might have had conversations with Jack. Given that the people Jack knew best seemed to know nothing, they returned to the City Hall building to see how the rest of the task force was proceeding.

It was just after ten o'clock when they got in, and Wells brought them up to date immediately. It was becoming increasingly clear that they needed a hit on the vehicle, he said, because without it there was no indication as to where Jack was heading, and time was getting away from them.

Suddenly, Max had a thought, and she pulled Cortez aside. "The magazines we went through from Jack's play house. We have all of those places cataloged that he studied for years. Do you think he may be heading to one of those other places? After all, Tulsa was one of the primary locations. Maybe we can find another escape plan there."

Cortez looked at Max and immediately reached for her laptop. "It's worth a look. We aren't doing any good just standing here."

Max and Cortez sat down together in front of the computer and pulled up the files with the magazine information, including a photo of the wall in Max's home. As they drilled through the files, Wells got a phone call and the whole room stopped, waiting for any indication that they had received a lead.

Wells glanced around the room as he finished the call, giving the team the nod they'd all been waiting on. "We've got the van, two hours from here in Arkansas. Nichols and Cortez, you're with me and Agent James. We'll fly from Tulsa. Prepare to leave. We don't know where this will take us or how long we will be gone. The plane will be on the tarmac waiting."

A quick stop at the hotel to grab their personal items and check out, and they were off to the airport. The flight to Fayetteville took just forty minutes, and upon their arrival they were met by the local Sheriff's Department, who led the team to the car waiting for them and then to the diner where Jack had left the van.

"The owner of the diner called it in after the breakfast rush. The van was there last night, but he didn't think too much about it until it was still there this morning."

234

Max checked the doors but found them all locked. She stood there with her hand still on the door handle stunned. Again, Jack Tyler was ahead of them.

After Wells gave the word, the sheriff pulled the lock from the driver's door with a crowbar. A quick search of the vehicle showed that it was completely empty, other than a box from a disposable cell phone. On the box was an associated phone number for the throw-away cell. Max immediately dialed the number, waiting for the third ring before the phone call was answered.

"Hello," Jack answered smiling.

"Dr. Jack Tyler?" Max asked, her heart racing a bit at the thought of speaking with Tyler.

"Yes, this is he."

"Dr. Tyler, we found your vehicle, and we know your whereabouts," Max bluffed, wondering if she could get him to offer any indication of where he currently was.

"Doubtful," he said confidently. "And who is it I have the pleasure of speaking to?"

"This is Detective Maxine Nichols of the Los Angeles Police Department, and I'm here with Agent Mark Wells of the FBI. Dr. Tyler, it would be best if you surrendered."

"Detective Nichols," he said slowly letting the words roll off his tongue, "are you the stunning woman I saw at the Beehive?" Not waiting for an answer, he continued on. "Perhaps turning myself in would be best for *you*, but certainly not for *me*. You see, I have things to do. I'm sorry to disappoint you, but have a good day, Detective Maxine Nichols. And give my best to your Hispanic friend." The line went dead.

Max stood, staring at the phone. She knew he was right. They did not have his location. His confidence was remarkable. She could hear the smugness in his voice, and at the moment she wanted to punch something. Wells and Cortez looked on as she shook her head, indicating that he hadn't offered her anything that would be helpful. "Nothing, but I could hear what sounded like the airport in the distance. He must be near an airport."

A crime scene team arrived to run prints on the vehicle and to look for any trace evidence. They still needed something material to connect Tyler to these crimes. Wells asked Agent James to interview the diner owner and the employees, to see if any one saw anything that might be helpful. After interviewing several people, Agent James came back out, shaking her head.

"So far no one remembers anything about the van or the driver of the van. I did get some information. There is a group of men that meet here every day about this time. Yesterday they sat next to the window where the van's parked. It's possible one of them may be able to provide some details. They should be arriving soon for their daily gathering."

"Great, make sure you speak to them the minute they start arriving," Wells requested turning back to Max and Cortez noting that they were watching the collection of evidence from the van. The evidence team had already recovered some prints on the steering wheel, and there was some trace fibers in the back of the van. The tech had said these appeared to be some sort of thread from clothing or a blanket. While this was happening, several cars had arrived, and the team was subjected to curious onlookers as the patrons rubber-necked trying to figure out what the commotion was all about as they made their way into the diner.

Some of these people were the group of older, male diners. They started arriving a few minutes later, and Agent James was quick to start speaking with them. After several minutes, she returned to the parking lot with a bit of news. "One of the men, Manny, sat next to the window said he saw a man park and then unload some luggage from the back of the van. He said the driver then went out front and waited a few minutes for a cab. The cab came probably ten to fifteen minutes later and picked him up. Manny said the driver was about six feet tall, wearing jeans and a white shirt, and a baseball cap, so he didn't see the color of his hair. Said the driver had on glasses. Not sunglasses, regular glasses."

"He's wearing a disguise?" Cortez asked.

"Possibly. It would make sense if he knew that we were on to him. We know he saw us at the salon, so he has to know we're trying to track him. Probably realized we were close to finding his house," Wells offered.

"Was the witness able to say anything about the cab service or which company it might have been?" Max asked, her mind running through the possibilities.

Agent James nodded, "Yes, he said the cab is the black one with the gold checkered triangle on the side, and the owner gave me some information. We need to get the logs to see who picked up here yesterday and where they took him."

Wells turned to the local officer. "Sheriff, can you assist us with this please? We need to know where the cab company took the driver of that van."

Max felt excitement growing. *We might have you yet, Dr. Jack Tyler,* she thought to herself. If they could figure out where he was headed, they could meet him there and catch him before he disappeared again.

The officer nodded. "You've got it," he said as he flipped open the cell phone. He punched in a number and waited for a moment, then started speaking. "Debbie, do me a favor and get a hold of the owner of the

Triangle Cab Company. What's his name? James? We need to know right away who picked up from the Bluestem Diner yesterday and where they took the passenger. We'll also need someone to interview that cabbie."

Max, Wells and Cortez all stood and watched anxiously listening to the one-sided conversation as the sheriff worked to gain information on who had taken a fare from this location.

The sheriff hung up and offered the information, "We're getting the cab driver's statement, but he said he took the driver to the rental center at the airport."

Wells and Max exchanged a look. Why would Jack rent another car? Did he know they were right on his heels, or was he just being careful? Was this the airport she'd heard on the phone?"

"Good work Sheriff," Max said, walking quickly toward the car. "We need to get to the airport right away."

Max, Cortez, James and Wells raced from rental counter to rental counter, asking for information on whether a Thomas Jennings had rented an automobile in the past twenty-four hours. Each counter showed no records of a rental by that name. Max showed the Avis rental agent a photo of Jack on her phone, and the woman shook her head, not recognizing the man in the picture. Looking down the row of rental counters Max saw Cortez, talking to a young male with a sassy attitude at the Hertz counter and then saw her head outside through the rental doors.

Finding nothing with her person, she walked towards the exit where she had seen Cortez leave and found her walking back in, "What ya' got?"

"He said that he wasn't working the day before, but the person at the exit might recognize the photo. I went out to see but got nothing out there either."

In the end, Wells requested a complete list of all rentals from the prior day, between ten in the morning and four in the afternoon. At a couple of counters, he met some resistance, until he said he would get a subpoena. He described the process of what would happen and how they would have to shut down until the FBI had reviewed all of their records. With this information, each of the counters offered their rental names and contact numbers.

Now, with a complete list in their hands, the three of them each took a page and looked through the names. Narrowing the list down to only the males, Max quickly honed in on the name Jackson Phillips. Jack ... son. This had to be the one. Showing Wells, she quickly returned to the rental counter, asking the agent if they kept copies of the driver's license. The agent shook his head, saying that they recorded the number, but didn't make a copy of the actual license. After further questioning, he was able to inform them that the rental contract indicated the car, a Chevy Aveo was a one-way rental that was to be dropped at the St. Louis airport.

Wells immediately called the bureau with the driver's license number and requested the information on the identification. A few minutes later, a photo was delivered to his email. The photo matched that of Jack Tyler. Wells dialed another number, snapping, "We need to be in the air to St. Louis in thirty minutes."

After thanking the Sheriff and his team and letting him know they would be in touch, the team headed to the private runway across the jet bridge from the rental center, where they'd landed two hours earlier. Thirty minutes later they were in flight to St. Louis.

Chapter Thirty-Seven

Jack hadn't slept well and rose early, ordering another meal from room service and spent the morning replaying his conversation with the pretty Detective. It had left his mind racing over the details again and again. He wasn't really sure if she was bluffing, but he was pretty certain they could not have traced him that quickly. The uncertainty left him anxious and restless. He needed to leave but was safer here than roaming the airport for any more time than was necessary. Deciding it was time to start getting ready, he headed to the shower.

After showering and packing his items, he sat waiting for the departure time. He'd spent some time watching the news and now knew that the police had raided his home in Oklahoma. They had found his surgery room and the freezer. Oh well, so they knew who he was, but based on the brief report, they did not know where he was and seemingly had not gone completely national with their findings yet. They must be trying to sneak up on him, hoping that he wouldn't hear what was happening. He knew he needed to get out of the country soon. After the phone call with Detective Maxine Nichols, it would be a national search soon if it was not already. He had to get on that flight and out of the USA.

Once the flight crossed into international space, they wouldn't be able to touch him. Jack had been very careful in his search of areas to travel, and had chosen the Cayman Islands because they were in British Overseas Territory and didn't have an extradition treaty with the USA. Once he was on that plane, he'd be on his way to safety.

The phone call from Detective Maxine Nichols had been a fun distraction from the waiting. It had let him know that they were onto him and had confirmed that he had no options but to leave soon. Of course, he had no way of knowing if the beautiful detective had been bluffing when she said they knew of his location, but he strongly doubted that they could have tracked him that quickly. Still, it was definitely time to get moving.

Jack left the room, wearing his glasses and ball cap pulled low over his brow. He tossed the room key on the counter on his way out. He'd requested the shuttle the night before, and it was waiting for him on the curb out front. After loading his items, the stout, balding shuttle driver asked him for his airline information and made the short drive over to the terminal, dropping Jack on the curb and assisting him with his bag. Jack slipped a $5 into the man's hand, drawing a big toothless smile from the wrinkled face. He could tell the man had worked hard his whole life and he appreciated that kind of discipline.

Then Jack followed the signs to the flight departures and checked in for his flight at the self-check kiosk counter, scanning his passport. Opting to carry his bag on, he continued to the security checkpoint, checking the display monitors on his way. His flight was on time and due to board in less than an hour.

He made his way through security, offering boarding pass and passport as requested, and removing money from his pockets. He slipped off his shoes and deposited these items along with the ball cap in the tub. He laid out his laptop in another tub and pushed all the items onto the security belt into the metal detector. He waited patiently as the two people in front of him took their turns going through the body scanner. At the direction of the gloved airport TSA agent, Jack stepped into the body scanner and raised his arms placing his thumbs in the center of his head. His heart raced, as he stepped through, placing his feet on the mat with the pre-drawn out shoes waiting until he received the all clear. Given the okay he collected his belongings, slipped back on his shoes and followed the signs that indicated the direction of his boarding gate. Arriving at his gate, he checked the monitor, which indicated that boarding would begin in ten minutes. He took a seat and waited for them to start.

Chapter Thirty-Eight

During the flight to St. Louis, Wells had the Bureau checking all departing flights the prior day and through the next twenty-four hours for any manifest showing a ticketed passenger name, Thomas Jennings, Jack Tyler or Jackson Phillips. If Jack Tyler was traveling from the St. Louis airport under any of these names they would have that information by the time they landed.

"If Tyler hasn't left the area yet, we'll have the flight grounded," Wells explained to Max and Cortez.

"What if he's gone already?" Cortez asked.

"It depends on where he's gone, honestly."

Max knew what Wells was referring to. Some areas were off limits to the USA, due to treaty agreements. If he'd gone to one of those countries, it would be impossible to extradite him. "Certain places outside of the USA won't give him back," she said quickly. "Let's hope we're ahead of him."

Max could feel her stomach churning as the time in the air seemed like an eternal wait. No one spoke during the flight, but she could occasionally feel Wells looking at her. She was careful not to allow their eyes to connect. Her feelings were all over the place. During the flight she struggled with the feelings that vacillated between the anxieties of tracking Jack, the possibility of actually being this close and finally catching him, worrying that somehow he might once again be a step ahead of them and slip away before they arrived, and the feelings she had for Wells. She continued to try to throttle those feelings and struggled to understand what they really meant. With Jack in cuffs she could relax and then she only needed to work through her feeling for Wells. He had said they needed to talk once this was settled. She tried to picture that conversation, but she could imagine it going in two very different directions and pushed those thoughts back again.

Chapter Thirty-Nine

Jack looked up as the airline gate agent began the flight announcement. "Welcome to Delta Airlines Flight #4673. We'll begin boarding for our flight to Grand Cayman, beginning with our 1st class and premier passengers, through gate #43. Please have your boarding pass ready to help make the boarding process go smoothly. We do have a full flight today, so please place small items under the seat in front of you and only one roller bag in the overhead storage compartment."

Jack stood and made his way over to the gate and handed his ticket to the ticket agent. The slim woman, with her blonde hair swept up on her head, smiled at Jack, accepting his 1st class ticket. "Welcome to the flight. Mr. Phillips."

Thanking her, Jack took his boarding pass back and headed down the jet bridge. After entering the plane, he stowed his bag in the overhead compartment and placed his laptop under the seat in front of him, so he could retrieve it during the flight. The flight attendant approached him and offered him a drink, but he smiled and answered that he'd have one once they were in the air. He settled into his seat, trying to not fidget as he waited for the door to close.

The other passengers poured onto the plane and took their seats one by one. Jack watched, looking at the wide variety of people passing him. Apparently the Caymans were a destination hot spot for families, as several children passed him. He wished that he could have taken Hope with him, but he settled his thoughts, reminding himself that he had to do this in order to have the future with her.

Chapter Forty

When the flight landed in St. Louis, Wells received word that a passenger manifest showed a passenger by the name of Jackson Phillips on a Delta Flight. The time of the departure wasn't available, but as they exited the plane, they were to be met by a Delta representative. Wells found out that the woman would be waiting for them on the tarmac with the flight information.

Max wasn't sure what this meant but was grateful that they would have immediate information when they got off the flight. They had to be on time to stop this man.

Exiting the plane, they found a small black woman waiting for them. She extended her hand and introduced herself. "Agent Wells, my name is Darlene Jefferson. I understand you're interested in a passenger by the name of Jackson Phillips." She nodded acknowledgement to the others.

"Thank you for meeting with us, Ms. Jefferson," Wells replied. "What can you tell us about the flight he's booked?"

"Unfortunately, that flight departed on schedule. It's already entered international airspace, and we're not able to recall a plane once it has crossed over into British territory. I am afraid you're too late, sir."

Wells looked at Max. "I understand, Ms. Jefferson. Thank you for your cooperation."

Max stood there on the tarmac with the wind from the planes blowing her hair into her face, forcing the rage she felt down deep inside her. The bastard *had* gotten away.

Chapter Forty-One

Jack hadn't fully relaxed for the first two hours of the flight. He'd watched anxiously until the airplane monitor showed when they crossed out of the USA and then finally ordered Vodka on the rocks. Sipping his drink, he reclined his 1st class seat and popped open his laptop, deciding that he could now watch a video. Finally able to enjoy himself, he reveled in the fact that his plan had worked. Hope was safely waiting for his return, and he was out of the long reach of Detective Maxine Nichols and her attractive Hispanic partner. Where he was heading, not even her friends with the FBI could get to him. Jack put his ear buds in his ears, ordered another drink and settled back in his seat. When the time was right, he would return, reunite with his wife and enjoy the rest of his life protecting her.

Chapter Forty-Two

Wells could hardly stand the pained look on Max's face. Neither she nor Cortez had spoken since Ms. Jefferson had delivered the news. There were a lot of loose ends to wrap up, and it would take weeks before all of the evidence was fully processed. Both Max and Wells had to inform their supervisors. There would be a massive amount of reports to file and interviews to conduct. All of the forensics on each of the bodies in both California and Oklahoma would have to all be completed. There would be questions from peers, and there were the emotional aspects to deal with, accepting the fact that they had been too late.

Both Max and Wells knew that Dr. Jack Tyler had escaped them for now, but they also knew he would not be satisfied. There was no way this man could refrain from killing. He had successfully restored Hope, but he was unable to take her with him. They could only assume that he'd disposed of her somewhere. What was more, they knew with absolute certainty that if he wasn't able to keep this one, he would have to have another one. It was only a matter of time before he was forced by desire or need to take another life.

Deciding it was too late to return to California or Washington tonight, everyone agreed an attempt at a good night's rest was in order. Checking into a nearby hotel, Wells left the women alone for a while as he checked in with headquarters and updated Detective Adair in Oklahoma.

No longer on the hunt for a serial killer, the women all decided to order a bottle of wine. As they sipped their drinks each one began to relax, slowly shedding the reality that their guy had gotten away. They shared some personal stories, getting to know a little more about Agent James through the conversation.

Wells returned to the table and joined them in a drink. They sat sipping wine and nibbling on food until it got late. Agent James was the first to excuse herself from the table, turning in for the night, followed shortly thereafter by Cortez. They said their good nights, though Wells and Max stayed on for a while longer.

Once the ladies had left them alone, Wells offered, "I know you're disappointed."

"I am," she acknowledge without even trying to deny it. "I mean damn it, Mark, we were so close. We *have* this guy, we just can't touch him."

"Yes, we have him. But guess what? He'll come back at some point, and when he does we'll arrest him."

"You might, but I'll be back in California, working some highway shooter case."

"Hey, we got you involved this time, right?"

"Yes, but it won't be that easy in the future. The colder my case in California becomes, the less likely it is I'll be allowed to stop, drop and roll to chase Jack Tyler around the country."

"Ever think about joining the FBI? Then you'd get to chase guys like this all the time," Wells asked, his wine glass half raised to his mouth and his eyes fixed on her beautiful face.

Max laughed out loud. "What? You're kidding, right?"

"Not really. Max, you have great skills and an instinct that can't be trained. We need good agents like you."

"You *are* serious?" Max said considering what he was saying.

"I'm dead serious. Think about it."

Max watched Wells for a moment before taking another sip of the wine. She was on her second glass and starting to feel a little tipsy. Deciding she needed to head up to her room, she started to excuse herself when Wells grabbed her hand.

"Stay with me tonight," he murmured.

"Mark, we shouldn't."

"Why not?" he asked, looking into her green eyes.

Standing up, he offered her his hand and walked her to his room.

Epilogue

It had been three weeks since Max returned home from St. Louis. The chief had praised her efforts and simultaneously ripped her for being unsuccessful in apprehending Dr. Jack Tyler. She and Cortez had started a weekly "girls" night at Max's house on Fridays, when schedules permitted. Cortez was completely unrelenting on her teasing of Max on the topic of Agent Mark Wells, but Max shut her down every chance she got. Privately, she had to admit that the man was fully under her skin.

That final night in St. Louis, after a couple of glasses of wine, she'd found herself in his room and again in his strong arms. When he'd taken her hand, her body immediately began to respond to his touch. Once his lips touched hers, she was filled with an intoxication that had nothing to do with the wine and everything to do with his strong, clean and manly scent. After she succumbed to his kiss and her hands found the muscles in his arms and stomach, there was no turning back. Their kissing had led to at first passionate lovemaking, followed by tender and gentle kissing, and an exploration that left no parts of their bodies unexplored. After hours of releasing into each other the energy they had channeled towards finding Jack Tyler, they had slept together, bodies intertwined.

The next morning, Max had stared in amazement at Mark as he slept, then covered his chest with light kisses until his blue eyes locked on her face. A smile had crept across his lips. It was a smile of comfort and contentment. In the end, after promising each other that they would not leave things as they had the first time they connected, they'd been forced to peel away from each other in order to prepare for their individual return flights home.

Since returning to California, Max had focused her attention on a new case and had shared endless hours of conversation with Mark on the phone. Each call ended with his niggling at her to cast her application into the FBI. She left every one of those calls torn between her emotions, her career aspirations, the unknown, and her own fears of commitment to a relationship.

Now it was Saturday morning, and she was preparing a light, healthy breakfast, with plans of following it up with a good run to get her body moving. She always enjoyed the burn of a good workout routine of any sort, and it sounded like exactly what she needed today. She was pouring coffee when the doorbell rang. Surprised to have an early morning visitor, she wondered if Cortez had forgotten something the night before.

They'd spent the prior evening sipping wine, talking about the men on the force, and occasionally speculating about what Jack Tyler was up to now.

When she opened the door, she was surprised to see Mark Wells standing before her with a lopsided grin on his face. "I was in the neighborhood, and thought I would swing by to see if you have time for breakfast," he said.

Max returned the smile and stepped forward, taking his hand and pulling him through the door.

***

A warm breeze came off of the ocean, causing little white caps on the glistening water in the Caymans. Jack sat with his now-tanned legs stretched out in front of him, sipping on a rum punch. Having restored Hope, he merely was biding his time until it was safe to return home to be reunited with his wife.

He'd been enjoying his time on the island but was beginning to get that feeling again. He wouldn't be able to fight it much longer, as only Hope's presence and the role of a surgeon had helped him resist the urges. He'd been noticing certain tourists lately … people who would be easy picks – those that frequently over indulged in alcohol. They would help tame the darkness and hold him until he could return to the United States. It was just a matter of time, not much longer.

He'd been tracking the news in the States, and his story had all but dwindled off. Based on this, he'd decided to wait at least one more month before returning. Until then, he'd enjoy his time here in the sun, while getting to know a couple of those overly intoxicated tourists.

Settling back in his chair, he took another sip of the sweet rum punch and smiled at his good fortune.

The End

Acknowledgement

There are several people who helped make this book possible. First, thanks to my partner, Lorea and to my children Maima and Akins for their patience while I spent hours absorbed in allowing my mind to take this journey. I also must thank my mother, Joyce Knupp for her honesty and encouragement as the first reader, editor and critic. She gave the nudge to keep writing.

To my editor Hollie Zunun, I thank you for what you brought to the final product, especially for your ideas and suggestions on the storyline. You did an amazing job of correcting my punctuation and challenging me all along the way.

A very special recognition goes to Jim Martin, a friend, co-worker and author of A Madman's Song, for generously sharing your discoveries on self-publishing. Your input saved me endless hours and made me realize I could do this. Read his book too, it is wonderful! Thank you so much!

FINDING FAITH

By

Valerie Knupp

Dedication

This book is dedicated to my mother Beverly "Joyce" Knupp who gave me the love of reading. My mother, who is an avid reader and my biggest fan, patiently waited on each section of this writing. She read carefully, offered valuable input and candid opinion. The quality of this writing is in part due to that input, and I am forever grateful. I love you, Mom!

Prologue

The body was wrapped in plastic, his signature incisions carefully concealed. He dropped the body into the hole, depositing the clothes along with it. She had been a feisty one, an island girl with a reputation for men and booze. It had been so easy, and he had enjoyed his time with her, taking several days before ending his pleasure and her pain. The past few months had been spent entertaining – in his special way - two tourists and three islanders, counting this one. This would be the last kill. Oh, people would die, certainly, but it would not be intentional, rather due to circumstances not within his control. It was time to return to the States. Time to reunite with Hope, and finally time to begin building back the life he had lost so long ago.

After completing the task of burying the body, followed by checking his surroundings, he returned to his car. He had picked up a used vehicle just to get him by during his time here in the Caymans. Three months. The time had both flown by and dragged on. But now it was time to go.

The flight back to the States had been uneventful. Jack had settled into his seat in first class, enjoyed the luxuries the ticket price afforded him, and waited anxiously for his flight to arrive in Houston. The few months in the Caymans had been refreshing, as was apparent by his tanned body and face. His mind, on the other hand, remained tormented by the waiting, sometimes drifting to thoughts of Detective Maxine Nichols. Patience, he wondered if she were as patient as he. This was an area that he never relished, though over time he had become good at controlling his desires, and was able to resist moving only on impulse. His skill in this area was driven by a vital instinct to survive and not be caught. Patience, he liked to joke that there was only one kind of patients, those in hospitals. This had always drawn a laugh from whomever he had used the phrase on.

Patients. Yes, it will be nice to get back to doing what he was good at, and what he had been born to do. Those months in Tulsa, working as a manicurist under the guise of a gay man, had certainly served the purpose. And it had given him the perfect cover, allowing him to escape, but that was not the lifestyle he was accustomed to. And his skill as a surgeon, a prided physician, was clearly needed.

As the flight carried him across the ocean, he considered his plan. It was well thought out, and he was more than ready.

Chapter One

The connection from Houston to Fayetteville, Arkansas seemed to take hours. The short flight in reality, felt as though it was taking hours as his anticipation of retrieving Hope from the storage facility mounted. He planned his arrival early enough that he could take a taxi to a car dealership where he could purchase a vehicle. His last time in Arkansas he had gotten by in a rental but he no longer needed a rental. He was ready to settle down.

The flight landed on schedule. He collected his baggage and headed out to the curb, hailing a taxi to be taken to the local Toyota car dealership. While in the Caymans, he reached out to his contact from Los Angeles and had received the documentation required to ensure his true identity, Dr. Jack Tyler, would remain unknown. Returning to the States under this new name, Dr. Jackson Taylor, ensured that he did not appear on any flagged lists that might have the authorities waiting to greet him.

Upon arriving at the car lot, he paid the cab driver and collected his belongings, while noting that the sales person was already heading his way. For three months he had spent plenty of time considering his position and the persona he needed to establish. The car he would purchase needed to support that perception. After looking through the car inventory of both used and new vehicles, he elected to settle on a Toyota Sequoia that was only a year aged with low miles. He knew this vehicle had plenty of room in it for towing and storing his precious cargo. He had used this model plenty of times in the past.

After a couple hours of negotiation and spending time with the finance department, he was exiting the driveway just before four o'clock with all the necessary paperwork in hand. He immediately went to a tag agency and registered the vehicle, receiving a license plate that he would install later when he got to the storage facility.

Next, he stopped at a QuikTrip gas station and purchased several bags of ice. He would need these to protect Hope for the trip they would make overnight, and he would replenish them as needed. Even though it was fall now and the trees had already turned colors he still needed to make sure her body was properly protected. With the ice purchased, he worked his way through the city anxious to get back to the storage location where he had left Hope three months prior. As he drove the adrenaline in his body soared in anticipation of seeing his lovely wife again. She had waited so patiently to be reunited, and the excitement nearly overwhelmed him. He forced his mind to close back in on the streets in front of him. It was now dark and after eight o'clock. The timing should be perfect. The

259

darkness would provide the perfect shroud for him to clear out the storage unit and leave undetected.

For a fleeting moment he worried. What if Detective Maxine Nichols and her Hispanic partner had found his storage? What if Hope was not there? What if the preservation of Hope had failed? He startled himself when he shouted out loud, "Stop it!" He knew his plan was solid, but he would not feel safe until he was at the unit and could see for himself.

Forcing his mind to refocus on more positive things, he considered his new life. He had already secured his new position in a small rural town in Illinois. There were a few formalities to settle, but he felt confident his plan was solid. He had purchased a home, via the Internet from his safe haven in the Caymans. He had transferred money into an escrow account and paid cash for the home. Then he'd secured an office on the main street of the town, abandoned and in desperate need of someone with his exact skills. He'd researched everything carefully and was certain his life was going to be perfect again. He just had to pick up Hope and then get them to their new home safely.

He pulled into the storage facility, keyed in his special code on the security pad, his heart raced as he waited for the gate to swing open. He advanced through, watching it close behind him, working his way back to the far corner of the storage facility. His eyes scanned as he passed each row, making sure he was alone. He spotted a moving van parked in front of a storage unit, five or six rows away, and decided that was not a threat. Those people were focused on loading their furniture and not him.

He pulled in front of the storage unit. His heart beat increased as he remembered the lucky number 7373, and considered what was inside. He backed the vehicle up so the rear of the newly purchased SUV was close to the door and out of the sights of the security cameras. He exited the vehicle.

Chapter Two

Three months had passed since Dr. Jack Tyler had slipped through Maxine's fingers. She had raced across the country with her friend and co-worker, Officer Lorraine Cortez, and FBI Agent Mark Wells. They had connected Jack to killing six people in Los Angeles and six more in Oklahoma.

The Oklahoma killings had helped them understand that after losing his wife and daughter in a terrible car accident, Tyler spiraled out of control in California. Then he had gone on a mission to restore his wife, by piecing parts of women together. He had literally removed the face from a TV anchor-woman that had strongly resembled his dead wife. The hands and feet had been stole from other victims. Others were killed either out of the necessity to quell Jack's need to touch the internal organs of his victims as the life left their bodies, or because they had somehow gotten in the way. Dr. Jack Tyler was a troubled man, a sick and sadistic killer.

As the team closed in on him, he ran departing the country to the Cayman Islands, where they couldn't extradite him. They had literally missed him by a couple of hours. His plane had already crossed international waters by the time they arrived at the airport in St. Louis, where Jack had cleverly planned his escape.

The weeks following these events had brought both joy and despair. Max still found times to study the information they had on Jack. She knew it was only a matter of time before he would return to the States and potentially kill again. Her desire to apprehend him had not faded, but rather had been masked in the desire and love that she had found in the long distance relationship she developed with Agent Wells.

Her waking hours were spent working new cases in the homicide division and talking with Wells into the wee hours. On days off when their schedules allowed, they took turns flying in to see each other, either at her bungalow in Los Angeles or his home in D.C. The times together were laden with laughter and passion.

The times apart were focused on their respective careers. Mark had been encouraging her to apply to the FBI Academy. She had recently submitted her application to the program and was now waiting to hear if she had been accepted. She knew her chances were good, given his recommendation, her successful career record and a degree in Criminology. Despite not apprehending Jack Tyler, Max was known as a closer in the homicide division of the LAPD.

Max realized that if she were accepted to the program, her life would change monumentally. She would need to relocate to the

Washington D.C., Virginia area. She would be required to live on the Quantico campus while undergoing twenty weeks of intensive Special Agent training. If this would actually happen, she and Mark had already discussed what the arrangement after training would look like. They agreed not to live together at first, allowing their relationship to grow, and ensure after time wore on that they truly were meant to be together for the long haul. Mark hadn't lost focus on finding Jack Tyler either, and they often discussed the progress or lack of progress as it was.

Mark was helping her in the effort to apprehend Tyler by using the capabilities of the FBI to establish some flags with the customs department. Should Jack re-enter the States as Dr. Jack Tyler, or his known alias, Thomas Jackson, the FBI would be notified immediately. So far nothing had flagged, and she grew increasingly concerned that Jack was smarter than their security alerts and would slip back into the country undetected, only to start killing again. Every day, she asked herself the same questions. Where are you, Jack Tyler? Are you already back? If you have Hope with you, will you be able to avoid hurting people? How long could Hope last in her current state? The last question always caused a shutter to crawl up her spine.

Chapter Three

Jack opened the door with both exhilaration and fear consuming his body to the point that sweat beaded on his brow. His nerves received their first wave of calm, as he felt the cool air waft over his body; the opening of the door exposed the cold temperature from within the frozen storage unit. The power had not failed, and the unit was cold. He walked in, closing the door behind him and preserving the required temperature.

Unaware of the chill inside, he walked forward to the shelf where he had carefully laid his beloved wife. He was overcome with emotion as he saw her laying there waiting for him. He swept her up into his loving arms. Tears flowed down his cheeks as he held her. He rocked her, unaware of the grotesque seam lines that outlined where the face, hands, and feet had been sewn into place. He was unaware of the effects the cold environment had on Hope's body. He pulled back to gaze into her eyes, "I promised you I would return, and now I have. I have returned to you, and I promise to never leave you again." He kissed her gently on the lips, his tears flowing, and a smile crept over his face. He felt peace inside. Finally, he was free. Free from the fear he had faced for months. His plan had worked!

***

The body lay on the shelf as he held it so closely, pale and blue from being stored away for three months in the cold storage facility, gazed back at him through the grotesque eyes, a pair of eyes that he inserted into the head of one of his victims. He had surgically removed each eye from the screaming woman, who he later killed. When he found a woman that had eyes with the characteristics of his deceased wife, Jack had taken that woman. Then he had surgically removed her eyes while she was awake and stored them until the moment he could place them into the perfect face.

The eyes were permanently opened. They seemed to stare back at him through the milk frost covering. The stitches that circled the hairline, hands and feet, and the fact that the face was not perfectly placed onto the head, making the whole body difficult to look at, repulsive to anyone else, were matters Jack was oblivious. To him, she was his wife Hope and perfect in every way.

***

Unsure of how long he had been holding her, he forced himself to pull away, suddenly aware that he needed to get moving. Staying here with the vehicle parked out in front of the door was not safe. They had a long drive ahead of them and a new home to establish.

He quickly began taking the items from the storage unit out to the vehicle. He had prepared clothes and bare essentials and his special tools. As he carried the boxes out to the car, he felt light. It would be nice to have all of his tools available to use again and to use them the way Hope had encouraged him to use them. Not in the way he had been forced to use them.

Inside the storage unit, he retrieved the tarp he had used to bring Hope here. Returning to his vehicle, he was careful to not allow the cameras to capture him. He opened the back of the vehicle and spread the tarp out on the floor. He stacked the ice around the area, leaving room to lay Hope down, and then returned inside. Grabbing the frozen blankets that had embraced his wife the past few months, he wrapped her tightly, completely concealing her body. The blankets would serve as added protection to preserve her as they traveled to their new home.

He prepared to return outside again, carefully looking all around before stepping out of the storage unit and into the night. He carried Hope and laid her down amidst the bags of ice, allowing them to fully embrace her body. He ensured the ice was carefully tucked all around her before covering her completely with the tarp.

He returned to the unit one last time, taking a quick look around making sure he hadn't left anything behind. Turning off the lights, he closed the door behind him and headed to the car. Once inside he drove to the office and deposited the lock in the box next to the door. He exited the storage facility and made his way through the city to the highway, heading north. It was nearly six hundred miles to Heyworth, Illinois, and it would be a long night. But what waited for him at the end of this journey was a life filled with joy and happiness. He knew because he had lived it before.

Making his way across the states, he was very cautious to not speed or do anything that might bring attention to his vehicle. He stopped to get fuel, coffee and a sandwich, and to replenish the ice. Hope was traveling well, and he was overjoyed with the idea of having her near him again.

As he drove Jack talked to the body in the back of his vehicle, telling stories of the house he'd picked out and the town where they would live. "Heyworth is a small community, a village by legal standards, with only 2800 people. It is the home of the Hornets. The town boasts of the typical small town pride of its students' success in sports. It's a big farming community, corn and soy beans mostly. In the summer, they hold the annual Hay Day festival, which is complete with carnival rides and a parade. You are going to love it there, darling." The night spent traveling had been fairly easy, and he was enjoying the time with his wife again. As he drove he gently teased her for being so quiet.

Jack pulled into Heyworth the next morning. Before heading to the real estate office, he doubled checked his cargo making sure that if anyone peered in, nothing would seem unusual. Feeling confident, he continued on and pulled in front of the local realtor's office. There was only one car out front, and he assumed it was the person he had worked with on the purchase of the house and the lease of his office. All he needed to do was get the keys.

Jack exited the vehicle and entered the office causing bells to jiggle that were hung up over the door frame. As he faced the room, he was greeted by an older, fairly rotund man who had quickly appeared from another room in the back. "Good afternoon, you must be the Dr. Jackson Taylor. I've been expecting you. Wasn't sure how early you would arrive in town." The man offered Jack his hand and carried a huge smile on his face.

Jack accepted the offer and shook his hand, "Just rolled in. You must be Dale. Glad to finally meet you," Jack said, returning the smile. A smile, he knew, warmed the soul of anyone he came into contact with.

"Well, I've got the paperwork and keys all ready for you. I'd be happy to take you out to the house and show you around. Give me just a minute to grab my keys, and we can head out."

Jack paused. "Dale, I really appreciate that offer, but you know I have a couple of things I need to do. I've been up all night and furniture won't arrive just yet. I really don't want to inconvenience you. How about I call you later and have you come by if I need help with any of the appliances or anything?"

"You sure, Doc? It really is no problem at all. I'd be pleased to show you around."

"I really do appreciate it, but yes, I'm sure. I want to check out the office too and take a quick tour around the town. You know I'm going to have to get to know people pretty quickly. Got to build up my client list." Once again, Jack applied his brilliant smile.

Dale nodded his understanding and moved back behind the large desk that took up most of the office. He opened a file cabinet and pulled out a large folder. He handed it to Jack. "I made you a complete copy of all of the paperwork from the transaction on the house. There is also a copy of the office lease. These are the keys to the house," he said as he handed Jack the keys. "This other set is the keys to the office. You'll find on the house key ring a key for the basement entrance and a key for the barn. They each are labeled."

Jack accepted the folder and the keys, checking out the labels on each one. "This is great, Dale. I can't thank you enough."

"It really has been a pleasure. You know the whole town has been awaiting your arrival. You won't have any problem building up your practice here. We have all been in need of a local doctor ever since Dr. Perkins moved away. He did the opposite of you, left for big city life," Dale laughed, sincere in his comment.

"I am certainly more than ready to slow down and get back to some of the simpler things in life. I truly appreciate you talking me up around town and helping to get my name out there."

"Well, you let me know if you need anything. Anything at all," Dale offered before walking with Jack towards the door and shaking his hand one more time.

"Be careful what you offer. I may just have to take you up on that." Waving good-bye Jack headed out to his car.

After climbing back into his vehicle, Jack headed through town. He saw where his office was located, but he opted to head out to the house. He needed to get Hope settled in before he could explore too much more.

He arrived at the house and pulled down the long driveway that wrapped around a big circle, lined with blooming hedges. The blooms were starting to fade as fall had clearly arrived, and it was time for the leaves to start dropping. Jack had purchased a big, white farmhouse with a wrap-around front porch. It was beautiful and sat on two acres just outside of town. It allowed just the right amount of privacy. Jack required privacy, lots of privacy.

He exited the vehicle, took the keys from the folder, and headed up the front steps of the porch. He inserted the key labeled "front door" in the lock and opened the door into the front entrance. He had studied the photographs online so many times in the past few weeks that he felt like he truly was coming home. He wandered the large rooms, taking in the nuances of the older home. The house was appointed with wood trim around the floors and ceilings, hardwood floors throughout, and a large kitchen with plenty of storage. He approached the mud room, just off the kitchen and near the back door, and discovered the inside entrance to the basement. This immediately drew his attention and reminded him of his time in Oklahoma. He had enjoyed some good times in that basement. And it had been the place where he had restored his Hope, taking the first steps to re-establishing the life they had cherished before the accident.

The accident... He hated it when he thought of that fateful day when his wife and daughter had been stolen from him, the ugliest, most difficult day of his life. That single event had led to a year of destruction for him and others. The first year he had been lost in his hurt, and as a result he had reverted back to the manner in which he dealt with pain as a boy.

Pain. He seldom thought of it. He avoided letting his mind travel over the days when his mother allowed those men to hurt him. His father always traveling left his mom lonely, and she frequently allowed men to follow her home. Some of those men were not so nice. Jack had emotionally degraded by the age of ten and took his pain out on others. Others, that came in the form of animals, wild animals that lived in the woods behind his home or the occasional neighboring pet.

That was all before Hope had saved him. Hope, his childhood best friend. Before she had caught him in the woods with one of those animals and vowed that together they would make it work. She convinced him that they could turn his pain into a positive thing. Jack had told her everything.

She was the only person he had ever trusted with his ugly secrets. That horrible day in the woods Hope had seen him with the cat still in his hands. She had him clean up. Then they had gone to the play house, and while he cried, she had held him. It was then that he told her everything. He told of the sexual abuse of both his mother and her frequent partners. How she would make him join her in bed whenever his father was out of town, sometimes just the two of them, his mother making him do things with his body and mouth. Other times it would be with a stranger she had brought home from the bar in town. He would be forced to watch them and sometimes join. A few of the men had hurt him.

In that moment, Jack and Hope had become forever linked to each other. They were linked by a secret that two young kids should never have had to keep, by a love that grew from that secret, and by a plan to eliminate the need for Jack to kill. It had worked, until that day. Until that drunk driver took her and their daughter Faith from him. But now, he had her back, and he would not ever let anyone separate them again.

Jack forced his thoughts back to the present and checked the time on his watch. Where had the time gone? The furniture should be delivered any time. He had taken some time to order the basic needed items. He could fill the house up more as he settled in, but for now he needed living room, bedroom, and dining room furniture. And he needed a freezer, a big freezer. Realizing he was still standing at the top of the basement stairs he searched for the light switch. Dale had helped him get the utilities turned on. He needed to get all of that set up too, but for now the power, water, and gas were on. He would visit the utilities company today, if he had time.

Descending into the basement he was pleased to see the layout was similar to what he had in Oklahoma. The rooms were separated and the basement even had a small bathroom. He checked the outside door access. The access was not his favorite part of the house. He preferred no one be able to enter his home without him knowing, but he had not been able to find one that only had an indoor entry. He specifically liked this home because the rooms were decent sizes, and the basement entry opened through double doors. This allowed for larger items to come in through them. He smiled when he saw it in person, remembering the struggle he had when trying to get the freezer set up in Oklahoma. He was barely able to get the freezer down the stairs. This was going to be easy. He made a decision that the freezer would go in the corner, left of the door. He was having a stainless steel table delivered as well.

He thought about the table for a moment. He shouldn't need to use it. He ran a series of questions through his head. If I don't need it, why did I order one? Does the table make me feel like I am in control? Am I worried that I will need to use it to maintain Hope?

Not able to find quick answers to these questions, he shrugged and entered the last room, finding it equipped with a shower head at one end of the room with a drain in the floor. The room was a pretty good size. It appeared that someone had used it as an extra bath. There were ample shelves lining one of the walls, making the perfect place to store his medical supplies. The lighting was good, and the walls were all lined with a shower enclosure material making the entire room washable. Good, I don't have to do that part myself. All of this made him very happy, though he knew deep inside he should not be. He should really have no need for a room like this. Even still, he mentally pictured a guest tied to the table. He could see his hands deep inside the cavity of a body. As he pictured this, he imagined the feeling he would have as he held each of the critical organs in his hands just as death came. He made up his mind. He would set the room up just like an operating room, just like he had in Oklahoma.

Talking out loud he stated, "No more, Jack. You won't need this anymore. You have Hope again to help you do positive things."

With the inspection of the basement complete, he started to ascend the stairs, and as he did so he heard the sounds of a motor and assumed it was the delivery truck. Glancing at his watch he thought, perfect timing. He needed the freezer installed so he could get Hope inside and properly cared for - and soon. He passed through the dining area and living room.

Jack looked out and saw a large truck backing up to the house. Heading out to greet the driver, Jack exited the front door and saw a big man headed towards him from the driver's side cab of the truck. "Mr. Taylor?" The man asked, his muscles rippling under his tight uniform shirt.

"Doctor Taylor. Yes. Thanks for being on time," Jack acknowledged as he approached the truck.

"No problem," the man responded as he began rolling up the back door of the big truck. They were joined by another man of equal size. The delivery men pulled out the ramp that was stored under the back end of the vehicle. Walking up the ramp they began pulling out dollies that had been neatly stored on the inside wall of the vehicle with tie down straps. Using the dollies they began pulling items off the truck, setting them out on the lawn.

Jack led them inside and carefully pointed out where each item went. Couch and love seat along with two end tables and a coffee table were delivered into the living room. Appliances were appropriately placed in the kitchen and laundry areas. The bedroom furniture was delivered into the master. A smaller bed was delivered into the guest room. Jack had no idea when he would use that, but he felt it necessary to make sure his home looked well appointed. Finally, the most important item came off the truck and was set out on the lawn. The freezer. Jack went over to the basement doors and unlocked them with the keys Dale had given him earlier. The two men followed him over to assess the situation before returning to the freezer. It was large. The men carefully strapped it onto a double appliance dolly then hauled the heavy load over to the doorway. They wrestled with it until they had it successfully sitting inside the room. It cleared the door frame by only a couple of inches on either side. Inside it took up the full corner next to the door, soaking up every inch of space from the floor to ceiling.

As the men returned to the vehicle to remove the television and a kitchen table, Jack focused on getting the freezer plugged in. He installed the shelves inside the unit lining one side, and then removed all of the packing materials. He set the temperature and double checked the working operation of the internal lights. Everything seemed to be in working order, and in a few hours it would have totally cooled to the desired temperature. He had the men deliver a few more items to the basement. The stainless steel table, which he had delivered into the shower room, a couch, a smaller flat screen television, and small table he had placed in the middle of the room near the freezer. He'd hang the TV later.

The men finished and loaded their items back into the truck and handed him a delivery receipt to sign. Jack quickly signed off and thanked them, anxious for them to leave, so he could bring Hope into their new home.

After allowing the appropriate amount of time for them to truly be gone, Jack pulled the SUV near the basement door. Checking his surroundings, he quickly opened the hatch on the vehicle and gently lifted Hope from it. He carried her inside and took her directly to the freezer. He entered with her and closed the door behind him, flipped on the lights and carefully laid her down inside on the shelf.

The space inside was small, but that was okay. Touching Hope's face, he determined her body temperature was cold enough until the freezer got to temperature. He certainly enjoyed being near her and for a moment he considered if he could sleep inside here with her. Deciding against it, he sighed knowing he would have to be satisfied with less time than they had before. It didn't matter. In fact, he would have plenty of time with her, and their life was going to be perfect here in Heyworth.

Double checking the temperature, he was pleased to see it was cooling quickly. Before he exited the inside, he kissed Hope and held her briefly, while promising to spend some time with her later. Closing the door behind him, he made sure the latch closed completely. He had several things to do, including picking up some groceries and checking out the office. He decided to go get something to eat, look at the office, and come back to rest for a while.

Jack headed back towards town. As he drove he enjoyed the rural setting with the massive expanse of the corn fields. The land was so flat he felt like he could see forever. The horizon seemed to be never ending. Like the life he and Hope would have here in Heyworth...never ending. He turned onto Main Street and pulled in front of the office that sat next to the local drug store.

Exiting the car he walked up to the office and inserted the key that was labeled for this door. The door swung in and exposed the front lobby of what had all the makings of a doctor's waiting room. The furnishing were modest but in good shape. The back office had three examination rooms and a small operating room for minor surgeries. Nothing serious would of course be done in this office. Those situations would be saved for the nearby hospital. There was acceptable equipment to take blood samples and perform minor x-rays.

Jack had plans in the next few days to meet with the Director at the hospital. He would offer his services there, which would likely get him a bit more time involved in the more critical care needs. He needed to have opportunities to really dive into surgeries that allowed him to relieve his dark impulses. It would be through those releases that he would be able to keep the urges under control.

Taking a final tour of the office, he decided it was completely satisfactory and had everything he needed to get started right away. Locking the office door, he stood outside on the sidewalk and looked up and down the street. There were few people about. Middle of the day, middle of the week, most people would be working. He saw a sign for a diner and realized how hungry he was.

Jack headed toward the sign situated a few doors down from his office. When he entered the door chimed causing the few people inside to turn to look at him. He nodded at them, and read the sign that said "please be seated," he found a seat at a table in the corner next to the window.

Within a few minutes he had a steaming hot cup of coffee and had ordered from the menu. Now he sat back and relaxed. A few minutes passed while he enjoyed the peacefulness of his surroundings. The server returned to the table to offer a refill on his coffee.

Pouring the brown liquid into the cup, Jack could feel the server eyeing him. He decided it was as good a time as any to start getting to know people. "Nice place you have here."

"Yes. We like it. I don't believe I have seen you around here before. Just passing through?"

"No, actually I just got into town today. I bought the farmhouse outside of town. Jackson Taylor," he offered, relying on the charm he had carried ever since he was a small child. "Nice to meet you, Sarah," he said reading her name tag.

Sarah was immediately taken by his smile. "Oh yes, well, welcome Heyworth, Doctor. The whole town has been awaiting your arrival. We need a good doctor here. Dale has been talking all about you."

"Dale? He has. Has he? Well, I will be sure to thank him for putting in a good word for me."

Smiling, Sarah excused herself to check on his food. A few moments later she returned with a large platter piled with eggs, bacon, hash browns, and toast. Setting the plate down, she filled his coffee cup again, telling him to enjoy, gave him a wink and then disappeared back into the kitchen.

Jack enjoyed his breakfast while watching the patrons and Sarah interacting with them. The typical small town familiarity was ever present. Finishing his food he thanked Sarah, and paid his bill, making sure he tipped her appropriately. He departed the diner and stepped back into the sunshine. The fall air was crisp but clear and refreshing. Jack headed back to his house. The food had been filling, and he was immediately aware of how tired he was. The groceries would have to wait.

Over a month had flown by since Jack moved into the farmhouse. He'd spent the first few days gathering up the rest of the necessary items for his house. This included getting the shower room fully set up as an operating room complete with all the necessary operating supplies. He'd shopped in Bloomington where there were a couple of malls to choose from. He'd opened his office and started taking clients. He'd successfully connected with the hospital, and they'd accepted his offer to be on-call for any emergency surgeries. The paperwork Jack's contact had given him was flawless. No one questioned his medical license, and he had the skills to more than support the role. The fact was, he was under-challenged here, but it was safe and a great place for Hope. It had been a very productive time.

Jack's evenings were filled with visits to the basement. He would remove Hope from the freezer and set a lovely dinner table. He prepared wonderful meals for two, and afterwards he moved her onto the couch and held her for hours while watching TV. He ignored the fact that she never ate any of the food...couldn't eat any of the food. Sometimes he would make love to her before returning her to her resting place, back inside the freezer.

He was satisfied with the way things were, completely oblivious to the grotesque condition of Hope's preserved body. His experimental chemical combination of embalming and taxidermy was working well. Though he was required to keep her cold, the combination allowed for periods of time out of the freezer and provided some flexibility, including the ability to move her arms and legs. There were some signs of decay, but otherwise the body was holding up well. He would dress her and occasionally wash her hair, always being careful not to allow the body to become too wet, especially around the incision lines.

They had a simple life. But he could tell there was something bothering Hope. She seemed sad at times. He knew what was bothering her. Like he did, she missed Faith, their beautiful daughter who had perished in the accident. He told her it would be okay. He wasn't really sure how, but he intended to make her happy. He had to make her happy.

***

Jack was afforded the occasional opportunity to conduct surgeries at the hospital. There had been a combine accident with one of the local farmers, and he had to remove the man's spleen. There had also been a car accident that caused some internal damages to a teenage boy. A tragedy since, unfortunately, Jack had not been able to save the young man. Despite the fact that he had worked diligently for several hours trying to stop the internal bleeding and even had successfully repaired the injured internal organs, which included a perforated lung. After the boy had nearly bled out, he stabilized momentarily, but the damage was just too great. Jack held his lungs as they filled with air for the last time, feeling both failure and euphoria.

It was these events that had held the darkness at bay. Jack was able to keep from using the stainless steel table and was thrilled that his plan was working. Having Hope back in his life had saved him. He no longer needed to kill innocent people. Being a surgeon had been the plan to keep him from killing when they were just twelve years old. Hope's plan. A plan she came up with that day when she caught him with the cat in the woods. It had worked before, and it was working again.

Jack couldn't be more pleased. If only Hope was as happy. Her sadness pulled at his heart. He couldn't bear knowing she was in pain and knew he had to do something to make her happy again. He just wasn't sure how.

Chapter Four

Max received her acceptance letter from the FBI Academy and gave notice to the LAPD. She'd enjoyed a couple of going away parties with co-workers and friends, packed up her belongings, and hauled a U-Haul across the United States. She allowed herself a week off with Mark, and they enjoyed time exploring more in depth the Washington, D.C. and Virginia areas. For now she'd placed her belongings in storage, keeping with her only what she would need at the Academy. She wouldn't need much as the program didn't allow for much free time. She planned on graduating at the top of the class and wouldn't allow anything, including Mark, to distract her. He was fully supportive and also knew the next weeks would be little to no time for them to spend together. Maybe a dinner or something here and there would be all they would have time for.

One of the hardest things for Max to do was to say good-bye to Officer Cortez. They had spent many hours together, and formed a strong friendship through the course of tracking Jack Tyler. Cortez had successfully applied to the detective's program and received a well-deserved recent promotion. Max leaving was creating an opportunity, which Cortez would fill very well.

The night before Max left, she and Cortez went out and enjoyed dinner and wine. They parted ways with a respectful nod that only the two women would understand. Only the two of them understood what they'd shared during the endless hours of staring at the murder board Max had made in her home prior to going on the manhunt to find Jack Tyler. The murder board had been an important part of beginning to understanding what was driving Jack. The details on that board had helped Max and Cortez put together the reason for Jack's killing spree in Oklahoma. Their many Friday nights at Max's house, drinking wine and studying that board, had helped in determining that Jack was fighting to restore his life. He was doing so by, literally, putting together a replication of his wife from the bodies of several other women. They would later learn that he had kidnapped women while hiding under the guise of a gay man who worked at a nail salon. He'd murdered women and had stolen body parts that appeared to match those of his deceased wife, Hope. The suffering some of his victims endured was unspeakable. He'd literally put together a body that he believed was his wife. Then, he'd taken that pieced together body and ran with her. Jack had boarded a plane to the Caymans, successfully eluding capture. And did what with his restored Hope? No one knew. This fact tormented Cortez in the same fashion it tormented Max. Within that torment and the loss in the failed capture, a lasting bond was formed. Max would definitely miss Cortez's friendship and her skill as a partner.

Max placed her house on the market, but it had yet to sell. Before leaving for the Academy, she gave her sister Power of Attorney, allowing her the ability to accept an offer and make the transaction on her home, so she would not have to worry about this while in training. This detail allowed her complete freedom to focus on nothing else but successfully completing the training with high marks. Feeling good about her decisions, she started the program with little else to worry about.

Max was immersed in the training at the FBI academy. She found the regiment both exhausting and rewarding. Several of the people enrolled had dropped under the academic and physical pressure. The Academy had about a sixty percent graduation rate, and this class was shaping up to be about the same. Despite these startling facts, Max was excelling. Her prior experience and exceptional physical shape was slowly moving her to the top of the class. There was little time for much else, but in her spare time she stayed connected to Mark.

"Hi, how are you holding up?" Mark asked when he finally reached Max on the line.

"Good. Tired, but good. How 'bout you?"

"Good here too, though I miss you."

"I miss you too, only one more week until graduation. Thought it would never get here. Now it seems crazy that it is here so soon. I'm looking forward to seeing you and working again. She paused. "Mark, I still keep mentally working the Tyler case. I can't shut it off."

Mark listened as Max confessed. He was pained by the torment he knew she would carry until Jack Tyler was brought to justice. "I still have the traps set. Though I hate to admit it, he has likely re-entered the U.S. by now, and we didn't catch him. He's clever and good at creating new identities."

Max proceeded cautiously, "I think we missed something. While I was in one of my training exercises, it dawned on me that we should have been looking for where he would have hidden the body he created."

"Max, honey, do you really think he kept the body? Wouldn't it make more sense that he buried it somewhere before leaving the country? He knows he can kill again and make another one. I guess I assumed that, since we caught up to him forcing him to run, he dumped the body with plans to come back one day and start over."

"I know that's what we all assumed. We believed we would never find the body, that he buried it somewhere, and then one day he'd return and do it all again. But, in my class, they were talking about a case. It was mob related and in most senses not really relevant, but we got onto the 'God Complex'. Anyway, none of that matters except that the un-sub reminded me of Jack. I don't think he would be able to part with the body. He believes it is Hope. He also believes he let her down once before. When the accident actually killed her, he believes he failed her and because of that he will never allow anything to hurt her again. Mark, I don't think he could just let her go. He put that body somewhere, and he planned on coming back to it when it was safe. In my mind that leaves only one possibility. Store it." Max stopped, letting Mark take in everything she just said. Continuing she said, "And there's the empty padlock box".

Mark considered her theory. "I see what you're saying. If he has already returned then he retrieved that body and took it wherever he planned on going next, but, if he hasn't yet returned and if we can find where he stored the body, we might be able to get him when he comes back to pick it up."

"Mark, there's more." Max hesitated before continuing on, "He's not done. He will only be satisfied with Hope for a while. What I'm saying is there is something still missing. Mark, he doesn't have his whole life back. He hasn't found Faith yet. I think he will look for her." She stopped and listened and could tell by the silence on the other end of the phone that Mark was obviously struggling with this idea.

"Max, that is a total different victimology. He's never hurt a child." He paused then added, "At least as far as we know. It's not typical for a serial to change who they hunt. That would be very uncommon."

"I know, but I don't think Jack fits the typical mold. He isn't specifically a gain or power killer. He really doesn't fit any of the five types. He is organized for sure, and he may be anti-social. But he is quite capable of fitting in. He proved that by working as a highly respected surgeon in California, and he was able to change his persona to fit in as a gay man in Oklahoma. Jack is a chameleon. I believe he is a hybrid of a gain/control killer. Also, thirteen percent of serial killers do, in fact, change their victim type." Max paused again. "I'm just saying, I think he is unusual, and these are some things we should be thinking about."

Mark was quiet for a minute. "Okay, when you get out of training we can work this a little on our own time. If we come up with anything then we can take it up the chain of command to see if we can make it active again. Deal?"

"Deal. Now what was it you were saying about missing me terribly?" Max joked, trying to return the conversation to a tone that was more typical for her and Mark.

After exchanging some small talk for a while, the two agreed to hang up for now. Max would graduate from the Academy in a week, and then they could resume the life they had agreed on. Max had an apartment already rented for after graduation. She owned her place in California, but she didn't want to buy a house until she knew where the relationship with Mark was going.

Before hanging up, Max told Mark she loved him, "Wells, my heart and lips will see you in a week. Be safe."

"I love you too, Max. Don't get hurt. See you in a week."

The week went by fast. Max continued striving to hit the timed exercises. Her mind worked over her theory on Jack Tyler, and it was often her thoughts and frustrations while thinking of him that forced her to push through some of the grueling exercises. Graduation day came soon enough. Mark came to watch her be sworn in as 'Special Agent Maxine Nichols'. Following the graduation they left together and went to Wells's house where he had planned a private dinner. They talked, drank wine, and ultimately fell into each other's arms, enjoying every moment, until sleep took their sweat-covered bodies.

Chapter Five

Jack was just finishing up with Mrs. Blum, an elderly woman that seemed to find reasons to come in for a check-up. He gave her discount prices and sometimes just talked with her. She was eighty three, and the biggest thing wrong with her, other than a bit of high blood pressure and occasional arthritis, was loneliness. He put a hand on her shoulder, "Now, Mrs. Blum, you go home and be sure to take your medicine every day, and you come see me if you have any problems. Right now you are as strong as an ox."

"Okay, Doctor Taylor. I just worry, you know. I don't want to get down in my chest."

Jack patted her arm and smiled at her old school reference to bronchial illnesses as he walked her towards the front. "No charge today. Okay, just take care of yourself and be careful out there. It is starting to get chilly."

Watching her walk out, Jack turned to find his front office assistant behind him with another file in her hand. She was a young woman who was attending nursing school and worked for him keeping his medical records. She was talented and eager as well as responsible. She also did not pry into his life. "Thank you, Mary. Who do we have next?" Jack asked, flipping open the folder.

"A little girl. Her name is Jessie. She is having some flu like symptoms."

"How old is she?" Jack inquired while scanning the chart.

"She just turned six," Mary answered. "She's in examination room two."

Jack nodded and headed towards the room, tapping lightly on the door before entering. Upon opening the door Jack was stopped dead in his tracks as he saw the little girl from behind. Her wavy, blonde locks dropped below her shoulders. His heart dropped, Faith?

Faith would be nearly seven years old now. The young girl turned to face him, and he realized then that, no, this was not Faith but another little girl who looked so much like her from behind. This little girl had brown eyes and olive skin. Faith had blue eyes and light skin and she had the same long golden hair. Just like Hope and just like this little girl. Gathering his composure, Jack applied a smile to his face that he really did not feel. He introduced himself to the mother who sat in the chair across the room and then turned back to the young girl. Knowing that children can be easily scared by strangers, and especially doctors, Jack knelt down to eye level with the girl. "Hi, I am Doctor Taylor. You can call me Doctor

Jack. I understand you aren't feeling so good today. I'm hoping I can help you feel better. Would you like that?"

The little girl nodded. Her eyes were big with uncertainty.

"Well, okay, so I'm going to need to take your temperature. It's really easy. All I need to do is swipe this right across your forehead," he said holding up the modern thermometer. "Want to see me do that to mommy first?"

Still uncertain, the girl watched as Jack ran the thermometer across the mother's forehead. Then she looked at it with Jack as he showed her the reading. "See. Now can I do the same thing to you?"

The little girl nodded, still a bit apprehensive.

Jack ran the thermometer across her forehead and read the output. 100.2. She had a fever. "Now can I look in your mouth? I'll let you stick your tongue out at me."

The girl, feeling a bit safer now, giggled at the idea of sticking her tongue out at the doctor. She nodded at him.

Remaining at eye level with her, Jack had her open her mouth and repeatedly stick her tongue out, making it more of a game than an examination. This further put the little girl at ease. As he examined her, he noticed red bumps on the inside of her throat. "Does your throat hurt when you swallow?"

The little girl nodded.

"I bet it does. You have some yucky red bumps in there making it sore. How about I get you some yummy grape syrup, kind of like the stuff you put on pancakes, which will help those feel better?"

"Okay." The little girl giggled again.

"Yeah, okay I'll tell you what, while I get this set up with your mommy, why don't you go see about picking out a sucker or a little toy out front? Mary can help you, okay?"

Before he could even finish, Jessie jumped down from the examination table and ran out the door off to see what goodies lay in store for her out front.

Jack explained to the mother that he wanted to give the girl syrup for sore throat pain and some liquid antibiotics. He felt the girl would be better within a couple of days. After writing a prescription, he followed the mother out to the lobby where Jessie sat with a pink sucker. "Did you pick something out?" Jack asked, smiling again at the little girl.

She nodded and stood to take her mother's hand.

"Can you promise to be a big girl? I want you to drink your syrup and listen to your mommy. You should feel good in a day or two. But if the syrup doesn't help you come back and see me. Okay?"

Heading out the door swinging her sucker, the little girl stopped before leaving, turned back and said, "Thank you, Doctor Jack." She giggled once more, and then she and her blonde waves were gone.

Jack felt the tightness in his chest again. He realized just how badly he missed Faith. He had forced himself to not think about that any more, focusing only on Hope. Now, he understood what Hope must be wanting. Deep in thought, he laid Jessie's folder on the counter for Mary to process the billing and file. Heading to his office in the back, he sat down and searched for a solution. He and Hope couldn't have any children. That wasn't possible. Or was it? Could he find Faith and bring her home to Hope? Several minutes later Mary interrupted his thoughts, letting him know that he had another patient.

After seeing two more patients, Jack let Mary go home. He turned off the lights and locked up before leaving. Traveling through town, the buildings and homes passing him in a blur as his mind returned to thoughts of Faith and how much he was certain this would make Hope happy. Arriving at the house he went inside, deciding he must have a talk with Hope.

First, he fixed dinner and brought the two plates down to the basement, setting them on the table. He opened the freezer and removed Hope, settling her down at the small table that served as their dinner table. Joining her he began eating. After he'd finished most of his dinner, he began the conversation he had decided was necessary to have with his wife.

"Hope, I know you have been sad lately. At first I admit I didn't understand why and was almost hurt by it because I thought you would be so happy to finally be back together. But, today I saw a patient, a little girl, and from the back she reminded me of our little Faith. It was at that moment that I realized what it was that has been troubling you. I miss her too, Hope. I have an idea. I know the accident left you unable to ever have children again, but I was thinking that I could bring Faith home to you." Jack stopped for a moment, waiting to see what Hope's reaction was. He could tell she was listening by her intent stare.

She wasn't resisting the idea so far, so he continued on, "I know you only want me to use my skills for helping people. That was the commitment we made when we were kids, and except for the time when we were apart, I have kept that promise. That was only because I was so lost without you, but once I figured out how to find my way back to you, it has been like the good days in California. I was thinking that if I could bring Faith back, it would have to be without causing pain. I've never hurt a child, and I wouldn't…I would…I will make sure no one suffers. Besides, wouldn't Faith be happier with us, her real parents?"

Jack paused as he waited for Hope to consider the idea. He watched her closely and didn't see any signs of anger or disappointment. In fact, she appeared to be smiling. He was sure of it. She loved the idea and agreed that Faith would be happiest with them! Now he had to find Faith and bring her home. He owed it to Hope to make everything perfect for her again.

After finishing dinner, Jack cleared the table and took the dishes upstairs placing them in the dishwasher. Then he returned to the basement, moving Hope to the couch where they could cuddle and watch some TV together. He continued to talk of his plans and how soon they would have their little girl home with them again. That night he slept peacefully and dreamed of a little girl with long, golden locks flowing past her shoulders, a little girl that looked so much like her beautiful mother.

**

Jack awoke feeling refreshed and with a new sense of purpose. He decided to drive into Bloomington for the day and found himself sitting in the parking lot of Miller Park, overlooking the playground area. Children were swinging, sliding and climbing. Jack watched and thought. This would have to be different. Bringing Faith back home to Hope was not going to be as easy as walking up behind an adult. Children were closely watched. He watched the children, but then he watched the parents. There was no way he could just walk up to one of these little girls, like the cute one with long blonde hair flying out past her shoulders as she rode the swing higher and higher. No way. The parents were too attentive, and even if they weren't, there were simply too many adults around, adults that could be witnesses. This would not work. Finding Faith was going to be more difficult. But, she should be home with him and her mother. A child belonged with his or her parents.

For a moment Jack got distracted by a little boy sliding down the slide. His heart pulled for a moment as he remembered one of the last conversations he had with Hope. They had just started talking about having another child, both openly talking about how wonderful it would be to have a son. That was not in the cards now. But, finding Faith, yes, that must happen. He must find a way.

Thinking of another possible idea, Jack backed out of the parking space and pulled through the park and back out onto the road. He worked his way out of the neighborhood and down Morris Avenue. Then he wound his way east until he was on Oakland Avenue and pulled over on the side street a block away from Irving Elementary School. Looking at his watch, he read two-forty five. Perfect. He would wait.

About twenty minutes later, buses began pulling into the parking areas and lining up. Jack watched in anticipation. Another ten minutes passed, and soon children began flowing out the doors. Cars pulled in and through after retrieving the children. Children walked across the campus and climbed onto the buses, and then some headed off down the various streets. Walkers, young children entrusted to walk the few short blocks to their homes. Jack pulled out from the street and circled the block. Children weaved their way through houses and streets some in groups and some alone. He was appalled by the fact that any parent would allow their child to walk alone. Not his Faith. Never!

Deciding he had learned and seen enough for the day, Jack made one more circle around the block and then headed back home. He had some research to do. How many schools were there? And, exactly how many little girls walked home alone every day? Faith was here. He knew it, and he couldn't wait to tell Hope about his great day.

Arriving home Jack immediately went downstairs to the basement. He entered the freezer and lifted Hope, bringing her to her place at the small table. He was bursting with excitement. "Hope, I think I have found her. It will take a little time. I thought she was at the park, and then I realized it wasn't right. Then, I realized she should be in school, and sure enough she is there somewhere. I just have to find out which one she goes to. I'm glad the people who have been caring for her at least had the good sense to keep her in school. She won't have lost any time. She will be exactly like when she went away. It will be exactly the same, Hope, you, and me, and our baby girl all together again. Hope, darling, it is going to be perfect again." Jack stopped, trying to catch his breath.

The body stared back at him, the eyes a blue gore, the head slightly tilted to the left where the hairline sat just off center. Jack kneeled in front of her and placed his head in her lap. "I promise you Hope, it won't be long now. Just give me a little time, and we'll be a family again, just like it used to be." he pulled her arms up around his neck and wept into her dress.

Jack looked up and realized he was still on his knees in front of Hope. How long had he been there allowing her to comfort him? He really had no idea. He rose from the floor and leaned in, kissing Hope tenderly before lifting her up and taking her back to the freezer. "I love you, and I will be back soon. I have some research to do." Another quick kiss on the lips, and he closed the door behind him. Each time he had to leave her he felt sad, but having her here with him and near was enough. Once Faith was home, it would be perfect again. He had to find her. To begin he needed his laptop.

Heading upstairs Jack felt renewed. He had a plan; now all he had to do was execute it. He sat down at the desk in the office and turned on his laptop. Once the system powered up, he pulled up the Internet and began a search on schools within thirty miles of Heyworth. The result didn't work, so he searched again on McLean County elementary schools. This time the query gave him a result of thirty public schools. Of course, there were also private schools, but after thinking through he felt very sure he could find Faith with this list. The link had a map attached. Jack clicked the link and was pleased to see it brought up a map of all the schools. He enlarged it and printed it out. Yes, this will definitely work, he thought. All he needed now was to spend time looking for his daughter.

He thought about his schedule at the doctor's office. He wondered if he could adjust his office hours slightly so that he could spend some mornings and some afternoons away from the office. Maybe he would open some evenings to accommodate his patient's schedules better, which would also free up his time to search for Faith. Yes, this might work. He would have to talk to Mary to see if she could adjust her schedule too. He would talk to her tomorrow.

Looking at the clock, he was surprised to see it was already nine o'clock. He needed to make something quick for a light dinner, so he could turn in early. Tomorrow was the start to finally putting the rest of his life back together.

Before logging off of the computer, Jack thought of another thing. He wondered what Detective Maxine Nichols was up to. He hadn't searched on her for a while and felt it was important to know what she was doing before taking the next steps. Typing her name in the search bar, he was surprised to find at the top of the page a new story showing her receiving her graduation certificate with the FBI.

Jack sat back in his chair staring at the page. *What are you doing, Special Agent? You now live in Virginia?* He continued searching further for her name and performed a people lookup. It showed her new address for free, but he needed to pay to find more information. Pulling out the credit card that contained his new name on it, he paid the $9.99 fee to receive a complete profile report on Maxine Nichols. A few minutes later he had a lot more information on her, including prior addresses, age 34 and single, no divorces. For another $9.99 he could get a complete report on family, employment, and social security. He sat there for a minute and decided that having every bit of information on her was a good idea. Paying the additional fee, he waited as the results generated. With the report complete, he printed it out. He read it thoroughly, thinking about the information. "Well, Special Agent, I guess I need to keep an eye on you," he said out loud.

Logging off, Jack put the report printouts into a file folder and placed it under his laptop, then headed into the kitchen to make a salad. He returned downstairs to share it with Hope. He sat her on the couch, and as he ate he explained what he had found out about the schools and his discoveries on Maxine Nichols. Finishing the salad he spent some time just talking to Hope. Having her near and just being able to talk to her was calming. He could sense that she was still sad, but bringing Faith home to her would make everything better. He stayed with Hope as long as he could. Before heading upstairs to bed, he placed her back in the freezer, vowing to return her daughter to her soon.

Chapter Six

Max woke in the morning as the sun rose and peeked in through the curtains. She looked over at Mark sleeping peacefully and would have sworn he had a grin on his face. She thought to herself how he was clearly proud of himself, and well, he should be given the way he made her feel. The memory of the night before made her smile too.

Crawling out of bed, Max grabbed his shirt, pulling it on over her shoulders. It hung several inches below her hips, covering her buttocks, draped over her frame and accentuating her muscular legs. She moved through the house to the kitchen where she started a pot of coffee. While waiting for it to brew, she went and grabbed her laptop computer and fired it up at the kitchen table. Within minutes the smell of coffee filled the room. She grabbed a cup from the cupboard, smiling at how organized Mark was; each cup facing forward, handles turned to the right. This was something that she liked. He was neat. Things in his life were in order. Pouring a cup of coffee, she returned to her laptop on the table and pulled up the Internet.

There was one piece of evidence that had been bothering Max and she had an idea. The CSI team in Fayetteville had found a single clue in the vehicle Jack abandoned at the diner, an empty box that had contained a padlock that was wedged between the passenger door and the seat. That box had been burning in Max's mind ever since.

With her laptop booted up, in the search engine, Max typed the words 'cold storage St. Louis'. The page loaded with over 800,000 hits. Revising her search she changed it to read 'cold self-storage St. Louis'. This time she got 150,000 hits, but she noticed in the first page there was a Yellow Pages listing that showed thirteen self-storage businesses offering temperature controlled storage. There was no way to know where Jack would have stored the body he had created, Fayetteville, St. Louis, anywhere in between. Shrugging she had to start somewhere. "This is manageable," she said out loud.

"What is manageable?" Mark asked as he wrapped his arms around her from behind, nuzzling her neck with his mouth.

"Must you sneak up on people?" She barked at him as she jumped.

Giggling, Mark continued to nuzzle on her neck. "Sorry."

Turning to him she kissed him. "Want some coffee?"

"Changing the subject?" he asked, peering over her shoulder at the screen.

"Not at all, just following my hunches, and I know you do want coffee," she teased back.

Sliding off the chair, Max went to the cupboard and pulled another cup down off the shelf and poured Mark some coffee as he looked at the Internet search. Returning to the table, she handed him the cup. "I'm thinking I can contact each of these places and send over a photo of Jack to see if any of them remember him. He definitely would have rented the unit himself. No way could he allow anyone to do it for him."

"I can help with this, but I want you to be cautious about getting your hopes up as this is just one city. There are a lot of cities in between Tulsa and St. Louis. I think we should check Fayetteville for sure too and then maybe any other major towns in between. They are likely the only ones that will have self-storage with refrigeration. He would also require a lot of privacy. Those that don't meet those requirements we can cross off."

"I agree. Then we just map it out, just like I did with Cortez. We were able to identify Tulsa as a likely place he would move to, and sure enough that is where he showed up." Max felt a twinge of that familiar excitement and hope. That feeling both encouraged and frightened her.

She was determined to find Jack. She both loathed him for killing people in the painful manner in which he did, and she felt saddened by his tragic life and losses. She still wondered what had caused Jack to begin killing as a boy. She knew something in his home life forced him to that point, and she was pretty certain that it was way more than the absence of his father. His mother's drinking was the likely contributor, but Max could barely dare herself to think of what all had happened to little Jack Tyler in those dark, drunken moments. She was certain none of it was good, and it would have been in those times that he had slowly come apart. It was only because his childhood friend, his sweetheart, the love of his life that he had been successful for so long. Hope had successfully led him into the light. Then the accident stole her and their child from him. Max often tried to imagine his pain. She felt compelled to find him, and she vowed internally that when she did, she would try to understand him. She needed to understand him. She needed answers. Max sat back down at the table in front of the computer next to Mark to resume her search.

They spent the next hour filtering for various cities between Tulsa and St. Louis for self-storage units that offered refrigeration. They were able to eliminate some of them because of the unit size. Some were too small, some too large. Some seemed too far off the route Jack would have had to follow to arrive in St. Louis as quickly as he had. This had narrowed their search down significantly.

Mark offered to supply the resources to get the photo out to each of the locations on their list. It was a simple process to mass email or fax, and with any luck they might get a hit. If the body was still in storage, then it was just time until Jack returned. If he had already returned to the storage unit, then they would at least know that he was back in the States.

With the list completed, they agreed to stop for the day. They headed off to the shower so they could go out and get some breakfast before going to the storage where Max had placed her furniture while in the academy. They needed to make the best of their time. In a couple of days, they would both return to work. Max would get her assignment soon, and Mark was already working an international human trafficking case. He had managed to get a couple of days off to help move her into her apartment and celebrate her graduation. Their time together would be stretched again as they settled into a normal routine. For today the goal was to get her moved into the new apartment.

The two worked together loading items into a small rental van Mark had reserved while Max was finishing the academy. They worked steadfastly until all the boxes and the few items of furniture Max shipped were placed inside the one bedroom apartment. To Max it felt strange and exciting all at the same time. She was basically starting completely over. Essentially she had an opportunity to reinvent herself. Things with Mark were going so well, and she truly enjoyed him in every sense. The passion they shared was fantastic, but it went far beyond that. For the first time in a very long time Max could see a future that included someone besides herself. Beginning to unpack the essentials, Max watched as Mark worked to hang a couple of pictures on the wall after gaining her approval of their exact placement. His strong body and slightly crooked smile warmed her as she set cups and glasses out on the counter. It was getting late, and she was feeling hungry. She asked Mark if he was up for ordering in Chinese food, and just as she was about to dial, her phone rang. It was her sister's number calling from Los Angeles.

"Hey, what's up, sis?" She asked into the cell phone.

"Hey, glad I caught you. I think we have an offer on your house. I wanted to run the details by you before telling the agent to accept. It's only two thousand under your listed price, and they are not asking for anything big on repairs or closing costs. Seems pretty straight-forward to me, especially in this economy."

"Really? Wow, that was fast. I was afraid I would have to carry that mortgage while paying rent for a year."

"I know. The couple seems solid. They have a little baby and need the space. They have already been pre-approved and have a good source of money for the down payment. The agent showed me their pre-approval documents. I think you should do it, Max. I can have the offer emailed over to you to look at but wanted to call you and let you know it was on the way."

"Great! Do that. I'll take a look at it and call you back as soon as I am done," Max said.

"Okay, check your email in a few. It should be there soon. Oh and, Max… I miss you."

"I will and me too." Max hung up the phone, a little saddened by the sudden reality of the house sale and obvious distance from her sister, even though in recent months they had not spent as much time together as they should have. Now it wasn't even possible, and that reality made it more difficult.

Mark watched as Max reached for her laptop and walked over to her, wrapping his arms around her waist and pulling her close. "You okay?"

"Yeah, I mean it's kind of weird, you know?"

"I'm sure. I wish there was an easier way for you to be an agent, us to be together, and both be near our families." He continued to look into her eyes, trying to comfort her with his gaze. "You're going to be a great agent, Maxine Nichols."

"Thanks," Max smiled back at him and gently kissed him. "Well, let's see how great this offer is, huh." Pulling away, Max booted up the computer.

An hour later, they sat at the built in bar, eating from little white boxes with chopsticks. After finishing dinner, they carefully reviewed the offer on her house then Max returned the call to her sister, giving her the go ahead to accept. The sister's chatted for a while about the Academy and graduation then ended the call with an air kiss through the phone while vowing to talk no less than once per week.

Feeling satisfied from the savory food, Max lead Mark to the bedroom to set up the bed. Agreeing on unpacking in the morning, they planned on staying at the apartment for the night, teasing that they might as well break in the new place. With the bed properly made, they settled into each other's arms on the fresh sheets, making love until they each fell into a deep sleep, exhausted from the day of moving.

Chapter Seven

Jack woke refreshed and ready to get started on his search for Faith. He showered and headed into the office, contemplating his discussion with Mary about changing the hours. He thought she would be okay with it but worked out the request in his head.

Arriving, he noticed that Mary's car was already in the parking space she often occupied. Perfect, he thought. He would be able to talk to her before any patients arrived. Entering the office he greeted Mary right away and proceeded back to his office to drop off his things, power up some of the equipment and turn on the lights. With everything ready for his patients, he walked up to the counter. "Hey, Mary, I've been thinking," he paused waiting for her to look up. With her eyes on him now, he applied the smile he knew no one could resist. "Most of our patients work during the day, and I think we need to reconsider our hours. I would like at least a couple of days a week to be opened later, but then close during the afternoon hours and open back up from maybe five thirty until seven. This will allow people who work or need to pick up their kids from school to have some additional options. What do you think?"

"Oh, well I had never really thought of it, but it does kind of make sense," she said still obviously processing the idea. "It could actually help me too. I have trouble sometimes getting my own little girl from school."

Mary was young, but Jack knew she had a child that she had very young. He respected her for working so hard to make sure she cared properly for her child. Smiling, he asked, "So, do you think it would work?"

"I think it's a good idea. I'm in."

Jack continued to smile. "Great, what do you think? How soon before we should do it?" He was trying to encourage her to choose to do it soon.

"Well, I guess that is really up to you. Looking at the schedule, we don't have that many afternoon appointments right now, so we could just work through those and not take any more. Are you thinking every day or just a few?"

Jack paused. "Let's try every day and see if it works for our patients. If it doesn't, we can always scale back." He was really thinking he wanted every day to look for Faith, but he couldn't allow Mary to know this. He also had some commitments with the hospital for emergencies and surgeries, and he needed that too. He knew that without the occasions to operate on people at the hospital, he would have to do something else to keep the darkness away. He was trying really hard to not allow the darkness to take him. He promised Hope that he would do everything he could to not have to hurt people. He planned on keeping that promise as best he could. After asking Mary to make new signs for the front door and to change the voice recording on the answering machine, he waited for his first client to arrive. The rest of the day was routine.

Just as they were about to close, he got a call from the hospital. There had been a tractor-trailer overturn on the highway just outside of town. The driver had internal injuries.

Responding to the hospital's summons, Jack raced over to assist. The driver was suffering from massive internal bleeding. Jack had the man rushed into surgery. In the room, Jack worked feverishly to stop the bleeding. His adrenaline raced as he sutured severed arteries. The blood continued to come, and the patient's breathing was labored forcing Jack to explore deeper, ultimately discovering a perforated liver. After several hours the man was finally stable, and Jack felt both relieved and light. The darkness was once again pushed back. Jack left the hospital a local hero and feeling very safe. With so much good news to share he would have a great evening with Hope. Everything was working out so well.

***

Over the course of the next couple of weeks, Jack adjusted his patient visiting hours, allowing him some freedom to search for Faith. He'd carefully stocked the house for a small child. He filled the cupboards with all of Faith's favorite foods and the medicine cabinet with everything she would medically need for any minor illnesses. He installed a deadbolt on the basement door, bought a padlock and chain for the outside doors, and bought a small futon bed and set it up in the basement. He felt he was ready now.

It was mid-afternoon, and his office had closed at one o'clock. He bid Mary a good afternoon and told her he would see her back at five thirty. He drove out of town and headed towards Le Roy. The past few days had been somewhat frustrating as he had visited several schools throughout McLean County to no avail. Each day he sat outside of the school watching as children made their way onto buses and down sidewalks towards their homes, but he had not seen anyone who even resembled Faith. He knew he had to be patient but frustration boiled in him as each night he returned home to Hope and explained how he had been unsuccessful in finding their daughter.

Pulling along the curb under a large elm tree on the street just south of the school, he waited. School would let out soon, and maybe today would be different. Jack considered his options and made a mental checklist of the items he had brought along with him. His medical bag behind the seat was properly packed with a syringe filled with 5cc of Chloroform, gloves, booties for his shoes, a cover for his hair, and rags. The back of the vehicle had a tarp stowed in the small compartment, and the seats had been laid completely flat, just in case today was a good day.

He thought about the Chloroform. The dosage had always been perfect for an adult. He would have to be cautious with a small child. Maybe Faith would recognize him and just come along with him. That certainly would make things easier, though he feared she had been away from him for a while, and the family she had now would have surely made her believe they were her family. Well, no worries, he had the syringe to help him until she really could understand.

A bell rang out from the school, causing him to sit up in his seat. He watched closely as the children exited. Then just as he was about to give up, he saw her. The long blonde locks bounced past her shoulders, her thin little legs poking out beneath the blue dress that he was certain, matched her eyes perfectly. She walked across the street near the buses, and he feared she had boarded one of them. But then, he saw her walking down the street. She walked along, her backpack bobbing along as she jumped the sidewalk careful to not step on the cracks. Jack smiled. He remembered that game. Only, he *always* stepped on the cracks. As he walked along he had always prayed his mom would break her back. Had that happened he would have been free from those things she did to him.

Returning his focus to the small girl, now fading off in the distance, he forced himself to stay put for just a bit longer. The buses were starting to pull away, and the parents that had come to pick up their kids had slowly come and gone. The area was nearly empty now, with only a few cars remaining in the parking lot. Jack assumed those were the school staff, teachers, principal, maybe even janitors or cooks.

Deciding he had waited long enough, the girl no longer in his sight, he started the car and slowly pulled away from the curb. His heart pounded in his chest at the very idea of having his beloved daughter with him once again. He could hear the increase in his heart rate pounding in his ears. His hands trembled, and he had to force himself to calm down. He made his way down the street following the path the little blonde had taken. His eyes scanned the street and fear started to well up in him that he had lost her, the very thought of losing her again crushing in on him, and just as he nearly gave up, despair filling him, he spotted her.

The little girl now carried a stick and occasionally stopped and poked at a crack or something on the ground. Her blonde hair shone brightly as the sun shimmered off the curls. She continued down the street, and the houses became sparse. Yards became bigger, forcing the houses farther apart from one another. An empty lot sat at the end of the block.

Jack rolled his window down and listened. He could hear the little girl singing a childhood song to herself as she walked. She was coming close to the empty lot. He looked both ways in his mirrors and thought; if he could pull up into the lot just after she enters, she really won't have anywhere to go. Then he could talk to her, and hopefully she would easily come with him. Reaching behind his seat, he pulled out the syringe and rag and stuffed them in his coat pocket. His heart raced. He had never tried to take a child. *What if she runs? What if she screams? Calm down.* He told himself.

Jack slowed down and rolled up as the girl walked into the lot. He pulled his car in front of her, got out, and walked over to her. "Hi. Can you help me? I'm kind of lost."

"Hi," The little girl replied a bit shyly.

"You aren't lost too, are you?" He waited. He smiled his huge, most welcoming smile, hoping it would put her at ease.

"No, I'm not lost. Where are you lost from?" She asked so innocently.

"Well, I was supposed to meet a teacher at the school, but I must have taken a wrong turn. I'm new here, and I'm trying to get my little boy Bobby enrolled in school today. Maybe tomorrow when he starts you can be his first friend?"

"Oh. The school is that way. Where is Bobby? Can I say hi to him?" Her eyes turned to the car, looking to see if her possible new friend was inside.

"Sure, he's waiting in the car. We drove a long way, and he fell asleep. I can wake him." Jack turned toward the car and could sense the girl following him. He reached his hand in his pocket and depressed the syringe into the rag. He then went to the back door and opened it, blocking her view with his body. "Bobby, hey buddy, wake up. I have a friend for you to meet. She is going to help us find your new school."

The little girl came up behind him. He stepped back so she could look inside the car. And as she leaned in, he wrapped his arm around her, forcing the rag over her mouth and pushing her inside. She struggled briefly but had no chance against his strong arms. Once she stopped moving, he pulled the rag away, being careful to not allow it to stay too long over her mouth. He quickly covered her with the tarp, took a look around, and then got back in the car. As he backed out of the lot, he scanned the area to be sure nothing had dropped on the ground. He drove away looking in all directions. The street was quiet. The first car he saw was coming towards him after he had turned the corner. His mind wondered if later that person would remember seeing his vehicle. He doubted anyone would remember merely passing a random car and quickly shrugged it off focused on getting back home.

Returning to the house, he was surprised when he pulled into the driveway and saw a vehicle. His heart raced. *What is someone doing here? I have to get rid of whoever that is right away.*

Scanning the yard and house he saw a stout man on the porch and recognized Dale, the real estate agent. His mind calmed a bit as he realized that Dale was likely only checking up on how things were. He mentally scanned all the rooms inside the home, quickly making sure there was nothing out that he didn't want Dale to see. Deciding everything was fine, he pulled up behind Dale's car, not wanting Dale to have any reason to walk near or around his vehicle. He glanced into the back seat and noticed one of the little girl's shoes poking from under the tarp. He quickly covered it, then exited the vehicle, and made his way up to Dale.

Trying to not show his irritation at the unexpected visit he smiled broadly, "Dale, to what do I owe the pleasure of this visit?"

"Hey, Doc! Was nearby, thought I better stop in and check on you, see if everything is as expected. You doing okay out here?" Dale's eyes swept the house and acreage.

"Doing, just fine, Dale thanks for coming by. Settling in pretty well, got almost everything unpacked and even got a few pictures on the walls. You want to come in?" Jack offered, hoping the man would decline.

"Oh, no, I don't want to intrude. But, I did want you to know that I hadn't abandoned you." Dale laughed a hearty laugh.

"Hey, never even entered my mind," Jack laughed back. "I truly do appreciate you stopping by. Thought I was going to have to call you the other day. In the next couple of weeks I'll have to figure out how to light the pilot on the furnace. Nights are getting a little chilly, figured I better be getting ready for it. I had the propane delivered the other day. So, other than that pilot, I think I am all set."

"Yeah, sometimes these older homes are a little tricky. Any time you need anything, give me a holler. I can help you out, or I can for sure tell you who around these parts can, and who you can trust. How's the office setup going for you?"

"It's going great, starting to pick up a little. Seems like people are starting to hear I'm in town. Word of mouth is the best advertisement. I'm sure you know how that works."

"Sure do. People like us rely on every referral we can get. I'm glad it is all working out, Doc, and I'll certainly keep telling people you are in town." Dale started heading towards his car.

Jack positioned himself between the two vehicles, ensuring Dale didn't get any closer to his SUV than necessary. "Well I sure do appreciate the free marketing, and I'll certainly return the favor." Jack continued to smile, despite the nervousness he felt inside.

"Fair deal, Doc. Fair deal. Well, I best get going. Let me know if you need anything. I'll come back out in a few days and light that pilot." Dale got inside his vehicle and waved as Jack stood and watched him pull away.

Not wanting to look suspicious, Jack went inside and watched from the living room windows until he was sure Dale was gone. Once certain, Jack headed to the basement where he opened the door so he could easily bring the girl inside, he took one more look outside before heading back to his vehicle. Arriving at the car, he could hear quiet murmuring from the back. The little girl was waking up. He needed to hurry.

Pulling the tarp away, he lifted the small bundle of blonde curls and carried her into the house from the same way he had come. He kicked the basement door closed behind him and carried the little girl to the couch. Gently laying her down, he stood back and looked carefully at her. He had little time to study her when they were in the abandoned lot near the school, now he could look her over to see if she was really his little Faith.

She was so beautiful lying there, still groggy, occasionally rolling her head from side to side, but she had not yet opened her eyes. He knew her head would ache for a while after she woke up. He gazed at her a moment longer, then decided while she was still out, he needed to prepare a few things.

First he locked the basement door. Next, he went outside and put the chain and padlock that he had bought a few days earlier on the exterior doors from the outside. Returning inside he got some water and two children's chewable Tylenol. He grabbed a snack sized bag of Oreo cookies and a glass of milk then returned to the basement.

The little girl was sitting on the couch, her eyes wide when she saw him. "Hi. Remember me?" He asked.

"Where is Bobby?" The little girl asked, still obviously believing that the man had a little boy.

Jack was surprised by the question. "Oh. He is not here right now," he lied.

"Where am I?"

"You are home now, Faith."

"My name is Cindy, and I want my mommy," The girl demanded, now appearing afraid.

"I know you do. She's here, and she wants to see you too."

The girl's eyes grew wide. "She's here?"

296

"That's right, honey. Your mommy is here, and she is so excited to see you too. How about you eat these cookies and drink some milk. I think your head hurts, right?"

She nodded while rubbing her forehead with her left hand.

"I'm sorry about that, but it'll feel better soon. And then you can see your mommy. Take these pills and eat these cookies, and it will help real soon."

The little girl took the pills and cookies. She looked at him, and he could see the fear in her eyes. The look saddened him, but he was sure as soon as she was back with Hope all would be good.

With the cookies and milk finished, the little girl was becoming more active and more demanding. "Where is my mommy? When can I see her?"

"Are you feeling better, Faith?"

She nodded her head bobbing up and down ignoring the name he called her.

Obviously her headache was starting to clear. "Okay, let me bring her to you," Jack offered.

He went to the freezer and opened the door. The little girl watched him carefully. He lifted Hope and brought her over sitting her next to the girl on the couch, he spoke softly, "Faith, this is your mommy. I know you may not remember her yet, but she has missed you terribly."

The little girl's eyes grew wide and her mouth flew open. Terror covered her whole face as she saw the grotesque body next to her, and a blood curdling scream escaped her mouth.

Chapter Eight

After Max accepted the offer on her house there had been a lot of paperwork to sign and review, but now things were settling down. It was just a matter of waiting for the sale to close and the money to free up. Max would clear enough money to put down on a new house, if that is what she decided to do. All of that would be contingent on how things continued with Mark. So far things were perfect. Everything had fallen into place, and a routine had begun to form. Some nights they spent at his house, and other nights they tucked into her apartment. They each had plenty of time on their own too, as their schedules were not always in sync.

Max received an assignment to work a drug trafficking case. A group of traffickers were responsible for the primary distribution of crystal meth between Chicago and Mexico. There might be a point where Max would need to travel for a day or two to Chicago, but so far she had been able to work the case, consisting primarily of research, from the Quantico offices. Mark was busy on his own case, but they took advantage of every moment when they could be together.

Mark requested resources that could work the list of self-storage locations. So far, thirty-five locations had been disqualified. These locations had verified never having rented a unit to anyone matching the photo of Jack Tyler that had been submitted to the storage facilities for confirmation. There were still another nine that had not yet responded. Max remained hopeful that they would learn something even if it was that the unit had been rented to Tyler, but was now vacant. At least Max would know if he was back in the States.

During her free time, she set up email notifications just like she had done when she was tracking Tyler in California. She established two different search criteria. The first was for young females between the ages of five and eight, murdered with similar injuries to those of the murders in Los Angeles. It was this exact search that had ultimately led to her being notified about the bodies found in Oklahoma. And it was from that notification that she and her partner Lorraine Cortez had worked with Mark in tracking Jack Tyler across Oklahoma through Arkansas into Missouri until they had lost him as he departed across international waters. It was also through that process they had proven he was the un-sub for all twelve murders in California and Oklahoma.

Jack's signature incision was very specific. He possessed a high level skill having been a well know surgeon. The cut goes from the neck to the pelvis, straight through the core of the navel. There would be circular flaps on either side of the incision, and the body would have been opened up with rib spreaders to allow room for him to place his hands inside the body, while he felt the organs as death took the victim. The precision for both the kill and the cleanup were very specific. Max was hoping she could get lucky again. *Will you kill little girls, Jack? Will you kidnap one and hold her hostage?*

Not sure of whether Jack would actually kill a child, Max set up the second search which would notify her of recent reports of missing children or abductions of blonde haired, blue-eyed girls, five to eight years old. The hard part of each of these searches was that Max had no idea where she was looking. She made the search to cover the entire USA. The toughest part of it was the waiting game.

Max reached for the phone and dialed her LAPD partner and friend. When the line was answered, she said, "Cortez, hey what's up?"

"Max. Girl, how the hell are you?" Cortez replied and Max could tell she had a big grin on her face at the sound of her friend's voice.

"I was working some angles on Tyler, and well, of course that made me think of you. Damn, it's good to hear your voice. How is LA?"

"You know. Cloudy in the morning, warm in the afternoon. Cool at night unless the Santa Ana's are blowin'."

Max laughed, "Not exactly what I was lookin' for, but okay I get it."

"You said you are working some angle on Tyler. What's up? Do you have a lead?"

"Not really. Call it a hunch."

"Okay, lay it on me."

Max spent the next few minutes telling Cortez of her theory on the storing of Hope's body and the idea that Jack may try to find Faith, seeking out little girls that match her description.

"Wow. Max, do you really think he will change his M.O. and start killing kids?"

"I don't know, Lorraine." She replied, using her former partner's first name.

"Well, keep me posted on your searches. We still need to nail this guy." Switching gears she asked, "How is Mark? And, how was training? I wish I could have made your graduation."

"Yeah, that would have been nice. Mark is great." Max blushed considering the two way meanings that could have held. "I mean, you know he is fine."

Cortez laughed a hearty laugh. "Yeah, I know what you mean alright. I'm glad it's working out with him. I thought the two of you were never going to admit the way you felt for each other. So, is Quantico cool?"

"It's pretty impressive. Training was a bitch, but I feel great. I learned a lot. It was actually through a case study that I came up with the ideas on what Jack may be up to. What about you? Any men in your life? And, how is the detective gig going for you?"

"No love life for me yet. Too focused on work to get involved. Work is good. The Chief seems to think I was your instant replacement and is constantly bustin' my ass."

"That is a good sign. It means he likes you, and more importantly, it means he trusts you. The more he hangs up on you the more you are part of the team." Max thought back to the number of times Chief Harding had hung up on her before she had finished speaking.

"Okay, if you say so. But, damn, it's frustrating."

Max was laughing again. "Well, we've got to find you some big strappin' Mexican to call your own. As for the Chief, I know what you mean."

"A Mexican man. Really? You don't know anything about me, Max. I need me a big strappin' black man."

Max thought for a second. "Well, if I'd known that I would have been workin' on hookin' you up with Detective Oklahoma. He was hot. What was his name again? Adair? That Mohawk was hot."

"Don't I know it! You were too focused on Tyler and Wells to see that one slipping' by," Cortez teased. "Don't worry. If the right man comes along, black, Mexican, or purple, I'll let you know."

"You damn well better!" Max teased her friend back. "Well, I probably better let you get back to whatever you were doing. Mark will be coming over soon, and I need to make something for dinner. Stay in touch, and if I get any leads on Tyler I'll let you know."

"Alright. Talk to you soon."

Max hung up and headed to the kitchen to begin making dinner.

Chapter Nine

Jack could not believe Faith's screaming and disrespect for her mother. He became very angry. "STOP IT! Stop your screaming now! You will not act like that towards your mother."

The little girl continued to scream as she pushed her body as far away from the horror of the dead body and the scary man as the couch would allow.

Jack had never hurt Faith, but in his anger he slapped the child. The action caused the screaming to stop, but tears flowed down her cheeks as she kept her eyes closed tightly, refusing to look at her mother.

"Faith, I'm sorry I slapped you, but you cannot disrespect your mother like this. She has waited over a year for you to come home, and this is what you do. What have those people done to you?"

The little girl opened her eyes. "My name is Cindy! I want my mommy! I want to go home!" Her eyes darted around the room looking at anything except the body that sat propped next to her on the couch.

Jack had enough of this behavior. He grabbed her by the hand and dragged her over to the futon on the other side of the room. "I have to go back to work. Maybe a little time to think will help you straighten out your attitude. I won't have you acting like this toward your mother. Can't you see how sad you made her? Oh, and don't even think about trying to get out. The doors are locked with chains on the outside, and there aren't any windows. When I come home, we will try again reuniting you with your mother. I would think you would be happy to finally be with her again. You think about that while I'm gone." Jack left the girl on the futon and went back to tend to Hope.

"Darling, I'm sorry. I know our little girl would never act like that. These people must have brainwashed her. Don't be sad, Hope. We will work this out. I promise you. I'll be home soon, only a couple hours." Jack kissed her tenderly as the little girl watched on in horror. Then he lifted Hope carefully and carried her back to the freezer.

Closing the door he turned back to the little girl. "Don't bother your mother while I'm gone. She doesn't need any more stress. Do you understand me?"

The little girl nodded her head as she pushed herself as far back into the corner of the futon as she could.

Jack looked at her, disappointment filling his eyes. "We'll do better when I get back home. I'll make your favorite food for dinner. Maybe that will help you to remember."

Jack climbed the basement stairs, leaving the lights on. At the top of the stairs he closed the door behind him and locked the deadbolt, securing the little girl inside.

***

Jack drove to the office, his frustration finally dissipating. He could not believe Faith and her outburst at seeing Hope. *What had those people taught her?* Oh well, he would take care of his patients, then return. He would make her favorite, macaroni and cheese, for dinner and see if that helped her settle back down. He thought about the basement while he drove, considering if there was any way Faith could get out. There were no exterior windows, and with the chain on the doors outside and the deadbolt on the inside door, he was certain there was no way for her to escape. Feeling confident, he tried to relax before arriving at the office.

He walked inside and found Mary already behind the desk. "Good evening, Doc. How was your afternoon?" Mary asked.

"Hi, Mary. It was eventful. I got some stuff taken care of," he replied trying to not show his frustration. Trying to prevent her from asking any more questions, he continued on, "What's on the lineup for us the next couple of hours?"

"Well, remember little Jessie from the other day? She's still not quite feeling up to par, so her mother is bringing her back in."

Jack tried not to react. He remembered little Jessie and her funny lopsided smile and pretty blonde hair. It was Jessie that had made him realize what kept Hope from being completely happy. Yes, he remembered Jessie. "Oh, okay, well I may need to give her something else. Is anyone else coming in?"

"Yes, one patient with an allergy issue and another person with either allergies or a cold, I'm not sure which. We should be booked perfectly, and we didn't have to turn anyone away. I think these new hours really make sense. The patients really like it."

"That's great news. I'm glad it's working out so well for all of us." He thanked her then headed back to his office to prepare for his first patient. A few minutes later, Mary let him know that Mrs. Wilson was in room # 1. She was the first person with allergies. A few minutes later, she was on her way with a recommendation and prescription.

Next, Mary informed him that Jessie and her mom Tina were in room # 2. He was surprised to notice that his heart raced a little bit at seeing the little girl again.

He opened the door and peeked inside. "Is that little Jessie back to see me?"

As he entered the room, Jessie giggled.

"So, what is this I hear? You're still not feeling good?"

She shook her head back and forth.

"Can you tell me what's happening? Does your stomach hurt?"

She shook her head again.

"Does your head hurt?"

She shook her head.

"Does your throat still hurt?"

She nodded.

He showed her the thermometer. "Can I run this thermometer across your forehead again?"

"Yes." She finally spoke shyly, her throat obviously sore.

Jack swiped her forehead and read 99.6, a mild fever.

"Can I look inside your mouth? I'll let you stick your tongue out at me again."

She giggled a little, the edges of her mouth turning up at the corners. Then she stuck her tongue out at Jack and laughed out loud.

Jack took the tongue depressor and played the game he had played during her last visit. He saw the red spots in the back of her throat again and was disappointed that the oral antibiotics were not working. He was going to have to give her a shot to get her moving forward a little faster. He hated the idea of that because she had started to trust him, but he really didn't have any choice.

"Okay, Jessie, you know I'll be honest with you, right?"

She nodded. "Yes, Doctor Jack."

"Well, remember I told you that you had some bad spots in your throat, and I had hoped that the grape syrup I gave you would help to make it feel better? But it just isn't strong enough. You need something that has the strength of Wonder Woman. Do you know who Wonder Woman is?"

"Yes, she is a super hero, but a girl one."

"That's right, Jessie, and she is really strong. You need a medicine that is strong like that, and the only bad part is that kind of medicine only comes in a shot. Now I know that sounds scary, but have you ever gotten a flu shot before?" He glanced at Jessie's mom for confirmation. She nodded.

"Yes, but I don't like shots."

"I know. No one likes shots, not even me. But sometimes it's the fastest way to get better, so we can play with our friends again. Do you understand?"

"I guess so."

"Okay, if I promise to not let the shot hurt and I promise to let you pick out your own Band-Aid, will you try to be real brave, so we can make you all better soon?"

Jessie looked at her mom. "I guess so," she said, sounding as if she was not sure.

"I'll be right back, and we'll get you out of here real fast." Jack winked at her and left the exam room.

He returned a moment later with a syringe. "I got the smallest needle, not more than getting a splinter in your finger. See?" he said, showing her how small it was. "Now the easiest way to do this is to face your mommy, and it will be over before you even know it. Ready?"

Jessie nodded then turned her head as Jack raised her sleeve over her shoulder and wiped the area with an alcohol swab. Really quickly he inserted the needle into the muscle in her upper arm and depressed the plunger slowly enough to not hurt. Just as quickly, he removed the needle. "Done."

Jessie looked back at her arm and smiled. "That didn't even hurt."

"Well, that, my dear, is because you are so brave."

He let Jessie pick out her Band-Aid. She chose Hello Kitty. Realizing the scary part was over a smile flashed across her face. Jack told her to go see Mary to pick out her sucker, and then he turned to her mom. "She should get better within a couple of days now. If she does not, bring her back again. We may need to take a culture of her throat, but I think this will knock it down." Following the child's mother, he walked back out to the front lobby. As he handed Mary the file he said, "No visit charge today, Mary."

"Thanks, Doctor," Jessie's mother said. An obvious appreciation shadowed her face that he assumed was caused by financial strain.

Jack leaned down to eye level of the little girl. "Jessie, you get better fast now. Promise?"

Jessie looked back at him and giggled, then made a crossing motion with the finger on her right hand over her heart.

"See you soon."

"You too, Doctor Jack." A quick smile flashed back at him and then the bundle of blonde curls was gone.

Jack watched as the door closed then turned back to Mary. "Who's next?" he asked with a smile.

Mary let him know the last patient was due in ten minutes, so he went back to his office to wait, asking Mary to let him know when the patient arrived.

Jack finished with the patients and headed home. Entering the house he proceeded through the living room and straight into the kitchen. He went to the pantry and pulled out a box of Kraft macaroni and cheese. This was Faith's favorite, and he hoped that the gooey, cheese covered noodles put her into a better mood. He could not stand the idea of Faith rejecting Hope. He knew deep inside that Hope looked a little different, but she was still his beautiful wife and her loving mother. He stirred the powder and milk into the noodles and let it cook while he made some Kool-Aid. Cherry. Also, Faith's favorite. He dished out three plates and poured a glass of wine for him and Hope. Placing everything onto a tray, he went to the basement door and carefully balanced the tray as he unlocked the door. He peeked inside before swinging the door open, making sure that Faith did not try to push her way out. He carried the tray down the stairs and set it down on the table. He looked around and saw that Faith was asleep on the futon. Before waking her he went back upstairs, pulled the door closed and locked it.

Then he descended back down the stairs, moving quietly across the room. Opening the door to the freezer, he lifted Hope and sat her at the table, then placed one plate and glass of wine in front of her. Then he went to the futon and gently woke Faith. "Honey, wake up. Daddy is home, and I've made your favorite dinner for you and Mommy."

The little girl woke up, her sleepy eyes obviously confused by her surroundings. Jack took her hand and pulled her up. It was then that she saw the body sitting at the table, and her eyes grew big again.

"Come on, honey. Mommy is waiting. I made your favorite, macaroni and cheese," Jack coaxed her gently.

The little girl looked from him to the table. "I don't like macaroni and cheese."

Jack turned and looked back at her. "What?"

"It makes me sick. I hate it. You are not my daddy, and that thing over there is *not* my mommy."

"What did you say?" Jack could barely control his anger. This little girl was not his Faith. He knew in that moment that this girl was wrong, all wrong. As he looked at her, he realized. Her hair, though blonde, was not quite the right shade. He stared at her, he could see now that her eyes were not the color of Faith's. They were darker and did not have those little flecks that matched her mother's. She had somehow tricked him. He took her by the hand and dragged her into the room with the shower and closed the door. *Think, Jack. Think!*

He returned to Hope. "Hope, I've made a terrible mistake. I thought this little girl was our Faith, but now I can see that I have been tricked. Our Faith would never act this way. I'm sorry that I brought you the wrong little girl, but I now realize it may take more time to find Faith. I can't take this girl back to her other home, Hope. Not if I am to keep you safe. Not if we are to stay together forever. I know I promised not to hurt anyone, but Hope, I don't see any other way than to make this girl go away. She has been so awful to you. She doesn't deserve kindness. Hope, please tell me you forgive me for finding the wrong girl. Please tell me you understand that finding Faith will be harder than we originally thought, and it may take time to find *our* little girl. I'll find her if you give me time." Jack leaned forward, staring into the grey, frosted and decaying eyes of the face in front of him.

He waited, and then suddenly he could tell. Hope knew he was right. This was not their daughter, and it needed to be dealt with. Jack felt a burning in his chest. He was riddled with disappointment, and yet there was an excitement that welled inside him too. He knew what he must do now. Kissing Hope, he told her how much he loved her and then carried her back to the freezer. Then he headed into the shower room which had now been fully converted into a surgical operating room. Now he knew why he needed the stainless steel table. Fate had known he would need it after all.

Entering the room, Jack found the small girl backed deep into the far corner. He looked at her with disdain. "You know you shouldn't have tricked me. You're not my daughter. I was wrong, and I'm sorry. I won't keep you here much longer."

Jack locked the door behind him then proceeded to the wall on the other side of the room. Next to the shelves was a small apartment sized refrigerator, and inside it was an assortment of vials containing different medications. He looked at the vials and selected one with a label that said Atricurium. *Perfect,* he thought as he considered the use. This specific medication was a general anesthesia that provided muscular relaxation during surgery. He usually did not like to introduce any medications. He never really paid too much attention to the pain he inflicted on a person, but he would keep his promise to Hope. He would not hurt any children. He took a syringe off of the shelf, inserted it into the vial, and drew out 25mg. He pulled on gloves, booties, and a full set of scrubs that he retrieved from the shelf.

Jack approached the little girl, the little girl that was not his Faith. Taking her by the arm, he pulled her over to the stainless steel table. He told her to be quiet and he promised to not hurt her. She fought him some, but he was so much stronger than her. Soon he had her strapped to the table, her arms secured with zip ties. He did the same with her feet. Once she was strapped down, he injected the anesthesia into the vein in her arm.

She cried until the injection took effect. But then, she calmed down and now rested peacefully. Jack went into motion. He felt the excitement that always presented when the darkness consumed him and he allowed desire to take over.

First, he removed the zip ties and the little girl's clothing. With her sedated he would not need to keep her tied down. He didn't bother with re-applying them after the clothing was removed. He reached for his rolling surgical cart and pulled it close to the table. His stainless surgical tools on the tray shined under the light, all laid out in a row. He looked at them and the small body lying before him, considering which tool would be best for the job. He chose a #5 scalpel and made an incision down the middle of the small chest, through the abdomen and to the pelvis. He made two circular incisions, allowing the skin and tissue around the abdomen to flap back. Next, he took the bone saw and cut through the chest plate and ribs. As the blood pooled around the little girl's body on the table, he laid down the bone saw and stuck his gloved hands inside her body, feeling the heart and lungs. Jack held her internal organs as the last pulses ran through them. He felt relief and euphoria.

Standing back, he stared down at the small body in front of him. His eyes drifted to her face and landed on her mouth, that viscous mouth, that mouth full of hateful words. Suddenly he knew what he needed to do. He picked up the scalpel and made a clean incision around the lips, swiftly removing the origin of the evil comments made against his precious Hope.

Tossing the mouth onto the tray, he forced himself to pull away. He stood back, and he looked at his watch. It was after ten o'clock. *Good*, he thought. Now he had to consider how to dispose of the body. Unlike in Oklahoma, he had not pre-planned any of this. He also was not sure about simply burying her. She was a little girl. For the first time ever, Jack felt a bit of remorse. Not for his actions, certainly not guilt. What was this emotion? Empathy, he decided, empathy, for the parents. He knew what it was like to lose a child. He knew the hopelessness that came with the loss.

It was then that he realized he needed to do something different. It was riskier, but it was the right thing to do. He would return this child to her family. First, he needed to thoroughly clean her. He picked up the suture needle and began stitching the wounds shut. After he carefully closed the incision down her torso, he sewed shut the tissue that remained where her mouth had once been. His lips curled into a smile. *She won't disrespect Hope again*. Next, he began the process of bleaching the body.

Then, he carefully wrapped it in a surgical sheet, and laid it on the concrete floor outside the door in the main room near the couch. Returning to the room, he bleached the walls and floor, then stripped off his clothes and bleached his whole body.

Still dripping wet, he lifted a small jar from the shelf and filled it with a combination of saline and formaldehyde, then dropped the child's severed mouth inside and sealed the lid shut. He took the jar over to the freezer and placed it on the shelf. Returning to the surgical room, he disposed of his scrubs in the laundry basket and rinsed himself once again under the shower at the end of the room. Satisfied that he was clean, he dried off and headed upstairs to get dressed. As he selected his clothing he was careful to choose items that were least likely to transfer fibers.

Returning to the basement, he pulled on gloves and redressed the body in the clothes she had come in. He carefully rewrapped it in a fresh surgical sheet. Then he lifted the body from the bare floor and carried it out to the SUV. He covered it with the tarp that had covered Hope just weeks ago, then climbed in and headed back towards Le Roy.

Jack always drove the speed limit, but on nights like tonight, nights when there was a body in his car, he had a heightened awareness to obey all the rules. He pulled into Le Roy just after midnight. The town was quiet as he drove to the area where he had followed the little girl. He returned to the street where he had first spoken to her. Killing his lights about a block before pulling into the empty lot he cautiously looked around. None of the houses nearby had any lights on inside. It appeared everyone was tucked away in their beds. He pulled on gloves and a hair cover wanting to be sure he left nothing behind. He got out of the vehicle, partially leaving his door open ensuring he didn't make any unnecessary noise. Making his way to the back of the vehicle, he quietly opened the door, and pulled back the tarp. Then he lifted the body out. He carried it over to the edge of the lot where there was a row of flowers. He placed the body face up next to the flowers making sure the surgical sheet wrapped around her like a cocoon, fully covering her. He quickly returned to the vehicle, softly closed the back door, climbed in and pulled away.

Once he was about a block away, he flipped on his headlights. As he drove he pulled off his gloves and hair cover and shoved them in the bag behind the seat. He didn't see another vehicle until he was nearly out of town. As he drove, he found himself hoping the child was found soon. The feeling was new for him.

In the past, he had always buried his bodies in a remote area, intentionally slowing the discovery. This was different though. No family should wait to mourn the loss of their child. He could control that, and he would not make a parent suffer any more than he had to. His own heart tugged as he remembered the day he had lost Faith. He breathed a sigh of relief as he returned home, feeling safe as he pulled into the circular driveway. Immediately, he went directly to the basement. Looking around, everything seemed in order. He began cleaning up the dinner now long cold and dried up.

Tomorrow he would continue his search for their *real* daughter. Realizing he had been too excited about the plan, he decided that he would be more careful next time, ensuring he studied the child a little more carefully. He knew what to do now. It was just a matter of time before he would have his family all together again.

Jack was exhausted from the stress of the day. He quickly said good night to Hope then made his way upstairs, dropping into bed and falling into a fitful sleep. Images of Hope's face shrouded in disappointment and of Faith calling out for Daddy plagued his dreams.

***

Jack woke the next morning feeling somber. Despite his mood, he was certain that he knew what the right course of action was now. He realized he had been over zealous and finding their perfect little girl was not going to be as simple as pulling up to a school and there she would be. It would take more work than that, and it would take time. He was okay with that. After all, perfection takes time. He knew this. He had searched hard and restored Hope. Faith would take the same amount of effort and focus. He was more than willing to dedicate as much time as necessary to finding his daughter and bringing her back to Hope, so they could all be together again.

He had to go to the office for a few hours then he could resume his search. He already knew where he was headed. There was another small town outside of McLean County called Eureka. The answer was in the meaning within the name; he should have known it all along. Faith would be in Eureka. He knew it. He had been so focused on staying within the county that he had nearly missed the clue. It was in the name. So obvious that he nearly missed it.

***

The morning in the office had been mostly uneventful. It seemed a few folks in the town had flu like symptoms, and he spent most of his time taking temps and handing out prescriptions. The afternoon had no patients booked, so he and Mary agreed to close for the rest of the day. This left him lots of time to head over to Eureka and see what the small town was all about.

He took Highway 74, enjoying the forty-five minute ride. Looking at the clock, he smiled as he realized he would get there just as school was letting out. He would have just enough time to check it out a little bit and find a perfect place to park. He drove into town making his way up Main Street and made a right onto East Crugar Avenue.

The elementary sat along the south side of the street. He followed the street past the school, looking through the windows of the classrooms that faced outward, and wondered if he would find Faith within. He thought so. He followed the street around and made a left at Darst, another left onto Eureka Avenue, and then a left onto Major Street. From here he parked underneath one of the big trees where he could see while he waited. It was almost time; the buses were already out front and were blocking his view. He changed his mind and pulled into a driveway and turned around, retracing his steps back down Darst and onto Crugar. He pulled over on the north side of the street. From here he could see everything, including the kids coming out of the school. He would even be able to see the kids getting onto the buses.

He didn't have to wait long. The bell rang, and the doors swung open as kids poured out. He watched for a few minutes, and then he saw her. His heart leaped. She was small and blonde. Her shoes had those blinking lights in them just like he and Hope bought for her. Her hair was a little longer. He stopped, doubting it for a minute, but then he realized, of course it had been over a year. He watched as she gingerly climbed up the steps onto bus #11. She stopped inside to talk to the driver. Jack could barely see the man driving, but he saw that whatever she had said to him had made him smile.

Jack continued to wait as the school emptied out, and the buses filled up. Then one by one they started their engines and pulled away. Jack would have to follow the bus and hoped that he would be able to do so without raising suspicion. He would just have to see. As the bus pulled away, he pulled out too. They were going the opposite directions, so he cut up Maple and waited at the corner of Eureka and Maple to see where the bus went. He never saw it come up the street, so he assumed it went the other way. He turned and made his way back to Darst. There he caught a glimpse of a bus as it turned right. He sped up to try to catch up to it and saw it again, this time making a left onto Main Street. He made his way along the road until he was able to come close enough to see the bus number on the back door. It read #11.

Jack smiled, the tension he hadn't even realized had been building in his neck and back slowly relaxed. He slowed, making sure he was one car back. The bus continued along past the cemetery and then made a left onto 4H Park Road. The car Jack was following turned as well, and so did he. About a mile down the road, the bus made its first stop, letting three young children out. It then continued on for another half mile or so and stopped at another farmhouse; two more children got out. Pulling out again, the bus made a third stop and then turned onto County Road 1600. The car Jack had been following turned left when the bus turned right. The next stop was at the end of a very long driveway. The bus doors opened, and Jack could see the little girl with the blonde hair making her way through the bus. And then she exited, waving at the driver. She checked for mail in the mailbox and then started down the long drive. Jack watched as the bus pulled away. Then he followed the little girl into the driveway as he reached behind his seat and pulled out a syringe and a rag.

Easing up beside the little girl, Jack rolled down his window. "Hi, there, can I give you a ride up to your house? I'm heading that way."

The little girl looked at him warily. "I'm not supposed to talk to strangers."

"I know, and that is very true. But I'm not really a stranger. I have a package I'm taking up to your house. It might even be for you."

"Oh? What is it?"

"I don't know. It's just a box to me, but it has this address on it. Do you want to hop in? We can take it up there together. I'm going straight to see your mommy or daddy."

Jack could tell the idea of a package was just too much for the little girl to resist. "Okay, but we have to tell my mommy."

"You bet, right away. I promise." Jack reached across the seat and opened the door for the little girl as she ran in front of the car to get in on the passenger side. Looking around Jack checked the mirrors. They were in the middle of fields. The corn had already been plowed under, and he could see there wasn't a soul in sight.

The little girl got in and immediately turned away to fasten the seat belt. As she did so, Jack wrapped his arm around her neck and slammed the rag soaked with Chloroform over her mouth. She squirmed against his chest for a few moments, but the chemical won the battle. Jack quickly unbuckled her and then got out and lifted her into the back of the vehicle. The Chloroform should last all the way back to Heyworth, but he didn't want to take any chances. He wrapped her hands, feet, and mouth with duct tape, then covered her with the tarp. He knew what to do this time. He would not have a disrespectful child talking to him or Hope. He would be sure this time. With her concealed he climbed back in the vehicle and backed out of the driveway. He made his way out onto the road. The GPS system led him through the country all the way to Carlock, where he could once again get back on the highway. Jack took his time, driving carefully. A song came on the radio and he hummed along with the tune enjoying the natural beauty of the countryside as he made his way home.

Chapter Ten

Jack went to the basement door and unlocked the padlock then pulled the door open. He returned to the SUV, looking all around making sure he was alone. He opened the back and carefully uncovered the girl, then lifted her out. She was just beginning to wake up but was groggy enough to not resist him as he carried her inside. He took her through the door and went directly to the operating room. He laid her on the stainless steel table then quickly returned to the door and locked it, making a mental note to reapply the padlock on the outside later.

He went back into his surgical room and, almost tenderly, removed the tape from the girl's hands and feet, applying zip ties to each and attaching her to the table, so she could not move. He'd done this many times before, but his victims had been adults. The last girl, well, she had not been respectful to Hope, and he could not allow that to happen. Not ever!

In fact, he needed to talk to Hope. She needed to support the next steps. There was only one way they were really going to find their one and only Faith.

He stared down at the small child and smiled. She was now awake and trying to talk to him, but the tape on her mouth prevented anything intelligible from coming out. Her eyes were wide with fear and confusion. She struggled unsuccessfully to move against the ties that bound her. Jack looked her over from top to bottom. Her hair and nose were just right. Her eyes were the perfect color of blue, light with little flecks in them, just like Hope's and just like Faith's. Her mouth was all wrong, the shape of the lips were too thin and turned down at the corners just slightly. Jack went out of the room for a moment and retrieved a tape measure. She was a little too tall, her legs too long and a little too thick.

The little girl's eyes followed Jack as he inspected her body. He knew she was scared. He knew what it was like to be a child and be scared of a man doing things to you. He would never hurt her like that. Never!

"I know you're scared right now, and I'm sorry for that. I know that feeling, and I promise you I won't let you stay scared. It won't be too long. Just try to relax now." Jack watched as the little girl listened to him. He couldn't be sure, but he thought she relaxed just a little.

He left the girl on the table and went back into the main room of the basement. Then he walked over to the freezer and opened the door, flipped on the interior light, entered, and closed the door behind him. Hope was inside seated on a chair in the middle of the small freezer where he had left her. Jack knelt down in front of her.

The body in the chair sat slightly lopsided, the head dipped to the left, and the mouth was slightly agape. There were areas that were starting to show discoloration, but overall the chemical concoction that Jack had used to preserve the body, while allowing it to remain pliable, was holding up well. To him it was his wife, his beautiful wife, and having her back in his life drove him. He could not, would not survive without her.

"Hope, honey, I've started to bring Faith home, but I was wrong about it. I have to find her, just like I had to find you. I know I told you I wouldn't hurt a child, and I meant it, Hope. I won't hurt her. I will never let a child suffer. I will make her sleep, Hope. And slowly I will bring Faith back to you, our beautiful daughter. She will be perfect in every way. I now know exactly what to do. I need to know that you understand that this is the only way. I can only do this with your support. Like always, Hope, we do this together. You've helped me since we were children, so I know that with your blessing, we can bring our baby girl home to us. I no longer want you to be sad, and having Faith home will return the joy to your eyes."

Jack sat back and looked up at the odd, garish face staring back at him. A few moments passed, and then he knew. Hope was smiling at him. He could see the joy in her face at the idea of having Faith back. As always her eyes told him that she was supporting him and helping him know the best way to lead his life, their life.

He remembered the promise she had made to him years ago. It was in the letter she had given him when they were just twelve. The words from that letter were forever burned into his mind. He had read it hundreds of times. She had given him the letter the day after finding him in the woods with a dead cat in his hands. That day, he was so certain that the only person he knew that truly loved him was going to walk away from him forever. But, she didn't walk away. Instead she took him by the hand and helped him embrace the darkness. She helped him turn all that hate for his mother into something good. The next day she returned with a letter, and in her small handwriting, she had made her vow. He read that letter so many times that every word was committed to memory. Though he had left it in his play house, safely tucked away for no one to find, he could close his eyes and read every word of the scrawled message.

Jack,

I know you are scared. I am too but I know together we can be stronger. I wont let you down. I have an idea on what we need to do. You will have to promise me that you will listen to me and fight hard to stay with the plan. One day we will be together and you will be special. We can use the play house to study and prepare. You will have to work hard and you will fight to be good because you are good. Then one day when we are all grown up we will go away together and live happily ever after just like in the farie tales. I believe in you and us and will always love you like you always love me. We have to keep this secret. No one else can ever know. I brought you some books today. You need to start to study these and let the pictures help you. Let me help you. One thing you have to promise is to never hurt anything again. I will help you together we will be strong.

Your Best Freind Forever Hope

Even the spelling errors were burned into Jack's mind. Those were the most precious parts of the commitment Hope had made. When he thought of that letter his heart would drop to his stomach. It was that butterfly feeling that had allowed him to follow Hope's plan, and for the first time in his life, he had known what it felt like to be loved. Then when Faith was born, he had known love in its purest form. A tiny child born from the love he and Hope shared, nurtured, and grown. Every day with Hope and Faith had been perfect. He wanted that again.

He remembered how a day later, he guessed because of their youthful shyness, they had never actually spoken about the letter. Instead, they had gone just off the path from the house and had carved their initials into a heart in a tree. From that day on, they were inseparable and spent every free moment working on their plan.

Again, today they were silently agreeing on a new plan.

Kissing his wife tenderly on the lips, he promised to bring back their Faith, committing that Faith would be home for Christmas. They would celebrate as a family again.

Standing, he gave her one final peck on the cheek and then exited the small space, shutting off the light after unconsciously checking the temperature. He closed the door and double checked that it was closed properly. Shivering slightly, he headed back to the surgical room.

Once back inside, he stared down at the child who by now was fully awake, and at the sight of him, she began to struggle against the zip ties that held her tightly to the table. Intentionally ignoring her eyes that seemed to plead with him, he went to the small refrigerator and removed the vial of anesthesia. He extracted a small dose, and then masterfully injected the dose into the nearly invisible vein in the little girl's small arm. It was only moments before she fell into a deep unconscious state. Relief swept over him. Now, she could simply become the subject of his dark desire and an important element in the mission of restoring his darling child.

He worked to remove her clothes first and then looked over her nude body, careful not to allow his eyes to spend much time on her private parts. Sub-consciously he agreed with his earlier assessment of her attributes. A final assessment determined which of those attributes were perfect and those that did not meet the requirements of matching his daughter completely. He decided what he must do.

Preparing for surgery he pulled on scrubs and gloves then quickly went to work. He selected the scalpel and cut through the soft tissue all the way around each of the legs at the top of the thigh. He carefully rolled the girl from side to side to make the perfect incision. Using the bone saw, Jack removed each leg from the torso, just below the point where the joints connected and below where he could feel the pulse. He selected the location for two reasons. First, it would be easier to reconnect more appropriate limbs later and second, to reduce the blood spatter caused from spurts that would likely happen from severing too close to an artery. He worked diligently to complete a perfect transfemoral amputation on each leg. Once the limbs were successfully removed, Jack elected to leave the skin flap open. In a traditional amputation, he would suture the flaps closed over the smoothed out bones to accommodate a prosthetic device, but he would need these flaps later.

He'd been so fixed on the surgical process that he hadn't paid much attention to the amount of blood loss, and he intentionally didn't provide any source for blood replenishment. The young girl had died sometime during the procedure, but Jack was not sure when that had taken place. The blood loss was immense. He was sure however that he had taken the appropriate measures to ensure she had not felt anything.

Jack looked at his work and took a few moments to clean up some of the blood, using the shower sprayer to wash down the body and head of the little girl, pushing her hair away from her face. After rinsing off the legs, he set them aside on the shelf while he considered his next steps.

With her rinsed clean he looked at the washed face of the little girl, and picked up his scalpel again. He made a small and smooth incision all the way around the outline of her lips. Then, he carefully cut through the tissue underneath removing her mouth resulting in a hole in the girls face, exposing teeth and gums. He dropped the flesh from the mouth onto the surgical tray to later place into a jar of saline and formaldehyde for preservation. Once again, he stood back and admired his work. What remained of the little girl was perfect. A smile crept up on his face. *Yes, this is starting to look like my little Faith,* he thought to himself.

An hour or so later, Jack completed the cleanup of the surgical room. He bleached the body, himself, the walls, and the floor twice, making sure all traces of the blood were washed away. Then he carried the torso of the girl into the other room. With complete tenderness he laid them side by side on the shelf inside the freezer with Hope cradling Faith in her arms. The sight brought tears to his eyes. He wept tears of joy as he realized that soon he would have his family completely together again. Leaving them together, he returned to the surgical room and pulled on a fresh hair cover and pair of latex gloves.

Gathering up the girl's clothes, he placed them into a plastic lawn bag along with the two amputated limbs. For several minutes he stood there in the middle of the room, his body nude, considering his options. Then he knew what he must do. He pulled on the clothes he had worn earlier. Still wearing the hair cover and gloves, he carried the bag out to the SUV and pulled the tarp over it.

Remembering the padlock on the basement door, he walked over and reattached the chain and lock. Though there was no one inside that he needed to keep in, the extra lock made him feel that his family was somehow safer. Checking the time on his cell phone, he decided that he had time for dinner at the diner in town, and it would give him a perfect cover. It was almost eight o'clock. The diner would be closing soon, but being seen locally at this time was certainly a good thing. Locking up the rest of the house and pulling on his jacket, he shoved the hair cover and gloves into his pocket and headed to his vehicle and into town.

Walking into the diner, he waved hello to a few people he recognized as he slid into a booth in the corner. There weren't too many people in this late. An older couple sat in the opposite corner, and a family he recognized sat at a table in the middle of the diner. The boy had been brought in the prior week for treatment of a strain he had gotten during a football game. Another group sat against the wall that he couldn't fully see. Sarah, the waitress, came up to him carrying a pot of coffee. "Well, look what the cat dragged in. How are you doing tonight, Doc?"

"Good, Sarah. How about you?"

"Livin' the dream, Doc, livin' the dream."

Jack smiled at the woman and nodded for the coffee to be poured. "Yes, please, though it will likely just keep me awake."

"I know what you mean. Do you know what you want tonight? We have catfish on special, or I can bring you a menu over, if you would like."

"Catfish? Hmmm that sounds really good. Don't think I have had a good catfish dinner in a while."

"It comes with fries and a salad."

"Perfect. Ranch dressing will work for me."

"Comin' right up," she said smiling, tossing her head as she walked away.

Jack was just about to take a sip of his coffee when someone popped out of the corner. "Hi, Doctor Jack," a young voice said, followed by a giggle.

Jack turned to look, and there was Jessie. "Well hi there, Jessie. You scared me," he teased. "Are you feeling better now?"

She nodded, her eyes dancing. "The medicine worked."

"Well, I sure am glad to hear that."

"I'm having ice cream. It feels good on my throat because it is all better now."

"Ice cream? Well now that really sounds like a treat."

Just then Jessie's mother walked up. "I'm sorry, Doc. She just had to come over and say hi to you."

Jack waved his hand at the woman. "It's no problem. At least she isn't afraid of me anymore."

"Yeah, I guess that's good," the mother agreed. "She's feeling much better now. That last trip did the trick. I promised to bring her out for ice cream once she felt better."

"I'm really glad to hear that. But, don't hesitate to come see me if anything else comes up."

"Oh, we will for sure. Thanks again, Doctor Taylor."

"Bye, Jessie. See you soon, okay? And you be good for your mommy." Jack waved as the mother and daughter headed out the door. Jessie tossed him a brilliant smile just before the door closed behind her.

He took a sip on his coffee as Sarah sat his salad down in front of him and hit his coffee with a splash to refill his cup. "Catfish will be out in just a few."

Jack suddenly realized how hungry he was. He couldn't remember if he had eaten today and knew that it was important to take care of his health. He had to be healthy for Hope and now for Faith too. He mentally promised to take better care of himself. Just as he was thinking about this, Sarah returned with a plate of food and some more coffee. She set the plate down and asked if he needed anything else. He looked over the plate and nodded acceptance at the platter in front of him.

All this fried food was certainly not healthy, but it sure did smell good. As he ate he considered his options on a healthier lifestyle. Even in Oklahoma he had maintained his workout routine and now realized that he needed to get back at it. Though he was still in excellent shape, he knew it would only be a matter of time before that was no longer true, if he didn't make a focused effort of it. Picking through the fish and avoiding any small bones, he decided that he could use the smaller room in the basement for some gym equipment. He could workout in the mornings before work or even in the evenings when Hope and Faith were watching TV. Tomorrow he would work on ordering some equipment and getting the room setup. For now, he was going to enjoy the food.

The older couple left the restaurant as Jack was finishing his meal, and now he was the last in the place. Apparently, the family had left at some point while he was deep in thought. Sarah returned with the coffee one more time, which he declined then handed her a credit card to pay for his meal.

After running the card, she returned it to him to sign the slip and collected his plates from the table. "Don't be a stranger, Doc. It's good to see you in here again."

"I won't. Things are settling down a little now. Getting into more of a routine, you know?" He smiled his generous smile, white teeth flashing and, no doubt, warming her heart.

Sarah returned the smile and headed into the back part of the kitchen. Jack felt good, full, and content. He headed out into the night air.

In the kitchen at the diner, Sarah talked to the cook, an older man named Sam who had worked there for more than fifteen years. "Sam, I am telling you, they don't make men like that one anymore. He is a fine specimen, for sure, handsome, charming, and smart too." Sarah stood, shaking her head as she watched through the serving window as Jack backed away.

Through the lights inside the diner, Jack could see Sarah and the cook watching him, so he pulled out as if heading towards his home. Then once down the street, he turned and headed towards the highway and back to Eureka. He retraced his steps to Carlock and through the country, back to the very place where the bus had let the little girl off. By now it would have been reported that the girl was missing, so he was careful as he got close to the road, watching for any indication of police.

Far in the distance, he could see a single flashing light. It must have been up at the home. The lane was at least a quarter mile, maybe even a half mile long. Jack killed his headlights then pulled up near the mailbox that sat next to the road. He climbed out of the SUV, pulled on the latex gloves that he had shoved into his jacket pocket, and gathered the bag from the back. He set it next to the mailbox, and then he climbed back in and drove away. Once he was a good mile down the road, he turned on his headlights and headed back home. He didn't see another vehicle until he was nearly to Congerville, a small town that sat between Eureka and Carlock and a good fifteen miles from the little girl's home. With the distance between him and the girl's home he began to feel confident. His plan was working. A peace enveloped him in a tight embrace much like the darkness wrapped around the night.

***

By the time Jack returned to the house it was late. He was tired but wanted to check on Hope and Faith. He locked the front door behind him and then dropped his keys on the coffee table before heading down the stairs to the basement, first going into the surgery room to look around and ensure everything was spotless. The room had a heavy lingering odor of bleach, but he did not notice. The stainless steel table, where the young girl had laid earlier, shined bright under the strong lighting. The floor and walls were clean, and everything seemed to be in perfect order. Jack smiled slightly as he flipped off the light and closed the door behind him. He headed over to the freezer and pulled open the door. Reaching inside he flipped on the switch, and his heart pulled at him as he saw his lovely wife and the beginnings of his daughter, lying together in a tender embrace. Tears dampened his face as he walked in next to them in the small space.

"Hope, I told you I would bring her to you. I can see how happy you are. Faith baby, Daddy is right here. Soon we can all be together. Christmas is coming and we'll celebrate. I promise you we will have the most glorious Christmas ever." Jack leaned over and gathered the pair in

322

his arms, cradling them for a few minutes. He gingerly kissed each on the forehead before telling them good-night. Turning out the light and closing the door Jack wiped away the tears that had dampened his cheeks and headed upstairs for a night of peaceful sleep. His dreams were filled with images of Hope, and Faith opening gifts while sitting around a beautiful Christmas tree that nearly filled the living room, while gifts bulged from underneath as they all smiled joyfully at one another.

Chapter Eleven

Max had been working her case and had made a trip to Chicago to assist in a stakeout that, unfortunately, had been a complete bust. Someone had tipped off the dealers, and the suspects had cleared out before they got there. She returned to Quantico exhausted and frustrated that they had not been successful.

Upon returning home, she discovered that Mark was off on his own case. She settled into her apartment after soaking in the tub for a while. Trying to relax, she poured herself a glass of red wine, nestled into the pillows on her bed and booted up her computer.

Max was hoping that the queries she had set up would deliver some information on possible scenarios that might help her find Jack Tyler. Instead she found information from the people Mark had asked to work the self-storage searches, and her eyes grew large as she read through her email. There was a message from a manager of a self-storage in Fayetteville, Arkansas, acknowledging that a person resembling Jack Tyler had, in fact, rented a refrigerated self-storage unit. That unit had been vacated more than two months ago. "Damn it! Jack, you have been in the States for a while now, haven't you?" Max pushed back from the computer, running her hands through her thick, wavy hair. *What are you up to? Are you killing anyone, Jack?*

Max slid off the bed and headed to her bathroom. She grabbed a scrunchie from her vanity drawer and pulled her hair back in a ponytail. Her mind was racing with thoughts of what to do next. Wishing Mark was home to talk to; she picked up the phone and dialed Cortez. When the phone was answered, Max couldn't contain herself. "Lorraine, it's Max. You aren't going to believe this. He's here. He's in the States."

"Girl, slow your roll. I know you are talking Tyler, but what's up?"

Max spent the next few minutes explaining the email she had received and the possible implications. Talking through her thoughts on what it could potentially mean was helping her know what she needed to do. "I'm going to pull out the magazines we had before and see if there are any more towns that jump out at me. Plus, we still have the list in order, and remember last time we did this, Tulsa was in our top three."

"Max, do you think having the frozen corpse will satisfy him? Or when decomposition sets in, do you think he will do it all over again?"

"I'm not sure. I just know he is so desperate to have his life back. I think he'll do almost anything. And, I am certain he won't be happy unless he has Hope."

"Max, you sound like you feel sorry for him." Cortez said, but it was more of a question.

"Look, I want this guy caught more than I have ever wanted anyone. But, I do feel bad for him. The promise those two kids made when they were so young and the way they successfully managed to keep Jack from harming anyone for so many years is impressive. If not for the accident that killed his family, I think he could have had a normal life. For that I am sorry, yes."

"I saw it too, Max. I do get it. But Tyler is a very sick man. He has to be stopped, and I doubt there is any chance that he can lead a normal life even if he believes he has Hope back in it. That body he put together won't last forever, nor can it keep him satisfied."

They sat each on their end of the line in silence for a few moments. Each contemplating the many implications of what Cortez had said.

"I know, Cortez. We have to find this guy before he completely melts down."

"Yeah, let's hope we aren't too late, already. And, how the hell do we find him when we have no idea what he is up to right now?"

"I don't know. I'm hoping one of my searches will turn something up. Unfortunately, that means he will have done bad things."

"How is your new case going?" Cortez asked, changing the topic.

"Oh, that? Yeah, that is frustrating too. You know, you worked a case like this one. Yours might not have been international, but I know it was a tough one. We keep showing up right after they have cleared out. It almost seems like there is someone on the inside telling them when to expect us."

"Any chance there is a snitch in the FBI or with the local PD?"

"Maybe. I hope that's not the case, but it certainly makes me wonder."

"Is there anyone undercover that might have gone under too deep?"

"Hmmm, now that is something to consider, for sure. Thanks for the tip. I'm going to have to check that out."

The two checked in on personal topics: how Mark and Max were doing, the sale of the home in California and how Max was adjusting to not being able to see her sister and nephew as often as she liked, as well as whether she was missing her parents. They moved off of Max and talked about Cortez. Max was excited to learn that Cortez had gone on a date with a firefighter she met at a scene of an arsonist that had been setting apartments on fire. So far the perp had not yet killed anyone, but Cortez was worried that he was escalating. Cortez said she and the firefighter were going out again the next weekend and said they had hit it off pretty well.

Max was disappointed that Cortez would not offer up any more details, but she vowed to tease her relentlessly. After laughing for a bit, they finally hung up, agreeing to talk again soon.

Max returned to the kitchen and refilled her wine glass, then decided to do some random ViCAP searches. She now had full access to the FBI systems, which gave her search capabilities that she hadn't had in local law enforcement in Los Angeles. She really wasn't even sure what she was looking for, but she knew she would know it when she saw it. The main ideas she had for finding Jack and the possible things he might be doing were already set up as searches that would auto email her any matches. Max paused for a moment, thinking just how much ViCAP - Violent Criminal Apprehension Program- applied to Jack Tyler. Max was sure Jack was up to no good. She just had to find something in this database that would lead her to him.

She sat back looking at the information in front of her. The list of missing children across the nation was overwhelming. Looking through data in the Missing and Exploited Person's database, Max discovered that approximately 800,000 missing children are reported each year, of which seventy-five percent are runaways or family abductions. In reality, there are only about 100 true stranger abductions. These were classified as Unidentified Subjects, usually referred to by the FBI as the un-sub. She knew from her research and training that two-thirds of the abductions in this category fell between the ages of 12 and 17. She could quickly rule those ages out. This gave Max some hope as she continued to scale back the data. The open cases that would fit the profile for Jack Tyler's daughter were quickly coming down.

Going on her hunch that Jack would want to find Faith, she started taking the data and separating out those cases of boys and girls, focusing her efforts only on girls. Next, she filtered out the teenagers and infants. She considered whether Jack would attempt to recreate Faith as a baby, or possibly younger than she was at the time of her death. He could try to turn back the hands of time in some way, as if to avoid the accident all together.

After a long pause while she played out the scenario in her head, she decided that he wouldn't do that, since he had not done that with Hope. He had basically put together a body of a woman, choosing victims that were the age and likeness at the time of the accident. She was certain that if he decided to do the same for Faith, he would follow the same path. Locking in on her decision, she continued to filter the data down to girls between five and eight years old. She was left with a total of thirty-four currently open and active cases. Finally, she looked at the cases that had been opened since the date the self-storage was cleared out. Now she was down to nine. Max printed out the list, which included last known photos.

She stared down at the photos that lay in front of her. Two had brown hair, one was African American, and one had short blonde hair. Faith had long blonde hair. Setting those four aside, she stared at the remaining five photos.

Max pulled out the copies she'd kept from the Jack Tyler case files, specifically looking for the list of cities from the magazines Jack had clearly studied in depth as a boy. Within those magazines Max and Cortez had compiled a list of most likely cities where Jack might settle down. Max had later rank sorted them based on the geographical surroundings. Her main focus had been on rural areas with quick access to a city. On that list in the top three was Tulsa, and sure enough, that had proven out, just not soon enough for Max to catch Jack before he got away. Flipping through one of the files, she pulled out the listing of cities from the magazines.

Max went to the linen closet and got out a sheet. Returning to the living room, she looked at the walls of the apartment and decided on the one behind the front door. Finding some tacks in her desk, she pulled a chair over and pinned the sheet up to the wall. She began to carefully arrange the pictures, potential cities that might be his hunting grounds, and case notes onto the sheet. She replicated the murder wall she had in California the first time she was tracking Jack. The chief had pulled her off the case, as it had gone cold, but in her own time Max continued to work her theory until it had paid off. After about thirty minutes, she stood back admiring the wall in front of her with a bit of disdain. She had the photos of Jack, Hope, and Faith, as well as the list of cities she had highlighted as potential hot spots for Jack to strike again - cities and towns where she was certain Jack had spent hours dreaming of as a boy. He read and reread those medical magazines, dreaming of a day when he and Hope would escape, and that is exactly what they had done, until the accident.

Max also added the photos of the remaining missing girls and indicated on them the cities they were missing from. Then she hung the map of the U.S. and added color push pins as points for each of the cities on the list. She separated her rank-sorted list into three and applied colors to each grouping. Red represented most likely, blue next, and yellow as least likely. As she looked on at the work she had done, the phone rang, startling her.

"Hello."

"Hey there, I don't have much time, but I wanted to check in." Mark's husky yet smooth voice came through the cell phone like music to her ears.

"Hi. You okay? Where are you?"

"Yes, we're all just fine. The team is coming in soon so I'll have to go. I'm in New Mexico. That's all I can say for now."

"Understood, getting closer?"

"I think so. We have a couple of good leads on the un-sub. I hope we can wrap this up and be home in the next couple of days. I'll try to call tomorrow. No guarantees. You take care, okay?"

"I will. Be safe, please."

"Ditto." The line went dead before Max could say anything else. She shrugged it off, knowing it was part of the deal. It would always be like this, and it would happen with both of them. But, she was okay with this arrangement, accepting that the time they did get together was better than not having Mark in her life at all. Setting the phone down next to her computer, she returned her attention to the sheet containing all of the information.

Staring at the photos of those little girls, she silently prayed that Jack had not hurt any of them. Considering the loss he had suffered and the means in which he was clearly trying to pull his life together with the restoration of Hope, she knew it was unlikely. She felt sad for a moment - for the children and for the young boy that Jack had been. *What happened to you, young Jack? What made you who you are?*

Max took the final sip from her glass of wine and decided that she needed to turn in so she would be in good shape for work the next day. She had another case to solve too. Before turning away she thought through her next steps. She would map out the distance between the missing children and her top possible locations to see just how close in proximity they were. Maybe this would give some direction on where Jack Tyler was now and what he was up to. *I will find you one day, Jack. I just hope I do it before you hurt a bunch of little girls.* With those final thoughts, Max headed off to bed for a fitful night filled with images of little girls running for their lives.

Her mind ran through all the possible things Jack would do to little blonde girls. She tossed in her bed when her dreams led her to visions of severed body parts and a beautiful, little, blonde haired girl reaching out as if pleading for help. When Max reached to her she saw the girl's hands were missing, and where they should have been, blood pumped from the nubs. Max sat up. She got out of bed and went to the kitchen to get a glass of water before returning to her bed to once again attempt to sleep. Drifting back off, her dreams this time took her to a tormented little boy. She could see him running from his home, the door slamming behind him as he raced off into the woods, where he caught and killed a rodent, then placed the bones in a small box that he hid in the floor boards of his play house. Max tossed in her bed again, the sheets twisting around her lean, muscular body.

Chapter Twelve

The morning sun rose early, casting a shine on the rich, black soil from the empty cornfields that had been plowed under weeks earlier. A light frost covered the perfect folds making the field look like perfect scoops of dark ice cream, indicating the wintery chill that hung in the air. The farmhouse became smaller in the rearview mirror as the police car made its way down the drive, the wheels stirring a trail of dust that appeared to settle on the frozen corn field. The officer driving the vehicle had been assigned to escort the woman away to stay with a family member while the house was thoroughly searched for the reportedly missing child. As was standard procedure in any missing or reported child abduction, the family was being carefully scrutinized. A key for early recovery is getting the husband and wife separated so they could each be interviewed without the influence of the other. The sheriff had encouraged the wife to leave with the officer, telling her to go and stay with her sister as the search of the home was clearly overwhelming, and she had nearly collapsed after several hours of questions and officers milling about the home. The husband was holding up better, and the sheriff really wanted to question him alone.

As the car approached the end of the driveway and prepared to turn right, the officer spotted something black and shiny lying near the mailbox. Stopping the vehicle he got out and started walking towards the mailbox. When he got a few feet away, he recognized the object as a large trash bag, the kind used for disposing of lawn waste. He returned to the vehicle and radioed back to the house. The woman in the car who had sat nearly catatonic until now was suddenly alert. She reached for the door handle.

"Ma'am, stay in the vehicle," he cautioned then finished providing his report through the radio back to the sheriff, who was still up at the house.

The woman ignored the warning and continued, pushing the door open and climbing out. She raced around the rear of the vehicle, causing the officer to drop the radio and dart around the front in an effort to cut her off before she arrived at the mailbox. He grabbed at her, but she pushed him hard against his chest and pulled away from his grasp, causing him to stumble backwards. She arrived at the trash bag before he could stop her. Her fingers, cold from the morning chill, fumbled with the cinch ties that bound the bag closed until her emotions drove her to dig her fingernails into the plastic. The officer recovered from the shove and arrived at her side as she forced a split in the bag large enough that some of the contents gaped through the opening. The sheriff's car slid to a stop, and as he poured out of his vehicle, he was greeted with a piercing wail from the woman as she fell to the ground, pulling the officer with her. The bag lay nearby with a child's small, bare foot poking out.

***

Jack woke early and headed to the office for a day pretty full of back to back patients. This was one of the days when he was grateful for the busy practice that was beginning to develop. It was keeping his mind occupied as he continued to consider how to finish the work of finding the rest of Faith. He could hardly think of Hope and Faith, so tenderly joined together, without smiling. Mary even commented on his chipper attitude today. He told her that he loved the cool weather and the promise of winter. That was a lie. He actually preferred warmer climates and missed California frequently but was truly happy anywhere Hope was, and now…with Faith coming home, he could certainly endure some winter weather. Besides it was going to make for having a great Christmas celebration. He only had a bit of work left to do with Faith, and then he would be ready for the holidays to come.

Wrapping up the day, he decided to go home and work out his plan for the next step. He really loved the way things had gone in Eureka. He knew the clue was right. After all, the name was a dead giveaway. The Greek origin of the word Eureka, meaning 'I have found it', was clearly the only clue he should have needed. As much as he would love to return there, he knew that was too risky. When he got home he turned on the TV It was just about time for the six o'clock news.

Jack sat and waited for any local news reports. As the programming ended and the news cut in, Jack was faced with a 'Breaking News' report. The anchorman went on to describe the grisly findings in the small town of Eureka and of another finding in Le Roy just a day earlier. Both missing girls were between the ages of seven and eight, both with blonde hair and blue eyes. When the report ended, the anchor speculated about certain aspects but clearly stated they did not know if these two crimes had been committed by the same person or whether there was any connection at all. Few other details were disclosed.

He smiled, knowing they were trying to find some connection between the two little girls, but there wouldn't be any. He was satisfied in two ways: first the bodies, or parts, as the case was for the second child, were home safe and sound with their parents, and second, he felt very confident that there was no way he could be caught. They would not find any trace evidence.

332

Leaning back in the chair he watched the report wondering what Special Agent Maxine Nichols would do if she were on this case. He was convinced she was the only one that might be able to find him.

Jack decided to make something quick and easy to eat. As much as he would like to have dinner as a family, it was not time yet. Tonight he would leave Hope and Faith together for some more mother daughter time, besides there was much to do before Faith would be able to come out and have dinner. *Soon*, he thought. But for now he needed to decide how and where he would find the correct parts to finish bringing Faith the rest of the way home.

With winter coming and the promise he had made to Faith to have a beautiful Christmas together, he felt pressure to move quickly. What if he couldn't find the perfect little girl to finish the plan? His heart raced a little, and as he succumbed to the worry, the darkness taunted him. His recent activities had been helpful in keeping the darkness buried, but right now it was weighing heavily on his mind. He closed his eyes and pleaded internally for strength to stay in control, for his wife and daughter.

Just then his cell phone rang; he looked down at the display. Recognizing the number he smiled, realizing everything was going to be fine and pressed the answer button.

"Doctor Taylor? It's Julie. I'm the nurse on duty tonight at the hospital, and we have an emergency. I was hoping you could come in right away."

Jack felt relief wash over him. "Of course, Julie, right away." He grabbed his keys and jacket, realizing that he needed a much heavier winter coat. He needed to go shopping to pick up some things for Faith too.

Driving to the hospital as fast as he could, he arrived in just ten minutes. Immediately upon entering the hospital emergency room, he went into action. There was a young female still on a gurney with several people working on her. She had major bruising on her forehead. The team was working to stabilize her.

Jack recognized Julie from the few other times he had come in to help. "What do we have?"

"A drunk driver, car accident, she sustained massive contusions, internal injuries and internal bleeding." She gave the vitals, indicating a weak heart rate and high blood pressure. "We are trying to get her stabilized, so you can take her into surgery to stop the bleeding."

"What happened to the drunk driver?" Jack's heart raced, anger immediately rising in his chest. Hope and Faith had once been stolen from him by a drunk driver.

"No," Julie said. "I must not have been clear. She," she said nodding at the woman on the table, "is the drunk driver. The couple in the other car didn't make it, died at the scene."

Jack looked up at Julie then his eyes moved back to the table. He pursed his lips together. "I'll scrub up. Let me know when she's ready. I'll meet you in there." Jack walked away and headed to the only operating room they had in the small hospital. His mind was reeling. Rage began to build in him. The woman in that room had killed two innocent people. *Just like…*

He removed a set of scrubs from the locker and pulled them on, and then he moved over to the sink where he thoroughly scrubbed his hands and nails all the way up to his elbows. He could not get his mind away from the thoughts of twisted wreckage and the innocent lives that had been lost.

A few minutes later, Julie entered the room and began to scrub too. Jack respected her. He had only worked with her twice before, but she had proven a good assistant in the operating room.

"She's stable for now, but it's touch and go. She's had a lot of internal bleeding, and she's still intoxicated." Julie shook her head in obvious disgust. This made Jack appreciate her even more.

Both fully scrubbed they entered the surgical room where the woman was being transferred from the gurney to the operating bed. "We'll have to anesthetize lightly due to the alcohol level," Jack said.

Julie nodded, administering the sedation. The woman was connected to all of the monitoring devices. Oxygen had been turned on through a mask that covered her nose and mouth, a bag of O-negative blood was connected to the vein in her right arm. She had dropped into a deeper sleep now, no longer just influenced by her injuries and the level of alcohol in her system. Jack stepped forward, requested a #5 scalpel, and made an incision down the center of her torso. He released a deep breath as the blood swirled out of the incision from the bleeding inside. The incision relieved some of the pressure on the woman's internal organs. The pressure alone could have been enough to cause her death. There was substantial damage to several of the internal organs. Jack smiled through his mask. His hands skillfully sought out the ruptured blood vessels. He sutured the tears as needed.

The beeping monitors indicated the woman's heart rate was dropping. Jack worked quickly, but he had no intention of allowing this woman to walk away from this table tonight. His hands explored more deeply for additional trauma, but he really was just buying some time. He knew the woman was losing the battle, and he was pleased about it. This woman had no right to receive this care, much less survive. Minutes later as his hands felt the woman's lung, the monitor flat lined. Of course, this was the moment Jack had been waiting for. He swore under his breath just loud enough for Julie to hear. She glanced his way. "We're losing her," he shouted out as if he cared. They worked for a few more minutes to try and revive the woman to no avail. Finally, Jack called time of death and stepped back.

Julie nodded at him, and after a moment she began detaching the monitoring devices and other equipment. She completed the patient chart that hung from the end of the bed and then covered the woman's face with the sheet. Jack left the room and went to the scrub sink to wash up. He pulled off his scrubs and sighed. He had done a good thing tonight, and the darkness now felt like it was a million miles away. Julie entered the locker room and nodded at him, unsure what to say. "She was just too far gone," she finally stated.

"Apparently so," Jack replied. He was still somewhat feigning frustration, though he felt none of it at all.

"Well, she didn't...," Julie faded off, shaking her head before finishing her sentence.

Jack looked at her. He was pretty sure she was about to say the woman didn't deserve being saved. He just nodded at her through the mirror they were both facing. "You did good work in there," he offered.

"Thanks. Sometimes situations like this make me question things - helping someone who I know destroyed lives today."

"I understand, but it's not our job to question. We just do everything we can to save lives and let the law, fate, or a higher power take it the rest of the way. At least that is my motto."

Jack was now fully cleaned up, and he stood looking at Julie in the mirror as she dried her hands. "I'll sign the chart and inform the family. See you soon, Julie." He gave her a final nod and went back into the surgical room to sign the chart, and then he headed down to the waiting room to give the woman's family the news of her death. When he started the trip home, he felt great. This had been a good day all the way around.

Jack arrived back home. It was late now, and he was tired. He recognized that he was also hungry. He never did eat his dinner, having gotten the call from the hospital just as he was getting ready to prepare something. He decided it was too late now and promised himself a healthy breakfast.

He wanted to go down and check on Hope and Faith, but instead he decided against disturbing them. Even so, the desire to be near them was too much, so he grabbed a throw blanket and went to the basement and lay down on the couch nearby the freezer. The feeling of being close to them was comforting. He laid there for a while and thought of the woman at the hospital and the good deed he had done tonight ensuring that she never hurt anyone again. The families of the couple she had killed in the crash would find some comfort in knowing that she had perished too.

The next day was Saturday. The office was closed. It pleased him that there would be plenty of time to develop a plan to bring the rest of Faith home. On that final thought, he dropped into a deep sleep.

Chapter Thirteen

It was Saturday morning, and Max was waiting for Mark to come over. He got in late the night before. He and the team had tracked one of the main players in his case and had apprehended him. After two days of interrogation they had finally broken him. He had given them enough information to capture two others as well. Now the lengthy legal process would begin, and hopefully with the two in custody, more of the operation could be shut down. Mark sounded beat. He told Max that they'd recovered fourteen girls and women, aging anywhere from twelve to twenty-four. They were still trying to gather more information on just how many woman and children had been sold by this group. The apprehension of these people and the possible recovery of more victims forced into prostitution would take months. Despite those facts, it had been a good trip, and Mark had described feeling really good about the apprehension.

Max was making breakfast when she heard a knock at the door. She went over and swung the door open and greeted Mark with a huge embrace. He returned the hug, enclosing her muscular yet lean body in his strong arms. "Well, now that is a greeting a guy could get really used to."

"I'm going to hold you to that," Max responded, placing her lips softly against his neck.

She leaned back and gazed up into his dark blue eyes. He returned the gaze then bent in and kissed her deeply. Their tongues swirled together, the warmth causing Max's heart to race and a heat to pass deep inside her body. After savoring the moment Max pulled away and led Mark by the hand into the room, closing the door behind her.

"Ummm, it smells great in here. You smell great too," Mark said, nuzzling her hair as she pulled him into the kitchen.

"Coffee?"

"Have you ever known me to say no to that?" Mark smiled at her as she reached for a cup from the cupboard over the sink.

"I fixed some breakfast. It's nearly done. I wasn't sure how late you would sleep, so I made a breakfast casserole." After handing Mark his coffee, Max turned on the oven light and peeked in at the egg, sausage, and biscuit mix. The cheese on top was bubbling perfectly. She grabbed the hot pads and reached in to pull it out and could sense that Mark's attention had drifted to the living room. She tried to play it cool as he turned back to her. She saw the surprise in his eyes.

"What is that all about?" She could hear the tension and concern in his voice as he nodded his head at the murder board that covered the sheet suspended on the wall.

Scooping out portions from the casserole dish as she spoke, Max began to explain. "It's how I work Mark, and how I think. I know you're not a hundred percent on board with the idea that Jack may be seeking to replace Faith, but I think it's a good possibility. And I need to know. We discussed how every good cop has a case that just won't let you go. Well this is the one for me. I know Jack can't stop killing. Perhaps now it even includes children. Or, he will kill again as soon as the body he put together as Hope decays to a point he needs to do it again. I want to catch him before we have more dead people. I know you never saw it, but after Chief Harding pulled me from the case in L.A., I built a board just like that one. It helps me think, and it brings new ideas to me. It was while working that board in the middle of my living room that I identified Tulsa as one of the top three most likely places for Jack to move to after he left California." She paused as she set his plate in front of him on the island bar and reached for forks.

"You know there is a chance that Jack use taxidermy methods on her, and if so, she will last forever. We found trace evidence of tanning chemicals along with many other things in that basement. It's possible he has created some crazy concoction that would preserve her forever. But there is also a chance you are correct," Mark conceded. "So... what has your murder board told you so far?"

Max motioned for him to follow her to the table with her plate and coffee in her hands. He took her lead. Settling down in a chair, Max began explaining the work she had been doing during her off time over the past few nights. "I have reprioritized the possible locations that Jack may go to next. I took Tulsa off the board as I think it's highly unlikely he will return there, but it also added some important facts about the places he might go, based off of what we learned in Tulsa. I originally thought he would go to a bigger city with rural settings in close proximity. He did that, but Tulsa was a bit smaller than my top two most likely locations, which were New York and Phoenix. So I have revisited this, and I now think he would go to a couple of smaller places including Baton Rouge, Bend, and Bloomington, IL. All of these places were in the medical magazines recovered from Jack's boyhood playhouse out in the woods. This makes these the top locations mentioned numerous times within those magazines matching the community size that somewhat match Tulsa." She paused to take a bite of the warm and savory casserole, waiting to see what Mark would say. When he said nothing she continued, "The photos of the little girls are a recent, narrowed search of missing girls. Last night I took some time to run the correlation to my key points. So far they are each too far away to be the locations I have identified. Jack has always stayed close to home. I can't picture that M.O. changing."

338

Mark listened intently as he enjoyed the casserole. "I understand your desire to catch him. I want him too. I just worry that if it takes a while, even years, or we have to admit maybe never, that it will eat away at you."

"I'm a realist, Mark, but I won't stop emotionally working this case until I know I have done everything possible to ensure Jack is stopped."

"Okay, how can I help?" He said, his eyes softening.

Max looked up, making eye contact with him for the first time since he saw the murder board on the wall. "You already are, by just supporting me."

She let a moment of silence sit between them before continuing. "I have ViCAP setup to send me any new reports. Basically it's a very narrow search to include only missing or murdered girls between the ages of five and eight where no family member is suspected. If murder is involved, I narrowed that search even further to include Jack's signature torso cuts and the body being cleaned with bleach. I set up the same search for women in case he has to replace Hope at some point. As new reports come in, I'll map them against my top ten cities. I know it's a long shot, but it worked before. You called about the Oklahoma murders, but I received an email against my search criteria too."

Mark sat peering over his coffee cup, then took a sip and set the cup down. "Eat your breakfast before it gets cold. It's way too good to waste. In fact I'm getting some more." Mark stood and walked back into the kitchen, helping himself to another serving of the delicious breakfast. He returned to the table and offered Max a refill of coffee before sitting back down. "How is your official case going?"

They spent the next hour talking through their respective cases, finishing the meal, and cleaning up the kitchen. As Max was wiping down the counter, Mark looped his arms around her waist, pulling her tightly against his chest and leaning in to kiss her neck. She spun around and leaned into him even harder. He lifted her up and sat her on the counter.

Max wrapped her legs around him and pulled him into her then pressed her breasts into his chest, feeling his muscles go taunt against her plump nipples. He moved his hands up her thighs and around her, pulling her up on his hips. She felt his body responding and drove her tongue into his mouth, the passion rising inside her. She had missed his touch the past few days and wanted him to take her. She pulled at his shirt, tugging it off over his head and dug her hands into the muscles in his back.

He responded by pulling away and slowly undoing the buttons on her shirt. He took his time, driving her crazy with the slow brushes across her breasts with his knuckles as he worked the shirt off. Mark smiled down at her knowing the slow pace was pushing her over the edge.

Mark lifted her off of the counter, her legs still wrapped around his hips. Kissing her, he carried her off to the bedroom where he spent the next couple of hours repeatedly bringing her to the edge, waiting until she could barely take the teasing any longer, before releasing with her. They napped for a while then woke and made love once more before deciding they needed to get out for a while. After taking showers, they headed out for a late lunch and long walk through the local farmer's market.

Chapter Fourteen

Jack woke up refreshed despite sleeping on the couch. He stretched out his long legs and rose to walk over to the freezer and swung open the door. Every time he saw Hope holding their Faith, his heart pulled. He was finally making his wife happy again. Not wanting to leave the door open longer than necessary, he blew them kisses and closed the door. Heading upstairs, he went straight to the kitchen and began preparing himself a healthy and hearty breakfast.

Feeling energized from his meal after clearing up the dishes, he began considering where he should continue the search for Faith. He searched the map of McLean County and came up empty. Nothing was jumping out at him. Becoming frustrated he decided to move on to something else that needed done. He needed to get some winter clothing, and he wanted to buy a few things for Faith. Both Hope and Faith loved clothing, and he wanted them to have what they needed for special occasions. Following the Christmas Eve tradition they had always observed, he would get them each new pajamas which they would open on Christmas Eve. And then he would get each a beautiful new dress for Christmas Day to wear during the fabulous dinner he planned to prepare. Renewed with excitement he decided to head to the mall in Bloomington. He needed some fresh air and he was hoping being out would help him understand where he should look for Faith next.

Gathering up his jacket and keys, he checked all of the doors and then headed out. Before leaving he verified the stock in his medical bag behind the driver's seat. Realizing he did not have a syringe of Chloroform, he returned to the basement to fill a syringe with 5cc. *Just in case.* Jack locked up again and headed back to the car.

As he drove he continued to consider where he might find Faith. The last one had been so obvious, as the answer was right there in the name of the town. Eureka, meaning "I found it," had been a clue. *Would there be another clue like that?* He thought of the town near Bloomington called Normal. *Could that mean something, a normal life again perhaps?* Deciding this had enough significance, he headed to the College Hills Mall that sat right on the border of Bloomington and Normal. The two cities had essentially merged into one over the years and were often referred to as twin-cities. *Yes, this could mean something.* His mind drifted to Christmas Day. He needed to get some decorations too. He would make everything perfect. He suddenly felt especially cheerful. He turned on the radio and was pleased to hear *It's a New Day* by Will.i.am piping through the speakers. Jack sang along to the chorus.

Arriving at the mall, he circled it looking at the store names. He ultimately decided it didn't matter, and he settled on a parking space in the middle of the parking lot near the main entrance, which placed him in the center of the mall. Exiting his vehicle he headed inside to look for the items he had come in search of.

Jack wandered the mall for a while people watching. His mood dampened as he saw families enjoying the shopping experience together. He knew this was something he would never do again with Hope or Faith. They both had loved the times they would go out to the mall in California. He remembered how Faith always wanted to spend time at the little playground in the center of the mall.

He went into Macy's and made his way to the men's section. Hope had always helped him select his clothing, but that would not be able to happen again either. His mood began darkening further. He tried to shrug it off, telling himself that he knew what Hope would pick out for him. He walked along the pathway between the various sections until he came to the winter coats. He spent several minutes contemplating the choices and decided on a trench coat. It was lined and waterproof, perfect for both rain and snow. He picked up a pair of winter gloves too and some funny pajamas that had the Grinch from the Christmas movie *How the Grinch Stole Christmas*. He thought Faith would think they were funny on him, and the idea made him smile.

Next he headed to the women's section and picked out some pajamas, also in the Grinch theme that had feet in them. He knew Hope was always cold, and these would help keep her warm. *Not too warm*, he thought. Then he looked at dresses and could not find anything he thought was extra special, so he worked his way to the children's section. He walked through until he found the girl's clothing. About that time a female employee approached him, "Is there anything I can help you find today, sir?"

Jack was pulled out of his thoughts and looked up to find a pleasant looking woman with a warm smile on her face. She looked to be about forty and seemed genuinely interested in helping him with his selections. Forcing himself to allow her to enter the private space he had been in just moments ago, he responded with a large smile, "Well, Delores," Jack said reading the nametag pinned to the lapel of her suit jacket. "I'm selecting some things for my wife and child. I was really hoping you might have some pajamas for my daughter that had the Grinch on them." He hoped to keep the theme for the whole family. He knew Faith would like it if they all matched.

"Sure, I think we do over here," Delores said as she started to lead him to the other side of the checkout kiosk. She looked through a specific rack and pulled out a couple of choices. One had the feet in them just like Hope's, and he thought that would be perfect.

"What size does your daughter wear?"

Jack paused, his mind racing for a moment. He hadn't considered that Faith was not nearly complete, and the choice he made on the rest of her parts would have an impact on the size of clothing she wore. Then his mind settled down; she would be the size she had been because he would find the perfect match. He looked at the two pajamas the woman was holding up. "I think this will do just fine," he said selecting the smaller of the two.

"Is there anything else you are looking for today?"

A part of Jack wanted to get out of there and away from the inquiring woman, but instead he forced himself to stay calm. *Always in control,* he silently said. "Yes, actually I'm looking for a special dress that my daughter can wear for Christmas dinner. I want to surprise her and her mother. I looked in the women's section but didn't seeing anything quite special enough," again he smiled, his charisma obviously putting the woman at ease.

"Oh, we have some lovely dresses for the holidays for both girls and women over here." Again, Delores led him through the store. They arrived at a section that was filled with holiday dresses. "Is this what you were thinking?" She waved her hand towards the array of dresses hanging in the section.

Jack gazed over the area. His eyes landed on a brilliant red dress that had just the right amount of sequins. He walked over and touched the material. It was satin, and it shimmered under the bright lights of the store. "I think my wife would love this dress, actually. Do you have this in a size six?"

"I believe we do. Let me look." Delores went about finding the right size and pulled out one and let Jack inspect it a bit further. "What do you think?"

"I think it is perfect," he replied.

"Would you like for me to put all of this at the checkout while we look for a dress for your daughter?" Delores smiled at his hands full of the pajamas, coat, and gloves.

"Yes, of course. Thank you."

After taking the items from Jack's arms to the register, she returned and began helping him look through the racks for a dress for Faith. Jack noticed a woman and her child nearby. The little girl looked to be about Faith's age, and she was dazzled by a certain dress on the rack, asking her mother if she could have it *pleeeaaase!*

Jack smiled at the exchange and then noticed the girl was wearing tights like a ballerina would wear. They were tight against her legs, showing the clear definition and tone. Jack tried to look closer without being obvious. The mother was resisting the repeated pleas to get her that dress. Jack continued to look through the rack as if he was interested. He worked his way closer to the girl. He needed to get nearer to her to really look and see exactly how tall she was. The dress she was so in love with was pink with sparkles and a big bow in the back. Just as Jack got next to her, her mother took her hand and said, "I told you no. We can't afford that dress. Now stop this, and let's go."

The little girl looked up at Jack as she was pulled away. Her face was filled with a frown, which would never do. But, her legs. Oh, yes he was sure. As they walked away, Jack held up the dress the girl had been so adamant about having. "I think that little girl convinced me this must be the right one," Jack told Delores. "How can I possibly go wrong?"

Delores smiled and took the dress from Jack. "I don't believe you could," she said smiling.

"I think that will do it for me today."

"Okay, well let's get you taken care of."

A short time later, Jack found himself leaving Macy's with several bags and searching for the mother and the little girl. His eyes darted through the crowds. The store was at one end of the mall. He had watched them leave, so he knew the general direction they had gone. He worked his way along, considering what the mother had been looking at. He realized that he had seen her earlier but had paid little attention. *Jeans*, yes she had been looking at the jeans. It was the little girl who had worked her way to the dresses, based on that he began paying special attention to the store fronts that boasted jeans on sale. He also considered the comment she made about money and discounted the Lucky Brand store, knowing full well she could not afford those jeans. He saw an Old Navy and thought it was a good bet. He wandered inside, casually looking around and stopping at the clothes racks here and there. He pretended to be looking for certain sizes or styles, but his eyes were scanning the aisles. Then he saw them coming out of a dressing room. His heart leapt. Deciding he needed to not stand out to the mother, he could ill afford to be remembered. He left the store and walked into the Footlocker next door. He stood there in mock interest of the window display, showing off a variety of very brightly colored tennis shoes, as he waited for them to exit Old Navy.

From the corner of his eye, he saw them come out. The woman pulled the child along with her by the hand. Based on the sullen look on the little girl's face, it appeared that she had not yet gotten over the dress.

The mother was carrying a bag, with the words Old Navy clearly printed on the side. Jack hoped this was a sign that she had gotten what she came looking for and would soon leave the mall. They wandered into the food court and got some ice cream. Jack wondered if this was the bribe the mother had offered the little girl in an effort to curb the rift between them. The thought made him recall a time when Faith had wanted something at a store and threw a bit of a tantrum. He too had succumbed to bribery to help her get past it. The memory made him feel warm inside. *Soon it would be perfect again.*

It was late afternoon by now, and the mother and daughter had visited several other stores and collected more bags. Jack continued to follow them throughout the mall, being sure to stay far enough away that they never noticed him. He had taken notice of the mall security cameras and avoided those as well. He wasn't really sure what he was going to do yet, but he knew that he should be careful just in case. Finally, the mother headed toward the mall exit. The little girl followed, occasionally becoming distracted by a sign, a toy, or another child.

Jack was pleased to see them head out the same exit that would place him near his car. He exited the doors and paid very close attention to where they were heading as he hurried to his SUV. He quickly placed his bags in the back, leaving the back door unlatched. He pulled out the pink dress the little girl had wanted so badly as an idea formed in his head. Once inside the car, he reached for the syringe from the bag behind his seat and stuffed it and a rag in his pocket. He quickly navigated his vehicle through the lot and made his way in the direction he had seen the woman heading.

Jack spotted them still walking to the back of the lot. The little girl was lagging behind, and the mother was focused on the vehicle. Jack looked at the rest of the parking lot, *empty*. He pulled up behind the little girl, and as he got close to her, he rolled the window down and showed her the dress. He depressed the syringe plunger into the rag. The mother arrived at her car and was busy putting the packages into the vehicle. The little girl saw the dress, and a huge smile crossed her face. Jack opened the door, and as the little girl came to him for the dress, he dragged her into the vehicle, covering her mouth with the Chloroform covered rag.

He softly closed the door and shoved the child onto the floorboard; before the mother turned around he drove down the row and headed out of the parking lot. He hadn't given the girl much of an application of the chemical, and she wouldn't be out long. He would have to find a place to take care of her, but first he needed to get far enough away.

He exited the mall and pulled out onto College Avenue and headed toward the highway. He got to Veteran's Parkway and heard a slight moaning coming from the back. He made a left at the light that headed him towards the airport, then pulled into the parking lot and remained far away from any other cars. Getting out and opening the passenger door, Jack leaned in and applied the still damp and chemical soaked rag over the girl's face for a second time. She squirmed slightly against the pressure, and he knew it was because the chemical was likely burning her throat and nostrils. He went around to the back to get the tarp and duct tape, so he could carefully cover and secure her after she had completely relaxed. A few moments later, with the girl properly stowed away for the travel back to Heyworth, he put the pink dress back in the bag then climbed into the driver's seat.

He needed to get out of town quickly. He was confident no one had seen him, including the mother. She had been far too busy with her packages to notice that her daughter was being taken away. But there was still no need to test fate. He knew the mother would spend a certain amount of time searching the parking area and then would go back inside the mall, thinking the little girl had somehow gone back in. When she didn't find her, it wouldn't take long before she panicked. Then police would be crawling all over the entire area. He wanted to be far away from here before that happened. There might even be an Amber Alert issued, and he wanted to be back safe in his home if and when that happened. He would watch it on the news to see if there was even the slightest indication that someone had seen anything that could even scarcely be tied to him.

The sun was starting to go down. Jack smiled; this was good. The sun set would totally slow the police down. He thought of Special Agent Maxine Nichols. She would never stop. *Would she?* Had she stopped looking for him? He made a mental note to run another search on Maxine to see if there were any new updates he needed to know. In the meantime, there was work to be done. As the sun made its final appearance for the day, Jack pulled into the driveway.

Unloading the small framed girl from the vehicle, he carried her into the house. Not bothering with the basement door and padlock, he just went straight through the front door and made his way down to the basement. She was still out of it, so he laid her down on the stainless steel table. Her hands and feet were secured. She was not going anywhere. He decided he could tie her down after unloading his shopping purchases.

Just as he finished stowing the tarp and duct tape back in the compartment, he saw headlights turn into the driveway. His eyes darted to the house. Too late, the door was still open. His mind quickly took steps through the house. He had closed the surgical room door and the basement door. The little girl was bound. Her mouth was covered, and she was still out. It was okay. He pushed the packages he was going to get from the vehicle back inside and closed the hatch. He couldn't be seen with women's and children's clothing. He shivered slightly in the night chill as he squinted against the lights pulling up next to him. Once his eyes adjusted, he saw it was Dale, his real estate agent.

The car pulled up next to him. The engine was killed, and Dale got out. "Hey, Doctor Taylor, I decided I should come out and check on you. They're calling for the first hard freeze tonight, might even get some snow. I thought you could use some help firing up the old furnace."

"Oh, I knew it was getting cold out but didn't realize it was going to drop that low." Jack pushed down his annoyance and displayed a big welcoming smile. In his mind he was picturing the layout of the basement. The furnace was back in the far corner of the extra room. He had planned on making a gym in that room, but so far he had not had the time. The rest of the basement was tidy. The freezer was the only thing that might be a worry. But he could explain that away easily enough. "I think I can probably figure out the pilot," he said hoping to dissuade Dale.

"Ah, it's no problem. I told you I would stop back by. I probably should have just done it the last time I was out here. These older homes can be a problem sometimes. Come on; let's go have a look at it." Dale was already heading to the front door.

Jack couldn't think of a way to discourage Dale, so he followed him into the house. "Okay, well I sure do appreciate this," he lied. "I'm sure it wasn't in the contract."

Dale laughed his hearty laugh. "Well, not directly no. But I like to be sure all of my clients are taken care of. Besides you are our town doctor. What kind of a guy would I be if I didn't take care of our local physician?"

"Alright, alright," Jack said as they stood in the doorway, his hands to his sides, fingers splayed, showing surrender.

"Well, okay then let's get that thing fired up, so you can sleep in a cozy house tonight." Dale headed toward the basement, obviously very familiar with the layout of the house.

Jack followed him, his adrenaline racing as he considered whether the little girl would be waking up. She wasn't secured to the table yet, and he worried she would make noise in that room.

"The furnace was updated a few years back. The tricky part is the placement of the whole unit. The way the ductwork was laid out prevented it from being a little easier to get to." Dale worked his full body down the stairs. At the bottom he continued straight ahead to the extra room and pushed open the door then flipped on the light.

Jack looked around the basement as he followed Dale. Nothing was out of order. He listened closely as he passed the surgical room. When he heard nothing he felt relieved.

"Smells like bleach down here. You been doin' some cleaning?" Dale asked.

"Oh, yeah, I scrubbed down the other room. It smelled a little musty. Call me crazy, but as a doctor I like that very sterile smell."

Dale chuckled and shook his head. He seemed to buy it.

Inside the room Dale removed the cover on the furnace and adjusted the knob to light and pumped the igniter button. He had to push his thick body into the small space between the wall and the furnace and, at a very odd angle. After a few tries, Jack heard the whoosh of air as the pilot ignited. He felt a whoosh of air from his own lungs, not realizing he'd been holding his breath wanting this to go quickly. "There we go," Dale said. "Got 'er."

"Well, I'm glad you came to do that. It might have taken me a while to figure it out. I'm sure I'll have no problems now that I have actually seen it being lit. I can't thank you enough." Jack smiled not feeling the sentiment of his words.

Dale replaced the cover and said, "Let's go up and make sure the thermostat is set properly. It's the programmable type. So you can set it for when you are gone during the day and have it set to kick on before you get home to warm the place up in advance."

They started to head up the stairs again with Dale leading the way. Jack could see him looking around and tried to hurry him along.

"Looks like you are pretty well set up here. That's a mighty big freezer you've got."

"Well, I have it for two reasons. One, I store medical supplies in there, and two; I bought a half a side of beef. Figured it was easier to do that then go out and shop once winter hits."

"Nothing better than fresh meat."

As Dale got near the top of the stairs, there was a slight bang from the surgery room. Jack intentionally tripped on the stair to cover the noise.

"Whoa, be careful. I'd hate for the doctor to be out of commission because he fell down the stairs.

"Yeah, I'd have a hard time explaining that one, wouldn't I?" Jack laughed as he continued up the stairs behind the realtor. He quickly closed the door behind them.

Several minutes later they had the thermostat programmed. "Can I make you a cup of coffee or tea to show my appreciation? It's the least I could do for all your help," Jack offered silently hoping Dale would say no.

"You know, coffee sounds wonderful. Have to make it quick though. The missus is at home waiting on me."

Jack made two cups of coffee in the Keurig and flipped on the TV, wanting the noise to soak up the silence in the house. Dale took a seat on the couch and within minutes the men were chatting as they sipped on their coffee. The TV flashed a breaking news announcement with an Amber Alert banner along the bottom. Dale and Jack stopped talking while the news reporter spoke about a child being taken just before dark from the parking lot of the College Hills Mall in Normal. He indicated that several people had been questioned, and they were waiting to talk with the estranged husband who was wanted for questioning. Jack struggled to not smile when the reporter said that part.

"These days people fightin' over their kids like that," Dale piped in. "I don't understand 'em. Just hope if he took her, he didn't hurt her."

Jack just nodded, not fully trusting himself to sound appropriately concerned.

"Well," Dale said setting his cup on the coaster in front of him, "I guess I need to get going. My wife will send out the posse if I don't get home pretty soon. I think you're all set now for winter, but call if you need anything." He stood to leave.

"I'll do just that. I really appreciate the house call tonight," Jack joked, walking Dale to the door.

"Talk to you soon, Doc." Dale waved as he headed out the door and into the night. Jack flipped on the porch light, illuminating the outside and aiding Dale in his effort to get to his car. With a final wave, Dale pulled away and disappeared down the drive.

Jack waited for a while before he headed out to get the shopping bags from the SUV. He needed to be sure Dale was long gone. Carrying them inside, he took everything but the bag containing the coat and gloves downstairs. At the bottom of the stairs, Jack walked over to the couch against the wall next to the freezer and laid the bags down. He opened the one containing the pink dress. He had an idea. Carrying the dress with him into the surgical room, he slowly swung open the door. The little girl was now awake and had wiggled her way off the table. That must have been the noise he heard when Dale was there. She had worked her way into the corner despite the hands and feet being taped together. She had obviously been working the tape on her mouth, as it was hanging lopsided from her lips. *Good thing Dale left*, Jack thought.

"Hi. I know you're scared, and I'm sorry for that. You really helped me out today. You see, I was struggling with picking out a dress for my daughter, but you helped me," Jack said holding up the pink dress. "You really wanted this dress, right?"

The little girl stared at the dress from across the room without ever moving or acknowledging her desire to have it.

"So, because you are being such a big help to me, I was wondering if you wanted to try this dress on?" Still holding the dress up, Jack waited. He laid the dress out on the steel table and approached the little girl. He picked up a scalpel off of the tray and leaned down as the girl recoiled from him. He cut the tape from her wrists and feet and then gently removed the tape the rest of the way from her mouth. "Put the dress on if you want to try it. I'll give you a few minutes." Jack walked back out of the room and closed the door.

After giving her a few minutes, he opened the door to check on the little girl. She stood in the middle of the room wearing the pink dress, but once again backed up against the wall, shrinking in his presence. Jack looked at her then realized she could not see herself in the dress. He walked out again and returned with a mirror that typically hung on the back of the guest bathroom door. He took it over and leaned it against the wall then stepped back allowing her access.

The girl shyly moved closer to the mirror while cautiously keeping an eye on Jack. She admired herself and forced back a smile. After a moment she began to feel a little safer and turned from side to side, admiring herself from different angles.

"You look very pretty," Jack said. "I'm sorry your mommy told you no when you asked for the dress."

At the mention of her mother, the little girl looked at Jack for the first time. "Can I go home now?"

"Not quite yet. There's still something I need from you." With the dress on Jack could fully see her legs. They were lean yet muscular in all the right ways. Yes, they were perfect. "Before I can let you go home, I just need a couple of things." Jack walked over to the small refrigerator and pulled out a small dark bottle. The little girl watched him warily as he took a syringe and injected the tip into the vial, extracting 5cc. "If you want to go home, you need to let me give you this shot." Jack watched her as she stood there with her eyes round, staring at the needle. "I know it's scary, but I promise you it will not hurt. I promised my wife that I wouldn't do anything to hurt you, and I never break promises to my wife."

The little girl stood staring at Jack with tears rolling down her cheeks as Jack inserted the needle into the vein in her right arm. She didn't even struggle. "You are a brave little girl, and now you can live like a princess forever. Your mommy would be so proud."

***

The little girl felt herself getting sleepy. Her eyes were becoming heavy. Fighting away the feeling, she could still see herself in the mirror. The man didn't look like he would be scary. His blue eyes seemed to smile at her. But he was scary. He brought her here and taped her hands and feet and put the icky tasting tape on her mouth. Suddenly she felt like she was flying. She could see the beautiful, sparkly pink dress flying through the air and something shiny, though she didn't know what it was. Then she was floating, and there was a castle and a white and purple unicorn. The castle doors opened, and the unicorn rode her inside and to a special room that was filled with stuffed animals and Barbie dolls. There was a beautiful bed with four big posts and a glittering white canopy. She was so tired now. The unicorn brought her next to the bed where she laid down in the soft fluffy blankets. Her eyes closed as she began dreaming of her life as a princess.

***

Jack went into the freezer and carefully inspected Faith. He needed to refresh himself on exactly where the legs had been removed. Completing his inspection he returned Faith into the arms of Hope, and then gently kissed each of them on the head before returning to the surgical room.

The little girl dropped fully into an unconsciousness state while Jack pulled on his scrubs. He carefully removed the dress and put it back on the hanger. He was pleased that he had given her a moment of happiness while ensuring that her parts were the appropriate match. The legs were truly perfect. Now that she was asleep, he could really inspect them. They were the perfect shape, tone, and color. He inspected the small narrow feet and tiny little toes. *Oh, yes, they are perfect.* Right down to the tiny little nails on the pinky toes. Just like Faith's.

Prepped and ready, Jack began the surgical removal of the legs. He made lines with a marker first, working to make sure that he removed these legs in the precise manner in which he removed the legs from Faith's body. He needed to make sure he could match them up so that he could attach them and make them look very natural. He worked meticulously again, completing the perfect transfemoral amputation on each of the legs. As he

351

completed the process, he washed and dried the legs and then carefully wrapped each with gauze at the point of where it had been severed.

He walked the legs over to the freezer and laid them inside on the shelf opposite Hope and Faith. He closed the door and headed back to the surgical room to clean up what was left of the child and the room. As he started washing down the girl, he realized that he had been so focused on the surgery the he hadn't even noticed the point when she had died. That didn't usually happen, but it happened twice now, and it made him wonder if bringing his family back could really help push the darkness away for good. He had been able to do it before, and it seemed the closer he got to having both Hope and Faith back home with him the less driven he was to succumb to his needs. He couldn't allow the idea that the incident at the hospital with the drunk driver had anything to do with the lack of interest in killing right at this moment. Because that would mean he would have to admit the darkness was not something he could consciously quell without a lot of opportunity in surgical settings to temper it.

Jack checked the time. It was twenty minutes until ten o'clock. He finished cleaning, including a bleach shower for himself, threw back on his clothes, and then bound up the stairs to catch the evening news. He needed to know what the status was at the mall.

Jack settled into the chair next to the front door, turned on and stared at the TV. The station was still set to the same channel that had run the report earlier when Dale was still there. The news was just starting. Jack turned up the volume and leaned forward. A couple of minutes into the newscast, the word "update" flashed across the bottom of the screen, and a picture in the top corner next to the reporter's head showed the parking lot at the mall.

"The scene at the College Hills Mall remains grim as police and DHS continue to investigate the report of a child who went missing earlier today from the mall parking lot. At around four thirty today in this parking space," the reporter indicated the space she was standing near. "Chelsea Simpson, 32, was returning to her vehicle after spending a few hours shopping inside the mall. As she placed her packages inside the back of the vehicle, she lost sight of her seven year old daughter, Ashley. When she turned around, Mrs. Simpson says her daughter was gone. Police are reviewing parking lot cameras and will investigate all vehicles seen in or around the area during this time, but so far they do not have any hard leads. Police are asking for you to call 309-423-7899 with any information."

Jack leaned back and relaxed. He had been watching so intently that he barely moved even to breathe. Getting up out of the chair, he turned the TV off and laid the remote on the coffee table. He walked down the hall to the office, turning on his computer. He waited until the wireless connected, then he logged on to Google and searched for Chelsea Simpson. After a few minutes he was able to find an address in Normal. He jotted it down then thought about timing. Things would be hot around this address for a while. Deciding he needed to wait at least a couple of days, he checked his patient schedule for the upcoming week and decided Tuesday night would be a good night. Assuming, of course, the news died down around the story. Before signing off he made a quick check for Special Agent Maxine Nichols. He spent a few minutes and did not find anything new that he did not already know. He took this as a good sign. Maxine was not up to anything that would indicate his family was at risk. After logging off he headed back to the basement to store the remains of the child.

Removing plastic from the shelf, he rolled out a long sheet on the basement floor then carried the body, less Faith's new legs, over and laid her gently on the plastic. Then he rolled the body tightly and secured it with duct tape on each end. He placed the bundle into a black lawn and leaf garbage bag and cinched it shut. Next he carried the bag to the freezer and placed it on the shelf next to the legs. Tomorrow he would continue the work on Faith. For now he needed to get some rest so that he was in good form.

Jack woke very early filled with excitement, as the reality of his accomplishment to bring his family back together set in. He prepared a quick, healthy breakfast and had a couple cups of coffee, then made his way to the basement to begin the important task of attaching the legs to Faith. On Christmas day they would dance again just like they had before. He remembered how Faith would place her feet on top of his, and they would dance around the living room in their California home as Hope watched on. Laughter had filled their home, and it would again soon. The memory made him smile and sparked an increased excitement in his heart.

Opening the freezer he carried the legs into the surgical room and laid them onto the shelf next to the stainless steel operating table. Next he unwound Hope's arms from around the torso of Faith, lifted her up and carried her into the room, laying her down on the table. He returned to the freezer and knelt next to Hope. "Honey, I had to take her away from you for just a while, but when she returns she will be more complete. We're getting so close, and soon we'll be able to behave as a total family again. I'll be back in a few hours to show you. Your beautiful girl is coming back to us a little at a time." With that he kissed Hope tenderly before closing the freezer and moving back into the surgical room to start his work.

He began by preparing the chemicals from the shelf. He would apply the same chemical procedure as he had on the cat that had been his final test animal, where he had finally perfected the process. He used the same process later on Hope. After years of experimentation, he successfully found a way to preserve a body in a very natural state while allowing it to be just pliable enough that he could enjoy spending time with his subject. It was through this process that he had been able to enjoy dinners and even short overnight stays with Hope over the past few months. Before he could spend quality time with his daughter, he must attach the legs to Faith's torso. He stood examining her. He had yet to find a perfect mouth, but that wouldn't stop him from performing the tanning, embalming and cryonic combination today.

He dressed in scrubs and completely washed for the procedure. With everything prepped and only the best of sutures ready, he began the laborious process of reattaching the legs. Using the skin flaps that he had left on the torso, he was able to stitch through and cover the majority of the seam, making the legs look as natural as possible. He attached every muscle, vein, and tissue, performing the surgery in the same manner as he would if he were reattaching a limb on an accident victim with the hope of restoring complete mobility. While all of this was not completely necessary, he would only perform the best work possible for his daughter. He worked methodically and focused for several hours until the procedure was complete on each leg. Then he stood back and admired his work. His eyes scanned over the whole body now, and he pumped the legs at the knees to ensure there was the mobility he desired. His mouth turned up at the corners and tears welled in his eyes as he saw his little girl lying on the table before him. Forcing himself to gain control, he returned his focus back to the rest of the process.

Jack worked at the exact formula, and as he worked he continued to test the balance between rigidity and a supple, natural feel. He had to get this right. Any errors would mean that Faith would not last, and he needed her to last for years to come. For a moment his mind wandered to Faith growing up and going off to college, marrying, having children of her own. At first the realization that this would never happen brought a heavy sorrow to his heart, but then he recognized that she would never leave him again. He would have both her and Hope forever! With these thoughts, joy overwhelmed him and without realizing it he wept. Tears streamed down his cheeks. He thought it was sweat and wished he had a surgical assistant to mop his brow, but for this intimate event he would be on his own. He lifted a towel from the tray and wiped his face, then returned his focus to completing the process.

A couple of hours had passed since Jack began the preservation process, and finally he had the look and feel he desired. Faith was now properly preserved, yet pliable. He would be able to move her so that she too could enjoy dinners at the table. He had missed those nights with Hope the past few weeks, but soon they would dine as a family. He smiled, warmth creeping over him.

Completing the process Jack spent the next few minutes washing the body using the least amount of water possible. He patted her completely dry, and then he washed and blow dried her hair.

With it all combed out and styled, he went to get one of the outfits he had bought at the mall while he was following the mother and daughter. He would save the pink dress for Christmas day. On that day both Faith and Hope would be dressed in the very best. It was only three weeks away now. He needed to decorate the house and get a tree with all the trimmings. Maybe Tuesday while he was in town, he thought.

He carefully dressed Faith in a little jogging outfit that had Hello Kitty on the jacket. Of course, it too was pink, as that was her favorite color. He wondered why it was so common for little girls to like that color so much. *Is it genetics or marketing that makes them love it so?* Deciding it really didn't matter, Jack shrugged to himself as he zipped up the jacket. Next, he put white socks on her small feet.

After she was completely dressed, he looked down at her and decided that even though he had work to do on her smile tonight, they could all have a family dinner. His heart sang at the thought of it. He would make her favorite macaroni and cheese, and this time there would be no crying or refusing to enjoy it. His Faith would love it the way she always had.

For now he needed to get her back into the freezer with Hope. He knew Hope would be missing her and would be excited to see how things had turned out. Faith had also been out of the cold for quite a while, and it was important to ensure she never got overheated. Jack lifted her up and stood her facing him, with her feet on top of his shoes and her head tilted back toward him, he stared into her eyes and realized he had his daughter back again. "Daddy is here, Faith, and I promise I will never let anything happen to you again. Not ever. All I need to do is find your smile, and then we can live happily ever after, just like in the stories."

Gliding her across the room to the freezer, Jack opened the door and was thrilled because he was certain Hope smiling at him as their daughter walked in to join her. "She's beautiful, right, Hope? I told you it was all going to be okay, and now we're all together again. If you can just give me a little more time, I'll find our daughter's beautiful smile, and then she will be perfect. Oh, and did I show you the dress I bought for her?" He laid Faith down again in Hope's embrace, and then he ran to retrieve the pink dress. "Look, Hope," he said when he returned, holding the dress up. "She'll look so beautiful. And don't worry; I got you something special too. But, you'll have to wait though. It's a surprise." Jack laughed at his own teasing. "Tonight we will have a special dinner for Faith coming home." At that moment Jack's cell phone rang. The sound shocked him out of his reverie, and for a moment he was annoyed. He realized though he had to keep his composure as he looked at the display and saw it was the hospital emergency number. He answered the phone, applying the appropriate amount of friendliness, "Dr. Taylor."

"Hello, Doctor. It's Julie at the hospital. I'm so glad you answered. Listen we have a young man that was brought in that just suffered a terrible farming accident. His leg has been mostly severed and we don't think we have time to transport him if we want to save it."

Jack listened intently, and after getting some more specifics on vitals and how long since the accident occurred, he agreed to be there as quickly as possible. Hanging up the phone, he turned back to his wife and child. "I have to go for now, duty calls, but tonight we will have some family time together." With that he bestowed a kiss on the cheeks of each then closed the door and pulled off his scrubs as he headed upstairs.

Within minutes he was dressed and sporting the new winter coat and gloves he had purchased. He stepped outside and was grateful for the warm clothing. It was clearly winter now, as was evidenced by a thick frost covering the ground despite the late morning sun shining brightly. He drove as fast as the slick roads and speed postings would allow and pulled into a spot at the hospital, taking long strides to get inside. Upon the doors swooshing open and the warm air hitting his face, he was immediately directed to the operating room. A few others were already prepped and waiting on him to scrub. An anesthesiologist was on duty and had already sedated the patient. Jack was able to go right to work.

The twenty year old had been caught in a plow, and his right leg had been partially severed. There was a lot of damage, but some of the tendons and nerves were still intact. Jack began reattaching the damaged limb, which had been appropriately packed with ice. The irony that Jack was called in to restore a leg did not go past him.

The surgery was long, and the prognosis for a full recovery was moderate. But there was a chance that this young man would walk on that leg again. With the procedure complete, Jack washed and then went out to speak to the family. He explained what he had done to try to repair the damage and was completely candid about the work that lay ahead. The road to recovery, if successful, would be a long one, but there was a chance. People always liked hearing that there was a chance. Jack assumed it was far better for them to hear there was a chance; which meant there was still hope. Jack smiled. *Yes, there was Hope.*

With his work done at the hospital, Jack decided that he would stop by the diner and get some lunch. It had been a long time - over six hours - since he had eaten breakfast, and he could definitely use some more coffee.

When Jack walked into the diner, a few people clapped. Jack was surprised by the reaction and did not know what to think. Then he realized the town was already a buzz about the young man's surgery. Small towns sure had a way of getting the word out. Jack smiled and nodded off the compliments and handshakes offered as he made his way to a booth. This was certainly turning out to be a great day.

Sarah approached him smiling with a pot of coffee in her hand. "That was some good work you did, Doc. The whole town is aware that you likely saved Sammy Blunier's leg."

"Thanks, Sarah, but there is a lot of work to do before we'll be able to declare victory, only time will tell whether the procedure worked. There's still a lot of risk."

"Well, if you hadn't come to Heyworth, there is no doubt he would have lost his leg for sure. I can't tell you how much we all appreciate you. Now, what can I get you to eat? I'm sure you worked yourself up an appetite."'

Jack smiled, amused at the comment. *You have no idea*, he thought. "I'd love some of that catfish I had a while back. Any luck getting me some of that?"

"You bet. Coming right up. Fries and coleslaw work for you?"

"That would be great."

After Sarah walked away, Jack took in the whole crowd. He was getting to know more people all the time, and he hoped he would be able to stay around here. But that would all depend on Maxine Nichols, he supposed.

As he glanced around the room, there were still a few appreciating nods sent his way, and then he noticed Sarah talking to little Jessie's mother who was sitting at the counter. The women were talking closely, and every once in a while, they would glance back over at him. He could only imagine what they were saying and had never really considered that anyone in town might consider him available. He wasn't sure, but he thought Jessie's parents were divorced or had never married. He only saw her name on the medical chart, and now that he thought of it, he realized she never wore a ring. Trying to remain closed to whatever womanly game they were up to, he focused on his cell phone, checking his upcoming appointments on his calendar. He could feel the women still occasionally looking at him, and he threw them a friendly yet uninviting smile. He looked around a bit and noticed Jessie was not with her mother, and for a brief moment he felt disappointed and then wondered what that was all about. Deciding it was only due to the fact that he had won over her fear, he continued looking at his cell phone until his food came.

The smell wafted up to him, and he suddenly realized just how hungry he was. Sarah poured him a refill and glanced back at Jessie's mother. They both grinned, and he knew for sure they were up to something. He would have to avoid or address it at some point, he was certain, but for now all he wanted to do was focus on his food, devouring every bite.

After he finished and Sarah had collected the empty plates, a man he did not recognize approached the table. He appeared to be older, though it was hard to tell through the weathered lines in his face, placed there from years of hard work in extreme conditions. He stood tall and muscular and wore a pair of thick, tan bib overalls. "I'd like to thank you," the man said through his pride.

Jack looked up and made eye contact, then stood to take the man's thick hand. "I don't believe we have met," Jack said.

"I'm Jed Blunier, and that boy you helped today is my grandson, Samuel."

"I see. He has a lot of work ahead of him, and you know there are no guarantees." Jack did not want to give false hope on just how difficult this could be. The slightest infection could put the leg at jeopardy, and that was assuming the nerves actually healed properly.

"He's a strong boy, and he'll work hard. You at least gave him a chance and I thank you for that."

"It's what I'm trained to do, sir."

With that the man nodded one last time then walked away. Sarah returned a couple of minutes after Jack had reseated himself. "Your tab is paid today, Doc."

"Really, who do I need to thank for that?"

"Oh, a little bird took care of it and asked I not say."

Jack nodded. "Well, I wish I could properly thank whoever it was."

"Just consider it from a thankful community and leave it at that."

"I guess I have no choice then," he said smiling. Before leaving Jack tossed a few dollars on the table for Sarah. Even though his lunch was covered, he still needed to take care of her. As he left he felt Jessie's mother watching him. He waved goodbye. Driving away from the diner, he wondered who had picked up the tab. *Was it Samuel's grandfather, or was it Jessie's mother? Or...someone else?* Deciding he might never know, he proceeded home, looking forward to an evening with his family. *Oh, that sounded so nice. My family. Yes, I have my family, again.*

Chapter Fifteen

Max spent the morning with Mark and returned home promising herself that she would straighten up the apartment today. Over the past few weeks she had been working long hours. And any time off with Mark was spent mostly at his house. She pushed a rogue lock of auburn hair behind her ear and looked around the apartment. The murder board on the wall didn't really help to make the place look less cluttered, but she could not take it down. Recently, she had added one more photo of a missing girl that might fit the criteria that Jack would likely be looking for, but so far there still was not a child from any of the cities that she considered the highest potential places for him to settle. She stared at the photos, and for a moment she questioned whether she was even on the right track. But her instincts told her that she was. It is just a matter of when. *Jack, how patient are you?*

As she considered that question, she wondered if he were more patient than she. Shaking her head she turned to assess the rest of the apartment and where to start with the cleanup. Heading to the bedroom to collect the clothes from the hamper so she could get her laundry started, she was startled by her cell phone ringing. Looking at the display, she didn't recognize the number. A quick assumption was that it was work related. She jumped immediately into her role as she answered, "Special Agent Nichols."

"Agent Nichols, my name is Daniel Zimmerman. I'm a Crime Scene Specialist in the state of Illinois. I saw your search notice on ViCAP, and well, we have a couple of cases that seemed like they just might fit your search."

"I'm listening," Max said. She immediately grabbed a pen and paper and started taking notes.

"We've had two girls that fit your criteria in the past few weeks. Normally, I would say they don't really match the same M.O.," he said, referring to the modius operandi, or the manner and method in which a crime is committed.

"I don't understand, if they don't match, why the call?"

"Well, it may just be instinct. Both girls are the right age range, hair coloring, all of that is a match. One girl had been snatched on her way home from school. She never made it home. Later that night she was dumped back along the route where she had been taken, basically the body was returned to the site where we believe she was abducted. The other girl…was taken also after school, right out of her driveway out in the country. We believe the perp followed her school bus because we know she made it that far." He paused for a minute as if gathering his thoughts.

"Then either late that night or early the next morning a bag was delivered out at the end of the driveway of the home. Special Agent, it contained the girl's legs."

Max's head reeled as she turned her attention back to the murder board in her living room and stared at the photo of Jack Tyler. "Was the rest of the body ever found?"

"No, it wasn't."

What was being described to Max did not fit what she thought Jack would do. Her mind worked to process the possible scenarios that would even remotely match Tyler to these girls. "Where did you say you're located?"

"I'm in Illinois. The girls were taken from two different counties, which is another inconsistency. McLean County and Woodford County, but Agent Nichols, there's more…the first girl, the way she was killed. She was cut down the torso, through the navel and basically had butterfly flaps in the skin mid torso. Someone had taken their time with her. I did a little reading on your Dr. Tyler case, and it is very consistent, including the precision of the wounds. The other girl… the legs were precisely removed, no hesitation marks and with a tremendous amount of skill. Skill I believe only someone from the medical industry would have."

Max almost felt lightheaded. This was it, no doubt. Only Jack Tyler, or a copycat, would do that. *But why would he take the girl back? Why would he take the legs back? Jack, what are you up to this time?* "Dan? Was the body or the legs cleaned?"

"Yes with bleach, thoroughly."

"Can I reach you back at this phone number?"

"Yes. Oh and Agent Nichols. There is another girl missing right now. She has been gone for almost forty-eight hours."

"I'll be in touch." Max hung up without even waiting for a response and immediately dialed Mark.

The phone rang three times, and she was afraid it was going to voicemail. Then she heard his voice. "Hey, I thought you were going to spend the day cleaning."

"Mark, he's at it again, three missing girls, two dead, in Illinois." Max was speaking in excited short sentences.

"Whoa, slow down Max, where?"

Max spent the next couple of minutes explaining to Mark what Dan Zimmerman had told her. "Mark, what do we do now? I have to be on this case and I know this is out of my pay rank being so new to the Bureau. But this is mine."

Mark nodded. "Max, I'll do what I can, standby." He disconnected the line, and she stood there staring at the line for a moment before she

362

began pacing back and forth across her living room. Each moment seemed like an hour. She walked over to the map, and it felt déjà vu. She had done the exact same thing last time. Last time… the time when Jack had gotten away. *Not this time, Jack. No way, you are not getting away with it again.*

After ten very long minutes Mark called back. "Okay, I've requested your reassignment. We'll have to wait for approval. In the meantime, I contacted the McLean County sheriff's department and shared our theory. They're reaching out to the CSI that you spoke with to get all of the details. I should hear something within the hour, and then we can leave."

Max listened to all of this and was nearly afraid to ask, "What are the chances that my assignment will be denied?"

"I think it's likely given your history with the subject that it will be approved. I explained that you're the only one that has ever made contact with Tyler. Max, assume you're leaving and pack while you are waiting."

"Okay." She hung up the phone and headed to her bedroom to prepare for a trip to Illinois, though there wasn't much to do. As an agent with the FBI, you pretty much were ready to go at any time. Your assignment could require you to travel at the drop of a hat. Agents typically had a bag ready to go and only had to add climate specific items. Max grabbed her FBI issued trench coat. It was lined and warm.

A while later her phone rang again. This time it was her unit boss. "Nichols, I understand that you wanted reassigned to a child abduction and murder case in Illinois. Unfortunately, we don't have the resources to allow that to happen at this time. Agent Wells will be assigned lead on that case but will be taking a different team from his unit."

Max's heart raced. "Sir, with all due respect, I'm very familiar with the subject in the case. I tracked him while I was with the LAPD and…" Before she could complete her sentence he interrupted her.

"I understand all of that; Agent, however our resources are limited, and we need to ensure our case loads are covered appropriately. You have done extensive work on the case you're on, and I need you ready as we are closing in on our guy."

Max was stunned. She could not believe what was happening right now, but knew protocol enough not to argue further and simply accepted the direction. "Yes sir."

"Thank you, Agent Nichols. I'll see you in the morning." The line went dead, and Max had to resist the urge to throw her phone. She immediately called Mark but was further frustrated when his voicemail picked up. For the first time since joining the FBI, Max regretted her decision. Tyler would be apprehended, and she would not be there to question him, see him face to face and have the opportunity to fully

363

understand the man. *Are you really a grieving husband and father? Or, are you just a sick, sadistic killer?*

An hour later Mark called, "I just heard. Max, I'm so sorry."

"I can't believe it, Mark. I *have* to be on this case!"

"I know how you feel, and I promise you if I have anything to do with this, we will catch Tyler this time. Max, I have to go. We're leaving in less than an hour."

"I know. Mark, please keep me in the loop. I have to know what's happening. Don't leave me for days without knowing."

"You have my word. I'll update you whenever there is a single break. I'll talk to you soon." With that he was gone. Gone to go chase the killer she should be chasing.

Unable to shake the frustration Max decided to go to the gym to spend some time beating a boxing bag around. She worked the bag until she could no longer lift her arms, then climbed onto a treadmill and ran for over an hour. Her mind kept returning to every possible scenario of capturing Jack Tyler. These visions included, finding him just as he was about to cut into yet another child, finding him inside a freezer with body parts all around him, and a final vision of her sitting across from him in an interrogation room, his boyhood good looks smiling at her as he explained why he had done the things he had done. It was the final vision that made her push on through her workout. This vision was the one she dreamed of every day since Tyler had flown off into the night on a plane bound to a non-extradition land.

Max ran faster, pushing herself to the maximum. Her heart rate pumped until the adrenaline finally began to settle and her frustration, which had turned to anger now, settled down into an ungrateful acceptance that she would not be able to enjoy any of the possible scenarios. Finally stopping the treadmill, she stepped off and made her way to the locker room where she showered and dressed in FBI issued sweats. As she was about to leave the locker room her phone rang. It was her boss again.

"Still want that assignment?"

Max was confused and thought she had heard wrong, "Sir?"

"Illinois? Still want it? Agent James had a family emergency and won't be able to travel. She has agreed to let you take her place on the plane. Still want it?"

Max wanted to say 'more than anything' but refrained from it, knowing it would not represent well. "Yes, sir, I certainly do."

"Can you be at the airstrip in 20 minutes?"

"I can, sir." The phone disconnected, and Max raced out of the gym and to her car. Her apartment was only five minutes away, and her bag was packed. All she needed was her service weapon and credentials. She drove as fast as the limits would allow her, collecting her travel items from her apartment, and then proceeded to the airstrip. She wasn't really sure how she had managed it, but she arrived in just over eighteen minutes. Mark was waiting for her beside the plane. He grabbed her duffle bag and boarded just ahead of her. They took their seats, and the door closed.

The next few minutes were spent introducing the members on the plane. Two of them were agents Max had met when she worked the case in Oklahoma when she was still a LAPD detective. Each of the agents nodded at her as she settled in. There was one other member that Max had not yet met. The man appeared to be in his early thirties. He was tall and lean with sandy brown hair. He introduced himself as Agent Fields.

The plane was in the air before the introductions were even completed, and Mark passed out case files. The next hour was spent covering the files in detail. Each member of the team provided his or her individual perspectives. Mark gave out the assignments, so they would be fully prepared when they hit the ground. Mark and Max would head to Le Roy to meet with the local authorities where the first body had been found. This body was the most like the cases Tyler was known for. The other agents would go to Woodford County and meet with the local authorities where the legs had been discovered. Each of the families had to be interviewed, and then there was still the issue of the current missing girl, that had been taken from the mall and had not been recovered. The police in Le Roy had agreed to allow the FBI to set up their investigation headquarters in the police station.

As they prepared for the landing, Max's mind covered all of the information they had so far. Photos of the body and legs had been sent over. Her stomach lurched at the idea of these little girls being cut apart, and her desire to capture Tyler grew with each photo and each detail. Mark looked at her over his own copy of the case file. Their eyes met for a moment, and she could see the relief in his eyes that she had been reassigned to this case. She hoped whatever the family matter was that had prevented Agent James from coming on this trip was not too terrible. Max made a mental note to contact her when she returned. Agent James had worked this case in Oklahoma as well and, most certainly, wanted to see Tyler brought to justice nearly as much as Max did. The rest of the flight was spent waiting in anticipation of what they would find once they landed.

Arriving at the Bloomington Airport, they were met with vehicles waiting on the tarmac. The missing girl, that was possibly still alive, had everyone's nerves jangling. Max knew that her chances to survive were slim. It had now been nearly two days since her disappearance, and she knew that if Jack's mission was to reassemble some grotesque, cobbled-together version of his dead daughter, he would not keep the girl long.

With Mark driving the vehicle, the two sped off in the direction of Le Roy while the others headed towards Eureka. They passed miles of wide open land, where just weeks earlier corn well over six feet would have danced in the breeze. The fields were now tilled under, showing the dark soil, clearly rich with nutrients topped with a light dusting of snow. There was a vast expanse as the view and the earth seemed to fall off of the horizon. A lot like Oklahoma, Max thought as she considered the similarities of Jack's choice. The soil was much darker here, but the open farm land displayed many similarities.

It was quiet as they drove. Finally, Max spoke, breaking the silence. "Any idea what the family emergency was with James?"

"Apparently, her mother is not doing well. She wanted to stay close just in case, and truth be told…I think she knew this one was your case."

"Well, I hope everything is okay, but I was about to go out of my mind."

Mark smiled, glancing over at her. "Really? I would never have known." He returned his eyes to the road as they entered the town of Le Roy.

The town was quaint. There were typical mid-western streets lined with unique homes dating back a hundred years or more, some with sweeping porches. Others had now been converted into apartments. There was a Dairy Queen, which made Max smile as she considered growing up in such a simple lifestyle. They pulled onto Main Street, which consisted of old brick buildings. Several were vacant. Some contained businesses, including a café, bar and quilting shop. Finding the police station, Mark pulled the car into a slot right in front of the steps leading to the front door. Max was out of the car before Mark could get his door opened.

Entering the building they were faced with old marble floors and a stout looking man sitting behind a desk about twenty-five feet inside. They each flashed their credentials, and Mark asked to see Sheriff Carter. The officer pulled his thick frame up off the stool he had been perched on and led them through the building towards the back. Entering a room on the left, he told them to settle in. The room contained a white board, a long rectangular table, and several chairs, but otherwise it was fairly institutional looking. Holding up his index finger, he indicated that he would be right back. He left them alone. They each set down their laptop bags and began setting up their investigation room. Mark began taping the photos onto the wall, including crime photos from Jack's earlier victims. He would use these to display the similarities in the cases. A moment later the officer returned, followed by a tall, lanky-looking younger man. The second man introduced himself as Sheriff Carter, shaking hands with both Mark and Max.

"I understand the FBI thinks we have a serial kidnapper, possibly serial killer on our hands." It was more of a question than a statement, but he continued without waiting for an answer. "I have to tell you, it would be a mighty big surprise for around these parts." His comments indicated to both Mark and Max that he had doubts, and those doubts might make it more difficult to work with him. Mark immediately went into the collaboration mode.

"With all due respect, Sheriff, if the recent dead children are in any way related to our subject, there is no doubt you have a serial on your hands. Our purpose is merely to help determine if that is the case or not, and if so, stop him before more innocent people are hurt. We appreciate you letting us join you in this search."

The sheriff looked at Wells, obviously assessing the genuine nature of his comments. Wells held eye contact until the sheriff nodded acceptance of the information. "Okay, let me get my team, and you can show us what makes you think our murdered girl is connected to your killer."

"Of course," Wells responded, nodding to Max to walk them through the series of photos that she now continued to hang on the board.

Once several other officers joined the room, Max began outlining everything that had happened with Jack Tyler. "Our subject is Dr. Jack Tyler," Max stated pointing at Tyler's photograph. "About a year and a half ago, his wife, Hope, and daughter, Faith," she said pointing at those two photos, "were killed in an accident by a drunk driver. Tyler fell apart. We later discovered that he had begun his killing with animals as a child. This was discovered by Hope, his childhood friend who helped him turn his desire into good by becoming a surgeon. They later married and had a child. He was a well-respected, highly skilled doctor in California. Tyler left the California area after his dump site was discovered. In that location we found the bodies of six people. Each was killed with a precision possessed by only someone with extensive training. The incisions are specific, and we believe this is what connects Tyler to your case. Tyler relocated to Oklahoma, where he continued to kill, but this time he changed his focus. He began killing woman, with the exception of a couple of men that got in his way. He was focused on putting together a replication of his wife, Hope. These women were pieced together. Tyler took various parts that most resembled Hope." Max pointed to the respective photos. "Eyes, torso, hands and feet, face." She stopped as she watched everyone's eyes move across the photos before she continued, "Tyler fled with the body. We believe he put the body in cold storage. He left the country for the Caymans and hit international air space about an hour before we caught up with him. We were unable to extradite him, but now we believe he returned to the USA under a new, unknown identity. We also believe he may be focused on finding his dead daughter, Faith. While he had never killed a child before, to our knowledge, he may not be satisfied with just having Hope. We believe he is trying to put the pieces of his life prior to the accident back together again." Max stopped and turned to Wells.

"Officers, if you look at the incisions on the body of the child you found, the wound is remarkably similar to that of the bodies of many of Tyler's other victims. As Agent Nichols described, there is a precision in Tyler's cuts that cannot be accomplished without training. This is his specific signature, and it's doubtful it could be mimicked to this precision by anyone other than Tyler." Wells paused.

Max picked back up the explanation, "The fact that in Woodford County there has been a recovery of legs from another female child matching the characteristics of Faith makes us believe that Jack may have abducted these children, and things did not go well. Later, he may have decided that the only way to bring back a perfect match to Faith will be through the same methods he used in restoring Hope." Max stopped again, having completed the theory they were operating within.

A tall, muscular, blonde haired, thirty-something, officer with a closely cropped beard spoke next. "Wouldn't the wife's body decompose to the point that he would be required to replace her?"

Wells answered, "This is an interesting aspect in the case. In Tyler's home in Oklahoma, there was trace evidence of three chemical components including the solvents used in embalming, formaldehyde, and methanol. Additionally, there were other chemicals known to be used in preservation efforts in cryonics, including liquid nitrogen and liquid oxygen. And then finally there was trace found for the chemical tannin, which is used in the process of tanning. Our analysis suggests that Dr. Tyler has come up with a chemical composition that will preserve a body in a more lifelike state, providing it's stored properly most of the time, in temperatures just above freezing. It's possible Tyler has come up with a solution that can last months or even years."

Max noticed a few eyebrows raised and heads shake. "Tyler is sophisticated, charming, and the loss of his family sent him back to the days of a boy killing animals in the woods. But his training has enabled him to create a replica of his wife, and now he may be working on the same for his daughter. Tyler is a narcissist, and he believes what he is doing is right."

Another officer in the back of the room asked the next question. "Is there any sexual attack or motivation?"

"No," Wells responded. "As a child Tyler took his time to explore the inside of his victims, in these cases animals that he could easily capture. It appeared that he had some fascination with the internal organs and their function. As a surgeon he was able to satisfy his needs and control his urges to kill, until the accident."

Max picked it back up again. "It was Hope who kept him grounded. In a childhood letter to him, she indicated that she had a plan and that together they could overcome his need. Their plan seemed to work as long as he could operate on people, allowing him to legally and respectfully explore his patients. When Hope died, his world crashed in, and in his despair and anger, he went on a killing spree. Then he came up with a plan to bring her back and gain control of his life again."

The tall, blonde officer spoke up again. "So, what are we looking for?"

Wells responded, "He may be in the medical profession again. He's been able to obtain a number of identities, and he blends in well. His charm wins over the hearts of the people with whom he surrounds himself. He will continue to kill until he has completed the task of putting his family back together. If he is unable to work in the medical profession, he will continue to kill because he has urges that he cannot control. He could be in this very community or a neighboring one. He'll drive a practical vehicle, a van or an SUV that will blend in easily but allows him the space to conceal his victims. He is confident and will easily stay one step ahead."

"Do we have any idea how closely he follows the investigation?" the sheriff asked.

"I have spoken with him once. As we tracked him through Arkansas, we found the package for a disposable phone. When I contacted him, he was quite confident that we would not catch him. Unfortunately, he was right. This tells me that he knows enough, and he won't be easy to catch." Max held eye contact with the sheriff until he looked away.

"We need to get moving," Wells added. "It's important that we see the location where the child was left, and we want to speak to the parents. The smallest detail could be important. And let's not forget, there is another missing girl." With that comment everyone began to dissipate.

The sheriff waited for the others to leave the room. "Let me give them their assignments. Then we'll head over to the drop site and the home

369

of the girl. The parents are a wreck. I think the father has been drinking since they got the news. I'm not sure he'll ever turn the corner. Poor guy blames himself for letting her walk home."

Neither Wells nor Max said anything. They had seen it before. A child goes missing, and the parents fall apart. They waited patiently as the sheriff gave instructions to his officers then followed the sheriff out into the daylight. Max quickly pulled her jacket tightly around her. The air was even cooler here than it seemed in Virginia. She had trained through the fall at Quantico, and winter had rolled in. Christmas was just days away now. The air here in Illinois was more severe, somehow piercingly cold.

"Supposed to snow tonight. We've gotten a few frosts and light dustings, but if it comes in as expected, it will be the first big one of the season. Expect we'll have a white Christmas. I sure hope that missing girl is some place warm and we find her safe long before the holiday." The sheriff looked up at the deceiving blue, clear sky. Max's gaze followed as she and Wells walked with him through the parking lot to begin the short trip across town and the painful conversations with the little girl's parents.

Chapter Sixteen

Over the past couple of days, Jack had purchased decorations for the house and had taken advantage of a day when the sun shined brightly, masking slightly the cold temperature, to put up lights on the eaves of the house. He kept a close eye on the news and had caught a glimpse of former Detective Maxine Nichols, now a Special Agent with the FBI. He understood now. She had gone to the Academy, and as a result she had been able to continue to track *him*! He watched the television closely, using the features of the DVR to replay the scene, pausing on her and her male associate.

He remembered her saying to him, "I'm here with Agent Mark Wells of the FBI. Dr. Tyler, it would be best if you surrendered." She had seemed so confident that day on the phone. It seemed so long ago. She was beautiful, and that confidence was displayed in the way she carried herself. *What does Mark Wells mean to you, Special Agent?* Jack tried to see if there was anything he could read in their behavior, but the view of them was too quick. They were walking into the home of the first girl, the girl who had deceived him and totally disrespected Hope. The mere thought of that little girl made anger rise in his chest. Forcing his thoughts to *his* little girl, he smiled, his little Faith, so perfect, so beautiful. Tears threatened to fall from the edges of his eyes. The love for her, for his family, overwhelmed him.

He'd had a long day at the office and then had been called into the hospital for a man who had suffered a heart attack. He'd successfully placed two stents, reopening the arteries and stabilizing the man. He came home tired yet feeling good. The surgery provided him with the opportunity to push back the darkness that had been taunting him ever since he removed the legs of the last little girl. He had been so tempted to do other things to her. He had wanted desperately to put his hands inside the body, even after it was dead. But he forced his feelings into check for two reasons: first and foremost, to keep his promise to Hope, and second, to stay focused on completing the work on Faith so the family, *his* family, would be whole again soon. He knew this was the only way to keep the darkness in control forever.

***

It had been two days since Jack had seen the federal agents going into the home of the dead girl. He felt confident that enough time had passed for him to deliver the body of the girl from the mall to her home.

371

He pulled on gloves and collected the black bag containing the partial remains and the girl's clothes from the freezer and headed out to the SUV, depositing the bag into the back of the vehicle. He walked around to the driver's door and shook off the chill that had quickly settled into his bones. He started the vehicle and turned on the defroster to clear the frost that had glazed the windshield. As a hint of warmth started to fill the inside, he headed down the driveway, making his way to Normal. As he drove through town toward the highway entrance, he saw the diner up ahead. His bones felt stiff and cold inside his body.

Suddenly, he pulled into one of the many open spaces in front of the building. It must be a slow night, likely because of the weather. He decided a hot cup of coffee would be nice for the drive. He climbed out of the vehicle, his shoe crunching a left over chunk of slush, now turned ice. Shaking off the wetness, he glanced in the back of the SUV before heading into the diner.

The chime announced his entrance. Sarah looked up from behind the counter. A big smile crossed over her face. "Well, look what the cat dragged in," she said, calling out her favorite greeting. What on earth are you doing out in this cold?" She glanced to the corner of the diner, causing Jack's eyes to follow.

In the last booth near the window, Jack saw Jessie and her mother tucked into the booth together. He recalled the mother's name from Jessie's medical chart as Tina. He noticed there were no other customers on either side of the room. The mother and daughter seemed to be playing a game or coloring. Tina looked up. A big smile spread across her face when she saw him looking her way. Jack waved at her then turned back to Sarah to order the coffee to go. Before he could get the order out, he felt arms loop around his legs, "Hi, Doctor Jack!"

Jack, surprised by the sudden contact, looked down and saw little Jessie clinging to his leg, looking up at him with a huge, crooked smile that was missing a tooth in the bottom front. "Well, hello, Jessie. How have you been?"

Letting go, she stood back. "I'm fine, Doctor Jack." Right then Tina walked up and handed her bill and some cash to Sarah. Jessie continued, "My mommy said she hoped we would see you again."

"Jessie!" Tina scolded, a blush quickly rising in her cheeks. "I'm sorry. She has a way of saying all the right things." Her eyes dropped away then shot to Sarah who let out a chuckle.

"Don't worry, Tina. Kids have a way of doing that. In fact, I am flattered." Jack said, placing his hand across his chest.

Sarah gave Tina her change and offered Jack his coffee, "On the house, Doc."

Jack took the cup and thanked her, then turned back to Jessie. "How is school going?" he said, leaning down to face level.

"It's okay. I don't like reading."

"Well, I bet you will one day, when you learn all the amazing places you can go when you're inside a story." He glanced at Tina and winked.

Jessie giggled. "You can't go inside a story." She laughed, and that crooked smile covered her face again.

"Sure you can. You can fly a plane, ride a horse, or drive a car, even though you're not old enough. You can even be a great mommy, just like your mommy. Inside stories you can be and do anything. It's like magic." He stopped, watching her face. "Will you make me a promise?"

"Okay," she answered with a little bit of uncertainty.

"Next time you're reading a story, try to pretend that you are the person in the story. Then *you* will be inside the story, and you can feel the magic. Deal?"

"You're funny, Doctor Jack." She giggled and hid behind her mother.

"Yeah, I am a little funny." He agreed with her and tapped her gently on the nose with his index finger.

Tina glanced at him and mouthed, "Thank you."

He winked then turned back to Sarah. "You sure I don't owe you anything for this?" He raised the Styrofoam coffee cup.

Sarah waved her hand at him and smiled. He thanked her again and turned to leave.

They said their good-byes to Sarah, and all three turned to leave at the same time. Jack held the door for Tina and Jessie, the cold air pushing in and causing him to shutter. Tina pulled her coat tightly around her and held Jessie's hand, thanking him for the gesture as she dug in her purse for her keys.

Jessie turned to him one last time, obviously not bothered by the cold air. "Doctor Jack? You should meet us to eat sometime. We have hotdogs and French fries, and they're *really* good."

"I'm sure they are fantastic, Jessie. Maybe we'll do that sometime." Jack could tell Tina was embarrassed and wishful all at once. He smiled at her, hoping he gave the appropriate influence to temper her discomfort without being overly encouraging. She returned the smile.

"Drive safe. These roads are still a bit of a mess," he said.

Tina nodded as she corralled Jessie into the car. Jack hoisted himself into the SUV, closing the door on the wind that seemed to cut right through. Glancing over to Tina's car, he waved. Tina waved back and Jessie pressed her nose against the window, offering that little toothless grin again.

Jack let Tina pull away first, then he backed out. He headed home. Somehow his plans had changed. He wouldn't be going to Normal tonight after all. Tonight the bag in the back of his vehicle would need to wait. *Tonight was not the right night*, he suddenly knew.

The mirror, mounted inside on the windshield, displayed a temperature outside of 20°F. Yes, it was truly cold outside. He guessed the wind chill had it close to zero. Ignoring the cold that had settled back into the vehicle, his mind worked through the plan that was forming in his mind.

As he drove he realized it was only a few days until Christmas, and he hoped for a white Christmas. Tomorrow he would pick out a tree and decorate inside the house. It would be beautiful and perfect for his family. He just had a little more work to do to complete the process of finding Faith and bringing her all the way home. He could not wait to see her smiling face once again.

The snow they had received two days prior had been cleared from the roads, and temperatures had risen above freezing the day he hung the lights, helping melt it off. Now, the headlights shone on the sides of the road, displaying the dirty snow, soiled from the plows and salt. Jack didn't like the appearance. It reminded him of the darkness, unlike the new fallen snow that was pure and clean. He peeled his eyes away and focused back on the road, paying close attention to the ice patches that remained, not yet having melted away. The drive back to the house was quiet. Jack didn't even turn on the radio, enjoying the peacefulness of nothing but the wheels churning along.

Pulling back up to the house, he balanced his coffee as he got out. The short trip had not afforded him a chance to even take a sip of the hot brew. Lifting the bag out of the back of the vehicle, while still balancing the hot coffee, he returned inside. He set the coffee on the table next to the door, then flipped on the light, and locked the door, feeling grateful for the warmth inside. He took the steps to the basement two at a time, crossed the floor, opened the freezer, and placed the bag inside on the shelf adjacent to Hope and Faith. For a moment he paused, admiring his nearly completed family. He realized that during the past few weeks he had not been able to spend as much time with Hope as he had before…before he started looking for Faith.

For a moment he felt sad, but then he relaxed because he knew that once he completed the plan, they could all be together every day. Right now Faith needed Hope. He leaned in and ever so tenderly embraced the two bodies, pulling their entwined, nearly frozen, bodies close to his chest. He held them, somewhat losing track of time, and without any realization that tears were rolling down his cheeks. Finally, he pulled away. "Hope, I'm close. I figured it all out today, and you'll be proud of me. I promise you. I will make you proud, and our daughter will be complete. Our family will be complete. By Christmas day everything will be as it used to be. As if we never lost any time. I love you so much. Both of you." He pushed back a lock of hair from Hope's face. Then he brushed his lips across the top of Faith's head, completely unaware of the gaping hole in her face where a mouth should be. Pulling away he gave one last glance at his family and closed the door as he walked out, locking the cold back inside.

He unconsciously shivered. Then he remembered the coffee and made his way back upstairs, retrieving the cup from the table, grateful it was still mildly hot. He sipped down the liquid, enjoying the warmth and rich flavor. He sat on the couch and clicked on the television. It was now almost ten o'clock. *Good, the news will be on soon.* He turned up the volume and waited.

***

The newscaster opened with a story on holiday shopping safety tips. Then there was a series of snippets of what was coming up. Jack leaned forward in his chair when he heard it would include an update from the FBI and a plea from the child's mother. Before they covered that story, they flashed a quick update on the coming weather and cut to commercial. Jack continued to sip on his coffee while he waited anxiously to see what the FBI would have to say. With his cup nearly empty, the commercials ended, and the newscasters, Edward Johnson and Jenny Klaus, reappeared on the screen. "After two days of searching for any clue into the disappearance of a seven year old girl from the College Hills Mall, local authorities and the FBI met today with reporters outside the scene of where the child was last seen, with a message from the child's mother." The camera broke away from Klaus and showed the live video scanning the crowd outside the mall. Jack leaned forward, his eyes fixed on the screen. A podium had been set up with two microphones.

Jack recognized the tall FBI agent Maxine had told him about. Yes, that was Mark Wells, and then there she was, standing behind him just to the left. Wells stepped up to the podium and spoke for a minute, but Jack heard nothing Wells was saying. His eyes never left the image of Maxine Nichols.

He watched her every move, her eyes scanning the crowd and the way she pushed the hair that blew across her forehead behind her ear. Then

375

suddenly she was moving towards the microphones, guiding another woman that Jack recognized as the mother he had followed through the mall. Only, the woman looked different now. Older somehow.

With Maxine holding the woman's arm, she stepped in front of the microphone and began her plea for the quick return of her daughter. She begged the crowd that had formed, as she stared directly into the camera and asked for her child to be returned before Christmas. "Please? Christmas is just a few days away. Bring my baby back home. Let her go." She broke into tears and Maxine led her back away from the cameras towards a car that waited in the background. Agent Wells thanked the crowd, and then the screen returned to the newscasters who expressed their remorse and immediately went into a breaking news story about an apartment fire near the college.

Jack leaned back in his seat and took the final drink from his cup. He stood, clicking off the television. "Don't worry, Agent Nichols. The little girl will be returned before Christmas," he said out loud as he headed to the bedroom. He needed rest. The next couple of days were going to be critical. He had a lot of work to do to get ready for Christmas.

Chapter Seventeen

Max led the woman away from the podium and to the car that waited to whisk her away from the reporters that shoved microphones in her direction while pushing at the police protection that held them back. She was reminded of vultures pushing to rip away at their prey. Those people cared nothing of the pain this poor woman, a mother wrought with grief, was going through. They cared only of their story, and it didn't even matter whether the child was found. Max wondered if they would actually like it even more if the child was delivered in a sheet like the girl in Le Roy, or maybe they would like it even better if she was in pieces like the one out in Eureka.

Inside the safety of the car, she offered the only comfort she could to the woman, warmth from the heater and the promise that they would not give up looking. They dropped the mother off at her home and helped her work her way through the crowd of reporters that had already gathered there, assuming she would return home after the press conference. Max hoped the plea was enough, but she knew Jack. And if Jack in fact had the little girl, she was likely already dead. *Why haven't you delivered her, Jack? Where is she, and what awful things are you doing to her?*

Back at the Le Roy police station, Wells asked for briefings on any new findings. "Agent Fields, where are we in Eureka?"

Fields leaned forward, his sandy hair falling across his forehead as he parsed through some papers. "We got some preliminary information from the coroner. Based on the decomposition of the legs, it appears the girl died between four and eight hours of being taken. The legs had been removed with perfect surgical execution that only a trained surgeon could have performed." He stopped for a moment, making sure Wells did not have any questions, then continued. "The CSI team said there was evidence of bleach on the bag, but they found no prints or residue that might indicate where we would find our un-sub. The bag is a known brand and sold at any grocery. The coroner confirmed the bleach on the legs. These all are consistent with the previous known offenses of Dr. Jack Tyler." He paused again. "The parents did not recall anyone or anything out of the ordinary in the weeks prior to the girl going missing. We talked to teachers and the bus driver. The teachers have not seen anyone around the school that stood out, nor had the child been behaving any differently. The bus driver said he thought there may have been a car following him, but he could not recall the make or model, couldn't even really say how long the car may have followed him or where it may have turned. That's all we have."

Wells nodded to the next agent, and he began his report. "There has been nothing found in the parking lot or surrounding areas that would help us understand which direction the subject may have taken the child. We just received all of the tapes for every angle in the mall parking lot and the stores. We have a lot of work to do to find the mother and child on those tapes, and to see if we can find anyone in particular following them. If we get lucky, we get a car and license plate. Unfortunately, they were parked far enough out in the lot that I'm not optimistic it will net anything." Concluding his report he paused and looked around the room at Agent Wells, Max, and the others.

Wells nodded at Max to begin her report. She looked around the room and pushed a lock of her auburn hair behind her ear. "The body in Le Roy also had been washed with bleach. The coroner has confirmed the incisions and damage to the internal organs are consistent with those of Tyler's prior victims. He compared the reports from the victims in both Los Angeles and Oklahoma, and the murder is consistent with two exceptions. The fact that this is a child and there was the use of an anesthesia. If Jack Tyler is involved in these murders, these two variables are new, and we don't know why he would evolve. We don't expect him to feel remorse, and we are not even certain he would be capable of it." Max stopped and turned back to Wells.

"There are enough consistencies in these murders to certainly consider Jack Tyler as a person of interest in these crimes. As for the disappearance of the other girl, we have nothing that tells us if these crimes are even related. We need to work quickly on the video tapes. Those may be our only chance of finding out whether there's a connection, but more importantly, returning the girl home unharmed. Please split the tapes up and begin going through them as quickly as possible." Wells turned away and faced the Sheriff.

Max realized that thus far the team had hit dead ends on the body of Cindy and the bag containing the severed legs. There was no trace evidence left behind and no way to know if the missing girl was associated with the dead bodies. *What are you doing with the rest of the body, Jack?* Max tried to shake off her thoughts. She knew she needed to remain objective, as it was the only way she would be useful and help the team in the recovery of the missing girl and the apprehension of whoever was killing these children. They had been here for two days already and had made no headway. Max grabbed a couple of the surveillance tapes that had been copied onto DVDs and popped one into the drive on her computer. She began the tiring yet important process of studying the grainy recording showing the cars pulling in and out of the parking lot at the mall.

The entire day and the next were spent studying the recordings. License plates were checked against the sexual predator database to exclude any known sex offenders. Even though the murdered child had not been sexually abused, there was a possibility that the missing girl had been taken by a predator and was not even related to the murdered girls at all.

The sheriff walked into the room, his long frame taking up the door way. "We've had another child abducted."

Everyone's eyes turned to him. The sheriff continued, "A male, eight years old, went missing this morning from the Eastland Mall. The case is very similar to the missing girl from the College Hills Mall abduction. The two malls are just a few miles apart," he said for the benefit of the FBI agents. "The boy was with his mother when he disappeared. He has not been seen since."

Max could not believe what she was hearing. *A boy? Jack would not need a boy. This could mean none of this is related.* Max made eye contact with Mark. She knew he was reading her mind. There is no way this fit.

Wells stood up, his eyes shifting away from Max. "Let's get units there now. We need to interview the mother and witnesses. Sheriff get a warrant for the surveillance videos both inside and outside the mall. Let's go."

Max was nearly frozen to the spot. Her mind was still reeling from the thought of a male child missing. *This was not Jack. No way.* Could it be a coincidence, or had she been wrong about this whole thing? In her gut she knew Jack had abducted and killed those two girls. She knew what he was doing. He was finding a way to fill the void of Faith. He was putting her back together. *But, this boy?* Pulling herself out of the chair, she grabbed her coat and followed the rest of the team already in motion.

The ride to Bloomington was mostly quiet. Max and Wells didn't speak. They were accompanied by Fields and Adams. Fields read off the notes the sheriff had provided. "The woman's name is Debbie Lindsey; the boy's name is Paul. The father and mother are divorced, and the father lives out of state in Indiana."

Max listened, but her mind was still processing what this meant. She was anxious to get to the location and speak to the mother.

Pulling into the mall parking lot, the area was already roped off with yellow crime tape. Reporters approached the car as it pulled up to the area. The foursome exited the vehicle, and Wells immediately said, "No comment," as soon as the questions started flying. Pushing their way through the crowd, the team approached the local police. "Where is the mother?" Wells asked.

The officer pointed to a woman who was sitting inside a police cruiser. The door was open and exhaust poured out of the tail pipe, making an ominous fog from the cold air. The woman was wrapped in a blanket, but was obviously shivering. The temperature had dipped into the twenties, and there was a light wind that bit through layers of clothing.

Wells immediately started giving instructions, "Fields, Adams, get with the crime team and see what they know. Any witnesses get their statements. We'll talk to the mother and find out what stores they visited. Then we'll need to interview the employees of those stores to see if anyone remembers anything. Once we get the surveillance tapes, we need to get on those right away. We have a good chance on this one. These first twenty-four hours are crucial."

Both Fields and Adams were in motion before he could complete his instructions, and Max immediately headed towards the woman in the blanket, slowing her pace as she neared the police cruiser. Wells followed. Max glanced back at him, and he nodded to her. They both knew the mother would respond better to another woman.

As Max approached, the woman looked up at her, a new tremor shuddering though her body. Max showed her badge and introduced herself, "Debbie, Mrs. Lindsey? I'm Special Agent Maxine Nichols. You can call me Max. This is Special Agent in Charge, Mark Wells." The woman looked at Max, glanced towards Wells then started to cry.

"I know this is difficult, but we need to ask you some questions."

The woman nodded.

"Can you tell me what time you realized your son, Paul, was missing?"

Debbie seemed to be thinking. "It was around five."

"And where exactly were you when you realized it?"

"We had just come out of Old Navy, and then he was gone."

Wells called Fields on his cell phone. "Old Navy, see if anyone saw anything." He clicked his phone shut and turned back to Max and the mother.

"....anyone following you, or anything out of the ordinary?"

"No. I never saw anyone. Paul let go of my hand for just a minute, and then he was gone." The woman took a deep, shuddering breath.

"I know this is hard, but was there anything specific Paul wanted to look at in the store or any stores Paul specifically wanted to go into that maybe you didn't get a chance to go to?" Max refrained from saying, "you wouldn't let him go into," knowing the choice of words could upset the woman.

Debbie thought for a few moments. "He wanted to get a pretzel."

"Okay, good. That gives us some place to look. Do you think it is possible he went to see if he could get a pretzel?"

"I don't know, maybe?"

Max noticed the woman failed to make eye contact with her throughout the interview. Thinking this was a bit strange Max knelt down so that she was eye level. "How long have you and Paul's father been divorced?"

Now the woman raised her head. She looked at Max briefly then looked away. "Why?"

"It could be important. When was the last time you heard from Paul's father?"

"Paul saw his father over fall break. Thanksgiving." Still the woman failed to make eye contact.

"Debbie, I know this is tough, but do you think Paul's father would try to take him?"

"He doesn't want to pay support, always blaming me for things. I don't know, maybe."

Max glanced back at Wells, he nodded for her to keep going with this line of questioning. "How can we contact your ex-husband? We need to reach him right away."

Debbie reached for her purse and pulled out her cell phone. She scrolled through the numbers and then showed the display to Max. Max handed the phone to Wells, who immediately dialed. The call went to voicemail. Wells left a number and message for the father to contact the FBI immediately. He shook his head at Max.

Max returned the phone to the mother and continued, "Is there any other way to reach him? We really need to rule him out."

The woman scrolled through the phone again and offered Max the phone number for her ex in-laws. "This is the number for his parents."

Fields suddenly walked up to Wells. "Sir," he said pulling Wells off to the side. Once they were out of earshot of the mother, Fields explained, "A witness at the Old Navy said the mother was kind of rough with the boy. She reported seeing the mother pushing him along. Said she thought the boy must be throwing a tantrum. Thought he seemed sullen and quiet. I thought you would want to know."

Wells had been secondary with the mother all this time, but with this new information, he stepped up. "Ma'am, was there any issue with Paul while you were shopping today?"

Surprised, Debbie looked up at him. "No! Why?"

"We need to know if you were having any issues with him. Maybe he was mad. Or, you were mad? Sometimes children misbehave in the store."

"No, he just wanted that pretzel. That's all."

While Wells asked the questions, Max dialed the number Debbie provided. A man answered the phone. "Good evening, sir. Is this Mr. Lindsey?" After confirmation she continued, "This is Special Agent Nichols with the FBI. I'm trying to locate your son Paul Lindsey."

"Paul? Why? What is this about?"

"Sir, I hate to be the one to inform you, but your grandson, Paul Jr., is missing. We need to talk to his father. Do you happen to know where he is or how we might reach him?"

"He told us he was going to be out of town, but I don't know where he was going. He travels with his job sometimes. He never really says where. Usually it's Chicago."

"Sir, if you have any way to reach your son, we need him to call us." Max gave the man a phone number and disconnected the call.

"Debbie, have you and your ex-husband had any issues lately?"

"When don't we have issues?" She shook her head.

"What kind of issues?"

"We fight over support, visitation, Paul's new girlfriend, you name it."

"More recently, has anything been especially challenging?"

"I told Paul I did not want Paul Jr. around that woman. I wasn't going to let him go there for Christmas."

"Okay, Debbie. Thank you. Do you have a recent photograph of Paul?"

Debbie dug through her purse once again. "This is the most recent. It's about two months old."

Max stepped away from the woman and joined Wells. "I think the dad may be involved. We have to find him and fast."

Wells flagged down the sheriff. "Can you get an APB out on the father and his vehicle? We need to find him." The all-points bulletin would ensure, wherever Paul's father was, they would pull him in. In the meantime, Wells took the photo over to the media and asked them to get it out as soon as possible for the missing boy, knowing that if anyone had seen him, the fastest way to recovery was through the media. Then he gave the photo to Fields to have copies made and get some to Agent Adams. He instructed Fields to use the photo to interview the pretzel shop employees and to canvas all the stores along the way.

***

Jack decided to have dinner in the basement near the freezer. He was missing time with Hope, but it was still too soon to take her from Faith. He knew Faith needed her mother right now, more than he needed Hope. But, he could be near. After a workout in the furnace room that he had set up with some free weights and boxing bag, he showered then made a healthy meal.

As he sat down in the chair to watch some TV and eat his dinner, he realized he was tired. It had been a long day followed by the workout. He was tired, yet he felt good. Things were working out perfectly. He sat back in his chair and took a sip of a Coke Zero. He loved the bubbly drink. It was one of his two vices. He enjoyed coffee too. He knew everything in moderation was okay and allowed himself these occasional indulgences.

He began flipping through the stations, hoping to find some updates on the investigation of the missing child. He stopped to take a bite. The local station was playing a talent show. Then suddenly there was breaking news. An Amber Alert flashed across the screen. Jack sat forward in his chair. *Oh, this should be good.*

To the right of the reporter on the screen, a photo of a young boy was displayed. His blonde hair swept to the side, and his blue eyes sparkled with mischief. The reporter continued to explain that the boy had gone missing from the Eastland Mall. Then a live report showed another reporter bundled up in a big coat, the wind blowing her hair across her face. Jack was no longer listening. The camera panned across the parking area just outside the mall entrance and stopped, showing a woman sitting in a car. It was obvious the woman was being interviewed. Jack quickly hit the pause on the DVR and leaned even closer. *Special Agent Maxine Nichols, there you are.* Jack stared at the frozen screen where Max kneeled, interviewing the woman in the car. *What is the mother telling you, Special Agent? That she lost her child too? That she failed to hold his hand tight enough?* Jack smiled, leaned back in his chair, and took another drink from the Coke Zero. *Now what, Special Agent Nichols?* Everything was working out perfectly. He couldn't be more pleased.

Chapter Eighteen

For several hours the police and FBI agents combed the entire mall for any witnesses or clues as to the boy's disappearance. Max felt certain that Jack was not involved in this particular abduction, and her instincts told her that the father and maybe even the mother were involved. She just hoped the boy was found safely, and soon, so they could get back to tracking Jack and the missing girl.

Wells had the facility management come in with blue prints of the mall, and even air ducts were searched. Every point in the mall was searched; they came up with nothing.

The mother was taken home, and orders were placed to add traces on her phones in case she received any phone calls. No one thought a ransom would be requested, but if Debbie was involved in any way, or if the father was and he tried to make contact, they could try to trace his call.

Now they were waiting. Max despised waiting more than nearly anything. Some of the team returned to Le Roy to continue looking through videos for the missing girl. Others set up camp in the mall, reviewing those videos. Wells set a rotation schedule for the agents to get some rest, as they had been going non-stop for nearly three days.

"Christmas is just a few days away. If we don't get some leads soon, I'm going to offer for the agents to go home." Wells told Max when they were standing alone.

Max glanced at him, and before he could say anything more, she jumped in. "Not me, Mark. I'm staying until we have something solid. If this boy is part of crimes perpetrated by one un-sub, then we will know it can't be Jack. He would have no reason to abduct a boy. It would have to be completely random." Max stopped at that thought. It would not be the first time Jack had killed randomly. Maybe that was what this little boy was all about.

"Okay, I'm pretty sure the others will want to be home. They all have families. Your sister will miss you. We were supposed to go visit."

"I know, but she also knows the deal. My job has always interfered with my family life. She will understand, and after we catch the un-sub, we can grab a weekend in California." Max smiled that flirtatious smile that she only offered him when they were alone or no one else was around.

Wells returned her smile. He admired the dedication to the case and job. "That's what I thought you would say."

With the local police and Fields covering the mall and the mother's home, they returned to the investigation headquarters back in Le Roy.

During the drive they discussed what they knew about the boy. Max outlined her suspicions with the husband, the fact that he had not yet called and no one seemed to know his whereabouts.

"I agree the disappearance of this boy does not tie to Tyler very well, but he has killed randomly, although never a child that we know of. When he killed in Oklahoma, it was with purpose, with the exception of his second victim, Gary. That was purely an opportunity kill. All of the killings in California were random, but none were children. We need to find both of these kids. If he has changed his MO, he could have killed one child during his search for Faith and then decided he liked the way it made him feel. That might be enough to make him do it again. If that's true, gender may not matter. We have to find these kids, and soon, if we hope to recover them alive." Wells squinted through the glare of the sun rising and flipped the visor down. The road curved, positioning the sun off to the side again, and he relaxed.

As they pulled into a space in front of the PD building in LeRoy, Max said, "I'm going to help with the focus on those tapes when we arrive. If these are related, and we can get a lead on the girl, we find the boy."

***

Nearly six hours later, Wells's phone rang. "Wells." He listened for a few moments and glanced at the team working through the documents, witness statements, and videos. "We are on our way." He hung up the phone. "We have the father. We don't know if he has the boy, but his car is at a farm house just outside of Bloomington." Wells was already pulling on his jacket. Max immediately followed suit, and they headed out the door with some of the others behind them. Wells drove as fast as the ice patches in the road would allow. He rattled off the address to Max, so she could navigate. The trip to the location took them about thirty minutes, and as they pulled onto the driveway that led up to a two story farmhouse with a big red barn off to the right, they assessed the situation. There were several local police cruisers on site already waiting for them in the drive. Wells navigated the car up to the front and parked.

Stepping out of the car, they approached an officer who was already heading towards them. Wells asked, "What do we know so far?"

Max was right behind Mark, as were several others. The officer in the driveway, a bald man that stood a good six foot four inches tall with shoulders nearly as broad as the barn in the distance, began his report. "We got notified by a neighbor that the father's car had been spotted here. This is a rental property that no one has lived in for a while. The property is owned by the man's grandparents. They still raise some dairy cows out here."

"Have you tried to make contact?"

"No, sir, we have not. We waited for you to arrive."

"Has there been any movement inside?"

"Nothing, it's been totally quiet."

Wells checked the time. It was nearly two o'clock. It would be unusual for anyone to be sleeping at this time of day.

The officer must have read his mind. "You would think he would be awake and should have seen us out here, especially if there's a child in there too."

"Do we know if there's a phone inside?"

"Nothing connected. Already checked that. Grandparents don't spend much time here anymore, and they weren't expecting their grandson here."

"Okay, thanks. Can we get a couple of people around the back? My team will go in."

Wells and the team headed up to the front of the house. Once they were in place across the corners of the porch and on either side of the door, Wells knocked loudly on the door. They waited. No answer. "Paul, we know you're in there, and we believe you have your son. We know you don't want to hurt him. We just need to see that he's alright. Come out and talk to us."

There wasn't any noise except the rustling of the leaves on the ground in the midday breeze. Wells pounded again. "Paul, we're coming in now. Don't do anything you might regret. We just want to talk with you." Waiting a few seconds and still no movement inside, Wells turned the knob. It was unlocked. He pushed the door in and pulled his gun from his holster. He slid inside with Max right behind him, the others following. Inside was a large foyer. The curtains were closed, making the house dark and somewhat difficult to see. Wells flipped on a switch he found in the entry way. Light cast across the room and displayed a spacious formal living room with a grand fireplace to the left. The room was clear.

Max moved to the right, which led into a dining room, and beyond that was a hallway that led to the kitchen. A set of curved stairs led to the second floor. With her Glock leading the way, she cleared the dining room, and then turned to the hallway. She pushed doors open as she cautiously moved from one room to the next.

The last room on the right was the master bedroom. There was a glow on the floor indicating a light was on inside. She turned the knob, staying to the side of the door as she nudged it inward. Pausing, she listened. Hearing nothing, she slid her body sideways through the door frame with her gun trained on the room, anticipating movement. She pushed on into the main part of the room and stood facing the bed where a male body lay with blood splattered on his chest and face. Seeing his dark hair, her pulse raced for a moment. *Could Paul be one of Jack's aliases?* That thought had never occurred to her until now.

Moving forward she could see his face and immediately realized the body was that of the photo they had been shown for identification purposes. It was the father of the missing boy. Checking his pulse, she confirmed he was dead. "Wells, in here," she called out. Her eyes scanned the room looking for the boy. Fear filled her. *Had he killed the child too? Was he a family annihilator?*

She checked the rest of the room, including the closet and bathroom. Nothing. *Where is the boy?* Lying next to the body on the bed was a note. She pulled gloves from her pocket and slid them on as Wells and the others entered the room. Lifting the note she was careful to not touch anything but the edges. She read it out loud. "I'm sorry. I didn't mean to do this, and I can't go to jail for kidnapping. Paul"

Dropping it into an evidence bag, Max handed it over to a Crime Scene Investigator that entered the room. "The boy isn't here. The note indicates that he took the child, but where is he?"

"Search the entire house. Look everywhere, closets, and crawl spaces; don't miss a spot. He may have hidden because he was scared. Call out to him as you go," Wells directed. Within minutes the house was filled with sounds of doors opening and people calling out to Paul Jr., as they meticulously looked for the boy. Thirty minutes later, after going through all of the rooms, including the basement, they had not found the child.

Max was getting worried that he had done something to the boy, when suddenly she thought of the barn outside. It was cold, but what if Paul had wanted to protect his son from witnessing his father's death? She raced through the house. Wells had seen that look before in Oklahoma when they were in Jack Tyler's house. He immediately followed her.

Max raced to the barn and slid open the big rolling door. The daylight flooded the hay covered barn floor. Birds in the rafters fluttered at the sudden commotion. "Paul?" Max called out as she made her way through the barn, looking in the milking stalls as she worked her way forward. She was just about to give up when she came to the last stall at the rear of the barn. She swung open the door and was surprised to see a sleepy boy sitting up and rubbing his eyes. "Hi, Paul," she said, recognizing the boy from the photo Debbie had given her. I'm Maxine. Your mommy asked me to come find you. Would you like to go home now?"

The boy stretched his arms over his head, shaking off the sleep as he nodded. He stood brushing the hay off his clothes. "Where's daddy?"

Max ignored the question. "Paul, what are you doing sleeping in the barn?"

The boy looked around, seeming confused. "I don't know."

Agent Wells and the others came into the barn and watched as Max gently coaxed the boy along. "Paul, what is the last thing you remember?"

He seemed to be thinking for a moment. "I was with my daddy. We drove for a while. He said we were going to go away for Christmas."

"Do you remember coming to this house?"

The boy shook his head.

"Okay, well let's go find your mommy. She's really missing you. Okay?"

He nodded his head again and took her hand as she led him back through the barn and outside.

An ambulance was arriving in the driveway, and the little boy looked scared at the sight of all the police cars. "Don't be scared. There were just a lot of people looking for you today. We thought you got lost at the mall."

Max walked the boy out to a patrol car. She had a brief chat with a female officer who would take the boy to the hospital to be examined and checked for drugs or any other signs of abuse. Max explained to Paul that the nice lady was going to take him to the hospital just to make sure he was alright, and his mommy would meet him there.

Wells looked at Max, "Great job."

Max sighed. "I'm so happy he's okay. I was starting to get really worried that either his father or Jack had done something to him. He's going to have a long road ahead trying to understand all of this."

"Yes, he will, but it's better than the other outcome. You said, 'or Jack'? You don't think the father killed himself?"

Max paused. "It looks that way, but could that be what Jack wants us to think?"

Wells nodded his head, understanding what Max was suggesting. "We'll need to interview the boy after he has been checked out medically. It's odd that he has no memory of how he got into the barn, plus, the fact that he's sleeping in the middle of the day."

Just then a news van pulled in the driveway. The reporter nearly jumped from the vehicle before it could park. "Special Agent, have you found one of the missing children?" The blonde in a tight, red dress and a mid-calf, trench coat asked, shoving a microphone forward.

"Yes, we have recovered the male child that went missing yesterday from the Eastland Mall," Wells answered.

"Does this mean the two mall cases are or are not related?"

"We do not have any reason to believe these cases are related at this time, but this is an active investigation."

"Has there been an arrest made in the case?"

"The boy is safe and is being reunited with his mother."

"Agent Wells, was the boy's father involved?"

"No comment." Wells began walking towards the house. Max followed.

The crime scene analysts were bagging and tagging evidence throughout the house. Wells approached the nearest analyst and asked who was in charge of the evidence collection. The young man directed him to another man in the master bedroom. The man was a CSI by the name of Robert Sythe. The master bedroom had several markers placed around the room. Sythe was kneeling over the body when Wells and Max entered the room.

"Robert Sythe?" Wells inquired as a way of interrupting the man without startling him. "Special Agent Wells, have you checked the hands for GSR?" Wells referred to gunshot residue that should be found on the father's hand if he in fact held and fired a gun.

"I swabbed and confirmed GSR," Sythe answered.

"I'd like to be sure that we have a handwriting comparison to ensure authenticity of the note," Max said.

Sythe stood and faced the pair. "Do we have reason to believe it would not be a match?"

Wells replied, "We need to be very thorough. There are other missing children. We want to be sure there is no doubt what happened here today."

Sythe nodded his understanding. "I'll confirm the GSR findings and do a preliminary handwriting assessment and have results for you in the morning."

"Please call us the minute you have results," Wells said, handing him a card. He thanked Sythe before heading out.

They worked their way back through the home and went outside, then pushed through the reporters to the car.

Once inside the car, Wells navigated through the media and other police cars. There would be a lot of evidence collected by the local police and crime scene analysts, but for Mark and Max, the most important aspects would be whether Paul Sr. fired the gun, if the boy had been drugged, and if the handwriting on the note was a match. An absolute confirmation that the father had in fact committed suicide was critical to understanding whether Jack was involved.

Wells headed the car towards St. Joseph's Hospital where the female officer had taken the boy. They needed to interview him more thoroughly. Although Max was not confident that he would know any more about how he ended up in the barn.

They arrived at the hospital and found the boy in a room in the children's ward. His mother had already arrived and was sitting next to him on his bed. There were others there too. Max assumed the older couple were grandparents. On the way to the hospital, Mark and Max had agreed that Max would take the lead on the interview with the little boy. She had built a rapport with him in the barn, and Wells felt confident that he would open up to her the most.

Entering the hospital room, Max greeted Paul. "Hi Paul, remember me, Maxine?"

Paul nodded and smiled. "You found me in the barn."

"That's right. Do you think it would be okay if I talked to you for a few minutes?" Max looked at Paul's mother seeking approval first.

Paul nodded again. Debbie moved over to allow Max to get a little closer to the boy's bed.

"Are you feeling okay?"

"Yeah, I think so."

"At the barn you told me you remember riding in the car. Now that you're awake, do you remember anything else about how you got out in the barn today?"

Paul shook his head.

"That's okay. When you were in the car, can you remember if it was daylight or dark outside?"

"It was dark."

"Can you tell me one more thing? Do you remember if there was anyone else in the car with you?"

Paul shook his head. "No, just me and Daddy."

"Okay, thank you, Paul." Max looked at Wells. He shook his head, acknowledging there was nothing the boy was going to remember.

"Paul, would it be okay if I talked to your mommy for just a minute?"

"Can I watch cartoons?"

"Well, that is up to your mommy, but I bet she'll let you."

"Sure, honey. I'll be right back," Debbie said, leaning forward to kiss the small boy on the head.

Max waved good-bye to Paul and followed Debbie into the hospital corridor. Once outside, Wells took over. "Debbie, we need to know if Paul was drugged in anyway, and we're seeking your permission to have the results of his examination disclosed to us."

Debbie looked a little concerned but responded, "Sure." She walked over to the desk at the nurse's station. The nurse looked up and Wells flashed his badge to her. "With the mother's permission, we need to see the results of the tox screen on the boy in room 201,"Wells said, referencing the room number on the wall outside Paul's room.

The nurse called for the attending physician. After a couple of minutes, a young woman appeared wearing a white doctor's jacket. "Hello, I'm Doctor Rice."

"Special Agents Wells and Nichols, we're following up on the report that the child might have been drugged. We need to know if that is true, and if so, what drug was used."

Doctor Rice nodded. "The patient was sedated with a high level dose of Benadryl. He had four times the normal dosage. For that reason we're keeping him overnight just to make sure it passes out of his system with no issues. He does seem to be doing well."

"Were there any other drugs or any other signs of abuses, physical or sexual?"

At that question Debbie's head popped up. "Paul was crazy, but he would never do ...that to his son."

Wells regarded her closely, "We have to ask, Ma'am. I know it's difficult."

Doctor Rice jumped in, "There were no signs of any physical abuses at all. The child is just fine in every other way."

"Thank you, Doctor."

With that Doctor Rice walked away and Wells turned back to Debbie, but before he could speak Max jumped in. "Debbie," Max laid her hand on Debbie's arm, "Go take care of your son. We're done here."

Debbie looked up at Max then over at Wells and nodded. "Thank you."

Mark and Max walked away from the boy's room and returned to the parking lot, working their way through the snow to the vehicle. The car had already cooled back down, by the time they climbed back in, forcing Wells to crank up the heater, in an effort to hurry and take the chill out of the car. "It doesn't appear Jack is involved in this case. We'll know for sure in the morning when we get the GSR final results and the handwriting analysis."

Max agreed with Mark and settled in her seat as they headed back to Le Roy. They both needed some rest, and they needed to get back working the other leads on the case. They had lost nearly two full days working the case on the missing boy, and while they were happy the boy had been found safely, they also knew the chance of the missing girl being found alive was unlikely.

Rest would have to come first in order for the two to continue working effectively. They headed to the Holiday Inn in Le Roy. They checked in several days ago but had barely been there. Only Fields and Adams had taken turns resting.

As they pulled into the parking lot, Mark asked, "Stay with me tonight?"

Max looked at his face. His eyes showed exhaustion and desire. She knew how good it would feel to roll up in his arms, but the risk was too great. "Mark, I would love that, but you know we can't. You're the Special Agent in Charge, and our relationship cannot compromise this investigation." She could see the disappointment in his eyes, but he nodded.

"I know. I just…"

Max took his hand. "Let's find the girl, find Jack, and get home, so we can cuddle in our own bed."

Mark smiled, leaned in, and kissed her gently, "Deal."

They exited the vehicle with large, fluffy snowflakes landing on their jackets and quickly coating the ground. They made their way across the white, slippery parking lot, inside and headed to their respective rooms after wishing each other a good night's sleep and agreeing to meet at six o'clock.

Max entered her room and removed her coat, draping it over the chair at the desk. Kicking off her shoes, she regretted her decision to not spend the night with Mark, even though she knew it was right. After freshening up in the bathroom, she pulled off her clothes and settled into an oversized FBI t-shirt and a pair of boxer shorts. She dropped into bed, set the alarm on her cell phone, and laid there. Her mind replayed the past few days. As much as she wanted to fall immediately to sleep, she could not help thinking that she missed something. Walking through every moment since the airplane landed in Illinois, Max knew she was overlooking something. With the nagging feeling pulling at her, exhaustion dragged her into a deep sleep.

Chapter Nineteen

Jack spent the past couple of days getting things ready for Christmas day. The special holiday was now only two days away. He had the house completely decorated. There was garland and lights. He had even gotten a train to run around the base of the tree. He had a few patients scheduled for the morning, and then the practice was going to be closed until after the holiday.

There was more to do. He still needed to finish the work on Faith. He had been hoping circumstances would align perfectly to the plan, but he was beginning to worry. Time was close. He might have to change his plans if things did not naturally line up. Suddenly, he had an idea.

***

After spending the morning helping patients through a variety of common cold symptoms, irritable bowel syndrome, and high blood pressure, Jack closed the office after wishing Mary a happy holiday. But before leaving he gave her a five hundred dollar bonus. The gesture caused her to give him a huge, spontaneous hug. She left saying she would be going to the mall. It was going to be the best Christmas ever. Jack smiled. Helping her made him happy and he felt light hearted. Locking up, he turned and made his way across the snow covered street to the diner. He hoped his good deed with Mary would provide him with the kind of karma he needed.

Jack pulled open the diner door, stomped the snow off his shoes and stepped inside to the warmth. True to form he was greeted by Sarah in the usual manner. "Well, look what the cat dragged in. Doc, what are you doing out in this weather?"

"Just closed up, Sarah, I thought I would get some lunch before heading home." Jack looked around the diner, and his heart jumped just slightly as he saw a group of people to the left of the diner door. At that table sat Tina and Jessie. This was better than he had thought it would be.

Jessie jumped up from the table and ran over to Jack, throwing her arms around his waist. "Dr. Jack!"

"Well, hello, Jessie. How are you doing?" Jack asked, returning the hug.

"I'm good. We're having lunch with my grandpa and grandma."

"I see. That sounds like a lot of fun."

"Come on. Eat with us." Jessie pulled on his hand, leading him toward the table where her mother and the others sat.

Jack felt awkward, as he felt himself being dragged to the table. "Jessie, your family is enjoying their time together," he stated, trying to disconnect himself from the little girl's offer.

Tina, Jessie's mother, spoke, "Please join us. We just ordered, and there's plenty of room." She waved her hand at the two tables that had been pushed together and the extra chair that sat at one end.

"Come on, son, grab the chair." The man with a full head of white hair said. His deep voice had an air of authority that seemed to resonate through the diner.

"Thank you, sir," Jack said, accepting the offer when he realized there was no getting out of this. "I'm Jackson Taylor."

Tina jumped in again. "Doctor Taylor. He's being modest."

"Doctor, well, son. We heard you made Jessie feel a whole lot better. No need to be modest here. You should be proud of your accomplishments."

Tina completed the introductions, and Sarah came over with a pot of coffee. She took Jack's order. Jessie insisted on sitting next to Jack. He looked at the little girl; her crooked little smile capturing his eye. The conversation at the table was comfortable. Jessie asked him to draw with her, and he spent a few minutes drawing pictures of Santa Claus until the food came. Jack was enjoying the time, being part of the family. He knew he would soon have this all back. Excitement rose in his chest.

The group finished their meals and rose to leave. Jessie was vowing to build a snowman when she got home. Jack enjoyed listening to Jessie tell how she was going to make the snowman and which items she would use for the nose and eyes.

After settling the bill, they waved their good-bye to Sarah and headed out into the cold. Jack helped Tina's mother into the car and gave Jessie another hug and then stomped through the snow to his SUV across the street.

Getting into the vehicle he waited, watching the family load into the cars. Tina and Jessie got into a different car than Tina's parents. Jack watched the older couple drive away. Then Tina backed out and waved at him as she passed. He waited a little bit longer then pulled out heading the same way Tina had gone.

He followed he made sure he stayed far enough back that he would not be noticed. He couldn't help but think about that beautiful, crooked little smile, Faith's smile. He was not sure how he hadn't noticed it sooner. But when she wrapped her arms around him that night a week or so ago at the diner and gazed up at him, he had known. It was right then that he had decided not to take the other girl's body home. Instead, he realized there was more to do, and little Jessie played a big part in it.

He watched as the car pulled nearly out of sight as he kept plenty of distance between him and the car in front of him. The snow crunched under his wheels as he made the turns, mimicking what Tina's car had done. He saw the car turn onto a street. He was pretty sure was a cul-de-sac. He lay back, keeping the car out of sight, and then slowly made his way to the street, peering down to see if he was right. He saw the car pulling into a driveway. It was the last house on the left, but there was a cross street at the end, not a cul-de-sac after all. He saw that the house next door had a For Sale sign in the yard. He drove on by, thinking about his options.

Deciding to pull around to the next block to see what it looked like and what access was like from there, he followed the street around. On the back side of the road there was an open lot with no home built yet. The street backed along the side of Tina and Jessie's yard. Jack was able to pull his vehicle along that street and have good visibility to the yard. There was no fencing and he was certain Jessie would come out soon to play in the snow if she was going to do so today. She had seemed pretty excited about making a snowman. He hoped she did just that. While he waited he contemplated just how he would get her to come with him. He just needed to get her in the car. Once she was there, he had everything he needed.

He watched the yard closely, his eyes barely moving or blinking as he waited. Then there was a sign of movement. The door opened, and both Tina and Jessie stood in the doorway. Tina waved as a bundled up Jessie leapt from the porch into the snow covered yard. She stomped around for a while then moved closer to the side yard where she began the process of trying to roll snow into balls big enough to erect into a snowman like creature. She was struggling and ended up with a lot of little snowballs, none worthy of being the snowman's body. Jack decided it was time. Knowing little children she would not take long before she gave up or became too cold to stay out any longer. He saw Tina peek at her a few minutes after she came out, and he hoped she would not look for her again for a few more minutes.

He climbed out and made his way through the snow over to where she was playing. "Hi, Jessie," he said quietly enough that he could not be heard inside the house. He definitely did not want Tina to hear them talking. That would ruin everything.

"Hi, Doctor Jack," she said, throwing him that perfect crooked little grin. "What are you doing here? Did you come to help me build my snowman?"

Perfect, Jack thought. "Well, I was about to go home when I thought you might need some help. Would you like to come with me while

I go get my little girl, Faith? She can help you. She's really good at building snowmen."

"You have a little girl?"

"I do. We could go get her and come back, and you two can play."

"Okay, but I should tell my mommy."

"Oh, I already did. I called her first. She said it was just fine. Come on. Let's hurry so we can get back soon. We don't want it to get dark, before we can get back."

"Okay," Jessie said running up and taking his hand.

Jack smiled, taking her hand and leading her to the SUV. He helped her into the backseat and buckled her seatbelt, then went around and got in.

"You know I'm supposed to ride in a car seat, right?"

"Yes, I know, but I promise to be very careful and drive super safe." He smiled at her in the rearview mirror. Again, she offered him that crooked little grin. His heart jumped.

The snow was coming down hard now. Jack was pleased, as he knew this was going to cover the tracks he and Jessie made when they walked across the yard. Very soon it would be hard for anyone to know which direction Jessie had gone.

Jessie talked to him all the way to his house. As she talked his mind was considering what he must do once they got to the house. He needed to get her inside right away. Tina would know she was missing very soon, and he needed to be at his house when that happened. He anticipated a search party would be called. He would need to participate in order to not raise suspicion. But he knew this was a good thing because he could even possibly help turn the search in another direction. Plus, he would know if they brought in the FBI.

Things were going to move very quickly now. He needed to hurry. After they pulled into the driveway, he helped Jessie out and walked her into the house. She, of course, immediately asked where his little girl was. He told her to wait just a minute while he got her. But, he first wanted to make them each a cup of hot chocolate, so they would be really warm once they started to make the snowman. Jessie smiled at the idea.

Jack popped two cups of hot water in the microwave. Then he asked her to sit down, and he told her he would be right back. He went to the basement, looking back to make sure she was not following him. He returned a few moments later with a sedative in his pocket. He dropped the pill into one of the cups, and he finished making the hot chocolate then he placed the hot drink in front of her as he talked. "Faith was taking a little nap. She is getting her snow suit on and will be up in just a minute. You two will get along perfectly. You remind me of her, you know."

"I do?" The little girl smiled as she licked marshmallow from her sticky fingers.

"Yes, you do. You have the same funny little smile." Before Jack could finish his sentence, Jessie was starting to fall asleep at the table. She had finished about half the cup of hot chocolate, which had been enough to knock her out. He lifted her small body and carried her down the stairs and into the surgical room, laying her gently onto the stainless steel table. He removed his coat.

He knew he did not have much time, so he went to work quickly. Pulling on his scrubs and gloves, he hooked Jessie up to an IV, providing her with antibiotics and a general anesthesia that would not react badly to the sedative she had already been given. This would be different. There was no need to kill Jessie, and he would not take pleasure in feeling inside this little girl. In some way he cared for her. He just needed Faith's mouth...

Starting right away, he slipped her out of her jacket and gloves, then lifted the #5 scalpel and made an incision around her mouth, removing the lips, tissue, and flesh that covered her teeth. He retrieved a jar from the shelf and filled it with formaldehyde and saline to store it until he had Faith ready. With the mouth safely stored, he went to the freezer and removed the two jars containing the mouths that he had removed from the other girls.

Holding the jars up to the light, he studied each mouth, choosing the one he felt would most appropriately fit. Making his final selection, he laid the mouth out over the opening he had created and began stitching that mouth in place onto Jessie's face. He intentionally did not use the best sutures and did a fairly poor job. It pained him to not do his best work, but he was counting on being able to correct that all later.

He took the remaining mouth from the second jar and placed it into a baggie, and then carried it over to the freezer. Inside he pulled back the cinch on the garbage bag that contained the body parts of the girl from the mall and dropped the lips inside. Pulling the drawstrings tight again, he closed the door and returned to the surgical room. He poured the solution from the jars down the drain rinsed them, replaced the lids and then set the jars back on the shelf.

He was just finishing up when his phone rang. He knew what that call would be. He ripped his gloves from his hands, dropped them into the trash as he reached into his pocket, and pulled out his cell phone. "Dr. Taylor," he said into the small speaker on his phone.

"Doc, it's Sarah up at the diner. Listen, Tina's daughter Jessie has gone missing. Some of us are getting together to help search. She can't have gone far, but with the snow and all. It's very cold out there and..."

Jack could hear the fear and concern in her voice. "Sarah, say no more. Where is everyone meeting?"

"Here at the diner. Will you join us?"

"Of course, give me just a few minutes. I'll be there." Jack hung up.

Okay, show time. Jack shoved the phone back in his jacket, removed the IV from her arm, and wrapped her back into her coat and gloves. The wound around her mouth looked bad, but he knew he could do so much better. And he would, but he must hurry. He zipped her coat to her chin, removed his scrubs, and carefully washed up. Then he pulled on his coat and lifted her from the table to carry her up the stairs. Before heading outside he pulled back the curtain, looking to ensure no one had approached. Seeing the drive empty, he grabbed his gloves from the table where he had tossed them when he came in and took her out to the vehicle. He laid her down in the back and covered her with the tarp.

He got behind the wheel and made his way through the snow, which was much deeper now than it had been when he came home just a little over an hour ago. Starting the vehicle he headed out of the driveway, his tires making long tracks in the snow behind him. He worked his way into town, watching closely for any police or even possibly FBI. If Special Agent Maxine Nichols came to town he would have to go quickly. He was almost ready if that was required, just final details now.

He made his way past the diner on an adjacent street, looking to see how much activity was there. The local police cars were out front. It looked like everyone was still gathering. *Just as I thought you would.* Jack smiled. He continued on and made his way to the hospital. He realized earlier that he would not be able to return Jessie to her home. He certainly wished he could, but he had an even better idea.

Approaching the hospital, he worked his way around towards the emergency entrance. No one was near the door way. The small hospital did not have any security cameras. He had paid special attention to this a long time ago. He pulled up right where the ambulances would enter. He knew the desk was set in behind the double sets of doors and he could be here for a few moments without being seen. He opened the door, got out without closing it, pulled open the back, and lifted Jessie out. He carried her bundled body over near the door, propped her up against the wall, and walked back to the SUV. He got in and drove away.

He watched his mirror. No one had seen him come or go from the hospital. Now he made his way around the streets so that he would come up on the diner from the direction of his home. He pulled into one of the parking spaces and waited just a few moments, assessing the people inside the diner through the window. Everyone inside was local. Jack sighed and opened his door to go inside and join the search party.

When he entered he was greeted by handshakes and nods. He assumed this meant he was part of the local team now. He liked that idea but knew it was likely short lived. He knew Special Agent Maxine Nichols would not let him stay here. She was close, he could feel her. As he joined the room, the sheriff was talking.

"We'll divide up into teams, working our way across town, knocking on doors and pushing through the snow. Tina says Jessie was not out there all that long. But with the snow now, she may have gotten cold, maybe got turned around and then out of fear sat or laid down somewhere. The snow would have covered her quickly, and we need to find her." He began dividing the teams up, gave a description of the snow jacket and pants she was wearing, and then started moving everyone out of the diner to head out to look for her. Sarah stayed behind, vowing to keep hot coffee, tea, and cocoa coming until she was found.

Jack accepted an invitation to ride with Dale. They worked their way over to Tina's house. The search party began making its way through the thick snow, paying special attention to any lumps or unusual bumps in the snow. Jack saw only a hint of the path he and Jessie had made when he had taken her away from the house earlier that day. As they continued to search, knocking on doors, and looking in yards, they heard the sheriff over the bull horn. "She's been found! She's been found!"

Jack glanced at his watch. It had been nearly an hour since he left her at the hospital. Following Dale and the others, he trudged back to Tina's house. She was sobbing; her mother holding her while her father was helping her into her coat. The sheriff walked up to Jack. "Doc, we need you. She's at the hospital. She's cold, and… there's something else. She's been hurt."

"You don't mean…?" Jack asked, putting on his most concerned face.

"No, not like that, someone cut up her face."

Gasping, Jack shook his head. "Dale, can you take me back to my vehicle? I'm going to need it."

Dale was already heading to the car. "Sheriff, tell the family the doc will meet them there."

The drive back to the diner was quiet, and Dale drove as fast as the car would allow. He pulled up next to Jack's SUV and let him out.

"I'll do my best," Jack said before closing the door.

Getting into his own vehicle, Jack sighed. It was going as planned, but he felt relieved to be alone again. Backing out he slid a little on the snow. He pulled away his wheels fought the thick, white powder that continued to fall.

***

The warmth of the hospital greeted Jack as the doors swooshed open when he entered. He went to the first emergency room and found Julie leaning over Jessie, who had been settled into a bed with a hospital gown. Her big snow jacket was lying on the table across the room.

Jack joined Julie and immediately starting taking vitals. "Any signs of frost bite?"

"No, she's lucky. We found her fast after she was brought here. Her vitals are strong. She was sedated somehow. We're going to run a toxicology screen on her and should have those results soon, so we can know what medication we can give her. It looks like her mouth was removed and then reattached. There are no signs of any other abuse or assaults."

This was just what he had wanted them to believe. *No one would ever suspect that this wasn't her mouth. No. In fact, this was her mouth. The other mouth was Faith's.*

Jack began inspecting the incision. "This needs to be redone. The mouth has been crudely reapplied. I can do this and reduce the chance of scarring. Get antibiotics going immediately, and then run that tox screen. I'll go talk to the family." Julie nodded as Jack left the room.

Jack knew that requesting the antibiotics before the tox screen would cover the antibiotic he had given her. The anesthesia he gave her would get lost in the Benzodiazepine that he used in the first sedative. The tox screen would come up with the equivalent of what was commonly known as Rohypnol, or a Ruffie.

In the waiting room, Tina and her parents, as well as a good amount of the Heyworth town's people, were anxiously waiting some news. When Jack approached Tina jumped from her chair.

Jack took her by the arm and led her a little away from all the others listening in. Her parents followed. "She's going to be okay. She doesn't have any frost bite, and all her vitals are strong. She was not sexually assaulted."

Tina sucked in a deep breath.

"But she was injured. Her mouth has extensive injuries. She also seems to have been sedated. We're running a tox screen to see what was used. Then I'd like to take her into surgery as soon as we can to repair the damage to her mouth. I feel very confident I can leave her nearly scar free."

"Oh, God." Tina nearly collapsed. Her father held her up.

"I need your permission to do this."

"Tina, let the doctor do his work," Tina's father's smooth voice calmly coaxed her.

"Can I see her?" Tina asked, her hands still shaking.

"Of course, but I caution you, it looks worse right now than it will later. Also, she's asleep and rest is the best thing for her right now." Jack led Tina and Jessie's grandparents to the ER room where Jessie rested.

About thirty minutes later they had the results of the toxicology screening on Jessie. The results showed that she had been given Rohypnol, a well-known street drug commonly known as a Ruffie, the date rape drug. The only other medications in her system were the antibiotics that had been administered at the hospital. With this information secured, Jack was free to prep Jessie for surgery to repair her mouth.

He went to see Jessie's mother and found the family around her bed. Requesting to speak with them, he explained that there was good news. Jessie had been drugged in a way that she would not likely have any memory. She might not even remember playing in the snow at all. He also explained that timing was critical to repairing her wound. The sooner they began the work, the sooner the healing could begin, and the less likely there would be scarring. He asked for permission to operate right away. Tina signed the consent, and Jack went to the operating room to prepare.

Inside the locker room, he got ready and then scrubbed while Julie was preparing to assist, and Jessie was being brought to the operating room. Jack was feeling really good. After he made Jessie look great, Faith's mouth was waiting for him at home. As soon as he was done here, he had a couple more things to do before tomorrow. He couldn't believe how quickly the past few weeks had flown by. The weeks spent searching for Faith had passed so quickly he had almost lost track of time. But, everything was working out so perfectly. Tomorrow was Christmas Eve things were coming together just how he had imagined.

Chapter Twenty

After repairing Jessie's mouth, Jack left the hospital to return home and gather the legless body of the girl that he still had stored in the freezer. There would be no more delays, tonight he would be returning home the girl he started to take home several nights earlier.

He drove through the darkness until soon he saw the city lights coming into view. He made his way along the route following the GPS instructions to the address that he pulled from his people search of the girl's mother. As he approached the street, the voice and map indicated he was just a couple of quick turns from the house. He was careful to check his surroundings. It appeared the street was asleep, now well after midnight. It had been a long day. Approaching the address, he was on high alert. He would need to be quick and quiet.

Continuing down the street, his eyes searched through the darkness, squinting in an effort to read the numbers on the mailboxes that sat near the curb.

Finding the correct number, he scanned the mirrors for any movement. There did not appear to be anyone awake. All the houses were dark, and there were no cars parked along either side of the street for as far as he could see. He was looking for any signs that might have indicated a police surveillance vehicle. No, it seemed he was alone.

Killing his headlights Jack pulled next to the mailbox, opened his driver door, walked to the rear of the vehicle, opened the cargo hatch, lifted the bag, and placed it next to the mailbox. He gently closed the hatch, not even certain it had fully latched, but ensuring he did not make any noise. Sliding back behind the wheel, he quietly clicked the door closed and pulled away. Jack waited until he reached the end of the block before switching on the headlights. He drove away and slipped off into the night unnoticed.

As he drove snowflakes began to fall. Jack smiled, taking the fresh flakes as a sign of a new beginning. A clean slate. Ebullience filled him. Even with the snow falling, making the road slick and challenging, the drive home was filled with beauty and wonder. It was Christmas Eve, and today was going to be a beautiful day.

Pulling into his driveway, Jack was greeted by the twinkling of the Christmas lights he had installed, the timer set to operate from dusk until dawn, appropriately turning them on along the eave of the house as desired. The effect was magical as the lights reflected off of the fresh snow that now blanketed the front lawn, sparkling like a million diamonds. He sat for a few minutes in front of the house just enjoying the sight before heading inside where sleep would take him quickly.

***

Jack was greeted in the morning by sun peeking through the bedroom curtains. He flipped the covers back, slid into his slippers beside the bed, and rose to look out on a yard covered with about a foot of snow. It was beautiful, exactly what he imagined. His feet padded down the hallway to the kitchen where he put a Starbuck's Pike blend into the Keurig and then began preparing an omelet filled with fresh vegetables and cheese. The room filled with a wonderful aroma, and he thought of the fresh smells he would enjoy tomorrow as he prepared the Christmas meal for his family.

For a brief moment, sadness overcame him as he realized Hope was no longer able to make the pies and stuffing. He had always so enjoyed the holidays, working together side by side in the kitchen. Forcing himself to not focus on the negative side of his situation, he thought of all the joy to come and turned his attention back to his meal, scooping it out of the pan and onto a plate, that he carried to the dining room table, then he retrieved the perfectly brewed coffee and sat down to enjoy his creation.

Forking the last bite into his mouth, he washed it down with the last of his coffee then stood to clear away the dishes and clean up the kitchen. With everything back in order, he made his way down to the basement. He had some work to do.

Opening the door to the freezer, he felt his heart catch, as once again he was taken by the gentle beauty and the tenderness he saw in the way Hope was cradling their daughter in her arms. He almost hated tearing them apart, but he had one final step to complete the process of bringing his daughter back home to his wife for good, where she would never have to let go again.

Kissing Hope, he gingerly removed her arms from around Faith and lifted his daughter. "Come on, honey. Come with Daddy. Mommy will be waiting for you to come back."

Backing out of the freezer, careful to not hurt Faith, he closed the door and carried her into the surgical room. Placing her onto the stainless steel table, he studied her mouth, making sure he was certain on the perfect alignment. Basically, he thought, he would be essentially performing the exact same surgery he had less than twenty-four hours earlier on Jessie.

He returned to the freezer to retrieve Jessie's mouth that he had safely stored until he could conduct the surgery. "It's time, Hope," he said to the cobbled together body that lay on the shelf, one arm dangling to the side. He lifted the arm and carefully placed it across the torso. "I have one last step, and then our daughter will be home with us again. I know it's taken longer than we had planned. I know it was harder than we thought it would be, but I've done it, Hope. You'll see she is going to be perfect again. Our beautiful, little girl is perfect, just like before." Jack stared into Hope's eyes and then smiled. "I love you, darling. I'll bring her to you as soon as my work is completed. Tonight we'll enjoy our Christmas Eve, and tomorrow will be just like always." With that he kissed her and then lifted the container that had the mouth stored in it and closed the freezer behind him, returning to the surgical room.

Jack pulled on gloves and prepared the sutures. He spent a few moments getting the alignment of the mouth perfect then began the process of reattaching it to the face of the body he had created.

Once the mouth was sewn in place, Jack stood back and looked at the face. His eyes then drifted down the entire body, he studied everything. Realizing he had messed up her hair as he carried her, Jack retrieved the brush from the counter behind him and tenderly brushed her hair. "Faith, you're so beautiful, and your mother is going to be so proud. We have missed you so terribly." Jack continued to look down into the eyes of the body that lay before him. The dead and sullen eyes gazed back at him. The mouth was sewn on into a crooked smile and the teeth showed partially through the lips, making the face take on a garish snarl. "Tonight is going to be so special, and guess what, tomorrow is Christmas, your favorite day of the whole year."

He finished brushing her hair. Satisfied with the way she looked, he once again lifted her and carried her out of the surgical room and back to the freezer. He wanted so desperately to just spend the day with both of his girls, but he needed to go and check on Jessie. Once he confirmed her healing was going as expected and talked one more time with Tina, he would be able to release Jessie. The only things he really worried about now was infection and making sure the flesh and tissue growth was beginning as expected. Mostly, he wanted little Jessie to heal nicely. After all, she had been such a good donor for Faith. There was really no reason why she would not have a normal life. He anticipated very little scarring, and he was certain no one would realize the mouth he had attached to her was not hers. Well, unless when the other body was found, the authorities connected the two cases, then, of course, there was nothing he could do about that.

Laying Faith down again next to Hope, he looked at his wife and said, "Well, darling, she's now complete. I think she looks exactly as she did before..." Jack faded off before completing the rest of that sentence. Ignoring the pain those memories caused, he changed his thought. "Isn't she lovely? Our little girl is here for Christmas. Tonight we'll sleep in our new pajamas and drink hot chocolate just like always." He stood staring into Hope eyes and then continued, "I'm glad you're as happy to have her home as I am. I know how sad you've been, and now as much as I hate to do so, I have to go to the hospital and check on a little girl. I won't be long though, I promise, and then we can begin our celebrations." Jack waited until he was certain Hope understood, and then he gave each of his girls a quick peck on the cheek. Before exiting the freezer, he double checked the temperature.

Satisfied that everything was fine, he closed the freezer door and returned to the surgical room to clean up. Once everything was sparkling and back in its rightful place, he returned upstairs to shower before heading to the hospital for a final check-in on Jessie.

Jack arrived at the hospital a little before eleven o'clock. The morning had gone by fast, but things were going exactly as he had planned. He and his family were going to have a wonderful Christmas together. The mere thought of having a day with Hope and Faith by his side, carving turkey and feasting on pies caused tears to well in his eyes. *Everything really is perfect*, he thought.

Jessie was in a room on the second floor of the small hospital. He parked and then made his way using the stairs rather than the elevator. Arriving at the nurse's station, he chatted with the nurse, a middle aged woman named Candice. It seemed Julie had the next couple of days off for the holidays. He asked for the chart and then continued down the hall to room number 214.

When Jack entered the room, he was pleased to see Jessie sitting up in her bed. Her mouth was swollen, but in all other ways, she looked just like the happy little girl he helped in the recovery of a very serious bout of strep throat. Tina was at her side, and cartoons were playing on the TV that was mounted on the wall across the room. Elephant wall border wrapped around the walls, an obvious effort to make it comfortable for a child.

Approaching the bed Jack smiled at Jessie, "How is my favorite patient doing today?"

Jessie mumbled through the swollen lips, "Okay."

"You know you gave us quite a scare yesterday."

The little girl tried to smile, but winced slightly.

"I know it's a bit sore right now, but I promise that will get better and you'll be back to teasing me any day now." Jack winked at her. "Now, can I take a look at your boo boo to see how it's doing? I promise I won't make it hurt."

Jessie nodded her head.

Jack pulled out his pen light and gently looked at the incision around the lips. The sutures were all still intact, and there were subtle signs of healing. "Wow, this is looking really good." Jack leaned back and looked down at the little girl. "You know how brave you are?"

"Yes," Jessie whispered, barely moving the lips that were sewn to her face, displaying that spirit that he had always enjoyed about her, though she still looked sad.

"That a girl," Jack encouraged, enjoying the feeling he had with knowing he was not only this little girl's hero, but quite possibly the whole town's hero.

"You know you're going to be just fine in a few weeks."

Still looking sad, Jessie stared down at the sheet that covered her small frame.

"Guess what? How would you like it if I said you could go home for Christmas?"

Jessie looked into his eyes, and again she winced as she tried to smile at him. She was clearly delighted with the idea. "I thought Santa wouldn't be able to find me," she whispered shyly.

"Well, I personally know that Santa can always find the good children, but let's get you out of here so you don't have to worry about that. How does that sound?"

Jessie nodded again then hugged onto her mother who had remained seated on the edge of her bed.

"Okay, well let me start working on your release. You're going to need some medicine to help you heal fast."

Jack patted her on the arm, then nodded at Tina and left the room to get the paperwork to release her to go home. He smiled as he walked down the hospital corridor, oblivious to the dull color of the walls and floor. He was pleased that his plan had worked perfectly. The Ruffie had left Jessie with no recollection of him taking her from her yard or of him promising to take her to meet his daughter. As he filled out the release paperwork at the nurse's station, he reveled in his accomplishment. Breathing deeply he sucked in the heavy antiseptic smell that filled the hospital. To most the smell was offensive and unsettling but for Jack it always made him feel calm. Completing the release paperwork, he graciously accepted the nurse's compliments on the restoration of Jessie's injuries. Yes, it truly was a good day.

Chapter Twenty-One

Max woke with a start, slapping at the alarm on the nightstand next to the bed. Rolling over she rubbed her eyes trying to wake up enough to read the time on the clock. The digital numbers illuminated in a bright green 5:00. *Damn*, she thought. It felt like she had just fallen asleep. Maybe she had just fallen asleep. Stretching her lean legs out, Max pulled the covers up around her neck, feeling the chill in the room. She still hadn't gotten used to the cold weather. Having only lived in the Washington D.C. area for a short while, her blood was still used to California living.

Now fully awake, her mind began rolling through the events over the past few days. She still had a lingering feeling there was something so simple she had not thought to check. It was as if she could feel Jack near. She knew they needed a break and soon, or he would slip away again.

Her body shivered, though she was not sure whether it was from the cold or her thoughts. She allowed her mind to think about the last time she and Mark had made love. Her lips curled into a crooked, lopsided smile. The warm memories were motivation enough to force her to roll out of bed and into the hot shower.

Stepping out of the shower with a towel wrapped around her hair like a turban and another wrapped around her body, she could hear the chirping ring tone that told her Mark was calling. Her mind immediately realized that it meant something had happened, as they had a plan to meet downstairs, and he would have no reason to call. Clinging to her towel, she padded across the carpet, cringing at the thought of the hotel carpet on her bare feet, and punched the answer button on her phone. "Mark? What is it? Is everything okay?"

"It's the missing girl. Her body was discovered. The mother came out of her home to head to work this morning and found a lawn bag next to the mailbox. You know what was inside. The legs are missing and so is her mouth. The crime team is already there."

"He's doing it again, Mark. The sick bastard is putting his dead daughter back together."

"We don't know that for sure yet. But, I agree with you, I think you're right. We have to prove it. We will prove it, Max. How close are you to being ready?"

"I just need to get dressed. Give me ten minutes." Max hung up the phone and hurried to pull on her clothes. She quickly dried her hair with the hairdryer that was in a bag under the vanity in the bathroom. Forgoing the unnecessary makeup, she pushed on shoes and slid into her shoulder holster containing the FBI issued Glock, then pulled on her coat and headed downstairs.

She met Mark in the hallway, and they entered the elevator together. Once the doors closed, Mark leaned into Max and kissed her. Max responded. She could never resist his kisses, his touch. They pulled away just moments before the door opened. Mark was still facing Max, and he smiled at her, his blue eyes sparkling. Max looked back at him and saw both love and concern in his gaze. "Let's find him, Mark."

Mark nodded at her as they exited the elevator and made their way to the area where the hotel offered continental breakfast. There was an omelet, cereal, fruit, and muffin station. They each grabbed a muffin and coffee then headed out the door to the car.

The snow continued, even after they had gone into the hotel, and was thick in the parking lot. The remaining team members had left the day before to be with their families for Christmas. They were scheduled to return the day after the holiday. Max silently hoped they wouldn't need to come back. She envisioned getting the break they needed, putting Jack in cuffs before they had a chance to return, ending this chase once and for all. Of course, she knew this was a long shot, but still could not help being wishful.

Mark navigated the car across the parking lot and out onto the road. The trip back to Normal was slow going. With each mile Max felt her frustration growing. The crime scene team was already on site, and Max quietly prayed that they would find some kind of clue. Not that she was necessarily a religious woman, but they definitely needed something linking Jack to these crimes. They also needed something indicating where he was specifically. She hoped for a fiber, a print, tire treads, anything that would help send them in the right direction.

Once they got onto Highway 55, Mark placed a call, seeking the results of the GSR and handwriting analysis of the suspected suicide from the prior day. Both Mark and Max were certain the tests were going to confirm the suicide, which would close the case and prove there was just a very unfortunate coincidence that had delayed the investigation into the missing girl, but had a mostly favorable result. The boy was found unharmed and was now safely back with his mother.

"Mark Wells, good morning. GSR was confirmed? Do you have the handwriting analysis yet?" Mark glanced towards Max and nodded affirmation. "Those results were fast. So, the coroner's preliminary cause of death will be suicide by gunshot? Thank you for rushing the results. I'll need a copy of the report for our case file." Mark hung up the phone. "The test results confirmed suicide."

"I didn't think it was Jack. Though had he pulled a stunt like that to throw us off, I wouldn't have been surprised either. Mark, I just know he's killing these little girls. He's putting Faith back together just like he did Hope. He's in this area, and we need to find him soon."

Mark took another sideways glance in Max's direction. "I agree it's very likely, but we need something to prove it. Until we have that, we have to be open to other suspects too. We don't want to become so focused on Jack that we overlook important details. We should start getting some results on the severed legs discovered in Eureka. If we can match tool marks and cuts with Jack's prior victims, it will certainly be something specific to start associating to Jack's MO."

Max nodded, though she was really hoping for more than just tool marks. Silence filled the car as they made the rest of the trip, arriving thirty minutes later to the address where the young girl had lived. Picking out the address was easy, as the street was blocked and yellow crime scene tape marked off about a hundred yards in every direction of the mailbox in front of the house. The pair flashed their credentials and ducked under the crime tape to join the investigation.

The coroner had already arrived and was studying the bag and the contents inside a makeshift tent that allowed for coverage of the torso from the curious neighbors and press that had already started to gather. Even the frigid temperature was not a deterrent to keep people inside and away from the scene. Mark and Max ducked behind the sheet and witnessed the torso laying out on a plastic tarp on the ground. It was obvious the legs had been removed and were not present on the plastic, therefore missing. The coroner was photographing the body of the child under the high intensity lights as Max leaned in to see what was the point of his focus. Max felt her stomach lurch as she realized that he was studying the girl's face. There was tissue lying on the plastic, next to a baggie and an evidence marker. That tissue appeared to be a pair of lips. Forcing her eyes away from the items of the tarp, she introduced herself to the thin, spindly man with the camera, "Special Agent Nichols. What do we know so far?"

The man paused, the camera still at his face. He lowered the device and turned toward Max obviously sizing her up. After assessing her, he also took in the other person in the tent, clearly deciding he was out-numbered by the agents.

He set the camera down, and introduced himself, then began delivering his initial assessment. "Greg Silverson, Chief Medical Examiner. The child has been positively identified by the mother who had the unfortunate experience of finding the bag containing the body this morning. The trash bag appears to be a basic lawn and garden bag found in nearly every home. We'll know more after the crime scene team does an analysis on color and ply, but I don't expect it to be too helpful. The child's legs were severed expertly, as was the mouth. The incisions are clean. The mouth was sealed inside the bag inside a baggie. "After a more thorough assessment, I'll have a better idea on what types of tools were used."

Max nodded her thanks to Silverson. "How soon will the CSI team have the bag for prints?"

Looking back down at what remained of the small child's body, Silverson wiped the sleeve of his white lab coat across his brow. "I'd say fifteen minutes before I'm ready to tag everything for transport. They'll take what you see here, including the plastic tarp, to ensure we don't miss anything."

Wells handed him a business card and asked to be contacted with any new information as soon as possible. Then he turned to Max and ducked around the sheet, back into the early morning light. Making a few inquiries they were led to the lead CSI, a woman by the name of Hannah Cole. After making sure the team would expedite the results and ensuring they checked every inch of the trash bag for finger prints, Mark and Max checked in with the local detectives. The team filled the pair in on the mother's statement of how she found the bag near the mailbox.

They agreed there was not much more they could do until the medical examiner could tell them if the severing of the legs and mouth was consistent with the other child. Or whether the type of tool used could be identified, which would hopefully begin to tie these cases directly to Jack Tyler, They decided to head back to Le Roy where at the investigation center they could focus on what they had learned so far and continue the process of trying to find links for these cases to the cases from California and Oklahoma.

Back at the police station, the two settled in at a table that was set up in the middle of the room. It was covered with various files and boxes containing the photographs and evidence from each of the prior abductions and murders.

Max started putting all the information in chronological order and began taping the photographs on a white board that covered one of the walls in the room. Under each photograph she wrote the name of the child, the date of the abduction, and the date the body or body parts were recovered. Then she finished it off with all of the known details. After she had completed the work, she stood back and looked at the board. Her eyes followed the photos, and she considered the development between each event.

The first child, Cindy, had been dumped complete, except her mouth was missing. She had incisions down the front of her torso, consistent with the precision and manner in which Jack was known to kill his victims. For Max this was enough of a tie to Tyler. Her attention was drawn to the photos of the dump site, causing her to reconsider her initial thoughts. No, she was not dumped; she was *delivered*. The child had been sedated prior to the mutilation of her body. This was not consistent with Jack's prior killings. Max added these details under the photograph.

Only the legs of the second child had been delivered. The torso had still never been recovered. The results from the tissue samples indicated that there was a similar method of sedation used on this child. The limbs had been removed with precision consistent with someone with training. Again, Max added these details to the board under the second child's photograph.

The third child was delivered to her home with no legs. The mouth had been removed and delivered in a baggie. They would have to wait for the tissue results to confirm whether or not the child had been sedated prior to the severing of the limbs or whether the wound marks were consistent with the others. *Consistent with Jack.*

Standing staring at all the information on the board, Max could not help but mentally ask several questions. She did not realize she was asking them out loud. "Are you done, Jack? Do you have a whole child? Is this it? Have you found Faith and restored your daughter from these children? Why are you removing the mouths? Did these children talk back to you? Did you panic, or did you feel remorse. Is it possible you made a mistake?"

Mark had been observing Max as she had been focused on applying the information on the board. He listened as she asked the questions and smiled in appreciation of her internal drive and style for working through the evidence. The more he listened to her, the more convinced he was that she was on the right track. This was beginning to look more and more like the work of Dr. Jack Tyler. Even though there were plenty of differences in these killings from those of his prior murders, there were enough commonalities that Mark too was convinced. To her it was becoming increasingly clear that Tyler was responsible for the death of these children, and was on a mission to rebuild the body of his dead daughter, Faith.

Max looked over, sensing that she was being watched. Her eyes met Mark's and locked for a moment, then she turned her attention back to the board. Next, Max put the location of the abduction, and discovery site. One thing stood out to her. In two of the abductions the child was returned to the place where the abduction was suspected. In the case of the other child, she had been abducted from the mall and recovered at her home. *Why?*

Underneath the photo, Max wrote 'he's watching'. Unless the child had offered up her address, which given her age and the emotional state she would have been in, it was unlikely. Jack must have been watching the news and had obtained the name of the mother, which had been released by the media.

Max walked over to her computer and performed a Google search of the name of the mother and quickly received several results for the address where the body had been delivered. It was that simple. He heard the name on the news and knew exactly where to get the address so he could *deliver* her home. *Why is this important to him?* Max wondered.

The next several hours Max and Mark continued to work quietly, occasionally sharing a glance or a comment. Each focusing on certain details as they waited for more information from the medical examiner's office. The room had been so quiet that they both jumped slightly when Wells's phone rang. He glanced at his watch and noted it was nearly three thirty. The day had flown by. "Wells," he said into the phone, switching it to speaker phone so Max could hear.

The voice on the other end came back through the small speaker loud enough. Max grabbed a pen and notepad and began taking notes. "Silverson here, I have some more information that I thought you might find interesting."

"Go ahead," Wells said.

"So far, the crime team has found no prints on the bag or the baggie. They also did not recover any fibers. This guy is careful. I've been focused on the body, and I can tell you the amputation is near as perfect as I have seen. This guy is definitely medically trained."

Max jumped in before Silverson could say any more. "Thanks, but this is not much more information than we had yesterday."

"There's more, Special Agent Nichols, I presume?" He said sounding a little annoyed at not knowing he was on speaker phone.

Max shrugged at Wells and rolled her finger around in a circle, indicating she wanted Silverson to get on with it.

Silverson waited just a moment, and when he did not get a response, he continued with his report. "The most important finding is that the mouth recovered with the body is not a match."

"Are you saying the mouth is not a match to the body?"

"That's correct. The size and shape is different, and I performed an HLA test, which matches protein markers. It is a test often used in finding donor matches for transplant recipients. I performed a low level detail test, and it was a negative match. To confirm my findings, I matched blood type. It too was negative. Both conclusively indicate the mouth is not a match to the body. The mouth delivered with the body, does not belong to the body."

Wells immediately began explaining to Silverson, "We have another child that was murdered, and the mouth was removed. It was not delivered with the body and has never been recovered. We need to have the same tests performed to see if the mouth belongs to that child. That child was found in Le Roy; we need to perform a comparison to that body immediately. Can you coordinate that?"

Silverson paused. "You do realize it's Christmas Eve?"

"Yes, I do understand. But we have children being killed. The subject is skilled and has unlimited financial resources. I fear we don't have much time to catch him."

After a long pause, Silverson responded, "I'll see what I can do. Give me a few hours."

Wells thanked him and disconnected the line. Looking at Max he could read her eyes and the concern behind them. "We'll get him, Max. We will," he said, offering encouragement he was not quite feeling.

"What if there are others, Mark? Could we be looking at this incorrectly? We were assuming the mouth matched the body, but it didn't. Now, we are assuming it will match the other body. What if it doesn't? Could there be more victims? Have we looked in a broad enough geography?"

Wells thought for a moment. "Let's spread the search over the state of Illinois, just to be sure. Although the speed of the kills would suggest there isn't enough time, but at least we'll be working through any open cases while we wait to hear back from Silverson." He dropped back into the chair in front of his laptop and immediately started typing away.

Logging into the NCIC website, Max started to query searches for missing female children between the ages of five and eight in the State of Illinois criminal database. Again, silence filled the room as they worked.

After a couple of hours poring over recent criminal reports, Max pushed back from her computer, stood and walked over to the table at the back of the room to make a pot of much needed coffee. Mark pulled back from the table as well, stood up and stretched. The police headquarters was quiet. Everyone seemingly had left to go home to have dinner with their respective families and ring in the holiday.

Max poured them each a cup of coffee and offered one to Mark who had walked up behind her and nuzzled the back of her neck briefly. Turning to face him, she smiled, locking her gaze on his blue eyes. The moment was nice. "Merry Christmas Eve, Special Agent in Charge Wells," she said, tossing her long, wavy hair back.

Wells loved when she did that, and the smell of her hair tugged at his senses. "Merry Christmas Eve to you too, Agent Nichols, not exactly how I envisioned our first Christmas together, though I should know better than envision anything, given the nature of this job."

"I have to confess, I have not bought a single gift," Max said, thinking about the actual holiday that would come tomorrow.

"Neither have I," Mark admitted as well. "Can we agree to have our own Christmas one week following our return home?"

"Sure. But why do you want to wait a week?" Max looked at him puzzled.

"Well, I do need a couple of days to shop, ya' know."

"Oh. Got it," she laughed." The moment settled between them. Max took a long draw on her coffee and said, "I guess we'd better get back at it."

"I guess so," Wells agreed and turned back towards the table where the computers sat.

Another hour and a half passed before Max about jumped out of her chair. "Mark, look at this!"

She turned her computer screen to face him. It displayed a newspaper clipping that had run in the local paper in Heyworth just that morning. The criminal report would not yet have hit the database, which is why it had not come up earlier.

Mark's eyes scanned the page. It was a story of a little girl that had gone missing and had later been dropped off alive at the local hospital. The article was brief and focused on the fact that the child had been found. It lacked details of the abduction, but there was a single line that said she was stable, yet sustained injuries to her mouth. Before Max could say anything, Wells Googled the Heyworth Police Department's phone number and was already calling.

Chapter Twenty-Two

Christmas Eve had finally come. After releasing Jessie from the hospital Jack spent the early part of the day shopping for Christmas dinner and finishing all of the decorations. By mid-afternoon the house was glowing with lights and garland, gifts were wrapped and under the tree and he had most of the preparations for the meal ready. Tomorrow he could focus just on his girls. It was going to be glorious. Tonight they would open their pajamas, eat chili, and bake cookies—just like they always did. Jack hummed as he worked.

It was now dark, and he lit candles for the table. The house glowed with twinkling lights everywhere. It was perfect. Finally, with everything ready Jack headed down to the basement. Tonight, for the first time ever, he would bring his whole family together upstairs. People in town would all be spending time with their families, and he felt it was the perfect time to enjoy life the way it was supposed to be. Together and free.

Jack opened the freezer door and moved Faith to the side then gently lifted Hope. He carried her up the stairs and placed her at the dining room table. Kissing her, he told her to wait a minute while he went to get Faith. Heading again down the stairs, Jack returned to the freezer, this time lifting Faith and carrying her up to sit next to Hope at the table. The candles glowed on their faces, highlighting the grotesque features and dead eyes, making the scene even more chilling. Jack just smiled at the pair, his heart bursting with joy at the idea of having the family back together again.

Chattering to them about the evening plans, he prepared bowls of chili for each of them. The smell was wonderful, as the savory dish had been cooking in the crock pot all day.

After Jack finished his food, he teased both about the little amount they had eaten. He got up from the table and busied himself with the dishes, all the while talking to the women in his life about the glorious plans for the future now that they were all together again.

With the dishes cleared away, he hurried back to the bedroom and brought out the gifts he had packed containing the pajamas. "I bet you thought I forgot," he said as he made his way back to the table. "I could never forget our fun and important traditions. This year I've picked the Grinch for our pajama theme. I hope you both love these." Jack set the packages in front of each body and then carefully opened Faith's first. He beamed as he held the pajamas in front of her. "Okay, sweetie, Daddy will help you get dressed in just a minute. Let's see what Mommy got."

After the gifts were opened, Jack gingerly dressed each body in the pajamas, careful of the tanned skin and areas that contained sutures. Then he pulled on his own pair. Feeling a little silly, just as he had in years past, he chuckled at how silly he looked, but he knew it made the girls happy. And right now that was all that mattered. In his Grinch PJs, he began to bake the cookies a tray at a time, and when the first batch came out; he placed them on a cooling rack while he got the icing and decorating kit ready. Once the cookies were cooled, he began decorating them, sitting right next to Faith explaining to her how to use the frosting tips and glitter without making a mess.

Jack leaned back from the table and looked at the decorated cookies sparkling in the candle light. He glanced from Hope to Faith and back again, and tears welled in his eyes, as he was over joyed with the sight. He was having Christmas Eve with his family again, something he thought might never happen. Life was so good.

Soon he realized it was getting late, and Faith needed to get to bed so Santa could come and bring her surprises for the morning. "Hope, I'll tuck her in and be right back," he said, winking at his wife. Her dead eyes stared straight ahead, her face now sunken in slightly on one side.

Lifting Faith, Jack carried her back down the stairs and placed her in the freezer, kissing her on the top of the head. "Now go right to sleep, darling, so Santa can come. It's going to be a magical day tomorrow. Sleep tight and don't let the bed bugs bite."

Once back upstairs he opened a bottle of wine and poured two glasses. He sat next to his wife and continued to talk to her about the wonderful evening and the future he planned for them. After drinking two glasses of wine himself, he invited his wife to join him in the bedroom. It had been a long time since they had been able to be together, with Hope needing to be there for Faith. But tonight, they could be together again. His heart raced as he kissed her passionately and carried her to the bedroom.

***

Jack awoke alone in his bed. He naturally reached to the side of the bed that Hope had always occupied throughout their marriage, but his hand only found cool sheets. As the sleep left him, his mind cleared, and he remembered that he had been required to return Hope to the basement during the night. Knowing that he must preserve her body, he had reluctantly returned her to the freezer after their passionate love making. While knowing they would never be able to spend a whole night in bed together again, he smiled at the memory of their night.

Christmas Eve had been perfect. He had his family again. Things were going so well right now, and he could not wait for the Christmas Day festivities to begin. With those thoughts he flung his feet over the edge of the bed and slid them into his slippers. He rose and stretched his muscular, nude body then made his way to the shower.

Clean and refreshed, Jack pulled on his Christmas pajamas and shook his head at the silly way he looked in the mirror. He went to the kitchen and made coffee and began a tea pot of hot water to make hot chocolate for Faith. Then he went around the house and turned on all the lights that had turned off by the auto timers he had set to go off at midnight. He retrieved the doll that he had purchased as the gift from Santa for Faith from the front closet where he had hidden it on the top shelf. It was dressed in all white with glitter on the little bodice. Faith had a doll similar to this one that she had carried with her on the day of the car accident. If she could only ask for it herself, he knew Faith would want Santa to bring her that doll more than anything else. He set the doll out in front of the tree. The smells of coffee and cocoa filled the room as he set out cups on the coffee table for himself and his girls. He placed a plate of cookies on the table, and then looked around. Everything was beautiful. It was time to start the holiday with his family.

Jack went to the basement to bring Hope first. She always wanted to see Faith's expression when she saw the tree and her Santa gift. Soon he had Hope upstairs and seated on the sofa near the Christmas tree. "Good morning, sweet heart. Merry Christmas. I told you today would be perfect. Everything is ready. Faith is going to have an amazing day." He leaned in and whispered in her ear, "Last night was amazing. I love you. Are you ready for me to get Faith?" Gazing into her sullen, murky eyes he was convinced that she had confirmed her readiness to get the day started. He kissed her on the cheek.

He started to head downstairs, but suddenly he remembered something. Returning to the kitchen, he took a small plate out of the cupboard, ate a cookie over the dish, leaving the appropriate amount of crumbs, and then filled a glass with milk, and drank most of it. He carried both over to the hearth and set them down in plain sight, under the stockings that hung beautifully between the swags of garland and twinkling, white lights. He had packed the stockings with bags of mixed nuts and socks a couple of days previously and now added an orange and apple to each, following a tradition that had passed down from his father's side of the family.

Looking around again, he nodded. Now it was perfect.

Taking the stairs to the basement two at a time, he went to the freezer again. "Good morning, Faith, Merry Christmas. Guess what? Santa came and brought something special just for you. Mommy is upstairs waiting for you. Come on. Daddy's going to take you upstairs."

Jack lifted the body of the child. Her head rolled to one side as he carried her up the stairs. He was careful, ensuring he did not bump her along the walls as he climbed the stairs, rounded the corner, and entered the living room. Jack smiled as he placed his daughter next to Hope on the sofa amongst the sparkling lights and Christmas glitter. The room looked beautiful, and Jack's heart swelled as he looked at his family. He went and got the gift that he had previously placed under the tree for Faith from Santa. Carrying the beautiful doll over to Faith, he placed it on her lap and wrapped her arm around it.

Next he gathered up the stockings for both Hope and Faith and laid them out in front of each of them. One by one he pulled out the items and laid them out, displaying the contents. After a few minutes, he had emptied the contents and he had shared the contents with both Hope and Faith.

Finally, he pulled out the boxes from under the tree. Both Hope and Faith had a large box with a big red bow on top. Inside contained the dresses he had picked out the night at the mall. As he opened each box, he held the dress up in front of each of his girls. They looked stunning, and he could feel their excitement at the beautiful gowns. After enjoying the beauty of his wife and daughter, Jack pulled hangers out of the closet next to the front door and hung the dresses up for later.

He turned back to his family, and a huge smile covered his face at the sight of Hope and Faith sitting together on the couch, surrounded by the boxes, wrapping paper, and stocking contents. The lights from the tree and other decorations made a special glow on each of their faces. He couldn't believe his good fortune. Here he was on Christmas morning enjoying the day just like he had before the…accident. Life was finally good again. He had successfully restored Hope and found Faith and brought her home to his wife.

After soaking in the scene in his living room, Jack carried Hope and then Faith over to the dining table, so he could enjoy them nearby while he worked in the kitchen. He prepared croissants for breakfast and then began preparing the Christmas meal.

He worked diligently talking all the while. "You two are going to love what Daddy is making for Christmas today. I got us a turkey and a ham. There not very big ones, given how little you girls eat lately, you women always worrying about your waistlines. I also got stuffing, rolls, yams, and cranberries. Oh, I mustn't forget mashed potatoes and gravy and both pecan and pumpkin pies. Okay, you caught me; I did cheat on the pies," he said glancing at the bodies sitting at the table with their milky eyes permanently staring at him. "I bought them. But I got them from the diner. These were freshly baked by Sarah. So, I think it counts as homemade."

As Jack talked he laughed at his own jokes, truly enjoying the life he had created. "You'd both like Sarah. She's a very nice lady. She would love the two of you too." For a brief moment, he felt sorrow flow through his heart. He knew deep down inside Sarah would never be able to meet his wife and daughter. However, he was determined not to allow such thoughts to ruin this perfect day, he forced the acknowledgement out and focused on the meal he was cooking.

Soon the house was filled with incredible smells. At nearly twelve o'clock, Jack paused from cooking and said, "Okay, Faith, it's time for you to take a nap. I don't want you to be tired for tonight. I have a big evening planned for our family dinner." Jack stood looking at the garish bodies still sitting at the table. "Honey, why don't you join Faith?" he said speaking to Hope. "You look tired too. Then after your naps it will be time to finally put on those beautiful dresses. I can't wait to see you. You're both going to look amazing."

Jack lifted Faith and carried her through the living room to the basement and back to the freezer. Returning upstairs, he collected Hope and returned her to the freezer, placing her next to Faith. He stood looking at his family.

"Oh, of course, honey. Daddy will get her for you." Jack raced back up the stairs again, returning to the dining room table. He grabbed the doll Santa had brought Faith and quickly returned to the basement, taking the doll into the freezer and carefully wrapping Faith's arms around it. He smiled down at his daughter and gave her a quick kiss on the forehead before kissing Hope on the lips. "Okay, rest well. When you wake up dinner will be ready, and it's going to be so wonderful."

Jack turned, unconsciously double checking the temperature on the freezer before closing the door behind him, and once again returning upstairs to check on the food. Everything was coming along as planned. It should all be ready around five o'clock. He originally planned to have it all on the table by six. He glanced out the front window and saw the snow glistening in the sun. It was truly a beautiful day.

While the food continued to cook, Jack went to the master bedroom and selected his own clothing. He pulled out a dress shirt that would perfectly compliment the dress Hope would be wearing. Then he picked out the tie Faith had given him on the last Christmas they had spent together. It wouldn't necessarily quite match, but that didn't matter. Wearing it would make Faith very happy, and that was what was important now. Jack took the dresses down to the basement, so he could get them ready when their nap was over. The night was going to be wonderful, and he could hardly wait.

Chapter Twenty-Three

After waiting for several minutes, Wells was finally connected with the Heyworth Police Chief. He spent the first few minutes explaining that he was the Special Agent in Charge of the investigation of several abducted and murdered little girls. After listening to Wells, the Chief acknowledged being familiar with the cases, but he was confused about how this had anything to do with his small town.

"You had a missing girl who was recovered alive, but we think there may be a connection," Wells explained.

"Oh. Yes, young Jessie. She wasn't missing all that long. So far we don't have any real leads. She can't remember much."

"We would like to meet with the investigative officer and possibly talk to the little girl and her parents."

"I'd be happy to have you come out, so we can share what we know. Obviously, we would rather not upset the child if we don't need to."

"I understand, but she may be the only person alive that has seen the subject. If we are going to catch this guy before he hurts another little girl, we need to move quickly."

"It's Christmas Eve, but come on out. We can share everything we have in our file with you. After that I'll see what I can do about the interviews."

"Thank you, Chief. We'll be there within an hour." Wells hung up the phone and turned to see Max grabbing her coat. Following suit he pulled on his coat, and the two headed for the parking lot. They returned to the hotel to check out and then began the short trip to Heyworth.

Max could feel how close they were. She felt absolutely certain that Jack Tyler was near. This may be just the lead they needed to catch him. If the little girl could remember anything, it just might be enough to lead them to Jack before he could hurt anyone else.

The ride to Heyworth was spent discussing the approach with the Heyworth Police Chief. Knowing he was resistant, they agreed they would need to take it slowly if they were to gain his approval. Of course, they could push it, but it was easier to work with the local police than force their way in.

Upon arriving in Heyworth, it took Wells just a few moments to locate the Village Hall where the Chief of Police said they could meet. The small building hosted all of the community support functions like street and public works, along with fire and police. Pulling in front of the brick building, they exchanged a glance, their eyes locking for a moment, before they exited the vehicle and approached the entrance to the building. The door swung open, and they were greeted by a large man with thick limbs that looked like tree trunks. He had a serious face with permanent lines between his eyebrows. "Welcome to Heyworth, Agents. Chief Stark. Come on in."

Entering the building they found themselves in a lobby facing a counter. It appeared as if during working hours this area would be staffed with clerks that took payments for the local utilities and minor traffic fines. Chief Stark lifted a section of the counter that swung up on a hinge to grant access to the back offices. Wells and Max followed the chief to the back and entered an office that was moderate in size and was filled by a large oak desk and two oversized chairs that the chief offered to the agents to occupy.

The walls were covered in news clippings of successes for the local high school Hornets football and basketball teams. Max recalled in her research of Eureka, the town of the second abduction, that their team name was the Hornets also. Why this stood out, she was not sure. It just seemed strange that two towns not all that far from each other had the same mascot. She thought about the towns, how Jack was making his selections. *Eureka, it means 'I found it'. Was this what attracted you, Jack? Did you find meaning in the name? A sign maybe?* Forcing her thoughts back to the room, Max heard the chief on the phone asking someone to join them. She hadn't seen anyone else in the building and was wondering where the officer had been.

A few moments later, a young officer in a tan uniform entered the room. Max quickly assessed the officer: mid to late twenties, tall, dark hair, strong jaw, slightly over-weight and held a serious look on his face. He was obviously trying to assert himself, and it was coming off as defensive. Max smiled internally, remembering what it was like as a young officer to be asked to consult with the FBI. It could be tough being confident, yet not coming off cocky or overly defensive.

"Special Agents Wells and Nichols, this is Officer Ryan," Chief Stark offered. Mark and Max shook hands with the young man. "Ryan was the officer first on the scene when little Jessie went missing. He was also first on the scene at the hospital when she was discovered outside the emergency entrance. Ryan, tell the agents what happened that night."

"Yes, sir," Ryan replied before pulling out a small note pad from his pocket and flipping to the middle of the pad. "We got the 911 call from the mother. The child, Jessie, had been outside playing in the snow, and when the mother decided it had been too long and the snow was coming down too hard, she went outside to tell her to come in. Her daughter was nowhere to be found. After searching the yard areas, she panicked and called it in. I arrived at the home six minutes after the call came in. I spent approximately ten minutes with the mother and confirmed the child was not in the home or in the yard area. That's when I called for a search party. We assembled at the local diner and within the hour had a large group of volunteers over at the child's home. We began a door to door search checking garages, cars, basements or cellars. Basically, we requested that the volunteers ask to see any place where we thought a child might hide or go to get warm. With the snow accumulation, there were no tracks telling us the direction the child had gone, making the search difficult." Ryan paused for a moment while he flipped a couple of the pages back and forth before he continued.

"I received a call from the PD dispatcher telling me to get over to the hospital, that the child had been found. I asked one of the volunteers to escort the mother, and I went ahead, as I was not sure what condition Jessie was in. Upon arrival the hospital personnel were working on warming her back up and prepping her for surgery. Her mouth...," he paused seeming to gather himself. "Her mouth had clearly been removed and sewn back on. It looked horrible. All these long threads hanging out. I interviewed the person that found her. Basically, she had been laid at the ER entrance. It seemed whoever took her tortured her for some reason, but had no intention of letting her die."

Max asked, "How many people were in the search party?"

"Oh, I guess about fifteen to twenty."

"Did you record the names of the people in the search party?" Wells inquired.

"No, but I bet we could get a list together pretty quick."

"Was there anyone in the search party that did not belong?" Max continued to inquire.

"Oh. No. Everyone was from town, locals that all know Jessie and her mom. We're a tight community."

"Has there been anyone in town lately that seems to be hanging around, an outsider?"

Ryan and Chief Stark traded a look and both shook their heads.

Chief Stark spoke, "No one from our town did this. No one from around here would hurt Jessie."

"Okay." Wells said, holding his hand up palm out. "You understand we have to ask. It wouldn't be uncommon for the un-sub to inject himself into an investigation."

"I understand," Stark accepted.

Wells pressed on, "We'd like to talk to a couple of members of the search party, and then we would like to talk to Jessie. She may remember something now that some time has passed. Anything she tells us may help us find who did this."

Chief Stark began to protest, "Look, that little girl has been through hell. How can this help her? I don't think I can let you do that to her, dredging up all those horrible memories."

Max responded, "We understand how terrible it seems to put a child through the ordeal again. But we have a person out there that has killed several children, and we believe this is related."

"You told me that on the phone, but those children were abducted and killed. They weren't returned to the local hospital. I'm not seeing the connection."

"We haven't shared all of the details about the murders with the news, but the first child had her mouth removed. It has not yet been recovered. We believe our subject is abducting little girls that have the general characteristics of his dead daughter, and he's taking parts of them that resemble her and slowly rebuilding his child." Wells hesitated to say the rest. "It's possible that the mouth Jessie had sewn on her is not even her own."

The blood drained from the young officer's face, and he looked like he might be sick.

"Oh, Jesus," was all the chief could say.

Max continued, "We'll need a DNA test of the mouth to see if it's a match to Jessie's DNA. During the interview, we'll allow the child's parents to be present if that helps Jessie feel safe, and we will only press on if the child is doing okay. You have my word that we will not push her too hard. But, she may be our key to catching this guy, and we have no idea if he's done with his mission yet. Which means time is critical because he could be thinking right now about the next child he will take."

"I'll have a few of the search party folks meet us at the diner first thing in the morning. We can go to Jessie's from there. I heard she was getting released from the hospital today and should be home. We can meet at ten o'clock. That gives a couple of the people who have kids time to watch them open gifts and then get back home before the Christmas meal. Sarah can have some coffee and pastries ready for us, I'm sure. You all will need a place to stay. I'll get you set up, just give me a few minutes."

Chief Stark made a phone call that included the appropriate amount of holiday greetings, and then he asked about providing rooms. After a couple of minutes, he thanked the person on the other line and hung up. "Okay, we have you all setup. Sarah has guest quarters in the back of the diner. It's clean and, hell, there's plenty of food on site. As long as you don't mind sharing a room, there're two beds and it has a full bathroom with a shower. It's kind of like a small apartment."

Mark and Max exchanged a look. "That will be fine," Wells replied.

428

"Well, let's head over there and get you settled in, looks like tomorrow is going to be a big day." Before leaving, the chief got Officer Ryan to start calling some of the people who had participated in the search party. "Set them up about 30 to 45 minutes apart, starting at ten. I don't want them all tripping all over each other or hearing what each other has to say. Let's try to keep this quiet. We don't need our town in a panic until we know what's going on." Grabbing his jacket and gloves, Stark led the two agents out of the building and asked them to follow him across town.

Wells followed the taillights of the police cruiser in front of him down the street and around the block, pulling into the space next to Chief Stark in front of the diner. There was a light on inside, but it was obvious the diner was closed. Chief Stark exited his patrol car and stood on the sidewalk waiting for Wells and Max to join him. Rapping on the door, he waited a moment. Then the door pushed open, allowing them entry. The threesome was greeted by a middle aged woman with a broad smile. The chief smiled back, "Sarah, sorry for the late intrusion and thanks for helping us out. This is Special Agents Wells and Nichols with the FBI. They're helping us try to figure out what happened to little Jessie."

Sarah nodded in response and turned her gaze to the agents. "Well, come on in out of the cold. I put a pot of coffee on and have the room in the back all made up. You're welcome as long as you need."

Filing in behind the chief, Wells and Max followed him into the warmth of the diner. The atmosphere was exactly what you would expect from a small town diner. Several booths lined the wall, allowing the diners to watch the town activities through the windows as they ate. Tables with vinyl covered chromed chairs sat in the middle of the room, spaced evenly across the black and white tiled floor. A long counter ran nearly the length of the restaurant, separating the diners from the pull-through serving window from the kitchen.

Sarah offered three cups of coffee; the chief declined. "If I don't get home soon the missus will have my hide. Have to at least make it before Christmas actually rings in. I'll be back in the morning before the others start to arrive. You all have a good night. Merry Christmas," he said as he made his way to the door and back into the night.

Wells and Max each accepted the warm brew and doctored their cups with the condiments that sat on the counter. As they sipped their drinks, Sarah showed them how to operate the lights and locks on the doors. "Okay, let me get you something to eat. I can't let you go to sleep hungry. The grill is not warm, but I could dish you a slice of meatloaf. It was baked a little earlier. It's still warm."

"We don't want to be any trouble," Wells offered. "Letting us stay here tonight is more than enough."

"Nonsense," Sarah said waving her hand for them to follow her as she led them into the back room, through the swinging door into the kitchen. Sarah pulled a couple of plates off the shelf next to the fry station. Peeling back some foil from a long tray that sat on the stainless steel table in the middle of the room, she grabbed a knife from an assortment that hung from straps along the wall and quickly slid it through the meat that was now releasing a delicious aroma. Max's stomach was already responding. It was only then that she realized she couldn't remember when they had eaten last.

Sarah placed a healthy portion of meatloaf and a large dinner roll onto each plate. "Sorry, it's not a well-rounded meal. I'll make sure you have a good breakfast in the morning."

Max took a bite of the mouth-watering food that seemed to melt against her tongue. "Don't apologize. This is amazing, and we don't expect you to cook for us on Christmas morning."

"Don't be silly. I live to feed people. It's what I do. The least I can do for you, trying to find the sick person that hurt Jessie. Poor little thing." Sarah shook her head as she busied herself, tidying up the kitchen and putting away the tray while the agents ate.

With stomachs full and the kitchen straightened, Sarah led the two into a room off to the left and behind the kitchen. "It's not much, but it ought to be comfortable for a night or two. Stay as long as you need. There are fresh towels in the bath, and you can help yourself to anything in the kitchen. I live right next door in the white house. If you need anything just come tap on the door. There's an extra key on the hook just inside the kitchen door. Should you need to leave, that will get you back in. I guess I can trust you with that, you being FBI and all," Sarah chuckled. "Alright I'm leaving now to get some sleep."

The agents thanked her and watched her turn and leave. Wells followed and locked the door behind her. When he returned he saw Max assessing their surroundings. The room was small but cozy. There was a small couch and chair, a console television that had clearly been there since the eighties, but apparently still worked because a newer DVD player was attached to it, as well as a receiver for satellite service. The other side of the room was taken up by two full sized beds. Next to the bed on the right was a door, which she assumed led to the bathroom. She looked up as Mark returned and gave him a big smile. "Well, Special Agent in Charge it looks like the Bureau will just have to get over the fact that we are sharing a room tonight. Merry Christmas," she said with a mischievous grin on her face, her emerald eyes sparkling as she dropped her belongings onto the chair.

Wells returned her smile and soaked in the playful look on her face. He approached her, taking her into his arms. Max returned his embrace, releasing a big sigh as she allowed her body to relax for the first time in days. Wells looked down at her. Their eyes met, and Max rose to her toes, her hands wrapping around his neck and pulling him towards her. Their bodies pushed together as their lips met. That warm familiar feeling filled Max immediately. She was always amazed at how quickly she responded to his touch, his kiss. She heard a quiet moan and suddenly realized it was coming from her. Mark softly played with her lips with his tongue then pushed between her teeth, allowing their mouths to explore causing passion to rise.

Max ran her hands down his muscular back and pulled his hips into her. He lifted her, wrapping her legs around his hips, and carried her over to the nearest bed. He gently laid her down and pressed the length of his body against hers. The kisses became even more intense. With one hand still holding her against him, his other worked to slip her shirt up over her head, and then he removed his own. Max's own hands pulled at his pants, slowly undoing them and working them over his hips and down his thighs. Moments later their efforts had rendered their bodies naked. They wound together becoming one, slow movements at first, then quickening. Max pulled Mark deep into her until they could no longer hold back, releasing together. Exhausted and satisfied their bodies still entwined, they dropped off to sleep quickly.

Max woke with a start. She looked over to see Mark was fast asleep. His dark hair tossed. A lone curl draped over his forehead. She smiled and pulled the covers up around him. She could tell it was still dark outside. Early? Middle of the night? Not being sure she decided to check her cell phone. Sliding out of the sheets, she padded in bare feet across the floor and retrieved her phone from the pocket of her coat which was still resting on the chair where she had dropped it. It was four o'clock in the morning…, Christmas morning. Not quite how she pictured the first Christmas with Mark, but last night had been amazing. Smiling, she set the alarm on her phone for six thirty and crawled back into bed, still time to sleep. Mark moaned slightly as she slid under the covers and wrapped her body around his in an effort to ward off the chill she had gotten in the few moments out from under the blankets. Her hand rested on his taunt stomach muscles. She laid her head on his chest and kissed him gently before dozing back off.

Morning came soon enough. The cell phone went off as planned at six thirty. Max opened her eyes and was greeted by Mark gazing down at her. "Ummm," she moaned. "How long have you been watching me?"

"Long enough to see just how beautiful you are."

Max stretched her body. Her lean muscular legs pressed against his as she pushed her breasts against his chest, the connection causing immediate arousal. Max slid on top of his body, straddling him and slowly working her hips against his. She tossed her long, wavy hair to the side and pulled him into her, drawing his head up, engaging in a passionate kiss. Once again they brought each other over the edge.

Their hearts raced together at first, then calmed. "We better get out of this bed, or we may be found by Sarah," Max joked.

Mark groaned in disagreement. "Merry Christmas," he said gently kissing her again.

"Merry Christmas, Special Agent Wells."

"We'll do something special once we end this."

"I'm going to hold you to that," Max smiled and then kissed his cheek.

"Okay. On three we get up together."

"Deal."

Together they said it, "One, two, three." Their feet hit the floor at the same time. Max gave him a mischievous grin, as they both rose out of the bed.

"Shower?"

Mark's eye brow raised and he glanced at the clock across the room. The hands in the shape of a chicken indicated it was nearly seven thirty. "We better not push it. You go first. I'll report in."

Max pushed out her lip in a pout. "Okay, but you owe me when we get home."

"Oh, no problem with that," Mark replied then leaned over and kissed her pouting lip. "I'll see you in a few minutes, Agent Nichols." He swatted her on the behind as she turned away.

An hour later, both agents were showered and ready to start the interviews with the volunteers that had helped search for Jessie the day she'd gone missing. They entered the kitchen as they headed towards the restaurant and found Sarah preparing eggs, bacon, and biscuits and gravy. She had coffee brewed, and upon seeing them, she immediately poured them each a cup.

"Well, good morning. I hope you were comfortable last night."

Max replied, making sure not to look in Mark's direction, "It was perfect. Thank you for providing us with a comfortable place to stay."

"The chief called. He'll be here in about thirty minutes. I thought you might like some breakfast. Least I can do to help you have a little bit of a Merry Christmas."

"We really do appreciate it, Sarah. And Merry Christmas to you too," Wells offered.

Sarah busied herself by finishing the food and dishing it out onto plates. "Here you go."

"This looks fantastic. Thank you for taking time from your family today," Max said.

"Oh, it's no worry. My husband passed away several years ago, and we never did have any young ones. So it's just me and this little town. I'm Momma to everyone, I guess." Sarah placed the plates onto the counter where the agents had each grabbed a stool and were sipping on their coffees.

Max smiled in acknowledgement of both the story and the food, and then dug into the savory looking dish in front of her. The night's activities had left her famished. Mark thanked Sarah and tore into his food too.

Before they could finish their meals, the bell over the door rang as the chief stepped in after stomping snow off his feet. "Boy, it's coming down out there again. Guess the kids get their wish for a white Christmas. I'm sure there will be some hills getting a work out later today. Good morning, Agents. I see Sarah has introduced you to some of her fine food."

"Yes, she certainly has," Wells answered, standing up to shake the chief's hand.

"Aw, sit down. Enjoy your meal. I just wanted to come up here and make sure we had our game plan laid out. We have Dale coming in first. He's our local real estate agent. He pretty much knows everyone and is real close to Tina, little Jessie's mom. Then we have four others coming in. I know you wanted to keep this under wraps, but I have to tell you, it won't take a moment after the first couple of people for it to get out. This town is tight, and people, well, they share." The chief slid onto a stool next to Mark and accepted a cup of coffee Sarah slid in front of him.

"Understood, we'll just need to move quickly. If anyone knows anything then we just need to work through each possible story to see if it leads us anywhere." Wells paused for a moment, choosing his words carefully. "Have you made contact with the child's mother?"

"I spoke to her myself this morning. I didn't want to unsettle the holiday. I told her we needed to talk to Jessie before too much time passed, and that other children were at risk." The chief sighed and shook his head.

433

"I sure hated to do that, but I knew that would get her to allow us to talk to Jessie today."

"We won't talk to her any longer than we need to. If there's anything she remembers about the un-sub, we'll get to it quickly, so they can get back to enjoying their day."

The room fell silent. The group finished their food, and Sarah offered them each refills. A few minutes before ten o'clock they saw a car pull up to the front of the building, and the driver made his way through the snow into the diner. The interviews were about to begin.

The bell above the door rang, and in walked a portly man, kicking snow off his boots and shaking it off his coat and hat. Sarah greeted him first, "Merry Christmas, Dale. Now get in here before you catch your death." She took his coat and offered him a cup of coffee.

Dale blew breath onto his hands, rubbing them together, and walked over to the table that Wells and Max had occupied. The chief was still sitting at the counter. Both agents rose from their seats to greet the man. After proper introductions Wells offered him a seat in the chair across from them.

"Thanks for coming in on this special holiday," Wells started. "We hope not to take too much time away from your family. We have a few quick questions."

"I'm sure happy to help in any way I can. And don't worry about the holiday, gets me out from under the missus's foot while she cooks. I just get my hands slapped anyway."

Wells began the interview asking, "First, can you tell us how you know Tina and Jessie?"

"Sure. I doubt there's anyone in this town I don't know, sold most of them their homes. After Tina's divorce she needed a small affordable home for her and little Jessie. Of course I've known Tina her whole life, sold her parents their home just outside of town. Tina was probably five or six years old then. I had just taken over the agency from my father at that time."

"Can you tell us about the day Jessie went missing?"

Dale shook his head. "It was a scary thing. I got the call that she was missing and then helped round up a few others. It was snowing real hard that day. I assumed she had gotten cold and crawled into some place to get warm. Until... she showed up at the hospital."

Max took over. "When you were helping with the search, was there anyone helping that is not a local? Or anyone that did not quite fit in?"

"No. Everyone in this town is pretty tight. It was all local folks."

"Did you go door to door or help with the ground search?"

434

"I was on door to door searches. We went around asking if anyone had seen Jessie and if we could check outbuildings, garages, anywhere she might have tucked away in."

Max continued the questions. "Did anyone seem uncomfortable in those homes, overly interested or uncooperative?"

Dale rubbed his hand over his face and leaned back in his chair. "Well, there is old man Tanner. He's always a bit uncooperative."

Max felt her first sign of hope. "What can you tell us about Mr. Tanner?"

"He lost his wife last year to cancer. He's been kind of isolated since then."

"How long have you known Mr. Tanner?"

"Oh, I think since I was probably ten or twelve. He's in his eighties now."

The encouragement Max felt moments before quickly dissipated. She glanced at Wells. "What about anyone else?"

"No, nothing stands out. Everyone let us check around, and some even came out to help us search."

"Did you see any passing cars?" Wells asked.

Dale thought for a moment then shrugged his shoulders. "Nothing stands out. I was focused on looking for any tracks in the snow or any clue that might tell us what direction Jessie had gone off in."

Max jumped back in again. "What about Jessie's father? Is he still in the area? Did he participate in the search?"

"That deadbeat hasn't been around for a long time. He left town after the divorce and hasn't been back even to visit Jessie."

"Any idea where he lives now?"

"Last I knew he moved up to Chicago. Name is Dale just like mine."

"Okay, well thanks for your time today." Wells handed Dale a card. "If you think of anything, anything at all that seems unusual or stands out, no matter how insignificant it might seem, please call right away."

Dale accepted the card, shook hands with the agents, thanked Sarah for the coffee, and after bidding everyone a happy holiday, headed back out into the snow. Just a couple of minutes after he pulled away, another car pulled up in front of the diner. The bell over the door chimed again, and in entered their second search party interview of the day.

At one o'clock the team stopped for lunch in between interviews. They had talked to three people so far and had turned up nothing unusual. Each person had pretty much told the same story Dale had shared. Nothing stood out. Everyone involved in the search was from the town. The heavy snow had covered tracks, and the houses they had gone to had been more than cooperative.

Max ran a searched for Jessie's father's name in the Chicago area and after a few minutes she had contacted him. She was shocked at his demeanor. He was clearly more concerned about not paying child support. Even after telling him about his daughter's injuries his only concern was about the money. After several minutes of convincing him that she could care less about the support payments. He was able to provide an alibi. He was working in Rockford on the day Jessie was taken. He worked at a restaurant and put his boss on the line to confirm that he had been there during the time Jessie was missing. While he was clearly a deadbeat dad, he was not their un-sub. Max was not surprised. She knew Jack Tyler was their man. They just needed to find him.

After enjoying a wonderful turkey meal that Sarah had prepared, complete with the traditional holiday sides, it was time to continue on with the interviews. Two hours later, after meeting with everyone Officer Ryan had setup for them to talk with, they had turned up nothing useful in finding who had taken and abused Jessie or anything that helped find the un-sub for the other abductions and murders. There was going to be no choice but to meet with the girl and see if she could tell them anything about her abductor.

With the last interview over, Wells called the chief, who then returned to the diner for a debriefing. The agents covered each interview and let the chief know they were unable to uncover any viable leads. Though the chief was not happy with the idea, he knew talking to Jessie was necessary. It was now nearly four o'clock in the afternoon, and after talking on the phone for a few minutes, the chief returned and requested to delay the meeting with Jessie until the morning. Jessie had gone over to her grandmother's house for dinner and would not be home for a couple of hours. The chief explained that it had been a fun yet emotional day for the child, and her mother did not want to over stress her as she was still healing. She offered to meet with them at nine o'clock in the morning.

Both Wells and Max were disappointed, knowing full well that allowing time to pass was not good. Max was becoming increasingly concerned that Jack had already completed his mission of putting his daughter back together, and patience was certainly not her strong suit. Wells looked at Max then returned his eyes back to the chief. "Nine o'clock will be fine. We'll allow the child the evening, but tomorrow we must talk with her."

Max started to protest, but Wells looked at her again. There was something in his eyes that told her to stop. The chief committed to them that he would return in the morning at eight forty-five. He said goodnight and once again left the diner.

"Why didn't you push?" Max was clearly frustrated.

Mark looked at her. "I understand your desire to move quickly, but we need the child rested. And if our thoughts are correct, we may need to have Jessie go get DNA tests."

Max nodded. She understood that Mark had no desire to have the little girl learn on Christmas day that the mouth, everyone believed to have been savagely severed then reattached to her face, might not even be her own.

"Tomorrow morning the team will return to assist us. If we get any leads, we'll be able to go in. That's the main reason to wait. I'm hoping we get something to go on. Something that will tell us where to look and even if Jessie can't help us, we'll have the full team to go through all the cases again. Maybe we've missed something."

Max nodded, though her mind was racing, before she could respond, Sarah walked back into the main part of the diner. "Can I talk you two into a slice of pumpkin or apple pie?"

"Sarah, you're truly spoiling us. I couldn't live in this town, or I would gain a hundred pounds," Max teased.

"Oh, I'm pretty sure a girl as fit as you obviously are is quite capable of not letting her body get out of control." Sarah ribbed back as she set two fresh pies in front of the agents and stood with a hand on one hip waiting for them to make a selection.

Both Mark and Max answered pumpkin in unison. For a few moments they all three laughed. "You two should eat pie and then enjoy the rest of your Christmas night. You've been working all day."

For a moment Max felt exposed. She had a good feeling Sarah knew there was more to her relationship with Mark than co-workers. She was even more certain when Sarah winked at them a few seconds later. "Well, I'm going to head out. Have a good night. Feel free to help yourself to whatever you need." Sarah headed into the back of the kitchen, and a few moments later they heard the back door shut and latch.

"She's on to us," Max said as she popped a bite of pie in her mouth.

"I know. Let's just hope she keeps it to herself. Not that I'm really concerned, but we don't want people focused on us and not on the case."

"So, do you have any ideas on how to spend our evening?"

"I'd like to drive the distance between Jessie's house and the hospital. Just want a sense for how far or how long it could have taken to abduct the girl and then deliver her to the hospital."

"I'm game, though it's already dark. We won't be able to see much tonight. It's snowed nearly all day. The streets will be slick."

"Hey, I'm used to snowy weather. No problem." Mark teased.

After finishing their pie, they went back to the guest quarters and gathered their coats. Retrieving the key Sarah told them to use, they exited the diner and headed out into the dark to get a quick overview of the small town of Heyworth, hoping to see something that might provide a clue. Tomorrow morning they would talk to Jessie, the team would return, and maybe they would get a lead.

Chapter Twenty-Four

The day was perfect so far. Dinner was ready, and Jack set a beautiful table. He only needed to get himself and the girls dressed for the special meal. Excitement flooded him as he double checked the clothes he had selected and headed down to the basement.

Hitting the bottom of the stairs, Jack's heart raced as he realized the plan he had been focusing on for nearly a year had worked perfectly. He did, in fact, have his wife and daughter back in his life, and he was...*happy*.

His breath caught as he put his hand on the freezer door and pulled it open. Inside his girls waited for him to get them ready for the evening. Removing Hope first, he carried her to the surgical room and laid her out on the stainless steel table. He slowly removed her Grinch pajamas and gently washed her body with cold water, making sure to avoid any sensitive areas where sutures were applied. He carefully dried her body completely. Then he shampooed her hair, and once complete, he blow dried and styled it. For a moment he reflected on his time at the Clary Sage School of Cosmetology where he had trained. He thought of Melody and some of the people he'd acquired friendships with during his time in Oklahoma. He smiled at the memory of how well the cover had worked for him.

Pushing the fleeting thoughts from his mind, he focused back on his wife lying on the table in front of him. Once Hope's hair was perfect, he lifted the dress he had purchased for her and slowly worked the dress onto her body. With a brush and some hairspray, he styled her hair in just the way she always wore it for him on special occasions. He slid on shoes that perfectly matched the color of the dress, and finally he applied some makeup. He then sat her up, slid her legs off the table and raised her up to face him with her toes touching the floor. She looked stunning; the dress fit perfectly. He stared at her, nearly unable to breathe.

"Hope, you look amazing." He hugged her close against his body and nuzzled her neck. "I can't wait to dance with you later. I'll put on some music for us."

Forcing himself to pull away, he carefully carried Hope upstairs and seated her at the dining table where she had sat earlier. Kissing her tenderly he brushed a stray strand of hair away from her eyes. "I'll be back in just a few moments. I love you, darling."

Jack turned and headed again to the basement and back to the freezer to prepare Faith the same way. He was more modest with her. Even though he was a doctor, the nudity of his young daughter had always made

439

him feel shy. He always wanted to be appropriate. Today was no different. As he bathed her he was careful to keep his eyes away from private areas and kept his focus on the sensitive sutured areas, making sure he did not get those areas wet. He shampooed her hair, carefully dried her body, blow dried her hair, then dressed her in her new dress. She looked amazing. He was certain she was smiling. Lifting her up he carried her over to a mirror on the wall and showed her how beautiful she looked.

"You look like a princess, Daddy's princess. Come on. Let's go show Mommy how perfect you look." Bursting with pride Jack carried her upstairs.

"Hope, look at our adorable daughter. Isn't she a princess?" Jack held Faith in front of Hope, who sat slightly at an angle at the dining room table, one arm dangling at her side. "Okay, let me get ready, and I'll join you in just a minute. Doesn't the food smell wonderful? He placed Faith in a chair at the table next to Hope. Be right back." Jack hurried himself to get ready, excited to return to the girls.

Completing the loop in his tie, he double checked himself in the mirror, smiling at his appearance. Slipping on his shoes, he closed the closet door, brushed the comforter smooth on the bed, and headed down the hall towards the kitchen. The smell of the food called to his senses.

Jack immediately busied himself by carving the turkey and putting all the side dishes into bowls. He carried the dishes out to the table where Hope and Faith sat waiting for him to join them. He noticed Hope sitting a bit awkwardly and adjusted her in the chair, pushing her seat forward, closer to the table. He laid her hand on the table, wrapping her fingers around the stem of the wine glass, and poured a red wine.

"This is a special year. It's a full bodied, earthy bouquet. You'll love it." He brushed the hair back from her face, looping the lock behind her ear. His eyes drifted to Faith who sat perfectly poised with a big smile on her face. "Look at our beautiful daughter, Hope. She's so happy." He smiled as happiness filled his chest. There was a special calmness that he had not felt for a very long time. "Okay, so who's hungry? I know I sure am."

After lighting the candles on the table completing the perfect ambiance, Jack began dishing food onto the three plates. Everything was beautiful. He was so focused on the food and his family and the total perfection of the moment that he didn't notice the car headlights flash across the front window. It was only when he heard the car door close did he realize he had a visitor. He knew that with his car in the drive and the lights glowing in the house, he would be unable to avoid answering the door.

Jack slid out of his chair and went quickly to the bedroom, removing a syringe of Chloroform and a rag from a medical bag that he kept tucked away in the closet. He needed to be prepared. As he stuffed the items in the pocket of his pants, he heard the doorbell, followed by a knock on the door.

Taking a deep breath and a glance towards the dining room table, Jack opened the door, blocking the opening with his body. Outside the door Dale stood with a large plastic bag in his hands the snow falling heavily around him.

"Merry Christmas, Jack, I know you don't have any family in the area, so I thought I'd come by and bring you some homemade food. The wife packed everything, even some pie."

"Dale, this is a surprise. Merry Christmas to you too, but this was not necessary. It's snowing so hard. You should be at home." Jack was trying to think of a way to turn Dale away, but the cold weather and the heavy snow was making it difficult. His mind working quickly he said, "I'd love to let you in, but I'm a little under the weather."

"Oh, well then let me come in and make this for you. Even more reason to feed you a good home cooked meal."

"Well, don't blame me if you end up needing a visit in my office next week," Jack said as he stepped back from the door, inviting Dale in. His hand slipped into his pocket and his fingers wrapped around the syringe.

"Oh, I'm too old and mean for a little flu bug to require me to go to the doctor, even if it is you." Dale laughed as he stepped through the doorway.

Jack used his body to block the view of the dining room as best he could and led Dale to the kitchen. As soon as Dale was fully in the house, the smell of food assaulted his nose. Entering the kitchen he saw the turkey in the pan and all the pots on the stove. He turned to Jack. "Looks like you've been cooking a bit yourself." As he spoke his eyes scanned the room and fixed on the dining room table. A gasp escaped his mouth. "What the hell?"

"Dale, meet my wife, Hope, and daughter, Faith." Jack's face showed both a sense of pride and a sinister smile.

"Jack? What have you done?"

Dale's eyes took in the scene: two bodies sitting posed at the table. Both had grotesque, fixed stares with milky pupils. The heads were slightly askew, each with obvious stitches. The woman's stitches were around her scalp, the face not quite properly aligned. The child's mouth was constantly agape in an unnatural laugh. Dale's mind suddenly clicked. That mouth, he had seen it somewhere. It matched the injuries Jessie had sustained. Turning to face Jack, he struggled for words. His heart raced as he fought waves of nausea that lurched in his stomach. Trying to remain calm, he decided negotiating was his only option.

"Jack, you need help, son. The FBI is here talking to people. They're going to figure this out. Let's go to them, Jack. I'm your friend. I'll help you," he said as he continued to watch Jack terror rising in his chest. Suddenly the reality of the situation seeped in and he knew his situation was desperate.

"The FBI, is here in Heyworth?"

"Yes, Jack. Let me take you to them. You can explain everything. They'll understand. We know you lost your wife and daughter. Everyone will understand. You just need to explain it to them. Come with me, Doc. I'll help you." Dale placed his hand on Jack's arm and tried to turn him to the door.

"Let me guess. Is it Special Agent Maxine Nichols?"

Dale stopped, surprised by the question. "You know Agent Nichols?"

"Let's just say we've spoken before."

"Well, good, that will make it easier to explain to her what happened here," Dale said, waving his arm in a sweeping motion at the dining room table. His heart was racing as he felt he was losing ground in convincing the man he had grown to respect as a friend, a trusted physician and skilled surgeon. He needed to get Jack moving towards the door and decided to head in that direction himself.

When Dale turned his back, Jack removed the syringe from his pocket and depressed it into the rag. He followed Dale towards the door, but before he got across the room, Jack slid his arm around Dale's neck and forced the rag over his mouth. Dale's hands reached up, attempting to pull Jack's hand away, but Jack was so much stronger. It only took a few moments before the Chloroform took over, and Dale slumped to the floor.

Jack pulled Dale's keys from the heavy man's pants pocket. He went through the dining room and before opening the door he grabbed another set of keys off the hook just above the light switch. He stomped through the snow to the barn and pushed the door open. Inside, sat a Toyota Tundra four-wheel drive. Weeks earlier he had bought and stored the vehicle - *just in case*. He swung the door open and pulled himself up into the seat. Firing up the engine, he slid the four-wheel drive button into the on position and navigated the truck through the snow to the front driveway. He opened the door, dropped out of the truck, and went to Dale's car, climbing into the driver's seat. He turned the car in the driveway and worked it behind the house, churning through the snow, and into the barn, being careful to stay in the truck's tracks making sure he did not get stuck. With the car stowed he, Jack closed the barn door behind him, and cold wind and snow blowing into his eyes, he returned to the house through the back door.

He walked to the place where Dale laid on the floor, still exactly as he had left him. Dale was not that tall, but he was a heavy man. Jack decided he could slide Dale down the stairs in a blanket. He went and got the comforter off the bed and laid it out next to Dale, rolling the big man over until he was centered on the blanket. Using the corners Jack pulled Dale down the stairs and into the surgical room.

Even with the bumping against the stairs, Dale didn't completely wake up. Once inside the surgical room, Jack lifted the man onto the surgical table and carefully removed his clothes, quickly cutting them away with the surgical scissors from the operating tray. Once the clothes had been completely removed, Jack used zip ties to secure Dale's hands and feet to the table. By the time Jack had him immobilized, the stout realtor was showing signs of waking.

Ignoring the mumbling that was coming from Dale, Jack went back upstairs and out the front door once again into the snow. The truck was equipped with a locked cargo cover that operated on a hinged system, allowing Jack to store items in the bed, while having complete privacy and security. He opened the hinged cover and laid down the tailgate.

Returning inside he lifted Hope from the chair she'd been sitting in and carried her out into the snow. He laid her gently in the back of the truck. He immediately returned to the house to bring Faith out as well. With his family in the vehicle, he closed the tailgate and shut the cargo cover, then went back inside.

Leaving the food and dishes scattered about, Jack turned down the lights upstairs then returned to the basement and re-entered the surgical room. He found Dale fully awake now and fighting against his restraints.

"Jack. What are you doing? You don't need to do this. You have friends in this town. I'm your friend, and I'll help you."

Jack looked at the man. He was clearly trying to negotiate his way off the table and back to freedom. As Dale was talking, a small ringing noise came from somewhere on the floor. Jack traced the sound to a pocket in Dale's coat and found a cell phone. The display showed that HOME was calling. Jack looked down at Dale. "You're going to answer this call and say everything is fine and that you might be a while. If you say anything else, I'll kill you, and as soon as I'm done with you, I'll go see the missus. Do you understand?"

Dale's eyes grew wide with fear. He nodded his acknowledgement to follow the instruction. Jack slid this finger over the answer bar and held the phone up to Dale's ear. He held his eyes on Dale's and nodded.

"Hey, babe, everything okay? Oh me, yeah the roads are bad, but I am fine. I made it to Jack's. Look, I may need to stay here a while. Don't wait up for me." Dale's voice shook a little as he spoke, but he kept going. "The Doc is under the weather, so I'm helping him out a bit. It'll take me a little longer, but I'll be home as soon as the snow lets up. I promise I'll be careful. I love you."

Jack closed the phone. "You did good, Dale. Your wife will not see me tonight." Jack reached for the duct tape from the shelf and placed a long strip over Dale's mouth. "Unfortunately for you, Dale, it seems you have managed to ruin the holiday with my family. I can't ignore that. But I do thank you for the tip regarding the FBI. That bit of information will help me protect my family. For that, you will be rewarded."

Jack turned away and opened the small fridge, retrieving a vial and syringe. He inserted the needle into the vial, suctioning out 5cc of liquid. Turning back to the table, he saw Dale struggling against the zip ties. His eyes were wide, face red, and blotchy spots were now covering his chest. "I can see you're distressed, Dale. You must calm down, or you'll have a coronary."

Jack held up the syringe. "This will take the edge off. I don't usually provide this privilege to adults who find their way onto my table. But...like you said, we *are* friends." Dale struggled even harder as Jack inserted the syringe into a vein in his right arm.

Jack watched as moments later Dale was awake, but relaxed. He could no longer fight, but he would remain aware of what he was seeing. Jack watched Dale's eyes follow him as he prepared. Removing all of his clothing Jack shivered slightly. His suit was ruined from the snow, and his socks were soaked inside his shoes. He shrugged; this held no importance compared to getting his wife and child to safety. He just had to finish up this one little detail. He pulled on scrubs to begin the surgical process.

Jack switched the light over the surgical table on and pulled the tray closer where he could see the assortment of tools. He lifted a scalpel and made a long incision down Dale's chest, through the navel to the top of the pelvic bone. As blood began to spill from Dale's body, his eyes remained wide open and tears flowed from the corners, but he did not move. He couldn't.

"Soon, Dale, this won't last long. That's good for you. For me, well, I would love to spend a few days with you. We barely got to know each other, but my family is waiting for me in the car. So, I must be going soon. Rest assured, I'll keep my promise about your wife. I have no

444

business here anymore." Focusing again on Dale's body, Jack cut two circular flaps, one on each side of the incision. Next he picked up the bone saw and began cutting down the incision, the saw chipping through the breast bone and ribs. The table pooled with blood now, and Jack pushed his hands inside Dale's body deeply until his fingers found the organs he so cherished.

It didn't take long until the heart stopped beating, and the blood stopped flowing. Dale had died with his eyes open, watching the entire process. Jack hadn't noticed. The euphoria consumed him. It had been so long since he had completely allowed himself the fulfillment of holding life as it leaves a body—a body he had caused the life to leave. It was different with the little girls. He had committed to Hope that he would not hurt them, and he had kept that promise. By fully sedating them, he had ensured they felt no pain.

Realizing Dale was dead Jack knew he needed to get moving. He would need to leave town before Special Agent Maxine Nichols found where he lived. It wouldn't be long before Dale was reported as missing, and the first place they would go would be to the last known place he had been. Jack's home. Yes, it was time to leave. Heyworth was no longer safe.

Chapter Twenty-Five

"I can't read these files anymore," Max said pushing back from the table. She and Mark had been reviewing the case files ever since the chief had told them they couldn't interview Jessie until the next day. He'd left them, then Sarah had left, and they had made their way through two pots of coffee and piles of paperwork and computer searches.

Mark stood and stretched. "I know it's frustrating. We'll find the lead we need, and we'll get him."

Max did not feel the confidence Mark spoke of, but she had hopes that the interview with Jessie would tell them something. Maybe she would remember where the subject…, Jack, had taken her or something he had said. Max hoped the little girl could remember the smallest detail, a smell, a sound, anything that might help them identify how or where to find him.

"It's after midnight. Let's get some rest. Tomorrow is an important day," Mark said, pulling Max to her feet.

Max settled into his arms, then pulled away to clear the table. Mark started putting the case files back together and closing down his computer. With everything stored, they headed back to the guest quarters and settled into the bed. Tired, they wrapped into each other's arms.

Max spoke first, her head lying on Mark's chest. I really have some shopping to do when we get back home."

Mark smiled and pushed a strand of hair away from her face. "This doesn't seem like Christmas, but I'm so grateful to be with you no matter where we are. You're the only gift I need."

"Aw, you're *soooo* sweet." Max slid up on his chest and gently kissed him then rested her head on his shoulder. Exhausted, it was only a few minutes before Max was pulled into a fitful sleep with dreams of children running away from Jack Tyler. Mark dropped into sleep right behind her.

The couple jolted to a start when Max's cell phone alarm sounded alerting them that it was six thirty. Mark stretched his strong, muscular body against Max. Her body always responded to his, and for a few moments they remained wrapped together enjoying the comfort of each other's warm bodies.

"I love laying here with you," Max admitted.

"I love laying anywhere with you," Mark added.

"But… we must get up. I just know Sarah will pop in on us any minute to make us some savory breakfast. I'm certain she's on to us, so we can't let her see us like this." Max pushed against Mark and rose to kiss him. Her hair fell forward, forcing her to push it to one side to keep it out of Mark's face. She giggled knowing she was tempting him. Pushing away, she slid off the bed and wiggled her finger for him to follow her into the bathroom. Mark's eyes soaked in her perfectly sculpted body and happily followed her into the shower.

Clean and refreshed, the pair dressed and prepared for their day. Mark called into the FBI headquarters while Max dried her hair. He hung up the phone as Max was pulling her hair back into a loose ponytail. "What's the word?" she asked.

"The team will be on the ground in Bloomington at noon. I told them to call to see if they should meet us here or back in Le Roy. We won't know until we've talked with Jessie. If she gives us any leads, we can have them join us. If not they can head to Le Roy and start working leads there."

Max nodded. She heard a tap at the door. As expected Sarah came a little earlier today. She started the coffee and was going to make something for them to eat. Max felt like she needed to get a good workout in and was looking forward to getting back to the gym at home. The food was amazing, but not exactly on a healthy diet plan.

An hour later, and again with her stomach full, Max found herself anxiously awaiting the next step. Her instincts told her they needed to move quickly. Failure to do so would either mean another child would get hurt or murdered, or Jack would again slip through her fingers. The thoughts made her slightly shudder.

"You okay?"

Looking at Mark's concerned face, she rubbed her arms. "Yeah, just the cold, I guess, and anxious to get moving."

"I know what this means to you." Mark looked at his watch. "The chief should be here any minute. Let's hope Jessie can remember something."

As if on cue, the chief walked into the diner. He walked over to where Wells and Max had been seated, but were now standing, and shook their hands. "Good morning, Agent Wells. Nichols," he said nodding to each. "Sarah, can we get cups of coffee to go? It's colder than a room full of ex-wives out there. Agents, ready? I spoke to Tina, uh, Jessie's mother this morning, and they're ready for us. There's only one stipulation. If Jessie gets stressed, the interview is over." He stared hard. His eyes darted between both Wells and Nichols.

448

"We understand and will do everything possible to make sure that doesn't happen," Wells reassured.

Sarah placed three Styrofoam cups of steaming, warm brew on the counter. They each prepared their drinks, snapping on the lids before slipping into their coats and pulling their collars up tight around their necks preparing to head out into the snow.

The minute the door opened the wind and snow stung their faces. The chief opened the doors to the cruiser. Wells took the front seat next to the chief and Max slid into the back for the short ride to Jessie's house.

As they traveled Wells spoke, "I want you to conduct the interview." he said to Max.

Max was surprised, but did not show it. She considered this for a moment then replied, "It may be best. She has recently been traumatized by a stranger who is likely a male."

Wells nodded, smiling internally. "Exactly, she may respond to you much more quickly, which will reduce any unnecessary stress."

Max just nodded and stared out the window for the rest of the drive. The snow was massive now. According the weather reports the small town had received nearly eight inches of snow overnight. She wondered if there would be delays at the airport. She pictured speaking with the child and began mentally preparing for the conversation as best she could.

After just five minutes of churning through the barely travelable streets, they arrived at Jessie's house. The chief pulled in front of the driveway but didn't risk pulling in. Max assumed, even though the cruiser was a SUV with four-wheel drive, he wasn't willing to take any chances of getting stuck.

The trio exited the vehicle and approached the house. Mark made eye contact with Max on the way to the door. She smiled, knowing he was wondering if she was okay with his recommendation. Max had worked a lot of different types of cases, but this would be her first interview with a child of a violent crime.

The chief rapped on the door, and Max could hear footsteps inside the home. A moment later the door swung open, and a young woman stood in front of them. She smiled, but Max sensed it was more forced than genuine.

"Come on in," she offered, stepping away from the door.

The chief stepped through first, followed by Max then Wells. Once inside, Tina took their coats and offered for them to have a seat in the living room.

Max took in the surroundings. It was a small home, but neat and cozy. There were a few toys in the corner and a doll on the coffee table.

The décor held a country charm with lacy curtains and oak furniture. Tina and the chief exchanged small talk for a moment. "Ma'am, my name is Agent Maxine Nichols, and this is Special Agent in Charge Mark Wells. We know this is difficult, and our intention is to take as little time as necessary. In order to make this easy, if it is alright with you, I'd like to talk with Jessie alone. You're welcome to be in the room, of course. And, if I could talk with her in her bedroom that might be the best way to make her comfortable."

Tina paused for a moment as she looked from Max to Wells and back again. "Okay, but please understand she's been through a lot. If it's too much for her, I'll have to ask you to leave."

"I understand, and I would do the same if I were her mother."

Tina's eyes met Max's and held for a moment. She stood and nodded for Max to follow her. Max looked over at Wells and the chief as she followed Tina across the living room and through an arched doorway that led to a hallway where there were rooms on either end and a bathroom straight ahead. They made a left and walked down the short hallway into Jessie's room.

The little girl was sitting on the bed playing with some Barbie dolls. She looked up as her mother and the strange woman entered the room.

Tina sat next to her daughter on the bed. "Jessie. This nice lady wants to talk to you about the day you got lost in the snow."

Jessie looked up at her mother, her eyes searching her mother's face, and then she turned to Max. "Hi."

Max had to physically focus on not reacting to the state of Jessie's face. Her little mouth was clearly stitched and scarred, yet she tried to force a smile.

"Hi, Jessie, my name is Maxine." Max kneeled down to eye level with Jessie. "You can call me Max if you want to. Most of my friends do. I'm with the FBI. Do you know what that is?"

Jessie nodded, "The important police."

"That's right. I heard you were a very smart young lady. I guess everyone was right. You have a nice room here." Max looked around at the pink vanity and shelves. "I bet you like the color pink."

"It's my favorite."

"I like it too." Max smiled and looked the little girl in the eyes. She wanted to show her that she was not afraid of the way she looked, and she needed to build trust with her. "You know the day you played in the snow? Can you tell me how far out in your yard you were playing?"

Jessie's eyes dropped down a little, and she pulled at a tuft on her comforter. "I was just playing in the snow."

"Did you go to the side of the house at all?"

Jessie shrugged her shoulders and shook her head.

"Okay. Do you remember seeing anyone? Or did you talk to anyone?"

"No."

"I want you to think really hard. Can you do that for me?"

"I guess so."

"Were there any cars parked on the street?"

"I don't think so. I don't remember any."

"How about what you do remember? Can you tell me the last thing you remember?"

"I don't remember anything. I went outside, but I don't even remember building my snowman."

"It's okay if you don't remember. Can you tell me the first thing you remember after going outside?"

"Waking up. I remember Dr. Jack checking on me and then telling me I could go home for Christmas."

Max felt her heart immediately race. "Dr. Jack?"

"He's real nice and funny. He fixed my mouth, and he made my throat better before."

Max looked at Tina. "He's the local doctor," Tina answered, sensing the question in Max's eyes.

"Okay, Jessie, you did really good today. And you know what? Each day is going to get better. Did you get these dolls from Santa?"

Jessie nodded and again smiled despite the pain she most certainly felt.

"Well, they sure are pretty. Will you promise me you will take good care of them?"

Jessie nodded. "I will."

"Thanks for talking to me today, Jessie. It was a very brave thing to do."

Jessie looked up at Max again, and her eyes with the little flecks of gray looked into Max's. "Do you have a badge?"

Max smiled. "I sure do." She removed the badge from her pocket and handed it to Jessie, letting the small hands explore the heavy, shiny metal.

Jessie's finger ran over the letters one by one then she handed it back to Max. "Will you catch the bad guy?"

Max felt saddened by her innocence and the depth of the question. She sensed Tina was on the verge of tears, but didn't dare break contact with Jessie. "I'm going to do everything I can to catch the bad guy. I promise you that."

Jessie studied her face again. Then her eyes returned to the tuft in the bed that her fingers had returned to plucking away at. She shook her head.

Max patted the young girl on the hand, thanked her once again, and turned to leave the room. Tina hugged her child before following Max back to the living room.

Once out of earshot of Jessie and back in front of the chief and Wells, Max asked, "What can you tell me about Dr. Jack?"

Chapter Twenty-Six

Jack looked down at Dale's dead body on the steel table. He had lost track of time somewhat and suddenly knew he must get moving. He pulled the shower handle that was mounted on the pulley over the steel table and began the cleansing process, carefully and thoroughly washing down Dale's body. Next, he removed his scrubs and he showered himself off. .

Jack worked meticulously cleaning his tools. Then he retrieved plastic sheeting from the shelf at the end of the room, carried it out, and laid it down on the rug just outside of the surgical room. Returning to the table inside the room, he cut the zip ties loose that had held Dale secure to the table then lifted him with a strain, carrying him with his feet dragging on the floor. He laid the dead man on the plastic. He rolled the body up tightly and grabbed duct tape from the furnace room. He kneeled to apply the tape to the roll, and then secured the body inside.

He returned to the shower and washed himself again until his skin was pink and hot. He scrubbed his fingernails with a toothbrush, and once satisfied, he washed the walls and floor with large amounts of bleach. Then, still naked, he left Dale where he was, climbed the basement stairs, and went to the master bedroom to dress. He quickly packed a suitcase, grabbing all the clothes and toiletries he would need to get him by for a little while.

With a suitcase packed and now fully dressed, Jack climbed back down the stairs to the basement and assessed the situation. He grabbed a moving dolly and straps that he had bought during one of his furniture purchases and laid it out next to the rug. He rolled the plastic-wrapped body onto the dolly and used the straps to secure it in place. Stressing his muscular body, he heaved the dolly up onto its wheels and dragged it a step at a time up the steep stairway.

The snow was too deep outside to take the dolly out, so he laid the dolly down. Returning to the basement, he grabbed Dale's clothes and the comforter he had used to drag Dale downstairs. Taking the stairs two at a time, he checked the time on the clock at the top of the stairs. Adrenaline pumped through him. It was morning. He had to get going soon. Time was running out.

He laid the comforter out next to the plastic-wrapped body and rolled the body onto it. He dropped the clothes on top of the pile, causing Dale's cell phone to fall onto the floor. Jack picked it up and shoved it into his pocket. Pulling on his coat and gloves, he checked to ensure he had his keys. Grabbing the comforter by the corners, he dragged the heavy body out to the driveway. After considering his options, he knew what he must do.

With Dale properly dealt with, he backed the Tundra up to the SUV and pulled out a tow bar from next to where the bodies of Hope and Faith rested. He worked to hitch up the SUV to the Tundra, ignoring the cold, which challenged his hands, and the snow that flurried in his eyes.

An hour later, Jack had the SUV properly hitched to the Tundra. He packed and loaded the medical supplies from the basement as well as clothes and necessities for Hope and Faith. Taking a final look around, he retrieved Faith's doll.

Once he had the final things packed into the truck all nestled in around the bodies of Hope and Faith, he returned to the house and went into the office where he retrieved his identifications from the safe that was concealed behind a picture on the wall in the office. He counted them. He still had three unique IDs. Each was complete with bank accounts, social security number, medical license, and passport. Reaching back into the safe he pulled out a bag. It contained two hundred thousand dollars in cash.

When he purchased the truck several weeks ago, he had done so under the name of Jake Thompson. He wouldn't be using that name though. Instead he would use one of his other identities Trent Jackman. He made a quick phone call. After answering some security questions and pressing several buttons, he had successfully transferred additional funds from his account in the Cayman Islands into an account he had previously established in the name of Trent Jackman, all untraceable. He stuffed the identifications and the cash into the small satchel that carried his stethoscope, a few syringes containing Chloroform, and a couple of rags.

He made his way through each room in the house, one by one turning out the lights and making sure he wasn't leaving anything he needed. He walked out the front door, locking it behind him.

He walked through the snow and double checked the lock on the truck bed cover then made his way to the driver's side, slapping his shoes on the side of the step as he climbed into the driver's seat. He turned over the engine and pulled away from the house. *Sorry, Agent Nichols, it's not our time.*

Chapter Twenty-Seven

Max stood waiting for the chief to answer her question regarding the person Jessie had referred to as Dr. Jack, but before he could answer, his phone rang. She waited as he took the call.

"How long ago? Where was he going? Okay, don't worry. We'll run out there and take a look around. I'm sure everything is fine. I'll call you as soon as I know anything."

The chief hung up his phone and turned back to Max. The look on his face told her something terrible was about to come out of his mouth. She was right.

"That was Dale's wife, Mary. She said that Dale went out to Dr. Taylor's house last night and never returned. He called her late and said that he made it there okay. He told her he would stay there until the snow stopped falling. She's been trying to call him since early this morning, and he's not picking up."

Max was becoming impatient.

"Who is Dr. Taylor? *And*, who is Dr. Jack that Jessie spoke of?"

"He's our local doctor, Jackson Taylor. He came into town a few months ago. Settled right in and has been doing some really great things for some of our folks, even helped with Jessie's surgery. Her face was…" He paused out of respect for Tina who had rejoined them in the living room. "He really did a good job helping Jessie."

Max and Wells exchanged a look, and Wells stood up immediately.

"Could we get our coats, please? Chief, we need to talk outside, and we need to go now."

The chief was already standing, and Tina was getting the coats. Max turned to her and thanked her while taking her coat. "We need to go now. Your daughter is a brave girl, and she's given us a lot of information. We may have more questions later, but I don't think it will be necessary. I'm sorry we need to leave so abruptly, but it's important."

Tina merely nodded. Her eyes were wide with worry and confusion. Max handed her a card and followed Wells and the chief out to the vehicle.

Once they were all inside the vehicle, Wells spoke again. "Chief, I believe Dr. Jackson Taylor is our subject. We believe a man named Dr. Jack Tyler who is wanted for several serial murders in two other states is committing the crimes on the children here in Illinois."

Max continued, "The initials are the same J.T., and he goes by Jack. These can't be coincidences. If Dale went out there last night and told him that we were in town, then Dale is in grave danger."

Wells's phone rang right as the chief fired up the vehicle. "Agent Wells," he said, his eyes passing back and forth between Max and the chief as he listened. "Good, we need you in Heyworth immediately. We have a lead on our Tyler. I'll text you the address. We're on our way there now."

The chief looked at Wells. His eyes grew wide. "I'll have Ryan meet us there."

Wells cautioned, "Tyler is dangerous. He's killed several people. We need to hurry. What is the address?"

The chief made a phone call to get the address of the house now occupied by the town's resident named Dr. Jackson Taylor. He hung up and recited the address to Wells who tapped it into a text message in his iPhone.

"The team should be here in about forty-five minutes," Wells said to Max.

Max felt adrenaline beginning to pump through her veins. *Jack, we have you this time.* She silently prayed that Jack hadn't done anything to Dale. As the chief made his way through town, Max stared out the window. Her mind raced through the many scenarios that could face them when they got to Jack's house. *Could all of this be a coincidence? Could this not be Jack Tyler? No way! This is him.*

The chief slowed the vehicle. "There's the house," he said pointing to a large farmhouse with a circular driveway that sat off the road.

"There are no vehicles in the driveway," said Wells.

Another police vehicle pulled up next to them. Ryan sat in the driver's seat. He rolled the passenger window down and nodded his head at the chief and the agents.

"Chief, I called for backups. We should have four more officers here is less than ten minutes."

Wells's phone chimed, indicating he had a text message. He pulled the phone out. "Our agents are ten minutes away also. Is there a back exit to this property?"

"No, the circular drive is the only way in or out by vehicle."

"What's the building at the back of the property?" Max asked, pointing to the barn.

"It's a barn. I haven't been out here since the doctor moved in. It's just a hay barn with a few stalls."

"The house looks like it has a full basement with a cellar entrance. Are there any other exits to the house?"

"There's a back door. It goes out from the kitchen area."

"When we go in, place an officer at each exit. Max and I go in through the front, with the team behind us. We place two officers at the barn. Once the house is cleared, we go to the barn and clear it."

The two vehicles sat in the middle of the road waiting while they talked through the plan until the other vehicles arrived. Everyone was briefed and given their positions. After pulling on the bullet proof vests the team had brought with them, everyone was ready. With the chief leading the way, the vehicles made their way down the lane. The officers and agents filed out of the vehicles and took their positions. Max pulled her Glock from her shoulder holster and released the safety. They approached the house with caution. Her heart rate increased as the anticipation of potentially finding Jack got closer to her reach.

With everyone in position, Wells rapped on the door. He and Max were on either side, flanked by the rest of the FBI team. The local officers held the positions around the parameter of the house. There was no sound or movement coming from inside the home.

Wells called out, "Dr. Taylor, FBI. Open the door now!"

There was still nothing. Wells looked over at Max, made a fist and pulled down, giving the signal that they were going in. He tried the door, but it was locked. He signaled again and kicked the door in. Max fell in right behind him, gun drawn, covering his back. They found themselves in a decent sized living area that was lavishly decorated for Christmas. Across the room was a dining table. Max made her way towards it. Her eyes scanned the table; it was set for three. The food hadn't been touched, neither had the two glasses of wine or the child's cup. Someone had interrupted.

As Wells made his way down the hall, Max rounded the dining room into the attached kitchen, followed by one of the other agents. The kitchen had recently been used to prepare the meal. Max touched the middle of the stove and the oven door as she passed, calling out "clear" as she continued. Neither was warm.

Following the path Wells had taken, Max made her way down the hall. Wells entered a room that was clearly set up as an office. She heard him call 'clear' as she made her way past him. She entered the room at the very end of the hall and found herself in the master bedroom.

The bed was made neatly, but was missing the comforter and other aspects of the room were in disarray. The closet door was standing open, and one of the nightstands was half opened. A master bathroom was off the room to the left. Drawers hung open, and some were emptied of their contents. She called out clear and retreated back down the hall to the living room as Wells called clear from the small room opposite the office.

Max returned to the living room and headed to the front door to let the officers know the house was cleared, when she noticed the stairs to the basement. She headed down the stairs with Wells behind her. She flipped on the lights and paused for a moment then continued. The main room was decorated as a den or extra living space, and in the far corner of the room was a large walk in freezer.

Max felt immediate déjà vu. It was nearly identical to the freezer found in the home in Oklahoma. She paused before making her way to the freezer and was almost afraid to open it. Fear of what she would find inside rose all the way up her spine. Swinging the door open with her gun ready, she let out the breath she did not even realize she had been holding when she found that the freezer was empty.

Wells called clear on a room half way behind her, and she turned to follow him to a door directly across from her. He swung the door in, and their sinuses were immediately assaulted with the strong smell of bleach.

The room was nearly identical to the one they had discovered in Oklahoma. The pristine stainless steel table in the middle of the room was all too familiar. The walls aligned with shelves were loaded with miscellaneous medical supplies. A small apartment sized refrigerator sat under one of the shelves. Wells swung it opened and found it empty. The room had obviously been recently cleaned, as was apparent by residual water on the floor.

Certain they had cleared the house, they went back upstairs and notified the rest of the team. Next, they needed to clear the barn. They made their way through the heavy snow. Wells pointed out to Max the tire tracks in the snow. At the barn entrance, the two agents pulled the doors back as Max and Wells, baring their arms, entered on the count of three. Inside they found a car. After a couple of minutes, the chief confirmed it to be Dale's.

The sun had come out and was pouring into the barn, casting rays of light, making the remnants of hay glisten on the floor. Dust hung in the air from the door being pulled open. Wells peered into the car and shook his head. He pulled out a latex glove from the pocket of his jacket and carefully opened the door then reached inside and popped the trunk latch. Max stood at the rear and with her Glock pointed directly into the vehicle slowly opened the hatch,

Another sigh of relief escaped her mouth as she acknowledged the trunk was empty. For the next several minutes, the team searched the barn before clearing the hayloft and each stall. Neither Jack nor Dale was anywhere to be found.

Max dropped her firearm to her side and clicked the safety back into place. Her mind raced. Jack would not likely take a hostage, so where was Dale? His car had been carefully tucked away. Max considered all of this. Then suddenly, an idea came to her. "Chief, what is Dale's cell phone number?"

Max already had her phone out and ready to dial. The chief gave her the number from his cell phone. She dialed and waited. The team of officers listened around the vehicle for a possible ringing from somewhere within the car. They were not rewarded.

***

Jack felt a buzzing in his pocket and reached in, retrieving Dale's phone. He smiled as he saw the area code was not local. He wasn't familiar with the 703 code that came up on the display, but he thought he knew what it meant. He slid his finger across the display, answering the call.

"Hello."

Max was hoping Dale would answer, but she knew immediately who she was talking to. Her pulse raced as she recognized the voice she had spoken to months ago just before they had chased Jack Tyler to St. Louis, narrowly missing him as he made his clever escape to the Caymans.

"Dr. Tyler? It's Special Agent Maxine Nichols."

"I've been watching you, Agent Nichols. Your career advancement is impressive."

"Thanks, Jack. May I call you Jack?"

"It is my name."

"Where is Dale? We found his car, so we know he's either dead or with you."

"Straight to business. So predictable," Jack made a clicking noise with his tongue. "I have a few questions for you, Agent Nichols. I saw you on the news. You didn't really think I took that little boy, did you? Hope and I always wanted more children. A little boy would have been nice, but I guess it just wasn't in the cards." He paused for a moment as if thinking. "Well, anyway."

"Dale? Where is Dale?"

"Maybe he went on a little vacation in my car."

"You and I both know that's not the case. His wife misses him. Jack, I know you know how that feels."

"Nice try, Agent. You and I are so much alike. Well, I need to go. I have a long trip ahead of me now. It's certainly been nice catching up with you again, Agent Nichols."

"No, Jack. You've got it all wrong. We're nothing alike."

459

"Really? We both set our minds on what we want, and we go after it. I'd say we're more alike than you'll ever want to admit. It's okay. I understand."

"Jack, it can't last, you know. The things you have done to those bodies. It won't last, and then what?"

Jack laughed. "You underestimate me, Agent Nichols. Tsk, tsk…Let's see if I underestimate you. What will you tell little Jessie? Will you really tell her that the mouth she carries is not her own? She doesn't really need to know. What will *you* do, Agent?" He drew the last sentence out, saying each word slowly with emphasis on the word "you".

Max was silent as she considered his question, but before she could answer, the line went dead.

***

"God, damn it!" Max nearly threw the phone.

Wells approached her. "Tyler?"

Max nodded at him, her frustration apparent.

"What did he say?"

"He didn't tell me anything about where Dale is. He was just babbling off a bunch of bullshit."

"It may seem like bullshit, but we need to go through it line by line as much as you remember. He may have said things that provide clues on where he is or where he's heading. Dale could be alive."

Max could feel the blood pounding in her head. She had him on the phone and no way to trace the call. She had gotten nothing from him, and because of it Dale would likely die, if he wasn't dead already. Reluctantly she followed Wells back into the house. The chief and the others followed.

As they walked Wells was ordering someone on the phone to put a trace on Dale's phone for GPS coordinates and he instructed the team to get Crime Scene on site. He hung up the phone and followed Max into the house. Then he asked her to go over the conversation with Tyler.

Chapter Twenty-Eight

Jack replayed the conversation in his head. He smiled at his challenge to her and knew he was right. But then… his blood pressure rose as he considered what the agent had said to him about his family. As he drove he was becoming more and more angry. The words she had said plagued him. *"Jack, it can't last, you know. The things you have done to those bodies. It won't last, and then what?"*

He shouted pounding his fist on the wheel, "Then what? I'll tell you what! I'll show you, Agent Maxine Nichols!"

Jack began scanning the road for a good place to dump the SUV and the cell phone. He needed to ensure he made it clear to Agent Nichols who was in charge. She couldn't control him. The mere fact that he had been able to restore his life was proof that no one and nothing could control him. The thought calmed him down. Flipping on the radio, he immediately began to sing along.

A few miles up the road, he saw a storage facility. Being the day after Christmas, he felt certain it would be closed. Perfect. He signaled out of habit and looked in his rearview mirror, nothing. No one ahead either. He slowed and pulled in. He smiled when he realized there wasn't a gate across the entrance. Following the rows to the back, he continued around so he was facing back out to the road far enough back that he wouldn't be noticed unless someone really was looking. Leaving the vehicle running, he got out and began disconnecting the tow bar. Minutes later, the SUV was separated from the truck.

Suddenly, he knew what he needed to do. He returned to the door of the truck, opened it reached inside and into his satchel pulling out a marker. He didn't have any paper so he leaned over to the glove compartment and pulled out the owner's manual. Removing one of the pages for logging miles and maintenance data he wrote in bold letters across the page. He stared at the words for a moment then smiled at it before taking it back to the rear of the SUV.

Closing the back he returned to the truck and pulled away, leaving the SUV sitting in the middle of the row in the storage facility. As he watched the SUV getting smaller in the distance he was reminded of the storage facility in Arkansas. He smiled realizing he would not be leaving his family behind this time. It had been incredibly painful to leave Hope behind when he was forced to leave the last time Agent Nichols threatened to catch him. Oh, but she had been a detective then. He wondered for a moment what happened to her attractive Hispanic sidekick. *Did you trade*

*her in for the handsome Agent Wells? Is he the reason you joined the FBI?
Or was I the reason you joined the FBI?*

Jack's thoughts consumed him for the next hour as he continued to make his way through the snow covered roads. He intentionally had decided to only travel the back roads, which made traveling slow. With the four wheel drive he was able to make his way without any real issue, but he worried about getting far enough ahead of Agent Maxine Nichols. *You can't catch me, Maxine. Not today. Not ever.*

Refusing to allow his fears to consume him, he returned his thoughts to his new life - the life that awaited him. He would need to make some changes. Most importantly he would need to find the perfect place for his family.

Soon a car approached him. It was the first vehicle he had seen since he'd pulled out of Heyworth. He sat upright in his seat. His breath caught as he realized it was a state trooper's car. The car was moving slowly towards him, and Jack's eyes fixed on the road, intentionally not wanting to make eye contact. He slowly reached behind his seat feeling for his satchel. It was easily within his grasp *if* he needed it. A few moments passed, and his breath released as the car moved past him and slowly disappeared into the wintery haze on the frosty window in the rearview mirror.

Suddenly he wondered what would happen if they put his picture out on the news. He needed a plan, and he needed one soon. He tapped the menu on the screen centered in the middle of the dash, then pushed through a few more buttons, pulling up the navigation system's mapping program. Balancing his attention between the road and the map, he hit the plus sign with his right index finger and zoomed out so he could see further ahead. He would go outside the town of Lincoln, and then the next sizable town would be Springfield. Certainly it would be easier to get lost in a big city. An idea began to form, but he needed a few things. He was certain it would work, at least until he had a more permanent solution.

Chapter Twenty-Nine

As the crime scene analysts worked their way through the farm house, barn, and Dale's vehicle, Max and Wells went through the entire conversation Max had with Jack Tyler. Over and over Wells asked the same questions until they had the conversation down on paper to a point where Max felt it was complete.

They were tracking the location of Dale's phone that Max called Jack on, and it wasn't long before they finally had some news. Agent Fields approached and informed the pair that the phone was showing at a location in between Heyworth and Lincoln. Jack wasn't far away.

Immediately the team was filing out, leaving the rest of the scene to the forensics team. Without four wheel drive the travel was slow and dangerous. They spent the whole time talking through the conversation Max had with Jack. She explained how he tried to compare her to him. How he had challenged her on if she would tell Jessie about her mouth.

Max considered all of this. He had taunted her. He was confident, certain that he was smarter. Certain that he was far enough ahead of them that he would again slip away. *Well, not if I have anything to do with it.*

The sheriff provided them with Jack's vehicle's make and model and he put out a statewide APB, referring to an all point bulletin on the vehicle. Additionally, Wells was working on a press release indicating Dr. Jack Tyler as a person of interest in murders across numerous states. It would air on the six o'clock news. Finally they would have Jack's photo out in front of the world, and it would hit national news. Within a few hours Jack Tyler would not be able to hide anywhere. He would not be able to fly out of an airport without being apprehended, and it wouldn't matter what his name was.

Max could feel adrenaline racing through every part of her being. Her instincts told her they were close, and she prayed that they would not lose him again. The slow pace of the drive to the location where the phone was registering was painful, and she found herself constantly replaying Jack's voice in her head. *No! We are not alike, Jack Tyler!*

After what felt like several hours pushing through the white mass of snow, the location of the cell phone was coming into view. Max could see a storage facility about an eighth of a mile down the road. *Jack, did you leave your family behind again?*

Wells pulled the vehicle over at the side of the road. "There is a possibility Tyler is in the building. We go in slow. We split into teams, cover the front, and clear the rows."

The team filed out of the vehicle and walked the rest of the way up the icy road to the entrance. Max and Wells took the middle front while the others went to either end of the facility. On Wells's command they worked two rows at a time. You could hear frequent calls of clear, then Max heard "here". Her legs couldn't move her fast enough. She rounded the corner of the row where the command had come from, and she saw an SUV parked. The agent was already moving in on the car.

There was no movement anywhere in or around the vehicle. Wells joined her and with their Glocks drawn, they continued to work their way until they were next to the SUV. She aimed her gun through the window into the front, and reached for the door handle swinging the passenger's side wide open at exactly the same time Wells pulled open the driver's door. Jack Tyler was not inside. Wells signaled to Max. She nodded, knowing he was telling her they needed to clear the rest of the row because Jack could still be here.

Within ten minutes they had cleared the storage facility. Wells was once again on the phone asking for the local police to assist.

Returning to where Max was standing he said, "We'll need a warrant, so we can search every storage unit. It's possible our suspect broke into one of these lockers and stored bodies in here. He can't take them with him on a plane, so unless he's planning on staying in the States, he'll need a place to store them."

"There's no refrigeration storage here, but it's cold enough right now to leave them here for now," Max added.

It wasn't too long before local police and crime scene specialists arrived and secured the area.

With the scene secured, Max returned to the vehicle and edged slowly to the rear of the vehicle. Frost had settled onto the windows obscuring the view enough that she couldn't quite see inside. With her gun tightly trained on the luggage area of the SUV she pulled open the back. A large roll of plastic stretched across the rear of the vehicle and her instincts told her they had just found Dale.

A note was attached to the bundle carefully tucked inside the plastic, obviously intended to be visible as soon as the discovery was made. In black marker it read:

464

SO ALIKE...
YOU KNOW I'M RIGHT!

"Damn him!" Max was furious. She stomped her way through the snow out towards the road. The snow had stopped a while ago, but there was still ample on the ground to make it slippery. And in her anger she nearly fell.

Wells followed her. "Don't let him get in your head. He's trying to make this personal, and it's *not* personal." He emphasized the word not. "It only becomes personal if you let him make it be."

"I know what he's doing. We have to get this guy."

Max had a defiant look on her face. Wells made eye contact with her and held her gaze long enough for her to realize the deep meaning behind his eyes. As the other agents and an officer approached, she pushed her hair behind her ear in a brisk frustrated move, took a deep breath, and spoke calmly.

"He's devolving. He no longer cares that we know he's our guy. This is the first time he hasn't tried to cover the crime or the body."

Wells looked away from her and to the rest of the team. "He is beginning to make mistakes. That gives us an advantage, but we don't have much time. He's smart. He's disappeared before. If we don't act quickly, we'll lose him again."

The officer, a tall, young man, with a thick mustache, spoke next. "He's in a big vehicle. Looking at the tracks," he pointed his finger along the path into the drive, "he towed that car in here. There's one set of tracks coming from the east with another smaller set following the same path. He went down that third row then made his way back up and left it right there in plain sight."

"He wanted us to find it. He wanted to send me a message," Max said.

"The tracks continue west," the young officer stated.

Wells looked at his watch. "Less than one hour and his picture will be out everywhere. He won't be able to hide. In the meantime, can you get all radio cars to be on the lookout for a van, large SUV, or pickup truck driven by a white male fitting our description?"

465

Chapter Thirty

Jack arrived in Springfield just before dark. He pulled into a Walgreen's parking lot, in what appeared to be a low income part of town. He was glad for this, as he assumed people in this area minded their own business.

Entering the store he was careful to not allow his face to be seen on the cameras. He spent several minutes in the store collecting the items he had come for, checked out paying cash, and without ever looking at the clerk, he exited the store.

Back in the truck, he began looking for a room for the night also in this part of town. He couldn't stay anywhere that more suited his tastes, at least not for tonight. Finding a room where you could literally pay by the hour, and realizing no one was going to report anything about anyone around here, he gave the clerk a fifty dollar bill that easily paid for the forty dollar a night room.

Returning outside he re-parked the truck in front of the room with the number twenty-two on the door, which matched the room key. The truck would be right outside where he could keep an eye on it to ensure Hope and Faith were safe. He desperately wanted to bring his family inside with him, but knew he must resist the temptation. If he wanted to get away far enough for them to be together again as a family in safety, he must be patient.

He grabbed his bag with his purchase, his satchel and overnight bag, and locked the truck, confirming it with a double chirp of the alarm.

Once inside the room, he took in his surroundings. The bed was covered in a green and blue comforter that had obviously seen better days. The gold curtains were faded from the sun, and the carpet was a dull orange color. Nothing about the room was comforting, but he wasn't here for comfort. And he had spent plenty of time in rooms just like this in California. His life had been filled with places like this during the dark time, before he had gotten his family back.

Dropping his overnight bag and satchel on the dresser stained with cigarette burns, he took the Walgreen's bag into the bathroom. He removed the scissors, hair dye, and make up. He looked in the mirror over the sink and slowly began cutting the sides of his hair. He worked away until he had removed all of his hair down to a close military cut. Removing the dye from the box, he carefully read the directions and mixed the two bottles together as instructed. He cut the tip from the applicator bottle and pulled on the rubber gloves that had been provided. He carefully applied the thick liquid to his whole head and smeared a little bit on his eye brows.

While he waited the twenty minutes for the dye to do its job, he cleaned up the hair that had fallen into the sink and onto the floor, and removed the remaining item, a disposable cell phone, from the Walgreen's bag before depositing the hair inside. Checking his watch he stripped out of his clothes and entered the stall. He stood under the shower head, and with the trickle of lukewarm water that came out, rinsed away the dye. Once the water ran clear, he grabbed a once white towel, now a dull light gray, from off the rack on the wall and dried off. He vigorously dried his hair then stepped out of the shower onto the aged tiled floor and peered into the partially fogged mirror. Looking back at him was an older man, slightly balding and grey. He smiled.

Now for the rest of the change, he opened the packages of makeup. He applied eyeliner and mascara. After a few minutes, he admired himself in the mirror, before him stood an aging man. He laughed. *I guess this is what Thomas would have looked like if he had stayed around long enough.* The thought made him reflect on his time in Oklahoma and the friends he had made there. He missed having friends. *I was just starting to make friends here in Illinois. Oh well, I have my family, and that's all that really matters. All I ever needed was Hope until we had Faith. That's all I need now too!*

Pleased with the transformation, he grabbed the bag and pulled out the belt he had purchased at the last minute. He stepped out of the bathroom onto the dingy carpet and rummaged through his overnight bag on the dresser, pulling out some fresh clothes. He would wear these tomorrow when he decided to move on. For now he needed to rest, and while the idea of the bed made his skin crawl, he knew what was best. He pulled on a pair of sweat pants and a t-shirt before sliding between the sheets. He retrieved the remote control from the bedside table, clicked on the television, and was surprised when the old console fired up. He flipped through a couple of stations, sitting bolt upright in bed as he turned up the volume. There on the screen was a news anchor sitting behind a desk followed by a photo of him on the screen.

His heart raced. He could barely breathe. Listening to the report, the anchor said that Dr. Jack Tyler was wanted for questioning in the murders across several states, including several deaths of young children and a realtor from Heyworth, Illinois. Anyone with information was encouraged to call a number listed at the bottom of the screen. Just below *his* photo.

Jack sat there staring back at himself until the photo went away and the news anchor moved on to another story. *Damn you, Agent Maxine Nichols!*

468

Wait... calm down. Jack got out of bed and went back into the dingy bathroom and stared at himself in the mirror. A sinister grin crept over his face. It was not, after all, his photo on the television. Not anymore.

Jack grabbed his laptop case, and returned to the bed. He lay back against the pillows, and booted up his computer. He searched the Internet for nearly an hour. Satisfied he'd found what he was looking for, he stored the information in his iPhone then powered down his laptop, returned it to the case and slid back in the bed. *Tomorrow will be a good day.* Within minutes he was fast asleep.

Morning came too quickly. He'd slept fairly well despite the occasional noise in adjacent rooms. Jack woke with a renewed sense of control. He knew exactly what he needed to do. He pushed his body out of the bed and quickly dressed in the clothes he had already selected. He freshened his makeup ensuring his disguise was solid should he see anyone. He cleared the room and quickly packed and then removed the bedding from the bed. He pulled back the curtain on the window before exiting the room. No one was around. Given the type of motel this was, he assumed most would sleep until afternoon, if they slept at all. People here were creatures of the night.

After gathering up his belongings, including the Walgreen's bag that now carried his hair shavings, he stepped out of the room, unlocking the truck. Not being able to resist, he took a quick peek at his precious cargo ensuring they were safe before opening the door and sliding into the seat. Before pulling away he punched the address into the GPS that he had stored in his iPhone the night before. The map immediately began locating the directions as Jack backed out of the parking space and made his way onto the highway.

Chapter Thirty-One

Max sat on the side of the bed of yet another hotel room. After finally getting the warrant and gaining access to the storage lockers, they searched one after the other but discovered nothing. Jack hadn't left the bodies behind, and while they knew he had headed west they'd lost the trail amongst all the other tire tracks about a quarter of a mile down the road. They had nothing and finally decided to call it a day to get some rest.

Max and Wells parted ways outside in the hall. The accommodations at the diner had been unique, and now that the others had returned, they needed to remain separated. He was in some other room somewhere on this floor. She wondered if he had slept better than she had. Her night was restless, her mind not affording her peace as she continued to replay the events that happened over the past week. There had to be something that would help her understand where Jack was heading. But despite her restlessness she had come up empty. Nothing was standing out.

The clock next to the bed read six thirty. She forced herself up and made her way to the shower. An hour later she was downstairs eating a continental breakfast and enjoying a rich cup of coffee. Wells had joined her, and now Agents Adams and Fields had joined the table too. The four began discussing the case.

Wells made arrangements with the Lincoln police department to set up a room where they could work the case. He coordinated for the files from Le Roy to be delivered to their new makeshift investigation room. Agent Adams was a serious sort and barely showed any emotion or facial expression. Max decided it was time to get in his head.

"So, Adams, you married, kids?"

"No." Adams replied without any change in facial expression.

"Why?"

Fields smiled and raised his cup to cover his amusement in Max drilling Adams.

Agent Adams looked at Max and studied her for a moment. "The job makes it difficult to keep a relationship. You'll see."

Max took a sip of her coffee, and as she sat it back down on the saucer replied, "You mean you can't find a girl that likes a guy that is never home, chases crazy killers, drug dealers, and human traffickers? Hmmm… seems like a catch to me." Her emerald eyes sparkled.

Adams studied her again for a moment, and then a hint of a smile curled at the corners of his mouth.

Wells and Fields both chuckled. Fields could no longer resist temptation and jumped on the bandwagon. "She's right. You're a real catch, Adams, one in a million."

They all laughed, enjoying the distraction from the challenge of the case for a moment. When the laughter died down, quiet settled over the group until Max broke the silence. "Any leads from the special news reports?"

Wells looked down at his coffee cup then made eye contact with her and shook his head. Max nodded in return, her mind struggling to come to terms with reality. *Nothing, we have nothing.*

Everyone finished their breakfast and left the hotel to make their way to the police headquarters. Several hours later they had photos displayed around the room. Victims' photos, photos of Jack Tyler, his wife Hope and their daughter Faith accompanied case records and a map of Illinois with pinpoints of where the killings had happened.

Max put up a map of Oklahoma and California and was applying pinpoints for each of the victims on each map. Fields stood behind her and considered her hypothesis. Max wondered if there was any path or pattern to Jack's kills which might help them understand where he was heading next. In the case of the Los Angeles murders, he relocated to Oklahoma, heading east. He continued east to Arkansas and then turned north to St. Louis where he boarded a plane and left the country. Could he be reversing his path, and if so, where would that lead? It wasn't much, but for now it was the best they had.

Wells was studying everything on the wall with an opened case folder in one hand when his cell phone rang breaking his obvious concentration.

"Wells," he answered. "We'll be there right away."

Max turned to face him, still holding a pin in her hand.

"We have a lead. A clerk at a motel just inside Springfield says Jack checked in there last night. We need to move. Fields, keep working Max's theory. Once you have it, map it in the computer and see if you can triangulate off the locations and predict where he might be heading. If Max is onto something, I don't want to lose time. When you're done, send it over our phones. By then we'll be at the motel."

Fields nodded. Max already had her coat on and was heading to the door. Adams and Wells fell in behind her.

The thirty-five mile ride to the motel was quiet. As they came into view of the city Wells finally spoke. "We go in slow. It's possible that he is hiding out at the motel. We have no way to know if he's armed, but we know he's dangerous."

Max jumped in, "And he will do anything possible to protect his perceived family."

Seriousness covered all of their faces as they saw the motel come into sight. It was the typical motel one would expect in the part of town where hookers and drug dealers conducted their business. Wells pulled past the motel and circled around the building to the back, providing them a full view of the parking lot. There were only three vehicles, and each seemed more typical of those driven by street thugs. Only one had a trunk large enough to potentially conceal a couple of bodies. Knowing Jack would be treating them as precious cargo the others were too small,

Wells parked to the north of the entrance, somewhat concealing their arrival. Exiting the vehicle they dropped into a line and approached the building from the corner without passing any of the guest room entrances or windows, slipping into the front of the motel lobby without drawing any attention. The door chimed when it opened, and a fiftyish looking man jumped up from the chair behind the counter. He was wearing a once white wife beater shirt, now covered in stains, delivered by an obvious variety of food and sweat. His eyes darted back and forth, a clear indication that he used drugs. Their sudden presence was obviously unsettling to him.

"Man, you guys shouldn't sneak up on a guy like that." As he spoke he rubbed at the stubbly, grey beard that sprouted haphazardly across his face.

"Agents Wells, Nichols, and Adams," Wells offered as a single introduction, and then continued on immediately. "We have a report that this man was checked into this motel," he said sliding a picture of Jack Tyler across the desk.

"Yeah, I checked him in here last night."

"What name did he use?" Max immediately asked.

"We don't really take names. He paid cash, and well, we don't have a log or anything."

"Did you see what vehicle he was driving?" Wells continued to counter.

"No. I never saw him drive anything. He must have parked down the way." The clerk pointed to the left of the door where most of the rooms were. His left eyelid had begun to twitch.

"Did he check out?"

"Well, I ain't actually checked the room. I kinda thought after seeing him on the tube that I'd just let you do that."

"Did you see him leave?" Max's frustration was starting to grow, but it was not detectable in her tone.

He just shook his head.

"Why did you wait to report this until this morning?"

"Man, I just saw it. I was watching Judge Judy, and it came on. I never saw the news last night. Fell asleep after things… settled down for the night." He hesitated on that last part, considering the implications of his nightly business.

"What room did you check him into?" Wells patiently asked.

"He had number twenty-two. You ain't gonna break down the door, are ya? I got a spare key." Before they could answer, he was already handing over the key.

Max took the black plastic key chain with the number 22 on it. Adams turned to leave, having stood patiently waiting for the go ahead for the questions to end.

As they exited the lobby, the clerk called out, "Hey is there a reward for this? You know cops coming in here ain't good for business."

Max looked back at the man, shook her head, and pulled the door shut behind her. He eyes were already scanning the lot. There was no vehicle in front of room twenty two.

They made their way single file along the front of the motel, passing several windows and doors, finally coming up to the room that matched the key chain. Flanking the door they drew their weapons. Wells called out, "FBI, open the door!"

A few seconds passed, and they heard no movement. Wells nodded to Max. She pushed the key into the door knob and turned it, forcing the door inward in one motion.

Wells pushed through the doorway. Max and Adams followed. The room was small and dark, taking only a few moments to clear both the main room and bathroom. Soon after Wells called for crime scene to come in and search the room. While they waited they made a quick assessment that showed that the trash cans were emptied and sheets and blankets removed. Jack had done a good job to conceal whether he had been in this room. Max was hopeful there would be some trace evidence to prove it was actually Jack that stayed here. But her senses told her this might be another dead end.

Chapter Thirty-Two

Jack left the motel early, not trusting that tweaker manager. He made his way across town, the morning traffic still light from the weather, people on long holidays, and kids out of school. The roads were now passable, but still slick.

He glanced at his face in the mirror and checked out his new hair. He had reapplied makeup before leaving that morning, forcing him to further step into the character he had decided would be a sufficient cover until a more permanent solution could be secured.

Following the map on his GPS, he arrived at his destination. It was daylight now, but there was no one around. He would have to wait, but he could wait inside. Stepping out of the vehicle, he retrieved the phone and his satchel then made his way up to the building. Pulling out a pair of gloves, he snapped them on then tried the door. It was locked as expected. He worked his way around the side and found a window. Before doing anything else he went back to the front and verified there was no security system. It was a small office, a one man show, nothing to worry about. Returning to the window, he picked up a small rock and tapped the corner just hard enough for the window to crack. He pulled the first piece away and used his hand to unlatch the hatch on the inside.

Climbing through, a few moments later he stood inside, his satchel in his right hand. He inhaled, the familiar smell immediately soothing him. He listened carefully for a few moments to ensure he was as alone, as he thought he was. Certain now, he moved carefully throughout the office, exploring the lobby and the back room. He resisted the temptation to run his hand over some of the tools. His eyes worked their way across each of the shiny items before he sat in the chair. He could rest here for now and wait. It wouldn't be long.

Jack dozed off in the chair, his satchel on his lap with his fingers clutching the handle. He was awakened by the sound of a door chime. He slid out of the chair and made his way across the room where he could see out the door and down the short hallway. Reaching into his satchel he removed a previously prepared syringe. He waited silently. One set of footsteps was all he heard coming closer. A slightly paunchy, balding man was making his way towards the door. Jack waited until the man came through the frame and crossed the room, stopping in front of the counter on the other side. Stepping forward, he closed the door in one quick motion, startling the man and causing him to spin on his heels to face Jack.

"What the…"

Jack walked quickly up to the man, and before he could react Jack injected the contents of the syringe into the man's neck.

The Ativan took effect quickly, and the man went slack. Jack dragged him over to the chair and pulled him up. He retrieved a roll of duct tape from the satchel and wrapped the man's arms and legs tightly to the chair. He would need to wait a while. The dosage was mild and would not last too long.

With the man secure, Jack went to the front of the office and sat at the computer. He typed out a sign that read *Closed for the holidays. Sorry for the inconvenience.* Jack grabbed the tape dispenser and went to the door. Opening it, he applied the sign, then closed the door and locked it.

Thirty minutes later the man began to stir. Jack waited, watching him closely. Once his eyes opened, Jack leaned in and spoke slowly.

"Good morning, Doctor. Sorry for such a dramatic start to your day. But you see, I need your services. I need for you to help me, and if you do I'll reward you handsomely."

The doctor's eyes were wide as he listened. He was obviously trying desperately to shake off the effects of the drug.

"I'll give you a few minutes longer to understand what I'm saying, but you see, I know things about you. You have a lot of debt. I can help you with that. When we're done, you'll no longer have those worries. Your debt will be free and clear. You'll make more money in a couple of days then you make all year. How does that sound?"

Jack could tell the cloud was lifting from his captive, and by the look on his face he seemed to be thinking about the proposition that was being presented. "I can see by the look on your face you're interested in hearing more about this." Jack turned to reach into his satchel that was sitting near the door. He pulled two large bundles of bills out and walked over to the chair again. Holding the bundles in front of the man he said, "There is fifty thousand dollars in each of these. You do what I ask of you, and it's yours."

The doctor's eyes flashed back and forth between the two stacks Jack was holding in front of his face. Sweat had formed on his brow, and he slowly nodded his head.

Jack smiled. "Good, I'm glad we can work together."

Chapter Thirty-Three

The search of the motel and questioning of the witnesses were all dead ends. Crime scene analysts recovered a ton of trace evidence, including a number of fibers and fingerprints, but it would take weeks to get the results of it all. And frankly, Max was certain that none of it would tell them anything new. Even if they proved Jack had occupied that room it would not tell them anything they didn't already suspect.

It had now been three days, and they had no new leads. Her theory on a possible pattern based on the geography of the killing spree Jack had followed had proven fruitless. There was no apparent pattern, or shape, or even a number consistency in the miles traveled. Jack had seemingly slipped through their fingers again, just as they had gotten close.

It all felt so familiar to Max. Needing to vent and talk to someone outside of the investigation that would understand how she felt, she called Cortez and had a long conversation. Max knew that only Cortez and Wells could really understand in totality the frustration of not nailing this guy. Cortez tried to convince her that they would eventually catch Jack Tyler, even though she shared her concerns and frustration.

Max's frustration led to remorseful feelings knowing that Jack would kill again, and it wouldn't be long. Though she was certain he believed that having his family with him again would be enough, she knew it wouldn't be enough. The bodies would eventually decay, and when they did he would kill again, maybe even start over again. The thought of this kept her awake at night, and every waking hour her mind worked through details naturally filed in her head. Still nothing jumped out at her.

"We're going to pull it in. There's nothing more we can do here." Wells sat looking at the team and specifically looking to Max for her reaction. He had told her the night before that if nothing new came up they would have to return to Quantico and work from there. Other cases were active and required their support.

Max tried to hide the way she was feeling. She knew Mark was right, but leaving felt like they were simply allowing Jack to disappear into the wind. At least last time they had chased him right out of the country. Her instincts told her he was in the country, and yet she had no idea where to look for him now. While there had been plenty of leads called into the tip line, they had so far proven to be just a bunch of crazies looking for quick fame or a free meal.

There was one thing Max needed to do though before leaving. She asked Wells to drive her back through Heyworth rather than flying out with the others from Springfield. Adams and Fields would depart in the morning, and Wells and Max would catch a flight out in the evening from Bloomington.

They began the process of tearing down the investigation room and wrapping up with the local authorities. The files consisting of the documents and photos that had continued to amass during the time they had been in Illinois were packed away into boxes and would be shipped back to Quantico.

Wrapping up, the group agreed to grab something to eat before turning in for the night. There was another light snow falling. It was not expected to interfere with travels and did nothing more than give the beautiful feeling of diamonds littering the ground. Wells drove through the falling crystals and pulled into the parking lot of First Wok. It had taken much bantering, but they had finally all agreed on a cuisine.

After making their way out of the vehicle and into the restaurant, they shook the snow out of their hair and off their coats. A few minutes later, they were seated around a table with carved chairs, drinking tea and sake. Soon the table was covered in a variety of dishes and little bowls of white rice they all could share.

For the first time in a few days, they enjoyed conversation about topics other than Jack Tyler. They laughed at Adams and his attempt to use chopsticks. Max grinned. "You know, Adams, you really are an okay guy." She teased him, having finally gotten used to his unusually uptight demeanor.

He smiled back at her. "Thank you, Agent Nichols."

Max nodded as she captured a bite of Mongolian beef between her chop sticks and stuffed it in her mouth. "My pleasure."

Finishing their meal, they sipped on the sake until it too was gone. Wells settled the bill, and they made their way back out to the vehicle. The snow had already stopped with just a light coating covering the ground.

Minutes later they were back at the hotel, and soon they all wandered off to their respective rooms. Wells stopped Max in the hall. "You okay?"

Max looked up at him. "Yeah, I mean we lost him, so no, but yeah."

"He messes up, and we'll get him."

"How do you always stay so positive? It's kind of annoying." She grinned at him.

"You'll get used to it. Assuming you stick around long enough."

"Oh, I'm not going anywhere."

"You ready for tomorrow?"

"Yes. You know I need to do this."

Wells searched her face. "I know." He brushed a wavy lock of hair from her brow and ran his finger down her chin. "Get some rest."

Max wanted him to kiss her, but she knew they couldn't here in the open like this while on a case. "We should have gone back to Sarah's tonight." She smiled up at him, locking her emerald eyes on his blue ones.

"That would have been nice," Wells acknowledged. "Stay at my place tomorrow?"

Max just gave him a teasing smile, turned, and started toward her room, tossing a flirtatious smile over her shoulder. Her long hair swayed with her body as she moved.

***

Alone in her room, Max tossed and turned, punching her pillow frequently throughout the night. Her thoughts vacillated between Jack Tyler and Mark Wells. She was anxious to get back home and settle into a routine. Well, as much of a routine as being an FBI agent allowed. But she would gladly keep traveling across the States if there was something to go on. When she finally drifted in and out of sleep, her dreams taunted her. Jack Tyler repeating over and over, "We are alike, you and I," as images of Jessie's sweet little face all twisted and mangled, laughed at her, through a big smile of sharp teeth and sutured lips.

Morning's arrival was a blessing, and Max got out of bed, eagerly rushing through her shower and dressing routines to get out of the room to be any place other than in her own head. Wells was downstairs when she got there, and she assumed his night had been no better than hers. She greeted him with a smile and immediately felt better seeing his blue eyes smiling back at her. It would be nice to be back in his arms tonight. She just had one thing to do first.

Agents Adams and Fields joined them, and they had a quick recap before parting ways with Max and Wells heading back to Heyworth. The roads were clear, and the sun was out. The prior night's mild snowfall had left everything looking crisp and clean, and the beauty of it was helping lift Max's spirits.

Wells reached across the seat and took her hand. The warmth of his strong fingers curled around hers, and she immediately felt that familiar tingle in her stomach. *How can this man make me feel so good so fast?*

They rode in silence for most of the way. Max began to feel anxious as they began to get closer to their destination. She was dreading this moment, but she knew she must take this step. Soon they arrived in Heyworth and made their way across the now familiar little town. They pulled up in front of Jessie's house and sat for a moment before Max took a deep sigh. "Let's do this."

Opening their doors they walked up the driveway and climbed the steps to the porch. Wells rang the doorbell and then stepped back. Moments passed before the door opened, and a puzzled Tina glanced at them, then stepped back and waved them inside.

Max started, "We're sorry to drop in like this, but we're about to head back to Virginia, and well, we have some information that is important to share with you."

Jessie was sitting at the table and popped up, coming over and hugging Max around the waist. "Hi, did you came back to see me?" She asked her question, hinting of part curiosity and part fear.

"I did want to come see you again. I need to go back to my home now and couldn't bear to leave without saying good-bye to you."

Jessie smiled and hugged Max tightly again. "I'm sorry you have to go."

"Well, me too, but I have to get back to my home."

"Okay."

"Jessie? Honey? Why don't you take Agent Wells and show him your new comforter and pillows?" Tina instructed her daughter, realizing Max needed to talk with her privately.

Jessie eyed Mark closely and then took his hand and led him toward her room.

Max could hear Mark as they walked away, talking to the little girl about how he would love to see her new bedroom items. Tina motioned for Max to take a seat on the couch, which Max graciously accepted.

"Please, Agent Nichols, I know you didn't come out here without a good reason. What is it that you needed to talk with me about? Did you find him?"

"I'm afraid we have not apprehended him, yet."

"The town is talking, so I know he killed Dale." Tina wiped at her eyes. "Are we in danger?"

"No. I don't believe so. In fact, I feel very confident that if our Dr. Tyler had wanted to do any further harm to Jessie or you, he would have done so. We believe that he actually cared enough to not hurt her any more than he did." Max watched as Tina winced at the idea that Jessie had not been hurt enough. "But there's more. I don't really know how to tell you this, other than to just say it. There were two other little girls that he killed, and well, he removed their mouths too. We have reason to believe that he took Jessie so that he could have her mouth. It's possible that the mouth Jessie has is from one of the other children."

480

Tina gasped and immediately began to sob. Her hand flew to her mouth as she sucked in, trying to catch her breath. Max moved over next to her and took her hand. "A DNA test would tell you for sure, if you chose to do that. It isn't necessary and might serve no good purpose, but I felt that you had the right to know and decide what you as a mother should do for your child. Tyler is an incredibly sick man. He is however a competent physician. Your daughter is healing."

Tina sat with her hand to her face, her trembling fingers covering her own mouth. She looked pale as if she might be sick. "I…I don't know what to do. What do I tell her?"

"I can't tell you that, but I'm sure you'll make the right decision, in time." Max's heart ached for this woman. She wondered what she would do if this were her child and a federal agent walked in telling her such a horror story.

Tina just nodded at her. "Are you sure he's not coming back?"

"I feel very confident."

"So you're saying he took what he wanted?"

Max hesitated then answered, "Yes, he did."

"Nothing makes sense anymore. I actually found him…," Tina's words trailed off without finishing.

"He is a charming and handsome man. There's no way you could have known. Things will make sense with time. It hasn't been very long. Let your daughter heal. She's amazing, and with your love she's going to be fine."

Tina nodded, wiping away the tears on her cheeks. "I need to freshen up. I don't want her to see me like this." She stood and disappeared down the hallway. A few minutes later, she returned just in time for Jessie and Wells to join them.

"Max, you must see this bedroom. It's really a little girl's dream. I bet you would even want it for your bedroom, a princess's palace for sure."

Jessie grabbed Max by the hand and pulled her from the couch and dragged her down the hall. Max followed willfully and fawned over the room, then followed Jessie back out to the living room. The little girl chattered away. It was amazing how well she was healing. She still had obvious wounds, but the healing was much better than just a few days ago.

A few minutes passed and Wells stood. "We really should be going."

Max stood too. "Come here, Jessie. Give me one more hug for the road."

Jessie gladly wrapped her arms around Max. Kneeling down to look the little girl in the eyes, Max pulled her close, "I'm so glad I got to meet you. You're a very special, brave little girl. If you and your mom ever come to Virginia, you call me so I can see you, okay?"

"Will you be coming back here?"

"No, probably not."

"Is it over?"

Max looked into the little girl's eyes. "It's over for you, Jessie. You don't need to be scared anymore."

Jessie searched Max's face and then hugged her again tightly. She released her hold, and Max whispered something in her ear, causing the little girl to strain out a smile.

Saying their final good-byes, Wells and Max stepped through the door and into the cold. The wind seemed to have picked up, and Max pulled her coat around her. Or maybe it wasn't the wind, but rather her need to close out the way the conversation with Tina had made her feel.

Back in the car, Wells headed through town towards Bloomington. He didn't say a word until they passed the diner. "I'm going to miss that place."

"I'll miss Sarah. You know she was totally onto us."

The conversation flowed for the next few minutes, and the mood lightened. Wells finally asked, "Are you okay?"

"Yes. Jack is wrong about me."

"I worry that you let him get in your head. You never thought there was anything to what he said, did you?"

"I needed to know he was wrong."

Wells glanced over at Max and nodded his head in understanding.

"What time is our flight?" Max asked.

"We meet our pilot at four o'clock" Mark answered. "We have time for lunch somewhere before heading to the airport."

They selected the airport restaurant where they could sit and watch the small planes land.

When Mark's phone rang, Max sat idle, listening to the one sided conversation, with increasing concern rising as she listened to Mark's tone.

He hung up the phone with a grim look on his face. "We have another body."

"What do you mean?" Max looked at Mark, confusion covering her face.

"A doctor was found murdered in his office in Springfield. It meets the M.O. We have to go. The pilot is going to take us now to Springfield instead of home. It's only a thirty minute flight. We can be there is a little over an hour."

"Why would he kill a doctor? I don't understand."

"I don't know. We won't know more until we get there."

482

Epilogue

Jack stood looking at himself in the mirror. He would have smiled if he could have, but the bruises and stitches still had a long way to heal. The doctor had done such a great job. The idea of earning a hundred thousand dollars in a few days had certainly kept him focused. The advance of ten thousand and a high dose of fear was enough to get him to agree to provide his services.

The reconstruction was fairly extensive. Insisting that he not be completely sedated had been a painful, but necessary choice. Jack needed to be aware enough to ensure the doctor did not renege on their deal, and if he did, be able to act before the authorities could arrive.

Jack sat in the chair enduring extensive pain as the incisions were applied and the modifications made. Afterwards he paid the doctor another twenty thousand dollars to provide the aftercare for two more days. The money and promise of such a large sum two days later had kept the doctor focused of course Jack had never intended to let the doctor live.

He left the doctor's office and started travelling not sure exactly where he was headed. All he knew was he needed much more time to recover. He had to get out of the state and find some safe retreat until he was healed.

Before traveling to far though, he had something he needed to do. He pulled out the disposable phone that he had purchased from Walgreen's and dialed the phone number he had saved days earlier.

The phone rang, and a familiar voice answered. "Agent, Nichols."

"You sound distressed, Agent. Having problems?"

"Jack?" Max snapped her fingers to get Mark's attention.

"Don't think of putting me on speaker. I'll hang up immediately, and I'd much rather talk for just a moment."

"Go ahead, Doctor."

"Well, I was wondering if I was right. Was I right Agent Nichols?"

"I'm sorry, right about what?"

"Don't play with me, Agent. I know I made you wonder about our similarities."

"Oh, are you referring to the note you left? Was that for me?"

"I didn't expect you to be so funny, Agent. I like that. Well, we don't have much time. So... how did it go?"

Max ignored his taunt to tell him about if, or how, she had told Jessie's mother about her injuries. Instead she chose to turn it around on him. "You know this has to end soon, Jack. How are the bodies holding up?"

Ignoring her question Jack continued, "You don't have to answer my question. It doesn't really matter. I already know that we share certain, uh... attributes." Jack intentionally applied emphasis on the word attributes as he continued to taunt her.

His playful banter and confident tone made Max's skin crawl. She tried to regain control of the conversation. "Jack? You know *I* am the one who is right." Max made certain she applied her own emphasis.

"My family is fine. Thank you so much for asking. I'll give them your hello. I just wanted to say good-bye, Agent Nichols. I'll be leaving now, and well, you won't find me." Sarcasm filled his voice. "Even if you did, you won't recognize me. I could be sitting next to you on the subway or plane, and you wouldn't even know it was me. Try not to think about me too much and I'll do the same Agent Nichols."

The line went dead. Max stood staring at the phone.

The End

Acknowledgement

My gratitude goes out to my editor and advisor throughout this process, Hollie Zunun. Every step of the way she pushed me to deliver quality and challenged me when the unexpected was too expected, forcing me to keep the suspense alive throughout this writing. Hollie, I am forever grateful that you have taken the twisted journey with me and the book's characters.

I am also grateful for my family. My partner Lorea for allowing me the time from our critically busy family life to dive into the world that Dr. Jack Tyler lives in. I also must thank my children Maima and Akins for their patience as my attention during movie night is frequently divided. Without your support I could never get the words onto the paper.

I quick shout out to Chris Snidow for the word for word look at every page. You rock!

Finally, to my mother and biggest advocate. I hope I make you proud. I love you!

CREATING CHANCE

By

Valerie Knupp

Dedication

Fam-i-ly

Noun - a group consisting of parents and children living together in a household.

      Lorea, Maima, and Akins, we are so much more than what is described in this definition. I dedicate this third and final book in the Jack Tyler series to each of you, because without your support I could never have gotten through this incredible journey.

      We are family, and to me the real definition means that we stand strong in the face of anything and everything. We protect our home like a fortress that holds our love, and we trust in each other even in the face of fear, anger, or hurt.

Trust

Noun – firm belief in the reliability, truth, ability, or strength of someone or something.

      To me the above better describes our very special family. I love you all very much!

Prologue

He stood looking at himself in the mirror. A smile crept up at the corners of his mouth. The doctor had done a fine job. A fine job indeed! The past three months had been spent healing. He had driven straight through from Springfield, IL to Scottsdale, AZ only stopping for gas, food, and ice.

It hadn't taken him too long to decide where to go. Scottsdale was certainly the perfect place to recover. Facial scars were not all that uncommon to elite residents and starlets undercover. Those who were so vain they felt compelled to stretch, nip, tuck, and pull at sagging skin. Skin drooping from age and sun, offended by close up cameras. Vanity had nothing to do with his reason for the change. Oh no, vanity was the last thing that drove him. Protecting his family was his only concern. He had to protect them. Keeping them together was his only motivation.

After arriving in Scottsdale he arranged for a three month lease in a house common for those seeking refuge during recovery. The accommodations included everything one could want. He arranged for groceries to be delivered as frequently as desired. At first the only thing he was lacking was a freezer. He made arrangements for one to be delivered, nothing elaborate this time. He couldn't risk it, just a simple deep freezer that could be stored in the garage. He didn't like it, but he quickly and frequently reminded himself that it was temporary and that the only thing that mattered was that he remained with his family.

For the three months he stayed mostly inside, except for spending time on the private patio. He spent many days next to the pool while sipping cold tea, wine, or the occasional Coke Zero.

Now looking in the mirror he knew it was time to move on. The scars were healed, and his new look was complete. He was pleased that the work, though extensive, was good. The raised cheekbones, widened forehead, and cleft chin had not taken away from the natural good looks that had always aided him. More importantly, with his new look he was not recognizable. The man that had gained unfortunate notoriety no longer existed.

In recent days he'd reached out to his contact in Los Angeles and gained access to another new identity. Additionally, he'd requested two new spares, just in case he needed them later. He knew one can never be too careful.

"So sorry to disappoint you, Agent Maxine Nichols," he said out loud as he continued to admire his new look in the mirror. Laughter exploded out of his perfectly re-shaped mouth.

Chapter One

Special Agent Maxine Nichols returned to Virginia after, once again, being unsuccessful in apprehending Dr. Jack Tyler. Since her return she had been assigned to a cargo theft case. There were millions of dollars in pharmaceuticals being stolen, and following each robbery the thieves seemingly vaporized into the night. They were highly efficient and capable of taking a tractor trailer rig in just seconds from a truck stop parking lot or distribution center. The operation was big and growing. The money from the drugs was then used to fund other activities like buying weapons.

The assignment was interesting and certainly something different from anything Max had worked on before, but in the back of her mind there was always the nagging feeling that she had missed something that could be the single piece of evidence that would lead her directly to Dr. Jack Tyler. An absolute professional, Max always worked her cases with purpose and drive. But her own time was dedicated to finding Tyler.

Upon returning from Illinois after finding the body of the cosmetic surgeon, Tyler's most recent victim, her relationship with fellow FBI agent Mark Wells had only deepened. They weren't working the same case right now, and at times their schedules were not in sync. But what time they did have together was intense, yet peaceful. Their love was growing, and Max was beginning to really envision a future with Mark. It was a strange reality for her to allow her mind to picture a future that included more than her career.

***

It was late at night, and Max sat with her feet in Mark's lap as they each respectively read through files and drank wine. Mark's current assignment was a pedophile case, and she knew it was weighing heavily on his mind. Tonight though, they both were scouring over the Jack Tyler files. Mark wanted to apprehend Tyler as much as she did.

It was odd to think that Tyler had actually brought the two together. Max remembered the instant attraction between them when Mark had come to Los Angeles to help provide a profile on a serial murder case she was leading. She was an LAPD detective then, and they spent long hours over a couple of days working through the case files. It was then that she started to fall for him.

493

Mark had to return to Quantico after delivering the profile. He left after a single night filled with passion. Months passed before they would be reunited when the profile they had developed had actually helped lead them to new murders in Illinois. Despite every effort to avoid getting close to him again, she found herself back in his arms.

Now she looked at him and rubbed her foot down his thigh, garnering a quick smile across his strong face. His deep blue eyes settled on the green of hers, and without saying a word they both chuckled. The comfort she felt in his presence was certain. Pushing a thick, auburn lock of hair back behind her ear, she returned her focus on the file in her lap.

Tyler's case was considered cold thirty days ago, and resources were pulled back. As a FBI most-wanted serial killer in multiple states, Tyler had effectively slipped through their fingers twice. A master of deception and a psychopath with narcissistic characteristics, he had proven to be unstoppable thus far.

Max removed her feet from Mark's legs and swung her feet to the floor to stand and stretch. She could feel Mark's eyes watching her as she left the room. She made her way down the hall and went and pulled a white sheet from the closet. She walked to the office and grabbed a small plastic cup containing pushpins and a roll of tape. She returned to the living room dragging the sheet behind her.

Mark looked at her, and she could tell by the look on his face he knew exactly what she was thinking. She pulled the love seat away from the wall then pulled a chair from the dining room table to stand on.

Mark laid to the side the file he'd been looking through and stood up. "Need a hand?" he asked smiling, taking one edge of the sheet.

"Sure," Max smiled. Her eyes connected with his again.

She was not sure what he would think and silently feared he might chastise her for falling into her former habits. Mark had not always supported the unconventional way Max would work a case. On more than one occasion, Max had used her living room wall as what was called a murder board. She lined the room with a white sheet and laid out the facts of the case by the order of events, displaying each detail of the grisly events. Then using the facts she would look for links, trends, and any missing elements that might help lead her to the killer. In this case Jack Tyler.

When Dr. Jack Tyler, a once prominent and well respected surgeon, killed six people in Los Angeles and buried them in shallow graves in the Malibu canyon hills, she used her living room to narrow possible locations where he had potentially relocated. His killing signature resurfaced in a burial site just outside Tulsa in the rural outskirts of a small town called Inola. Tulsa had been one of the top three locations Max had narrowed in on by using her living room wall murder board process.

She wasn't sure what else to do, but she knew she couldn't just keep looking at the files. With Mark's help, and after exchanging a knowing look, a few minutes later they had successfully hung the sheet on the wall to create a canvas for the murder board.

For the next hour, they pasted photos and created a timeline. When they were done they stood arm in arm looking at the morbid reality of the carnage Jack Tyler had left behind in his troubled wake.

The murdered included six in California, six more in Oklahoma, and five in Illinois. The last five slain included three young girls. The lives were all lost in the midst of Tyler trying to reinvent his family. Tyler's wife and daughter were killed in a car accident in California. Tyler began to fragment on that day.

Though they had never seen it, both of the agents believed that Tyler had used parts from his many victims to create replications of his dead wife and daughter. The evidence recovered indicated that he was using some crazy formula of chemicals to preserve the body through a mixture of embalming, taxidermy, and cryonics. Neither one of them knew how long the concoction would last, but Max feared that Jack would start all over if his formula failed.

Max also knew that they needed to find a lead somewhere in the middle of the evidence or from within the case documents accumulated during the investigations. She was certain Tyler no longer looked like Dr. Jack Tyler, given that his last victim had been a cosmetic surgeon who specialized in a wide variety of plastic surgery, and she knew this was going to make apprehending him even more difficult.

Just before leaving the trail cold Tyler contacted Max, taunting her as he'd done on a few other occasions. He told her that he could sit next to her on the bus or plane, and she wouldn't even recognize him. Max believed him and realized that they were going to have to outsmart him if they were going to catch him. And so far outsmarting Jack had proven to be quite difficult.

Chapter Two

Even though it was only late March it was already getting warm in the desert. Realizing the freezer could not travel with movers for two or three days in the heat. He also knew he couldn't trust the contents with anyone else. Jack decided renting a U-Haul truck for his precious cargo was the only way.

He needed to get to his destination quickly. He planned to drive straight through. The journey was just over four hundred and fifty miles. It would take over seven hours to make the drive, and that was with minimal stops. Thinking about it he figured it would likely take him eight or nine hours. He wasn't really looking forward to the drive, but the reward at the other end was going to be well worth it.

Jack took a few minutes to perform a final walk through of the rental home and before leaving placed the keys on the counter as the landlord had asked. Locking the door behind him, he stepped outside and double checked the hitch on the U-Haul to make sure the tow for his van was secure before pulling away.

He hadn't been out much since coming to Scottsdale, thus allowing his face to heal and ensuring he was not detected. As he navigated his way through the city streets out to the highway he saw the signs for Phoenix. He remembered his in-laws and wondered how they were doing. He knew Hope would love to see her sister Mindy, but well, that just wasn't possible. The thoughts suddenly made him feel melancholy.

Mindy had tried to come around right after the...accident, but he shut her out. He wanted nothing to do with her. She seemed genuinely concerned for his welfare, but when they were kids he never fully trusted her. She always seemed distant with him, and after the accident he was in no frame of mind to deal with family.

Even with all of his reservations about Mindy he couldn't help wondering how she and her family were doing. As he was passing through Phoenix he saw the exit that he and Hope had taken so many times when they'd gone to visit for the holidays or a long weekend. Hope adored Mindy. They were very close in age and often times were mistaken for twins. The visits to Mindy's house were always pleasant, and Jack found himself trying to remember why he ever distrusted her. Hope always told him he was just imagining things. With Phoenix growing in the distance he considered if she'd always been right.

497

The time spent driving went quickly despite the somber mood that had filled him as he left the Phoenix area. His feelings were further tormented when he found himself wishing his wife and daughter could ride in the front with him.

Crossing into California, Jack immediately felt his emotions begin to lighten. Jack pulled out of Arizona at just after two o'clock. The sun set before he crossed into California, but he never minded driving in the dark. He could almost feel the ocean breeze and the mountain air and was very excited to return to his home. It'd been far too long, and there were a few things he needed to know.

He imagined driving up into the Malibu Canyon, but immediately realized that was a very bad idea. Besides, there was nothing there anymore. He knew Agent Maxine Nichols had destroyed the site. He shrugged reminding himself that as long as he had his family none of that mattered. All he'd ever needed was Hope. She'd proven that to him so many years ago.

Feeling much better now Jack turned on the radio. He flipped through the presets until he landed on a song that was familiar and hummed along. Soon the city lights were an endless glow as city after city flew past him. He'd chosen to take Highway 134 to avoid any late night traffic on the freeways and finally was pulling through Santa Paula. The orange groves passed by, and Jack lowered his window to enjoy the fragrant air. Ahhh... yes, he was home. Well, he would be in less than an hour.

As he passed through Ventura, he could see the white caps of the ocean waves crashing near the pier. He finally made his way up the mountain road, gliding on the pavement in the dark through Oakview and finally pulling into the small quaint town of Ojai. His heart raced as he stopped at the light on Main Street. He wasn't expecting his feelings to be so conflicted.

He both felt elation and anguish all at the same time as he made the necessary turns along the all too familiar path. Even though it had been years since he had been here the vehicle seemed to know its way without any assistance. He followed the curve of the driveway just past midnight and sat staring through the darkness at the large house.

While in Scottsdale, Jack worked for weeks negotiating the purchase of the home in Ojai...his home. Returning to the place where everything began with Hope somehow made perfect sense.

For years all he'd ever wanted to do was leave this place, and now suddenly it seemed the only place he could possibly be. He could change things. With Hope he could do anything, and raising Faith here could take the demons away. He knew it was true. Certain it was the only way he looked forward to his new life.

Getting out of the vehicle, he approached the porch and inserted the key he'd already put on his key ring. The tumbler turned, and the door clicked open. He took a deep breath and stepped inside.

Chapter Three

Any evening that Mark's assignment drove a schedule that did not align to hers, Max spent the time combing through files, creating individual searches, and even working unusual possible scenarios.

Mark was still assigned to a serial pedophile case, and it was certainly taking its toll on him. She didn't know much of his case, but she was aware that a young boy's mother had arranged the sale of her son to a middle man known for selling children to pedophiles. Mark was working nearly twenty-four hours a day trying to find the boy before the pedophile took possession of the child and hurt him or before the boy disappeared for good.

Mark would occasionally wrestle around in his sleep, waking sweaty and out of breath. It wasn't like him. The man she knew was always strong and composed. She was beginning to worry. The case seemed to be getting into his head. He seemed to be falling into the trap he always warned her not to allow happen. "Don't let Jack get into your head, Max," he would say. She knew she was going to need to talk to him soon if he continued to struggle. She hoped they would catch the un-sub quickly. Then his mind could rest again.

Max decided she'd give him just a little more time, trusting him to manage through the case and whatever demons he was fighting. But she planned on keeping a close eye on him and would be there for him when he was ready to talk.

Turning her focus back to Jack Tyler, she realized that she needed some resources, and she didn't have permission to use the FBI databases to work on Tyler's case on her own time. She also had yet to build relationships with people working in data jobs. Being a fairly new graduate still in her first year she had not yet proven herself, or made the tight connections that she could reach out to when she wanted to look into something outside of her existing case.

Oh, sure there was a certain amount of granted respect just from having graduated the FBI Academy, but that alone was not enough to gain access to systems and tools or even people who would be willing to help on what was right now considered an inactive case.

She had an idea. Picking up the phone, she dialed a familiar Los Angeles number and waited half expecting voicemail to pick up. She was pleasantly surprised when she heard a familiar voice.

"Max? Everything okay?" Cortez asked.

"Hey, Lorraine, yes, everything's fine, just hoping to get some help," Max replied to her friend and old LAPD partner.

She and Detective Cortez were partners when Max first started working the Jack Tyler case while she was still a Detective in Los Angeles, California. The two women spent weeks studying the case files in Max's living room. They would sit around on Friday nights when they weren't working, drink wine, and stare at the sheet extended across the wall that contained the photos and case facts. It was on one of those Friday nights they had narrowed the cities that would be likely places for Jack to relocate. Sure enough, several months later one of the top three cities—Tulsa—was where Jack ended up and continued his killing spree.

"Okay, you know I'll help if I can."

"Well, I was thinking about the names Jack has chosen. I think there might be name combinations we could identify based on the names he has chosen so far. We could create a list of the most likely names he might choose. I need to know if there was a history on the names he's used in the past. Did the history start right when he moved to Tulsa for Thomas, for example, or did he buy a name with a history, and if so, where was that history? I don't know what that part will tell me, but the more we know about those identities the more likely we can figure out what new identity he might be using."

"It's not a bad idea, but why are you reaching out to me? Don't you have like a million data analysts and all kinds of FBI toys to do your digging around on?" Cortez teased.

"We do, but it's not my case and I don't have a go to person yet. That takes time. Bobby could do this, I'm sure. I just need him sweet talked."

Cortez gave a hearty laugh. "God, I remember you working him. He would start shaking his head right when he saw you coming, but he could never tell you no."

Max laughed too. "He totally busted my chops all the time," she said agreeing.

"I'm not sure I have the magic to get him to go around the chief, but I'll give it a try."

"Give Bobby my best." Max was still laughing.

The two women talked for quite a while longer, catching up on the latest in each other's lives. They laughed and before hanging up agreed to get together sometime soon.

Max smiled at the phone after they said their goodbyes. She truly missed Cortez. They'd been a good team. She loved Mark, but they seldom got to work together.

For a few minutes she remembered when the chief told her she would be taking Cortez with her on the Tyler case. Her initial reaction was negative. Max was used to working alone, and she liked it that way. Working with Cortez had changed that for her. By later working with Mark, she had learned how to work as a team and had come to realize the advantages of doing so.

Her mind drifted back to Tyler, and she hoped Bobby would come through for her. He'd worked magic for her many times in the past, but she was no longer part of the LAPD and knew she was asking a lot.

Chapter Four

As soon as Jack stepped through the door a familiar smell assaulted his senses. It was masked some by a new, pleasant smell. Over the top of the old wood, linseed oil, and furniture polish that was baked in over the years was a new smell of vanilla and cinnamon spice. The new smell was that of pies, cookies, and flavored teas. Jack found himself focusing on the newer smells. The old ones flooded him with memories that he'd spent years trying to forget.

Making his way through the familiar floor plan, he took the stairs two at a time. At the top on the landing he turned to the right towards the master bedroom. He paused outside the door, his fingers wrapped around the cool brass knob. His heart raced, and sweat covered his brow. The palm of his hand made the brass knob feel wet, making it nearly impossible to turn. Tightening his grip, he twisted harder and slowly pushed.

Stepping into the room, his eyes scanned his surroundings. He let out the breath he'd been holding. Things had changed. The bed was on the other side of the room. There was a small lamp on the table next to the bed, illuminating the room slightly. Jack slowly approached the bed and stared down at the frail body under the covers. The woman was asleep, her eyes closed and her frail, twisted hands clung to the blankets near her neck.

Jack clicked off the lamp and retreated back out of the room. No need to disturb her now. He needed to get the rest of the family safe and out of the U-Haul.

He retraced his steps back down the stairs, but instead of going through the front door he turned down the hall then took a left off the kitchen through the laundry room. He opened the door that led into the garage. Reaching inside he felt for the switch, flipped it into the on position, and flooded the garage with light.

He looked around. An older model Mercedes sat parked on the left side. A thin layer of dust covered the gold paint, an obvious indication that it hadn't been driven in a while. Gardening tools filled one corner. The familiar workbench lined the front wall, and miscellaneous items covered the opposite wall.

Assessing the situation, he descended the two steps that dropped him onto the concrete floor. Remembering where the outlets were, he looked between two stacks of boxes and began moving the one that more likely covered the place to plug in his precious cargo. Ten minutes later he had cleared a large enough space along the wall opposite the car for the freezer. This would have to do for the next few days.

Looking up he noticed there was a garage door opener that didn't used to be there. He glanced over to the wall next to the door and saw the activation button mounted next to the light switch. Walking over he pressed the button and waited for the garage door opener to raise the door.

Ducking under the door as it rolled over his head, he retrieved keys from his pocket and began methodically removing the tie downs that secured the van to the trailer. He pulled the stowed away ramps out from the backend of the trailer and verified they were flat on the ground before opening the door of the van. He climbed in behind the steering wheel of the van and slowly backed it off the trailer and onto the driveway.

Next, he removed the tow bar and hitch from the trailer, unwound the support wheel and dropped the trailer onto the driveway off to the side and out of the way. Climbing into the U-Haul, he backed it into the garage opening after properly lining it up, then he slid back out of the truck and walked around to the back.

He retrieved another set of keys from his pocket and pushed the silver one into the padlock that had secured the doors during the trip. He slid the latch open and pulled the doors apart. Grabbing the straps from under the tailgate he backed up, dragging the ramp out, and then he dropped it into place.

Jack climbed his way up the ramp and removed the two four-wheel dollies from the wall of the trailer, then lifted each end of the freezer onto the dollies. He slowly skated it down the ramp and maneuvered it over to the space he'd cleared. With the freezer in place he plugged it into the wall and immediately felt comforted when he heard the low hum of the compressor kick on. He really wanted to open the lid but knew better than do that right now. It was best to let the cold air stay inside until the entire system cooled back down. He slid his fingers along the lid and silently bid the contents good-night.

Reinserting the ramp into the trailer, he pulled the truck forward far enough that the U-Haul was no longer in the garage before rolling the trailer back in place behind the bumper and reconnecting the tow bar and hitch. He then wound the wheel back up into the towing lock.

Tomorrow he would return the U-Haul and trailer to the dealer down in Ventura. For now he needed some rest. Grabbing his suitcase, medical bag, and laptop bag from inside of the van he returned inside, turned off the garage lights, and found himself wandering through the house touching the familiar things. The furnishings had changed, but the fireplace was the same, the crown moldings, and the granite counter tops in the kitchen all the same.

Room by room he walked through the house until he came to his old bedroom. Of course all of his boyhood things were gone, but the light on the ceiling was the same. And when he finally settled down to rest he found himself staring up at the light fixture.

Memories flooded him. He thought of the times his mother would come into his room and wake him up, making him join her in her bed. Other times she would just climb into bed with him, sliding all over him. He lay there rigid, closing his eyes and trying to force those memories away. For a little while he began questioning why he'd come back here.

Then he remembered why he returned. This house would be a home again, and it would be filled with love. After all, this was where it all began. Different memories filled his mind. Memories of Hope, how they'd sat on the edge of his bed when they were fifteen, and he'd finally worked up the nerve to kiss her for the first time. That kiss had been the beginning of a new life for him. He remembered how nervous he'd been and then how shy he felt and how she had touched his hair afterwards. Their eyes met, and then they both giggled.

Suddenly, the room seemed happy again. It was with Hope that this would be a great place to live and raise their daughter. His mother could no longer hurt him. With that thought he drifted off to sleep.

Morning came quickly, but he rose with excitement. It was time to start rebuilding his life again. He was finally going to have his family with him, the months of waiting almost immediately faded into the past.

First, he needed to check on Vivian, his house guest. Making his way across the hall, he arrived at the master bedroom. Tapping lightly he turned the knob and entered to find the elderly woman awake leaning back against her pillows. She looked frail.

It had been years since Jack had seen her last. Her daughter, Suzanne, was frequently left to babysit him. He liked her just fine and she was always nice to him, but he was still pleased when she had died at the young age of thirty-three. More satisfying was the fact that there were no other living relatives. Vivian's husband died years earlier, and after having fallen ill she has had a caregiver for the past six months. It seemed she had advanced lymphoma. Jack contacted her lawyer and made arrangements for her health care in her final hours.

Under a different name he bought the house outright under a mocked up business name, citing interest in it from a historical perspective, wanting to make it into a bed and breakfast inn. He'd only been able to seal the deal after agreeing to allow Vivian to live in the home until she died. All of the transactions were untraceable and could not be linked back to him.

Jack was a man of his word. A matter he prided himself in. He would care for Vivian until she passed away. The people in the town of Ojai would think he was her long lost nephew—a son from a deceased brother who had fathered a child he'd given up his paternal rights to at birth. This too could be confirmed. He'd made sure the paper trail was air tight. Just in case…

"Good morning, Vivian," he said as he approached the bed. "I'm Tyler Thomas, your new caregiver and a licensed physician."

"Good morning," she replied in a soft whisper.

He looked down at her and knew she had little time. He felt both pleased and sadden by this realization. His ambivalent feelings were twisted by his history with Vivian. He remembered that she would often offer him cookies and milk as a young boy.

"I trust they told you I was coming?"

She merely nodded in acknowledgement.

"Can I get you some tea and toast this morning, Vivian? I thought our first day together I would spend some time getting to know what you need and want. I don't want to force things on you just because your doctor is saying this is what you should or shouldn't take. I'm a doctor too, and I want to be sure to give you the best care."

Vivian smiled, noticeable only by a slight lift at the corners of her mouth. "Thank you. Tea would be nice."

Jack checked her catheter, IV drip, and medicines that had been left on her night stand. He then walked across the room and opened the door of a small refrigerator and looked at the various medications inside. He administered the appropriate dosage from one of the vials into her IV drip and returned the vial back to the refrigerator.

"I'll be back with your tea in just a few minutes. You rest then we can talk." Jack patted the old woman on the arm before turning to leave the room.

"Have we met before?"

Jack turned back surprised by the question. "No, I don't believe so. Why do you ask?"

Vivian struggled for a moment before gasping out, "Your eyes." She laid back into the pillows, and her eyes closed.

Jack walked down to the kitchen and put the teapot onto the stove. His mind raced about the comment she had made. The old woman despite being on medication had recognized something in him—his eyes. He was sure of it. While he waited for the water to boil, he retrieved his laptop bag from where he had left it the night before and began powering it up.

The teapot began to whistle. He went to the stove, moved the water off the fire, and turned off the gas flame. Retrieving a teacup from the cupboard, he realized Vivian had her cups in a different cabinet than his mother had. He was pleased that she'd moved things around. Already the house was feeling like his. Not hers! Not his mother's.

Jack carried the tea up the stairs, careful to not spill any, and once again approached the large bed Vivian rested in. His footsteps caused her to open her eyes. He could feel her studying him. Smiling he said, "Here's your tea. It's pretty hot. You'll need to be very careful."

The woman continued to study him as she took the cup gingerly in her thin fingers and raised it to her lips. She sucked in a small amount into her mouth and then set the cup aside on the nightstand. "Thank you."

"You're welcome. Are you sure you don't want any food right now? You really should eat. I could bring you some chicken broth, Jell-O, or an Ensure milkshake. We have to keep your strength up."

"You're kind, but nothing now. Maybe later. The tea is lovely."

"I see there's an intercom here on the nightstand, so you can call me any time you need me, even if it's just because you'd like me to come up and read to you. I don't mind," Jack said nodding at the book lying next to the woman in the bed.

"I don't need much these days. Keep the pain away. Visit me occasionally. I think it helps."

"I'm here to care for you, and I'll do just that."

Vivian's eyes wandered over him. He knew there was a familiarity that she was remembering. Memories returned of the days he'd spent with her. She used to talk with him, asking questions and challenging his mind. She'd tell him how smart he was. He was counting on the fact that the meds were potent and her mind was too far gone to make any connections.

"You go. I'm going to drink my tea and then rest for a while." She lifted the tea cup. It was cooler now, and she could handle it a bit better.

"Okay, you rest. I'll be back in a while to check on you. Call me if you need anything." Jack pulled her blankets up for her. He smiled as he leaned over her, their faces very close together. He could sense her eyes on him.

Pulling away, he stared down at her then turned and headed out of the room. He was beginning to wonder if the work he had done was enough. His mind scanned the people over his life that would be able to recognize him. It would only be people who have spent a tremendous amount of time with him. There was no one else in Ojai. Teachers maybe would be the only risk, but many of them would have died, transferred, or retired.

Jack had few friends during school other than Hope, no one he was ever really close to, so he felt comfortable that with Hope's sister nicely tucked away in Phoenix, he should not be running into anyone here in Ojai that would recognize him, especially given the changes he had made. There was just one detail that would seal the deal.

Returning to the kitchen where he left his now fully booted up laptop, he logged onto the Internet and began a quick search. Within minutes he made a purchase for an overnight delivery. Sighing, he closed the computer and decided he needed to see his family. A little reassurance right now was necessary.

He entered the garage through the door off the laundry room. He flipped on the lights and immediately made his way to the freezer. Standing in front of it, he took a deep breath and lifted the lid.

Chapter Five

Mark returned home late and telephoned Max to let her know that he would see her in the morning. They were still living separately, though the only time they weren't together was when either was on a case and their hours didn't match up. They agreed to share time between their respective homes, except lately it seemed they were getting closer to living together.

Max continued to claim residence in a two bedroom apartment that she had rented after moving to the area to be near Mark. She was comfortable in the apartment for now.

After talking on the phone for a while they agreed that Mark would come pick her up around eight. It was Saturday, and they were going to spend the morning together. Max worried even though he'd said all the right things, but the stress was very clear in his voice.

Max went to bed after their call and found herself tossing and turning. Her mind was tormenting her both about Jack Tyler and Mark's obvious anguish. She didn't remember falling asleep but woke in the morning completely tangled in her sheets and with lingering, faint memories of her dreams.

Shaking it off, she untwined her lean, muscular legs and slid off the bed, heading directly to the shower. It was nearly seven o'clock when she got out of the shower. Mark would be there in an hour.

As Max got dressed, fixed her hair and makeup, she considered how she could address her concerns with Mark. This would be new to their relationship. So far they had never had a situation that caused any type of pull between them, at least not since they officially started seeing each other and Max had made the big decision to relocate to Virginia. They had gone months not seeing each other after their first passion encounter in California, but after reconnecting in Oklahoma their relationship had been near perfect.

Max had just finished a cup of coffee when Mark knocked on the door, and then used his key to come in. She grabbed another cup and decided that they needed to talk before they got out in the world where there were too many distractions. Mark came over to where she was standing in the middle of the kitchen and wrapped his arms around her, leaning in to sweetly kiss her.

Max could never resist his touch or his kiss and instantly fell into his embrace. She leaned into his hard body and returned his kiss, teasing him gently. Pulling back she brushed the one curl that always dipped across his brow, pushing it away from his eyes. Their eyes met and Mark pulled back looking down at her.

"Talk to me," she said deciding the direct route would be the best approach, go straight for it.

"It's a rough case."

"I get that, but it's getting to you. You always tell me not to let it get into my head. Mark, it's in your head. Talk to me, what's going on with you?"

After picking up the coffee cup Max set it in front of him. Mark nodded. Taking her hand, he led Max to the dining room table.

"Sit down. It's complicated."

"Okay," she said waiting for him to continue.

"We found the boy."

Max waited, unsure where this was heading. Her mind immediately went through the gambit of possible outcomes. Had the child been found dead? Was he alive but severely abused, tortured or...

"He's alive," Mark offered obviously reading her silence. "The pedophile had just taken possession of him. Needless to say he was terrified. We found two other bodies, both boys, both dead. The boy's fate was certain if we hadn't gotten to him."

"This is great news, Mark. I know you've been struggling with what would happen to him. What about the mother and the middle man?"

"The mother committed suicide. The guy she sold the boy to gave up the pedophile. He also is responsible for the sale of several other children, both boys and girls. We're trying to track down the other kids."

Max sat quietly listening, allowing Mark time to talk. When he seemed to come to a stopping point she inquired, "This case really rocked your world. Can you talk to me about that?"

"It did," Mark admitted nodding his head. "The boy, he was so scared. He held on to me. When we arrived he said, 'I knew the good guys would come.' He's only five."

"Mark, there must be more to this. Not that this isn't enough, but you've been distant and struggling ever since you began this case."

"Max." Mark stopped and seemed to stare off in the distance.

She pulled her chair closer and took his hand. "Talk to me, Mark."

He looked over at her. His eyes connected then looked away. "You've met my brother and sister. What I didn't tell you was I had another brother. His name was Thomas. We called him Tommy.

When I was twelve, Tommy and I rode our bikes down to the store on the corner near our house. We went inside, and I was looking at comic books. Tommy was in the other aisle picking out some candy. I don't really know how long I looked at those comic books. Old man Gus always let us come and hang out."

"All the kids in the neighborhood went there a lot. On hot days we would go and get an ice cream. Anyway, when I finally got done I went into the next aisle to tell Tommy it was time to go, but he wasn't there. I looked in all the aisles then went to get Gus. He was in the back room and came out when I called him. He helped me look for a few minutes. I ran outside and looked for Tommy's bike, thinking maybe he had gone on back to the house. It was parked right there where we left them." Mark stopped, looking into her eyes.

Max could see the torment in Mark's eyes. "What happened to him, Mark?" she prompted, holding his eyes with hers.

"After I couldn't find him, I raced home and told my mother. She called the police. Hours later, they found Tommy's body in a freezer in the back room of the store. Gus, it turned out, was a pedophile. Later, they discovered that he was responsible for several child abductions. Tommy had been raped before being strangled. They figured out that he was dead while I was still in the store. While I was reading those damn comic books, Gus was torturing and killing my ten year old brother."

Max could see the shame and anguish in Mark's eyes. "Mark, I am so sorry, but you were just a boy."

"I know. I also know that if I had paid more attention Tommy would be alive today. This case just drummed up all of those old feelings...old feelings of inadequacy and failure."

"When we first met you told me your father was a cop. You also told me that it ran in your genes. Were you talking about Tommy? Being in law enforcement, all the way to the FBI, is it about trying to get it right?"

Mark stared at Max then shrugged.

"Mark, this is important. You have to trust me with who you really are and what drives you."

"I guess so. My father kind of fell apart after Tommy's death. He was on his way to detective prior to his death. Afterwards he stayed a beat cop. His spirit was broken. My parents stayed together, but they swirled around each other rather than remain married. I've always felt like it was my fault. Of course they both tell me it's not, but deep down I know I could have prevented it."

"I think I'd feel the same way."

Mark's eyes darted up to hers again, locking in on the green. She could see relief flood over him. "I wasn't sure how to...," his voice trailed off.

"Mark, you have to know you can tell me anything. If we're going to share our lives and make this work, if we're in this for the long haul then you have to trust me, and I have to trust you, even with our deepest secrets, fears, and skeletons."

"My family never speaks of Tommy, and I've never told anyone about him before. Of course Quantico knows, because they know everything."

Max leaned in and kissed him. "I'm glad you trusted me."

"I do trust you, Max." Mark paused, took a deep breath then continued, "There's more."

Max leaned back so she could see his face. "Okay, what is it?"

"The boy," Mark nodded. "In my case, he has no one. He trusts me. I want to spend time with him, maybe even help until they find him a home."

Max thought for a few minutes, not sure how to respond. "Mark, I understand the connection to Tommy, but I'm concerned that you're getting too close. We're trained to not get connected to the victims in our cases."

"I know, Max. I really do, and I've thought about that, even questioning myself about why I want to do this. He's nothing like Tommy. He's blonde and small. Tommy was dark and tall for his age. I don't think it's because of Tommy, although I realize I could be just trying to rationalize it. I don't know for sure. I just feel like I left him. I just don't want him to feel alone and afraid forever."

"Can I meet him?"

Mark turned to her, obviously surprised by her sudden question. "Yes, I think you can."

"Let's do it. Let's go see him. Where is he?"

"They were putting him into an emergency foster home last night. I told him I would come see him today. I had to pull some strings to get that approved."

"Okay, so what do we have to do to ensure you can stay connected with him?"

"I'm not sure. I wanted to talk with you first before talking to the social worker about visitation. Once he's settled somewhere it should be better."

"Well, let's not worry about that now. Let's take him to breakfast if they'll let us."

Mark reached for his phone and was already placing a call. Max could see the stress slowly slipping away, and she felt relieved. She knew getting so personally involved was not the best idea, but she also knew she had allowed herself to get deeply involved in the Tyler case, and she didn't even have a personal trauma to justify it.

A few minutes later Mark hung up. "We can take him for two hours. The foster home is willing to let me see him periodically, but it's just a temporary home. They're trying to find him a permanent one. With his mother dead they hope he won't get bounced around too much."

"What's his name?"

"Heath. His name is Heath."

"Well, let's go get him. I'm sure he'll be glad to see you." Suddenly, Max realized the boy may not want to meet her. "How do you think he'll respond to me? Clearly his mother betrayed him. I'm sure he's too young to fully understand that, but there's likely a part of him that does understand it."

"He trusts me. I think it will be okay. I'll just have to talk to him first. Once I tell him that I brought a friend…"

Within a few minutes the couple was on their way to pick up the young boy. Inside the vehicle Max reached over and took Mark's hand. She had mixed emotions about the boy they were about to go meet. She knew supporting Mark right now was important, especially given the background he'd just shared, but she also worried that he was getting into something that might be bad for either him or the child. Deciding that she wouldn't be able to control this, she resigned herself to just being supportive of Mark.

Their ride was quiet, and then Mark pulled the car in front of a small house in an older neighborhood. He turned to Max, his eyes searched hers. As always it seemed he knew what she was thinking. "I know you think this is crazy. I just need to make sure this little guy is okay. Trust me?"

"I do trust you, and I'm here for you. Just let me know what you need and how I can help." Max paused. "Promise me you won't pull away, that you'll stay open with me."

"Deal." Mark kissed her gently. "Okay, let me go talk with him. I'll be back in just a few minutes."

Max waited patiently in the car while Mark entered the home. A few minutes later he came down the walkway with a small blonde haired, blue-eyed, beautiful, little boy. The child seemed to be tugging Mark along the path as he pulled on Mark's hand. In Mark's other hand was a child's safety seat for the car. Smart. She hadn't even thought about car safety.

Max watched as they came closer. The boy was smiling, and she found herself admiring his resilience. She shook her head as she acknowledged the amazing strength in character of a child able to rebound from unconscionable circumstances.

Mark opened the passenger door, leaned over to the child, and looked directly into the boy's eyes. "Heath, this is my very good friend Maxine. You can call her Max. That's what I call her."

Heath laughed. "That is a boy's name."

"I know. Cool, right?"

"Yeah."

"Hi, Heath, nice to meet you."

Heath looked at Max with a small amount of apprehension, taking about a half step behind Mark. "Hi."

"I was hoping, if it was okay with you, to go and have some breakfast with you and Agent Wells. I'm really hungry, and pancakes sound very good to me right now. I think they even have those with the funny face and strawberries on them."

Mark looked at Heath. "What do you think, buddy? She does look pretty hungry."

"Okay, I'm hungry too."

"Well, let's do it then, big guy."

Mark spent the next couple of minutes getting the child's seat appropriately setup in the back behind Max before Heath crawled up into the seat, and Mark buckled him in.

A few minutes later with everyone seat belted in, they headed off to the restaurant. Mark navigated through the streets thinking of a kid friendly restaurant and pulled the car into the IHOP parking lot. They piled out of the car, and with Heath holding onto Mark's hand, they went inside.

After settling into the booth, they ordered, and Max took the kids' menu and began coloring with Heath. After a few minutes he warmed up to her. Max looked up at Mark and saw him smiling at Heath and her chattering away to each other. She had to admit, being with Mark and Heath felt very comfortable. She'd never considered what the future would look like with Mark, but at this moment she could picture a family. She liked the way it felt and the possibility of the future.

The food came and Max set aside the picture they had made. Tearing into the food, and with sticky fingers from syrup and hot cocoa, Heath devoured the entire smiley face on his plate and some of what Max had ordered.

Once the food was gone the boy seemed to turn a little somber. He turned to Mark and asked, "Is my mommy dead?"

Mark looked a little surprised, but obviously elected honesty as the best policy. "Yes, Heath. I'm sorry, but it's true. She is."

Heath looked really sad, but no tears came. "Who will take care of me?"

"For right now the lady you're staying with will take care of you while we work to find a home for you for forever."

"Will I get a new mommy?"

Mark was clearly struggling, so Max jumped in. "Heath, Agent Wells can't answer that right now. But there are a lot of smart people trying to make sure you find a very good family."

"Can you be my new family?" Heath asked.

There was an air of innocence in the question that tore at Max's heart strings. She could see the fear in his eyes caused by the uncertainty. His mother had obviously never treated him well. Any mother who would sell her own child was not going to win mother of the year, but to Heath it was all he knew and as long as he had his mother, he had something. Before he learned of his mother's death, he had a semblance of safety. His five year old mind wasn't capable of realizing the magnitude of the danger his own mother introduced into his little world.

"Heath, it's not as easy as that. A lot of important people are working on making a good decision for you," Mark responded as Max tried to collect herself. Tears had nearly drawn, and she pushed hard to hold them back.

"You are important people, right?"

"We're people who care about you a lot. We aren't going anywhere. We'll be there to be sure this works out okay for you."

Heath nodded, but he remained quiet.

Mark paid the bill, and then the trio headed out to the car. Mark looked at his watch. "Hey, we have a few more minutes. It's a little cool out still, but the sky is clear. How about we go to the park for a little bit?"

For the first time since the conversation at the table, Heath looked up and smiled. "Yeah!" There was excitement back in his voice.

"Let's do it!" Max added as they piled back into the car.

An hour later they loaded back into the car after playing on slides, swings, a merry-go-round, and monkey bars. Mark had helped hold Heath up to the bars and guided him across. They'd both pushed him on the swings, and had taken turns going down the slide with him and catching him at the bottom. They'd all laughed a lot. It had been a good time.

Heath fell quiet again once they were back in the car and began their return trip to the house where he was staying. He stared out the window from his perch on the child safety seat. Max could see Mark checking on him frequently out of the corner of his eye. She knew Mark was worrying about returning him to foster care.

The car idled up to the curb in front of the white-sided house, and Mark killed the ignition and climbed out. Max got out too and waited as Mark got Heath out of the car seat. They stood on the sidewalk for a moment saying good-bye. Max was pleasantly surprised when Heath hugged her tightly. She whispered in his ear, "Stay strong, big guy."

Mark took the boy's small hand and the safety seat in his free hand and headed up the sidewalk.

Chapter Six

The lid swung open, and Jack stared down into the freezer. The body of his daughter, Faith—or at least his reproduced version of her—lay facing up, wrapped carefully in plastic, on top of Hope. He gently lifted the plastic-bound body and lovingly laid it on the floor of the garage. He gingerly unwrapped the plastic and stared at the exposed body, then breathed a sigh of relief after he examined her and found everything as he had expected.

Hugging the body he spoke, "Faith, honey, Daddy's here. I'm sorry you had to stay away so long. Let's get Mommy out here now, so we can all be together."

He gently kissed Faith on the cheek, oblivious to the incisions around her mouth where just a few months earlier he had sewn on the mouth from a little girl in Illinois that had been his patient.

The little girl, Jessie, had reminded him of Faith with her crooked little smile. He'd spared the girl only because he had become quite fond of her. After sedating the child he'd taken her mouth then crudely sewn on another mouth from one of his other victims. Before she had time to wake from the procedure, he left her at the door of the emergency room entrance.

When she was discovered he was called upon to help. He rushed to the hospital where he offered his expert services on a number of occasions.

After explaining to the family that the child's mouth had been removed and apparently sewn back on, he raced into surgery to reapply the mouth in expert fashion, making him, for a brief moment, the town's hero. Except... except for Special Agent Maxine Nichols forcing him to leave town to protect his family.

Pushing the memories from his mind and his focus back to his family, he returned to the freezer to retrieve his wife. Lifting the larger plastic-wrapped body from the bottom of the freezer, he carried it over to the floor next to where the grotesque, pieced together body of his daughter lay.

Demonstrating the same care he had shown just moments before with Faith, he unwrapped the body. He felt his head pounding and his heart racing. He couldn't believe his eyes, and as the reality of what he was seeing set in, rage filled him.

Stumbling backwards, he tripped as his foot tangled in the corner of the plastic from Faith's body. Laying in the middle of the floor was the body that he had spent so much time creating, the exact replica of his wife Hope, carefully preserved, and whom he had lavished with love and care for months, now lay crushed and flattened, beginning to fall apart.

In his rage, Jack grabbed anything in his path and threw it across the garage, slamming his fists against the drywall, driving holes into the wall and exposing the wooden studs. "NOOOOOOO! Hope, I need you. Hope!!!!"

Dropping to his knees next to the body, he scooped it up in his arms and rocked back and forth. Her still slightly frozen head rolled back to clearly show the decay and crushed check bone. His worst fear was coming to life—his beloved wife stolen from him again.

The voice of Maxine Nichols rang in his head, "It can't last forever, Jack, what you've done to those bodies." "Shut up, Shut up!" Jack shouted, placing his hands over his ears. He stared back down at the body. "Hope, darling, I am so sorry. I'll fix this. I promise you." Looking over at the child's body next to his wife, he turned Faith's head away.

He lifted Hope's body and carried it into the house to the kitchen. He laid the body down on the kitchen counter and grabbed his medical bag. "Think, Jack. Think!" he shouted out loud.

He returned to the garage and carefully wrapped Faith again. "Honey, Mommy isn't feeling well. I know we were going to spend some time together, but I need for you to take a little nap while Daddy tries to help Mommy feel better. I promise to spend some time with you a little later." Jack stood back and looked down at the body as he placed it back into the freezer and closed the lid.

Racing back inside he returned to Hope's side. He stood, contemplating what he could do. The body was badly decomposing; he could see that now. He couldn't think of any method to repair the damage that was already done. He considered Botox to re-inflate the areas that had become flattened, but instantly knew it wouldn't work. He thought of a more robust taxidermy approach, but knew it would leave the body hard and not lifelike. That would never do.

Jack knew of another process called Thiel soft-fix embalming. He'd never tried it personally, but his understanding was that the method retains the body's natural look and feel. For a moment he got excited at the thought of it, then realized it was too late. He would have needed to do that when he'd first begun the preservation process.

Suddenly, the gravity of the situation overcame him. He held the body and wept. Despair began to overcome him. He had no idea how he would survive now.

He had no idea how long he'd been standing there with his face buried in the dress Hope was wearing, his tears dry now. He was shocked out of his grief by the sound of the intercom buzzer and a frail voice requesting his assistance.

Pulling away he turned to the kitchen sink and washed his face with cold water then dried it with a paper towel before going to see what Vivian needed.

He tapped on the door before pushing it open. Stepping inside he spoke softly, "Everything okay?"

"Yes, I was just hoping to get some water or ice chips. My mouth is so dry."

"Of course, which do you prefer?"

"Ice."

"Sure. Is there anything else I can bring you?"

Despite his attempts to avoid her, Vivian looked into his eyes. "You look sad."

"Do I? I'm probably just tired. I'll get that ice for you."

"How much longer do you think this will last?"

"This?" Jack was surprised by the question. It certainly wasn't the first time he had a terminally ill patient ask that question, but for some reason it seemed different with Vivian asking.

"Me, just laying here day in and day out, sleeping most of the time away in between the pain, this is no life."

"I suppose that depends on the strength of your body and…mind."

"Or you?" Vivian locked her eyes on his.

"Let me get that ice for you," Jack said pulling his eyes away.

As Jack entered the kitchen his heart wrenched as he saw Hope, or what was left of her, lying on the counter. He averted his eyes, trying to remain focused on getting ice for Vivian. For the moment Vivian was helping him avoid what he knew he was going to have to deal with.

He retrieved a glass from the cupboard and let ice crush into it from the ice machine in the front of the stainless steel refrigerator. The appliances were all new, a much nicer touch than the old white ones his mother had. After getting a spoon out of the drawer and with the ice in hand, he retraced his steps back upstairs.

Tapping lightly on the door again as he entered, he crossed the room to the bed. Vivian had dosed but stirred as he approached. A slight smile crossed her lips as her eyes settled on him. He felt exposed by her and yet comforted all at the same time. He couldn't quite grasp the emotion he felt. There had been far too many already in the few hours he'd been awake.

He scooped some of the crushed ice bits onto the spoon and slid them into the old woman's mouth. She closed her eyes again, appearing soothed as the cool slivers graced her dry palette.

Opening her eyes again, she spoke softly, "You never answered my question."

"I'm sorry? What question was that?" Jack asked truly confused. For a moment he thought perhaps she had dosed deeply enough that she'd entered a dream state for a brief moment.

"Will you help me?"

"Vivian, that's why I'm here, I came here to care for you."

"That isn't what I mean." The woman began to cough.

Jack took a tissue from the side of the bed and swabbed at her mouth. Suddenly Jack understood. "No, it's not time yet, Vivian. Your body is still alive, and your mind, although weary, is still awake."

"When it's time, will you help me? When it's time?" Her eyes misted over, and this time they pleaded with him.

He struggled. He certainly had killed plenty of people, but not like this. Not when he...needed her. He couldn't, not now. He stood there avoiding her eyes then looked at her and nodded. Scooping another spoonful of ice, he looked at his watch as she sucked on the chips. It was time for her pain meds again.

After feeding her a few more ice chips he delivered morphine into her IV, and within a few minutes she dropped back off to sleep. He stood and stared at her. His feelings were all mixed up right now. Hope was dead and Vivian was alive. Nothing was making sense right now. And Faith, what about Faith?

Since Vivian was going to be asleep for a while he returned to the kitchen. He stared at his wife and suddenly knew what he must do. He went to his room and searched through his luggage, finally pulling out a white dress for Hope. He carried it downstairs and slowly removed the clothing she was wearing. He carefully slipped her in the white dress. When he was done he stood back, and his breath caught at the sight of her beauty. Tears ran down his cheeks.

Turning away, he went into the garage and looked around. In the far right corner he saw a shovel. Lifting it he went back inside. From memory he wound his way through the kitchen and out the back door. The door slammed behind him. The sound was so familiar. He couldn't remember how many times as a boy he had bounded down the step with the door slamming behind him as he went out into the woods towards his playhouse.

For a moment he got scared and wondered if his playhouse would even still be there. What if Vivian's husband tore it down? What if over the years it had fallen apart?

Forcing himself to calm down, he made his way through the overgrown brush. It was obvious no one had been down this path for a while now. The path was barely visible, the grass tall and vines wrapped around each other.

He used the shovel to help break through the dense brush, breathing a sigh of relief when he soon came upon the small playhouse, which has been nearly consumed with vines. He noticed that some of the vines appeared to have been removed at one point, and he wondered who'd been inside. Could it have been Vivian's husband before he died? At first he felt violated, but then realized it didn't really matter. He was home and no one would be going in there again.

Laying down the shovel, he began pulling at the vines, ripping them away from the house until finally he uncovered the door and windows. He took the shovel and cut through the vines around the base of the house, and after nearly an hour he was dripping with sweat as he stood back and stared. His childhood sanctuary was fully revealed. The small building showed some signs of age, but it looked just as he remembered.

With the playhouse unveiled, he pulled on the small door, which creaked as he tugged on the handle, until it swung open. Poking his head inside his senses swirled as memories flooded in from the smell. He could picture Hope sitting in the corner, cross-legged on the planked floor, her blonde hair pushed behind her ear on the right, her tank top falling off her shoulder, and her knees dirty from climbing trees and hiking through the woods. His heart tugged, and a lump formed in his throat.

Climbing through the door, swiping away cobwebs and dirt, he had to duck a little since he was unable to fully stand up inside, his height restricting him in the small room. He looked around and poked his head up into the small loft. His old cot was still there, but broken. He went to the other side of the room and bent down. From his childhood memory he tapped his toe against the old boards, then reached down and tugged on the familiar loose board, pulling the plank out. He peered down inside, but it was too dark to see. Reaching in, he felt around and only touched dirt. *Impossible.* Dropping to his knees he reached even further into the opening, feeling all around. Still he found nothing.

Unable to believe his treasures were missing, he quickly got up and began running back to the house. Going inside, he rushed into the garage and looked around until he found a flashlight. Clicking it on, he was pleased when the batteries didn't fail him, and at a near run he returned to the playhouse.

The door creaked, and the hinges whined against the years of no use. Inside he dropped to his knees again, shining the light down into the opening in the floor. Straight down he could see where the box that had contained his treasures had once been. The square imprint in the soil was obvious, but the box was gone!

"You bitch, Agent Maxine Nichols!" He was so angry he spat out the words. Suddenly he knew his sacred spot had been violated. Standing up, he shone the flashlight and peered into the loft. His magazines were gone too. The magazines Hope had given to him. Their magazines, their future, their plans–gone!

"You'll pay for this! I promise you that!" The rage was climbing in him. "I live here now, Agent. Just try to come back, I dare you. I'll be here protecting my family now."

With that and his adrenaline driving him, he retraced his steps back to the house. Inside he got a blanket from the hall closet and carried it to the kitchen. He laid it out on the floor and gently lifted Hope from the counter, laying her body in the middle of the blanket. He leaned down and kissed her tenderly, ignoring the mushy indention on her head.

"I love you, Hope. I'll always love you. I'll find a way for us to be together forever. Just wait, I need some time to figure it all out, but I promise you I will never give up. Faith needs you, and I need you." He wrapped the decaying, pieced together body in the blanket and then lifted her in his arms. He carried her out the back door towards the playhouse.

Upon arriving at the playhouse, he pulled the door open with his finger as he carefully balanced the bundle in his arms. He laid the wrapped corpse on the floor inside and then returned to the house where he retrieved a hammer, pry bar, plastic sheeting, and some nails from the garage.

With the supplies in his hands, he listened at the bottom of the stairs for a minute, ensuring Vivian was still asleep before once again heading into the woods.

Inside the playhouse he worked the floor boards loose until he had an opening large enough that he could drop through to the dirt below. Taking the shovel he began to dig. Tears rolled down his face. He dug until he had a hole four feet deep and five feet long. He laid the plastic into the hole and then climbed back out to retrieve Hope. He sat down with his feet dangling into the hole as he held her in his arms. He didn't even notice the boards digging deep abrasions in his back as he slid down into the hole until his feet hit the ground. He clung to Hope inside the blanket, protecting her as he tightly cradled her body.

He lowered her into the hole and wrapped the plastic tightly around the blanket, folding the ends around her head and feet to create a cocoon. For a long while, he kneeled next to her and sobbed. His heart was breaking. He wasn't sure he could survive without her. He also knew he didn't know how to care for Faith without Hope. He could barely acknowledge it, but he knew what to do.

Pulling himself back up onto the floor of the playhouse, he went back to the garage. He walked to the freezer and lifted the lid. He stared down at Faith. Inside he knew what to do, and it was killing him. "Faith honey, Mommy needs you now. I need some time to bring us back together again, but in the meantime you'll need to help take care of your mother. She's not feeling very well and having you will make her feel better."

Lifting his daughter from the bottom of the freezer, he carried her out into the woods and into the playhouse, slid down through the floor again, and laid the small plastic-wrapped body next to Hope. The sobbing that started when he first began digging continued, and there seemed to be no end in sight.

Jack lay down in the hole with the two bodies. He wept until he couldn't cry any more, feeling paralyzed by his grief.

He jumped with a start. Looking around he realized he'd somehow fallen asleep with his wife's and daughter's bodies wrapped in his arms. His fingers were coiled in a grip around the plastic, and as he uncurled them they ached from being so tightly clutched. He knew he couldn't prolong this any longer. He stood up and retrieved the shovel and began to slowly, pensively scoop the dirt onto the bodies.

Once he completed the burial of his family, he pulled himself back onto the floor of the playhouse. Methodically, he reinstalled the planks, nailing them into place, being careful to not crack the brittle boards. With the task complete, he looked around the playhouse and noted that if not for the shiny nail heads everything looked as it always had. His absolute most valued treasures were stored under those boards.

He headed back to the house, trying to ward off the desperation that was building. The darkness was swirling around him. It was everywhere. He knew what it meant, and he knew he wouldn't be able to fight it for long. Not without Hope. Not without his family.

Chapter Seven

After dropping Heath back off at his temporary home, Mark and Max returned to Mark's house and spent the day replaying the time with the boy. Over dinner Max decided to address with Mark the topic of the child's future. She needed to understand what he was thinking. Not really wanting to cook, they ordered in Chinese food from their favorite little delivery spot.

Max plucked vegetables out of the white container with her chopsticks and watched Mark consume an eggroll. She leaned back, dropping her chopsticks into the little tub. "What do you imagine with Heath?" she asked in her usual direct fashion.

Mark looked up from his food, chopsticks in mid-air. He set his food down and leaned back in his chair. "I don't know, Max. All I know is he needs someone in his court. I want that someone to be me...us."

"He's an amazing kid, but I'm not sure what you can do."

Suddenly Mark got up from the table and left the room. He was gone for a few moments and then returned. He walked over to her and took her by the hand, lifting her from the chair.

"When we returned from Illinois I went shopping for your Christmas gift. I bought you that necklace that I gave you, but while I was shopping I bought something else. I knew it wasn't the right time to give it to you, but I knew it would be one day."

Max stood looking at Mark, confused by what he was saying. "I don't understand."

Mark reached into his pocket and slowly knelt down on one knee. "Maxine, I love you. In fact, I have loved you from the moment I saw you get off your motorcycle, well, actually from the moment you removed your helmet and I saw you. The very minute I saw you, I knew my life would never be the same. I know we agreed to wait at least a year, but I don't need a year. I know I love you, and I know I want to spend the rest of my life with you. Maxine Nichols, will you make me the happiest man in the world and be my wife?" Mark opened the small box he'd been holding, exposing a beautiful teardrop diamond ring, the band glistening with smaller diamonds.

Max stood staring down at Mark, her emerald eyes glistening, his words causing her heart to race. She loved this man. There was no doubt in her emotions. She smiled and bent down to kiss him tenderly. "I love you too. Yes, Mark. I say yes." She pulled on his hands to raise him up to her level and settled into his embrace.

After a few moments Mark pulled back and removed the ring from the box. He took her left hand and slowly slid the ring on. "I wasn't sure what size, so I guessed. If it needs to be sized we can do it any time."

"Mark, shut-up and kiss me," Max said leaning into him, pressing her body against his, sliding her hand down his chest and across the front of his jeans, immediately feeling the response of her touch.

A small gasp escaped Mark's lips as Max slowly unzipped his pants and slipped her hand inside. She wrapped her other arm around his neck as he lifted her off the floor and carried her to the bedroom. They sank into the pillows as Mark expertly pulled her jeans away and slid her top over her head.

Her hands ripped at his shirt as the desire rose in her. His fingers played on her flat stomach. She felt like her skin was on fire with every touch. Wrapping her legs around him, she pulled him to her and pushed at his pants with her feet, slowly working them down his legs. He pulled back and slid her to the edge of the bed as his clothes dropped to the floor. Slipping his fingers into her thong he rolled the silky material down her thighs.

She worked her feet out of the material and locked her legs around his hips. His erection was full, and she could feel it against her stomach as she rose off the bed and embraced him, wrapping her fingers in his hair as she teased his lips with her tongue.

His hands explored her body, finger tips gently teasing her nipples and sliding down her waist across the tops of her thighs and between her legs. His thumb circled her wetness, causing her to rock forward. He pushed her shoulders back, kissed her neck and down her shoulders, lowering his mouth onto her breast and flicking her nipple with his tongue, then traced her muscular belly down to where his thumb continued to tease.

Max was starting to lose it. The teasing was driving her crazy, and she found herself nearly begging. "Mark, please I want you inside...." Before she could finish the sentence Mark slid his body on her, pushing inside and thrusting deep within. She arched her back and felt as if she would explode, her ears ringing. Their mouths met, tongues probing with unbridled passion.

Max began to rock, following Mark's rhythm as their bodies pulsed together. It seemed as though there were drums inside her head as they worked each other to total ecstasy.

Hours later and only after having repeated the experience in a tender, slow and purposeful manner they dosed off. Awaking famished and realizing they'd never even finished their dinner, Mark hopped out of the bed naked and disappeared down the hall. A few moments later he returned with the Chinese food on plates. He'd warmed the food in the microwave and returned smiling with chopsticks in hand.

Max sat up in bed, leaned back against the pillows, and pulled the sheet up under her arms. After setting the plates down on the bed, Mark left again for another minute, this time returning with two glasses of wine. Crawling back in bed, he shoved a bite of food into Max's mouth, playfully teasing her.

Max watched Mark devour his food and smiled at the realization of how much she loved this man. The reality of the proposal was setting in. They would be married one day, and this is how life could be. Her mind returned to Heath as she sucked a snow pea into her mouth. Although she didn't want to ruin the moment, she needed to know something. "Mark, why tonight?"

"Why tonight?" Mark seemed genuinely puzzled by her question.

"Proposing, why tonight? I mean, we were discussing Heath and how he fits into your future and then suddenly you proposed? Don't get me wrong, I'm thrilled and I love you. I see a future with you, but why tonight? Why when we were talking about Heath?"

Mark set his plate down on the nightstand next to his side of the bed and turned to her. Leaning in, he kissed her then began explaining, "I wanted to ask you at Christmas, but I knew it was too soon. I knew you weren't ready then. Now with Heath and all, I've seen over the past couple of months, I see you as my future, and I don't want to wait any more. I see kids with you, especially after watching you with Heath today. You were amazing, and I want that for the mother of my children."

"Mark, talk to me about Heath. Something happened with the two of you. What do you see happening with him?"

"I honestly don't know. I wish I could say. I wish I knew what I could do for him."

"I saw you with him today. It's more than you just wanting to help him. You feel responsible for him. You want to be responsible for him. I don't even know if you realize that yet."

"What are you saying, Max?"

"I'm saying he needs someone he can count on, and you imagine being that someone."

"Whoa, I never said that," Mark said holding his hands up and palms facing her in protest.

"You don't have to say that. It's obvious."

Mark stared back at her. He seemed to be absorbing what she was saying. "I don't understand. What are you saying, Max?"

"I'm saying you won't be happy without knowing for certain that Heath is safe. And...there's only one sure way to know he's safe."

Mark shook his head. "I still don't understand, Max."

"I'm saying you should apply for foster status and try to get him placed with you. Honestly, I think that has a lot to do with why today is the day you asked me to marry you. In your heart that's what you want, and you see us together as a family. A single man won't likely be granted custody, but a married couple would."

"Now wait a minute, Max. If you think I only asked you to marry me because I wanted Heath to come live with me, you don't know me very well."

"I didn't say that, but on an unconscious level, I do think it plays a role."

"Max, I'm sorry. I...I don't know what to say."

Max set her plate aside. "Mark, don't be sorry. I love that you feel responsible and care so deeply for that little guy." She took his hand and turned towards him, wrapping her foot over his leg and pulling him to face her. "I said yes. I already knew even if you didn't, and I said yes anyway. I love you, and if loving you includes Heath, then I still say yes."

"What do we do?"

"I don't know, but I think tomorrow you should call the social worker and find out what the chances are."

"Is it too fast?"

"Life is fast. Heath's life changed too fast. It's not necessarily the order which I pictured, but I know my life includes you. I love you."

"You, Maxine Nichols, are amazing. I have no idea how or why I got so lucky." Leaning over, he kissed her deeply then handed her plate back to her and fed her another snow pea before picking up his own plate and loading his chopsticks with rice.

Chapter Eight

Jack returned to the house and went in to take a shower. He felt totally spent. Physically, he was covered in dirt and tears. Emotionally, he was riddled with rage, fueled by despair and the feeling of failure. He turned the water on very hot and scrubbed at his skin as if somehow the scalding water could wash away the pain and anger of his loss. The vigorous cleansing left his skin feeling raw and sore. The tingling just made him more aware as if his skin itself was angry.

After toweling off he dressed quickly and then went to check on Vivian. Respectfully he tapped on the door before entering the room. For a moment his heart stopped as the old woman lay in the bed, and he thought that she too was dead. Suddenly he realized she was breathing lightly, and he sighed.

Checking the catheter, he emptied the contents of the bag in the toilet of the adjoining bath. When he flushed the toilet, the noise caused the woman to stir. She opened her eyes slowly and faintly smiled.

"Hello, Vivian. You've been resting for quite some time. Would you like the T.V. turned on?"

She nodded her head, and he picked up the remote control to turn on the flat screen that was mounted on the wall. He flipped through channels until she selected something.

"I'm going to get you something to eat. Ice is just not enough. How does some broth sound?"

Vivian shrugged.

"Is there something else you would prefer? Ensure? I saw that there was strawberry, chocolate, and vanilla in the cupboard."

"No, broth is fine."

"I need to check your catheter site. And can you tell me when you last had a bowel movement?"

"Do what you need to do." She seemed to be considering his question. "I think sometime yesterday. It was when James, my prior caretaker, was here."

"We need to get you onto your side for a while. I don't want you getting bed sores."

Jack pulled back the blanket, trying to allow the old woman as much dignity her plight would afford. Determining that the catheter was looking as it should, he slowly rolled her to the right and then adjusted

533

her pillows so she was more comfortable. With her situated and watching television, he left to make her some broth.

As he entered the kitchen he choked back the pain caused by seeing the bare counter where hours earlier his wife had laid. He forced his eyes away and went to work finding a can of chicken broth and a bowl that he could microwave to warm the liquid. With the broth hot, he collected a spoon and a fresh glass of cold water.

Carrying the items up the stairs, he entered the room and set the bowl and glass on the nightstand then took a chair next to the bed, pulling it up close enough where he could assist in spooning the warm broth into Vivian's mouth.

"It does taste good. Better than I thought it would."

Jack smiled. Seeing the woman eat made him feel better, as if there was hope. Hope, he needed to have Hope.

He could feel Vivian studying him again and tried to distract her by offering her some water.

"Why do you appear sad?" she asked.

"Me? You must be mistaken. I'm just tired from my trip," he lied. He wondered how she could read him so well.

"I see your sadness. It's okay."

Jack looked at her and ignored her comments, continuing to offer her broth as she could take it.

After feeding Vivian, Jack gave her another dose of pain medication, and it wasn't long before she fell asleep. He took the dishes down and put them in the dishwasher—another new appliance, modern conveniences that had not been there during his childhood.

The sun set and darkness blanketed the outside and filled him inside. He knew Vivian would likely sleep through the night. He decided to go for a drive. Grabbing his medical bag after pulling on a sweatshirt, he walked outside and realized that in his grief he'd failed to return the U-Haul and frowned at the inconvenience. Shrugging at the realization that it was only one more day, he decided he could return it in the morning.

He climbed into the driver seat of the van and navigated it past the U-Haul down the driveway and headed towards the beach. He watched as the mountains grew smaller in the rearview mirror and the city lights of Ventura came into view.

As he entered Highway 101 he could see the Ventura Pier and chose his location. He exited at Seaward and headed west towards the beach. Turning left on Pierpont he went to the end, entering Marina Park. It was getting late now, and there were few cars. Jack pulled into a space, rolled down the window. The fresh, salty ocean breeze wrapped itself around him. He waited and watched.

The sound of the waves crashing and then ebbing could be heard in the distance. He'd been here many times as a child and knew there was a jetty just over the small slope and past the ship that sat on the sand and served as a playground for the local children.

Within the hour the parking lot emptied out, and Jack reached into his medical bag, pulling out a rag, gloves, and a syringe that he always had prepared. He shoved the rag into his pocket as he exited and slipped on the gloves. Heading towards the sound of the waves, he pulled his sweatshirt hood up over his head. His eyes scanned in both directions. He could see a lone jogger far in the distance heading toward him. He slowed his pace and looked all around. There was no one else in sight.

The jogger was getting closer. Jack waited until the man passed, then he turned and quickly approached the runner from behind. He depressed the syringe into the rag, and just as the jogger realized that he was being followed, Jack swung his arm around the man's neck and slammed the rag over his nose and mouth.

Arms rose to fight, clinging at Jack's gloved hands, but the drug won and the arms lost the battle. Jack pulled the man up to a sandbar close to the parking lot then jogged over to his vehicle and backed as close as he could.

Hurrying, he returned to the man and lifted him, pulling him on his feet to the SUV. Opening the hatch, he pushed him inside. Jack folded down the back cubby and pulled out a large tarp that he kept stored in the van. Covering his victim, he closed the door, looked around confirming no one was around, slid into the driver's seat, and drove out of the park.

As he was leaving, he saw a BMW coming toward him. His timing was perfect. If he'd taken a few minutes longer the BMW would have been a problem. He knew he shouldn't take risks like this, but tonight the tingling in his skin was just too much. His loss today required action, and he was going to attend to it.

He removed the gloves as he drove, careful to obey all traffic signs. Jack followed the winding road back up the mountain and returned to his childhood home. He'd always dreamed of taking a person here, but he never had. Of course it was really his mother he had wanted to kill. All he had ever had the pleasure of experiencing here were a few small animals. Of course, that was all before Hope had caught him and made a pact with him. He shook his head, forcing the thoughts from his mind since they only deepened his anger as rage grew again inside.

Killing the engine, he got out of the vehicle after retrieving his medical bag. He went inside. He needed to assess a couple of things before bringing his visitor inside. Because of earthquakes it was uncommon for homes in California to have basements, but his home did. Built into the mountain, half of the home sat on a foundation, and the other nestled on top of a basement.

He went around to the entrance that opened from a mud room just near the back door on the main floor. Reaching inside the door for the light switch, he flipped it to the on position, flooding the entrance with yellow fluorescence. Descending the stairs he was pleased to see the area was free of clutter.

In the main room all that was there was an old workbench, that at one time had served as a laundry table. Next to it was a shelving unit that was now empty. Off to the left was a smaller room with a door. He remembered there was a shower in that room. His father used it after working in the garden. Another small room to the right contained a toilet and sink. He opened the door and turned on the sink then flushed the toilet. Everything seemed to still work. Satisfied, he climbed the stairs two at a time and stepped out into the night.

Grateful for the solitude of his childhood home, Jack easily got the man into the house undetected. He found some duct tape in the garage and stripped the man of his clothing, then successfully secured him to the workbench. He stood and waited, watching closely, eager and with anticipation of what would come next. A half an hour later, the jogger was beginning to wake up.

Jack watched as his captive began to wake. He could tell the jogger was confused. He watched as the man shook his head, trying to remove the fog. The jogger attempted to raise his hand but struggled, not coherent enough yet to comprehend that he was taped down. Jack didn't like the fact that the workbench was made of wood. The porous surface certainly was not ideal. He also didn't like the old oil and grease stains that covered the surface and legs. It was not the usual sanitary condition that he was used to, but it was going to have to do, for now.

He gently slapped his visitor's face in an effort to help him wake up. "Wake up, my friend."

The jogger's eyes opened wide, and Jack could see the instant fear in his eyes. "Help me," the man pleaded.

"Not likely. In fact, you're going to help me." Jack watched the man's face change from hope to desperation and then fear. "Today has been an especially bad day for me. But you're going to make it better. Oh, yes, I have a need that you will fill very nicely."

For a moment Jack was reminded of Benz, the car salesman from Oklahoma. He had spent days with Benz. That had been one of the most successful times in warding off the darkness. Oh, Benz had been nice enough, but he could have told people about Jack and that just couldn't happen. So Jack followed the man then brought him back to his house and kept him for several days. Jack smiled as he recalled his time with the car salesman. That was before he had Hope back with him. He knew all he needed was his family, and then everything would be okay. He would figure it out, but for now he had something to keep him calm, and this jogger was just the right thing.

The man stared up at him and began to thrash against his bindings. "You can't get away, so you might as well calm down." Jack picked up the medical bag that he brought in from the car, unlocked the hasp, and reached inside for gloves. He pulled out a small leather roll and unsnapped it.

Retrieving a leather case from his medical bag, he rolled it open across the jogger's chest. Four different surgical knives of varying sizes were exposed. After slipping on the gloves, Jack ran his fingers across the shiny instruments. "Eeny, meeny, miny, moe," he said as he carefully made his selection while watching the jogger's expression.

The man really began to struggle now, his eyes bulging from the sockets. "I can see you're scared. Well, I should warn you that this is going to hurt. As a matter of fact, it's going to hurt a lot," Jack said as he took the number five scalpel and made an incision all the way down the man's torso from between the two clavicle bones to the pelvic bone. As Jack made the incision, the jogger writhed against the bindings, arching his back and curling his fingers into fists.

He cut into the jogger's body, and blood began to pool onto the workbench. But Jack didn't notice. He was far too interested in his pleasure.

With the incision complete, Jack began to talk, "Today my wife and child died for the second time. Do you know how that made me feel?" He paused and leaned over close to the man's face.

The jogger, in an obvious effort to somehow get out of the predicament he was in, finally able to find his voice gasped out, "I didn't," then grunts and groans followed.

"No, it's true you didn't, but you'll help me get over my pain. I lost my precious wife, Hope, and our beautiful daughter, Faith." As he talked about his wife and child the anger began to build. His frustration took over, and before he could stop himself, Jack pulled the man apart and forced his hands deep into the cavity of the jogger's chest. He intentionally squeezed the organs inside, angrily twisting and pinching.

At first the jogger's heart rate increased. His body squirmed against the bindings, and he screamed out in pain, fruitless efforts. For a moment Jack wondered if Vivian could hear the cries but gave little more thought to it knowing even if she could hear there was nothing she could do about it.

The man's heart began to slow, and as it did Jack squeezed the organ almost gently as if giving it stability again before he pinched it hard one last time, forcing it into a spasm before it slowed and finally stopped.

Jack screamed in release of his anger as the man died on the table in front of him. He screamed at his inability to savor the moment and at the anguish and loss he'd suffered.

Minutes passed. He wasn't really sure how long, but finally he pulled away. The man was now dead in front of him with his spilled blood pooling on the concrete floor. Jack sobbed as he removed his hands from inside the pale body. There was so much frustration inside him right now that he could barely control himself, but then he realized that he needed to get himself together if he was ever going to be able to be with his family again.

Jack began to busy himself with the cleanup. This part of the process had become as much a part of the ritual as the act itself. His surgical training and perfectionist demeanor would allow nothing less than precision.

An hour later he had the man and his clothing bundled in a sheet that he got from the hall closet. He needed better supplies, but this would have to do for now. Tomorrow he'd get to unpacking. He hadn't moved much, but his medical supplies were necessary. Looking around he acknowledged that he needed to get this room set up much more thoroughly.

After securing the bundle with duct tape, he lifted the jogger over his shoulder and prepared to head off into the woods again one last time for the day.

Chapter Nine

Max was waiting for Mark to come by and pick her up for an appointment with the social worker assigned to Heath's case. They'd already met with an attorney regarding emergency guardianship. There were some challenges, for sure. The first being that they were not yet married, and the second was their unexpected schedules and the nature of their jobs. The meeting with the social worker was to see what Mark needed to do to get qualified as either Heath's guardian or as his foster parent.

Over the past few days Max had given considerable thought about the proposal and the possibility of Heath becoming a very important part of the life she would lead with Mark. It both thrilled and terrified her. Marriage and a child were crazy, she knew, but she also knew Heath had really not been given a fair shake. Mark adored him, maybe even felt responsible for him somehow.

A few minutes later, Mark knocked on the door and pulled Max into his arms the minute the door opened. "Ready to do this?"

"I sure am," Max replied, applying a kiss on his neck.

"No reservations? No concerns?"

"Of course, I have both, but that's normal. I don't have reservations to the extent that I think we shouldn't go to this appointment. I'm counting on the social worker helping us better understand what we might be getting into."

"You're so logical about this."

"We have to be, Mark. I also want to be cautious. I'm trying to not get my hopes up until I understand more, and you need to be cautious too."

"I know. I'm trying to be realistic too."

"Well, let's go do this and see what she has to say. What's her name again?"

"Dana. Dana Thompson. Heath really likes her. She's one of the good guys. I actually think she really cares about the kids she's assigned to."

"Sad that you even have to say that or that any social worker wouldn't have the kids' best interest at heart, but I know there are so many that face their cases as the numbers on the file."

Mark looked at her for a moment then nodded. "We should probably get going. Our appointment's in forty-five minutes. Traffic may be heavy."

Max nodded and grabbed her keys from the small table that sat next to the door. "Let's do this."

The ride across town was slow going, but they arrived on time for their appointment. They sat for a moment in the car holding hands, their fingers interlocked in a silent embrace, before getting out and heading up the walkway. They smiled at each other before Mark swung open the door.

Inside, Mark stepped up to the counter and checked in with the plump, strawberry blonde woman that sat behind the window. She asked him to have a seat and explained that they would be called back in just a few moments.

They took chairs facing the door that people use when coming from the back office. That also gave them the view of the exit. This was a typical trait of almost anyone in law enforcement. Having a view on the door and any potential threat became second nature, more habit than conscious thought.

After about ten minutes, the door opened and a short, thin African-American woman opened the door. "Mark Wells," the woman called out, looking down at a clip board.

Both Mark and Max stood and greeted the woman who led them down a corridor, making a left and finally to a door on the right side. "Ms. Thompson will be right with you. Please have a seat."

They entered the room. It was quaintly decorated with soft colors and modest furnishings. Max found herself thinking that at least it isn't the institutional setting often associated with social and government facilities. She remembered Mark saying the woman was one who really cared, and this seemed to show in the décor. There were a few hand drawn pictures on the shelf behind the oak desk that seemed to be from former clients, based on the scrawled thank you messages in crayon.

Almost as quickly as they could be seated, the door opened again and in bustled a woman who appeared to be in her late fifties or early sixties. It was immediately apparent that despite her age she was a ball of energy. She approached them quickly, taking Mark's big hand into her much smaller one. "Special Agent Wells, it's good to see you again." Turning her attention and her smile to Max she continued, "And you

542

must be the lovely fiancé I've heard about. Dana Thompson, it's a pleasure to meet you," the woman offered in introduction.

Max returned her smile and extended her arm, taking the woman's hand in her own. "I guess that would be me." Max hadn't heard anyone refer to her as a fiancé yet and suddenly felt shy and yet warm all over inside at the title.

"Please, get comfortable. We have a lot to talk about, and I want to make sure I answer all of your questions today."

The next hour was spent with Dana explaining to the couple how the social service system worked in the state of Virginia, which had jurisdiction over Heath. They were pleased to learn that an emergency placement could be made in the circumstance of abandonment or neglect.

In this case, both applied. Heath had been both neglected and abandoned by his mother. The father had been killed shortly after the boy was born, and there were no other living relatives. Heath would either have to be adopted by someone, or he would remain in the foster system until he aged out at eighteen.

Dana also explained the pros and cons of attempting to take on a child that had gone through the types of trauma that Heath had experienced. There was likely a need for long-term therapy, and there would probably be battles down the road as the yet unknown emotional traumas played out.

She explained the likelihood of a judge placing the child permanently with Mark. A single male was not good, but should the couple marry, she felt fairly certain they could apply for emergency placement, followed by temporary foster, and then ultimately adoption if that was the path they chose. In the meantime, she could allow visitation with Heath to ensure the connection was continuing to build with all three.

"You two need to really decide if you want to start your marriage off immediately with a child. I can almost guarantee you, Heath will no doubt present some challenges along the way. It won't be easy. These kids unfortunately just aren't easy."

Max jumped in, "We understand, and yes, we've been talking. That's all we've been talking about."

Mark added, "I think we have to decide if we're ready to be married right now so we can get the process going. Do you think our jobs will pose any problems?"

"As long as you can show proof that you can financially provide care for the child, I don't see that as an issue with placement. You might need a nanny or a relative that can provide care should both of you need to be out of state at the same time. Other people do it."

"How do we get started?" Mark asked looking over at Max for reassurance and getting the nod he was hoping for.

"You can take the paperwork with you now. That gets you started on the process of fostering. Either I or another social worker will come out and do home inspections. For emergency placement we come out first then make periodic stops in the first sixty days. Processing you should be pretty easy, actually, because all of the background checks and registration with CODIS are already complete through your jobs with the FBI. Sometimes that takes a while." Dana reached into the desk drawer to the right of her and began pulling out forms and putting them into a folder. Before she was done there was about a quarter inch stack of papers accumulated.

Pushing back from the desk, the energetic woman stood and handed the folder to Mark as he and Max rose from their chairs. "You can't take them back, you know. They're not puppies."

"We understand," Max replied.

"I just like my families to know what they're getting into. It seems all very romantic, but we're talking about a boy who has witnessed and experienced things no child should ever see."

"Honestly, we have no romantic notions. In fact, I think we expect this to be difficult," Mark offered.

"Well then, you have a lot of forms to fill out." Dana smiled at the couple. "I think you'd make great parents for Heath."

With that, she walked the couple back down the corridor and to the lobby. She handed Mark a business card and shook their hands, telling them to call any time if they had questions that needed answers.

Once back out in the car, they looked at each other. At first their gaze was just serious, and then smiles broke across both of their faces.

"So we have the day off. Let's do it," Max said.

"Do what?"

"Well, we're already downtown. City Hall has to be around here somewhere."

"Maxine Nichols, are you saying what I think you're saying?"

She smiled, displaying a mischievous lopsided grin and raised one eyebrow. Her head tilted slightly, and her green eyes twinkled in the spring sunlight in an obvious challenge. "I've never pictured myself having the whole princess wedding. Waaaayyyy too much attention for me," she said dragging out the sentence.

"You're totally serious?" Mark was stunned at her certainty.

"What about your family? My family?"

"My family will be pissed, and then they'll get over it," she shrugged and giggled. "I don't know your family well enough to know if they'll be pissed. That, my dear, will have to be your call."

Mark sat staring at her beautiful eyes and silly grin. Her confidence was unwavering in the moment, a trait that had drawn him to her from the moment they'd met.

He leaned in and kissed her tenderly, then started the engine and threw the car into gear.

Chapter Ten

Jack woke early. He felt better yet somehow disappointed in himself for not taking more time with the jogger. He allowed his emotions to get the best of him. He spent a few moments reflecting on the weeks after the…accident and how he had spiraled out of control. He had gotten drunk and lost. He couldn't let that happen again, or he would never be able to have Hope and his daughter back with him.

Last night after taking the jogger deep into the woods where he dug a deep hole, depositing the body and covering it with the soil, he returned to the house and carefully showered, making sure to remove any blood or dirt. Afterwards he made sure Vivian was set for the night and provided plenty of fluids and medication to get her through until morning. He spent about an hour reading to her until the medication took hold, and she fell into a deep sleep.

He threw his legs over the edge of the bed and forced himself to stand up. He needed to check on Vivian. Pulling on pants and a t-shirt, he went into the bathroom to freshen up before going upstairs to tend to her. He first went to the kitchen and prepared a cup of tea and an Ensure milkshake. He really needed to get something more than just ice and tea into her system. It was important to him to keep her strength up.

With the tea and shake on a small tray he found in the pantry next to the refrigerator, he took the stairs slowly, making sure not to spill anything. Outside of Vivian's door, he tapped lightly to announce his entrance before balancing the tray on one hand and swinging the door inward.

Vivian's small, frail body lay resting nestled into the pillows, but the sound of the door woke her. Her eyes fluttered open, and a slight smile curled at the corners of her mouth. "What time is it?"

"Oh, it's early, only a little after seven. I brought you some tea and a shake."

"Tea sounds nice."

"I really need you to try the shake too. I know it's hard, but you must keep your strength up."

"Why?" The woman's eyes seemed to plead with him.

"Because life is precious. You need to savor it."

"There is no value in it anymore."

"You are providing value for me."

The woman stared at him as if trying to assess whether he was telling the truth. Her eyes softened. "Tell me about you. Where were you before coming here?"

"Well, I've lived lots of places. Most recently, I was living in Scottsdale, Arizona."

"Tell me about it?"

Jack looked at her, studying the wrinkles around her eyes. Her blue eyes seemed to twinkle just a little. They were eyes that were filled with sadness. He assumed the sadness was a result of the loved ones she had loss. And there was pain in those eyes, both physical and mental pain.

There was a hint of something else in those eyes too, but he couldn't quite place what it was. Jack began to talk as he went about emptying the catheter and administering her medications. "It's very hot in Arizona. Air conditioning is a must. It's beautiful too though, or at least parts of it are. A lot of the buildings are the same color as the sand, so at times it can be very bland. But the rock canyons are lovely."

Vivian sucked on the straw Jack had placed in the shake, the effort nearly more than she could muster. With a ragged breath she prodded for more information. "Family?"

Jack realized she was seeking information about his past, and his mind raced on what, if anything, he could share with her. "I have some distant relatives that live in Arizona. I haven't seen much of them lately though. We weren't very close."

"You must fix that."

"Fix it? I'm not sure that's possible."

"You need to try."

Jack looked at Vivian. She forced him to accept her gaze and she nodded at him. "Okay, I'll keep that in mind. For now though I need to give you a bath, and we need to turn you again."

Jack began the process of gathering towels and a warm bowl of water. Then he gently sponged the woman, careful not to tear her tender skin. "I could go and get you some movies today. I have to run a couple of errands anyway. Do you have any favorite oldies but goodies that you might like me to pick up?"

"Gone with the Wind, my favorite," she rasped through her discomfort as he rolled her to one side.

"I'll get it for you. We can pop it in tonight." With a fresh gown on, Jack settled the small body back into the pillows.

"You're gentle."

"Well, I'm supposed to be gentle. My job is to provide you the best of care. Was my predecessor not gentle?"

"Not always."

Jack envisioned someone manhandling Vivian and instantly felt rage. The feeling unsettled him. It had been a long time since he'd felt any emotions about anyone other than Hope and Faith. Confused by the feelings, he suddenly excused himself and turned to leave the room.

"Movie tonight?" she asked sounding hopeful.

Jack turned back to face her. "Yes, Vivian, I promise," he said without facing her.

Leaving the room, Jack began to assess what he needed to accomplish today. He had to take the U-Haul back to the dealer. It was now after eight o'clock, and they should be open. He needed some coffee and hadn't found any in the kitchen. He saw a coffee pot, so he'd just need to stop by a grocery. He went to the bedroom to put on some shoes, grabbed his keys, and went out to the garage.

Looking around everything seemed to be in order. The hum of the freezer immediately caught his attention. He forced his eyes away from the reminder that his wife and daughter were gone, stolen from him again. He had to get them back. He wasn't sure how just yet, but he knew it was the only way he could survive.

Hitting the button to the garage door opener, he waited as the door slowly rose, letting the morning sunlight pour in. He walked outside, grateful for the beautiful day, and climbed in and slid behind the wheel of the U-Haul truck.

Pulling out of the driveway, he navigated the truck and trailer down onto Main Street. He went just a few blocks before pulling over next to a wide open space of curb. Climbing out of the cab, he locked the doors and walked across the street to the small bookstore that housed a quaint little café. As he opened the door he was greeted by the aromas of rich coffee and pastries. The barista welcomed him, and after a few minutes delivered him a steaming hot cup of coffee and a warm bagel.

He selected a table next to the window and enjoyed watching a pair of birds playing outside while he savored the coffee. He took a bite from the bagel, and his mind replayed the morning with Vivian. Suddenly, he knew what he needed to do. It was so obvious, but somehow she'd made it clear. He smiled as he finished off his breakfast and began mentally preparing how best to execute the plan to be reunited with his family.

Chapter Eleven

Mark and Max stood in the middle of the City Hall building. They obtained a marriage license and now were waiting for one of the authorized clerks to perform the simple ceremony. They were fortunate that in the state of Virginia a blood test was not required which could have delayed their sudden decision to marry today. The whole process was as simple as paying fifty dollars for a marriage license and filling out some paperwork.

Mark looked down into Max's emerald eyes. "You're completely sure about all of this?"

Max waved the marriage license at him and teased, "I wouldn't have this now if I wasn't sure, now would I?"

"That was only part of what I was referring to." Mark studied her face closely.

"I know," she replied, then leaned into him and raised up onto her toes to kiss him on the lips. Before she could say anything more, the door swung open, and they were joined in the foyer area by a plump man. The area was merely a large opening that was lavishly appointed with solid marble slabs.

The man that entered the room called out, "Wells and Nichols?"

The couple exchanged a glance and a smile, finding the formality of it amusing given the fact that there were no other people waiting in the area. Others had come and gone, but had walked on past to enter other rooms throughout the large City Hall building. There were people bustling about on their way to pay tickets, file land rights, or some other business.

Today they were the only couple waiting to be married. Max was relieved by this fact as it made it more intimate. On the way over in the car, she and Mark agreed that they would inform their respective families and have an official ceremony in a couple of months when things with Heath settled down.

Max hadn't ever really spent time fantasizing about her marriage like so many other girls. She'd spent her life imagining her life as a police officer solving crimes. She'd accomplished her dreams, and while she'd never dreamed of a fancy wedding with a flowing gown, she also hadn't imagined marriage in a court house either. The only thought she'd really ever given to her wedding day was that she wouldn't stand there and say "I do" unless she truly loved the person she was standing beside.

551

Today she knew the only requirement in her marriage dream was being fulfilled. She did, in fact, love the man she would be standing beside.

Mark answered the man's question, drawing Max out of the flurry of thoughts that flew through her mind. "Yes, I'm Mark Wells, and this is my fiancée, Maxine Nichols."

Max barely had time to get used to the title of fiancée, and in just a few moments it would change to wife. Letting out a small sigh, she stepped forward with Mark as she took hold of his hand.

They followed the man through the door into a small room with four straight back chairs, presumably for witnesses, a non-requirement in the state of Virginia. They'd decided not to have anyone meet them here, allowing themselves a little more time to decide how and when to communicate with their families and their colleagues. The door containing a small four by four inch window closed behind them, clicking shut and leaving the room nearly silent. There wasn't much else to the room. It wasn't more than fifteen feet long with a small podium standing at the other end.

"My name is Dennis Chamberlain. I'll officiate your marriage today. In my role I will sign the marriage register, and I will submit the necessary documents to the Clerk of the Court. Those will then be sent to Vital Records. Once Vital Records completes the processing, you will be able to obtain certified copies at any time. Do either of you have any questions?"

Mark looked over at Max and smiled. "I don't believe we do." Max merely shook her head.

"Do you have any special vows that you would like to say or read to each other?"

Neither Mark nor Max had even considered this. Max could feel her cheeks flushing a bit. "No."

"We have a few traditional vows that you can choose from." Dennis reached to the podium and lifted a book that looked as though it had been thumbed through a least a thousand times. He handed the book to Mark. "Take a moment to select those vows that best suit you or your respective religious affiliation."

Taking the book, Mark started flipping through the pages as Max looked on. After a few minutes they agreed on a set of fairly traditional vows. Max pointed to the page that said "Husband and Wife" as opposed to "Man and Wife." Mark nodded to her in immediate understanding. Max was definitely not a subservient woman, and those words suggested that the marriage was not a union of equal partnership, but rather one where the man was revered as superior to the woman. Max couldn't picture herself saying those words and meaning them.

Turning back to Dennis, Mark returned the book, pointing to the page they selected. Dennis looked over the page briefly and nodded. "Do you have a ring?"

Max removed the engagement ring and handed it to Dennis. Mark looked a bit hurt for a moment until he saw the huge grin on her face. She was amused by the lack of preparation. They both giggled and instantly joined hands, fingers interlocking once again as they turned to face Dennis.

"Do either of you have any last questions or comments?"

In unison they replied, "No."

"Okay, well, then let's begin."

"...I now pronounce you husband and wife. You may now kiss the bride."

Their eyes had been locked the entire time. As unplanned as this was, it couldn't have been more perfect. They were the only two people in the world during those few minutes. Mark had been holding Max's hands the entire time, and now he pulled her to him, sweeping his hand into the small of her back while his other hand reached up into her long auburn hair and cupped the back of her head to raise her head. He gently bent to her and delivered an intimate kiss. Still lost in the moment, they only pulled away when there was a sudden sense of discomfort emanating from their officiator.

"I love you, Maxine Wells."

"I love you too, husband." Max grinned at the sound of the words coming from her mouth. "Now, let's go figure out how we petition for emergency custody of that little boy we've been talking about."

Mark shook his head. A smile spread across his face, and his blue eyes sparkled. "Okay, but we have to have a honeymoon night before we can have children."

Turning back to Dennis, he nodded and immediately began to busy himself with the paperwork. After a few minutes he presented them with a certificate of marriage, a few other documents, and a receipt for his services which contained the record number. When it was all complete, he turned and smiled for the first time since he'd introduced himself. "Congratulations, Mr. and Mrs. Mark Wells."

"Thank you," Mark responded then turned to face Max. "Shall we, Mrs. Wells?"

"Yes, let's do this." Max couldn't believe it. She felt great. Life was good. Her career was going well. Mark was more than the perfect man she'd always hoped to find, and soon they would have a young boy sharing their lives.

They left the room and proceeded back out to the parking lot to the car. Once inside they kissed for several minutes before agreeing that they better get going if they hoped to catch the social worker and get the emergency custody paperwork started. They both hoped within a couple of days they could take temporary guardianship of Heath. More formal paperwork would follow, but once he was with them they'd know he was safe.

Chapter Twelve

Jack returned to the house after delivering the U-Haul, picking up *Gone with the Wind* for Vivian, and grabbing a few other items including coffee for the next morning. He walked the few blocks from the U-Haul dealership after turning in the truck and trailer.

It felt surprisingly good to be back in Ojai. He relished the opportunity to reinsert himself into the familiar town. The old haunts felt right somehow. The morning alone gave him clarity, and he figured out exactly what he would need to do to make things right here.

In the last couple of hours a plan had come to life on how he could get his wife and daughter back home. There was only one problem; he was going to need to leave for a few days. Reaching for his cell phone, he placed a call to the hospice agency that had been caring for Vivian prior to him coming into town and taking over.

After explaining who he was he said, "I was hoping you could provide care for Vivian for two or three days. I have a family emergency and need to go out of town suddenly."

"We could have her prior caregiver out there tomorrow morning. Is that soon enough?"

"Yes, that would be fabulous. What time should I expect him?"

After waiting for the time and agreeing on the final arrangements, Jack hung up the phone. With lots to prepare now, he needed to check in on Vivian and get busy.

Jack spent the next few hours getting everything ready for Vivian's care while he was gone. The frail woman slept, so he turned on soap operas which seemed to help keep her awake and alert. She needed to stay alert at times, or she would surely give up. He wasn't ready for her to give up.

Tonight he was going to make sure she got another Ensure shake down when they watched their movie. While he sat and talked with her he realized the excitement of his plan was making the darkness creep in. Unfortunately, in his sadness and anger the jogger had gone too quickly, and he knew his desires wouldn't be abated for long. Only with Hope in his life and when he was working was he ever able to control the darkness. Without either, there was no way he was going to be able to keep things in check.

He needed a table; that wooden workbench would never do. He could set the basement up the way he liked things—clean and sterile. If he was going to live here for very long, he'd need certain things. He went to retrieve his laptop, and while Vivian watched her shows he sat nearby ordering supplies online.

With the table, small refrigerator, and a variety of pharmaceuticals ordered he was confident he could entertain guests for quite a while.

When a commercial came on he broke the news, "Vivian, I need to leave for a couple of days."

She turned to him, her eyes searching his face. "Where are you off too?"

"I decided to take your advice and try to reconnect with my family."

"Oh? Good for you."

Jack looked back to the T.V. as the show resumed. He stood and checked her IV's, and after checking his watch realized it was time to administer her medication. He was trying to time the drugs to allow her to enjoy the movie later. At this point it was important to keep her medicated heavily enough to keep the pain away. Unfortunately, that meant she slept a lot. Within a few minutes she had dozed back off into a deep sleep. Jack collected the dishes and quietly left the room without turning off the T.V. in case she woke again soon.

When evening came Jack returned to Vivian's room with a shake for her and popcorn and a beer for him. He settled in next to her bed for the long movie. She tried a couple bites of popcorn, letting the buttery puff balls melt in her mouth. Surprisingly, Vivian remained alert through the entire movie and seemed thrilled with the experience. It was the most animated she had been since he had returned to the home.

When the movie ended, he tended to her medical needs and promised to see her in the morning before leaving town.

"Thank you."

"For what, Vivian?"

"For the movie and the time."

"It was my pleasure." Jack brushed a stray lock of grey hair away from her brow and pulled the covers up around her. "Good night, Vivian."

Morning came with early signs of the sun peeking through the windows. Jack rose and went to the kitchen to make some coffee. A few minutes before seven o'clock there was a knock on the door. Jack was in the middle of packing an overnight bag and stopped to go let his relief caretaker in.

Standing back from the door, Jack assessed the younger man as he entered carrying an overnight bag and medical backpack. Reaching his hand out to assist, Jack introduced himself. "Tyler Thomas. Thanks for coming back for a few days."

"Jimmy," he replied. "Not a problem. I'm still waiting on another full-time assignment, so this is good. This lets me make a few extra bucks until that comes through. Besides, the ole' lady is nice and easy to care for."

"I'll only be gone a couple of days." Jack turned to the man, placing emphasis on his words as he spoke, "Let me be very clear with you, that *ole'* lady is to be given the best of care. Are we clear?"

The thick neck of the caregiver, who looked like he'd rather be surfing than caring for an elderly woman, showed signs of stress as the artery in his neck popped out. "Yeah, man, I only meant..."

Before he could finish his comment, Jack interrupted him, "I think I know what you meant. She told me you can be rough with her. I don't expect to hear that when I return. I expect you to spend time with her, stay exactly on schedule with her medication, and be gentle. Are we clear?"

"Yeah, man, relax. I'll be good to her. I promise."

"Good." Jack smiled. The charismatic smile that had aided him throughout his whole life though now altered, still held its charm. Immediately the surfer was put at ease. Jack knew he'd already made his point.

The next hour was spent finishing his packing and making sure Vivian was all set. Leaning over Vivian's bed, he handed her a small cell phone. "This is programmed for you to call me by dialing 1 and the pound sign if Jimmy here is not being nice," he nodded at the surfer. "You call me, and I'll take care of everything. I'll only be gone a couple of days. You be strong while I'm gone, okay?"

"Go find your family. Don't worry about me. I'll be here when you return."

Jack nodded before giving Jimmy a final look and turning to leave.

Jack arrived in town just before sundown. The drive had been fairly easy. It was Wednesday, and aside from the lunch hour, he hadn't hit much traffic the whole drive. He decided he needed to get something to eat, and besides, that would allow time for the sun to fully set. To work well, he'd need darkness for the plan that he was envisioning. He tapped on the GPS system in the center of the dash and selected the restaurant icon, then scrolled down until he found something that looked appetizing.

For some reason, The Arrogant Butcher seemed interesting to him. He smiled and made the selection to start the directional mapping that would lead him there. It was only a few miles away in the downtown area. He took his time winding through the city streets. He rolled the window down after exiting the freeway and was enjoying the freshness of the warm spring air and the beauty of the sunset over the desert sky.

Once in the parking lot he navigated the vehicle into the first available parking space. He exited his vehicle, clicked the remote on the key chain to lock the doors, and weaved in between cars across the parking lot. Inside the building, Jack indicated a table for one and accepted the opportunity to sit outside on the climate controlled patio.

The menu had some really appetizing and unusual choices. He knew from the name that it was a good choice. He wanted a cocktail but decided against it, knowing he needed to have his total wits about him. Now was not the time to compromise and risk being anything less than alert. After all, the future of his family depended on tonight.

A short while later the server brought him the appetizer of black mussels, which smelled amazing. He tore into the bread that accompanied the savory dish. Then suddenly he became aware that he was being watched.

At first he began to get nervous, and then he realized it was merely a woman trying to capture his eye with innocent flirtation. He noticed she was a very attractive brunette. Her long legs folded perfectly and stretched out just right under the table to give him a preview of what the rest of her body would likely look like.

Oh, he'd love to spend some time with her. In fact, the darkness would love to take her before the meal even came, but no, he would not be distracted now. Hope and Faith were waiting on him. He turned his head away and stared out the window, hoping she would take the subtle hint that he was not interested in her that way.

Plates were cleared then more came, and Jack enjoyed his time at The Arrogant Butcher, all while not allowing the woman to overpower the irony of the evening. The scallops that he ordered were succulent, and he devoured everything on his plate. Then the dessert menu came, and he forced himself to ignore the sound of the options, as he wanted to be satisfied but not sleepy. He still had a long night ahead of him.

He was also taking a lot of pleasure sitting out in public without concern. By now most certainly Jack, the man he used to be, would have been noticed. Cops would have come plowing into the restaurant with anxious rookies wanting to make their claim to fame and seasoned detectives or FBI agents fighting over the notoriety of the collar. This new look had given him the cover he desired, and it was working quite nicely.

Jack paid the bill, scribbling his latest name on the receipt. He smiled as he saw it in print. Tucking the credit card back into his wallet, he stood and began the walk back through the dining area. He nodded to the brunette as he left. She was truly lovely, and he knew she was just as lovely on the inside too. But that was not meant to be. It was dark outside now, and the moon had taken on a nice glow. It was just after eight thirty now. He needed to wait a while longer. It was too early and definitely not safe to proceed right now.

Deciding how to spend some time, he climbed in the vehicle and backed out, immediately heading to the top of the edge of town. He had always enjoyed the night sky and total darkness sprinkled with brilliant stars that twinkled like diamonds floating in the air. It would only take about thirty minutes to get to the top, and then he could look down on the city and enjoy the evening until it was time.

Two hours had passed since Jack had left the restaurant, and now he felt certain it was safe to begin the descent back into the city. He wound his way back down the hill and then followed the familiar path to the modest residential area.

The homes on the block were mostly dark inside. One had a light on in what appeared to be the back bedroom. He slowed down as he approached and noticed the homes on either side were buttoned up for the night. The home he sought was as snug as a bug too. Jack pulled along the curb as he killed his headlights and studied the area.

Chapter Thirteen

One week after Mark and Max had tied the knot, Max laid in bed relaxing. Mark was in the shower, and she realized she'd been so consumed by the marriage and the efforts to try to gain guardianship over Heath that she hadn't had much time to think about Dr. Jack Tyler. It surprised her somewhat, and she had to admit it pleased her too. Not having Jack consume her every waking moment was almost a relief.

Mark had asked for a few days of vacation to work with the social worker, and it was beginning to look like they would be granted guardianship within a week. They both would need to appear in court, but the social worker and their attorney felt their petition would be granted.

Max always struggled with anything that she couldn't control, and the waiting seemed ridiculously long, even though it really had only been a few days. She also struggled with knowing Heath was in a foster home with a lot of other kids and not likely getting the support he needed right now. All she could think of was that he was such a little guy to have been through so much, including the sudden death of his mother. She wondered about his long term mental health and hoped that together with Mark they could offer him enough stability and love to get him past the scars that, no doubt, existed.

Max had an assignment later today that was related to her case, but this morning they were heading over to Mark's parents' house. They'd not yet told them of their sudden marriage and plans regarding Heath. It wasn't that they had delayed the conversation. It was simply that time had gotten away from them. They definitely needed to have the conversation soon, or risk causing a rift in the relationship Mark had with his family.

Hearing the shower turn off, Max stretched and forced her body out of bed to take her turn in the shower. Since the day at City Hall, she was staying at Mark's full time. She couldn't believe they were married. They would definitely have some work to do on the living arrangements soon.

Fresh out of the shower, dressed, and ready for the day, Max could hear noises in the kitchen and followed the sound that seemed to merge into fantastic smells. Mark was making a valiant effort to cook omelets. She smiled knowing he was trying to domesticate himself, when in reality chasing bad guys was way more his thing. Stepping in, she took the spatula and directed him to the coffee pot. A short while later they were enjoying omelets, coffee, and toast.

"Have you thought about Jack lately?" Max suddenly asked, as if it was the first time she'd mentioned the killer in a few months.

"I think about him some, yes. We both want him. Bad, but Heath has just seemed to consume me. I've really tried to think about my motives to ensure we have been smart. There's no turning back once we bring him into our lives full-time." He studied her for a moment. "Have you thought about him?"

"Sometimes, but I've been focused on you, the marriage, and Heath too. You know, when you were on Heath's case I was starting to get very worried about you. You seemed so lost. I understand why now, but at the time, I wasn't sure what was wrong and didn't know how to help."

"Have you called Cortez yet?" Mark asked, changing the course of the conversation.

"No, I need to. I'll call her in the car on the way to your parents' house. I need to see if Bobby has come up with anything for me."

Mark nodded as he popped the last bite of omelet into his mouth. "You think we're making the right decisions with Heath, right?"

Max looked up surprised by the question. "Mark, yes, we're making the right decision. I've been thinking. I'm going to have to change my ways a little. I can't have a murder wall in my living room."

"I know that's how you work best. We'll figure something out. Maybe we can setup your own room in the garage. That way we can keep it locked to ensure Heath stays out. If having a murder board is how we'll catch Jack, then we need one."

Max smiled and stood to collect the plates off the table. "We need to get going soon."

Mark glanced at his watch and grabbed the cups and loaded them in the dishwasher. Max turned to head out of the kitchen, and before she could get past the counter Mark grabbed her hand. "Ready to do this with my parents?"

"I think so. Will they be angry with us?"

"Angry, probably is too strong, but they may not be happy about it. I don't want you to worry though. I can handle them, and they really do just want me to be happy."

Max shrugged. "I'll follow your lead, but you owe me a trip to see my sister. In the meantime, you drive. I'm going to call Cortez while we drive."

***

A few hours later they were on the way back from Mark's parents' house. After the initial shock of the marriage had worn off, the visit had gone okay. Mark's father started to get upset, but Mark stood up for their decision and relationship. Mark's mother had wanted to see her son get married and was happy to hear there would be a ceremony with friends and family later.

Max had assumed they'd be more confused or concerned about Heath, but they seemed to have an instant understanding of Mark's draw to the young boy. Max watched the exchange as Mark explained the case, and how Heath had been recovered unharmed. She was surprised by their support of the unusual speed to a sudden marriage and family.

When they left the house, Mark's mother hugged Max tightly. Max returned the hug and promised to come back soon. They'd committed to keeping the parents posted on Heath's placement and agreed to bring him over to meet them as soon as they could.

On the way home Max took Mark's hand and began to fill him in on the conversation with Cortez. He'd heard one side of the conversation, but lacked some of the details, and she'd ended the call as they had pulled up to his parents' house, leaving no time to give him the update.

"Bobby has some names that are probable combinations that Jack might be using now. Cortez said he was not totally convinced it was viable data, but she was going to run with some of it and will send it over to me too."

"We could trace all those names. If someone is using the name and has recently relocated to a new area that would be a great first place to start." Max could tell Mark's mind was swirling on how they could use the data to find Jack.

"Oh, and she teased me relentlessly about getting married like we did."

Mark laughed out loud. "I'm sure she did."

"All she kept saying was, 'If you'd just listened to me.'"

"Well, we would have had more sex if you'd listened to her."

"What!"

"You barely even looked at me almost the entire time we were in Oklahoma. You were so angry with me."

"I wasn't angry with you. I was afraid to get close to you. I didn't want to get hurt. In my mind you were too serious and too handsome to not hurt me, and after our one encounter in California, I just didn't want to do that again."

Mark was grinning.

"Okay, I *did* want to do that again, but not just once."

"Well, I'm certainly glad you finally let down your guard."

"Me too, husband," Max teased.

"Did Cortez or Bobby have anything else?" Mark asked, directing the conversation back to finding Jack Tyler.

"No, that was it for now."

Mark's phone rang, interrupting their conversation. He answered the call and allowed it to pipe through the Bluetooth on the car speakers. "Agent Wells," he answered, assuming it was FBI related.

"Mark, it's Dana. Dana Thompson. I have some good news. I was able to get a meeting in family court tomorrow at one o'clock. Can you be there then? It'll need to be both you and Maxine."

Mark glanced over at Max and nodded. She nodded back at him, giving confirmation that she could arrange her schedule to accommodate the meeting. "Yes, of course we can both be there. What will happen at this meeting?"

"It should be pretty straightforward. The judge will review the petition. He'll ask you a few questions, and he'll talk to Heath. I'm going to meet with him to let him know what will be happening so he's not scared."

"Will he make a ruling on the spot?"

"Yes, he will. You should be able to take Heath home with you tomorrow."

"Can we see him today?"

"You could meet me over there. I'm heading there now."

"Okay, we'll see you there."

When Mark hung up Max said, "This is great news, Mark. Let's get my car. That way we aren't rushed. I have to report in at two o'clock, but I'd like to see Heath for a little while too. You'll be able to spend more time with him, if it's allowed, without having to rush to get me back."

Mark sped up the car a little to get to the house quickly. He pulled into the driveway and then leaned over, kissed Max on the lips, and watched as she swung open the door and got out. He waited until she started her own car before backing the car out of the driveway and heading towards Heath's foster home.

Chapter Fourteen

Jack waited longer, all the while considering his options. Finally making a decision, he rolled down the window before pulling the car away from the curb. He circled the block and parked half way down the street. While he was driving he listened carefully to the neighborhood sounds. He was specifically listening for any sign of neighbors being awake or dogs barking. Hearing nothing more than the normal comforting sounds of darkness he pulled over and listened again.

Reaching behind his seat, he pulled out a pair of gloves, three syringes of chloroform, and stuffed a roll of duct tape into his pocket. Sliding out of the van, he closed the door quietly, taking care not to make any noise. He silently glided up the sidewalk that lined the homes while he put on the pair of gloves. The street was silent and, short of the fluorescent lamps that lit the sidewalk every two hundred feet or so, the desert air was cool with stars dotting the clear black sky. A cool breeze came out of the west, highlighting the buzz he already felt on his skin.

His senses were on high alert. He felt totally alive, and he wondered why it had taken him so long to realize this was the only way he would ever really have his family back. He'd have to remember to thank Vivian for giving him the idea.

He approached the house and noticed the motion sensor on the porch light, so he slid to the right to avoid its detection. Outside the front door cloaked in the darkness, he rang the doorbell. His heart rate increased as anticipation embraced him. It was well after eleven o'clock now, and the residents would surely be sleeping or at least tucked in their beds.

Moments passed and then he heard footsteps. The door knob turned, and the door cracked open slightly. Jack could see his brother-in-law, Paul, in the light of the living room. However, Paul was struggling to see him on the darkened step. "Paul, good to see you. Sorry to stop by so late," he said pushing his way into the house and kicking the door closed.

Before Paul could respond or even fully comprehend what was happening, Jack pulled one of the syringes containing a fast acting sedative called methohexital from his pocket and plunged it into Paul's neck. His brother-in-law slumped at Jack's feet onto the floor.

A few moments later Jack heard a female voice call out from the back of the modest home. He immediately headed in that direction. He walked past two doors on the right side of the hallway, each adorned with letters spelling out girls' names, and another room on the left. The door was standing open, and as he passed he recognized it as the guest bathroom. From memory he continued down the hallway, knowing the room he was looking for was at the end on the left–the master bedroom.

He paused momentarily before entering. Pushing the door inward, he moved forward towards the bed. The room was dark enough that he could easily be mistaken for Paul long enough to do what he came for.

As he got closer the figure in the bed sat up slightly. "Paul, who was it?"

"It's Jack."

"Jack?" Delayed surprise filled her voice.

"I've missed you, Hope."

"Hope? Jack, how did you get in here?"

"We need to go right away."

"Go where? Jack, where's Paul?"

"He's sleeping. It's time for us to go home. Please hurry."

"Jack, what are you talking about? I am home."

"Paul let me in. I don't know why I didn't realize you've been here all along. I'm sorry it's taken me so long to come get you and Faith. Now, it really is important that we hurry. Please, get dressed so we can go."

"Jack, I'm not going anywhere with you." Mindy, Jack's sister-in-law and nearly an identical picture of Hope, reached and turned on the lamp on the night stand next to the bed.

"Hope, we must get Faith and go. We have a long drive ahead of us."

"Jack, I'm not Hope. It's me, Mindy, Hope's sister."

"I understand that you might be confused right now. That's okay. We have plenty of time to straighten this all out. But for now we need to go."

"Jack, you look different. The police have been looking for you. It's time to turn yourself in. Too many people have been hurt."

Realizing it would take her some time to adjust; Jack removed the second syringe from his pocket and approached Mindy. She was shaking her head and holding up her hands as he gently plunged the needle into her neck. "I'm sorry, darling. We can talk through all of this soon, but for now we have to get Faith out of here and go."

Mindy slumped over, her blonde hair spilling across the pillows. Jack brushed her locks away from her face and stared down at her. His heart raced as he realized how much he had missed his wife. He leaned down and kissed her. The warmth of her lips burned deeply, and he suddenly knew this was right. He would never need to store her away in the cold. They would be able to be together forever.

A smile crept over his face. "I'll be back in just a minute, sweetheart. I need to go get our daughter." Jack turned away from Mindy and returned to the first door in the hallway. Ignoring the letters that spelled out "Madison" on the door, he turned the knob and pushed in, immediately seeing a small bundle wrapped in the twin bed. He approached the bed and looked down at the child. Dark hair covered the pillow, and he recoiled and backed out of the room.

Continuing to the next door he repeated the process, again ignoring the letters that this time spelled out the name Allie. Inside the room he found the small treasure he was expecting. Blonde locks splayed out across the pillow, and light cream-colored skin shone like a beacon in the small amount of light that peaked in from the living room. Jack stared down at the angel. He wiped at the tears that flowed from his eyes.

Looking around the room, he saw a doll and a teddy bear. He lifted the child and each of the items and carried them out to the living room. Paul was still slumped on the floor. He'd have to deal with him in a few minutes. He searched the room and the kitchen until he found the car keys. He scooped them up and went out the door off the kitchen, which he knew opened into the garage. Pressing the button on the wall just inside, he activated the garage door opener. Sliding in the seat of the car, he turned over the engine and backed the car out. Depressing the button on the visor, he closed the overhead door and turned the vehicle down the street, leaving the lights off until he was around the corner.

Two blocks away, he parked the car, removed the garage door opener from the visor, and left the keys in the ignition. He could hope someone would steal it and take it all the way to Mexico, but it really didn't matter as long as he had time to get away.

Stepping out of the car he checked all around. He was still wearing the gloves, and felt certain there would be nothing connecting him to the vehicle. He walked along the streets until he was back at his own vehicle. Opening the door, he climbed behind the wheel, started the engine, and returned to the house, pulling into the garage using the remote. Once inside with the security of the overhead door closed behind him, he breathed a deep sigh. Now he could really start with his plan.

In Scottsdale he had traded the truck he used to escape Illinois and purchased a mini-van. He wanted to buy a SUV in the same model that he'd had in the past, but worried that it would somehow make it easier to track him, so he chose a mini-van. The seats folded flat into the floor which afforded him a lot of space. He had needed that before, and it would certainly come in handy tonight.

Opening the back hatch, Jack pulled the tarp out and laid it out in the back of the van, then went back inside the house through the same door he had exited earlier. Paul was still in the same position on the floor. It would be a while before the drug wore off.

He went to the master bedroom and lifted Mindy's petite body from the bed. He carried her down the hallway and out to the garage, gingerly laying her out on the floor of the van. She was wearing only a nightgown, and it slid up as he laid her down. He carefully pulled it down to cover her thighs. His eyes scanned her thin yet muscular legs. Hope always did have the loveliest legs. He forced his mind to focus on the plan. There would be plenty of time to enjoy each other later.

He turned and returned inside the house. This time he went to Paul. He stared down at the muscular man. He would love to spend some real quality time with Paul, but in order for his plan to work he needed to control his dark desires. Shrugging, he bent down and pulled the man up by his arms, slid his own arms around Paul's chest, and tugged him backwards, heels dragging on the carpet down the hall. Inside the master bedroom, he hoisted the man into the bed. He made sure he had a pillow under his head and covered him with the blankets.

Walking around to the side of the bed where Mindy had laid just moments earlier, he folded the blankets back as if someone had tossed them over as they exited that side. Looking around, he grabbed the purse that sat on the dresser and removed a pair of jeans and a blouse from the drawers along with the women's tennis shoes that sat next to the closet. He looked around and smiled. *Perfect*.

With Paul dealt with, he returned to the living room. The child was sound asleep. Unfortunately, he needed to be sure she remained that way, and though he regretted needing to do so, he knew he must make her sleep. Removing the last syringe from his pocket, he rolled the sleeping beauty to one side and stuck the needle into her neck. She moaned but responded with nothing more than that before she was locked into a full slumber that would last for a while.

Lifting the child, he carried her out to the garage and placed her next to her mother on the van floor. Oh, they were so beautiful he could hardly believe his eyes. His Hope and Faith were truly right there in front of him. They were even more perfect than he'd remembered. Not wanting to do so, but knowing there was simply no other choice; he covered the two sleeping beauties with the edges of the tarp.

After closing the door to the van he went back inside. He walked through the house and made sure nothing was disturbed. He returned to the child's bedroom and gathered clothes and shoes before returning to the living room. He retrieved the toys he'd set down earlier, and then before leaving he made sure the front door was locked and all the lights were off. He carefully returned to the garage, allowing the lights on the stove to illuminate the path, and slid back into the van. Pressing the remote control one more time allowing him access to the street, he backed out of the garage and onto the street and closed the garage door as he pulled away.

He retraced the route back to the car he'd left earlier two blocks away. With his headlights off he pulled next to the car and quickly got out and placed the remote back on the visor before driving away into the dark of night with the sleeping woman and child tucked under the tarp behind his seat.

***

Jack immediately left town, travelling for two hours before he pulled off the highway again. He chose an exit that was in a remote area to reduce the possibility of anyone seeing him. He found a lone gas station that was open and pulled off to the side, making sure that he parked far from any lights. Getting out of the van, he checked his surroundings. The station was in ill repair and wouldn't likely have too many vehicles pulling in. There was only one other vehicle in sight. The driver was pumping gas into the tank and should be on his way soon.

Keeping an eye on the other driver, Jack went to the rear of his van and opened the back about half way then leaned inside. He laid his hand on Mindy's leg to see if she responded to his touch, a sign that the drugs were starting to wear off. He needed to keep both sedated until he could get them back home.

Just as he thought he could travel for another couple of hours, Mindy groaned slightly. Convinced that he needed to give her more of the medication, he went to the side door and retrieved his medical bag. Inside he had four more syringes. Selecting one, he slid into the back seat and closed the door then pushed back the tarp to expose Mindy's head.

"Hope, you are so beautiful. I can't wait to get you home, our home where we can be a family again. It's going to be perfect."

Mindy moaned slightly again. "Honey, I know it's uncomfortable right now, but it will only be like this for a while. Then everything will be wonderful, just like it used to be." Jack comforted her as best he could then slid the injection into her neck, putting her back into a deep sleep.

While he was there he took a quick peek at Faith under the tarp. She too seemed to be sleeping peacefully. She would likely sleep quite a bit longer given her size. Deciding things were under control for now, he carefully covered them up and exited the van.

The patron who had been getting gas was long gone, and now Jack had the station to himself. Pulling up to the pumps, he decided now was as good of time as any to fill up. The next stop would be several hours. Leaving the van parked at the pump while the gas was flowing, he locked the van, listening for the chirps to indicate that the vehicle was completely secured, and went inside the station. A large cup of coffee was certainly in order. Driving for a minimum of another five hours before he made it back home was going to be difficult. He needed to stay clear and had already been up for going on twenty hours now.

The man working behind the counter was in his mid-twenties and seemed bored out of his mind. Jack paid for his coffee with cash, thanked the man, and turned to return to the car. He was nearly certain the employee would never remember him because he barely looked up from his cell phone the entire time. There were security cameras, but Jack could tell they weren't functioning. There was no red light indicating recording, and no motion sensors. The whole setup was a cheap ruse to deter would-be robbers. Jack smiled as he left the store. He could be comfortable that anyone looking for Paul's family would never know he rolled through here.

Removing the pump from the tank, Jack felt pretty reassured that he could make it to Ojai with only one more stop. He would wait a couple of hours before calling Vivian's caretaker to tell him what time he'd be back so he could go on home. Jack certainly didn't need anyone at the house when they arrived. His life was finally going to be exactly the way it was supposed to be again and he certainly wasn't going to let the surfer dude get in the way.

Back in the van and on the highway, Jack realized he needed to be very careful. He couldn't allow his excitement about the future to cause him to speed. Forcing himself to remain focused, he set the cruise control at the speed limit and settled back into the seat, sipped on his coffee and dreamed of the life he was about to enjoy. *Oh, life was going to be good again.*

Chapter Fifteen

The court room was small compared to the impression one would have from watching courtroom action on television. The only people present were Mark, Max, Dana, the judge, and Heath's court appointed guardian ad litem. Heath was brought in briefly. After about forty-five minutes of reviewing documentation and asking questions, the judge ruled in favor of emergency placement into Mark and Max's custody.

When it was done Heath was brought back in and was told that he would be able to go home with the newly-wedded couple. A huge smile covered his small face. Max realized it was the first time the boy had smiled that big since she met him. She watched as Mark hugged Heath and could tell a weight seemed to be lifted off his shoulders. Being able to help Heath was allowing Mark to settle the past.

Dana explained that a social worker would come by their home soon and periodically check in with them over the coming weeks. Bursting with pride, Mark and Max left the courthouse, each holding one of Heath's little hands in theirs. Heath chattered all the way back to the house and asked if they could have pizza. His random and simple conversation made Max smile, and Mark promised him pizza for dinner.

***

When they arrived home, Heath roamed the halls and bounced on the bed in the room that would be his. They had some decorating to do to make the room suited to a child, but Mark and Heath could work on that over the next couple of days. Mark was still arranging the sitter service. They had a lead on a nanny that was the sister of a fellow agent. It felt good to have a referral rather than trying to rely on a total stranger to care for Heath.

Max was frustrated that she was not going to be able to help make those arrangements, but her case was starting to heat up and they were close to narrowing in on the drug trafficking operation. The plan was to raid a drop and bring in people that could lead them to the organization that was heading the entire operation.

In some ways she felt overly conflicted. There were so many things to do, and new priorities were driving her now. She had her main work responsibility, her husband, and a child, and she wanted to have some time to run down the names Bobby had provided as potential leads on Jack Tyler. She was being forced to prioritize her life now in ways that were never necessary when she was single and with her career as her sole focus.

She was also seeing a softer side of Mark that was pleasing. When they met he was this totally serious, tough guy. It was sexy and all masculine, and now what she was getting to know was the layers and depth of the man she had grown to love. Those layers were going to provide the substance in their relationship that would enable her to remain in love and desire to stay with him forever.

After spending a while just settling into the house, Mark ordered pizza, and Max went to the bedroom to get comfortable. As she came back into the living room after changing, she could hear giggling, and she peeked around the corner to catch a glimpse of Mark holding Heath up in the air. The muscles that popped under Mark's shirt challenged the seams, and she realized that watching the way he interacted with Heath was the most attractive she'd ever seen him.

***

The days following Heath's court appointed custody were filled with new beginnings and learning how to care for a child and settling into a life of balance between family and work. Family had all been very supportive, and friends brought toys and clothes over. Soon Heath's room began to look like a child's kingdom.

On the surface everything looked perfect, but Heath often had nightmares. Max took turns with Mark going to him when he needed support. He would settle back down after a few minutes of comfort. He wet his bed at times, so they purchased plastic sheets to protect the mattress. Finally, after getting Heath added to the health insurance they began therapy sessions and were hoping to see some progress soon.

Max's case had turned up millions of dollars in the recovery of pharmaceutical drugs, and after an aggressive gun fight at a truck stop just off of Interstate I-40 they'd made a number of arrests and were now tracking the owner of a large pharmaceutical company located in California. She'd been lucky. So far there was only one overnight trip required, and the nanny recommended by their co-worker was working out very well.

Mark went back to full duty, and Heath started school. He was making friends and would come home filled with stories of other boys and playground antics. Things were settling nicely. Max notified her landlord that she was giving up her lease and, as time permitted, was slowly moving her things over to Mark's house.

Once Heath was tucked into bed, the passion that had first pulled Mark and Max together was stronger than ever. There was a familiar excitement that seemed to constantly sizzle between them. Life was good. They were happy, and things were going pretty well with the ready-made family.

Max took down the murder board in her living room at the apartment and began setting up a similar area in the garage at the house. They spent a day adding in a wall and door. The room was still crude, but it allowed Max to have the space to focus in the way that seemed to work for her. Heath wouldn't be allowed in that room. They agreed to keep it locked at all times.

Now that her family was stable and a routine was established, Max set up a desk and a computer in the room. She got home early and now had an hour before Heath would be home from school. She sat staring at the murder board stapled to the studs in the wall. She was considering the names Bobby had provided to Cortez. *Time for me to re-focus. Jack, where are you?*

Chapter Sixteen

Jack returned to California after giving Jimmy instructions to go home. He spent the next few days getting the basement established, fully furnishing the main room with a bed, TV, small kitchen table, and couch. He added a stainless steel table in the side room, setting up everything exactly the way he needed it to be able to take care of Hope and Faith while ensuring no one interfered with their safety.

He left Arizona with Mindy and her child and returned to California with Hope and Faith—his cherished family back together again. So far keeping them comfortable had been his only real concern. He knew it would take a little time before they settled in, and he really just wanted everything perfect for them. He was certain that he finally figured out the ideal way to have his life back.

Vivian continued to hang on, and it seemed Jimmy had taken good enough care of her that she hadn't felt the need to dial the phone number he'd given her. And now that he had his family back with him, there would be no reason for Jimmy's services again.

Early in the day he drove across town and followed Jimmy from the agency to his house. The fact was that Jimmy hadn't taken all that good of care of Vivian the first time around, and Jack knew he would not be able to allow that to pass. He was biding his time between feeding Vivian and caring for Hope and Faith. Waiting patiently until after midnight, it was time to pay Jimmy a visit.

"Hope," he said to Mindy. "I know we've always agreed to not hurt innocent people and that I'd use my skills for good versus simply feeding my dark impulses. But Jimmy is not innocent. He hurt Vivian when he cared for her, often not staying with her like he was supposed to, or leaving her far past the point of discomfort and in pain."

Mindy sat on the couch where he'd placed her, staring back at him. She could hear him perfectly but was not able to express her thoughts or feelings. No matter how hard she fought, the drugs won out, keeping her in an alert yet paralyzed state.

"You do understand, Hope darling, don't you?" Jack asked, his eyes pleading with her and waiting for a sign that she understood and supported his choice. "I followed him today. I know where he lives, and I believe he needs to pay for his transgressions."

Mindy couldn't respond, but Jack saw something in her eyes. A flicker, maybe even a sparkle and he knew. "Oh, thank you, darling. I knew you'd agree with me. Hope, I never want to disappoint you or defy the agreement we made when we were kids. I love you so much, and I only want what's best for you and our beautiful daughter."

He glanced over at the chair and smiled at the little girl he saw staring back at him. Her right arm dangled off to one side, and her blonde curls trailed over her shoulders. "She is so beautiful. Isn't she, Hope? Our adorable little Faith. Maybe one day we'll have that son we dreamed of. Do you remember talking about that?"

Not waiting for an answer that couldn't come, Jack leaned in and kissed Mindy, offering a deeply passionate kiss. Excitement filled him as he realized the enjoyment he felt in the warmth of the kiss. His Hope was truly alive, perfect in every way. He had finally done it, and he couldn't be more pleased.

Leaning back, he pushed a lock of hair out of Mindy's face and gave her another quick peck on the lips, then checked his watch and clicked his tongue inside his cheek. "I've got a couple of hours before I can leave. Do you think it's time I checked up on Agent Maxine Nichols? We certainly don't want her to ruin our plans. I'll be right back. Don't go anywhere." He chuckled and then turned and left the room.

A few minutes later he returned to the basement with his laptop. He plopped down on the couch next to Mindy. "It's so fun that you can do these things with me now. Agent Maxine Nichols has tried to keep us away from each other, Hope. We just can't let that happen."

Jack opened the lid to the computer and tapped away on the keys. With his wireless connected and Google open, he typed the agent's name into the search field. His first few attempts yielded nothing new, her graduation from the FBI academy being the most recent result. He tried a few different approaches and suddenly leaned forward as his eyes scanned the result on the screen.

"Why would a woman like Maxine Nichols suddenly get married?" His mind raced. "Do you think she's pregnant? Do you think while she was in Illinois trying to find me she laid down with Agent Wells? She married him at a court house, no ceremony, and no family present. Odd, don't you think?"

***

Mindy looked on, a steady blank stare cast over the screen. While she couldn't move, her eyes attempted to scan the page, searching for anything that might indicate someone was looking for her.

She saw nothing other than the small legal announcement of the union between Mark Wells and Maxine Nichols in the state of Virginia. She remembered the agent coming to her home in Arizona asking questions about her brother-in-law Jack Tyler. Mindy had been unable to provide details of his whereabouts. At that time she hadn't had contact with Jack for almost a year. She was stunned to hear they thought he might have been involved with the murders of six people that had been discovered in a grisly burial site in the Malibu canyon.

Despite her concerns about Jack's odd behavior as a boy, Mindy never thought him capable of murder. Now though, she knew full well of his capabilities. She had followed the news stories and knew he was connected to murders in three states. He killed children and was believed to have used the body parts of his victims to create replications of his dead wife and daughter—her sister and niece. The horror of that knowledge terrified her for the fate of herself and her child. Her eyes shifted to the little girl sitting across from her. Their eyes met momentarily, and she tried to comfort her in that moment. She was terrified and could only imagine how scared her young daughter was.

She shuddered internally at the thought of how Jack considered her to be Hope. It was true, the sisters had been often asked if they were twins, but the fact that he had gone so crazy that he believed she was Hope scared her. He had already shown signs of wanting intimacy with her, and she knew it was only a matter of time before he wanted more. And she would be unable to do anything about it.

She wondered what he had done to Paul and their other child. She prayed they were okay, but she feared Jack had killed them both. A lone tear escaped the corner of her eye and rolled down her face. She could feel it but was unable to wipe it away. Fear filled her, worrying that Jack would see it and become angry with her. She mustn't show weakness around him if she hoped to survive this.

She hoped that in time he would not sedate her. If she got the opportunity, she would work to earn his trust. She just needed the opportunity. For her daughter's safety, she would do whatever Jack wanted from her.

***

Jack continued to surf the Internet trying to glean any more information he could about why a sudden, private wedding ceremony for Agent Maxine Nichols had taken place. Several attempts at searching had given him no results so he decided to change the criteria and searched on Mark Wells instead. He was astonished by what he found.

In the legal notices there was a single line indicating a court appointed guardianship of a five year old male child to Mark Wells.

"Hope, she's not pregnant. They got married so they could take custody of a young boy. Very interesting, don't you think? I assume they couldn't do it while single and living together," he said as Mindy continued to watch the computer screen.

He searched in vain to find a picture of the boy. Deciding there weren't any images for him to find, he finally gave up, satisfied for the moment. *So, you got married and have an instant family, Maxine. With these recent events, have you forgotten about me? That would be too good to be true.*

Turning to face Mindy he asked, "Remember we were talking about having another child? We hoped that we would have a little boy, a playmate for Faith. We never got the chance. But now we're being given a second chance. It's funny how life creates chances. Don't you think, Hope? We're so lucky."

Jack stared into Mindy's eyes and mistook the fear that was clearly evident as approval of his comments. He smiled back at her, still ignoring the signs of terror that only her eyes could convey as she remained in a paralyzed state.

***

A few days passed, and all the while Jack could barely remove his focus from that boy. He had become so focused on the idea of having a son, which thrilled him, that he had not yet handled the situation with Jimmy. He was so envious of Agent Maxine Nichols. He imagined how rewarding it would be to have a five year old that looked exactly like Hope. A boy he could teach and play with in the woods. A boy who could enjoy the playhouse the way he had enjoyed it as a child.

In between fantasizing of having a son he began to slowly wean Mindy and Allie off of the drugs, allowing them to move around on their own, like the ability to take food and water. This prevented him from having to feed and water them intravenously as he had been doing up until now. He wanted to get to a point where they could care for themselves.

He spent hours building security features into the basement that would ensure they would not be able to escape as they became more mobile. Confident that over time he would be able to allow them to have full range of not only the basement but also the home, he patiently waited for signs of compliance to their new life as his wife and child. On a sub-conscience level he knew they were resistant, but consciously he convinced himself that they were his loving family and everything was perfect now. There was just one thing missing.

As Mindy became more capable of participating in daily life his attraction and sexual desire grew. He was missing the intimacy he always shared with Hope and even considered conceiving a child now. There was just one problem…He remembered that Mindy had some issues following the birth of her children and knew that she was not capable of carrying a child. Oh well, there were other ways. Soon a plan began to form. There were a few things he would need first so that he could proceed. Excitement grew.

"Hope, Faith, my lovely family, I have an errand to run. I'll be back soon. Maybe I'll pick up some food from Boccalli's. Hope, I remember how much you loved the lasagna. We won't be able to sit out under the trees and enjoy the stars like we used to, but we can enjoy the savory food. Faith has never had the pleasure of trying it, so that will be a special treat. Don't miss me too much. I'll be back soon." He nearly skipped out of the room after planting a kiss on the top of Faith's head and Hope's pursed lips.

At the top of the stairs he applied the deadbolt and the strong arm across the steel door he'd recently installed. The strong arm was essentially a steel bar that locked across the door, affixed deeply into the concrete wall making it impossible to push the door open from inside. The entire basement was assembled from concrete block set deeply in the ground. The door was the only exit point. With the deadbolt and strong arm in place, Jack was quite confident there was no way out.

After checking in on Vivian and finding her alert and watching *Judge Judy*, he left the house and locked up behind him. Winding his way through town, he decided it was a good opportunity to check in on Jimmy. Swinging the vehicle out onto Main Street, from memory he returned to Jimmy's house. Making the final turn, he slowed as he passed by the small single-story corner home, taking notice that Jimmy's car was sitting in the driveway. Jack smiled, a familiar feeling rippled through his body, the darkness wrapping in on him like a thick cloak.

Continuing down the road, he retraced the route back to Main Street, through town to Matilija Street, and pulled into the Radio Shack parking lot. He assessed his surroundings and felt good that there were only a couple of other cars in the lot. He hoped those were employees' cars. He exited his vehicle, closed the door, and approached the store. Entering caused a chime to announce his presence.

Jack was greeted almost immediately by a young, geeky looking man who appeared to be barely in his twenties. His large, thick framed glasses seemed to be a shield for the heavy acne that covered his entire face.

"Good afternoon, sir. What may I help you with today?"

Jack smiled. His allure and natural charm immediately engaged the young lad and put him at ease.

"I am looking for some security cameras, basically a monitoring system. Do you have anything like that?"

"We sure do. Do you want something that is just internal to your home or business, or a system that can be monitored by the local police and fire, as well?"

"I think just internal to my home. I want to be able to ensure my kids are safe." Jack smiled again. "Getting to those teenage years and having friends over more, you know how it is?"

The pimply faced man laughed and nodded. Jack assumed he didn't really know what it was like. He likely wasn't invited to participate in many of those events.

"We have a unit over here that provides monitoring for four rooms, and it can be viewed on your cell phone," the young man replied, leading Jack to the other side of the room and picking up a large box from the bottom shelf.

Jack listened as the pimply faced man awkwardly explained how the device worked. His interest was in the monitoring ability and the feed he would get to his laptop and cell phone. He needed the ability to see what was happening in the basement from anywhere.

"Is there any audio capability that comes with this or as an add-on?"

"You mean you would want to be able to speak through an intercom of something like that?"

"Correct." Jack felt compelled to continue with an example based on the blank stare he received through the thick glasses. "Imagine if my teenage son has a girl come over and things get a little too hot. I want to be able to tell him to settle down and send her home." Jack had to refrain from laughing knowing the picture was making the guy horny at the very thought of it.

A bit flustered, the sales clerk pushed his black framed glasses up on his nose and then quickly moved to another shelf, turning his back to Jack seemingly in an effort to regain his composure. "We do have this. It's not part of the video unit, but it can work in conjunction with it." He carried the box over to the glass checkout counter and set it down then flipped open the box to display the contents. He spent the next few minutes describing the contents and how they would work.

Jack learned that basically, speakers could be mounted to the wall and an app could be downloaded for iPhone or Windows compatible devices, allowing the user to talk through a speaker and into the room where the speaker is mounted. It could also be used as a room to room intercom.

"Can the person inside the home turn off the device? I definitely wouldn't want my son turning it off, basically overriding the point of it in the first place."

"No, sir, that's the beauty of it. You can set it up to be controlled from a certain device. So for example your laptop would be the administration device, and the setup changes require a password to override the configuration. It gives you complete control of what and how you want to monitor or interact with the intercom. The video system works the same way." Pushing his glasses up over his pimply nose again, the sales clerk seemed pleased with himself.

"Great, I think this will work perfectly for controlling my kids. I'd also like to install a front door intercom with a monitor. You know where you can see who is outside the home?" Jack said, pulling his wallet out of his back pocket prepared to make a purchase.

After a few more minutes of the clerk showing him a few choices, Jack selected the intercom system too. It was a last minute thought, but after the way things went down with Dale in Illinois he didn't want any surprises like that again. He needed to protect his family in every possible way.

The sales clerk seemed ecstatic with the purchase as he bagged the boxes. Just as they were finishing the transaction and Jack was signing his alias onto the credit card slip, the door chime rang announcing the arrival of another customer.

A tall blonde woman entered the store. Jack grabbed his packages by the handles on the bags and turned to exit. As he passed, the woman stopped him. "Hello. Do I know you?"

Jack stopped, startled by the exchange. "Excuse me?"

"I'm sorry, you just seem so familiar. I thought I might know you from somewhere."

"I don't believe so," Jack replied rushing to the exit.

Getting to his vehicle as quickly as possible, he placed the packages on the back seat and climbed into the driver's seat as fast as he could. Backing out, he headed down the street and slammed the steering wheel with his hand, shouting, "Damn it, damn it, damn it!!!"

Anger rose in him. That woman recognized him. He knew who she was. Her name was Rebecca Tillman, or Reb as she liked to be called. She and Hope had remained friends until their sophomore year when Reb had expressed her concerns to Hope about him. Oh, she'd gone on and on about him being odd, strange, or creepy even. Hope hadn't listened, of course, and had severed the friendship just before they had gone off to college together.

As he drove he wondered what would happen if she remembered where it was she knew him from. He could not allow that to happen. He would have to take care of it. Oh, he would have fun with that, for sure. Deciding she was more of a risk than Jimmy, he looped back towards the Radio Shack, and rather than pulling into the parking lot he stopped about half way down the street and pulled in behind a Mercedes Benz that was parked along the curb.

For a moment his mind flitted back in the past to Benz—the used car salesman he spent quite a bit of time with in Oklahoma. Benz had been the perfect house guest. Jack had certainly enjoyed his time with that man. Maybe Reb could offer the same type of pleasure. The corners of his mouth curled slightly at the thought of it.

A few minutes passed, and then he saw her. She exited the store carrying a small bag. He watched as she climbed into a Lexus SUV and backed out. As she started down the street, he waited until a car merged in behind her and then he pulled out.

Keeping her car in his sights, he stayed back far enough to not be detected. He watched as she turned down a side street, and he slowed before identifying the street was not a cul-de-sac. He followed her, watching the SUV closely as it weaved through the trees that created shadows on the street from the late afternoon sun.

He continued to hold back far enough that he almost lost sight of her, and then watched as she pulled into the driveway of a ranch style home that sat at a great distance off of the street. The home was surrounded by trees and an ample yard. *Little Ms. Reb, you've done okay for yourself. What'd you do? Sleep with the rich quarterback?*

As he passed he saw the mailbox at the front of the driveway. He noticed the numbers and the name Tillman in block letters across the side. *Interesting, you're not married. Still have your maiden name. Or, have it again. What happened? Did someone hurt you real bad?*

He continued down the street and followed the winding path until it met with another and then hooked his way back out of the neighborhood. Once he was a good distance away, he stopped on the side of the street and pulled out his cell phone. He Googled "Rebecca Tillman, Ojai, CA" and waited for his 4G network to deliver the results. A few moments later he had a few options to choose from. He quickly selected the option to run a background check and logged into his previously established account to keep track of Agent Maxine Nichols. When he set it up he had no idea how handy it would be.

Within a few minutes he had the details about Rebecca Tillman. The records indicated that she was divorced and the mother of a child that had died at birth. Maybe that was the reason for the divorce. She changed her name back to Tillman a year after the divorce. Jack clicked "yes" on an advanced search and learned that she was the only name on the title of the house she led him to. Her mother died three years ago, and her father resided in Iowa. All indications were she lived alone in that home. *Oh, it is going to be a good night.*

Jack drove out to Boccali's and picked up the promised food before returning back home. He spent some time with Vivian before going downstairs to enjoy dinner with his family. He prepared the table and then assisted Mindy and the young girl to sit down for the meal. Although each day Jack was backing off on the medication, neither was able to completely walk on her own. Within a couple of days they would be able to move more freely. He assisted them with the food, which surprisingly they each readily accepted. Hunger must have finally overcome their resistance to him.

"Hope, it really is good to see you with an appetite back. I've terribly missed our dinners together." Turning his attention to Faith, he smiled and brushed his knuckles gently against her face. She flinched slightly, but he didn't notice. "What do you think of the lasagna? It's almost like your favorite, macaroni and cheese. Don't you think?"

The scared child looked at her mother. Mindy grunted out, "Good," before the girl could answer. The child gave a quick nod, following her mother's lead. Mindy watched in terror then relaxed slightly as her daughter answered the question correctly.

587

Jack chattered away throughout the dinner to the two half-immobile people sitting at the table. When the food was nearly gone and the two slowed down their acceptance of the food that he spooned their way, he began to clear the dishes.

"Well, I need to begin the installation of the equipment I purchased. I selected several items that will absolutely ensure you are both kept safe. You won't ever need to worry about your safety again. I bought equipment that will allow me to see where you are and what you're doing at any time of the day or night, even if I'm not home." He looked back and forth between the woman and child. "Isn't it great, Hope? I never have to worry about you leaving me ever again. Never can someone take you from me. We'll be together forever."

Leaving Mindy to contemplate the finality of his last statement, Jack left the room. He spent the next few hours working diligently to setup the video monitors and intercom systems. When he finally had everything installed, he downloaded the recommended apps to his cell phone and laptop. With everything in place he began monitoring his captive wife and daughter in the basement. Since they were both still sedated, he lost interest quickly but was pleased with the manner in which he could check their status on his cell phone. Now he had a visit to pay to Reb, but before leaving he needed to ensure his family knew they were safe.

He unbolted the door and descended the stairs. He didn't notice the subtle shudder that ran through Mindy as she saw him enter the room. "Hope, I just wanted you to know I got everything set up. Look how cool this is," he said showing her the view on the cell phone, which now displayed him standing in the room next to her showing her his phone. "I'll truly be able to be with you no matter where I am. You'll always be safe now, Hope. Nothing can ever happen to you again. I just wanted you to know I'm watching before I go up to check on Vivian."

Mindy's head gave a slight snap at the name. "Oh, you didn't know she was here with us, did you? Yes, she's not all that well, but I'm caring for her. She's bedridden, pretty frail, actually. I'm doing the best I can with her. She resists eating some days, and so I'm focused on keeping her comfortable."

He smiled down at Mindy and saw a frown on her face. "Oh, don't worry, darling. I'm fine caring for all of you. I'm just sorry I have to divide my time. And I forgot to tell you, I saw your old friend Reb today. Remember her, that dreadful bitchy girl that tried to separate us? Anyway, she may come to visit soon. I think I'll invite her over." Jack laughed at the irony of his comment. "Okay, sweetheart, it's getting late. You need your rest, as does our little girl." With that he lifted her onto his feet by pulling her up by her arms and forcing them to drape around his neck. With her body pressed against his, he gazed down at her and passionately kissed her. Leaning back, he smiled and whispered in her ear, "Not now, darling, Faith is watching. Maybe once she falls asleep. I love you, Hope." He assisted her in walking across the room to the bed, laid her down, and kissed her again.

"Okay, Faith, time for bed," he said, turning to the child, lifting Allie up and carrying her to the couch to lay her down. After carefully covering her up, he kissed her small cheek and said his good-nights to each before leaving the basement.

He didn't really have plans with Vivian. She'd fallen asleep for the night long ago, but he didn't want his wife to worry about him being out in the middle of the night. She needed to feel safe in knowing that he was in the house with her at all times. He double checked the door to the basement, looked at the monitors, and checked the app on his cell phone before turning to leave.

Outside in the night his body tingled. He felt alive. Things were going so well. He just had a few loose ends to clear up before he could proceed with the rest of his plans.

589

Chapter Seventeen

Max got home before Heath returned from his afternoon Kindergarten class and before Mark returned from the office. She went in during the wee hours of the morning to meet with the task force as they monitored the drug company CEO. He had unusual comings and goings during the middle of the night, and they were trying to get a fix on what he was up to. There was some concern that he was rebuilding his trafficking network faster than they could gather enough evidence to prove he was the mind behind the entire operation.

Lately though, Max was spending a lot of time in the private room in the garage. She went in and locked the door behind her, making sure Heath wouldn't enter on accident. She was trying to make some sense of the names that Cortez had sent over. So far she came up empty. She worked through the list one by one looking for anything unusual, but given the fact that the names were somewhat common and that she had no idea where to look for Jack, it was a slow process.

The first thing she did was cross-reference the names against the locations that she had previously identified as the most likely cities that he would live in. This was still based off of the list she had put together when she first started tracking Jack after he killed six people in California.

The discovery of his magazines under his playhouse from when he was a boy in Ojai had been instrumental in creating the list. Later, he had in fact turned up in Tulsa, Oklahoma, the number three city on her list, and then again outside Bloomington, Illinois. She knew those cities held special meaning to him, and she hoped that she would be able to tie him to one of them again. If one of the names matched one of those towns and anything out of the ordinary jumped out, she just might have a lead.

She tried to narrow down the searches by sorting the names associated to the list in fewest to highest order, hoping she would get lucky and not have to work through the high numbers at the bottom. It was a long shot, but she had to try. Letting Jack Tyler remain at large just simply was not an option. Not realizing it, she said out loud, "I'm coming for you, Jack, and I will find you."

After going through the data, Max heard the door open to the garage. Glancing at her watch, she realized the nanny must have just brought Heath home. She decided it was time to wrap up for the day and saved all her files then turned off her computer.

When she opened the door she was startled to see Heath standing there. "Hi, Max. Whatcha doin'?" the boy innocently asked her, curiously trying to peer inside the room.

"Oh, hey there, big guy. I was just workin'. Whatcha' doin'?"

"Lookin' for you. Wanna play with me?"

Max chuckled, putting her arm around the small boy's shoulders and leading him away from the room, locking the door behind her. "Sure. How about we get a snack first?"

Heath smiled up at her, his crooked little grin glowing at her. He slipped his little hand into hers as they entered the house.

Once inside Max got them each a banana, Heath's favorite snack, and cut it up in little pieces. They sat face to face at the dining room table as they popped the mushy, white bits into their mouths while Heath chattered about his day. Max smiled at his resilience. Life had dealt him a very bad hand, and yet anyone looking at him right now would have thought he never suffered a sad moment. As she sat watching him lick his sticky little fingers, she felt grateful for having the ability to be there for him now when he needed someone the most.

A few minutes later the front door swung open and Mark came in carrying Chinese food. Heath jumped down from the chair and ran to him, nearly barreling him over. "Yea, chicken sticks," he yelled as he clung to Mark's waist.

Mark laughed at the greeting as he held the bags of food over the boy's head and out of the way of a possible spill. Once Heath settled down Mark leaned over to kiss Max, who had joined Heath at his side, then continued on to the kitchen counter to set down the bags.

"You don't like chicken sticks, do you, Heath?" Mark teased the little boy.

"Yes, I do," Heath answered with emphasis on his words in a sing-song way.

Max chimed in with, "I bet you don't want any since you just had that banana."

Heath gave her a look then said, "I could eat a whole chicken."

Max laughed at the assuredness the little guy presented. "I bet you could!"

A few minutes later the group offered the nanny the evening off and settled down to eat an early dinner. Heath practiced with his children's version of chopsticks with the shape of elephants at the end, and instead of being two separate sticks they were connected at one end, making it much easier for small hands to hang on to. Even still, as he tried to navigate noodles into his mouth, a good portion fell back onto his Sponge Bob plate and down the front of his shirt. Mark and Max exchanged a glance and each smiled at the certain mess that would be the result of the dinner selection. The small family continued to eat, chatter, and share stories throughout the dinner until the food was nearly depleted and Heath was sufficiently covered in gooey sauces.

Finishing off with the fortune cookies, Mark let Heath pick his own before handing one to Max and taking his. Heath attempted to read the words by calling out a few letters that he knew. For all of his struggles he was doing pretty well. He was able to recognize most of the alphabet and was progressing well ahead of where he needed to be to enter first grade.

Finally, after letting Heath attempt to read his own cookie Mark read it to him. "A new perspective will come soon."

"What does it mean?" Heath asked with obvious curiosity and excitement as if the fortune could truly predict the future.

"Well, it means that soon you will think about things differently," Mark replied.

"Oh." The boy was clearly thinking hard about the message. His young mind obviously churning. "Like being a big boy in first grade?"

Both Mark and Max laughed out loud. Mark replied, "Exactly like that."

Heath seemed satisfied and listened anxiously as Max read hers, followed by Mark reading his. They each explained what theirs meant, and once he was satisfied with the responses, they began to clear the containers and plates away from the table. Max started to do the dishes when Mark stepped in and offered to assist while she helped Heath with his bath. They often took turns with the household chores and Heath's care. Tonight it was Max's turn to handle bath duty.

With a sufficient bubble bath drawn at the perfect temperature, Heath settled deeply into the foamy water and played with a variety of toys that lined the tub wall. As he played Max sponged him clean, washing his hair with no tears shampoo. A half an hour later Heath was dried and dressed for bed, complete with a nighttime pull-up required for his bed wetting problems. They'd discovered early on that Heath wet the bed nearly every night. She'd be lying to herself if she said the bed wetting wasn't concerning. She could only hope that as the emotional scars healed this would improve.

Her mind drifted to Jack Tyler. He had been a bed wetter, she was certain. She thought about his abusive mother and his troubled life, how Hope at such a young age had reached into the dark torment and had given him a life preserver to cling to, and how that life preserver was snatched away so quickly. She smiled as she thought of Mark being the life preserver for Heath. Together they would give this boy something to cling to and keep the evil from coming after him again.

"Max, are you going to tuck me in and read me a story?"

She smiled at his innocent request that snapped her out of her thoughts of Jack and the horrible childhood he had endured. "You bet I am. Why don't you go pick out a story? I'll be there in just a minute."

Heath ran off down the hall to his room, and Max hurried to clean up the towel and clump of clothes that lay on the floor. When everything was back in place she followed the path the child had taken and found him kneeling in front of his small bookcase. He was holding the story of *Little Red Riding Hood,* and though she didn't really know why, the book sent chills up her spine.

Shaking it off, she chastised herself for having such strange thoughts over a children's story that she herself had adored when she was a child. Heath crawled under the covers and pulled the blankets up to his chin and listened, only occasionally interrupting her as she read the story.

When the wolf had been successfully conquered Max kissed Heath on the head. He wrapped his arms around her neck and whispered in his sleepy state, "I love you, Mommy."

Max's heart raced. This was a first, and she almost didn't know how to feel. They'd only had the boy a few weeks, but clearly he was settling in.

"I love you too, Heath," she replied hugging him tightly.

"Will Daddy come in too?"

"Yes, I'll send him to tuck you in too."

"I know what the tortune cookie means," he said, pronouncing fortune cookie wrong as he had always done. "It means I feel different for you. Good different." His eyes were starting to close and Max patted the covers around his sides before standing up to go and get Mark.

In the living room she found Mark tapping madly at his laptop. "Problem?" she asked.

"No, just finishing up something."

594

"Heath wants you to tuck him in, though I think he's already in dreamland."

"Right. On my way," Mark said, standing up and turning to the hallway.

"And, he called me mommy and you daddy."

Mark stopped dead in his tracks. "He did?"

Max nodded in confirmation. "He did."

A huge smile crossed over Mark's strong and almost always serious face as he turned back to the hall and towards the boy's room to say his good night.

Chapter Eighteen

Jack stood under Reb's bedroom window. He peered in long enough to determine that she had a small dog. There didn't appear to be any other movement in the home. Reb lived alone. Well, other than the dog.

He felt his pocket, confirming he had what he needed, and then slipped around the end of the house, his gloved hands checking windows. So far he hadn't found any open, but he wasn't discouraged and wouldn't let a few locks stop him.

By the time he decided it was safe to move forward it was well past midnight. He checked the monitors back at the house on his cell phone. Hope and Faith were sound asleep. He smiled at the peaceful scene.

Satisfied his family was fine, he continued along the side of the house, making his way back to the bedroom. He peered into the window and waited for his eyes to adjust from the cell phone glow to the darkness. After a few moments the pupils in his eyes adjusted, and he could see Reb snuggled into her bed. He watched carefully. The little dog was tucked in the fold of her knees.

Deciding it was time, he moved around the house to the furthest window from the master bedroom. He looked around on the ground and found a rock, then reached in his pocket and pulled out the rag he had shoved in there before leaving his vehicle. He wrapped the rag around the rock, and with one more look around, he tapped the rag-covered rock against the corner of the window. The glass gave way with a quiet shatter.

Jack stood there frozen as he listened for any movement inside. He heard a few small barks that seemed to start towards him then turned and went towards the back yard instead. Jack sighed then began removing the remaining glass fragments. Shoving the rag back in his pocket, he dropped the rock on the ground. After making sure there was nothing to get cut on, he pulled surgical booties and a hair cover from his pocket and put them on before hoisting his muscular body up through the window and dropping in on the carpeted floor. Glass crunched under his feet. He hovered and listened before moving. His eyes quickly adjusted to the light inside the home. It was dark, but a light shone in the hallway and a clock cast an eerie blue haze on the floor from the stove.

Jack could hear the dog barking outside and saw that there was a doggie door next to the back patio door. The flap was still swinging slightly. He treaded softly over to it and quickly slid the panel closed to keep the pet outside. He felt relieved that he wouldn't need to deal with the woman's pet. He wasn't interested in animals anymore. No, he had moved far beyond that dark pleasure years ago.

Reaching into his pocket, he pulled out a syringe he'd tucked away before getting out of the van and began slowly creeping down the hallway. Just outside the door he stood still with his back up against the wall and waited.

The dog continued to bark occasionally, probably wanting back inside now that the noise it had gone in search of had not been discovered. The woman remained still in the bed. Jack leaned in far enough to see which direction she was facing and found her back to him. He contemplated his approach briefly and then silently pushed off of the wall and entered the room.

Next to the bed he stood staring down at the woman—Reb. He hated her then, and he hated her now. *This is going to be fun*, he thought. He pulled the rag from his pocket, along with the syringe, and depressed the plunger into the rag.

"Hey, Reb," Jack said just loud enough to wake the sleeping woman. He watched as in her confused state she shook her head trying to make sense of what she was seeing. The surgical hair cover likely added further confusion. He could only imagine that her initial thought was that she was in the hospital. That was if she could make him out at all.

Well, plenty of time for her to catch up later. Right now, it was time to get Reb home where he could fully teach her all the lessons she deserved all along. He leaned forward to press the rag against her face and was startled when she shot out of the bed and lunged at him. Before he knew what happened, his vision was blurred from an intense pressure against his eyes.

Reb dug her thumbs deep into his eyes sockets, forcing him to drop the empty syringe as he grabbed at her wrists and slammed her back down onto the bed. Clinging to the rag in his hand, he slid his knee up under himself and used it to push hard down on her chest while wrestling her wrists into the hand that was free of the rag. She arched her back and tried to push against his muscular frame.

Finally, he was able to lock her arms under his while working her thin wrists tightly together. He could feel her pulse pounding against his thumb as he wadded the rag into a ball and pressed it against her mouth as he leaned even deeper into her abdomen, forcing the air from her lungs. The lack of oxygen caused her to gasp for a breath, taking in a deep dose of Chloroform. A few moments later her legs and arms went slack, and the wrestling match ended. She'd fought hard, but she was no match for his strength.

Being sure that she was completely unconscious, Jack slid off of her and stood staring down at her body, his face red from the struggle; his hand shook with anger. "That wasn't very smart, Reb my dear. You just sealed your fate. I might have been nice or at least gentle with you, but now you'll pay. We're about to have a whole lot of fun together."

Jack rolled her out of the bed, and with his adrenaline still pumping, he slung her over his shoulder. Her arms and hair dangled behind his back as he walked through the dark hallway to carry the woman to the garage. He lowered her to the floor by dropping the bundle with a thump. "Oh, that probably hurt. I'd say I'm sorry, but I'm not."

Jack left Reb laying there and went back into the house. Using the door to the garage, he entered through a small room connected to the kitchen. He cautiously slid through each room while searching for her purse. He found his bounty sitting in an office next to the master bedroom. Digging through the bag, his fingers curled around a set of car keys. Snatching them out, he turned and went back out to the garage.

Sliding in behind the wheel of the Lexus, he turned the key in the ignition and flipped the visor down to look for a garage door opener. Finding a programmable feature in the ceiling panel next to the rearview mirror, he pushed the button and smiled as the door began to open. Backing out, he pulled the car on the opposite side of the driveway, then exited and walked quickly to his own vehicle just at the edge of the property.

Jack looked around. The neighborhood was still quiet with the exception of Reb's small dog. He needed to let that dog back in the house so he would quiet down. Deciding he'd deal with that once he had Reb secure, he pulled forward and turned into the driveway, pulling his vehicle into the garage. The lights were on inside, so he quickly hopped out and walked around the front grill of the vehicle, and hit the remote mounted on the wall next to the garage door.

Protected by the privacy of the garage, Jack went back inside and opened the doggie door. He was faced by a small mixed breed dog. The animal immediately approached him, quickly demonstrating his lack of watch dog skills. Jack patted the small, wiry haired dog on the head then went back to the garage with the dog's nails clicking on the floor behind him.

Back in the garage Jack opened the back hatch of his vehicle and then walked back to the front of the garage and pulled Reb's body over to the back of the vehicle. He slid the end up into the back and then pulled the tarp out to carefully cover his new cargo.

The small dog was still hovering around. It sniffed at the blanket on the floor and whimpered slightly. "It's okay, little guy. She's just sleeping for now. Don't worry. Nothing bad is going to happen to you." Jack watched as he spoke to the little dog. His tail wagged and tongue draped to one side.

Jack went back inside the house for one more look around. Then suddenly he remembered something. He walked quickly back to the master bedroom, and once near the bed he knelt down, feeling around under it until he felt the syringe. Careful to not stick himself, he scooped it up then stood looking around in the dim light. Feeling confident that he didn't leave anything in the bedroom, he turned to leave. As he passed the office next to the master bedroom, he grabbed Reb's purse, then remembered the broken glass.

He carried the purse to the kitchen counter and set it down, then took a few minutes to look through various closets until he found the vacuum. He lifted the device labeled Eureka, which instantly triggered a flash of memories of the small town he'd found in Illinois.

Focusing, he turned and went back to the area where the glass fell in and was crushed into the carpet. He unwrapped the cord from the vacuum's handle and squinted through the dim light until he found a plug in the wall behind him. He plugged in the machine and carefully sucked up the debris, listening as the chards made pinging noises as they whirled up inside the canister. Once the noise subsided he looked at the locking hasp on the front of the vacuum and removed the canister. Carrying it into the kitchen, he looked through drawers until he found a grocery sack. He dumped the debris into the small plastic bag, being careful to not allow anything to fall onto the floor. Then he walked the canister back over to the vacuum to reinstall it.

Unplugging the item from the wall, he wrapped the cord back around the handle and carried the vacuum back to the closet where he originally found it. He walked back to the kitchen and lifted the purse from the counter, pausing briefly as his mind worked through each room. With the bag containing the glass still in his hand and satisfied that he left nothing else, he returned to the garage and closed the door behind him.

Hitting the remote on the wall, he lifted the little dog and carried him to the driver's side of the vehicle. He opened the door and set the small animal on the seat next to him. Starting the engine, he backed the car out far enough that he could pull Reb's car back in.

Jack quickly made the swap of the cars inside the garage, and then backed his vehicle out of the driveway and wound his way out of the neighborhood. When he was a few blocks away he sighed. "We're safe now, little guy," he spoke to the dog as he drove.

Within a few minutes Jack arrived back at his home and quickly tucked the vehicle away inside the garage. He went to the back of the vehicle and immediately pulled the woman out of the van, hoisting her onto his shoulder so he could carry her down to the basement.

The little dog followed at his heels as they entered the house through the garage. With the keys in his hand, he removed the bar from the basement door and unlocked the deadbolt. A step at a time he carefully descended the stairs, glancing into the room where Hope and Faith were sound asleep. The medication made them rest a lot. Neither one stirred at the sound of his footsteps. He continued to the room that he had prepared for his special surgical needs.

After depositing Reb onto the stainless steel table, her body making a thumping noise as he dropped her, he returned upstairs to secure the door just in case one of his family woke up. The little dog stood at the top of the steps waiting for him.

"Come on, you can do it. These steps aren't that big," he encouraged the pup as it danced back and forth working up the courage to take the first step.

Jack watched as the dog finally pushed against his fear and began easing his way down the steps.

At the bottom Jack patted the little dog on the head and praised him, "Good job. I told you it wasn't too hard."

Returning to the surgical room, Jack closed the door behind him, and he could feel the adrenaline begin to pump again. It had been a while since he'd been able to allow the darkness to rip through his veins, and he was very much looking forward to the euphoric release that came with his exploration. Reb was going to be especially satisfying. That little bitch had tried to ruin his life, and back then he'd ignored it. Now his patience was paying off.

601

Jack spent the next few minutes removing his clothes and pulling on scrubs. Properly dressed for the occasion, he worked Reb's clothes off of her, and once fully nude, he retrieved zip ties from the shelf on the wall and tightly secured her hands and feet to the table legs. With her fully fastened in place all he had to do now was wait.

As expected, a few minutes later Reb began to stir. Jack smiled as he watched her eyes flutter and try to open. He didn't apply a gag to her mouth, not yet. He wanted some time to talk with her first.

Reb rolled her head to the side as she tried to shake off the effects of the Chloroform. Finally, her eyes opened and scanned the room, stopping on his face. They grew wide.

"Well, hello, Reb. Remember me?" he asked.

Reb tried to talk, but nothing came out at first. Her tongue flicked across her lips. "Store," she managed to get out, her voice raspy and dry.

Jack laughed out loud as he realized she was talking about the Radio Shack. "Well yes, I guess you did see me there, but no, Reb, that is not exactly what I was talking about. We go way back, but you don't recognize me, do you?" He was nearly gloating in the success of the surgical modifications that had been made to his facial features.

Reb's eyes scanned his face. She was clearly confused by his comments. Jack leaned in closer. "Familiar," she choked out, fighting her hands and feet against the pressure of the zip ties which held her tightly to the table. Within moments she'd worked herself into frenzy and began to scream.

The little dog stood at Jack's feet and whimpered. Jack bent down and lifted up the little dog. Reb immediately stopped struggling when she saw her beloved pet. Her head began shaking furiously, and tears poured down her cheeks.

"Oh," Jack said, "I'm not going to hurt him. I like him. I think he likes me too." Jack looked at the little dog, and the dog took a quick lap with his tongue, landing a puppy kiss on Jack's nose. "See, he does like me."

Reb continued to fight against the restraints. "What do you want from me?" she forced out while continuing to study Jack. Her eyes scanned down and landed on his hands, and a hint of recognition sparked. He could tell she had seen something familiar about his hands. He had meticulously manicured nails with perfect half-moon crescents.

"I really don't want anything. It's just payback time," Jack said as he watched her eyes looking for anything to help figure out who he was.

"Payback?" Reb asked clearly puzzled.

"Think about it. I'll give you a hint. You tried to destroy my relationship."

He watched as Reb stopped fighting, and the wheels began to turn in her brain. Slowly a mild yet confused recognition came over her face as she seemed to remember. Her eyes dropped to his hands again. "Starting to figure it out?"

"Hope?"

"That's right. You tried to ruin the beautiful thing Hope and I had. But it didn't work, now did it? Today when I saw you, I knew you would try to ruin us again. I can't let that happen."

Reb stared at him, tears rolled from the corners of her eyes. Her eyes searched his face. "Hope... dead."

"Oh, she was, but I took care of that. She and our daughter Faith are asleep in the other room, sorry, but there won't be any reunion for the two of you."

Reb began fighting again as the realization set in that the man hovering over her was Jack Tyler, nationally known as a wildly insane killer. A shudder coursed over her. Jack could only imagine that she had read stories in the paper about him. He'd been pursued by the authorities in several states and had made national news.

"Well, about that reunion. I'm glad you know who I am. This is going to be so much fun for us." Setting the little dog back down, Jack pulled on a pair of surgical gloves, and then picked up a scalpel from the tray that hung suspended on an arm over the surgical table. Light glinted against the polished tool. Reb began to scream again, but Jack was too busy making his signature incision to notice.

Blood flowed out of Reb's body and puddled on the table at her sides. Jack throttled his desires. He desperately wanted to dive his hands deep into her body, but he knew if he did then the fun he planned on having with Reb would end abruptly. He couldn't have that since he planned on having a long relationship with her.

He looked down at the woman's nude body, and without allowing his eyes to explore the private areas, he assessed her condition and realized he needed to stabilize her. He went to work quickly suturing up the incision he made down the center of her abdomen.

A few moments later, he had stopped the bleeding. Although she had lost a fair amount of blood, and there was no doubt organ damage from his invasive probing, she would not die. He wouldn't allow her to die. Though she'd gone slack at some point and had fallen unconscious he wasn't aware of when that took place. He'd been too focused on his own enjoyment that he'd missed that moment.

Jack began cleaning up. He looked down and watched as the little dog lapped at a small pool of blood on the floor. His paws were now a bright crimson. Jack smiled. "Hey little guy, what are you doing?"

He lifted the small dog, rinsed him, and then toweled him off. Afterwards he rinsed the blood off the floor and down the drain in the center of the room. "Now stay out of stuff, okay?" Jack said setting the little dog back down.

Moving over to the other end of the room, he opened a small refrigerator that sat in the corner and pulled out an IV bag. He returned to the table and carefully inserted the IV into Reb's right arm, then hung the bag on a portable stand. He would hydrate her enough to keep her alive. After all, he wasn't finished with her yet. He double checked her breathing and was satisfied that even though her breathing was labored, she was stable. With that he pulled off his scrubs and deposited them in a laundry basket next to the door, then hosed himself down, scrubbing at his skin and washing himself thoroughly with bleach.

Finally, satisfied that everything was perfectly cleaned, he picked up the little dog and exited the room. A quick peek in on Hope and Faith showed they were still sound asleep. He wasn't sure what time it was, but he was tired and hungry. Ascending the steps, he unlocked the door and stepped onto the landing. Setting down the little dog, he closed the door and applied the bar across it, sealing in his family and guest.

After going to the kitchen, he immediately cracked several eggs into a skillet. The clock on the wall indicated it was three o'clock in the morning. He usually ate much healthier than this, never eating at this time, but his late night adventure left him famished. He scooped a couple of spoons of the fluffy yellow scramble into a small bowl and set it down for the little dog then quickly devoured the rest himself. The dog licked his chops and stared up at his new master, wagging his tail in approval of the snack.

Jack rinsed the dish he used for the eggs and filled it with some water, setting it on the floor again, allowing the small dog to lap up the liquid until he was satisfied. Placing the dish in the sink, he led the little dog over to the back door and let him outside. The dog watched Jack warily at first, then stepped out into the night. A few moments later he returned inside.

Jack patted him on the head. "Good boy. I guess I need to give you a name. I don't even know what kind of dog you are, but you sure are a scruffy little guy. Scruffy, that's it. Come on, Scruffy. Let's go check on Vivian and then it's off to bed for us."

Chapter Nineteen

Jack woke with a start. He looked over at the alarm clock on the bedside table. It was nearly ten o'clock. He started to sit up but felt a weight at the back of his legs. Looking down, he saw the small dog curled next to him. The dog's brown eyes looked into his, appearing eager to see what would be next.

"Well, good morning, Scruffy. We have to get moving. Vivian, Hope, and Faith need us." Jack lifted the little dog off of the bed and quickly went about getting breakfast ready for Vivian while the dog explored the house. He went up the stairs with the dog following right at his heels.

After tapping lightly on Vivian's door, Jack entered. She lay propped up on the pillows with her eyes closed. Each time he entered the room his heart jumped as he thought she'd passed, but then she'd stir slightly and he would smile as relief washed over him.

"Good morning," he said softly.

Vivian opened her eyes and smiled slightly. She looked around the room, her eyes settling on the small dog. "You have a friend?"

"This is Scruffy. He lost his owner recently and needed a new home."

Jack checked Vivian's catheter and vitals while asking, "How are you feeling?"

"Like a teenage girl," Vivian teased.

Jack gave her a disapproving look. "Seriously, how are you feeling? What's your pain level?"

"The same, I guess."

Jack administered meds to her and offered the tea he'd brought up. He spent the next thirty minutes trying to get a protein shake down her before she dozed off again. He tucked the blankets around her before quietly leaving her to rest.

The next stop of the morning was to check on his wife and daughter and Reb. Once in the basement, he was pleased to see both Hope and Faith were awake. For the first time he allowed the medication to wear off completely, so they were sitting cuddled together on the couch. When he entered the room they shrunk deeper into the cushions.

"Good morning. Sorry, I didn't mean to frighten you. No need to be afraid, but we do need to talk. It's time we started acting like a family again. I want to allow you freedom here." He swept his arm across the room.

The woman and child sat staring at him, their eyes wide with fear. It tore at his heart that they would be frightened of him, but he knew it was time for them to settle in. He knew how to make them more cooperative. Holding up his finger, he said, "Stay here."

Jack went to the surgical room and swung open the door. Reb lay still tied to the table. Her nude body was pale and her breathing labored. The incision down her torso looked raw and angry. Jack's breath caught as he saw her. His adrenaline immediately ramped up. Reminding himself he needed to focus on his family, he continued to the refrigerator in the corner. Swinging open the door, he looked at the vials in the cool interior.

Jack selected the bottle labeled Phenobarbital. He stared at the bottle for a moment and then closed the door, trapping the cool air inside. This would keep everyone in the right frame of mind so they could reconnect as a family. He certainly understood why this was so hard. They had been ripped apart. His wife and child had suffered severe trauma, and now they were healing. It would take time.

Returning to the room, he was pleased to see that neither the child nor mother had moved. Scruffy was on his heels as he went back and forth between the rooms and now stood at his side facing the couch. Jack approached, and while they had the energy to get to the couch, neither was willing to put up a fight as he injected them each with a mild dosage of the drug from the vial. They would be able to function but would remain passive and relaxed. This was the way he needed things to be until they got used to this arrangement.

"Hope, I love you so much," he said after removing the needle from Mindy's arm. She just watched as he brushed her hair from her face. "I bet you're getting hungry." Jack knew what he needed to do and went upstairs for his next task.

Within a few minutes he made breakfast and delivered it down the stairs. He helped them move over to the table, and they sat as a family to eat the food he had prepared. The woman and child ate slowly. Their navigation of the fork to their mouths was somewhat impaired by the drugs in their system.

Jack rose and left the table, quickly climbing the stairs. He returned a few moments later with his laptop. He opened up the computer and logged on. After a few minutes he successfully ordered a small refrigerator, electric stove, and a microwave to be delivered the following day. Tomorrow he would set the rest of the basement up to accommodate food and cooking. He needed Hope to begin resuming some of her duties of feeding and caring for Faith. The sooner she started acting like a mother again the sooner she would begin to realize this is where she belonged.

With the items ordered he decided that while he was logged on he would check on his favorite person–Special Agent Maxine Nichols. After a few minutes he was unable to find anything new on the beautiful agent. Next he logged onto a home page for the Phoenix news to see if there was any report on Mindy. He hated it, but he knew he needed to make sure his new identity was still protecting him. He could never let anyone get close enough to hurt his family again.

His eyes scanned the screen as he sat across from Hope and next to Faith. They continued to eat slowly as they watched him click away on the computer. Finally, his search found what he was looking for. In a headline that read "Husband/Father Suspect in Wife and Daughter's Disappearance," Jack skimmed through the article carefully and nearly laughed out loud when he realized the police believed that Paul had caused his own injuries to cover up a crime committed against his wife and daughter.

"Hope, this is perfect. Honey, we're safe. No one is even looking for us. We can relax and truly be a family."

Mindy's eyes met his. A mild tremor rushed through her, but Jack barely noticed. He was too focused on the story and elated by the report.

Hitting the back button on his search page, the screen returned to his lookup on Maxine Nichols. His eyes again scanned the page, and then he typed in Mark Wells and re-read the stories he read before about the little boy. Maxine Nichols and Mark Wells were the proud guardians to a little boy. Jealousy filled him.

He looked across the table at his wife and daughter, and a smile formed on his face. Life was going to be so good. He had a few things he needed to do, but suddenly he felt so happy about what the future would hold.

Later that evening after dinner, Jack sat for a while watching TV with his family. Scruffy took turns sitting on his lap and Faith's. It was cute to see her cuddled up to the little dog. It seemed to make her happy, and he wondered why he'd never gotten her a dog before. The day quickly got away from him, between taking Scruffy out, checking in on and caring for Vivian, and being with his family. It was evening, and the darkness was calling for him. It was time for his family to sleep and time for him to make another visit to Reb.

Hope and Faith were carefully tucked into bed for the night. Jack tucked Scruffy in with Faith, and then left them to rest and entered the surgical room. Reb lay on the stainless steel table. Her eyes popped open at the sound of him entering the room. "Well, it's good to see you're feeling better. You were a little under the weather earlier," he said referring to her unconscious state earlier.

Reb's eyes grew wide, and her feet started to twitch as fear pulsed through her nervous system. "You better keep yourself calm. You could cause yourself to have a stroke. You know, getting it all worked up."

Unable to calm herself, Reb's feet continued to twitch. "Well, I do understand your concern because you're right after all. What I'm about to do is in fact going to hurt like hell."

Jack snapped on gloves and slipped out of his clothes and into a fresh set of scrubs. Within moments and despite Reb's screams and pleas, he snipped and pulled away each of the sutures, depositing them onto the surgical tray. Reb arched her back against the pain as Jack slid the scalpel into the opening that just barely began to heal. Blood oozed out of the new opening. Jack slid his gloved fingers into the cavity and touched organs. Still he resisted the urge to push his hands fully into the woman's battered body, as he wanted to enjoy more time with her. Killing her now would be a disappointment.

With his immediate needs met, Jack once again stitched the woman's body closed and secured a new IV bag. Like before, Reb passed out from the pain at some point during the violation of her internal organs. Her breathing was labored, but once again she would survive. Jack knew the pain must be excruciating, but he didn't really care. Only once had he ever really cared about the pain he inflicted on his victim. He smiled as he remembered little Jessie. He had stolen her mouth, but let her live.

For a moment the memory made him feel sad as he realized the procedure had ended up being unnecessary a complete failure. Things hadn't gone as he had planned, but for a while Jessie had brought Faith back to him, long enough for him to realize he had been going about it all wrong. And now he'd found his real family.

Reb was once again stitched and resting. Exhausted from the adrenaline, he washed everything down the drain. His body washed and

610

clean he went upstairs to pull on some boxers before returning down stairs.

He moved Faith and Scruffy to the couch then slid in between the covers of the bed and pulled Hope to him. She was sound asleep and didn't respond, but it felt good to hold his wife again. Her skin was so soft, and her hair smelled of honeysuckle. He felt himself becoming aroused and forced himself to push those feelings back. He would wait for her to feel more comfortable. Relaxing, he let out a sigh and spooned against her. Soon he was fast asleep.

***

Mindy woke to the warmth of a body snuggled tightly against her. She felt lips kiss the back of her neck and for a moment she leaned into the feeling. Her mind clearing from sleep and drugs she suddenly realized where the warmth came from and rolled over to pull away. Her body went rigid.

"Good morning, darling. I hope you slept well. How does a good breakfast sound? I'll make Faith her favorite pancakes. Then later we're going to get some appliances delivered here so you can prepare meals yourself. I'll have to go out to get some groceries. I'll stock up everything. I want you to have everything you want."

Mindy stared at him. She wanted to gash his eyes out, but she couldn't seem to bring herself to have the strength to do anything but lay there paralyzed by her fear. Her mind felt like quicksand. She knew she needed to pull herself together for her daughter Allie, *Oh God, where is she?* Her eyes searched the room, finally finding Allie still asleep on the couch. There was a small dog wrapped in her daughter's arms.

Mindy's heart pounded deep inside her chest, and her head hurt. Jack lay close to her talking, but she really had no idea what he was talking about. *I have to get out of here,* she thought, but she had no idea how to make that happen when lifting her head off the pillow seemed insurmountable.

"Today, I'm going to start slowing down the meds so we can begin to act more like a family. I think you're sleeping too much. I want you to be able to care properly for Faith. She needs you. I know you experienced a lot of pain from the accident, but you should be healed now. After all it has been well over a year since that horrible day. You both have been through so much, but I promise you nothing but the best now."

611

He was still talking. *Did he say he was going to let up on the drugs?* If he did that, maybe she could find a way out of here. Where is *here*? She tried to find something in the room to help her understand where she was, but nothing looked familiar. She started to wonder about Paul, but she made her mind come back and focus as best she could on Jack.

Suddenly, Jack was moving. He slid out of the bed and leaned in, and he was so close she could smell him. He kissed her mouth and pushed his tongue between her lips. She wanted to wipe her mouth but struggled to raise her hand to her lips. Her mind recognized it would not be a good move. She would have to play along.

She watched as Jack left the room, and then returned a few moments later and forced a pill in her mouth. She swallowed reflexively, and the pill nearly lodged in her throat. He handed her a glass of water, and she sipped it slowly as the pill slid further down her throat. *What did you give me, Jack?*

Jack walked over to where Allie slept and patted the dog on the head. Then he leaned in and kissed her daughter on the head. She sighed when she realized that her daughter didn't stir and that he hadn't touched her. Thank God she was sleeping.

"I'll be back in a little while with some breakfast. I'm sure you're hungry."

She watched as he left the room. She could hear footsteps that sounded like they were going up stairs then a clicking and scraping sound. When she couldn't hear anything else, she forced her head up and worked her body up on the pillows. She needed to get up and get to Allie.

***

When Jack returned to the basement he found Hope holding Faith in her arms. Scruffy was sitting next to them wagging his tail. Jack smiled. He couldn't believe his eyes. He truly had his family again.

Jack set the table and then invited his wife and daughter to join him. He was glad to see they were able to walk to the table on their own. Neither spoke, but they did slowly eat the breakfast he had made them. He looked down and saw Scruffy looking up at him with wanting eyes, so he took a pancake and tore it into small pieces, feeding the small dog who took the food eagerly. Jack made a mental note to get dog food.

Clearing the table, he called the dog which followed him without question up the stairs. Locking the basement door behind him, he entered the kitchen and set the tray with the breakfast plates on the counter, then opened the back door to let Scruffy out. He watched for a moment as the dog scampered out into the trees.

Jack washed the dishes before checking on Scruffy and finding the dog patiently waiting at the door. As he was letting the dog back in, he heard a knock at the front door. With Scruffy following right behind him, he went to the door and found a delivery truck outside. He invited the driver to the garage where he had the appliances unloaded. He could handle taking the items down into the basement himself.

With the items unloaded and the driver gone, he made a trip up to check on Vivian and got her setup with the required meds and her daily soap operas. He hoped that soon he could share his family with her. It would be nice if they all could spend some time together.

With Vivian taken care of, Jack let Scruffy out once again before putting him back in the basement with Faith. He noted that his family was asleep again. The drugs were obviously still thick in their systems. Good, this was a perfect time to take the appliances downstairs. Retrieving an appliance dolly from the far corner of the garage, he strapped the refrigerator in place and muscled it through the doorway and slowly down the stairs one at a time.

An hour later Jack had the refrigerator, stove, and microwave set up in a mock kitchen at one end of the basement's main room. Things were really starting to look homey now. Satisfied that he had everything working properly, he secured the basement and made a run to the grocery store.

It felt good to be out of the house. The sun was shining, and the air was brisk. Occasionally he caught a hint of the ocean air that had managed to make its way up the mountain and into the Ojai valley. At the store he packed a cart full of items he knew his wife loved to use in cooking. He bought spices and milk and juices for Faith, a big bag of dog food for Scruffy, and a few dog treats and toys.

In the aisle that had automotive and other hardware accessories he searched for a padlock he needed for the surgical room. As Hope and Faith got stronger, he wouldn't want them entering that room. That was his special place. Even though Hope fully knew about his needs, Faith wouldn't understand, and it would most certainly frighten her. He needed to protect her. Her innocence was very important.

613

He bought special items for Hope, fragrances she liked for her hair and lotions for her body, and then picked up a couple of toys for Faith, including some crayons and coloring books. There were a few more things he needed, but he would have to get them at the hardware store.

Making another stop, he got PVC pipe, a utility sink, a shower head, and the appropriate hose connections. He could route water lines from the surgical room at the end of the basement into the smaller room and improvise a shower and kitchen sink for the girls. It wouldn't take too much to set it up. He considered a shower curtain rod, but thought about it again. He wouldn't buy anything that could be used as a weapon or tool.

Looking around the store quickly once more before deciding he had everything he needed, he paid and took everything outside and loaded it into the back of the van around the groceries. It felt good to get out, but he wanted to get back home to his family. Vivian was due for her medication, and it would soon be time for lunch. It seemed time flew by these days. Being back with his family, he was alive again. He drove through the familiar streets, and happiness filled him.

Unloading the groceries, he took them down into the basement and filled the refrigerator and the shelves that had in years past held his father's paint cans or tools. For now the shelves were a mock pantry.

Quickly connecting the electric stove in the corner of the soon to be makeshift kitchen, Jack popped a pizza in the oven while Hope, Faith, and Scruffy watched from the couch. The TV droned on in the background as he began fabricating the wall adjacent to the surgical room into a shower for the bathroom. He added a sink next to the stove and mounted the microwave onto one of the shelves.

The timer on the new oven dinged, and he was pleased when he saw Hope get up and take the pizza out of the oven. She worked slowly and with intense focus, as if it took all of her energy to do the menial task.

She got the pizza out of the oven and worked to slice it with the plastic utensils Jack had provided. Then she set the pizza and plates on the table and assisted Faith to her chair at the table. Jack continued to watch from where he worked.

With the items installed and plumbed, he tested the water flow, drainage, and pressure. They had both hot and cold water and would be able to comfortably shower now. The drainage wasn't perfect, but with concrete floors and block walls, it was good enough. The dishes could now be washed here too. No more carrying them up and down the stairs.

After placing two dog dishes on the floor near the stove, he filled one with water and one with dog food. Scruffy immediately ran over to investigate, smelling the food and gobbling away at the small kibbles. His tail wagged the whole time.

Jack washed his hands and joined his family at the table. Hope seemed to be settling in nicely. He smiled. It was good to see her doing some normal tasks of a wife and mother.

Finishing his slice of pizza, Jack pushed back from the table and thanked Hope for the delicious meal. He leaned back in his chair and studied the scene. Faith sat next to him and Hope was across the table. Scruffy was curled up next to Faith's chair. Across from Faith sat an empty seat. It was a table for four. Knowing Hope could care for Faith—at least her basic needs now—and with the surveillance in place, he knew what he needed to do. Jack went upstairs, secured the basement, and made a phone call.

***

Several hours passed before Jack's phone call was returned, and his head was buzzing with excitement. He could barely contain himself as he sat with Vivian watching some movie from the *Leave It to Beaver* era. She was thrilled that he stayed and watched the movie.

He'd already given her a bath and had made sure she was comfortable. He fed her crushed ice and held her hand as the pain medication took hold. Some days the pain was worse, and this was one of those days. For now she was at ease, and the movie was a great distraction.

Checking his phone to monitor the basement, he saw Hope and Faith watching TV together. Scruffy was sitting between them. Each had a hand on the little dog, gently patting his soft, wiry fur. His family was doing well.

The medication was coming out of Hope's body, and she was beginning to be capable of caring for Faith. For something to do after lunch he had encouraged them to take showers, so he checked in on their progress while he waited for his call. Hope had helped Faith wash her hair, so right now they sat there looking shiny. They each had a freshness that he could almost smell from two floors away.

He continued to sit with Vivian, but the noise from the movie was simply a buzz in the background of his mind. He was planning. He really couldn't believe his luck. The blood was pulsing through him at a nearly deafening rate. His ears throbbed, and the more he tried to calm down, the more excitement he felt at the possibilities.

"Are you okay?" Vivian squeezed his hand.

"Oh, I'm sorry. I guess I let my mind wander," Jack answered a bit startled.

"Thank you for sitting with me."

"My pleasure," Jack answered smiling at the frail woman.

"Is it time yet?"

Jack felt a tug inside his chest. Moments ago he was nearly exhilarated. That feeling was crushed under her simple question. It was a question with so many implications.

"Not yet, Vivian. I want you to meet my family first."

"Your family? I thought…"

"I know, but remember you told me to reconnect? I did that, and it's wonderful. You'll love them. There's only one problem. I'll need to move you. I'm going to have to make a little trip soon. Just a day, maybe overnight, but I won't be gone long. You can stay with my family while I'm away."

Vivian smiled. "I'm glad you worked things out. Family is important."

"Yes, it is," Jack said. He watched as Vivian's eyes drifted closed. Moments later her mouth opened slightly, and she took deep yet short breaths as she fell into sleep influenced by the illness and medications.

Jack stood and tucked her hand gently under the covers before he slipped his away. He watched for a few more moments then silently turned and exited. Once outside the room, Jack was again able to allow his thoughts to run wild in his head. The information his contact had given him was simply too good to be true. Opportunity was knocking, and he damn sure was going to answer.

Chapter Twenty

Mark surprised Max with tickets to go see her sister in California, eager to introduce Heath to his new family. That day had quickly arrived. The trip would be short, just a long weekend, but Max was thrilled to be heading to see her sister Shauna.

Max held Heath's hand while Mark presented their boarding passes and special firearms permits and guns to the airline agent. The agent highlighted each with a pen and scanned their identification with a strange purple light. He peered over his glasses, looking them over with obvious scrutiny, and then handed back the items before telling them to have a safe trip.

Putting the identifications away, Max dropped Heath's hand for a minute before continuing to the security checkpoint behind Mark. Heath asked a million questions about everything from why the man had the purple light to why they had to take their shoes off, and if the machine could see all of his insides. The last question made both Mark and Max laugh out loud—would he look naked when he went through the scanning machine? It took a brief moment to convince him that no one could see him naked.

They spent the next few minutes riding the tram and making their way to their boarding gate. Confident they had plenty of time, they agreed to get something to eat before the long flight to Los Angeles.

Heath shoved a chicken nugget in his mouth, chewed happily, swallowed, and then asked, "Will your sister like me? Can we go to the beach when we get there?" Shoving another nugget in his mouth, he bobbed in his seat anxiously awaiting an answer.

"Slow down, tiger," Mark said. "Max's sister will like you just fine. And, yes, we can go to the beach. It may not be right when we get there, but for sure it will be soon. Deal?"

"Okay, deal." Heath continued to pop nuggets and fries into his mouth and gobbled away at the food.

"Are you getting as excited as he is?" Mark asked Max.

"I am. It's pretty exciting to see my sister and for her to meet Heath."

"A lot has happened since you last saw her. You've moved, sold your house, graduated from the FBI, got married, and took in a foster son. You sure do know how to live."

Max laughed. "Yeah, well I think a couple of people helped me on this wild ride." She looked between Mark and Heath. They laughed with her.

After finishing their meal, the trio stood and followed the signs towards the gate. They arrived to find they were just ten minutes from boarding. Max encouraged Heath to walk with her to the restroom while they waited, and Mark took a seat near the gate.

Returning from their walk, Heath bounced on his feet as he anxiously anticipated getting onto the plane as the gate attendant started calling the boarding sections. The plane filled quickly, and they settled into their seats as Heath checked out the sliding window panel, the folding food tray, everything in the seat back, and finally settled down a little to study the airplane exit plan.

Unfortunately, they would have to do it all again before making it to their final destination because the only reasonable rates included a connection in Minneapolis. Fortunately for them, the layover was pretty quick, and her sister would be there to pick them up upon arrival in Los Angeles.

Max was really starting to get excited now about seeing her sister and her family, as well as meeting up with Cortez. The trip was entirely pleasure, but she intended on getting some time with Cortez and Bobby to go over some of the files they had been sharing back and forth on Jack Tyler.

There's no way she could be in L.A. and not see Cortez, much less avoid spending some time focused on Tyler. After all, L.A. was where it had all started, and while she had a lot of fond memories of L.A. for so many other reasons, the one that stood out the most, and because it was unresolved, was Jack Tyler's six buried bodies in the Malibu hills. She had to admit to herself that she would never fully rest until Tyler was either dead or behind bars.

She also wondered if he was still living with the decomposing bodies of what he obviously believed were recreations of his wife and daughter. The thought made a shudder roll through her body.

"Are you cold?" Wells asked noticing the tremor.

"No, just a chill I guess," she replied not wanting to tell him that she was thinking about Tyler in front of Heath.

Several hours later and after changing planes, they finally landed in California. The passengers wrestled luggage out of the overhead compartments and from under seats, and one by one each exited the plane. Heath continued to ask question after question, typical of a child's quizzical mind. Finally off of the plane, they worked their way through the throngs of people that bustled in every direction through one of the busiest airports in America.

Max texted her sister that they were on the ground and on their way out, and Heath's excitement seemed to grow with every step. "She's waiting just under the United Airlines sign at the curb," Max explained to Mark after receiving a returned text.

Mark nodded and pointed to the exit sign. "What will she be driving?"

"A white Lexus SUV," Max replied.

"What's a trexis UUV?" Heath asked, scrambling up what he had heard.

"It's a kind of car."

"Oh." He seemed satisfied for now and less excited when he realized it wasn't necessarily something really cool.

The doors slid open, and they were greeted with a whoosh of warm air as they stepped outside. Max searched the parking strip and then pointed at a few cars to the right where a woman stood waving from the rear of the vehicle. "There she is," Max said.

Within a few moments Max and her sister, Shauna, were locked in an embrace. As Max pulled away, she immediately turned to Heath and introduced the boy. "Heath, this is my sister, Shauna. Can you say hello to her?"

Heath shyly kicked at the ground before softly saying hello. Shauna kneeled down to eye level. "I bet you're hungry after your long trip. Would you like to go get something to eat?"

"Okay, I guess so, but can we go to the beach too?"

Shauna laughed. "I figured that was the first thing you would want to do. We just need to drop your things off at my house and pick up my son so you have someone to play with. How does that sound?"

Heath was smiling from ear to ear now and obviously very excited about the idea of having a playmate to share in the beach experience. He nodded his head up and down.

"Okay, well let's get going then."

They piled into the car, and Shauna wiggled through the heavy traffic and out of the airport. Heath talked the whole time until they arrived at Shauna's house, located just off of Santa Monica Boulevard. Max smiled at the sun and the ocean. It truly felt good to be back here. She watched as businesses flew by and thought of the first time she and Mark had lunch together.

Less than an hour later, the two young boys suited up for the beach with sand pails and shovels, they were on their way to Zuma Beach. Heath could hardly contain himself and was becoming fast friends with Max's nephew as they ate fruit snacks in the matching car seats Shauna had installed in the back.

Max and Shauna chattered almost as much as the boys while Mark sat and listened to the noise around him, enjoying the warm breeze that flowed through the window. It felt nice to be on vacation and not have a case hanging over his head. Heath's case had taken a toll on him, and this week here in California was certainly going to help wash out some of the pain that had come in the wake of working that case.

Shauna navigated the SUV into a parking space at the far end of the lot, allowing them some open beach space away from others. They piled out of the vehicle and unloaded a picnic basket and blanket from the back. The boys were already kicking their way through the sand with Max and Shauna calling out after them to slow down and to not go in the water until they all get there. Knowing Heath had never been to the beach before and wouldn't have any concept of the power of the waves, Mark chased after them to ensure they didn't go in.

Mark led Heath by the hand as he put his toes in the water for the first time. He squealed as the cold water splashed up his legs and pulled his feet deeper into the sand. The next hour was spent digging for sand crabs and playing with the strange, wiggly crustaceans, followed by building sand castles. They only stopped playing to eat.

***

Jack watched from his vehicle. His heart rate raced as he saw the beautiful, light haired boy playing in the sand with his dark haired friend. His eyes bounced between the child and Agent Maxine Nichols. *Oh, wait. Her name is Wells now, isn't it?* He couldn't believe the agent was back in California, but was relieved to see that it appeared to have nothing to do with him. He relaxed as the realization settled in.

When his contact had told him that the agent had flight plans to California, he was afraid she was onto him and was planning to sneak in on him when he least expected it. With the flight schedule in his hands, he had been at the airport and watched them arrive. He'd followed them to the house and assumed it was Maxine's sister but couldn't be sure. He watched as they had put the picnic basket in the back of the vehicle.

His eyes returned to watching the boy—a son. A son, just like he and Hope had talked about. They'd been planning to have another child, and he just knew it would be a boy—a little brother for Faith to play with. Jealousy of Max and her new family filled him.

Focus! He told himself, realizing emotions like jealousy were useless and even reckless. He continued to watch the family play until they started to wrap up the blankets and collect their items. Max toweled off the little boy, tousling his blonde curls. The boy laughed and danced about in the sand.

Jack's eyes scanned Maxine's muscular body. He'd almost forgotten how attractive she was. His eyes shifted to Mark Wells. He was the epitome of tall, dark, and handsome. Jack sized him up in comparison. Not that he wanted Maxine, no; he had Hope. And he would never be unfaithful. His devotion and commitment to his wife was for life. He wondered if Mark Wells would be dedicated to Maxine for life. *What would you do to keep her with you, Agent Wells?*

The family loaded everything into the SUV and backed out of the parking lot. Jack waited then pulled out behind them. He knew where they were staying and didn't dare risk being noticed. With two FBI agents riding in the car, he wondered if they would instinctively realize they were being followed and then notice that it was the same model of vehicle that had followed them earlier. He wasn't willing to risk this, so he dropped from behind and went a different route. It was time for him to get something to eat. Maxine and her family would likely go back to the house and spend the evening together. They were all covered in sand and salt and would need showers.

Feeling confident that he had some time, he drove down Santa Monica Boulevard and found a restaurant that looked appealing. It was time to check on his family back at the house. He was sure they would be fine or he wouldn't have left them, but he still wanted to check in with the video system.

While inside the restaurant and after placing his order, Jack logged onto the surveillance system through his phone and watched Hope, Faith, and Vivian through the various camera selections. He could see the main room where he had placed Vivian's medical bed.

Knowing that he had to leave, and not trusting anyone in his home, he had made the decision to move Vivian down into the basement where she could be with Hope and Faith. He had temporarily placed her on the couch while he relocated the bed. Once he had everything in place for her, he gingerly carried Vivian down stairs and introduced her to his family.

He watched the security feed as Hope checked on her and suppressed a smile, not wanting anyone to notice him. His family was doing just fine, and he would be home soon. His plan was to be home before Vivian needed any more medication. Just before leaving, he had given Vivian a pretty heavy dose of morphine and had added a morphine push to her IV where she could push the button herself when she needed to, without any risk of allowing her to over medicate.

Hope was doing exactly what he had expected. She was still moving slowly, but her motherly instincts drove her to care for Faith and Vivian. They needed her, and he knew she needed them too. It was those traits that he had always admired about her the most.

He flipped the camera to the surgical room and watched for a moment, being careful that no one could see over his shoulder. He saw Reb lying there attached to the table. He leaned in and saw shallow breaths and knew she was still alive. *Good.*

Confident that things were fine back at the house, he closed the app right as his food was delivered to the table. He thanked the plump server and turned his attention to his meal, suddenly realizing how hungry he actually was. He watched the sun setting outside through the windows while enjoying the food. His mind swirled about his family and the wonderful future ahead.

After a rich cup of coffee, Jack paid the bill and went back out into the night air. It was cooler, and the darkness smelled of fresh, salty ocean air. He felt as if he could hear the waves slapping happily against the sand, but he was actually too far to really hear it. The image made him feel alive, happy, and good. His senses were on full alert, and he was ready to execute his plan.

Once back inside the vehicle he relaxed back into the seat and waited. A while later he looked at his watch and saw that he still had time since it was only nine o'clock. To kill time, he logged back on to the surveillance app on his phone and observed his family. They were watching TV curled together on the couch.

After a few minutes Hope got up and checked on Vivian. Using his fingers to spread the screen, he zoomed in. He watched closely as Hope gently tended to the old woman. He waited and realized that she must have been satisfied because she returned to the couch.

Reaching behind the seat, he retrieved the ear buds that were carefully stored in the side pocket of his laptop bag. Plugging them in and applying the buds to his ears, he listened. They were watching a movie. He waited a moment then recognized some of the lines of *To Kill a Mockingbird*. Great choice for Faith.

Jack could remember watching that movie himself when he was about her age. He listened more closely and wished he'd installed some more robust speakers to support the video. He could hear Faith's sweet little voice slowly asking questions.

Closing the app again, he decided there was plenty of time to take a drive. He pushed the gear shift into reverse and backed out of the space, then propelled the vehicle forward out of the drive and headed towards the Malibu Canyon.

Thirty minutes later he was on his way up a familiar winding road. When he passed the entrance gate for Shalom Camp, his pulse raced as he neared the familiar spot. He recognized the spot as a large oak tree loomed over the road out of the darkness. He pulled the vehicle over onto the shoulder.

Reaching across the vehicle, he retrieved a small flashlight out of the glove box and clicked it on. Within moments he exited the vehicle, crossed the asphalt, and dropped off the opposite side of the road into the thick brush. It was obvious no one had been here in a while. He counted his paces instinctively until he was deep into the thicket. He stopped, knowing he was standing in the exact spot where he had buried six bodies over the period of a few months. He wished those bodies were still there, but knew... yes, he knew Agent Maxine Nichols – no – Agent Maxine Wells had stolen them.

It was cathartic being here right now, as he was beginning a new chapter in his life. Filled with emotions, he forced himself to move from the spot and return to his vehicle. Before getting in he reached under the driver's seat and pulled out a small tool box. Removing the screw driver, he went to the back of the vehicle and removed his license plate, then did the same for the front.

Getting back in the van he returned the flashlight to the glove box, the screwdriver into the tool box, and then fired up the engine to make his way back down the mountain.

He looked at the clock on the dash and noted the time now was after eleven. Perfect. By the time he got back down the mountain and to the house, it would be nearly midnight. He assumed the agents would tuck in early tonight given the long travel and day at the beach.

Forty minutes passed before he turned onto the street and pulled over at the end of the block. He watched the neighborhood for a few minutes. It was quiet. He assessed the house. There were no lights on inside. The street lamps illuminated the sidewalk by casting long, blue shadows. His eyes scanned each house along the path that led up to the two story brick-faced home where he watched the family enter earlier.

Every home had a perfectly manicured yard. The homes were better than middle class, and Jack suspected most of these people lived close to bursting at their financial means. Everyone in L.A. was always trying to compete with each other—nicest cars, most beautiful home, best schools or bodies. It was a bit ridiculous, really, and nearly always led to over spending and high debt.

He was grateful that his success had afforded him luxury and lack of need to worry about those silly competitions. No, his needs were fulfilled through caring for his family and the feelings he achieved when surgically invading another person's being. It was the fact that he both took and saved lives that drove him. Nothing material could even remotely compare to what he had accomplished.

Deciding the silence in the neighborhood was the perfect cloak of safety, he slid his car up the street, just in front of the house neighboring the one that was the point of his focus. He needed to be cautious since there were, after all, two FBI agents inside. He had to assume they were good with details like the make and model of a vehicle. He had intentionally removed the plates in case they woke. His vehicle was common enough that they would never find him without the actual plate. He made a mental note to put the plates back on before his return to Ojai later. He certainly didn't want to make any long trips without plates on. *No room for error.*

He reached behind his seat and pulled his medical bag forward, retrieving a syringe and rag. Before sliding out of the vehicle, he slipped on latex gloves and checked his pocket for his Swiss Army knife then quietly exited, softly clicking the door shut. Slipping up the sidewalk, he took a sharp turn up the driveway to the side door leading to the garage. It was a long shot, but he was hoping that it would be unlocked and make his job easier. Past experience told him that the side door was the most commonly forgotten exterior door.

His hand grabbed the knob, and he took a deep breath as he turned the knob. Giving the door a slight nudge, he stopped, shocked when it in fact pushed open. He slipped inside. The garage smelled of engine oil and soil.

Standing just inside the door with his back against the wall he listened. Every sense was tingling with excitement and anticipation.

Other than the normal sounds that any home would emit, it was silent. He needed to be most careful now. Taking a moment to let his eyes focus on the items in the garage he made a mental picture of everything in his path, on the floor and walls. If he tripped or bumped anything on his way in or out, it would cause a great deal of noise, and he couldn't afford any mistakes.

Slowly starting across the floor, he passed in front of the SUV that occupied one side of the garage. Then he passed a smaller vehicle shrouded in a car cover and based on its shape it appeared to be a sports car. He approached an interior door on the opposite side from where he just entered. He reached for the door knob and turned it, but unfortunately, it was locked.

He quickly overcame his disappointment and went to work on the lock with the smallest blade of his pocket knife. He had learned after a few times of not being really successful that he needed to bring small tools with him, which was why he always carried a Swiss Army knife in his pocket. It only took a couple of minutes before he had successfully turned the tumbler and was standing inside a laundry room.

Sucking in a deep breath he waited, listening again—still nothing. The house remained silent. Moving forward and paying close attention to every detail, he remained acutely aware of everything. Nothing had excited him in this way. Every minor noise resonated through the pounding of his heart in his ears–the sound of the refrigerator, a clock ticking, the house settling. He made his way through the kitchen guided only by his instincts and the glow of the moon shining through the light-weight curtains.

Finding a set of stairs that he could tell led to the second floor, he turned and climbed slowly, deliberately paying special attention to the possibility of any creaking steps. He paused for a moment when a fan kicked on somewhere in the attic. Recognizing it as the air-conditioning system, he continued on.

Arriving on the landing at the top, he followed the hallway until he found the first bedroom. The door stood slightly ajar. Waiting briefly once more, he allowed time to listen again. His ears tuned for every noise. *Can't be too careful.*

He knew he shouldn't but unable to resist the temptation, he slid through the small opening. Out of fear that it might squeak on the hinges, he turned his body sideways making sure not to touch the door. Inside the room he moved with slow, purposeful, light steps across the carpeted floor.

The curtains on the far side of the room were opened maybe an inch, offering enough moonlight that he could see the bed in front of him. He focused on his breathing, controlling it with small draws through his mouth. He'd learned through exercise routines how to not allow adrenaline to cause hyperventilation—a technique that had aided him in moments like these.

Slipping closer to the edge of the bed, he peered down at the two figures curled into each other. His heart raced as he stared down, his attention focused on the female. Her long, auburn hair cascaded out over the pillow. He knew all along that she was a stunning beauty, and seeing her in person confirmed it even in the dim lighting. This was a moment he had pictured time and again, but never thought would actually come to fruition. He had to quell the visions of his hands deep inside her body, touching and exploring. Oh, how good that would be.

Not able to resist the urges coursing through him, he reached out and almost tenderly touched the locks of hair that seemed to be caressing the pillow. His eyes darted to the man next to her, and imagines of him split wide open on a shining stainless steel table immediately entered his head.

Sliding his hand in his pocket, he removed the Swiss Army knife he always carried and gingerly folded open the scissor part of the tool. He leaned forward then very carefully lifted a few strands of the hair that splayed out on the pillow and made a small cut. The knife made a quiet snipping sound as the locks fell free and into his fingers.

The sleeping man stirred, pulling the woman closer to him, causing Jack to pull his hand back. *So protective, Agent Wells.*

Realizing he'd spent as much time as he could allow, he took one more gaze down at the lovely Maxine Nichols—or Wells, and slowly backed away from the bed, retracing his steps to the door and slipping out without making a single noise.

Once out of the bedroom, he re-oriented himself and noticed another door a little farther down the hall. This one stood all the way open. He paused briefly again to listen for any motion from the room he just left.

Satisfied that the house was still in rest, he entered the second room. He saw an airplane hanging from the ceiling and toys on the desk under the window on the far wall. Approaching the bed, he saw two small figures under the bundle of blankets. Scanning the first pillow, he saw a dark ball of hair and moved his eyes to the other pillow where his gaze landed on the lighter hair.

His heart was racing again. He wanted to reach down and push the hair back so he could see the child's beautiful face, but he knew better. Removing the rag and syringe from his pocket, he injected the liquid into the rag and then quickly and deliberately placed the rag over the boy's face while pressing his body down on top of him. In doing so, he managed to restrict the amount of movement to no more than if the boy had turned in his sleep. The other child stirred slightly, but did not awaken.

After being certain the boy was properly sedated, Jack lifted the boy from the bed and retraced his steps back down the hall, down the stairs, and out the garage door, intentionally leaving the doors wide open. He slipped back out into the darkness and to the van where he laid the sleeping child down in the back and shut the hatch. He got behind the wheel and drove off into the night without looking back.

Jack made sure to put good distance between himself and the house before pulling over in a parking lot to reinstall the license plates on his vehicle. It was late, and he certainly couldn't risk getting pulled over with the boy in the back of his van.

Looking around to make sure he was alone and seeing no one around, he secured the plates. But before getting back inside he took another syringe from his medical satchel and gave the child an injection of Rohypnol, commonly known as a Ruffie. The drug would help ensure the boy had no memory of what had taken place this evening, protecting both the boy and himself.

Knowing the child would sleep easily until he made it back to Ojai, he slipped the tarp that he carried in the cargo net over the small body, then got back in the van and traveled through the palm tree-lined residential streets to the freeway where he entered the ramp heading north. Within two hours he would be safely home. He smiled. Tonight had truly been one of the most important moments of his life.

Chapter Twenty-One

Max woke with a start as her cell phone rattled on the nightstand. For a moment she was confused, her surroundings not immediately familiar. She shook off sleep and reached for the phone that buzzed again, insisting on being answered.

"Nichols," she answered still using her maiden name.

"Hey, it's Cortez. Sorry to call so early, but we have an issue."

Max glanced at the alarm clock next to the lamp on the nightstand where her cell phone had moments ago rested and read five thirty-two. "Jesus, Cortez," she muttered just as her mind realized Cortez would not be calling this early unless there was a valid reason. She sat up, propping the phone under her chin as she pulled on pants, then slid off the bed and slipped into the adjoining bathroom.

"I got a call this morning from a missing person's detective in Phoenix."

Max felt her blood start to pump. "Phoenix?"

"Right, listen up. Mindy and her youngest daughter are missing."

Max was still trying to shake off the sleep and wasn't quite following. "Mindy?"

"Yeah, Max, as in Jack Tyler's sister-in-law."

"Shit."

"Shit is right. She's been missing going on three weeks."

"What the hell. Why wasn't I notified sooner?"

"Slow down, girl. I just got the call. Apparently, the local police didn't make the connection to Tyler and have been totally focused on the husband. He said he was attacked, and the other child was left sleeping in the home. He called the police and reported the wife and child missing. The police thought he staged the whole thing and have been trying to get him to confess. The scene was clean. It totally smells of Tyler."

Max was completely alert now. "Where and why would he take them? Mindy was never a big Jack fan. That could be really bad for her."

"I don't know why, and of course, we can't be sure. But I thought you'd definitely want to know. I was looking forward to spending time with you, just didn't think it'd be like this."

"Let me fill Mark in, and I'll call you back."

"Okay. The chief is not sure we have any jurisdiction in this case. There's no way or reason to know that Tyler is back in California. He could have taken them anywhere."

"I know. I'll call you back in a few."

Returning back to the bedroom, Max tapped Mark on the shoulder. "Mark, wake up."

"Max, what's up?" Mark sat up startled by the urgency in her voice.

"Jack Tyler's sister-in-law is missing. She and her daughter have been missing for nearly three weeks."

"What?" Mark asked, but was already slipping out of the bed.

"Cortez just called. She received a call from a missing person's detective in Phoenix. Apparently, they've been looking at the husband this whole time. And unfortunately, there's nothing connecting Jack to the case, but the detective thought it was too much of a coincidence and called me."

"Call Cortez back and ask if there's a place where we can meet and get the case details. Can your sister watch Heath for a while?"

"Sure. No need to wake the whole house. I'll leave her a note and have Cortez pick us up."

Mark pulled on clothes, while booting up his laptop and put on his shoes then pushed a stored number on his cell phone. "This is agent Mark Wells. We need everything we can get on the missing person's case for Mindy Prescott in the Phoenix area," he said referencing a file on his computer for the name. There's a child missing too. I want everything there is on the case faxed to Detective Lorraine Cortez at the LAPD."

While Mark was talking, Max was back on the phone with Cortez asking her to come pick them up. Cortez confirmed she'd be there in fifteen minutes.

Max went into the bathroom and ran a comb through her hair and brushed her teeth. Mark entered and stood beside her and took the other toothbrush from the travel kit. They spit into the sink in unison then shared a towel to wipe their mouths. Max grazed Mark's mouth with a gentle kiss then turned back out of the room and rifled through her luggage to retrieve her Glock 45. Even though they had come here on vacation, as an FBI agent neither of them traveled without their service weapons, even though it meant they had to gain special clearance for each flight.

Mark returned to the bedroom as well, and Max handed him his service weapon. Within five minutes the two were heading quietly down the stairs to go outside. Max turned toward the kitchen where she found a pen and paper and wrote out a short note to her sister to call her as soon

630

as she was up. Just as she was about to join Mark outside, she turned to find her sister Shauna standing there with her hand on her hip.

"Sneaking out? Have you had too much of me already?"

"It's a case. I'm sorry. Will you keep Heath busy until we figure out whether there's anything to the information we got?"

"Of course, do you need a car?"

"No, Cortez is picking us up in a couple of minutes."

"Okay, don't worry about Heath. I'll keep the boys busy."

"You're the best."

"Max, does this have to do with Tyler?" Shauna asked, concern showing on her face.

"Yes." Their eyes met briefly before Shauna nodded in acceptance and understanding. Max acknowledged that Shauna knew her well enough to know she could never rest until Tyler was captured or dead. Max gave Shauna a quick hug. "I'll call in a couple of hours to give you an update when I know more."

With that she turned and was about to leave when Shauna asked, "Did you open this door?"

Turning back she noticed the door leading to the garage was standing open. "No, I didn't really notice it. Maybe we left it open last night when we came in."

Shauna looked at Max then shrugged before closing the door. "Call me when you can and be careful."

"I will, thanks, sis!" Max said before crossing the living room and exiting through the front door where she joined Mark outside. He was on the phone again asking questions when Cortez pulled up to the curb.

The two agents walked quickly to the curb and climbed into the police issued Crown Victoria. Cortez sped away as they exchanged greetings.

Chapter Twenty-Two

Jack drove the van into the garage and closed the rollup door behind him. Within a few minutes he had removed the small, limp bundle from the vehicle and carried him inside, laying him down on the living room couch. Jack sat down next to the child, kicking off his own shoes. Exhausted and finally able to fully relax, he pulled a blanket Vivian had perfectly folded over the back of the couch and spread it out covering both Heath and himself then laid his head back. Sleep took him almost immediately.

Light shone through the kitchen windows and the glow poured into the living room over Jack's face. He woke and shielded his eyes with his hand then worked at the stiffness in his neck. He looked down at the boy lying next to him. He'd taken a Chance and it had worked out perfectly. *Chance ... yes it was perfect...*

Glancing at his watch, he was surprised to see it was almost noon. He'd slept longer than he'd wanted to, obviously needing the rest, but he needed to get up and get moving. Despite the discomfort of sleeping sitting up, he'd slept peacefully and knew it was because his family was now perfect. *Everything is going to be perfect from now on.*

Slipping his shoes back on and after spending a few minutes combing Chance's hair down with his fingers and straightening his clothes, and despite the fact that the child was still quite sleepy, he decided it was time to introduce him to the rest of the family.

Unlocking the door, he carried the boy's limp frame down the basement steps. At the bottom of the stairs, he approached the couch and laid the boy down before returning up the steps two by two to lock the door once more. He descended the stairs again and was faced with Hope standing there looking between him and the blonde boy on the couch.

"Jack? Who is this boy? Whose child is he?"

"Hi, honey. You're looking so much better. I'm sorry I had to leave you for so long. But I'm back now, and finally we can have everything we ever wanted."

Mindy's eyes grew wide. "I don't know what you're talking about."

"Hope, darling, I've brought our son home. His name is Chance. He's perfect, don't you think? Just like we always talked about" Jack approached Mindy and pulled her into his chest. He looked down at her. "Your heart is racing. Are you feeling okay?"

Pushing her hair away from her face and keeping her eyes away from Jack's gaze, Mindy replied, "I'm fine. I'm just surprised, that's all."

"Of course, it's a lot to take in—a new child, a brother for our little Faith. But finally we're all together, you, our children, Vivian, Scruffy, and me. All together here in this home, where we belong, where it all began."

Mindy averted her eyes. Her lip trembled slightly, though Jack didn't notice. "Yes, the way it's supposed to be," she said forcing the expected response.

"Chance should wake up in a little while. He's been asleep for quite a while. When he does wake he may be a little confused about where he is. This will pass in a few days. Soon he'll understand that we are his true family and that he should have been with us all along."

Mindy nodded, and Jack smiled accepting her approval. "I'll bring him along slowly. Hope, I can see worry in your eyes. Please, don't worry. He'll be fine, and Faith will help him settle in." Jack turned to focus his attention in the opposite direction. "How is she doing?" he asked, nodding towards Vivian.

Mindy's voiced hitched slightly, but Jack didn't notice. "She sleeps a lot. She asked for you earlier. I told her you'd be back soon."

Jack walked across the room to the bed where Vivian lay. He felt her pulse and brushed her hair from her forehead. Her breathing was a bit labored but steady. His heart tugged at him as he realized time with Vivian was limited. Forcing his mind back into the happy times, he looked towards the bedroom area. "Where's Faith?"

Mindy quickly walked over to him and stood between him and the bed. "She's sleeping. She'll probably wake up just in time to play with Chance." Mindy forced a smile and placed her hand on his arm, her fingers trembling slightly.

"Of course, well, no need to wake her, I guess."

Taking a chance Mindy continued, "You know, I'm worried about Vivian. We probably should have her in a facility where she can get full time care."

Jack's head snapped back in her direction. "Hope, do you think someone else can take better care of her than I can? She needs to be with people who care about her." Jack had never lost his temper with Hope, but he couldn't believe she would suggest such a thing. He felt his pulse pumping in his neck and had to concentrate to keep his temper under control.

Mindy recoiled slightly at his response. "Of course, you're right."

Jack reached out, not noticing how Mindy flinched at his touch. He lifted her chin until her eyes met his gaze. "Hope, I love you so much and now that we're all finally together, I just want to focus on our family. With Chance here we're finally complete. We have everything we dreamed of, and there's no reason Vivian can't share these moments. I know her time is short, and that's all the more reason for her to be with people who truly care for her. I know you have her best interests at heart, but I truly believe she is right where she needs to be."

Mindy blinked back tears and nodded. Jack leaned in and kissed her tenderly still holding her chin in his hand.

***

Mindy internally shuddered as Jack's lips closed in on hers. She closed her eyes and accepted his kiss. She'd tried to use the suggestion of moving Vivian as a possible means to escape. It hadn't worked. She'd taken a risk and failed.

While Jack was gone she had spent some time trying to find a way out, but with the cameras on her she'd been unsuccessful. She wasn't sure when Jack was watching and knew she had to be very careful. She'd been too afraid to take too many risks.

The cloud that had been in her head for…how long?…was finally clearing, though she knew the medications he continued to give her kept her from being totally clear. It was only while he was gone that the drugs really started to wear off. She glanced to where Allie slept and considered that a blessing. She could only hope they could get away before the fog cleared for her. She prayed her child would not remember any of this.

There was only one thing Mindy knew for certain; she would do anything she had to do to protect her daughter. Jack obviously believed she was her dead sister, Hope, and that her daughter, Allie, was her dead niece, Faith. Though she had always thought of Jack as odd, she knew Hope adored him, and she knew he had absolutely cherished her sister and their daughter. Knowing he would never hurt either of them gave her a bit of comfort. She had to play the role, whatever that took.

She had to ignore the images of bodies buried in the Malibu hills and in the country in Oklahoma; the horror of the children killed; and of the mouth removed from an innocent little girl in Illinois. She had to stay in the present. She most certainly knew what her brother-in-law was capable of, but she had to believe that as long as he thought she was his wife everything would be okay.

She stood frozen, facing the madman that had once been her sister's husband, and waited for his direction. She forced the trembling in her body to cease by focusing her mind on her daughter and making a mental promise in moments like these to think of Paul, she would escape. *Oh, Paul, I hope you and Madison are okay.* Choking back the images of her husband and oldest daughter, she couldn't help but wonder if Jack had killed them or if they were alive and trying to find her and Allie. Knowing she couldn't become distracted by despair, inside her mind she screamed out, "Stay focused on Allie!"

Suddenly, she realized Jack was talking to her and forced her attention back to him, willing herself to pretend to be Hope.

***

"Hope? Are you okay, dear?"

Mindy's eyes rose to meet Jack's. "Yes, I'm sorry. I guess I was just wondering how soon it would before Chance wakes up. I'm anxious to spend time with him," she lied.

Jack smiled and felt his body relax a little. "Well, we'll slowly encourage him. It may take just a little time."

"Well, for now I have a few things I need to do. Why don't you prepare us something to eat? I'll join you in a little while. Will an hour be enough time?"

Mindy briefly looked at him. "Sure." She started to turn away but was pulled back.

"I love you, Hope. I've always loved you," Jack said, his hands holding hers tightly and pulling her into him. He leaned in and kissed her passionately. Pulling away, Jack smiled then released her and turned to leave the room, heading towards the surgical room. "I'll be working, so please don't disturb me."

\

***

Jack unlocked and opened the door to the surgical room with the keys he kept in his pocket. He slipped into the room, closing and locking the door behind him. On the table Reb's pale body lay motionless. The jagged incision down the center of her torso seemed to glow in the sudden light.

Jack approached her and placed his index and middle finger on her throat. His heart rate increased slightly as he felt a weak pulse. He leaned in close to her ear. "I see you're still hanging on, Reb. For that, I thank you."

Reb blinked, obviously straining against the lights and struggling against the pain. "Good girl, wake up now. I'm sorry I wasn't here to spend time with you the past couple of days. I really would have liked more time with you, but I had something far more important than you to deal with."

Reb's head rolled from side to side. Her breathing labored. It was clear she was distressed. "I think it's time for us to rendezvous. Have I ever told you how much I always hated you? Well, never mind. That really doesn't matter much now."

Jack continued to riddle her with questions he knew would never really be answered. "Are you ready to have some more fun? Strange, isn't it? I hate you, and yet you have given me quite a bit of pleasure since you've been my guest."

Reb's eyes grew wide, and with the little bit of strength she had left in her body she struggled against the restraints that still held her arms and feet to the stainless steel table. Jack ignored her struggling efforts and prepared the room for surgery.

Realizing the lunch Hope was preparing should be nearly ready Jack looked around the room. Satisfied that he had everything prepped and despite the fact that his adrenaline was already pumping he didn't want to disappoint Hope. "Reb, I know you are likely anxious to get started and while I would love to oblige you, I can't let my lovely wife wait, but don't worry I won't make you wait long. I'll be back to see you later today."

Jack left the room locking the door, dropping the keys in his pants pocket, leaving Reb lying naked, cold, exhausted and filled with terror.

Mindy already had the table set and was just ready to dish food into bowls. She'd made a homemade soup and prepared a fresh salad, the room smelled amazing, of fresh herbs.

"Honey, you really do spoil us, this looks like a really great lunch." Jack said as he entered the room. Nodding to the couch he asked, "Has Chance started to wake?"

"No, Not yet," Mindy answered her eyes darting to the couch.

Chapter Twenty-Three

Mark and Max were greeted at the door by Chief of Police Harding who appeared to instantly stifle the pride he obviously felt in the accomplishments of his once young detective. "Well, look at you, Nichols. All grown up into a FEEB," teasing her with a nickname commonly used by local authorities for FBI agents. Everyone knew there was no love lost between the local and federal organizations, and though he would never tell her to her face, using his gruff exterior to hide his pride, Max could tell he was nearly bursting.

"Yeah, yeah, Chief. I see you're still a funny man," Max tossed back at him.

Immediately turning to business Harding asked, "Well, what do you think? Is your boy Tyler at it again?"

"Honestly, we haven't had much time to get caught up on the events around the Prescott abduction. I don't feel I can really answer that question yet." Max nodded towards her ex-partner. "Cortez filled us in a bit in the car on the way over." Just as Max was finishing her sentence, her cell phone started buzzing. "Excuse me," she said looking at the display. "It's my sister. It must be important."

Stepping away a few feet, Max answered her phone, "Shauna, is everything okay?"

"Max, I don't know. I can't find Heath anywhere. The garage door to the outside was open, and I've looked everywhere." Shauna was rattling as fast as she could and was obviously out of breath.

"Whoa, slow down. He's not in bed?" Max's mind reeled at what she was hearing.

"No, he's not. Max, he's not in the house or the yard. I've called for him outside. He's gone!"

"Okay, slow down. We're coming right back." Max hung up the phone and faced the group who had turned their attention to her as they clearly heard her side of the call. "Jesus, Mark. Heath's gone!"

"What do you mean gone?" Mark asked in his usual calm, but direct manner.

"Shauna went to check on him, and he's gone. The garage door is open, and he's nowhere." Max could feel tears starting to well in her eyes, and she forced herself to gain control. "We have to go back right now."

Cortez and the chief both were immediately in motion. "I'll get some squad cars over there to canvas the neighborhood," the chief offered.

"Max, it'll be okay. He probably just got curious and wandered off. Let's go!" Cortez encouraged.

Racing back out to the parking lot, they piled into the vehicle Cortez had used to bring them to the station. Before they could even get their doors closed, Cortez had slapped the temporary police lights on the top of the car and was pulling away with the siren blaring.

Cortez was an expert driver and navigated the city streets with ease, pushing people out of the way and respecting the urgency of the situation. The ride to the station had taken them nearly twenty minutes, but they returned to the house in just over seven.

As they were nearly to the house, a chilling memory hit Max. "Mark, the kitchen door to the garage was standing open before we left. Shauna asked if I'd opened it. We closed it without thinking too much about it. He may have already been gone when we left," Max said, her heart pounding in both her head and her chest.

Cortez screeched the car into the driveway at an odd angle, and they all poured out onto the lawn. Before they could even get to the door, a panicked looking Shauna raced towards them.

"Max, I don't know where he is. I'm so sorry!" The fear took over her and tears poured down her cheeks.

Max hugged her sister then pulled back. "Shauna, I need you to keep it together. You're going to have to tell us everything you can remember." Leading Shauna into the house, Max took her inside and lowered her onto one of the dining room chairs. Reaching for a note pad, she began to ask questions, repeating them over and over, attempting to stimulate any additional memories. Max knew sometimes it was just little details that helped.

Mark was in motion and began the process of having an Amber Alert released to the local radio, TV, and freeway notifications. Within the hour the neighborhood was crawling with police vehicles and officers who were going door to door searching yards and talking to neighbors.

When nothing turned up from the search, Max began to really panic. She couldn't imagine that Heath would wander off on his own. After all, they weren't in their home town, and where would he go? Terror filled her. Could someone have come into the home while they were all sleeping and have taken him? It seemed nearly impossible.

640

With no leads and nothing else to go on, Mark called for a crime scene analyst to come in and dust the doorframes and windows to see if there were any signs of forced entry.

Max had given Shauna a break, but now resumed her questions. She was trying to get Shauna to remember whether or not the garage exterior door had been closed and locked. They walked through the questions over and over again, but Shauna couldn't remember.

They talked through what she remembered. They had gone to the beach. She had been excited about the visit, and she couldn't remember the last time anyone had actually accessed that door. Nothing. They had a big, fat nothing!

Mark approached Max, and she could see the terror in his eyes. She knew he was thinking of Tommy and how this could not be happening all over again. He took her hand. "The Amber Alert is out. We'll find him," Mark said with a confidence she didn't personally possess. She nodded but wondered if he was saying that because he really believed it or because he needed to hear it for himself.

While they stood there together, the chief arrived on the scene. He could see the grave look on their faces as he approached. "What do we know?"

Mark responded, "Not much. Both the kitchen door and garage door were open. The kitchen door was open before we left to come to the station. If that's the exit point, it puts him out of the house prior to our departure. We didn't check on him because it was too early and didn't want to wake him. Shauna checked on the kids shortly after we left. She wondered if our leaving might have awakened them and was considering breakfast for them. When she entered the room, only her son was in the bed. Heath was gone. Assuming he'd wandered downstairs to play, she started looking for him. After searching the house she went outside, both the back and front yards, then into the garage. That's when she discovered the door standing open. She can't remember if it was locked or when the last time it was accessed. Her husband had left for work already, but he's on his way home. He may be able to help fill in the blanks on the door. In the meantime, the analyst you sent over is taking prints from doors and windows. We need to rule out whether an intruder forced his way in." The words hung in the air. Mark stood unmoving. His typically warm, blue eyes appeared frozen like ice on a pond, locked with the chief's.

"Okay, the Amber Alert is out and is running on every local station. It'll hit national news soon, and I think social media is already grabbing it." The chief paused for a moment. "Cortez," he barked, causing her to immediately appear from the next room. "What has the canvas gotten us? Do we have anything?"

"I'm sorry, sir. It was early. So far no one saw a little boy walking the neighborhood around dawn. School has started now, so it's getting harder as we're starting to get reports of sightings. We're working those leads, but so far they've proven to be other neighborhood kids."

"Max, where have you gone since you arrived in town? Is there anywhere the boy may have wanted to go back to?"

"The beach." Max turned to Mark, feeling hopeful for the first time. "Mark, do you think he would have tried to go to the beach on his own?"

Mark turned to the chief. "Can we get a canvas going on any route headed towards the water? He may remember what direction we came from."

"I'm on it, Chief," Cortez called out before he could even respond.

Harding nodded at Cortez then turned his attention to Max. "We'll find him, Nichols. Stay focused."

With that comment he was gone. Max knew him well enough to know he was on his way to apply pressure to the tip line and to the canvas. She tried to sigh, but her breath seemed to be stuck deep inside as if strangled by her rib cage. Her head began to throb, and then suddenly another terrifying thought began to edge its way into the outskirts of her mind. She refused to let it in, but it sat there as if taunting her.

***

The day had blown by and still there were no solid leads on how or where Heath had disappeared. Max felt as if her mind was crumbling around her, and she could see despair beginning to settle in on Mark. Shauna had all but turned into a ball on the couch, barely able to even care for her own child. Their beautiful world was crashing around them, and there was nothing Max could do.

It was beginning to get dark out, and everyone agreed to move to the station where they could start working the case in the manner they would if they didn't know the child that had gone missing. "You should stay here in case he comes back," Mark offered to Max even though he knew the likely answer he would get.

"Shauna is here. I need to keep working. We need to work the case, Mark. I feel paralyzed."

"They're going to isolate us. You know that. We're too close to be assigned to this case. They're going to continue to question us, and they should," Mark warned. "It's what I would do."

"I know. I'm okay with that too. It's part of it, and it helps keep them focused in the right places."

Mark stared into her eyes and resigned himself to their situation. "Let's go."

"Shauna, we need to go. We're going to the station. There's a lot we can be doing, and staying here is not going to help. Are you going to be okay?"

Shauna nodded as her husband brought her a glass of water. "I'll take care of her. We'll be fine," Shauna's husband reassured.

"They may want to ask more questions, but for now they feel confident either Heath left on his own or an intruder…," Max couldn't complete the sentence. She hugged her sister then turned to leave with Mark.

***

It was two o'clock in the morning before Max was able to be reunited with Mark. They were separated and questioned for hours. Finally, they had been cleared of any suspicion and were able to begin working with Cortez. They weren't allowed too much access, but the chief was allowing them to remain involved, keeping them well informed. The news was not good though. Two miles in each direction from the house to the shore had been under surveillance for hours. The Amber Alert tip line was lit up with callers, but nothing surfaced as a solid lead.

"They want you to do a press conference and speak out on the morning news. Top story. We need to make a plea. If Heath was abducted. His abductor may not see him as a boy, but rather an object. We need to change that. Both of you need to be there, but Max, you need to be the one that talks. Make it personal—he's a boy; he does boy things; he likes the beach; and cars—whatever applies."

Max nodded and turned to Mark.

The chief continued, "We've had a picture of Heath blown up and will have it beside you. Speak to that photo as much as you can and then directly into the camera. You know how to do this."

The next few hours seemed to crawl by. But when six A.M. rolled around, all the local news stations were gathered on the steps of the police headquarters. When signaled, Chief Harding led Max outside onto the steps with Mark behind. It was there that she delivered the speech of her life time.

"...If you have him, he's a little boy. He's been through a lot already, and we love him and miss him. You see, we took him into our lives because we need him as much as he needs us. He got to go to the beach for the first time just a day ago. He giggled at the sand crabs and the way the sand pulled away from him, squishing between his toes. Please, let him come home to us."

Throughout the conference Mark stood behind Max with his arm on her waist and offered a few final words for the camera. "He's our son. We adore him and want him home safe. I plan on teaching him how to ride a bike and to fish. Heath, if you see this you know we love you."

Chief Harding concluded, holding his hands up, "No questions," and guided Max and Mark back into the building.

Once inside Max broke down and cried for the first time. This was real. "Mark, what if...?" She stopped, unable to bring herself to finish her thought.

"What if what, Max?" he pressed her.

"What if Jack did this?"

Mark stared at her for a moment, a look of disbelief on his face. "How would he know we're here? How would he even know about Heath?"

"I don't know, Mark, but something is not right and my gut tells me he's involved somehow."

By now Mark had come to trust Max's instincts. So often when she had that feeling, she was dead on. He had not accepted her thoughts before and had later regretted it. With Heath's life in the balance, he could not afford to second guess her now.

"Chief Harding, Max has a theory. Tyler may be involved in this. We need a full team, and we need it now. I'm going to bring in some more agents from Quantico to assist. This is still your case, of course, but we have to align our teams. If she's right, we don't have a lot of time. Tyler has only left one survivor ever, and that victim is scarred for life."

Chief Harding stood facing Mark. Their eyes locked in a dead-on stare as the chief seemed to be thinking through everything Mark has just said. "Okay, Wells, you got whatever you need from my team. We'll find your son, and if that little bastard Tyler did this we'll take him down once and for all."

Chapter Twenty-Four

After lunch Jack had spent time with Hope helping cleaning up the kitchen and watching TV before returning to the surgical room. Inside the locked room with his scrubs on, he lifted the scalpel from the tray next to the table as Reb's eyes followed his hand. Her body gasped out a few ragged breaths as a single tear fell from her right eye and trailed down her shallow cheek. He ignored her and focused on the deep incision along the half-healed cut as he used the scalpel to tear through the flesh for a third time.

This time he merely sliced right through the sutures with little regard to the tiny wire-like strings. Reb was thrashing about now, but Jack didn't notice. He was far too focused on his process and what was to come. With the incision complete, he turned to the shelf behind him, lifted the surgical saw, and turned back. Using the tool, Jack sawed right through her sternum. He set the saw down and inserted a rib spreader into the opening and pushed apart her body, giving him access to a variety of prizes.

His heart thumped inside his chest, beating against his ribs like the flapping wings of a caged bird, as he slid his hands deeply into the cavity of her body and thoroughly explored her vital organs. His fingers sought out her heart and gingerly pressed around the beating organ. He reveled in the triumphant energy that flowed into him from within her body. He squeezed the slippery muscle, slightly driving an erratic reaction. The beating increased at first then slowed to a near stop. He squeezed again. This time the heart reacted wildly in his hands, and he rejoiced in the power and control he felt in the moment. His ecstasy came to an abrupt stop as the firm, yet soft treasure stopped reacting to his taunts.

Jack leaned back and looked down recognizing that Reb was now gone, and he felt both vindication and disappointment. She had betrayed him and deserved this. His disappointment came only from the realization that he would not be able to spend time with her again. He also knew the darkness would never let him be free.

Even though he had Hope back with him now, his family whole and very much alive, he still was missing his required use of skill that kept the darkness away. He couldn't ignore his impulses without having his surgical outlet. His mind wandered as he began to clean up. There was still Jimmy to deal with. After all, he hadn't treated Vivian right. With that thought he began to whistle softly.

The surgical room was restored to its normal sterile shine. Jack grabbed Reb's personal belongings and carried her ravaged body out of the basement, past Hope who watched with wide eyes. He didn't take time to acknowledge her gaze. Carefully locking the door behind him, he went through the kitchen and out the back door that gave access to the garage.

Jack grabbed the shovel from the corner of the garage while balancing the nude woman's body half-hoisted over his shoulder. He exited the back door of the garage and navigated his way through the underbrush and along the path to the play house. After a few moments, he decided the woman who years ago had nearly broken apart his relationship with Hope had no right to be buried near the bodies he'd once thought were those of his family, so he pushed past the playhouse he loved so dearly as a child and continued on deeper into the woods. When he arrived at the edge of the creek he stopped and looked around. Deciding this was as good as any place to bury the body; he dropped the frail corpse onto the ground and began to dig next to the narrow bank of the creek.

The soil was soft this close to the water, which made his job easier. It only took thirty minutes to have a hole dug deep enough to properly conceal the body. Using his forearm, he wiped the sweat from his brow, and after assessing the area, he lifted the body just enough that he could drop it into the dark space he had created. The body crumpled against the walls of dirt. He dropped in the bag containing her purse and clothes and began covering it with the soil he had just removed moments ago.

Ten minutes later he had the soil piled on top of the body. He took a few minutes to scatter leaves over the area to make it look more natural. Standing back and looking around, he noted that nothing looked as if it had been disturbed. With the task of burying Reb complete, he became relaxed enough to be aware of his surroundings. He could hear the creek trickling nearby and the birds chirping in the trees. Remaining perfectly still, he allowed himself time to enjoy the beauty of the area.

The sun was starting to set. Jack had spent more time with Reb than he'd realized and it was time to get back inside. Dinner would certainly be ready soon, and hopefully Chance was beginning to wake up. He'd slept a lot longer than Jack had expected and would, no doubt, have a lot of questions, and he certainly wanted to be there to welcome his son home. Turning away from the creek, he retraced his steps through the woods.

After entering the house, Jack went upstairs and took a shower and dressed in comfortable clothes since he wouldn't be leaving again tonight. The shower was refreshing, and exhaustion from the last twenty-four hours and sleeping on the couch settled into his body. Despite his tired state he felt peaceful. Reb had helped push away the darkness for now, and a complete calm seemed to be embracing him.

As he approached the basement stairs he was greeted by a wonderful aroma. He smiled, realizing Hope had prepared a family meal. It would be the first one with their son. Chance might not be feeling up to the task of eating right away, but even still it was the first one together as a whole family. His chest burst with pride and excitement.

He entered the basement and locked the door behind him, taking each step with purpose, and was met at the bottom by Hope. He was pleased to see she seemed alert and relaxed.

"I made a roast. I hope you like it."

"Thank you, darling." Jack leaned into her and swept her into his arms. He kissed her passionately. Her body felt warm as if teasing him. He suddenly was aware they were being watched and pulled back to find Faith looking at them.

"Mommy?" Faith looked at them and sounded confused.

"Faith. Honey, are you hungry? I know I sure am," Jack teased. He walked over to where she was standing and kneeled down to eye level. "Mommy made us a roast, and I bet it's the best we've ever had."

Faith just stared at him. He brushed a lock of hair away from her eyes and then turned to the couch where Chance still lay, though he seemed to be stirring.

"Has he been awake yet at all?" Jack asked Hope.

"Not yet. He's made a few noises, stirred a little, but has not yet awakened."

Jack turned his attention to Vivian and spent a few moments tucking the blankets in around her fragile body before saying, "Okay, well let's eat, and maybe Chance will wake up soon enough to join us." Taking Faith's hand, he led her over to the table. She went willingly.

***

Mindy watched as her daughter took Jack's hand, and she silently prayed that her small child would willingly accept the situation

649

they were in. Allie was finally starting to be more alert, and Mindy knew soon she would have to try to explain to her young daughter how important it was for her to just act the part that has been given to her.

Jack had carried that woman's body out past her earlier, and it was in that very moment she understood what she needed to do. Everything from here on out would be exactly as if she really were Hope. She had to make Jack believe she was Hope and live the dream he'd created in his head. He was obviously delusional, and she was certain that as long as she and Allie played their roles in his crazy fantasy, they would be safe.

Her mind kept returning to that woman's face and how the head twisted in a way that it had been grossly staring at her as Jack carried her body out of the room. That face. It was familiar, and it took her half way through making the meal for her to make the connection. That woman had once been Hope's best friend. She could remember when Reb had warned Hope about Jack and how strange he was. Hope had become very angry and had stood up for Jack. Seeing him carry her out of the basement terrified her beyond anything she had ever experienced.

Mindy could remember many conversations with Hope about Jack when they were kids still living at home. As teenagers she had warned Hope a number of times that there might be something not quite right with him.

A tremor ran down her spine as she considered what would happen if he realized she was not really Hope. For now his desire to have Hope back with him was over powering reality. Clearly, he knew he came into her home and took her and had the presence of mind to do that, but now he seemed convinced that she was Hope and that Allie was Faith. She had to keep it that way. Her life and Allie's life depended on it.

Realizing she hadn't been paying attention, she returned her focus to dinner. Dishing the meal onto the plates, she served Jack a good helping of the savory roast and potatoes. On the side she had prepared a fresh salad and mixed vegetables. Setting the plate in front of him, she watched as he smiled up at her. It took everything in her to return a smile that she hoped felt genuine.

Once all the plates were filled, Mindy took her seat. It was difficult to eat even though the food smelled amazing. Realizing she needed to look every bit the happy wife, she forced bites of the succulent meat into her mouth. The food did taste good, and knowing it was important that she keep her strength up, she ate nearly everything on her plate. She certainly didn't want to have a chance to escape at some point and be too weak, causing her to fail to save her daughter because of it. She would never forgive herself. Those thoughts allowed her the focus she needed to continue to eat and nourish her body.

She watched as Jack scooped mouthfuls of the food, obviously really enjoying the meal.

"Faith, isn't this delicious?" Jack asked breaking the silence.

Allie looked confused, and Mindy nodded to her, hoping she would understand to just agree. She nearly sighed out loud when Allie spoke, "I like it."

***

Pushing back from the table, Jack rubbed his stomach with his left hand. "That was by far the best dinner I've had in months. Thank you, darling." He stood and picked up his plate, as well as Hope's and Faith's, and carried them over to the small kitchen. "I do believe it's my turn to clean up. You clearly have done plenty lately, what with caring for the kids and Vivian. Why don't you take a shower and freshen up?" A flirtatious smile covered his face as he winked.

Mindy looked back at Allie, who had moved from the table to the couch next to the boy and turned on the TV. Returning her gaze back to Jack, she nodded in agreement and headed to the small bathroom. As she passed, Jack curled his arm around her waist and nuzzled her neck. "You make me so happy, Hope. I love you so much." He released his grip and swatted at her butt as she pulled away and continued across the room.

Jack busied himself with the dishes, and once they were all clean, dried, and put away he went to the bed where Vivian lay. He gently took her pulse and observed her breathing. She was stable but obviously weak. The medication offered her what comfort she could gain. Unfortunately, that meant she slept a lot. Her eyes fluttered open at that moment, and he smiled down at her. "Well, hello, sleepy head."

"You're back from your trip," she said in a barely audible mumble.

"I am. I'm sorry I had to leave you, but I wasn't gone long, only a day. Hope took good care of you, I'm sure."

"Hope?" A confused look crossed the woman's face momentarily before her eyes closed again.

"Sleep well, dear," Jack offered, though the old woman clearly had dropped back off into a medicated rest.

Turning his attention across the room, he approached the couch where Heath and Allie sat. "How are my two favorite children?" he asked, gaining Allie's attention. "What are you watching, Faith?"

The girl gazed at him for a moment as if she didn't quite understand the question then replied, "TV."

"Well, I know that, silly, but what show are you watching?"

The child's eyes returned to the TV nearly in slow motion. "A cartoon."

"Fantastic. I love cartoons. Can I watch it with you?"

She raised her shoulders in a subtle shrug. "I guess so."

"Do you remember how we used to get up on Saturday mornings to watch cartoons together?"

The child looked up at him, her big blue eyes connecting with his for the first time since he'd brought her to the basement. She nodded then turned her attention back to the TV.

"That's my girl." Jack pulled her close to him, requiring her to rest against his chest.

Mindy returned from the shower to find them somewhat cuddled together on the couch.

"Hey, honey. We're watching some cartoons. Why don't you join us?"

Heath stirred a few times on the end of the couch, and Jack slid the boy's small body closer to him and rested the child's head in his lap. Mindy joined them on the couch next to Allie, and Jack stroked Heath's hair.

After one hour and two cartoons later, Heath opened his eyes and stared up at Jack. "Well, look who's waking up. Hello, son."

The boy blinked his eyes several times and appeared to be trying to cast off what might be the remnants of a dream. He tried to sit up but was not able to muster the energy to do so, so he rested back onto Jack's lap.

"Hey there, take it easy, big guy. It will take you a little bit to wake up. Take your time. We're watching some TV together. Do you want to watch some too?"

The boy's eyes moved around the room and stopped on the bed on the other side. He tried again to sit up but once again wasn't able to compel his body upright.

"Are you hungry? Mommy made some really great pot roast. We saved you some."

The boy's eyes darted around at the word mommy, and then stopped on the woman at the end of the couch.

Jack followed his gaze. "That's right, Chance. That's your real name, and she is your real mother. I know that probably seems a little confusing. You see, we had to keep some secrets from you to keep you safe. But finally you're home with your *real* family," Jack said applying emphasis on the word *real*.

Heath looked at the little girl next to the woman, and then his eyes moved once again to the bed across the room.

"That's Vivian. You can call her grandma. I'm sure she won't mind. She's been a little sick lately, but she loves little boys like you."

Mindy watched as Jack spoke to the child in a soothing and convincing manner. Her eyes dropped down to Allie who met her gaze. The girl's eyes were filled with questions. Mindy slowly shook her head at the young girl. Allie's eyes dropped to the floor as if she understood the subtle warning.

Heath's eyes returned to the little girl. His head nodded slightly towards her.

"And, that is your sister Faith. You two have been apart for a long while now, but you'll be fast friends. Your job will be to watch out for her. Even though she's a little older, you'll be stronger. Brothers need to take care of their sisters. Do you understand?"

A small nod came from the boy before he looked back up at Jack, their blue eyes connecting with each other. Jack did everything he could to express comfort and safety to the boy in that moment. He felt the child's body somewhat relax and watched as he drifted back to sleep.

"He's had a long day. For that matter, so have I. Why don't we all turn in? Tomorrow will be a really special day." Looking to Faith, he asked, "How would you like it if Daddy makes special pancakes tomorrow?"

Allie looked up and gently nodded before dropping her eyes to the floor again.

"Good deal. Then let's get your bed ready." Jack stood and turned to leave, taking the stairs two at a time. The basement door closed, and he returned a few minutes later with a set of sheets, a couple of blankets, and two pillows.

"I got the fold-out couch because I just knew we were going to need some more space. You two are young enough that you can sleep

653

together for a little while. Of course later…well, we'll see how that goes. We have a whole house to grow into with time. You two want to give me a hand?" Jack set the bedding down on the floor.

Mindy and Allie stood, and Jack lifted Heath off the couch and then gave Mindy instructions on how to pull the couch out into a bed. A minute later the room was filled with a queen sized bed, aligned pretty closely to Vivian's bed.

"I know this is a little crowded, but it'll have to do for now," Jack said while looking to Mindy to put the sheets on the bed.

"Al… Faith, why don't you go get your jammies on," Mindy said nearly slipping up and calling her Allie.

Allie did as she was told, and as Mindy got the bed made, the little girl reappeared just as Jack was laying Heath down.

"Okay, honey, climb in," Jack said. He seemed to suddenly realize something and turned to quickly climb the basement stairs. When he returned he had a book in his hand. "We can't expect you to go to sleep without a bed time story, can we?" Jack lifted Allie into the bed and tucked the blankets up to her chin, then sat on the edge next to her, and opened the book filled with bedtime stories. He picked one and began to read. Within a few moments Allie dropped off to sleep. Jack turned to Mindy. "Look at our kids. Aren't they beautiful?"

Mindy nodded as she offered up a forced smile.

"Now, it's time for us to turn in." Jack reached out and took Mindy's hand in his as he led her to the room just off where the kids and Vivian were fast asleep.

***

Mindy's heart raced as she felt herself being led to the bed, which she had until now shared with her daughter in the dank basement. She was hopeful that Jack would be too tired for what she was certain he had on his mind. After all, he had been up all night and all day. Her mind reeled as she considered her options.

"Are you tired, darling?"

She jumped, his voice pulling her out of her thoughts. "Yes, it's been a busy couple of days," she replied hoping it sounded convincing enough.

"Me too," he answered.

Pulling back the sheets, Jack tugged at his shirt and pulled it over his head. Then he kicked off his shoes and socks and tossed his pants over the back of a chair, his keys fell out and landed on the floor next to his shoes. He stood before her in nothing but his briefs and Mindy's heart pounded even harder at the sight of his muscular body. Fear enveloped her, making her feel light-headed. Suddenly, she had an idea. "I'll be right there," she said as she went to the bathroom.

Inside the small room, she took a moment to regain control of her emotions, flushed the toilet, and then splashed cool water on her face. Feeling a bit more in command of her body, she slipped on the pajama he'd bought for her then opened the door and returned to the bedroom where her heart immediately took flight again, pounding wildly in her chest when she saw him in the bed propped up against the pillows.

She compelled her legs to move forward. Her mind focused on protecting Allie as she slid under the sheets next to the madman her sister had married.

Jack turned to her. "God, you're stunning."

She pulled the blankets up tightly around her neck and snapped off the table lamp beside the bed, knowing her eyes would give away her fear. Suddenly, a memory invaded her mind. She recalled how Hope would rub Jack's neck and back–something he seemed to really enjoy. She decided it might be the only way to protect herself, at least for tonight.

"You've had such a long day. Why don't you let me rub your back? You know how it always relaxes you." After making the offer she lay in the now dark room, unable to see his face and waiting with anxiety for his reply.

"Oh, that sounds really fantastic. I'm very tired."

Mindy felt his body rolling in the bed and knew he had turned on his stomach. Sucking in her breath, she turned to him, placed her small hands on his back, and began to pray that her touch would not deceive her. All she could think of as she began to move her hands over his broad, muscular back was getting her and the children out of here alive. Somehow she must find a way.

It wasn't long until soft snores filled the room, and Mindy began to relax. She continued to massage Jack's back for a few more minutes, wanting to ensure he was fully asleep. Finally, she moved as far away from him as she could, being careful to not stir too suddenly, and curled her body into a tight ball. She lay there wondering what she could use in the room to kill him. *Could she kill him?* She wasn't sure, but then thoughts of him hurting Paul entered her mind. She wept softly in the dark. Sleep eventually took her.

***

Jack stirred in the bed. His arm reached to the place where he knew Hope would be resting next to him. His fingers found a crumple of soft blankets and pillow. Opening his eyes, he scanned the room while blinking out the sleep and welcoming the morning light. His gaze rested on Hope in the small kitchen as his nostrils filled with the scent of bacon and coffee. A smile covered his lips, and his chest welled with love. Tears filled his eyes. Suddenly, he realized his dreams had become a reality. He truly did have his family back, and the proof of it was right before him.

Rolling over in the bed, he scanned the rest of the room and saw Faith already awake on the fold out sofa with her little head propped against the big pillows. Scruffy was wrapped around her and lifted his head when he saw his master moving around. His tail made several thumps against the sheets. Chance was still asleep next to the girl and the dog. Jack looked at the boy and thought that today he should become much more alert as the medication wore off from his system. That big breakfast Hope was making was certainly going to help with the absorption.

Sitting up, Jack swung his strong legs over the side of the bed then stood, rubbing his eyes and stretching his muscles out. Grabbing his shoes and keys he went straight up the stairs seeking clean clothes.

Returning to the basement he went to Vivian's bedside to check on her. She too was awake and seemed fairly alert this morning.

"Well, good morning, sunshine. You look pretty chipper today."

The old woman smiled up at him then struggled out a raspy, "Good morning."

At the sound of his voice, there was a loud clatter from the kitchen. Mindy dropped the spatula and turned to face him.

"I'm sorry, dear. Did I startle you?" He looked at her with obvious concern on his face.

"I guess I didn't hear you get up," she quickly responded while recovering the kitchen implement from the floor and quickly moving to the small sink to rinse it off.

Moving away from the old woman, he crossed to his wife and wrapped his big arms around her waist from behind. "You know I would never do anything to intentionally frighten you. I'm sorry. I'll be more careful."

656

Mindy stood in his embrace, frozen in place. "It's okay," she choked out.

"This breakfast smells amazing. You're really spoiling me."

"Would you like some coffee?" Mindy asked, pulling away to reach for a cup.

"That would be great," he replied, not noticing that she pulled out of his embrace. "Let me see if I can wake up Chance. I think the food will really help him." Jack turned back towards the kids and faced Faith. "Good morning, sweetheart," he said as he sat next to Chance.

Allie stared at him then managed a meek, "Good morning."

Mindy watched the exchange from the kitchen then turned back to the cup and filled it with coffee. She took the cup to Jack, setting it on the small table next to the couch.

"Thank you, darling." Jack smiled up at her.

He turned his attention back to Chance after giving Scruffy a few good scratches behind the ears. "Hey, buddy. Time to start trying to wake up." He shook the child lightly and then pulled the boy's small body next to him, cradling him against his chest.

The boy's eyes slowly opened. He blinked several times then his small fists came up to his face and rubbed in an obvious effort to wipe away the grogginess he clearly still felt.

"It's morning, and Mommy is making us a wonderful breakfast. You need to wake up so you can eat. Eating is going to make you feel a whole lot better."

The boy pushed his body up and sat up on his own. He looked all around, at first seeming confused, and then appearing to remember his short moment of being awake the night before. "Mommy?" he asked seeming confused again.

"That's right. There's a lot for me to explain to you. Do you feel good enough to stand up? We could take a little walk. Scruffy needs to go outside. Would you like to go with me to take him?"

Wide blue eyes turned to search Jack's face then shifted to the dog cuddled on the little girl who lay next to him on the bed. He nodded his head and began trying to push his body off the bed.

"Okay, take it easy, little guy. You might be a little bit wobbly at first," Jack warned as he watched the boy clambering to get off the bed. "Hope, honey, we're going to take Scruffy out for a minute. How soon before breakfast is ready?"

Mindy partially faced Jack then answered, "Ten minutes."

"Oh, perfect. We'll see my girls in just a few minutes."

Heath was now standing, while still rubbing at his eyes.

"Okay, I promised Faith pancakes so I'll mix those up real quick when we get back in. Come on, little man," Jack said while taking the boy's little hand and snapping his fingers for Scruffy to come with them. The wiry little dog happily bounced off of the bed and bounded up the stairs ahead of Jack and the child.

At the top of the stairs Jack unlocked the door. The deadbolt made a heavy clicking sound as the tumbler released from its hold. Then just as quickly, he locked the door behind him, sealing Mindy and Allie inside. Still holding the boy's hand, Jack led him through the house to the kitchen while on Scruffy's heels. At the back door Jack unlocked that too, and the dog immediately pushed through to get out into the sunlight. The morning was glorious with the sun already claiming the day.

"Let's take a little walk, and I'll do my best to explain everything to you. I know you're a little confused right now," Jack said leading the boy out into the daylight.

Following the dog, the boy walked with Jack through the woods along a half-beaten down path. Jack waited, allowing the sunlight and warmth of the day to provide some natural comfort before he began.

"First, let me start by telling you your real name. It's Chance, not whatever you've been called before. Also, I can finally tell you that I am your real father and Hope downstairs is your real mother. The little girl is your sister Faith. You see, when you were very young you were taken from us. I can't really explain why, but I'm sure people thought it was the best way to protect you. Now you're safe and back where you need to be. We're all safe now, here in this house."

The child stopped and looked up at Jack. His head tilted way back as he squinted against the sun that peeked through the trees. "Where's Mark?'

Jack hesitated for a minute then knelt down to eye level with the boy. "He is the one who brought you to me. You see, he was part of the whole plan—he and Maxine. The trip to California wasn't really a family vacation, but rather a plan to bring you back where you belong. They couldn't tell you because it wasn't safe to do so. There are still very bad people out there. Mark and Maxine love you very much, but had to keep secrets in order to get you back to me, your mother, and sister. Getting you home to us is all we've been dreaming of and what Mark and Maxine were required to do. It's their job as FBI agents to get kids back to their *real* parents," Jack emphasized *real*. "It's been a long time, and I couldn't be more proud of how brave you've been. I know there are times you've been alone and scared."

Jack stared into the boy's face. "Chance, we love you, and it has broken our hearts to be away from you for so long. But now... now we can really be a family, and no one can ever take you from us again."

Heath searched Jack's face and then suddenly was almost bowled over by Scruffy who eagerly jumped and licked at the child's face. Heath giggled and wiped at the wet kisses left on his cheeks. Jack laughed heartily with him, and soon they were both rolling around on the ground as the dog pounced on them.

Covered in leaves Jack stood up and pulled at the boy's hands, freeing him from the dog's continued tongue-lashing and lifting him onto his shoulders to give him a piggy back ride. "Are you hungry? I'm starving, and I bet that great breakfast Mommy is making is ready now."

Heath latched his arms around Jack's big shoulders. "Me too," he said still giggling.

"Come on, Scruffy. It's time for your breakfast too," Jack called out to the dog. Scruffy quickly turned hopping and jumping around and headed towards the house.

Chapter Twenty-Five

As soon as Mindy heard the door to the basement click locked, she went and sat next to Allie who remained on the couch absorbed in a cartoon on the TV. So far, Mindy was grateful that Allie seemed to have no recollection of meeting Jack. She was so young when Hope died and Jack hadn't really been around since having fallen apart following the accident.

"Allie, listen to me," the concerned mother said, making her small child look at her. "We are in danger here. You have been doing so good. In order to stay safe we're going to have to do whatever that man says. Do you understand?"

The little girl's blue eyes seemed dull compared to their normal bright and shiny glow that had always been filled with excitement and curiosity. She nodded her head, but said nothing.

"I know this is scary, but I hope someone will find us soon. In the meantime all you have to do is whatever that man says, okay? He won't hurt you as long as you play along. We can act like this is a game, okay? We'll pretend this is our real family."

Still staring up at her mother, Allie finally spoke, "Where's Daddy?"

Mindy choked back tears and forced a smile. "He's at home, and I'm sure he's looking for us every minute." Trying to keep her face from showing Allie her own concerns about her husband and other daughter's welfare, she pulled the little girl close to her, hugging her so tightly the child started to squirm.

"Mommy, you're hurting me."

"I'm sorry, honey," Mindy said letting her grip loose a little bit. "Now listen, the man will be back very soon. We have to play our game, okay?"

"Is that boy my brother?" Allie asked obviously confused.

"He is in the game. So just act like he is, okay?"

Mindy pulled back from the child and looked down at her again. The child's eyes stared up at her, and finally her little head nodded.

"Okay, now I have to make our family breakfast to make your pretend daddy happy." Mindy kissed her daughter on the head and then stood and returned to the makeshift kitchen. As she passed the bed she looked down at the frail old woman before continuing her duty of feeding the madman who had once been her sister's childhood friend and husband.

Chapter Twenty-Six

Max was exhausted. It had been twenty-four hours since Heath had been discovered as missing, and there was not a single sign of where he'd gone. They'd formed a search and rescue recovery room back at the LAPD headquarters, and she was suddenly surrounded by familiar faces from her days as a homicide detective on the force.

In addition, Mark had called in three of the FBI agents from the prior murder investigations from the Jack Tyler cases that had spanned across several states. She knew they had top talent and that they would not cease their efforts until Heath was found. She was struggling to keep her composure, and she could see the strain in Mark's face as well.

The task force already pinned up the details of what they knew, including photos of the open doors in the home. Crime scene investigators had searched Shauna's house from top to bottom, even crawl spaces and the attic, and found nothing.

They'd collected bits of evidence and fingerprinted every door frame and knob in the home, as well as taking prints from the entire family. It would take a few hours—maybe even a day, despite the chief's absolute demand that this had top priority—to get any prints that should not be in the home. Even then, those would need to be eliminated one by one as other friends of the family, repair people, or anyone that may have had access to the home for valid reasons.

Both Mark and Max gave their depiction over and over again of the events since their departure from their home in Virginia. They were repeatedly asked if there was anyone who may have shown a particular interest in Heath at the airports, on the plane, or at the beach.

Max began to feel chills run through her as she thought of her last conversation with Jack Tyler. He'd warned that he could be right near her, and she would never even know it. They knew he had changed his appearance by using a plastic surgeon's skills prior to killing the man and then vanished into thin air.

Wracking her brain she tried to picture anyone around them on the plane or sitting nearby in the airport that might have stood out or shown too much interest in them. She tried to remember every car at the beach, but she'd been so happy to be seeing her sister and nephew and to be watching Heath experience so many new things that she couldn't seem to conjure up any images that stood out. *Am I getting paranoid? Why would Jack take Heath?*

The white board had a timeline of events drawn out, a map of the area, photos of Heath, Jack Tyler, Hope, Faith, and of Mindy and Allie. As she sat and looked at the board she couldn't hold back her thoughts.

"It's a long shot, but we have to seriously consider that Jack Tyler has taken Heath and the Prescott's." She felt frantic and spoke cautiously, not wanting to inject her paranoia into the investigation. She'd already spoken this concern to Mark and the chief but now felt confident enough to speak it more broadly. She knew full well throwing ideas into the mix could cause long unnecessary distractions that could lead to delays in recovering Heath.

Her comments caused a lengthy discussion and no one really knew why Jack Tyler would take Heath. So far he had only been focused on what seemed to be the resurrection of his dead family. There was one question that everyone seemed equally concerned about and that was whether Tyler could have changed his focus to hurting Max. And why would he do that? They did all agree that there was no doubt he had focused on her during the prior investigation, calling her directly on more than one occasion.

Leaving the team to ponder the bomb she'd dropped, Max stood and stretched her legs and ran her hands through her thick hair. She felt like adrenaline was ramping through her veins. Anxiety was driving her every thought. She wanted Heath back and she wanted him right now, but had no way to just make that happen. Being out of control was maddening.

Mark and Cortez walked up to Max. Cortez handed her a cup of coffee. "It's not any better than it was when you worked here, but it's warm and there's caffeine in it." Cortez had a serious look on her face despite the subtle reminder of the terrible brew the LAPD was somewhat infamous for making. Her friend and former colleague almost always carried herself in strict professionalism on the job. Max knew her softer and funnier side from before she'd moved away because of the nights they had spent hanging out in Max's house drinking wine, talking smack about the guys in the LAPD house, and attempting to track Tyler's next move.

"Thanks, Cortez," Max said, accepting the Styrofoam cup and thinking to herself, *Oh great, more caffeine.*

"Do you have an update for us?" Mark asked.

"We don't have much. The Amber Alert has provided some tips, but nothing legitimate so far. There are techs on the phone, and we still have officers on the street re-canvassing the neighborhood and beach area."

Max nodded, noting the sadness in Mark's tone. Her heart tore as she remembered his story of the loss of his younger brother who was taken and killed by a neighborhood grocer when Mark was just a kid. She wasn't sure he could handle another loss like that, and she knew for certain he would feel responsible if something happened to Heath, just as he felt responsible for his younger brother Tommy's death.

"I know I'm close to this case, but my gut tells me Tyler is responsible for this," Max offered, knowing the implications of her words. So far no one Jack Tyler had taken had survived except for the little girl in Illinois, and even then he'd damaged her for life by cutting off her mouth and replacing it with that of another child he'd murdered. "We have nothing else, and while the Amber Alert is out we need to start focusing on Tyler. Have any of his known aliases been used in any way? We need to search everything, credit cards, prior bank accounts, passports—everything."

Mark nodded his head in agreement. Immediately taking charge and doing what he was best at, Mark seemed to shake off his own personal fears and stepped into his role of Special Agent in Charge. "We need to divide our efforts. Cortez, can we get the local team to focus on search and rescue efforts, while I align my agents around the Tyler theory? We'll get more done this way."

Cortez didn't even wait to answer. She turned and headed in the direction of the chief.

Mark looked down at Max before gazing at the white board and then called out to the team, "Jenkins, I want you working all past names Tyler has associated with. See if you can find anything. Everyone else, we need to focus our efforts on possible locations where Tyler might go, and we need someone to work on the possible names we have that Tyler might use next. Those are a long shot given we don't know where he might be, but if he truly is responsible for the abduction of the Prescott's, he's likely still on the west coast. That would put him in both Arizona and California in a very short period of time. Let's start our search in these two states then branch out from there."

Max jumped in. "I'll take the likely aliases. I have the file."

Without any more words, the small team went into action.

Chapter Twenty-Seven

Jack went into action when he returned to the basement and made the kids funny-faced pancakes adding them to the already fantastic breakfast Mindy had prepared. The dishes were washed and put away when Mindy asked Jack to go out and pick up some groceries, giving him a list of items she wanted. Jack was happy to oblige her request and didn't even realize that her motivation of the request was less about the need for any food items was and more about keeping him away from her and Allie. Even as he kissed her before leaving, he failed to notice the gasp she was unable to refrain from releasing.

Jack resisted the idea of taking Chance with him. As much as he desired having his son with him everywhere he went, he knew the boy was still settling in. After giving both kids a peck on their respective cheeks, he told them he would be home soon and then ascended the stairs out of the basement. Before departing the house he double checked all the locks.

The day was sunny and warm, causing him to smile at his good fortune. Everything was truly perfect now. Pulling the car out onto the street, Jack turned on the radio and tapped his fingers to the music as he drove. He arrived at the local grocery and parked the vehicle in the first available space before going inside.

Getting a cart, he started on the first aisle going through one by one collecting the items from his list. He rounded the corner of the fourth aisle and nearly stopped dead in his tracks when he saw Jimmy, Vivian's less than qualified former caregiver. Continuing down the row, he smiled when he got closer. "Jimmy, good to see you," he said insincerely while applying that natural charm that had always worked for him.

Jimmy looked up from the shelf he'd been focused on, a smile crossing his face. "Well, hello. How is Miss Vivian doing?"

"She's doing fine," he lied again, not wanting to disclose anything about the woman's condition. It took a lot of composure to maintain a pleasant look on his face when in reality he wanted to be anything but cordial.

"Well, good seeing you, man," Jimmy said smiling, and then returned to scanning the shelf where his attention had originally been.

"Yes, I'll be seeing you," Jack replied before continuing to gather the items on the shopping list. Walking through the aisles he could feel the sudden welling of darkness filling his entire being. His mind flashed to images of Reb laying on the cold stainless steel table, but even remembering his time with her wasn't helping his suddenly sullen mood.

Staring at spaghetti sauces, on every can and jar all he saw was Jimmy's face smeared with blood, the tomato pastes blending in with the images perfectly. Forcing himself to focus, he selected one of the sauces and placed it into the cart, then continued through the store getting all the items before checking out.

Placing his purchases into the back of the vehicle, Jack got in, closed the door, and sat in the parking lot for a moment trying to gather his thoughts and push back the dark feelings that overcame him after seeing Jimmy in the store. He mindlessly turned the key in the ignition, starting the vehicle's engine. A news story interrupted his thoughts. Reaching for the volume, he twisted the knob and listened carefully.

"The son of husband and wife FBI top serial profilers, Mark and Maxine Wells, has allegedly been abducted. The five year old went missing yesterday in the early hours. Local police and the FBI are working together, but at this time they reportedly do not have any solid leads. Because the Special Agents were the lead investigators in the case of 'Most Wanted' serial killer Jack Tyler, speculation is already swirling as to whether the serial murderer could be involved in the child's disappearance."

Jack was stunned at first, but then of course realized he'd known all along that the investigators would assume he was involved. He turned the rear view mirror towards him. He looked at his face, turned side to side, and smiled. No way would anyone recognize him. Feeling confident that he was safe from Maxine's clutches, temptation rose and an idea began to form.

Pulling out of the parking lot, he headed the car towards the Dollar General and pulled into one of the front row spaces. He exited the vehicle and clicked the remote to lock the groceries inside, and then walked into the store, making a left just past the register. Within a couple of minutes he had secured his item and stood waiting to check out.

Returning to the vehicle he looked around. He thought for a moment that he might be getting paranoid then shrugged it off, knowing full well that unlike what was depicted in the movies the police could not find someone by mere background noises on a phone call. Pulling his personal cell phone from his pocket, he first checked the video monitoring equipment and saw his family sitting together on the couch. Nothing seemed out of the ordinary. A perfect picture, so he felt confident he had more time.

He punched the button on his phone to bring up his contact list, and then reached inside the bag containing his purchase from inside the small convenience store. Quickly peeling off the packaging, he pulled out the disposable phone and went through the setup options. He punched in the numbers from the contact list in his personal cell phone and waited for the call to connect.

Soon his wish was granted. "Agent Wells," Max answered. The persistent ring jolted her away from the research she'd been focused on.

"I saw the news report, Maxine. It seems you have a new last name."

Snapping her fingers, Max stood. "Jack, so I do. What have you done with Heath?"

"Tsk, tsk. Why must you always go straight to business? You really should relax some."

Mark and the others quickly surrounded her, and Mark turned his own phone on next to hers in an effort to record the call. "Funny, Jack, but somehow my son being missing seems to have put a damper on my relaxation time. Now, why don't you tell me what you've done with him, and I can go back to vacationing?"

"Sorry, can't help you with that, but you know I must say that husband of yours really shouldn't leave such a beautiful woman and child vulnerable like that. It's truly a terrible thing, someone coming in and taking a child right out from under your noses."

"How do you know he was taken from under our noses, Jack? Maybe because you were there? Why not tell me where he is?"

"It's not becoming of you, Agent, to sound so... desperate."

"Jack, come on. You know what it's like losing a child. If anyone would understand having the need to get a child back home, it's you."

"Nice try, Agent." Jack laughed at her efforts.

"How is your family holding up? I'm thinking your pieced-together family rotted away. Not quite what you hoped for. Was it? Is that why you took Mindy and her daughter? Did you need a fast replacement?"

"My family is just fine, Agent. Nice talking to you. Don't worry that pretty, red head of yours. All is well. I do hope things work out as they should for you, Agent. It's always nice talking with you."

Jack ended the call and tossed the phone in the plastic bag along with the packaging. Then he placed the car in reverse and backed out of the space, pointing his car towards home.

Chapter Twenty-Eight

Max stood staring at the phone. "Please, tell me you got it."

"Detective Cortez, we need a trace on Max's phone. Can you arrange that? This isn't the first time Tyler has contacted her, and he may do it again," Mark said immediately going into action.

Cortez took Max's phone, and with a nod, left the room.

"Agent Adams, please get this recording captured and do everything you can to pull out anything that might indicate where it may have come from. Run trace on Max's cell as soon as Cortez is done. Maybe he got careless, and the call will lead us somewhere."

Adams took Mark's phone and immediately went to work on it after sitting down at the table and plugging the phone into the USB port on his laptop.

Max watched as Mark got everyone in motion. The room seemed to swirl around her. She pictured the bodies of the children in Illinois with their limbs removed, and her heart raced as her mind placed Heath's face on each one of them. She could barely stand, her legs feeling weak under her. Trying to gain her composure, Max placed her hand on the back of the chair near the table she had previously been sitting in and stabilized herself. There was a glass of water on the table, and she reached for it and raised it to her lips, letting the cool water into her mouth.

Mark was suddenly near her side. "Are you okay? You don't look well."

"I'm scared, but I'm fine," she replied not making eye contact with him, knowing he would be able to read her.

Mark nodded. "We'll find him, Max. We have to find him."

"I know. We just need to focus. Come on, let's go over the call."

Mark pulled the chair out, allowing Max to sit down which immediately made her head feel better. He sat in the chair next to her and was joined by Agent Jenkins. "Okay, let's walk it through. The first part of the call I didn't get, so you have to tell us exactly what he said when the call originated."

Max sighed and ran her hands through her thick, red hair. She felt something that she hadn't noticed before now, something about her hair in the back. She ran her fingers through her hair again, and this time she was certain something was wrong. She worked her hands down the strands along the back left side of her head.

"Max, are you ready?" Mark asked, seeming confused by her silence.

"Mark, look at the back of my hair. It feels like it's been cut. There's a part that feels short compared to the rest." She turned her back to him, allowing him access to the back of her head.

Mark pulled her hair back into his own hands and followed her fingers along the strands. His strong, thick fingers struggled to feel with the same nimble movements, but Max's hand led his to the specific area of her concern. He bent his head down to look under the locks and could see the blunt cut across the back of her hair. There was a strand about two inches wide that was clearly two to three inches shorter. It was difficult to see as it was at the back and slightly under the outer most parts of her hair.

Max turned back to face Mark and asked, "Well?"

"It seems like there is a two or three inch square missing." Mark responded, concern covering his face.

"Tyler said something about my red hair. I assumed he was referring to photos he'd seen or from the television coverage during our investigation. I know he's seen me before, but I think he was taunting me. Mark, my hair is cut!"

"If he cut your hair, it certainly means he was in Shauna's home, and it means...," Mark's words trailed off, unable to complete the sentence that this would no doubt mean Tyler had taken Heath.

"Who else could have done this?"

Agent Jenkins lifted Max's hair again and snapped a few pictures with a camera on her cell phone, and then emailed them to each of the members on the team.

Mark held Max's eyes for a moment then spoke, "We have to focus. Walk me through the whole phone call."

Max looked at Mark and could see the pain in his eyes. She knew he was torn between concern for her and the thought that Jack Tyler had been close enough to cut her hair. She couldn't help but wonder if he was holding it while talking to her right now. He always demonstrated his smug attitude when he called. He clearly knew he had the upper hand. *Heath, focus on Heath. It's just hair.* "Okay let's do this," she said with a focused quick nod of her head.

"Okay," Mark nodded at her and glanced at Agent Jenkins. "What was the very first thing he said? We really need to get the first part of the conversation down."

672

***

About an hour later they had gone over the phone call several times and were now replaying a cleaned version of the recording Mark had made from holding his own cell phone up to Max's phone. Max's side of the conversation was very clear. Tyler was harder to hear, and it was nearly impossible to catch any background noises that potentially would indicate where Tyler was calling from.

Max listened to the recording several times and filled in any gaps. Tyler never actually admitted being in the house, but the reference to her hair and then the cutting clearly indicated that Tyler was, in fact, responsible for Heath's disappearance.

Agent Adams confirmed that Tyler used a disposable phone, and it was untraceable. Once again, they had nothing.

Mark stopped everyone. "We have to go back to what we were doing. There's a lead somewhere. We just have to find it. In five minutes I want an update on what ground everyone has covered."

Cortez returned to the room while they were going over Max's statement. "I know it is unlikely Tyler will call again. He's smart and knows we will attempt to trace any new calls, but if he does call, the trap is set and we'll get him.

Though Tyler had not admitted or said anything that could connect him to the abduction and disappearance of Mindy and her daughter, he had them. Max was sure of it. She could only assume that something had gone wrong with the bodies he had so lovingly built. Her stomach suddenly rolled over at the thought of all the people that had died so he could make those pseudo replacements for his family. Now, he had moved forward to live replacements. She was certain of it. She could *feel* it.

"I believe he has Heath, Mindy, and Allie," she heard herself saying out loud.

"He's never kept hostages," Jenkins said, then nearly recoiled at the gravity of her words and what that would mean to her fellow FBI agents, specifically the boy's adoptive parents.

"Because he thought he couldn't. I don't mean not capable. I mean it never occurred to him. But Mindy and Allie, well, they're just too tempting, too much of a resemblance to Hope and Faith. My bet is those bodies, his little experiments, began to fail. He immediately needed to replace them. There were only two ways to do that: start over and hopefully perfect the process or find the very next best thing."

673

Mark nodded his head. "There's no doubt Mindy's a dead ringer for Hope." He turned to look at the white board and the assorted photos. The pictures of Hope and Mindy were remarkably close, as were the photos of Faith and Allie. "They both are actually very close, but how does Heath fit in?"

Max pushed her chair back and jumped up, grabbing a folder on the table opposite them, and then flipped through several pages. After several minutes she came and sat back down. "I can't find it, but I swear there was something Tyler said about a son. Maybe it's just my mind playing tricks on me, but something was said about him and Hope planning another child and how he wanted a son." She shook her head in frustration and concern that she might not be remembering something real.

Agent Jenkins spoke up, "We could ask the brother-in-law, Paul, if he knows whether Hope and Jack were planning another child. He may know. It's a start."

Mark added, "If we're right, I don't think he'll hurt them unless they try to get away or fight him in some way. Mindy knows he's a psychopath, so let's hope she's smart enough to keep him focused."

Max continued the thought, "She may be in more danger than the kids. If he believes she is his wife…" The idea hung in the air like a very thick cloud. Max knew if Jack thought Mindy was his wife Hope, there would be certain things he would expect from her, and if she couldn't deter him or comply with his demands she would be in eminent danger.

"What do we have so far?" Mark asked trying to get everyone back to tracking Jack, knowing it was the only way they would actually find him.

Jenkins spoke up first, "I've tracked most of the names against former bank accounts and social security numbers. Nothing pops. I'm working on credit report searches now. I should have each of those within the hour."

"Good," Mark said turning to Agent Adams. "What about you?"

"I've been triangulating off of the abductions sites and most recent activities while factoring in the time between the Prescott abduction and the time since Heath's abduction. He can only be in California, Arizona, Utah, or Nevada. He wouldn't have had enough time to drive into Oregon or New Mexico. I'm now trying to tie these out to the locations from the magazines Jack had as a child. We know so far he's stuck pretty close to those locations. Within a couple of hours I'll be able to state specifically where he is most likely located."

674

"We're going to have to narrow it down. That is massive geography," Max countered.

"I understand," Adams defended. "I'm working on it, trying to take the states within driving range since Heath's abduction and then narrowing in on the cities, which will narrow our search efforts."

Mark looked over at Max and could sense her frustration but continued to push, "Cortez, any luck with canvases?"

"Nothing has panned out. We've had several reported sightings from the Amber Alert, but all so far have been a bust. Additionally, we still have a foot patrol in the neighborhood conducting new and re-interviews as well as keeping a focus on the beach areas. Max's phone is set up to trace. If Tyler calls again, we'll trap him."

Max jumped in, "I've been working the potential names Tyler would choose next, based off the research Bobby gave us. I also have the history on prior names. The prior identities associate back to names of people that died as an infant. Those names were dormant with no social security information until Jack starting using them. " She nodded her head at Cortez, knowing she wouldn't have that information without her help. "The hardest part is narrowing the names down. The list is long for each. As soon as Adams has the cities narrowed, I can target those areas first. Then I can try to tie them back to a deceased infant of the same name."

"Okay, Adams. Pressure is on you." Mark directed, "Everyone focused."

With that direction they each went to their respective assignments. Everyone understood the gravity of the situation. Mark asked Cortez to get someone into an interview right away with Mindy's husband Paul. They needed to know anything and everything he might know about Jack's desire to have a son. All information Paul provided would be helpful in understanding what Jack might do next, or where he might take Mindy and the kids.

Max watched Mark make another call, after requesting Paul's interview, and petitioned another agent to be assigned to reassessing Paul and Mindy's home for any possible things that might have been overlooked in the original investigation. She knew it was a slim chance that anything new might be discovered, but realized Mark wasn't willing to take a chance on missing even the slightest detail that might provide a lead. Heath's safe return depended on every possible trace being carefully reviewed.

Max had to force her mind not to consider that Jack may have already killed the boy she had come to love dearly. If Jack was still creating people from the combined bodies of several victims, he may have wanted only certain parts of Heath. Her body shuddered at the thought and the images that came with it. Despite the terrifying feeling this gave her, she suddenly realized if this were the case there would likely be other kids missing too.

"Mark, we may be missing something. We need to focus on possible other missing kids. If Jack is creating a son rather than just taking one, there will be other kids. Let's face it; he killed people to restore his wife and daughter. So unless that process failed, he may follow it again." She swallowed heavily, realizing that she was suggesting that Heath may have been cut into parts to create the body of a potential son for Tyler's sick collection of bodies he considered to be his family. She winced slightly as she saw the look on Mark's face.

Mark's dark blue eyes flashed from torment to focus. "Okay, Jenkins, while you're waiting on the credit reports focus on possible other missing kids. Keep it specific to the areas Adams said are within scope. These would have to be very recent abductions. Keep the search narrowed, between the abduction of Mindy and her daughter and today. We can't know whether Heath would be the first child or not. Also, we should expect to see abductions, murders, or dumps of women or female children that match Faith's description. If his original creations have failed, he may have taken Mindy and Allie to start over."

Max's eyes met Mark's, and her heart tore. There was a sadness he couldn't hide. Cortez walked up and grabbed her by the arm. "Walk with me for a cup of coffee?" Max looked at her not wanting to waste any time, but she nodded and followed her friend and former partner to the break room.

"What's up?" Max asked, trying to hide her crumbling resolve.

"Just checking on you. How are you holding up? I'm worried."

Max shook her head. "I'm a wreck but trying to stay focused. Mark can barely look at me. I don't think I ever told you about his younger brother Tommy. Let's just say something happened to Tommy when they were young kids, and Mark feels responsible for his death. I know he feels responsible again. I'm not sure what happens to him if we don't get Heath back alive."

Max prepared a cup of coffee, and she could tell Cortez wanted to reassure her, but hesitated. She knew her hesitation was because the promises would be empty. Knowing Tyler the way she did, anything was possible. In fact, given Tyler's M.O. there was a really good chance that Heath was dead within hours of being taken.

"I appreciate it, Cortez. Let's just get Tyler and make this madness stop," Max said, balancing her coffee cup in her right hand.

"You got it. No getting away this time. Tyler is ours." Cortez patted Max on the shoulder as they headed back to the investigation room where the others were still working away.

Chapter Twenty-Nine

After hanging up the phone, Jack struggled to keep his composure. He replayed the call in his head and suddenly realized that he'd given Agent Maxine Wells a lot to think about. He smiled as he recognized that he never really confirmed anything about his involvement. The more he thought about the call, the more certain he became that there was no way the FBI agents would know how to track him. For a few moments, he felt good as he drove.

When he passed the grocery store he had been in earlier, he remembered Jimmy the surfer. He started thinking about the way that young man had treated Vivian, and the darkness seemed to close in again. He started thinking about his strong fingers wrapped around Jimmy's heart, and his mood lifted slightly.

Jack pulled into the driveway and navigated the vehicle up the curved path and then hit the button to open the garage door with the remote that was slipped over the visor. Inside with the door closed behind him, he retrieved his grocery bags and carried them through the garage and house to the basement door. Retrieving the key to the deadbolt from his pocket, he listened carefully for any movement while holding several bags in his other hand before he opened the door. Hearing nothing unusual he twisted the key in the lock, pulled the door open, and stepped through the doorway, closing the door behind him.

Descending the stairs he was pleased to see his family on the couch all cuddled together. Hope sat with Faith on her left and Chance on her right. Vivian lay nearby in her bed. It was a sight to behold. He could hardly believe his good fortune, his beautiful family enjoying the day together.

Chance saw him and immediately jumped up and ran to his side, as did Scruffy who had been lying near the couch on the floor. "What did you get?"

"Just some groceries, big guy, but I did get some donuts for a special treat, and some ice cream."

"Can I see what kind?"

"Sure, come over here and help me put the groceries away."

Heath hovered over Jack as he placed the items out on the small table and then slowly put them away. "Can we have pizza? I love pizza."

"Of course we can," Jack replied looking over at Mindy. "As long as your mommy says it's okay."

Mindy nodded. "Sure, we can. Maybe tonight for dinner."

Jack smiled at Hope. Her beauty always amazed him.

With the groceries put away, Jack grabbed the remaining bag that lay on the table and turned to Heath. "Chance, want to go with me to take Scruffy for a walk?"

The boy was bounding up the stairs with the small dog nearly as fast as the words came out of Jack's mouth. "Yes, can we walk in the woods again?"

"Sure, we can. I want to show you my playhouse from when I was a boy. You're going to love it. You know, that's where me and Mommy played all the time."

"Really?"

"Yes, really. Come on, I'll show you. Faith, do you want to come too?"

Allie pushed into Mindy and shook her head.

"She still seems a little tired. Maybe another day she'll feel a little better and want to go with you. You boys go and have fun. We'll be here when you get back," Mindy offered.

Jack smiled and nodded, not realizing Mindy's comments were intended to pacify his desire to have Allie go with him. He turned and followed Heath up the stairs. "Okay ready, Chance? It looks like it's just us boys."

"Ready!" Heath responded.

The man and boy slipped through the door behind the dog. Jack closed and locked the door then walked towards the back of the house. "Hold up, Chance. I need to get the shovel."

"What are you going to dig for?"

"I'll show you."

"Can I help?"

"Sure, buddy. Let me grab the shovel, and you can help." Jack smiled at his son, and his heart burst with pride. He retrieved the tool from the garage and returned to find Scruffy and Heath playing together by the back door. Scruffy immediately started hopping around anxious to go outside. "Hold on, Scruffy," Jack said laughing at the sight.

Jack pulled the back door open, and both the dog and the boy darted out into the sunlight. Heath quickly ran out into the woods and headed down the path. "Hold on, guys. Wait for me," Jack called out to them.

They wandered down the path, stepping over the brambles that seemed to try and wrap around their ankles. Heath ran ahead when he saw the small wooden building looming in the distance. "Is this the playhouse?" Heath shouted out with excitement in his voice.

"Yes, that's it. I spent a lot of time in there when I was a boy. Mommy lived down the road just a little. And she would ride over on her bike, and we would play out here for hours. The walls of that little house know everything there is to know about me."

Heath looked on at the building in amazement. "Can I go inside?"

"Of course you can. It's yours now. I hope you'll enjoy it as much as I did."

"I DO love it. It's perfect." Heath opened the door, the hinges complaining from lack of use over the years. He let the door close behind him and then stood and peeked back out at Jack through the small circular hole in the door. "Did you play games in here?" Heath asked standing on his tip toes to look through the opening in the door.

Jack considered this question, and his mind flashed to all the things he had done in that little building. "Well, why don't you come out here and maybe I'll start to show you some things I used to do. But first, we need to dig a hole. Still want to help?"

"Uh-huh." Heath came out of the building and anxiously stood next to Jack.

"Okay, let's pick a good spot."

"How do we know if it's a good spot?"

"Well, if you have something important enough to bury, then you better pick a spot that you can remember and that you are pretty sure no one else will ever find."

"What important thing are we burying?"

"We are burying a phone."

"Why are we burying a phone? Don't you need your phone?"

"This phone is a special phone, not my normal phone, and it's one I don't want anyone to ever know I had. Where do you think a good spot would be?"

Heath looked around. His eyes scanned the area. "Under the playhouse is a good spot."

Jack smiled. "You know, when I was your age I thought so too. I had some special things buried there, but someone found them, so I didn't find a good enough spot."

"Oh." Heath looked around some more. "What about under that tree?" He pointed to the east at a big oak tree that seemed to dominate the area.

Jack smiled. "Now that looks like a good spot. Let's do it."

They walked over to the base of the tree, and Jack dug the shovel deep into the soil, then handed the shovel over to Heath. Scruffy ran up and began digging with his paws, helping Heath out as the small boy struggled to manage the shovel covered in heavy amounts of soil. Jack's chest welled with pride as he watched Chance and the little dog digging away.

Seeing Chance getting tired, Jack stepped back in and helped finish the hole, giving it one last deep pitch. Then he lifted the bag containing the packaging and cell phone and dropped it onto the ground next to the tree. He pushed it into the hole with his shoe. He scooped a pile of dirt in on it, and then let Heath finish covering it up.

Jack stood back and looked at where they'd just finished and said, "Look at it, Chance. Will you remember it?"

"Yes," the boy answered.

"Will anyone else be able to find it?"

Heath looked around, and then his face fell. The mounds of dirt were uneven, and it was obvious the ground had been disturbed. The boy seemed sad when he realized that maybe he hadn't done a good job. "Yes."

"So what do we do about that?"

Heath looked around and then walked back to the tree and began putting leaves over the dirt. "Cover it up?"

"That's right, son. You got it. We have to cover it up so no one will see it."

Jack proceeded to help fill in the dirt with leaves and twigs. A few minutes later, he asked Heath the same question, only this time Heath stood looking up at him with a proud smile on his face.

With the phone properly buried and hidden, Heath ran off to explore in the playhouse again. Jack sat down on a fallen log nearby and watched as the boy and dog played. His eyes darted around the woods that he was so familiar with. He loved these woods, so many good memories here. A squirrel danced up and down on a nearby tree. Jack watched, his senses awakened by the twitching of the squirrel's tail.

Heath saw the rodent and pointed to it. "Look, Daddy."

"Yes, Chance, that's a squirrel. I used to play with those when I was a boy out here."

"You can catch them?"

"Well, I used to be able to. I would set up a little trap for it so I could catch it."

"Can we set a trap and catch it?"

Jack could see the excitement in the child's eyes. "Okay, but not today. We probably need to get back inside."

"Awww," Heath complained, but as Jack stood up he immediately followed him back to the house.

***

The day withered away. The kids watched some TV, and then Jack talked the whole family into playing a game together. Hope seemed to be more herself now, and he really enjoyed the time together. But as night started to set, he felt anxious, and it seemed as if his skinned crawled.

His blood felt hot inside his veins, and despite the happiness he felt, he couldn't seem to focus on his family. The darkness was starting to become demanding. Being in California was good; his family was good. But he was not practicing medicine, and without the outlet that he and Hope had designed for him to release the relentless desire, he couldn't fight the pressure that was clearly building. As dice lay on the table in front of him requiring his play, he could only see Jimmy's face. Each tiny dot appeared as a speck of blood calling him to action.

Struggling to maintain his composure, he wrapped up the game and then indicated to Hope that it was time for the kids to go to bed.

"Later I need to go out for a while," he explained to her, wondering what her reaction might be.

"Okay," Mindy replied.

Jack sighed with relief that she didn't challenge him on where he might be going. His mind flashed to the day in the playhouse when they'd vowed to work together to hold back the darkness. Today she seemed to understand and was not questioning him. He wasn't certain he understood her reaction, but was grateful nonetheless.

He began cleaning up the area and helped Heath get ready for bed. "Chance, I need to go to town and get you some more clothes and better things to sleep in. I'll do that tomorrow."

"Can I go with you?"

Jack pondered the child's innocent request. "Not this time, little buddy. We need to still be careful. I think we're safe now, but we have to be sure that all the bad guys are gone. I never want to be away from you again."

Disappointment filled the boy's eyes. "Okay," he said, accepting the explanation.

"I'll tell you what though, we can go out into the woods again. In fact, if you want to come out for a few minutes with me right now you can. I need to take Scruffy out." Jack hoped the compromise would help make the boy feel better.

Heath's eyes lit up at the offer. He was already heading to the stairs.

"Whoa, hold on, Chance. Let me finish helping your mother put our game away, and then we can go."

Mindy heard the comment. "You two go ahead."

"You sure?" Jack asked for confirmation. "I don't mind helping."

"It's okay. The dog needs to go out."

"Okay, thanks, babe." Jack leaned in and kissed Mindy on the cheek. "I love you, Hope."

"I know," Mindy replied as she continued to clean up the kitchen of glasses and dice.

Jack was so pleased with the opportunity to get out of the room that seemed overly stifling, that once again, he missed her subtle clues. A sliver of a shudder ran through her at his kiss, and there was a dull tone in her voice as she forced a response to his words of adoration.

"Come on, let's go," Heath said standing at the top of the stairs trying to open the door. Scruffy stood next to him with his paws on the top step, begging to get out.

"Okay, guys, I'm coming." Jack turned from Mindy and took the stairs two at a time.

Once out of the basement, Jack could almost immediately feel some of the weight removed from his body. The outside air cooled his skin and the night sounds helped calm the crawling feeling that had been racing through him for the last hour.

"Chance," he spoke. "It's important that you learn how to be safe in the darkness. Always listen to the night. It speaks to you."

"The night speaks? How?"

"Not in words, but in sounds. The sounds can tell you if there is danger or peace in the air."

Almost as if on key, a coyote bayed in the distance, followed by others in a near eerie frenzy as they chased their prey. Then as quickly as it started, the cries stopped in an abrupt and final, united scream.

"Those were coyotes. They're like wild dogs, and they're strong enough to kill a dog like Scruffy, or a deer, even a farmer's cow."

"Why?"

"They're just doing what comes naturally to them. Sometimes it's for food, and sometimes they do it because they just need to."

"Oh." Heath stood listening to the night. "Will they hurt Scruffy?"

"No, because we'll keep him safe. It's our job. Just like it's my job to keep you safe."

"How?"

"Any way we need to. When you're supposed to protect something, it's your job to do whatever it takes. I'll do anything to protect you, Mommy, and Faith."

Heath smiled up at him and slid his small hand into Jack's. "Are you really my daddy?"

"Jack stared down at the little boy. "Yes, son. I am."

Heath smiled. "I always wanted a real daddy."

Jack returned his smile and said, "Okay, enough exploring for tonight. It's time for you to get to bed. Come on, Scruffy." Jack called after the dog, which had stayed relatively nearby in the dark of the night. The little dog immediately responded and followed Jack back to the door.

An hour later with the kids fast asleep in bed, Mindy was sitting on the couch. Jack began, "Hope, honey. I need to go out for a while." He hesitated, hoping he wouldn't need to explain why he needed to go out, and was relieved once again when she didn't ask.

Before leaving he checked on Vivian, making sure her medication was set properly. He checked her bedding and made sure she was clean and dry, turning her slightly in hopes of keeping her comfortable and free of bed sores. Each day he seemed to be losing her more and more. This fueled the already burning fire inside. Once again the internal flame was itching in his veins.

Turning back to Hope he gave her a quick kiss on her cheek and left with a final message, "I'll be home soon."

***

When Jack left Hope, he was pleased. Pleased to have the time out of the dark basement. Pleased that he could take care of this annoying

685

burning that had now flooded his senses, and pleased that Hope had not pressured him about where he was going or how long he'd be gone.

He was such a lucky man, having a wife that was so sensitive to his needs. He began to whistle as he locked his family safely in the basement. Grabbing a jacket from a hallway closet, he went out to the van. He knew exactly where he was going. He had been there before.

Certain that he had the proper supplies in his doctor kit behind the seat of the van, he pulled the vehicle out of the garage. It was getting late—now after ten o'clock. For a small town like Ojai ten o'clock was button up time. The streets were nearly empty, and as he passed through the residential areas, the houses were cloaked in darkness. Street lamps gave the town the perfect glow. Jack loved the night time, the stillness that came with it and the fear most felt it held. Not him though, he felt empowered in the dark. Empowered and free.

He pulled the vehicle up in front of the house after paying close attention to the neighbors' homes. All were dark. Everyone had gone off to bed already. He killed his lights as soon as he turned onto the block, making certain not to disturb anyone.

He reached behind his seat to retrieve his gloves, booties, and a syringe. In the movies they always talked about the kill kit and showed all kinds of things. He smiled, guessing he was a simple man or maybe just a smarter one. These few items were all he needed.

Double checking that the dome light was turned off in the van, he removed the keys from the ignition, clicked the door open, and slipped out into the night. There was a light breeze in the air, and the neighborhood smelled of eucalyptus.

Approaching the house he followed the cobblestone pathway, avoiding the solar lighting that ran up the driveway. He noticed the moon was only a small crescent and was already considering what lighting source he might have inside. The challenge the total darkness presented did not deter him. In fact, it seemed to increase the adrenaline that was already pulsing into his muscles, senses, and breathing.

He pushed through two large Cannas, the leaves crackling against his body, and stood next to the fence separating the front and back yards. He could hear water running somewhere and decided there must be a koi pond in the back yard. Hearing nothing else, he depressed the latch with his gloved thumb, delivering a clicking noise that seemed to scream in the night. He paused and listened. Convinced the house was still, he continued through the gate and left it slightly ajar, not wanting to make the same noise again.

686

As he moved deeper into the yard, he peered through the first window along the side of the house. It was the kitchen. As he suspected the bedrooms were toward the back of the house.

He soon found the source of the running water noise, and as he expected there was a koi pond with a small waterfall running through it. In the middle it had a small island with a water-light. He would prefer it not be there, but it was dim enough that he continued on.

A window rose from the ground on either side of a sliding glass door that opened from the small patio that contained a glass-top table and cushioned chairs. The yard was covered in a multitude of flowers. Jimmy clearly had a green thumb, or he had a gardener that gave a lot of tender care to the numerous colorful plants that dotted the entire fence line.

Jack approached the window on the left of the patio door first and found it impossible to peer in. He moved over to the patio door and attempted to open it. Locked. He reached in his pants pocket and disappointment started to fill him as he realized that he had forgotten his trusty and reliable Swiss Army knife. He calmed himself and accepted that he would have to get in another way.

Next he went to the remaining window and peered through. The blinds were pulled open about two inches, enough to be able to see there was a bed and dresser. It seemed someone was rolled up in the blankets, and he could tell there was another door in the room, which believing it to be a bathroom caused him to draw the conclusion that this was the master bedroom and room where he would find the means to relief from the darkness that had nearly consumed him.

Returning to the second window, he gave it a gentle push and felt it give slightly. Not wanting to make any noise while trying to force it, he went back to the master room window and peered in again. He noticed the lump in the bed was still in the same position. He continued on around the corner of the house and found a door that had eight rectangular square windows in it.

He could see into the garage. Turning the knob, the door opened and granted him access to the inside. There was a workbench with several tools on it and several containers of surfboard wax. The wall on one side had three different surf boards, each a slightly different shape. Saw horses filled the main part of the garage floor. This was Jimmy's apparent workshop for his surfing hobby.

Jack could barely see inside the garage, but the adrenaline seemed to be enhancing his vision just enough that he could see a door. Watching his step, he moved cautiously towards it, and reaching out, he took the knob in his gloved hand and twisted. His breath held as he anticipated it to be locked. He had to resist laughing out loud when the door opened, and he realized he wouldn't need to use his trusty and missing Swiss Army knife after all.

Pushing the door inward slowly, he listened carefully to both the inside of the home and the hinges of the door, hoping neither would betray him. The door squeaked almost immediately, which forced him to pause. He turned around and looked closely at the workbench, and then after squinting in the darkness, he saw a shelving unit on the opposite wall that seemed to contain paints and sprays.

Once again carefully watching his steps, he approached the shelf and scanned the items on it. On the second to the bottom shelf he found what he was looking for—WD40. Lifting the blue and yellow can, he carried it back to the door and depressed the small red button two times on each of the hinges. Setting the can down on the workbench, he pushed slightly on the door and relaxed as the door opened quietly inward.

He stood inside, just left of the kitchen, in a small laundry room. The home had subtle lighting by the illumination from the clock on the stove, microwave, and DVD player. The subtle lighting was all he needed. He passed through the kitchen, glancing only for a moment at the living room until he found a hallway.

Controlling his breathing, he took gentle steps down the carpeted hallway and approached the bedroom to his left. He was very certain the room was the master and where he needed to go, but he had been unable to assess the other room and wanted to be sure his assumption that it was unoccupied was accurate. The door stood open. He stepped in and looked closely at the bed. It was an obvious guest room, and tonight there were no guests.

Turning, he crossed the hallway. He heard something and froze. There was movement inside the bedroom. Then he heard a flushing sound. Jimmy was awake. He would wait until his prey settled down again, recessing back into the safety of the empty guest room. A glow came from under the master bedroom door. At first, he worried a light had come on, but then he recognized that it was the soft glow of a phone.

For several minutes the light remained on. It went off, and the room went quiet again. It seemed Jimmy was texting or using the Internet and now had returned to bed. Jack silently exhaled, forcing himself to wait a few more moments. He needed Jimmy to be nearly asleep. He couldn't afford a repeat of the situation he had with Reb. She had surprised him, and one thing for sure was he learned from his mistakes.

He also knew Jimmy was an avid surfer and would therefore have superior upper body strength to Reb. The burning sensation of the darkness that was raging inside made him feel irritable. While he waited he considered his approach in the room. Tilting his head slightly, he could hear a low buzz. He was unable to determine what the source was, but he was certain it was some sort of small appliance. Focusing harder, he heard slow breaths, the kind that comes with the first stages of sleep. It was time.

Chapter Thirty

The hallway had a slight, fading blue hue that was cast from the lights, illuminating the time on the stove in the kitchen. To anyone else it might have seemed ominous, the glow casting odd shapes that seemed to bounce back off the doors that lined the narrow path leading to the source of Jack's obsession.

Jack stepped out of the dark room and into the blue cast, allowing it to devour him. He silently moved toward the bedroom door where he could hear the rise and fall of sleep-filled breath that grew louder with each step forward. *REM sleep, the best time to approach.*

He paced his own breath to match that of his sleeping prey. Stopping in the doorway, he allowed his eyes to adjust to the subtle lighting of the bedroom before moving closer to the bed. A clock on the nightstand glowed 11:18 in huge lime green digital blocks. His eyes shifted back to the bed. There was a large bundle that faced the opposite wall. As he inched closer to the bed, his shoes silently stepped on the medium napped carpet pile.

As he stood over the sleeping bundle, he reached his gloved hand into his pocket, pulled the syringe and rag out, and instinctively inhaled before pressing the plunger to squirt the toxic sedative into the rag, ensuring he didn't inadvertently inhale any of the fumes. He leaned in, and in a quick movement forced the rag over the face of the sleeping man. Then just as quickly, he pressed his right knee into the man's back as he wrapped his left arm around the man's neck. There was a short struggle before the man went limp in his arms.

"Good boy, Jimmy," he said as he shoved the rag and syringe back into his pocket, careful to not allow the needle to come in contact with his skin. "Time for us to have some fun."

Jack got Jimmy prepped for the ride back to the house. He wrapped him in the blanket from the bed so he wouldn't need to carry him more than necessary. He dragged the bedding to the floor and grabbed two ends of the blanket containing the unconscious man and pulled, dragging him down the hall and back out through the living room. He looked around until he found Jimmy's keys. He continued through the house, letting the blue glow direct his way and his senses guide him back to the garage.

Jimmy clearly parked outside. Assessing the garage he decided there was room to open the garage and pull his van in. There was plenty of room, all he needed to do was move the saw horses out of the main part of the floor to clear the way for his vehicle. He looked around and found a small step stool and opened it just under the garage door opener. Stepping up, he was careful to not allow his booty-covered feet to slip as he reached above his head and turned the light bulb out far enough that the light would not come on when the garage door opened.

Returning the stool to its rightful place, he pushed the button on the wall and watched as the overhead door curled open. The sound of the small chain-fed motor seemed deafening in the silence of the night, and his pulse quickened.

He quickly walked out into the night and down the driveway past Jimmy's vehicle and to his own van sitting under a tree at the curb. Climbing in, he started the engine as he pulled the door closed with a gentle click. He nudged into the garage without turning on his headlights and squeezed in between the saw horses and surf boards. After shoving the gearshift into park, he climbed out and quickly hit the button on the overhead door, locking himself back into the safety of the home.

Jack took a moment to calm his breathing before heading back into the house to collect his prize. As he was about to begin dragging Jimmy the rest of the way through the house, there was a knock at the front door. His heart rate immediately increased. He slid his back up against the wall and considered just ignoring the loud rapping at the door. Thinking better of it, he went to the door and opened it slightly while keeping his hands from sight, knowing the gloves would raise concern.

"Hello," was all he could think of offering to the skinny man that stood before him. Jack sized him up quickly. His clothes were disheveled, hair slightly askew, he had a stubbly beard and looked to be in his sixties, but Jack guessed he was much younger.

"Oh, hey, I was looking for Jimmy," the man said rubbing nervously at his beard, seeming surprised to find Jack at the door.

"He's not home, went on a nursing gig. I'm watching the place for him for a couple of days," he lied.

"Huh," the man grunted out as he looked out at the car in the driveway, the grey whiskers on his chin jutting out.

Realizing the car was a problem, Jack quickly offered an explanation, "Some kind of special thing, two of them had to go. His co-worker wanted to drive. I think the patient was a big guy with some special needs. Jimmy said it would take two of them to lift him. I dropped him off at his co-workers house then came on up here."

The guy grimaced a little at the description of the supposed patient. "Oh, okay. Well, I saw the garage open, and Jimmy has never opened it to pull in so I got a little worried."

Great, nosey neighbor. "Well, he should be home in a couple of days. Can I leave a message for him?" Jack threw on his most gregarious smile and continued, "I'm sorry, I didn't even ask your name."

"No. No message. Name is Ron. I was just checking to see that everything was okay."

"Sure, I understand. You can't be too careful these days."

"How is it that you know Jimmy?"

Jack thought quickly before answering. "We surf together." He stopped short of trying to explain where they would catch waves together as he didn't want to take a chance on getting it wrong since he was not sure if nosey Ron would know Jimmy's favorite spots.

Ron rubbed his grey chin hair with spindle like fingers and dirty nails stained with nicotine. "Well, glad everything's okay." He turned to walk away then turned back. "What'd you say your name was?"

"I don't believe I did, but it's Sam," he lied again, not wanting to give out his real name.

"Well, nice to meet you, Sam. I live just over there." He pointed to the house directly across the street. "If you need anything, just let me know."

"Ya know, I just picked up some beer, want to come in and have one?" Jack asked following an impulse. He was taking a chance, but temptation overcame him.

Ron had already started to walk away but turned back. His eyes assessed Jack, and his tongue darted out of his mouth, flicking quickly across his lips. "Oh, what the hell. Why not?" He smiled as he stepped forward. Jack gambled on the origin of the man's ruddy complexion, obvious heavy smoking habit and thin frame. Ron clearly liked alcohol as much, if not more, as he liked being the nosey neighbor.

This was going to be good. *Two in one night?* Jack could feel an unprecedented excitement begin to run through him. This was going to be almost as good as cutting Maxine's hair, he thought as he stepped back from the door and opened it just far enough for Ron to enter.

Pushing the door closed, he snaked his gloved hand around Ron's neck and locked Ron's arms down in a tight squeeze with his other. With his arm bent at the elbow, Jack applied pressure against the man's carotid arteries. From his medical training he knew this would

693

cause cerebral ischemia, or loss of blood flow to the brain, and the lack of oxygen to the brain would quickly drop Ron into unconsciousness.

The neighbor's fingers reached up to Jack's arms, and he swore through his teeth in his initial surprise. It took only moments before he started to lose the battle against the much stronger, fit man who held him tightly in a grip that certainly must have felt like death was eminent. Ron fell limp on the floor.

Jack knew this condition was only temporary and turned to the garage where he could retrieve the duct tape he carried in his bag. At the passenger side of the van, he reached across the back seat and dug his hand in the bag, curling his strong gloved fingers around the tape before re-entering the house.

Thirty-five minutes later Jack was pulling back into his own garage with a double bounty. He felt almost intoxicated. He'd never had two guests at one time. Even when working in the emergency room in his early days as a resident doctor, he always focused on one patient at a time during surgery. Sometimes it was back to back, for sure, but never in the same operating room at the same time.

Jack got out of the van once the garage door closed fully behind him and walked around to the back, opening the compartment where the two men laid side by side. Jimmy was still unconscious and rolled inside the bed cover, while Ron was awake again but unable to do little more than struggle against the tape that bound his legs, arms, and mouth. Seeing Jack, Ron began to struggle more, as if his anger would somehow help free him.

"Hello, Ron. Sorry about the tape, but you see, you really shouldn't spend so much time spying on your neighbors. In fact, it really is bad manners. Don't worry though. We'll get you out of that tape soon enough. Just sit tight for a minute." Jack did not wait for Ron to answer. He knew full well that not only he couldn't answer, but also that whatever he would say, even if he could, would be just spewing of rage and unreasonable pleas.

Jack pulled at the rolled bedding and got Jimmy to the end of the van before yanking him down onto the floor of the garage. He went and opened the door to the house before tugging Jimmy up the two steps and towards the kitchen. Jimmy's head bounced inside the blanket as he went up each of the steps, causing the man to moan slightly. Jack watched him closely for a moment before dragging him through the house to the door

694

near the basement entrance. Certain that Jimmy was still out of it, he left him lying there and returned for Ron.

Again, the man reacted to Jack's presence, kicking his bent knees. Jack laughed at him as he saw sweat covering the man's brow, knowing that sweat was the tell sign that Ron was afraid. Jack couldn't help but enjoy the feeling he got in knowing he held the man's fate in his hands. Ron had, after all, nearly caused him major issues tonight.

Pulling Ron toward him by the ankles, the skinny man kicked at his hands. Jack decided he wouldn't take any chances and went to the side of the van, opened the door, and retrieved his medical bag. He opened it and reached inside taking a moment to collect what he was looking for.

With a syringe in his hand, he pulled Ron closer and injected the clear fluid into the man's boney arm. Moments later Ron relaxed, and while he was wide awake he was unable to respond any more to Jack's touch. Ron no longer could flinch at Jack's approach or kick as he tried to carry him away. Jack slid him from the van and lifted him onto his shoulder. The man was monumentally lighter than Jimmy and was no challenge for Jack's strong body.

At the basement stairs, Jack dug with one hand to get the keys out of his pants pocket so he could open the basement door. Fumbling with the small key, he slid it into the lock and lifted the bar away while balancing Ron against the wall. Pulling the door open, he rebalanced his load and headed into the nearly dark basement.

The kids were sleeping, and he looked for Hope. He saw her slender frame in the bed. He stood at the bottom of the stairs for a moment, hesitating and thinking about the door being open at the top of the stairs. After deciding everyone was asleep, he went quickly to the surgical room.

He struggled with the keys again. He picked the smaller one and again fumbled a bit with the lock until the key engaged. With the door to the surgical room open, he went in and dropped Ron onto the steel table before turning to head back up the stairs to retrieve Jimmy.

Jack glanced again at the kids and Hope; no one had moved. After a quick check on Vivian he went back up the stairs. Jimmy was just starting to show signs of consciousness, so he knew he needed to hurry. Sliding the bedding down the first few steps until it cleared the landing, he closed the door and locked it, depositing the keys back into his pocket with a double check of the door to ensure it was locked securely.

He stepped over the bedding roll and pulled the heavy lump down the remainder of the stairs to the bottom and across the floor. The roll banged against the couch, causing a thumping noise until it finally cleared the tight space. Jimmy groaned again. Jack was sweating, his brow damp, and his body filled with heat, yet he felt chilled on the outside from the cool night air.

Jack was faced with making a decision. For the first time ever he had two house guests, and with both inside the surgical room he tried to decide what he wanted to do first. He had been thinking about Jimmy for a while. However, Ron had really tried to ruin things for him, and that deserved punishment. Then an image of Vivian not being properly cared for crossed his mind, and he knew what he must do.

Jack left the men in place and went back to the stairs, trying to be quiet while taking the stairs two at a time. He retrieved a small chair from the main kitchen upstairs and brought it to the basement. He locked the door again and hoisted the chair up over the couch as he passed. Taking the chair into the surgical room, he put it in the corner facing the table, then lifted Ron up off of the table to place the man in the seat. Ron reacted in the only way he could—his eyes wide and darting all around.

Jack took a roll of duct tape from the shelf and secured Ron's hands and feet to the chair, ensuring he couldn't fall to the floor. With Ron in the perfect viewing position, Jack pulled the blanket away from Jimmy, and then lifted him off the floor, struggling at first with the younger man's weight. Finally, Jimmy's body position was just right so he could pivot him up onto the table.

Jimmy was really starting to come around now, and Jack realized he needed to secure him fast. He cut Jimmy's clothes away from his body and rolled him from side to side to pull the clothes free. With the clothes removed, Jack secured the surfer's hands and feet to the table with white zip ties.

Looking over at Ron, Jack smiled as he saw the gaunt man staring on. He felt a prickly chill cover his skin. The sweat was slick, and his tongue darted out, sliding over his lips. They tasted of salt. He slipped out of his own clothes and pulled on a set of scrubs, a hair net, and gloves. Just as he was ready to begin his procedure, he heard a noise and turned to see Chance staring at him. In his rush to get Jimmy secured before he became fully alert, he had forgotten to close and lock the door.

Chapter Thirty-One

Mindy watched as Jack left. She waited a while before deciding she really needed to take a chance and see if there was any possible way of getting out. She knew Jack had the room rigged with cameras, but she had a feeling he was going out to perform the crazy things for which he was wanted by the FBI. She was starting to feel desperate and not sure how much longer she could keep up the façade of a loving wife. It was risky, for sure. If she happened to get caught, it could be the moment that she caused two innocent children to be killed. She was banking on the fact that he was focused on wherever he was going or whoever he was going after, and it was now or never.

She went up the stairs and listened closely at the door. The house seemed silent, and the floorboards were quiet. Usually she could hear him walking across the floor overhead and depended on her deep memory from her childhood to tell her which room in the house he was in. Her mind would follow him from the kitchen to the living room or garage, her mind's eye tracing his steps with each creaking board.

For now it was quiet. She assessed the door and saw the locks on the inside and knew he was carrying those keys with him at all times. She pushed against the door; it didn't give at all. This obviously was not going to be a good solution for escape, and her spirits dampened. Retreating back down the stairs she realized that she needed to assess the other areas of the basement. Moving to the back part of the basement, she knew there was another room, but since she had been afraid to leave the confines of the area that Jack had defined as their living quarters, she had no idea what was there.

Slipping past the couch where the kids slept, she moved her hands along the wall, struggling through the room lit only by the television glow. She felt a door and wrapped her hand around the knob. Holding her breath, she slowly gave the metal handle a twist. Nothing. The door was locked. She shook the knob again. Even though her mind knew there was no use, she pushed then pulled. "Damn it!" she swore under her breath.

Continuing to feel along the wall, she found nothing else, and then wondered what she could use as a weapon. Maybe when Jack returned she could attack him, maybe when he was sleeping. *I could kill him in his sleep. I just need a tool to do it,* she thought to herself.

Searching a piece of furniture that appeared to be an old laundry table that sat at the end of the narrow nook past the door, she squinted to assess the items on the table, including a small wrench. It wasn't much, but it might work. She took it and continued the rest of her search. There was nothing else she could use. She thought about the items in the kitchen. Nothing would work. Jack had provided all plastic utensils.

Inside the bathroom she looked around and saw the toothbrush. She'd seen on TV how you could make a knife out of it by melting the end and shaping it into a point. She wondered if she could do this without Jack noticing that it was gone.

Moving from the bathroom to the bedroom, she slid the wrench deep in between the mattress and box spring, then stood there wondering if he would find it. She looked around the room, trying to consider a better hiding place, but found nothing. For a minute she considered hiding it in Vivian's bed, but knowing Jack checked her bedding regularly, she reconsidered. For now the bed seemed the best solution.

Her eyes traveled along all the walls and then the ceiling. There seemed to be nothing in terms of a way to get out. Then she noticed a gap in one of the ceiling tiles and wondered if there was some way to get up there and force her way out through the floorboards.

Considering the time, she decided she better not push her luck tonight. Jack might be back soon or decide to observe the video and see what she was doing. She couldn't take any more chances, not tonight. But before she gave up she noticed a pair of Jack's pants on the chair. He had tossed them there when he had gotten ready for bed the night before. She walked over to them and hesitantly lifted the pants from the chair, reaching into the pockets.

Her hand recoiled when she felt something strange. Overcoming her apprehension she reached in again and pulled out the soft silky item from inside. She choked back a scream when she realized that she was holding a lock of auburn red hair. Unable to contain her repulsion, she shoved it back in the pocket. There was something else in that pocket—a Swiss Army knife. She wanted desperately to take it but resisted, certain Jack would know it was missing. Despite a trembling that had consumed her, shaking her to the core, she reached in each of the other pockets but found nothing else.

Unable to fight the churning in her stomach she returned to the bathroom and wretched in the toilet until she thought her guts would come out. When the waves finally subsided, she washed her face and brushed her teeth and got ready for bed while still considering how she could make a weapon. One thing she did resolve to do was pretend to be asleep when Jack came home.

Terror filled her as she lay there with the covers pulled tightly around her neck. She wondered if he had seen her looking around and, if so, what he might do to her. Or worse, to the kids. A new terror flooded her as she started to wonder if he would try to wake her, and she silently prayed he would simply never come back at all.

She dozed, drifting in and out of sleep, trying desperately to stay awake, wanting to be aware of what was going on around her. But sleep pulled her in. Her mind flitted through images of severed bodies, the horror of Jack on her, kissing and pawing. Sorrow filled her as her dream crossed over to images of Paul's dead body ripped apart in the living room of the loving home they had shared.

She woke with a start just as she was nearly pulled into a torturous vision of her beautiful eldest daughter…The door opened at the top of the stairs, and she froze. Trying not to hold her breath, certain she would soon hyperventilate, she waited.

There was a thumping noise as Jack came down the stairs, and she had to resist the temptation to turn and see what that noise was. She could hear Jack's breathing, almost a grunt, as if he were struggling. She had heard that noise before. *When was it? Was it when she was drugged, and he brought Vivian's bed downstairs? Yes, that was it.*

He was bringing something down the stairs. She was sure of it. *But what would he be bringing down here in the middle of the night?* Instinct told her it wouldn't be good, and she prayed the kids wouldn't wake up. Whatever he was doing she was certain would terrify them. Remaining still, she continued to listen with her eyes squeezed shut and her hands clutching the pillow in tight fists.

She heard the door at the back of the basement being opened. The very door that she herself had tried to open earlier. She began wishing she could see in there. *Maybe there's a window.* He returned up the stairs, locking them in again. *Damn.* Subconsciously she wished he would forget.

Her mind drifted to the wrench that lay just beneath her. Could she hit him when he came to bed? Her heart rate climbed again, and she had to mentally focus on not allowing her breathing to accelerate. A tear fell from her eye onto her pillow as the fear started to overcome her. *Focus, Mindy!*

She could hear shuffling noises and then a door close. She expected Jack to come out and head towards the bed, but instead it was quiet. Then she heard strange noises, groans followed by a man's voice that said something. "Dude?" she thought she heard from the forbidden room. There was a clanging sound, then mild laughter—Jack's laughter. *Oh God, he has a man in there!*

For several moments she wished Jack had just kept her sedated. But then she remembered the kids. They needed her to help get them out of here alive. Allie was barely herself, and Heath seemed to like it here. He believed Jack's story and was easily being tricked into believing that Jack was his father.

Swallowing hard, she tried to focus again. It seemed to be quieter now. She wondered if Jack had killed the man, and she felt almost certain he probably had. Her mind returned to the idea of the wrench under the mattress.

Chapter Thirty-Two

Max sighed, pushing back from the table and computer that had occupied her time for the past two or three hours. She stretched and pulled her long red hair back from her face, wrapping her thin fingers tightly around the thick tresses. Her fingers paused for a brief moment on the shortened strands.

Mark walked up behind her. "Cortez has something to share. She thinks she might have a lead."

Max didn't need to hear more. She was on her feet and moving to the table across the room in front of a projection screen that was already being lowered. Cortez was standing next to it, and as she saw her former partner her chin dipped towards her chest in a silent nod. Max knew this meant she was onto something and was about to show the first hint of a lead they had so far. Everyone gathered around the table and waited for Cortez to begin.

"Jack Tyler was born and raised in Ojai Valley, California. He lived there until he went to college but never returned. We believe he was a very abused boy, the perpetrator his own mother. A week ago this woman," a photo flashed up on the projector screen, "Rebecca Tillman, went missing. There has been no sign of her since. Her car was found around the corner from her house in an unusual place. Her dog is also missing. The pet was her companion, and at first family members thought maybe she had gone on a trip, taking the animal with her, but now she's been gone too long and with no contact. Her employer says she never called in when she was supposed to report to work. This is totally out of character for her."

Max stood looking at the photo. This woman looked nothing like Hope. The only link so far was that she disappeared from Ojai. Not getting the connection, she started to object, but before she could do so, Cortez continued.

"Rebecca went to Ojai Valley High School with Hope and Jack. In fact, until their junior year Hope and Rebecca were close friends. I talked on the phone with Rebecca's ex-husband. He and Rebecca married shortly after high school after dating all through school. He claims that Rebecca warned Hope to stay away from Jack, that there was something off about him, and after that Hope wouldn't speak to her anymore."

Max shook her head. "Why would he go back to Ojai? He wanted to get away from there. He and Hope basically bolted as soon as they could and never looked back."

"That's a flaw in the theory, but it's pretty ironic that Jack is on the run. We think he's in California or Arizona, and now a friend of Hope's from high school has vanished. A friend of Hope's that betrayed Jack."

Max took it all in. "I need to see her house." Her eyes moved to Mark.

"Cortez, you and Max go to Ojai, check out the house, and interview neighbors. Agent Jenkins, check for any other missing persons in or around Ojai—male, female, and children."

Jenkins looked up. "Sir, I have something to report too. The credit reports have just come back on all of Tyler's prior aliases. There's a single hit. He ran a people search on intellicus.com, must have forgotten that his account was established under the name he used in Illinois."

"Who was the people search for?" Wells asked.

"I'm trying to get that information but had to request a warrant. They wouldn't release it without it. I'll have that in the hour."

"Let me know the minute you know who he was looking for. Is there any way to trace where the transaction came from?"

"We're searching the IP address, but so far have not been able to trace it. Although, the last known address associated with the credit card was in Illinois. We'll know a lot more as soon as we can get the information on the account."

"We need that information now!" Mark barked, and then tried to catch himself by resuming the control he normally possessed in his tone. "Agent, push them. We need to move."

"Yes, sir." Agent Jenkins went back to the table she had been working at and immediately starting punching numbers into the cell phone.

"We may be onto something, and I need a full team. Agent Adams, go to the hotel and get rest. I need you back in four hours fresh."

"With all due respect, sir, I'd rather stay."

"I appreciate that, but I need to keep this team going twenty-four seven, and I can't do that if no one rests."

Adams nodded his head, though the disappointment at the order was clear on his face. He wouldn't argue. Wells was a good and well trusted leader. He began packing his laptop and stood to leave.

Cortez walked over to Max. "I'll have a car in ten minutes out front."

Max merely nodded as she returned to the table and began collecting her things. Leaving her files behind for the others, she made eye contact with Mark, who stood across the room giving a few additional instructions to the team. He finished the conversation and walked towards her, taking her by the elbow and leading her out into the hallway as the others tried not to watch.

They stood just looking at each other for a few moments, neither willing to say anything. Max broke the silence. "I have to see for myself if anything looks like his work."

"I know. I also know no one will recognize it better than you. But…"

Before he could finish she filled in his words. "I'll be careful. It's not like Jack is going to be waiting for me in her home."

"I know."

"If he has Heath, and he's near his old stomping grounds, I'll know." Max leaned in and kissed Mark on the lips, ignoring protocol. Right now she only cared about finding Tyler and saving Heath. "If that bastard has our son…," the words trailed off as Max controlled herself from letting the rest of the words trickle off her tongue. "I'll call you later as soon as I can. Let me know if anything else pops on the trace that Jenkins has going."

"Max…no heroics."

She tilted her head in an agreeable nod, causing her thick hair to topple to one side, and then turned and walked out the door.

Chapter Thirty-Three

"Daddy, what are you doing?"

Jack turned around, facing the small boy and kneeling to eye level. "Hey, buddy. What are you doing awake right now?" Realizing how frightened Chance could be, he quickly decided to address what the boy was seeing. "You know Daddy is a doctor, right?"

The boy rubbed at his sleepy eyes and nodded his head.

"Well, I got called for an emergency. That's why I had to go out late, and now these men need my help. Come on now, I need you to go back to sleep so Daddy can work real fast."

Heath's eyes were wide as Jack turned him out of the room and pulled the door closed behind him, blocking the child's view. Leading the boy back to the bed, he lifted him up and tucked him back in.

"I'm sorry if that scared you. Surgery can be very scary, but it has to be done. Now, can you be a big boy and go back to sleep?"

Heath nodded, in the low lighting his blue eyes took on the color of the dark sky as he stared back into Jack's eyes.

"Good boy. Don't go in there again, okay?"

Heath nodded once more.

Jack sat next to the boy a little longer, pulling the covers up to his chin. Jack's hand brushed the locks of hair away from the boy's eyes, and he leaned in to kiss the small soft forehead. In a few moments Heath's eyes began to close. "I love you, little man," Jack said before rising to return to the surgical room.

Inside the room again, Jack turned the lock in the door, securing himself and his captives inside. *No more interruptions*. His skin seemed to sing with anticipation. This was truly a new and exciting event. He couldn't wait to watch Ron witness the true beauty of his work. He thought for a moment how, at first, he had truly been annoyed with Ron for knocking on the door, and now how thrilled he was to have him sitting here in the room with him.

A tray hung suspended over the table like an arm baring a platter of shiny offerings. Jack lifted the #5 scalpel and turned it over in his hand, the glint of the metal casting a reflection against the tray.

He paused briefly considering how he would handle Jimmy first then Ron. He certainly liked having a guest for longer than a few hours, and with two of them he had options. With his mind made up, he turned to Jimmy. The surfer was finally awake, *perfect timing*.

"It's about time you woke up," Jack said with a sinister sneer under his face mask.

"Dude!" Jimmy shouted out.

"Quiet now. My family is sleeping. If you can't settle down I'll have to silence you a different way."

"What do you want, man? You're nuts."

"Nuts? Maybe. It's all relative, don't you think?"

"Whatever, dude. Let me outta here."

"Let's talk about that, ole' Jimmy boy. Let's talk about how you treated Vivian. How about this... I ask you a question, you tell me the truth the *first* time," he applied pressure on the word *first*, "and maybe I will consider some leniency."

Jimmy squirmed against the ties but suddenly stopped. "What? What do you want to know?"

"Okay, question number one. Did you ever leave Vivian in her soiled bed longer than should be expected?"

"What the f...?"

"Jimmy, answer the question now or I'll...," Jack swiped the scalpel across Jimmy's chest in a sweeping motion indicating the cut he would make.

"Okay, okay, dude. Yes."

"Yes. What?"

"Yes, I left her too long," Jimmy seemed defeated, his voice shaking now.

"Tsk, tsk. I knew it. Question number two. Did you ever ignore her ringing bell when she clearly needed your assistance?"

Jimmy began to squirm again. "Fuck you!"

"Such foul language, Jimmy. That might be question number three if you don't hurry up and answer me now."

"Yes. Alright, sometimes I waited. Now let me go." Jimmy was attempting to flail now, the fog from the drug really starting to dissipate from his mind.

"Good boy, Jimmy. For telling me the truth, I'll show you some mercy. I think I'll let you die tonight rather than keeping you around for a few days. After all, I still have ole' Ron here for that."

Jimmy's eyes followed Jack's gaze, his head turning to the far side of the room. Seeing his neighbor, Jimmy arched his back and hissed in anger, "You son of a..."

Jack laid the scalpel down and snapped up the duct tape in one quick sweep and slammed a wide strip across Jimmy's mouth. "I'm

706

sorry, but you are really starting to annoy me, Jimmy. First, you mistreat a poor defenseless old woman. Then you rudely attempt to wake my family up." Anger bubbled up inside Jack at the thought of how Jimmy had treated Vivian. He'd known it all along, but now he knew for sure. Jimmy was about to pay dearly.

He took another long strand of tape and wrapped it over Jimmy's forehead then around the table to secure his head in place. A final strip was wrapped in the same fashion completely around the table to cover Jimmy's mouth. The struggling surfer was immediately silenced to no more than grunts and groans. His hands were bound in tight fists, and his feet wobbled back and forth as if they were waving for someone to assist.

"I'm actually a bit surprised at your reaction to seeing ole' Ronnie boy over there. I'd think you would be glad to be rid of the nosey ole' fool."

Jack took a look around and laid the tape back on the tray and retrieved the scalpel he had laid down so abruptly. He took a deep calming breath and said, "Now, where was I?" With that, he made a long incision right down the middle of Jimmy's torso.

As the blood began to spill out of the wound, Jack looked up and locked stares with Ron, whose eyes popped in his paralyzed body. "It is lovely, isn't it, Ron?" Jack asked as he watched the silver table take on a new crimson shine. "Oh, and I've just begun. The best parts are coming. Just wait, you'll see."

With those comments hanging in the air, Jack continued. He took the ribs spreader and pushed it down into the opening, pushing the bones apart and exposing the organs that were the focus of his quest. His hands entered through the new opening, and he had to consciously remember to include Ron in the process. He looked over at his guest and smiled, noted only by the pinching at the corner of his eyes.

"See, it's beautiful in here. I'd let you feel for yourself, but well, I hate to share." Jimmy pitched and pushed against the obvious pain brought on by no anesthetic during the massive invasion into his chest cavity.

Jack could feel the cool of his gloves quickly turn to silky warmth. A coppery smell began to fill the air. He breathed in the thick fragrance and held it inside. The air of the room seemed to immediately calm the nerves that had been jangling inside him all day. Finally, he was beginning to get some relief from within.

His fingers felt past the ribs and in between the lungs until his strong fingers looped around the muscly heart. Thump, thump,

707

thump…thump……..thump, the beats faded as he squeezed. He pulled back, relaxing the pressure. Thump, thump, thump…thump……….thump, he squeezed again and again until the beats came much less frequently, and then finally stopped.

Jack took a few moments to explore some of the other vital yet less fascinating organs. Replacing the scalpel on the tray, he left a bloody stain and picked up the small scissors. Reaching back inside the lifeless body, he snipped away at the atria and ventricles, and then the fibrous value flaps until he cleared everything to hold the delicate muscle in place. He tilted and turned the muscle until he lifted if from the chest cavity. He stared at the magnificence of the organ. Carrying it around the end of the table past Jimmy's head, he approached Ron.

Holding the organ gently in his hands, he displayed it in front of the terrified man's face. "I told you it was beautiful. Would you like to hold it?" He stared at Ron's face, the eyes bugging out of the skinny, weathered face. "No? Hmmm…too bad. You're missing out on something incredibly marvelous, but your choice, I suppose."

Returning to the other side of the table again, Jack laid the muscle back down in the middle of Jimmy's gaping chest. He studied the man for a moment. "Well now, I bet you wish you'd been a bit nicer to Vivian, don't you?"

With that he began the process of cleaning up the bloody mess. He clipped away at the duct tape and zip ties until Jimmy's body was free from the stainless steel table. Jack rolled the body onto the blanket on the floor. Jimmy's head met the cement through the blanket with a thick thud. "Oh, that would have hurt. See, I did you another favor."

Ron's eyes dropped to the body on the floor, and he watched as Jack rolled his neighbor into the blanket then carefully secured the ends with duct tape. Opening the surgical room's locked door, Jack lifted a long roll of heavy duty clear plastic from the shelf next to the door and stepped out into the main room to roll out a long strip. He sliced the plastic free from the roll with a scalpel from the tray then stepped back in the room. He then lifted the blanket and placed it into the middle of the plastic sheeting. He rolled the blanket up inside the plastic sheeting and duct taped the ends. Now the blood was secured inside the plastic cocoon.

Leaving the bundle in its place, Jack stepped back into the room and locked the door again behind him. For the next hour Jack worked furiously to clean the room, including the floors and walls, and the surgical tools, as well as his own body, putting everything back to their glimmering state. When he was satisfied he dressed then turned and looked at Ron. "Tomorrow will be your turn."

He lifted the seemingly frozen man and laid him out on the table, cutting away his clothing. After securing him tightly to the table with zip ties, he left the room for the last time that night, leaving Ron in the dark with the visions of Jimmy's brutal death dancing through his mind.

***

Mindy lay frozen in place. She could hear the muffled terror from the room at the back of the basement, and she knew what Jack was doing. She'd heard him come in and saw him carrying in the bundle and then a man over his shoulder. She had to resist all temptation to get up when Chance had gotten out of bed. Her desire to protect the boy from seeing what he would likely see was overwrought with the fear of what the kids would do if he killed her. She knew she needed a plan—and soon.

As she lay in the semi-dark room with her eyes pinched closed, her mind raced trying to consider what Hope would do. Clearly her sister had married this madman, and she knew deep inside that Hope would never allow him to just kill random people. Her sister had been loving and kind, not the wife of a crazy killer. Obviously, Hope had somehow managed to keep him from doing these horrible things. *But how?*

Chapter Thirty-Four

Max slid into the passenger seat of the police issued vehicle that Cortez checked out for their hour and thirty minute trip to Ojai. Max felt like she could breathe for the first time in hours. The cool, fresh early morning air felt great, and suddenly she felt alive and … *what was that feeling? Hope?* Yes, she felt hopeful.

"What do we have?" She jumped right into working the case doing exactly what she did best—catching bad guys. It felt good to be back in L.A. and riding with Cortez. She loved the FBI, but this was familiar and familiar seemed incredibly important right now.

"Photos from the house and lab reports," Cortez said handing a file that sat in the middle of the seat.

Max took the file and began flipping through the pages. After a few minutes of silence, Cortez waited just letting her take it all in, and Max finally spoke, "What are the chances of him returning to Ojai?"

Cortez seemed to be really contemplating the question before answering. "What is there to return for?"

"Exactly. Why go back, for what? What is there for him? His family is dead, and the memories are all painful." She paused to think. "Except those of Hope."

"Right and those kids ran from that place as fast as they could. So, why go back?"

"I don't know," Max admitted. "I hope we're not chasing a red herring. Heath doesn't have time for us to just be running around looking for Tyler in some place. I won't forgive myself if I've allowed Tyler to get me so focused on him that I lose sight of Heath."

"I'm with you, Max. It doesn't make sense, but then what does Tyler do that makes sense?"

Max flipped through the file again. She looked at a couple of photos from the high school year book. Jack, Hope, and Rebecca were all in one picture together. The caption under the photo read, "Friends for Life." There was some irony in the caption. She tried to read Jack's face in the photo. It seemed a mixture of love and distain. Oh yeah, he hated Rebecca. She could see it, almost feel it from the photo in her hand.

The wheels turned under the car, and palm trees were replaced by the dry hills of Calabasas. Max watched out the window, her mind processing all of the information. Heath had been gone for nearly four days now, and they really had nothing. Internally, she cringed at the reality of the time that had passed. She couldn't stop her mind from thinking about the children in Illinois; Jack didn't keep his victims four days. With the kids, he had killed them almost immediately.

New palm trees started to come into focus as they approached Thousand Oaks. She found a small amount of hope in remembering beautiful little Jessie—the little girl that Jack had actually shown compassion by allowing her to live. He had severely injured her before leaving her at the emergency room entrance. She hoped if he had Heath that in some way he would connect with the boy, and she could find him before Jack had time to hurt him.

The pair descended the smooth snake-like Conejo Grade, a steep seven percent drop that would deliver them into the Oxnard Plain and the Camarillo Valley. The 101 Freeway was skirted with a runaway truck lane to help big rig drivers avoid certain death should their brakes fail to handle the push of the inertia from the combination of the speed, grade, and weight of the eighteen wheeled vehicle. Max stared at the strange necessity that had always intrigued her.

She loved the natural beauty of California and rode silently in awe of the sparkling lights that lay out below her. The sun was just starting to rise, and both women remained quiet until they were climbing again, this time into the Ojai Valley. It was unusual for the two women to ride without talking. But then nothing was usual right now. Normally they would have picked the possibilities apart, tearing down Jack Tyler's thinking bit by bit, but each stayed inside her own head for the majority of the drive.

Cortez broke the silence as they slid past Oakview, a sleepy little town of four-thousand, that sat between Ventura and Ojai. "How do you want to play this?"

"Who's meeting us?"

"The Ventura County Sheriff's department, Ojai sub-station."

"So, we get Barney Fife?" Max sneered, referring to the overreacting blowhard from the American classic *The Andy Griffith Show*.

"I hope not," Cortez offered, not sounding too certain. Looking down at the folder that Max had placed back on the seat between them, she said, "Captain Kennard."

"We're meeting him at the house or the station?"

"The station, but he knows we want to go right over to the house. He wants to go over all the interviews. Neighbors, you know."

"Right, Barney Fife," Max rolled her eyes.

Cortez burst into laughter and Max joined her. It felt good to laugh. She hadn't let out any emotion other than stress and fear for days now.

Their laughter fell off as they pulled into the quaint, beautiful town of Ojai. The town typically known for its shopping, majestic, mountain views, spa treatments, and great food suddenly took on an ominous feel. The car grew quiet again as Cortez navigated down the main street towards the police sub-station.

Cortez pulled the cruiser into the first available space in front of the adobe style sub-station and looked over at Max. "Ready?" Cortez studied her former partner's face, the stress obvious in the deep lines around her eyes that were not normally present.

"Yeah, let's do this," Max replied pulling on the door handle and stepping out of the car into the morning sunlight. The air was still brisk, typical of California mornings. The air was refreshing to the strain that Max had felt throughout the entire drive. She took a moment to allow the cool morning to settle the feeling that had covered her since shortly after getting into the car. Taking a deep breath, she headed towards the building with Cortez on her heels.

Inside the building they were greeted by a desk sergeant who, immediately upon introduction and request to see Captain Kennard, picked up a handset on the old-style phone that sat next to him on the desk and spoke briefly. Hanging up, he offered a quick nod and said, "He'll be right up." He motioned that they could take a seat in the chairs that lined the hallway. Both remained standing, enjoying the stretch of their legs from the long drive and also demonstrating their sense of urgency.

Moments later, Captain Kennard presented himself. Shaking hands with both women, he asked them to follow him back to his office. He was in his mid-forties and sported a thick, dark mustache that matched his thick hair and served as a cap to his full lips and broad smile that exposed excessively white teeth.

Max wondered if those teeth were caps or dentures, thinking they were inconsistent with his age. There was an obvious strength in his stance. His tall frame was supported by broad shoulders, coupled with a serious look in his grey eyes that helped dispel the earlier concerns of meeting up with Barney Fife that she'd so freely joked about in the car.

After closing the door, he led the women over to a conference table that sat at a ninety degree angle to his desk, which was directly ahead inside the room. The conference table was surrounded by six executive style chairs, and the table was lined with a number of photos and documents. Without offering a seat, he began explaining what they were looking at.

"Rebecca," he started then corrected himself of an obvious familiarity with the missing woman. "Ms. Tillman has been missing now for going on ten days. She has been a member of this community her entire life." As if justifying his earlier use of her first name he explained, "This is a small town, and everyone knows each other if you're around for any time at all. I actually graduated just a few years before her and was friends with her ex-husband."

Max's eyes narrowed in on some of the photos, the rumpled bed sheets, the vehicle parked along the street, and the yearbooks opened to expose some photos of Rebecca throughout school. Her eyes stopped on photos of Jack and Hope Tyler.

"Did you also know the Tyler's?"

"I did. They were all freshmen when I was a senior. Jack was a pretty good football player and got to dress for varsity, which was fairly unusual for a freshman." Kennard tapped a captioned photo of Jack catching a football. The caption underneath read *"Freshman-Tyler goes long for a 43 yard touchdown against Buena Bulldogs."*

Max looked at Kennard, locking his grey eyes in her gaze. "What did you think of Jack Tyler?"

Kennard seemed to consider his words before answering. "He was a bit unusual, I guess. He didn't really seem to have a crowd that he fit in with. He and Hope were somewhat isolated, and I think that got worse as they got closer to their senior year. Jack was very focused on getting into medical school, and I think most of us chalked up his isolation to that drive. Hope clearly supported him a hundred percent. They were very close, really inseparable."

"What can you say about how Ms. Tillman fit into Jack and Hope's relationship?"

"Every indication was that Hope and Rebecca really parted ways in the middle of their sophomore year. I was a senior, but the rumor mill had it that Reb stepped over the line voicing her opinion about Jack to Hope. You know making comments like, he isn't right for you. The kind of statement that immediately caused Hope to severe the friendship. I guess back then everyone just saw it as your typical high school girl drama."

Max nodded then continued to look at the photos, picking up one of the bedroom in Rebecca Tillman's home. "What about forensics? Any fibers, DNA, or blood left in the house or car?"

"Nothing, both are clean. We've run prints on all doors and windows, the nightstand, door jambs, and we pulled fibers from the bed, floor, and car. So far everything matches clothing and prints of Ms. Tillman, her ex-husband or family members."

Max lifted another photo. "Broken window?"

"Yes, everything would indicate that she left on her own, except for that."

"Debris?"

"None."

"How soon can we go over to the home?" Something about these photos was bugging Max.

"We can go now. I'll drive you over."

Max turned and was already half way out the door. Cortez immediately turned as well, causing Kennard to react quickly and obviously surprised by the sudden departure.

When she got outside, Max stopped to wait for Kennard to catch up and then followed him to his police cruiser. He led the way around to the side of the building and pointed, indicating which vehicle they were going to. Max climbed in the back to allow Cortez to take the front seat since she stood a good four inches taller. Really she just wanted to think, and being isolated to the back made her feel like she could do that.

The trip over to the house took no more than five minutes, travelling just a few blocks across Main Street and up onto the hill. Max assessed the house as they pulled up. Nothing stood out specifically about this home versus any other. There was nothing specifically lavish that might attract it more than others on the block for a robbery that might have gone bad. It did sit on the corner, which could isolate it a bit more, making it a little more desirable, but the landscaping of the house two homes down would indicate to a robber the possibility of more valuables inside. *If I were going to rob one of these homes, that is the one I'd pick.*

All three officers exited the vehicle and walked up the small pathway to the front door. There was still crime scene tape around the entry. Max stopped Kennard before he ducked under the tape. "Show me the window first," she requested.

Max followed the captain around to the side of the house to the window that was broken out. She reached in her vest pocket, pulled out gloves, and slid her hands inside. Cortez and Kennard followed her lead. Looking around the ground, her eyes landed on a medium sized rock that lay off to the side. Her gaze travelled to the window, and she stepped forward, mentally accessing her height to the window. She reached up to the window and determined she could hoist herself through it if she really wanted to, despite the fact that it was at eye level to her.

Turning to Kennard, she asked, "How tall are you, Captain?"

He looked at her and responded, "Six-two."

Comparing him to Tyler she asked, "Do you think you could easily hoist yourself through that window?"

Kennard stepped forward. "Easily."

Max bent and looked at the wall below the window. There were no obvious scuff marks or abrasions indicting that someone had recently climbed through this window. She took a closer look at the ground and then asked the captain to retrieve the rock in an evidence bag.

Satisfied that she'd seen everything she needed to out here she said, "Okay, let's go inside now."

Cortez stayed behind for a moment longer looking over the ground more closely. The ground was very dry, and even their footprints did not make imprints where they had just stood. Turning away, she followed Max and the captain back around to the front of the house.

After dipping under the tape Kennard opened the door with a key he retrieved from his pocket. An eerie silence filled the rooms inside. The door closed behind them adding to the strange aura as the morning light was blocked out.

Max stood still, her eyes scanning the room. She looked at pictures on the walls and book shelves. The house was homey and yet somewhat sterile too. In the kitchen there was a set of small dog dishes, one about half full of dog kibble and the other water. "Any sign of the dog?"

"No, that's been a bit of the mystery. It's as if they both disappeared off the face of the earth."

"Would she leave the dog behind if she left on her own free will?"

"According to her ex-husband, no, she took the dog with her everywhere."

"What do we know about him? Is he a possible?" Cortez asked, suggesting that he might be a suspect in his ex-wife's disappearance.

"He has an alibi for several days around the time she went missing. He was actually out of state on a business trip in New York, was seen in several meetings and during evening functions, making it unlikely that he was involved. The timeline wouldn't allow him to fly back from New York and get back to meetings by morning. We checked flights in between the two cities, and there was nothing with him on the passenger list except for his flights to and from the meetings on his original itinerary."

"She was first reported missing by her employer?"

"Yes, I know him. As I said, this is a small town. He called worried and asked if we would just check it out. When we got no answer at the house, we called the ex and other family members. No one had talked to her in a few days, but that was not reported as unusual. The main concern was the no call, no show to work. At first we just assumed it was a scheduling misunderstanding, but after a couple more days of no contact we started a more in-depth investigation. We gained access to the home and found the broken window and what appeared to be a quick exit from the bedroom." Waving his hand around the room, "She was pretty tidy, so the mess of a bed seems out of character."

"What about her purse, keys, and cell phone?"

"All missing, cell phone goes straight to voicemail as if the phone is turned off or dead."

Cortez jumped in, "When did you make that first attempt?"

Kennard stood thinking for a moment. "She'd been gone for a few days."

Following Cortez's thoughts Max questioned, "So the phone could have lost its charge by the time you made the first attempt?"

"Yes, but her boss tried to reach her before that and got the same result."

Max continued to slowly walk through the home, following her instincts to the area where the window was broken. She stood facing the broken window. Based on the size of the window, it seemed unlikely the woman, Rebecca Tillman, would leave it broken. The nights were certainly cool, and it would be impossible to ignore it or have it go unnoticed.

Without approaching, her eyes scanned the wall and then the floor. There were no scuff marks on the wall and no apparent glass on the floor, but she noticed something else. The carpet seemed to be vacuumed in a pattern inconsistent with the rest of the house. She turned to look behind her and followed the pattern up the hallway and into the living room. In every place but under that window the vacuum tracks moved north to south. In this area they were east to west, as if someone had vacuumed only that area.

"Cortez, we need to find the vacuum."

Cortez's eyes followed Max's. "I see it. Foot prints in the middle are probably from the crime team, but there's a definite vacuum pattern."

Kennard stood behind Max and followed her eyes. "We didn't catch that," he said in obvious disappointment.

Cortez left the room, and from somewhere else in the house called out, "Got it!"

Max took a step back, forcing Kennard to back away so she could leave the room. Following the sound of Cortez's voice, Max found her standing in front of a closet where she lifted a Eureka vacuum out and stood looking at it. The cord was neatly wrapped around the handle. No one had wildly put the unit away. Max knelt down and popped open the canister lock and pulled the cylinder out. She held it up to look through the clear hard plastic. "It's empty."

Opening the lid, she looked deep inside. There was the typical dust residue but no visible glass. "We need this checked for prints and glass fragments. If there are fragments or residue, we need to see if there's a match to the window. Let's see if there was an intruder that tidied up. At least we'll narrow this down to her leaving on her own or potentially foul play," Max said handing the canister to Kennard.

"I'll put a rush on it."

"Have the rock analyzed too for any glass fragments while we're at it," Cortez said.

Kennard pulled his cell phone out of the holster on his belt and punched in some numbers. He gave some pretty direct yet basic instructions before hanging up and snapping the phone back into its case. "I'll have someone here in less than ten minutes to take this to the lab. We can get a preliminary report by the end of the day."

Knowing the typical delays in getting forensics, Max contained her reaction to the end of the day. It would be lucky if that really happened, and although she knew that, it was difficult to wait. She wanted those results immediately so she could know if there was truly foul play, though her instincts already told her the answer.

Proceeding on through the house, the team continued their journey down the narrow hallway. Max pushed open the door to the first room on the right and found what appeared to be a guest room. A quick scan of the room told her it hadn't been disturbed any time recently. The bed was perfectly made, there was nothing out of place, and a light layer of dust lay on the nightstands. The carpet was perfectly brushed in the same consistent pattern with the rest of the house, except for the spot under the broken window.

The room on the left was a bathroom. It was nicely appointed. Max looked at the items on the sink, and it appeared this was not the bathroom primarily used by Rebecca. She continued on, and at the end of the hall found the master bedroom.

The door stood open. Max stepped in the doorway scanning the room. Like everything else in the house the room was tidy, except for the bed. The bed covers were very disheveled. Not just rumpled, but pulled way back and hung half off the bed. Either Rebecca Tillman had a very restless night, or something had disturbed her and a struggle had occurred.

Moving into the room, Max walked over to the closet and opened the door. She stood facing a good sized walk-in closet. Stepping inside she studied the contents, considering the clothes on the hangers and shoes on the floor. Her eyes scanned a few small boxes and then landed on the luggage in the corner. Her eyes narrowed in on the tag on the handle. She walked over, careful to not touch anything else, and read the tag. It was from a recent trip out of state. *You didn't leave here on your own did you, Rebecca? You would have taken your luggage.*

Cortez went deeper into the master bathroom, and as Max closed the closet door she said, "Toothbrush, brush, blow dryer, tooth paste, hair spray, and make up right here. And…there's a small travel bag with travel toiletries in the bottom drawer."

"Luggage in the closet recently used. This lady didn't go anywhere on her own. She was taken."

"I agree," Cortez confirmed.

"Look at the bedding too. If I'm getting out of bed, I throw the covers back, away from me. These are dragged off the bed."

"She could have had a lover in there with her," Cortez countered.

Max nodded, accepting the idea as an alternative solution and began talking it through, "She brings him home, things get frisky, and it goes south. They struggle, he knocks her out." She continued the theory, this time shaking her head, "But no blood, hair, fibers." Turning back looking for Kennard, who had stepped away from the room, Max called out, "Hey, Captain? Did the forensics team check the sheets for fluids?"

Kennard returned to the doorway. He nodded. "Yep, nothing but a little sweat."

Max thought for a minute. "Could have used a condom?" Could be her sweat, early menopause?" She asked sharing possible reasons for the lack of any fluids and justification for the sweat.

Cortez shrugged her shoulders and nodded her head, accepting either possibility.

Max returned to the bathroom and looked in the small waste can next to the toilet. Empty. "Did crime scene collect the trash?"

"I don't think so," Kennard answered.

Cortez was already in motion. "Kitchen," she called out over her shoulder.

Max and Kennard followed her and watched as she opened the cabinet under the kitchen sink and removed the waste can that sat nestled in under one side of the sink. Inside there were a few items, a couple of envelopes from the mail, a sales flyer for Walmart and an orange peel. "No condom, no glass."

"Let's check outside. Has the trash been picked up?"

Kennard replied, "I'm not sure. It comes on Tuesdays and Fridays to this street, but unless Rebecca had it out at the curb it would still be there."

The three went outside and looked inside the trash can. There was one bag, and after a careful look through the bag it didn't appear to contain anything out of the ordinary. So far nothing hinted of a boyfriend or a spontaneous lover.

The more they looked around the more Max was convinced the woman had been abducted. The person was clever and thorough, leaving nothing behind. That smelled of experience. The kind of experience like Jack Tyler had, but so far she had nothing to tie him to this case and no reason to believe he would come back to this town. In fact, everything she knew about Tyler led her to believe that he wouldn't come back here ever.

"Okay, I think we've seen enough here," Max advised. "We need that forensic work back as quickly as possible to see if we can prove there was a disturbance. Until that comes in we've got no more than we had before. But from what I see, she didn't plan on going anywhere."

"I'll lean on them and get you the report the minute it comes in." Kennard offered referring to the lab work Max was demanding.

Kennard had that stern look in his eyes again as he spoke, and Max got the feeling that he was able to get results when he wanted to.

She was glad about that and felt a little more comfortable thinking he might just be able to get them back tonight.

The return ride to the police sub-station was quiet, and when they arrived Max thanked Kennard for his help. She provided him with her business card and asked him to contact her immediately with the results or if any new information came in. They all shook hands before the two women returned to their car.

Max turned to Cortez, "Drive by Vivian's house. Let's make a house call."

Cortez looked at her. "You think he'd go back to that house?" Cortez continued before Max could answer. "Besides, she would recognize him. Even with the plastic surgery. Surely she'd call us the minute he left."

"No, I don't really think he'd go back there. But if he did, he'd want to look around. Maybe there's something there that he'd want to retrieve. Who knows? I agree, she'd recognize him, but we never told her what he'd done. We only told her that we were worried about him. She might not realize how dangerous he is." Max thought for a few seconds then finished off with, "It's a long shot, but it's all we got."

Cortez shrugged in agreement. "Well, I could use some of that fresh squeezed lemonade."

Max smiled at her, remembering the woman's sweet demeanor and hospitality when they had visited her during a previous attempt to find Jack Tyler.

Cortez backed the car out of the space and turned in the direction of the Jack's childhood home. According to Vivian she moved into the home that Tyler inherited and then sold because he had no interest in returning to the house. By then he was living in Los Angeles with a thriving medical business.

The streets were lined with bougainvillea and jacaranda trees, creating a beautiful blooming tapestry. Despite the heavy mood from their earlier time inside Rebecca Tillman's home, the natural beauty that filled the town helped to calm the anxiety in Max that seemed to be rising with each passing hour.

Cortez navigated the cruiser into the curved driveway. The home was as beautiful as Max recalled. Pulling in front of the walkway to the front door, Cortez stopped the car. They stepped out of the vehicle, again being embraced by the cool breeze and the warmth of the sunshine. As they walked up the sidewalk, something stood out to Max. The lavish foliage showed obvious signs of poor care. Nodding her head at it for Cortez to notice, she approached the door and rang the bell.

Chapter Thirty-Five

"Agent Wells," Jenkins approached with a report in her hand. "You're going to want to see this."

"What do we have?" Mark asked turning towards his fellow agent. Jenkins was a highly competent agent. She'd passed the FBI Academy with high marks in her class about five years previous.

Her creamy, dark skin and high cheek bones outlined serious eyes. "I got the report back from the credit card. Jack Tyler performed an Internet background check using intelius.com." She paused, an obvious hesitation in her voice. "Sir, the Internet search was on Rebecca Tillman."

Mark took the report from her hands, his eyes scanning the details on the page. A serious look covered his face, obvious by the deep furrow that sat like a canyon between dark brows hooding his tired blue eyes. Looking up at Jenkins he offered a mere, "Thank you," before reaching for his cell phone.

Dialing Max's number, he grew frustrated when it went straight to voicemail. It wasn't like Max to turn her phone off. Knowing Ojai was located in a valley nestled into the mountains, he wondered if she was having reception issues. *Or could it be something else?*

"Agent Jenkins, please brief the team on your findings. I'll try Cortez's line." Wells was already dialing. Once again the call went straight to voicemail. *It must be a reception issue.* Now in motion, Wells left the room and made a left in the hall, then followed the marbled tunnel to the chief's office.

Following the sound of the barking loud voice, Wells found Chief Harding standing in the middle of the room shouting into a phone. It was obvious he was chewing on someone about a press related issue.

Seeing Wells approach, Harding ended the call abruptly. "Agent Wells, is everything okay?" His solid jaw jutted out to the left, obvious concern covered his face. "Do we have something?"

"We do. Jack Tyler conducted a background check on Rebecca Tillman—the missing woman from Ojai. Cortez and my wife went to investigate the woman's home. Neither is answering her phone. Do you have the name of the contact from the Ventura Sheriff's Department?"

"One moment," Harding turned away and in a brisk walk carried his large frame over to a desk across the room. He returned immediately with a folder in his hand. Wells could see Tillman written in a scrawl across the tab.

Flipping the file open, the chief scanned the page, his thick finger sliding over the paper. "Captain Kennard. Number's right here."

Wells punched the numbers in his cell phone as Chief Harding rattled off the area code followed by the seven digits. Two rings later an electronic phone system answered, and Wells listened and made the proper choices that would guide him to the desk sergeant. Within a minute he was connected to Captain Kennard.

Skipping the formalities, Wells was very direct. "This is Special Agent in Charge Mark Wells of the FBI. Earlier today you were to meet with Agent Maxine Wells and Detective Lorraine Cortez. Are they still with you?"

Kennard hesitated briefly, "Agent Wells, yes. They were here, but they left over two hours ago."

"Did they indicate where they were headed?"

"Not specifically, but I assumed back to L.A."

"Was there anything specific identified during their time with you?"

"Yes, a few things. We collected a few more items. The canister of the vacuum was already empty when we found it, but Agent Wells wanted me to have it checked for glass fragments to see if there was a match to the broken window."

"Have you received those results?"

"Not yet. They won't likely come in until later today. I've got a rush on them, but it's not easy to get any forensics on a same day turnaround."

"I understand," Wells acknowledged. "We're going to need your help. We now have information showing that Jack Tyler did, in fact, have an interest in Rebecca Tillman."

"Certainly, what can I do?" Kennard responded, sucking in his breath.

"I'm going to get a flyer faxed over to you. It is a likeness of what we believe Tyler may look like today, given recent plastic surgery. We need to get it circulated to stores, likely places where Tyler would have to shop if he were staying somewhere in Ojai. My team and I will be there as soon as we can."

"You got it," Kennard answered, and before he could say any more the line went dead.

"Thank you, Chief," Mark said turning back the Harding. "We're going to have to get to Ojai as quickly as possible. Tyler may have Tillman there, and knowing Max, if she figured any of that out she may be following that lead on her own."

"I'll send two of my team to assist. One of my detectives is in this too." Harding turned, and Wells began the walk towards the investigation room. He could hear Harding barking out orders.

The trip to Ojai was clearly the longest drive of Mark's entire life. As they passed through Ventura, he watched the waves slapping angrily at the sand, seemingly peeling it away much in the same way Tyler peeled opened his victims. He turned his head, changing his gaze to the opposite side of the freeway. His eyes soaked in the mountainside that was speckled with expensive homes, packed tightly together like pushpins set into the hills.

His gaze fixed on a tall cross that stood high above the city like a beacon protecting everything below. The cross gave him an eerie foreboding feeling as if it were specifically warning him. He punched Max's name on his cell phone again, hopeful she'd pick up, but unfortunately, he got the same response—direct to voicemail.

Chapter Thirty-Six

Jack buried Jimmy's torn and ragged body deep in the woods near the creek, close to where Reb was laid to rest. After showering and obsessively bleaching and scrubbing his body clean he fell into bed next to Mindy. He didn't even realize she was actually awake when he leaned over and kissed her cheek before dropping into a blissful sleep.

Morning came quickly since his late night escapades kept him up most of the night. He was rattled awake by Mindy preparing breakfast and rolled over to watch her in the makeshift kitchen. For a moment his head was a fog of mixed visions floating between Jimmy and Ron, then of Heath coming into the surgical room. He turned over to look at the couch. The kids were still asleep. He flipped back over to Mindy. *Oh, Hope, you are so beautiful.* The sight of her in the kitchen—her blonde hair cascading down her back, thin legs, and tight buttocks— made his heart tug in his chest. It was so good having her back with him.

As he watched he heard the rustling of the sheets from the couch, and a moment later Heath stood staring down at him. "Good morning, Chance."

"Hi, Daddy," the boy said rubbing at his sleepy eyes.

Jack pulled back the covers and pulled the boy under the blankets, snuggling with him. "You cold?"

"No," Heath said, nestling into the man he believed to be his father.

Mindy looked over at Jack and the boy. Jack smiled at her. *Life is perfect.*

"Did you fix the sick man?" Heath innocently asked.

Jack studied the boy closely. "No, buddy, I wasn't able to this time. He was a very sick man, and sometimes when people are too sick, they just can't be saved."

Before the boy could ask more questions Scruffy jumped at the side of the bed, bouncing like a pogo stick in an attempt to get up on it. "Oh, look who needs to go outside. Want to come with me?" Jack asked.

"Okay," Heath answered, immediately climbing out of the bed.

"Okay, okay, buddy. I hear ya," Jack said to the dancing dog as he swung his feet over the bed and started to pull on the pants he dropped next to the bed after his nighttime hike into the woods. They had some dirt on them, so he carried them over and dropped them into a laundry basket near the bathroom. Then he retrieved another pair from the back

727

of the chair. As he lifted the pants, his pocket knife fell and spun on the floor. He quickly retrieved it and dipped it into the front right pocket. As he did so his fingers were enveloped by silky threads, and he smiled as he remembered clipping hair from Agent Maxine Wells's auburn head.

Pulling the strands out of his pocket, Jack stood staring at the rich ginger locks, his fingers sliding over the silky hair. Realizing he was being watched he looked up. Mindy was staring at him. He shoved the hair back in his pocket and flashed a warm reassuring smile at his lovely wife.

After he finished dressing, Jack helped Heath pull on play clothes and shoes, and then he let Hope know they'd be back in a while. He crossed the room to be by Hope's side and looped his arms around her waist. "Do you know how much I love you?" Not waiting for an answer, he spun her to face him and leaned to kiss her. "I love you, Hope," he said before placing his mouth on hers and slipping his tongue between her lips.

Feeling a tug at his shirt, he pulled away. "Daddy, let's go."

He leaned in and kissed Mindy again. "Okay, okay, buddy," he said to the anxious child. "We'll be right back," he said to Mindy with a smile before releasing her and following the running boy and dog up the stairs. He didn't see her wipe the back of her hand across her mouth in an effort to clean away his kiss.

With the door to the basement secured, the man, boy, and dog took their usual wander through the thick underbrush. New paths were starting to form from the recent visits out into the woods.

Holding Jack's hand as they walked Heath asked, "How do you become a doctor?"

Jack stopped and turned to look down at the boy. If he had any doubt that this boy was truly his son it vanished in that single question. Kneeling down he was subjected to wet slaps from Scruffy's tongue, but Jack laughed and patted the little dog. Focusing back on the inquisitive boy, he responded to the child's question, "Well, it takes a lot of work. For me, it was something I had to do. I need it even more than I like it."

"Can you teach me? I want to be a doctor." The little boy's eyes searched Jack's face with a sparkle that reflected hopeful excitement.

Jack stood looking at Heath, his mind filled with delight. His boy wanted to be just like his father; pride filled every ounce of him.

"I practiced a lot when I was a boy. I was about your age and a lot like you." Leading the boy around to the side garage door, Jack pulled from his pocket the keys he carried with him and unlocked the door. With Heath following closely behind, he went inside the garage and spent a few minutes gathering the necessary items to take back outside.

"Okay, if you're really going to be a doctor you first have to learn all about the anatomy of living beings. The anatomy is the things that are on the inside, like the heart that makes your blood pump and the lungs that help move the air through the body so it can breathe. You have to know how all those things work. Then once you know that, you can learn about how to fix those things if they get broken."

Heath listened intently and followed Jack back out into the woods. "What are we going to do?"

"We're going to build a trap."

"How?"

"I'm going to show you, but first the most important part of a good trap is a good location. You have to find a spot that will allow you to catch something quickly. Jack began walking around and started explaining how to identify the right spot. He talked about animal droppings and showed Heath how to determine if the droppings were from small or large animals.

A few minutes later Jack selected a spot and began compiling the items he retrieved from the garage into a makeshift trap. He was surprised at how quickly it came back to him.

Jack showed Heath the importance of making sure the hinge functioned properly, or the animal could easily get away. He explained how to choose the bait for the trap. For this trap he used dog food.

"Make sure you place the food way at the back. The animal will usually set off the trap when they try to get the food. It will climb in to get the food, and when they do they will bump the prop and the top will fall, catching them inside the trap." Jack demonstrated using his hand knocking the prop over and causing the trap to drop to the ground, leaving his hand still inside and with the cage over his wrist.

Pulling his hand back out, he reset the trap. It was ready and set to spring. Jack promised to make a better one if Heath actually liked learning about the animals. "Okay, we've been gone for a while. We better go back inside. We don't want Mommy to get mad at us for being late for breakfast."

Before going back to the house, Jack leaned down with his hands on his knees. "Son, there are two more things you must know. Not everyone will understand why you need to do these things. Not everyone wants to be a doctor, so there is no way they could know what it feels like to want that. The other thing you have to remember is that you never use your family pet for your studies. Do you understand?"

Heath nodded. "Will it take a long time?" the boy asked with excitement filling his voice, glancing back at the trap.

"It depends, but we can come back out later and check it."

***

The morning was spent not only eating the breakfast Mindy prepared but also watching morning cartoons. The whole family piled on the couch with Heath sitting on Jack's lap.

Mindy watched closely at how gentle Jack was with the boy and felt a wave of relief in that, but she wondered how she was going to get the children away from him before something terrible happened. She knew he had killed a man last night, and she feared the little boy had seen it. He seemed fine today, and that scared her almost as much as Jack scared her.

Her thoughts often moved to the weapon under the mattress, but she couldn't figure out how to use it without putting the kids in jeopardy. If she attacked him and somehow he over-powered her she'd be dead, and then the kids would be left alone with him. She couldn't take that risk. And Vivian, the poor woman, she nearly gasped at the thought of Vivian. She sucked in her breath as an obvious sigh to mask the gagging she felt in her throat.

Allie sat tucked tightly under her arm in a protective snug. Mindy was worried about her. Her darling little girl hadn't spoken in days. A subtle nod when spoken to was about all she offered. The thought of the trauma her daughter was enduring made her stomach lurch. She struggled to not allow the fear to pull her into absolute despair.

While Jack was doing whatever awful things in that room, she had laid in bed and had prayed her daughter would not wake up to hear the atrocities. Through the darkness Mindy had seen Jack carry a bundle up the stairs, and she could hear the crinkling of plastic. As he had approached the top of the stairs and the door opened, letting light in from the second floor, Mindy had dared to look, and her eyes had burned with

730

tears as she saw Jack lugging the long, rolled bundle on his shoulder through the door.

She had known what he had done, and her mind raced—a collage of images of escape, killing him, vivid images of her demise, the torture he would certainly level against the children one day, and a search for how Hope had managed his needs for so many years. She racked her brain through their childhood and remembered the intense focus Hope had suddenly pushed on Jack to become a doctor. She searched through the memories of the years past and finally determined that had begun sometime around seventh grade.

She decided to take a chance. If she could just get him to stop killing it would buy her time and stop the kids from more exposure to his insanity.

"Jack." She jumped, startled at the sound of her own voice. "I think you should try to get on at the hospital."

Jack turned, his eyes searching hers. "I'm so enjoying our time together though, darling. I wasn't there for you once, and I won't make that mistake again."

Mindy tried to think how to respond. "I know you worry about us, but I need you to be strong. You know, like we always planned. People need you, and you need them. You're such a skilled doctor." She took a chance, silently praying that her hunch was right. She held her breath, and her eyes dropped, expecting a rage to flow from the devil that sat near her on the couch.

Jack watched her. She could feel his eyes on her. "Okay, you're right, Hope. You're right, you've always been right. Tomorrow, I'll call tomorrow and see if there are services I can offer."

Mindy let her breath out. She found herself waiting and then words began to flow naturally out of her mouth, driven purely on instinct. "I think it's best—for us, for the kids."

***

Jack didn't like disappointing Hope. She was right, but he feared that if he wasn't with them he would be unable to protect them. He knew that she didn't like the way he handled his darkness when he wasn't working. Whenever he was working and able to perform surgeries, he was able to keep the darkness at bay. It was, after all, how they had lived for so many years. *Before*…He couldn't finish the thought. The accident was no longer part of their reality. They'd beaten it and had his family

731

back, and even more now he had a wonderful son who he knew was going to make him proud. *Yes, he had a son.*

He had some unfinished business though. Ron was in the surgical room, and tonight he would allow the darkness to take him one last time before returning to a respectable profession. He knew allowing the darkness to drive him was dangerous and felt torn between protecting his family from danger and placing himself in danger. His thoughts tormented him, and he felt restless.

Getting up, he went over to Vivian and pulled a chair beside the bed. He talked to her, check her, and held her hand, taking great care to make her comfortable. Unfortunately, even tending to her didn't temper his restless feeling.

"Come on, Chance. Let's take Scruffy outside," Jack said standing and patting his leg to get the dog to follow him.

Both the dog and boy hopped off the couch and were right at Jack's side. The dog jumped around like a bouncing ball, his pink tongue flopping from one side of his mouth, hopping up the stairs as his furry little legs drove him towards the door.

After they were out of the basement and out of earshot of Hope and Allie, Jack said to Heath, "What do you think, Chance? Will there be anything in our trap?"

The boy was practically running towards the door. "Let's go see, Daddy."

Outside of the house Heath pulled on Jack's hand as he ran to the place in the woods just a few feet from the trunk of a large oak tree. The very oak tree that Jack and Hope had carved their initials into the day she'd caught him with an animal in his hands and covered in blood. The sun peeked through the canopy of trees, creating a patchwork of sparkling leaves and shadows.

Jack pulled back on the boy's hand to slow him down. "Hold on, buddy. We have to go slow. No need to scare our prey."

Approaching more slowly now, Scruffy suddenly stopped, and wiry hair rose on the middle of his spine. He began to growl and bark, pouncing side to side around the small trap.

"Scruffy!" Jack barked out commanding the little dog to back down.

Jack approached, still holding Heath's hand. Inside the makeshift trap a small rabbit sat frozen in fear. The terrified animal breathed rapidly, and its eyes were wide and unblinking. "It looks like we got something."

"A bunny," Heath said with a wide smile on his innocent little face.

"Yes, a bunny."

"Can I pet it?"

"Of course, but hold on though. We don't want it to get away."

Jack knelt down next to the trap with his knee resting on the ground, and with one hand he lifted the trap door and slowly reached in to capture the rabbit by the scruff of the neck. The rabbit kicked its back feet wildly at the air as it was lifted off the ground. Dropping the trap door, Jack wrapped the rabbit in his arms, securing its feet and calming it down. Within a couple of seconds it settled in his embrace, unassumingly trusting.

Heath reached over and placed a small hand with plump little fingers in the soft fur. A big grin covered his face.

"Okay, ready to practice?" Jack asked. "Do you want me to show you how I practiced being a doctor when I was a little boy?"

Heath's eyes took on an almost sparkling green hue in the midday sun. There was naïve innocence in his nodded response.

Standing up, Jack carried the rabbit with Heath and Scruffy following behind. The small dog hopped up and down trying to get a good smell of the furry creature.

Jack walked across the yard to the small playhouse and stepped onto the platform while still holding the animal by the loose fur around its neck. He balanced the rabbit in one hand and pulled the door open with the other, then stooped in through the small door and let Heath inside with him, shutting Scruffy outside, much to the dog's disappointment.

Dust rose from the wooden floor and danced in the air in the stripes of sunlight that peeked through the small cracks in the slats of the wood. Jack kneeled down on the playhouse floor while maintaining his grip on the scrap of the rabbit's neck, setting the animal down.

Heath watched intently. Jack reached his free hand into his pocket and pulled out the Swiss Army Knife then plucked the largest blade open with his thumb. A peak of sun glinted off the shiny metal as he looked at Heath.

"This isn't the best, but it's all we have right now. Ready?"

Ten minutes later the boy sat staring down at the matted fur of the beautiful animal. Tears streaked his face. Crimson blood had already begun to dry on his small hands, making them feel papery and stiff. "Why did it die, Daddy?"

Jack looked at the boy and saw the disappointment in the death of the animal. "I know it's hard to understand, but if you want to experience life as closely as we just did, sometimes your patient will die. But if you practice long enough, you'll learn how all those parts inside work together, and then you'll be able to learn how to fix those parts when they become broken."

Jack stood up slightly hunched over in the small playhouse. He lifted the dead animal. "Come on, we need to bury it and then go clean up."

Heath followed Jack as he went to get the small shovel, and then walked with the man, stuffing his small bloody hand into Jack's as they trudged a little way into the woods. Heath stood watching as Jack dug a small hole, laid the animal inside, and then covered it back up.

Silently they went back towards the house. Jack called Scruffy away from the grave of the rabbit, where the little dog sniffed and pawed at the ground. After putting the shovel away, they went back into the main kitchen. Jack pulled a chair over to the sink and stood Heath on it, and then turned on warm water. He tested the temperature and helped Heath rinse the blood from his little fingers and watched as the water rushed down the drain—first red, then quickly replaced with clear bubbles from the soap he applied. Jack then washed his own hands until all the crimson blood was gone.

When both had dry hands, he lifted Heath off of the chair and held the boy in his arms for a moment. "You will make a wonderful doctor one day. Daddy's proud of you. You did really good today."

The boy smiled slightly, a hint of confusion and pleasure in his eyes. He wrapped his tiny arms around Jack's neck and laid his head on the muscular shoulder. Scruffy whimpered at their feet.

***

Allie didn't speak the entire time Jack and Chance were gone. She sat on the couch and stared at the TV, but Mindy couldn't tell if she was really watching any of it. Chance, she wasn't even sure if that was his real name or some crazy idea Jack had concocted. It was the only name she knew him by and couldn't just think of him as just a boy.

Mindy took a chance and went to the room at the back of the basement—the room where Jack had taken that bundle. Despite her fear, she tried to open the door. Her heart pounded so loudly in her ears that she had to force back a scream. The rattle of the door handle made her jump, confusing the noise she had made with what she thought was Jack returning too quickly. She stifled a chuckle at her fear then tapped on the door. *Jesus, I'm going crazy.*

She thought she heard something inside, so she placed her ear against the door and called out, "Hello?"

She listened carefully, and was sure she could hear a muffled groaning. *Oh, God, there is another person in there.* Stepping away from the door, she walked over to the bed and slid her hand in between the mattress and box spring. Her fingers wrapped around the wrench. *It's still there.*

She stood when she heard footsteps overhead. He was coming back. Her eyes darted to Allie on the couch, and she could see her daughter's fingers rapidly fidgeting with the fringe of the blanket. She had been calm until now. Her heart wrenched inside her as she watched her daughter's terror manifest in repetitive motions.

Food, it's time for food again. She heard water running above, and she quickly moved to the kitchen, opened the small refrigerator, and pulled out some chicken and vegetables.

Mindy couldn't help but notice there was something strange about the boy's behavior after he and Jack returned with the dog. He was sullen and quieter than normal. He seemed slightly withdrawn from Jack, too. He joined Allie on the couch and quietly watched TV.

After they ate, to her relief, Jack left the basement for quite a while. While he was gone she sat near the kids and placed her arms around each, trying to offer them assurance that she herself didn't feel. Heath soaked into her side, but Allie seemed completely withdrawn.

When Jack returned he was showered and had on fresh clothes. He went to Heath and suggested the boy take a bath. He lifted the child from the couch and out of Mindy's arms and carried him off to the shower. Soon the boy was freshly dressed and smelled of shampoo. Mindy wondered where the fresh clothes came from. She assumed based on the tags that Jack had shopped for them during one of his outings.

The day wasted away. Her thoughts were like a ping pong ball dancing across the table trying to find a way to escape the certain slamming of the paddle. No matter how hard she tried, she couldn't find a way to escape from the hold Jack had on her. With each passing moment fear rose in her, and she felt like she was slipping away.

Jack waited for the children to fall asleep then encouraged Hope to go to bed. He explained that he had something to finish up before attempting to start work again. He didn't explain any further knowing full well she wouldn't approve. There was nothing he could do to stop this anyway. He certainly couldn't just let Ron go. The man had seen far too much.

Flipping off the lights and leaving only a slight glow in the room from the subtle lights of the kitchen appliances, he walked around the couch into the darker corner of the basement and unlocked the surgical room door. Inside the room with the door closed and locked behind him, he flipped on the lights, shedding a brilliant glow over the secured, naked man on the table.

The paralyzing drug had worn away, and Ron was now fully alert. The presence of his captor sent him into a violent flutter like a bird with broken wings.

"Calm down, Ronnie boy. You wouldn't want to hurt yourself, now would you?"

A hissing sound escaped from Ron's nose as he attempted to breathe through the tape that held his mouth closed and head tight to the table. Bloody tears around his wrists and ankles indicated that he'd obviously been working at the zip ties.

"It's not worth your struggles. No one can hear you and you can't get away. But I think you know that already, don't you? Let me ask you, Ron. How was it watching me work on Jimmy? Did you enjoy it as much as I did? It is truly amazing. Life, I mean."

Jack leaned over close to Ron's face. He talked slowly and watched Ron's eyes grow large; the pupils dilated from fear. His head shook in a mild tremor. Jack briefly wondered if he was cold, but ultimately decided it didn't matter.

As much as Jack wanted to spend days with Ron, like he had with Benz in Oklahoma and Reb here just days before, he had made a promise to Hope, and he planned on keeping it. There was nothing, including his darkness that would get in the way of making Hope happy. He would return to the days of managing the darkness through his surgical skills, making his explorations specific only to moments in the effort of trying to save people. That was the arrangement he and Hope made all those years ago.

Jack pulled on a full set of scrubs and inhaled deeply, and then lifted the scalpel from the tray. He ignored Ron's thrashing and bouncing against the zip ties and pain as he took his time ripping through the man's body, exploring all the slippery organs and toying with the heart as he worked it to the edge of death then pulsed it into a throbbing beat between his fingers. It finally failed after several minutes of the torment and lay stalled in his hand.

Wiping sweat from his brow, he realized he had lost complete track of time. Peeling his hands out of the center of Ron's chest, he went through the cleaning ritual he'd so perfectly mastered over the years. He hosed everything down including his own body that was now striped of the scrubs. Once he was satisfied that the room had been restored to its pristine state, he packaged the man for a plastic-encased wooded burial.

The morning was greeted by a sparkling sunrise and a light breeze. Jack got up early to go upstairs and shower. Today he would keep his promise to Hope and call the hospital to see if there was some way he could assist with emergency or surgical procedures. He knew his ability to control the demanding urges could only be tempered with rightful opportunities to get inside the patients' bodies. He also knew he would try to keep his promise to Hope. He wanted to make her happy. All he ever wanted was to make her happy.

Deciding the best approach was to go to the hospital in person, Jack dressed appropriately, gathered the documents to support his latest identity, including his medical license, and with everything in a folder he set off to talk to the hospital director.

Two hours later Jack returned to the house. He had secured an agreement to work on-call for any major emergencies. Then he had stopped by the grocery to pick up a few items and was excited to get home to Hope to tell her the good news.

As he started to pull into the driveway he saw a car pull in ahead of him. Something told him to not follow it. He passed the house slowly and watched as the car stopped. Two women got out. One of the women was Agent Maxine Wells, the other her attractive former Hispanic partner. He'd seen them both before in Oklahoma when he'd hidden in the back room posing as Thomas the nail salon employee.

Blood pounded in his ears as he considered his options. Parking his van on the street, Jack reached behind his seat and grabbed his medical bag. He slipped out of the van and quietly closed the door with a slight click of the latch and worked his way along the driveway through the trees. Rounding the corner of the house he heard the door bell ringing.

He slipped inside the house through the back door and went directly to the front door. Punching the button on the intercom he asked, "Yes?" in a very low voice, staying behind the door almost entirely.

"Hello, is Vivian home?"

"She's not doing well these days. She's resting."

"We certainly understand, but it is very important that we speak with her," Max said while holding her badge in front of the camera eye.

"FBI, oh my," Jack said maintaining his low voice and trying to sound overtly surprised.

"May I ask who you are?" Max asked.

"I'm Vivian's caregiver, Jimmy. Vivian has cancer," Jack lied.

"Well, we really do need to see her," Max continued to prod.

"If you can give me a few moments I can see if she is feeling up to guests."

"That would be great," Max said glancing back at Cortez.

Jack clicked off the intercom and returned to the garage. He wrapped his fingers around the hammer in the tool box that sat just inside the door and retrieved two syringes from inside his medical bag before opening the front door, intentionally staying behind and out of view.

Max stepped through the doorway first followed by Cortez. Jack swung the hammer down on Cortez's skull. There was a loud crack, and she slipped to the floor. Max started to swing around and reach for her weapon, but Jack dropped the hammer and swept his arm around her neck. His other hand plunged the needle of the syringe into her neck.

Max pulled with all her strength at the arm that coiled around her, but was rapidly taken by a haze of quick flashes of Cortez lying like a crumpled rag on the floor with a crimson halo surrounding her head.

Chapter Thirty-Seven

The cruiser finally pulled into the town of Ojai, and though Wells continued trying to reach both Max and Cortez, neither phone answered. Each attempt went directly to voicemail. Wells was becoming increasingly concerned that something was wrong. It wasn't like Max to not check in or keep him updated with the status of her findings.

He gave instructions to the remaining team back at the Los Angeles precinct to continue working their plausible theories, and he brought Agent Jenkins and two detectives with him. He was beginning to wonder whether he had made the right choice or if he should have brought even more agents with him. He had a feeling he was going to need them.

By the time they arrived at the sub-station where Captain Kennard told them to meet him, it was late afternoon. The sunny day was beginning to show signs of ending as the sun was slowly setting behind the mountains they had passed through. It would soon be dipping into the salty ocean, the waves lapping away the last signs of light.

Wells knew that nightfall would make their search more difficult, and he unconsciously prayed for Max to call and explain that they had been out of cell coverage. He looked down at his own cell phone as he exited the car and saw that he had three bars. His brow furrowed with deeper concern.

Kennard met them inside. Apparently, he had been waiting for them to arrive. After brief introductions Kennard asked, "Any word from Agent Wells or Detective Cortez?"

Wells shook his head. "Have we received any leads from the distribution of the photo?"

"Nothing so far," Kennard replied. "It's being circulated. We've gotten it out to nearly every store. If the likeness is right and he's in this town, someone will see him. It's just a matter of time."

"I'm afraid we don't have time."

Wells's phone rang, and he reached to retrieve it, hoping it was Max returning his numerous calls. Disappointment filled him when he saw the call was coming in from Agent Adams.

"Wells," he answered abruptly.

On the other end Agent Adams began speaking, "Sir, I think we may have something. I've been researching the names that the L.A. analyst, Bobby, gave us as probable aliases Tyler might use. With the focus on Ojai, I decided to narrow in on that city, and one of the aliases recently purchased a home in Ojai. Sir, it happens to be the home that Jack Tyler grew up in." Adams stopped, waiting for further direction.

Wells listened carefully. "Adams, good work. Send me the address."

Hanging up the phone, he turned to the others. "We've got something. Tyler may have returned to his childhood home. Captain, are you familiar with the house?"

Chapter Thirty-Eight

Max couldn't feel her body. She could see everything that was happening, but was unable to move, speak, or feel anything. She watched in horror as Jack carried Cortez away. She lay on the floor and could see a tremendous amount of blood. A cloying coopery smell filled the room. She tried to shake the fog from her brain and out of her limbs, demanding that her body respond to her commands. *Nothing!*

Trying to force her brain to function again, she worked through what had happened. A man had come to the door and let them in; she didn't see his face. A loud crack, and when she turned to see what it was, it was too late. Cortez was on the floor, and *oh God, all that blood!*

He said something to her. *What was it?* Her mind was a clutter like a child's closet. *"Well, hello, Agent Maxine...Wells, is it now?"*

Jack! That son of a bitch hit Cortez with something. Her eyes darted around, and she looked far to her left past the blood. On the floor next to where Cortez had been just a few moments before was a large claw hammer.

Her eyes slammed shut. *Think, Max. Damn it, think!* She felt despair starting to creep in. The lack of mobility and control of even her own body weighed on her. She had imagined this day over and over—literally hundreds of times over the past year and a half—but never had it ended with her on the floor like a shell with eyes. *How could you have been so stupid? Why didn't I call Mark and tell him where we were going?* Her muddled mind was a flurry of questions, ridicule, and accusations. None of which was going to help her or Cortez now.

She heard a noise. A door opening, keys rattling. She wanted to scream out. Maybe Vivian was here and would hear. She could hear shoes walking towards her, heavy shoes—shoes of a man. Then she saw them and pants, then hands reaching for her. Suddenly, she was being dragged up from the floor.

"Agent, how are you feeling? I think your pretty detective is feeling a little bit like Humpty Dumpty right now. Hmmm, I guess we'll see if I can put her back together again. How would you like to watch?"

Jack reached into Max's pockets and retrieved her cell phone. He slid his thumb across the screen while balancing her under his arm and her hand draped around his shoulder. She could see him scrolling through the phone.

"Well, good, you've made no recent phone calls or sent any text messages. This should mean we have some quality time together. It does appear someone has been desperately trying to reach you though. Oh, well they'll just have to keep trying. You know I've been looking forward to officially meeting you. Though your lock of hair is certainly nice, it's not nearly as lovely as you are in person." He stared into her eyes, pure evil piercing her.

Lock of hair? He had taken my hair. That means...Heath!

She tried to move her arm again, but little more than a twitch of her fingers came out. *But they did move. Didn't they?* She wasn't quite sure. Suddenly, she was being dragged again, and then carried.

She watched as Jack powered off her phone and opened a door. She heard keys again, and then it felt like she was falling, and then level again. She was in a room; it was darker and smelled damp. She could hear a TV, cartoons playing, the sound of another door opening and shutting, bright lights, and then, *OH, GOD, NO!*

Cortez was lying on a metal table. She had a huge cut on her head, and her hair had a dark matted stain. She wasn't moving. Fear filled Max—fear of Cortez being dead, fear of not being able to save Heath if he was still alive, fear of dying and never seeing Mark again.

She was slammed down into a chair. Her head rolled back and hit something hard. She knew it should hurt, but it didn't. She watched as Jack used duct tape to attach her arms to the chair.

"Well, Agent, what shall we do now?" Jack asked her with a mild laugh in his tone. "It would appear the lovely detective is in a bit of trouble here, wouldn't you say?"

"I just bet that you've wondered over and over again, what it's like to be me. You know, there are no words that could describe it. You really just have to experience it. So, why don't we do this together, huh? What better way for you to get to know me?"

With that Jack turned away from Max and began removing Cortez's clothes, snipping them away with scissors. He rolled her to the side, causing her head to flop at an odd angle with her body.

Max closed her eyes. She refused to watch this. She would not give Jack the satisfaction of making her witness his madness. Suddenly, he slapped her, but she didn't feel it. Her eyes flew back open, and her head jerked with the movement.

"Agent, you must stay with me. I really do want you to participate. Now don't close your eyes again. Or...well, let's just say, you won't like it."

A few moments later Max could feel tingling in her hands, feet, and head. The effects of the drug were beginning to wear off. She wanted to wiggle her fingers and toes but resisted the temptation, not wanting him to know that the feeling was coming back into her body.

"Now, where were we?" Jack asked as he finished removing Cortez's clothing. Next, he pulled on scrubs and gloves. He maneuvered closer to him a tray that seemed to dangle in space over Cortez's body and lifted up a knife with a curve at the end.

"Do you like this one?"

Shaking his head, he put it back down. "Not my favorite one either, though quite handy for the right circumstances." He lifted another smaller knife that looked like a scalpel to Max's untrained eyes.

"Do you prefer this one?" He stared at her, waiting as if she could actually respond to him.

"Yes, a good choice indeed, one of my favorites. It's a #5 scalpel, quite ideal for this sort of procedure. You are catching on so quickly, Agent."

With that, he took the scalpel and made a long incision down the middle of Cortez's abdomen. Max choked back a scream. Her throat seemed to close off and nearly take her breath away. Her mind wanted to kick and writhe and fight against her bindings as she wanted to lash out at him, protect Cortez, and kill him, but her body did not respond.

All of a sudden there was a loud noise. The door slammed open, and in a flurry of motions, Jack swung around as a woman–*Mindy!*–attacked him and hit him with some sort of a tool. *A wrench she hit him with a wrench.*

Max watched in horror as she saw Jack sprawl to the floor. The scalpel went flying, and the two bodies intertwined in a frenzied wrestling match on the floor. Jack rolled over, holding his head as a gaping wound became visible above his brow.

His arms swirled around the woman. "Hope! What are you doing?" His body crushed down on top of Mindy's small frame.

Mindy was screaming, kicking, and clawing. "I'm not Hope! She's dead. She's been dead for almost two years now!"

Jack clambered to his feet and yanked Mindy off the floor by her arm, then pulled her against his muscular chest.

Max watched as Jack held the woman tightly against his body. He spun her with him, her arms still grabbing at him and her legs swinging in efforts to kick away. Opening the small refrigerator, Jack reached in, but Max couldn't see what he retrieved before he dragged the struggling woman out of the room.

Forcing herself forward, she began trying to rock the chair. Her body was still struggling to follow basic commands, and her efforts were fruitless. She could hear grunts and kicks from the room outside, then a child's scream of, "Mommy!" followed by a few more sounds of an obvious scuffle.

"How could you betray me, Hope? I've always loved you. Everything I've ever done was for you and our family."

Max listened as she heard deep guttural sobbing—the kind only experienced through deep loss or death. As she tried to rock the chair over again by compelling her body to lean forward, she heard what sounded like furniture moving. *What the hell are you doing, Jack?*

Max wanted to scream out to him to distract him away from Mindy and the child, but her voice wouldn't work. Her mouth barely moved at her demand. She assumed the child was Mindy's daughter. It sounded like a girl. *Right?* Could it have been Heath's voice? She felt like she was going crazy, her mind playing tricks on her. Had she heard a child scream at all?

Suddenly, it was eerily quiet. Jack's heavy sobbing stopped, and there was no movement at all. Max listened intently, but all she could hear was her own heavy breathing and a hammering of her pulse in her ears. Her eyes drifted momentarily to the table where Cortez lay. She tried to see a rise and fall of breath. Uncertain, she took her eyes away. She was not able to accept the amount of blood that had pooled around her friend's body. *Come on, Cortez. Stay with me*, she silently pleaded. She leaned forward again, fueled by the desire to get Cortez out alive. *I'm going to kill that son of a bitch and get you out of here!*

744

Chapter Thirty-Nine

A police officer approached and spoke quietly with Captain Kennard as Wells stood impatiently waiting for an answer to his question.

Kennard turned to Wells. "Yes, I'm familiar with the Tyler home." Before Wells could say anything else Kennard continued, "We also have a hit on the photo we're circulating. A clerk at the Radio Shack said the man in the photo bought a bunch of monitoring equipment for his home. My officer interviewed him. Kid was very specific, said he remembered it well because it was his biggest sale all month."

"We need to get to the Tyler home immediately. Can your officers assist?" Wells asked.

"Certainly, Agent, but sir, there's more." Kennard continued not waiting for the go ahead, "My officer showed a picture of Rebecca Tillman to the clerk, and he said she was in the store right behind Tyler, bought a package of batteries."

"We need to go. Captain, please have your team meet outside in five minutes." Wells was already turning to his team to give the orders.

Outside the air was cool and night had fully settled in now. Wells gave the instruction on how they would approach the Tyler home. He and Agent Jenkins would approach from the front. Captain Kennard and two officers would cover the other exits. They would go in with no sirens and lights out. There was no way to predict what Tyler would do if he knew the police were surrounding the home.

With the instructions clear, everyone loaded into the police cruisers and headed towards Jack Tyler's boyhood home. Wells, usually calm and cool, could feel his heart racing. He feared his wife and son were both dead or even possibly would never be found. He squeezed his eyes closed, preparing for what they would find when they arrived at Jack Tyler's house.

The police cars lined the street rather than pulling into the drive. Wells pointed towards the van that sat on the street and asked Kennard to radio it in to see who it was registered to. Within moments they had the answer; it was the same alias that had bought the home. Tyler's vehicle was sitting on the street.

They began making their approach. The police cruiser that Cortez had checked out of the motor pool that morning was sitting in front of the house, driving Wells's heart to race even faster. He gave the hand signal for the teams to move around to the back of the house. He hesitated just long enough to give everyone time to get into position before approaching the front of the house with Agent Jenkins behind him.

At the front door Wells noticed the intercom and the camera that would allow anyone inside to see who was at the door. He reached out and turned the knob. To his surprise the door opened. Using a flashlight, he scanned the area in front of him and saw a large pool of blood on the floor just inside. A hammer lay just off to the side.

Signaling to Jenkins, they moved forward and silently cleared the room they were in. They continued forward by passing through a dining area and into a kitchen. A back door was visible. Wells clicked open the door to allow Captain Kennard and his officers in. He motioned towards the front of the house to the stairs that led to the second floor.

Wells pointed to another door and swung it open. It led to the garage. They cleared this room as well while two more officers filed into the home. They worked room by room. Just as Wells was beginning to think Tyler had taken Max and Cortez somewhere else, the beam of his light flashed over a door that seemed to have something mounted on it. Moving forward with his Glock pointed and ready, he saw the door had a mount for a bar to secure it closed. The bar was leaning next to the door against the wall. Motioning again to Agent Jenkins, they stood on opposite sides of the door as Wells pulled it open. His light flashed onto a set of steps that descended into a dimly lit room below.

Taking the first step, Wells began the descent into the basement, cautiously expecting to be attacked from below. Near the bottom step, he saw Max lying on the floor with a shiny object in her hand. Resisting the desire to race towards her, he knew he needed to secure Tyler before he could provide her any assistance.

Scanning the rest of the room, he saw a small kitchen table at the back. He felt himself gag as he saw the macabre picture of what seemed the perfect family seated for dinner, except for the body of a white haired elderly woman showing obvious signs of rigor and the way the small girl's head sat oddly to one side—a younger version of the woman sitting next to her with her mouth agape. And the way the small boy, *his boy,* sat slumped forward with his arms dangling at his sides.

746

For a moment he felt like he was a boy all over again with that familiar feeling of failure overwhelming him. He had failed Tommy all those years ago, and now he had failed Heath. He stood frozen in the spot, and from somewhere in the room he heard Agent Jenkins calling for medical support. At the head of the table sat Jack Tyler. His head cocked sideways, and his eyes plumped open. A strange grimace splayed over his face as if he were laughing.

Wells pushed forward, approaching the strange dinner party. He went first to Tyler, his training forcing him to ignore his desire to go to his son. With his Glock trained on the source of their year-long manhunt, he placed his fingers on the man's neck. He felt nothing. "He's dead," he called out to the others that were now filling the room.

Fear covered him as he turned to Heath and reached forward to feel for a pulse. His knees almost buckled as he felt a beat. Fearing he imagined the *thump...thump,* he kept two fingers against the child's neck. After being certain he turned to Jenkins. "He's alive. We need medics right now!"

Kennard appeared from nowhere and was already confirming that the other child was alive as Wells turned to Mindy Prescott. "The kids and mother are alive!"

Wells finally turned to Max and found an officer already talking to her. Her eyes were open, and the officer was trying to remove a blood-covered scalpel from her hand.

As he kneeled down to Max she whispered, "Cortez."

***

Moments later the entire room was filled with light, as medical personnel began working on each person. Max was lifted onto a gurney, and as she was taken from the room her eyes found the grotesque picture at the dining room table. Jack Tyler's gaze seemed to be taunting her. She could hear in her head the words he had once said to her, *"You and I are so much alike."*

Chapter Forty

Max and Heath had been rushed off to the hospital. Both were confirmed to be in stable condition, so Mark was torn between going with them since Rebecca Tillman was still missing.

The team continued to search every inch of the home and room by room the reports came back as cleared. Wells walked outside and stood in the dark night and listened to the rustle of the trees. His instincts told him that the wooded area behind the house held many answers. As he was waiting on the cadaver dogs to arrive and help search the property Captain Kennard approached, "Agent Wells, we have another problem."

Mark turned to face Kennard. "What is it?" A grave look fell over his face.

"Two more people are missing. A local caregiver and his neighbor both have not been seen or heard from in two days."

"Do we have reason to believe it's connected?"

Kennard nodded. "Apparently the caregiver, a man named James "Jimmy" Noland," Kennard said looking at a small notepad, "was Vivian's caregiver for nearly six months."

"When will the dogs be here?" Mark asked.

"Should be here within five minutes," Kennard answered.

Headlights lit the trees and flashed across the house before stopping in the driveway amidst all the other police and medical vehicles. The driver exited the car followed by a passenger, both dressed in full police gear. The two moved to the back of the vehicle, and the driver opened the hatch to allow two large German Sheppard dogs out.

Wells and the team surrounded the handlers, and within minutes Wells split the officers and agents into teams. The back of the property was the obvious area to search first, so after spreading out the two assigned teams began their search.

Flashlights waved in the dark, and the underbrush crunched beneath the feet of the officers. Mark was working with the team on the west side of the property, and about half way into the thicket the dog began to report, barking wildly at the base of a tree.

A forensics team was standing by for recovery efforts if there were to be any and immediately approached the barking dog.

After carefully securing the area around the tree and setting up flood lights, the crime scene analyst took a number of photos before beginning the removal of the loose soil that showed signs of having been recently disturbed.

The removal of the soil didn't take long before a small animal was lifted from the makeshift grave. Laying the animal out on a sheet of plastic, it was obvious the creature had been killed recently. A close assessment disclosed that it was a rabbit and that it had been essentially gutted. Its internal organs hung through the hole in its abdomen.

The analyst spoke first, "Looks like it was slit open with a sharp implement. No jagged edges. Precision."

Mark turned back to the handler. "Keep looking." He stood there for a moment staring at the mess on the plastic sheet and wondering why Tyler would have resorted to killing animals again.

Agent Jenkins spoke, "It doesn't make sense, does it?"

"No, it doesn't, unless he thought he could temporarily temper his urges."

Agent Jenkins nodded, her dark skin accented in the flood lights.

The two agents turned back into the dark thicket to follow the rest of the team that had resumed the search. A few moments later Mark could hear water trickling and realized there must be a stream or creek just ahead.

The dog began to report again, and then another dog baying could be heard off to the east and back closer to the house. "Agent, please go to the other team and radio me with what they've got. I'll stay here."

Two hours later there were flood lights illuminating two more areas on the property. Four bodies had been recovered near the creek—three males and a female. It would take some time for positive identification, but Wells assumed that Rebecca Tillman and the two local men would be identified. The additional man was unknown.

Under the child's playhouse were two more bodies. It was the same playhouse Max and Cortez had reported finding animal bones and the magazines that had been instrumental in tracking Jack Tyler to Tulsa, Oklahoma over a year earlier.

This grisly discovery was the obvious first attempt Tyler had made at restoring his family, and in actuality they were several bodies combined. He had murdered people, and using the body parts, put together replications of his wife and daughter. The process he had used to preserve the bodies had obviously failed, and it was then that he abducted Mindy and Allie to start the process all over again with the closest representation of his wife and daughter he could find.

Mark stood with the other agents around him as they watched the careful recovery of the bodies. By morning the team was tearing down flood lights and bodies had been moved to the morgue for autopsies and identification.

Two days later fingerprints confirmed the female to be Rebecca Tillman and two of the men as James "Jimmy" Noland, Vivian's caregiver, and Ronald Camp, Jimmy's neighbor. Based on the preliminary time of death it appeared they had been killed within hours of each other. The other body was identified as a missing person from Ventura, a jogger that had gone missing from the beach weeks earlier.

Lots of forensic evidence was gathered, including a small bag containing glass fragments from Tyler's own trash. Mark was certain these glass fragments would match the glass from Rebecca Tillman's window. There was no disputing Tyler's skill at being able to elude police and cover up his crimes.

Mark couldn't find any solace in Tyler's death because he knew there were many more killers out there working right now who were just as clever as Tyler. In fact, he already knew there was a case that was going to be handed to him and the team almost immediately upon return to Virginia.

752

Chapter Forty-One

It had been two weeks since Lorraine Cortez's funeral. Max was released from the hospital the day after they had entered Jack Tyler's home. She'd gone to see Cortez's mother to express her sincere condolences. She left there feeling like she had handed over an empty bag of words. Nothing could bring Lorraine back to her mother, and nothing she could say could change that fact.

Most days she just felt guilty for keeping Cortez involved. She had left to go to the FBI. She could have left Cortez out of the entire thing, but she had continued to involve her, sharing her theories and asking for assistance.

Mark had filled her in on the discoveries out at the Tyler house. He'd brought her the files to read, shared the photos with her knowing full well she wouldn't rest until she could understand all of the events that had taken place while she was in the hospital. Her eyes had carefully studied every photo, each numbered in the order in which they had been discovered.

Mark continued to tell her that Lorraine wouldn't have had it any other way. The final report indicated that the continued focus and professional tracking had left Jack Tyler nowhere else to run, and in the end Max and Cortez together had helped drive Jack Tyler to commit suicide by giving himself a very lethal dose of anesthesia.

Max took pleasure in knowing Tyler's death would save the government a ton of money by not keeping a madman on death row, eliminating the endless appeals that no doubt died with him. But she felt like in the end he had won.

He had prevented her from getting into his head, asking all of the questions she'd wanted to ask, gaining the answers she desperately needed. He had stopped her from the pleasure of taking his life, killing him and having the satisfaction of knowing that she'd prevented him from killing any more innocent people. Taking his own life had stolen from her the ending she'd pictured so many times and stolen her friend… her *best* friend.

Though Tyler had administered a potentially lethal dose of Rohypnol, Mindy and Allie had been discovered soon enough, and the doctors had been able to reverse the intended effects. They were released after spending a couple of days in the hospital and had returned to Arizona to put their lives back together. Max had met with Mindy once and learned that Allie still hadn't spoken since their rescue. In the hospital Mindy had been reunited with her husband and daughter, and Mindy and Paul were beginning therapy to help Allie overcome the trauma from the time spent in that basement.

The autopsy on Vivian indicated that she had been dead for over a week. It turned out that she was actually Jack's biological mother, Janice *Vivian* Tyler. Jack's father apparently knew his wife wasn't capable of managing the house, and with Jack's older sister Suzanne dead, his father had left the real estate to Jack. The elder Tyler must have assumed Jack would care for the home and his aging mother, but instead Jack had left his mother and the home behind. She had remained in the home and remarried shortly after Jack had moved away. Vivian married a man named Donald Wilson soon after the senior Tyler died, and Vivian's new husband later purchased the house from Jack.

Max felt nothing but anger at the thought that she had missed the important detail of Vivian's name. They'd never run a background check or any other research on Vivian or Jack's parents, and as a result never made the connection that Vivian was the very same Janice Tyler the old woman had so openly spoken of during their visit with her over a year earlier. Unfortunately, less than five years later Vivian's new husband passed away, once again leaving Vivian alone to care for the home on her own.

When Max and Cortez had first gone to visit Vivian while trying to find Jack, the pleasant old woman who Max now knew was suffering from dementia had entered a place in her life where the illness had changed her. It had changed her for the better, and there was nothing suspicious in her story or in her demeanor that raised concern, but even still Max could take no comfort in the thought that the connection could have changed the course of the investigation and Cortez would be alive today.

Further research into Vivian's background uncovered a history of schizophrenia and long periods of her being on and off of medication. They had come to the conclusion that when off of the medication she would perform horrible acts on little Jack Tyler, but in her elder years she was a kind woman who politely offered even unexpected guests lemonade and openly shared stories of other's transgressions, seemingly unaware she was speaking about herself and her own family.

The theory in the FBI's official report indicated that Jack was unable to cope properly with the abuse he had endured at his mother's hand as a child, had fragmented, and had begun killing animals at a small age. With Hope's love and guidance he had been able to keep it together, but after her death he had fragmented again and had fallen into a murderous abyss.

Why he returned to the home was anyone's guess, but they assumed like so many abused children, he seemed to forgive Vivian for the things she had done to him. He was a boy that was unable to accept that his own mother could hurt him the way she had for all those years.

Heath surprisingly seemed to be doing pretty well. He also had been released from the hospital after spending just a couple of days. He'd asked about the little dog that had been found lying next to Jack Tyler's feet. It was taken to animal services and after discussions with Rebecca Tillman's family, who had admitted they did not want the animal, Mark had requested to adopt the little dog and surprised Heath when he'd gotten out of the hospital. Max hoped it would help the boy's recovery.

And after returning home, they immediately got him into therapy. Max knew it was going to take time to get him to understand all the things that had happened to him. They knew Tyler had told him lies about being his real father, what his name was, so many lies, and Max worried about him not knowing who to trust.

The situation brought her and Mark even closer together. He had obviously been able to put away some of the childhood demons that had plagued him his whole life. Mark had been able to save Heath unlike his brother Tommy, and there was a noticeable calm over him. The close reality that Max could have died in that basement along with Cortez drove an even richer appreciation for the time they had together and the future they would share.

They were committed to giving Heath the love and support he would need. She just hoped in time he would be okay and wondered what the long term effects would be of those days in the basement with Jack Tyler.

Max sat on their back porch sipping coffee in the morning sun while Scruffy laid quietly at her feet. She felt grateful that she would return to work tomorrow. The idleness of being at home seemed to feed the guilty feelings that would swell over her like the tide on a jetty during a hurricane. Her mind replayed those final hours over and over.

Going back to see Vivian had been her idea. Cortez hadn't seen the point in it. Yet it was there that the yearlong hunt for Jack Tyler had ended, and there where Cortez would sustain injuries too severe to recover.

A single tear slid from her eye as she recalled Mark telling her that as Lorraine took her final breath in the ambulance, she whispered to the medic a final request to, "Tell Max we got him."

Max brushed away the tear. The sun shined on her auburn waves as her finger twisted at the strands of hair that remained a couple of inches shorter than the rest, and a small smile crossed her lips as she whispered into the wind, "Yes we did."

Epilogue

Max watched Heath playing under the trees towards the back of the yard. He seemed good as he bounced around in between the sunshine and shade. It was really amazing how resilient he was.

The little boy certainly had been through more than any person, much less a child, should ever have to endure. She felt grateful and a sense of pride at his strength.

A sudden eerie feeling came over her as she watched him crouch down and stare in fascination at a small squirrel. There was something strange in his ability to stay so incredibly still, a focus not natural to a boy his age. He began to creep towards the small animal as if ready to pounce. When he got too close, the snap of a twig scared the squirrel, and it scampered away. Its tail twitched as it leapt onto the tree and scurried up to a limb safely out of the boy's grasp.

Heath remained crouched down. His head turned to peer up into the tree while he continued to watch the animal for several more seconds. The squirrel clicked at him in a teasing manner.

Heath turned around and saw Max watching him. Did she imagine it, or was there something different, something dark in his eyes? He gave her a crooked little grin and wiggled his chubby little fingers at her. Her mind flashed to a picture from the files. Photo # 1 showed a dead rabbit lying on a sheet of plastic with a gaping hole down its center and its internal organs hanging out. A chill ran down her spine.

The End

Acknowledgements

Hollie Zunun, my editor, you are the very best!!! Without you I am not sure I would have ever gotten all three books on paper. Your input has been invaluable!!!

Shout out to Mom for giving me honest feedback throughout each of the Jack Tyler stories.

My "work world" colleague Patrick Plunkett for the shameless plugs he throws out for my writing efforts every chance he gets.

Chris Snidow for the final touches after Hollie and I have exhausted every chance to get it right! Your keen eye is very appreciated!

My family, I love you!

About the Author

Valerie Knupp lives on seven acres outside the Tulsa area near Inola, Oklahoma. She loves to travel and is an avid reader of anything with a grisly plot. When not doing one of these things, she enjoys spending time around the house with her partner and two adopted children. Restoring Hope was her debut novel and it was always with the vision of a trilogy wrapping up with Chance.

To my loyal readers, thank you for taking the Jack Tyler journey. I hope these pages have evoked a number of emotions, from empathy to rage.

If you find any errors while taking any Jack Tyler journey, want to provide feedback and comments or just want to stay up to date on what the author is working on please visit:

www.thrillersbyknupp.com

www.ingramcontent.com/pod-product-compliance
Lightning Source LLC
Chambersburg PA
CBHW052337020726
47503CB00001B/6